Transgressions

Transgressions

The Iowa Anthology of Innovative Fiction

Edited by Lee Montgomery,
Mary Hussmann, and David Hamilton

Foreword by William H. Gass

UNIVERSITY OF IOWA PRESS Ψ IOWA CITY

University of Iowa Press, Iowa City 52242
Copyright © 1994 by the University of Iowa Press
All rights reserved
Printed in the United States of America

International Standard Book Number 0-87745-474-4
Library of Congress Catalog Card Number 94-60574

Printed on acid-free paper

01 00 99 98 97 96 95 94 P 5 4 3 2 1

PREFACE AND ACKNOWLEDGMENTS

The inspiration for this collection of fictions occurred during my tenure as a student at the Iowa Writers' Workshop. As an older student with a background in art, I was stunned by how many of my colleagues so readily dismissed works by authors such as William Gass, Bob Coover, and Donald Barthelme, among others part of the "experimental" or "metafiction" movement of the sixties and seventies. I knew certainly that "experimental" work was still moving forward somewhere and felt it critical that a publication such as *The Iowa Review* present this work in a special issue.

Many contributed to this issue's success. Special thanks go to *Iowa Review* editors, David Hamilton and Mary Hussmann for considering the idea in the first place; William Gass and Robert Coover for their early support and willingness to work with us in assuring its outcome; Douglas Messerli from the Sun and Moon Press and Curt White from the Fiction Collective Two for recommending the writers who were working with non-traditional narrative forms; and finally and most important are the writers themselves whose work within these pages will most certainly shock and dismay while serving as a stubborn reminder that many a reckless future awaits other rebels wherever they may be.

Lee Montgomery
Topanga Canyon, CA

Introduction: Anywhere but Kansas
William H. Gass

I WAS NEARLY TEN when my parents gave me a chemistry set for Christmas. It came in a handsome wooden box and contained a rack for test tubes, as well as niches where vials of powerful powders might be kept. There was a little packet of sensitive paper (litmus, I think), a knobbed glass rod, the obligatory manual, a metal loop for suspending a test tube over a flame, a conversion table (ounces into spoons), and suitably exciting poison labels. Dreams flew out of that box when its lid was lifted: dreams of bombs and poisons, of plots described in disappearing ink, of odors distressful to the weak. I set up a small lab in the basement and there I performed my experiments. "Performed" was the right word. "Experiment" was not. For I didn't follow the booklet where it led, or listen to its lectures. I slopped about, blending yellow with white and obtaining brown, mixing crystals with powders and getting dust, combining liquids with solids and making mud.

Later, in high school, I would take chemistry the way I took spring tonics and swallowed headache pills. Although I broke beakers and popped little pieces of potassium into puddles of water to watch the water fly, I did occasionally manage to obey tutorial instructions as well, repeating experiments which others had long ago undertaken. My predecessors had asked their questions of Nature with genuine curiosity, and waited, like an eager suitor, her reply. My method displayed a different spirit, which was to fudge my procedures in order to obtain the result already written in the chemmy books. I was not being taught to experiment, or even to repeat experiments. I was being taught to cheat.

An experiment, I would learn much later, when I studied the philosophy of science in graduate school, had to arise from a real dissatisfaction with existing knowledge. There was a gap to be filled, a fracture to be repaired, an opening to be made. Nature's interrogator had to know how to ask the correct question, and to state it so clearly that the answer would be, in effect, an unambiguous "yes" or "no," and not a noddy wobble. Every experiment required a protected environment and an entirely objective frame of mind. The results should be quantifiable, and the process repeatable. Every successful repetition spoke favorably for the quality of the first occasion. Furthermore, experiments were never carried out against the rules, but were performed, like surgery, always well within them, otherwise they would not be recognized as experiments at all.

What is generally called "experimentation" in the arts, more nearly resembles my ignorant and youthful self-indulgent mess-making. I was acting out a fantasy, not learning anything about chemistry, and while every smelly substance I concocted had to have been made according to chemistry's laws, I did not know those laws, nor could I have learned them from anything I was doing. And how many botches have been excused by calling them the results of the experimental spirit? We have to imagine an artist wondering what would happen if she were to do this, try that, perform a play in silence, omit the letter "e" in three pages of French prose, construct a world of clothes-hanger wire, color walls with cow manure. Having found out, though, then what?

A good experiment is as perfect and complete as the Parthenon, but the word, in popular speech, is derogatory, as if the experiment were going to be on the audience. Experiments, moreover, even if elegant and crucial, are admired for their results—the "yes" or "no" they receive—and (except for specialists) not for their procedures. We don't want to read interrogations, we want to read results.

Critics, patrons, academicians, characteristically insecure and immature beneath their arrogant demeanors, are devoted to rules and definitions of decorum. Scarcely has an innovative form, a daring method, a different point of view, established itself than its codification begins: it must be given a catchy name (and labeled "experimental" perhaps, at least avant-garde, or something even trendier such as "existential," "absurd," "metafictional," "minimal," "surreal," "post-mod"); next, its superficial qualities are catalogued (it looks to the future in this respect, remains unchanged in that, returns to the past right here, but seems, at another point, content with the status quo); its cultural links are then explored and evaluated (does it reveal the sorry *Geist* of the *zeit*? does it express malaise? is it symptomatic of some social sickness? is it toughly feminist? is it resolutely gay?); finally it will be given a fresh critical vocabulary, a new jargon to fit this latemost fad like a cowboy boot pulled over a golfing shoe. Since, and sadly, by the relentless use of commandments and plenty of otiose rhetoric, the latest craze can be put in place as quickly as an ugly tract gets built; it is therefore repeatedly necessary for writers to shake the system by breaking its rules, ridiculing its lingo, and disdaining whatever is in intellectual fashion. To follow fashion is to play the pup.

Many fictions which appear to be "experimental" are actually demonstrations. When Galileo dropped his proofs from Pisa's tower, the proof was purely in the seeing. To demonstrate an equal fall for both a lead and paper ball, he'd have had to put Pisa's tower in a vacuum tube and monitor the competitive descent of his samples with instruments more precise than any he had at hand. But that was not the point: the point was the persuasion of the eye and the subversion of a backward principle. If Doctor Johnson claims you can't write a satisfactory poem about a coal mine, the poet is, of course, called upon to write it. Disgracing one more rule won't dissuade everybody of the view that art is made by recipe, because the constitutionally constipated will begin drawing up additional regs at once; but it will encourage the intelligent suspicion that neither by breaking nor abiding is quality achieved.

So "subversive" is often a good name for some of these fictions. Between my muck-about basement days and the discipline provided by my high school class, I enjoyed an interlude as a bomber. With sulfur from my then neglected set, a little potassium nitrate purchased from the pharmacist, and charcoal scraped from any charred board, I discovered that I could make gun powder. By filling pill capsules also obtained at the drug store with my gray mix, and slamming the whole thing with a stone, I could make a very satisfactory bang. It provided me with an exhilarating sense of power. It wasn't long before I was coating wet string with my concoction in order to make a fuse. However, I was open to experiment: sometimes I wet the string and sometimes I made a paste and sometimes I soaked the string in the grainy mixture. Then a toilet tube packed with paper and powder was set off with a sound so violent it shouted of my success.

"Make it new," Ezra Pound commanded, and "innovative" is a good name for some kinds of fiction; however, most newness is new in all the same old ways: falsely, as products are said to be new by virtue of minuscule and trivial additions; or vapidly when the touted differences are pointless; or opportunistic, when alterations are made simply in order to profit from perceived improvements; or if applied like a brand, and meant simply to mark a moment, place, or person off from others, and give it its own identity however dopey.

You may be the first to open a play with the word *merde*; or the first to write of America because you discovered it; or the first to detail the production of ball bearings; or be brave enough to say straight out that, actually, the emperor's new clothes are tacky; or be accounted a pioneer because no one had described, before you, how it is to die of a bad disposition. Perhaps your poem on the taste of sperm will cause another sort of sensation. However, innovation that comes to something is nearly always formal. It is the expression of style at the level of narrative structure and fictional strategy. When we describe a writer's way of writing as individual and unique, we are referring to qualities it is often impossible and always unwise to imitate—Beckett is simply Beckett, Proust Proust—but original as their voices may be, they are not, just for that, innovative, because innovation implies the beginning of a new direction, whereas the style of late James (which I have the good taste to admire) has realized its completion and signifies an end.

The style of *Finnegans Wake* was certainly new and inimitable, but it was the cyclical structure of the work which was innovative; it was the polyphony of the text, the principle of the portmanteau, the landscape of the dream, the text's extraordinary musicality, which provided that wealth of stimulating possibilities for other writers.

There is something to be said for just getting away from it all. Writers begin as readers of a driven and desperate kind. Over the hills and far away, Lady Castlemain is meeting her beau beneath a blooming . . . what? . . . chestnut tree; Horatio Le Paige is pitching his last game, the bases are jammed, his arm is sore, the crowd is on his case, the catcher has called for an illegal pitch, which may be his only way out; Baron Pimple has caught Miss Tweeze without her duenna. Readers begin by wanting to be anywhere but here, anywhere but Kansas, and, when those readers begin writing, a good many of them will want to write anything except what they've been reading, not because some of what they read wasn't wonderful, for once upon an unhappy time it took them anywhere but Kansas, but because such writing had become its own Kansas now, and represented dullness and repression and the damnably indifferent status quo. Anything if it's not normal narrative . . . anything but characters given sunken cheeks and a hard stare, yes, better the Tin Woodsman, better the Bert Lahr lion, but also anything other than the predictable plots and routine scenes, neat outcomes, and conventional values . . . anything but Oz. Transportive fictions make sure of that. Their originality may be secondary to their denial of everyday; their subversive qualities secondary to their profound desire to be anywhere else, anywhere that hasn't Aunt Em, anywhere not over that sentimental rainbow, anywhere so long as it's not to a sequel.

Many times metafictions, because they caressed themselves so publicly, behaved more like manifestos than stories. They were more "explanatory" than "experimental." Instead of showing that something could be done by doing it, they became tutorial, emphasizing technique; teaching the reader how to read; admonishing him for his traditional bourgeois expectations; and directing his attention to art instead of nature, to the reality of the work instead of the reality of the world. That has always been a lesson more than hard to learn, for most people prefer to duck the difficult tedia of daily life, and ask that their experience of the wider world be filtered through layers of sensational detail and false feeling—hence neither living right nor reading well.

Exploding toilet paper tubes had been such a noisy success, I moved on to lead pipe. Into a piece I had found which was about six inches long and half an inch in diameter, I packed plenty of powder, tamping it down with the wooden handle of a small screwdriver, and then closing up both ends with thin, minutely folded, layers of cardboard. Set off by fuse alongside a neighbor's house where I stuck one end in some soft ground like a flare, it exploded with a smoky roar that could be heard for blocks, and fragments of pipe flew everywhere, a large shard penetrating the wall of my friend's front room. I ran as if riding the wind. I believed I heard sirens—police after me? firemen to the house? my father rising toward the higher elevations of his rage? Ah, we do like to fancy our books are bombs, but bombs, we need to remember, in order to make a great show—do their damage, prove a point, teach some slow wit a lesson—have to blow themselves to bits and pieces first.

When learning to play any instrument well, to wrestle, lift weights, dance, sing, write, it is wise to exercise. Try describing a hat in such a way the reader will realize its wearer has just had her dog run over. Practice putting your life into the present tense where you presumably lived it. Do dialogue—let's say—between a hobo and a high class hooker, then between an ambulance chaser and a guy who sells scorecards at the ballpark—let's say—about the meaning of money. Between pints, get the arch of the dart down pat. Shoot foul shots day in and rim out. Pick a sentence at random from a randomly selected book, and another from another volume also chosen by chance; then write a paragraph which will be a reasonable bridge between them. And it does get easier to do what you have done, sing what you've so often sung; it gets so easy, sometimes, that what was once a challenge passes over into thoughtless routine. So the bar must be raised a few notches, one's handicap increased, the stakes trebled, tie both hands behind your back. Refuse the blindfold, refuse the final cigarette, refuse the proffered pizza. Do dialogue in dialect: a Welshman and a Scot arguing about an onion. Hardest of all: start over.

Of course, if you feel you have mastered at least some of your medium, you can improvise—take its risks and enjoy its pleasures. Now you trust yourself to go the right way like a roach to the kitchen, as if by instinct: taking off from an idle word, a casual phrase, a small exchange between disillusioned lovers, a notion about narrative time you got while reading Bergson, an item in the morning paper; then letting the music lead, a surprising association rule, or a buried meaning rise raw and green and virile as a weed, until the rhythm of the sentence settles in, the idea begins to unfold like a flower, time finds itself without hands, a character begins to speak in an unfamiliar tongue, and the shape of the scene is in front of you—nothing to it—you modify the metaphor, vary the normal flow of feeling . . . yes, it is certainly lovely, the facility between give and go, the rapport you have with your material, ease of flow . . . yet one person's grateful pee is not another's—that's a law about all calls of nature— accordingly, the improviser must be careful to make his modulations, like those riffy moments in music, so splendid they shall not seem contrived, and the best way to do that is to contrive them.

As the reader will surely see, some of the stories in this collection are honestly experimental, a few are demonstrations, others are designed for subversion, not a small number teach, one or two are truly innovative, and I detect signs of improvisation here and there, the energy of exercise, satire's smile, fantasy's furbelows and feathers, novelty's enterprise, the sweat of concision; and, of course, most pieces are a mix of this or that, with even a little of the calm and customary to cool the dish. The intention I rather prefer, among this quiver load of paranormal approaches, is the exploratory, although the word suggests surgery, and as a label is no more suited to the totality of its subject than "innovative," "subversive," or "experimental" are.

The explorer sees in front of him an unknown territory, an unmapped terrain, or he imagines there must be somewhere a new route to the Indies, another polar star, gorgons alive and well amid jungle-covered ruins, mountain views and river sources grander than the Nile's, lost tribes, treasure, or another, better, way of life; because he is searching, not inventing; he is trying to find what is already there: regions of life as neglected as his own history, themes as far from general attention as a cavern at the bottom of the sea, structures as astounding as those which show up stained in tissue slices. Explorational fiction records an often painful and disappointing journey, possibly of discovery, possibly of empty sailing; yet never toward what may lie out of sight in the self, since that is what improvisation discloses, but of what lies still unappreciated in the landscape of literature—implications unperceived, conclusions undrawn, directions everyone has failed to follow. The spirit of the explorer may be indeed to scalpel society and show its rotting organs, nor is every implication nice as toast with tea; however the key to this kind of fiction is that the chest, which the existence of the key suggests, must be (or be believed to be) there in six feet of sand beneath the bolt-scarred tree. In that sense, exploration is the work of a realist, however fanciful that reality may seem to those encountering it for the first time.

Maybe we can pun our way to another genre, in as much as labels seem to matter more than their jar. The prefix "ex-"apparently has to be there, since we already have the "explanatory," the "experimental" and "exploratory," as well as the sweat from "exercise." Nevertheless, we ought not to be tied tamely to the past. How about "innoversive fiction"? I like the "metamusical" myself. "Excremental" belongs to Joyce. "Minnovative" describes a movement whose small moment has come and gone. "Exploramental" makes me think of "florabunda," though I do fancy "post-cynical" and could easily find a use for "metafutile." Remember when all we had to worry about were the Yellow Press, Blue Movies, and Black Humor?

I could see a plume of gray smoke when I looked back toward my imagined pursuers, and my legs grew longer through every lope (I had experimented, I had made my exclamation point, and I was now being taught), nor did I begin to gasp for breath and feel my blood beating hard in my head, until I had run right out of my neighborhood and saw a strange little shop and strange houses of one story, strange streets lined with

shallow ditches, lots of transplanted Christmas trees, a strange black
boat-tailed bird, strange absence of lamps, and felt I had found a country
where every noun began with "strange" and "and" was its only connective
. . . my boom had blown me farther than the pieces of its pipe . . . to a
strange, yes . . . to a strange strange lampless land.

Before the Days of Dreaming · *Kathy Acker*

O:

"How can I do this? Begin.

"Begin what?

"The only thing in the world that's worth beginning: the end of the world."

O, being a whore, had to find the origin of whoredom.

.   .   .   .

Alexandra, one of Cleopatra's friends, had loved Cleopatra so deeply that she had tried to persuade Anthony to be both kind and gentle to his paramour's children.

In order to please Alexandra, the first princess, Herod the Great had made her seventeen-year-old son into a priest. The boy was beautiful. Herod drowned him.

Of this Alexandria, no longer anything remains.

O remembered the poet saying that Alexandria is replete with men who are sick, solitary, and prophetic. All those who have been deeply wounded in their sex. When O came to Alexandria, the air was as dry as the wings of insects. There were neither male solitaries nor male prophets. For such men are found only in the white world and that world has died.

Here, O thought, lies the center of all prostitution.

.   .   .   .

O began to dream that she was in the whorehouse for which she had been looking. She wasn't anywhere yet. She had already passed by "The Brothel Of The Virgins."

O:

"I entered the most famous whorehouse in Alexandria.

"These are the names of some of the whores:

"Whore #1, Ange, 21 years old, politically mature, a professional imagination, a sweetheart only when she comes into contact with children, or with anyone (men, women, or other categories, sedentary, semisedentary, and nomadic) uninterested in money. Ange lucidly believes in the progress of this country.

"I HAVE NEVER FORGOTTEN HER.

"Two years ago, Ange was put into the prison of M____. There, though still lucid and generous, she was broken. I saw her bruises.

"Thus, in shit begins the new world.

"Whore #2, Barbara, in older days left Egypt for France in order to continue her studies. Classical ones. Some days off the ship in the harbor of Marseilles, to her consternation she learned that she would have to do whatever she would have to do in order to survive there, and so she returned to her activities of the night. What I am saying is that in order to earn the right to education in the western world, it was necessary for the whores who were not from the western world to be at war and to continue teaching themselves.

" 'You fuckers.' Said Barbara. Finally sick of whoring; every morning, to earn her right to education, she got up at four, in order, for the rest of the day, to work her ass off in the shipyards of Midnight-by-the-Sea. A machine cut off her right foot; despite that or in despite, whenever possible from then on, she came to the aid, effectively and materially, of those whose social origin was named <u>Misery</u>. Misery due to exile. Exile, whose other name is <u>Delayed Death</u>, is the fate of all those who live in the realm of racism.

"Barbara, now known as St. Barbara, again inhabits an Alexandrian whorehouse.

"Whore #3. She sleeps all the time. Her name is Louise Vanaen de Voringhem. While she's sleeping, her record player blares. Not that she's got anything against music. But she has to sleep because she's been so worn down by work.

"Some day Louise Vanaen will have to get up, and one day she did. Because her body wanted to wake. Immediately she walked toward the source of her music. Suddenly she was thrown to the ground and cut in her left eye. A neighbor, one of the many Algerians Armenians Bedouins Egyptians Vietnamese surrounding the brothel, hearing screams which he recognized as unusual, ran over to the house, gun in hand. In order to defend herself, with this neighbor's help, she mortally wounded her attacker by cutting off his balls.

"For this reason, Sister Louise was inculpated of voluntary homicide. For this reason: she was Arab and her rapist was white. Since only her natal family was allowed to visit her there and they lived far away, Louise Vanaen dwelled in solitary for many years.

"Her family was poor.

"In her prison, the whore Louise Vanaen began to dream of a revolution, a revolution of whores, a revolution defined by all methods that exist as distant as far as is possible from profit.

".   .   .   .   .

"Louise wrote this to her sisters:

" 'These pages smell of women.

" 'I perceive more clearly during sex. All the lips, all the fists: it's necessary to have the deepest discipline so that all these, so that everything, can be seen. In the brothel where women are talking, where the women are cooking, lips on lips, hands on hands, all the world is at peace.

" 'In these rooms of sleep and of dream,' she continued in another of her letters which will become famous after history has gone to sleep, 'we will walk around, brushing by each other, touching each other without actually touching, there we shall affirm everyone, even flesh that is bourgeois, the flesh that likes to be done but not to do, the flesh that is the object of desires.'

"From these letters, St. Barbara developed her political theory of religion: Every revolution starts in a church or in the place of the church because churches and brothels do not have windows that lead to what lies outside. And so are refuges to all the shipwrecked of the world.

"To you, Barbara, courage. Courage for all of you, the generosity that inhabits prostitution."

"I've been so tired lately," Lulu, another prostitute complained, "that nothing turns me on."

Ange replied, "That's the fate of all of us who are prostitutes."

Lulu and Ange decided to masturbate so they could find a reason to live.

Lulu, starting to masturbate: "My mind's all over the place so I can't do this right now."

After some time had passed, she said, "No. Not now."

Ange, who was doing the same thing, muttered, "Me too."

Lulu: "Now we're entering the night."

Entering the night resembled entering a room. Entering through the narrow doorways, the room could be glimpsed. The halls' walls were pale green (a lighter green than the color of the walls of most of childhood). Lulu: "Here's a toilet. No, I don't want a toilet. Now, turn the door's handle and walk in. It's necessary to sidle in sideways.

"Why did I just stop feeling anything? . . ."

In order to live, Lulu needed to be in the realm of sex.

Lulu:

"Body, talk.

"While I masturbate, my body says: Here's a rise. The whole surface, ocean, is rippling, a sheet that's metal, wave after wave. As it (what's this it?) moves toward the top, as if toward the neck of a vase, it crushes against itself moving inward and simultaneously it increases in sensitivity. The top of the vase, circular, is so sensitive that all feelings, now circling around and around, all that is moving, are now music.

"Music is my landscape.

"Deep down, at the bottom. Whatever is bottom is so deep that it is spreading away from its center. . . . Toward what? Opening up to whom? Opening up only to sensitive. Sensation is the lover.

"If I could move down there, down this rabbit's hole, I would never stop coming

"never never

"and I want to come and come and come

". . . why? . . .

"The middle ring or the ring around the middle of the shaft is doing most of the feeling, but now it's slipping downward. If this tunnel, which the ring's slipping down, becomes rigid, there won't be any more sensation. No sensation is nothing. If this tunnel becomes rigid, there'll be nothing. I must make my world out of nothing. Relaxation's opening the field, but I don't dare, I'm holding back, open to being a rose; a rose unfolds again and again until the nerves drive the flesh into pure nerves; they are; I'm closing again (becoming rigid): these are the rhythms of the labyrinth.

"The vibrations (pleasure) are taking over. Now any desire to stop . . . oh yes, there it goes; this disappearance of it causes laughter; laughter is a threshold that's soon reached.

"As soon as I went over this threshold, for the first time I began to play; I was opening and opening to the point that I could touch being pure nerves.

"In the realm of being pure nerves, to touch is to be touched: every part of mind, body, and feeling is relaxing so much that sensation has domain. When I came, the spasms traveled all the way down the funnel until its bottom where there was an opening. Then or there, everything disappeared; the world or everything became more sexual.

"My hole opened up into only opening; the vibrations intensified.

"Soon this world will be nothing but pleasure, the world in which we live and are nothing but desires for more intense and more intense joy.

"I want more now, I want every rose, all the major rows down there, but something is always going over. Again again. An animal. It would always come again: the animal claw."

Thus Lulu entered the labyrinth.

She taught the whores to do this and all of them began to masturbate regularly.

Lulu said, "I want to talk about being a criminal because that's the only thing that makes sense to me."

Ange says to Lulu:

"Today I had to come by reading pornography.

"First, I took any book and just opened it. I was only going to read a few sentences until I became wet enough for my dildo to slip easily into my cunt. But the first sentence I read was about a woman who was beautiful and older seducing a very young boy who was just so hot for her that he would have come even if she had done nothing. This sentence turned me on to such an extent that I couldn't remain at the edge of the text, I had to enter into the words and this entering, as I sat there with a dildo up my cunt, I think that that must look ugly, was a moving into the halls, with all their walls, there, of my rising sexual energies. I don't think that this space which I was now in was my body . . .

"I wasn't in a body, but in a place.

"In my cunt, there's a little animal, a type of fish, but it's a mammal. A weasel-cat. The weasel-cat, who's hungry, is sticking out its tongue . . .

"And so I came without language.

"My whole cunt is now this animal who's becoming hungrier: mouth opens more widely, the clit is a tongue which licks, laps, is tapping like a foot, tapping what's outside as if a floor. Eyes lie above this tongue. All my sensations are a sky. I could no longer talk. As soon as I stopped talking, everything turned white and the waves that were approaching, slowly, steadily, and very strongly, solid, solid, transformed into my blood, then into my bones; whatever had been the rhythms of my body inside my body were now rhythms outside. This is the meaning of <u>mantra</u>. The final orgasm will occur when my brains are making mantra."

Lulu says to Ange: "I would smear the whole world with sperm."

Here finally are the days of the beginning of happiness when the heat and the yellow are dry. When the spine's bottom rises up from its body:

"No," says one whore, "I'm not going to masturbate today because inside my cunt, the well where all is bottomless, has come out so far, as if an animal is moving out of the hole, that I'm turning inside-out. I'm scared. I'm scared . . . that if that happens . . . god knows what might happen, I'll never be able to stop coming so it'll have to be a new kind of world . . .

"But I don't know if I can give up the pleasure of masturbating even for a day."

St. Barbara was the first callgirl to tell a client to go get fucked so that she could continue masturbating:

"Old-Filthy-Husband-Who-Kills-Off-Wives (this was a common term for 'husband' in Alexandria as in many of the third world cultures who lacked the benefits of contemporary civilization), Old-Scum-Tongue-Who-Can-Only-Lick-Off-Wives, under whose armpits lies pollen, Azzefonian, you're just about to depart for the seas of Europe. Right?"

"Right," Azzefonian answered.

"Well, those waters stink of the dead cunts of white women or the cunts of dead white women and other strange fish that cause diarrhea, whereas our cunts, O Legba Eleggua La Flambeau La Sirène, O Legba You who are truly us, our cunts are made from the sun and out of rubies. Cunts to whom we gave birth in the foyer of the end of the world. Our cunts are knives in our fists and the insides of our thighs are becoming darker.

"Come inside; come inside."

Azzefonian, in love with white, went off to Europe.

Finally free of johns, the whores, now alone, spewed out bits of ink, words in ink, sexual or filthy words, words that were formed by scars and wounds especially those of sexual abuse, those out of childhood. All the women bore their wounds as childhoods. Therefore, words apocalyptic and apostrophic, punctuations only as disjunctions, disjunctions or cuts into the different parts of the body or of the world, everything priced and priced until, finally, all the numbers disappeared and were displaced by the winds:

Ventre, vente, vent.

These were only some of the elements of whore writing: all will never be named, for both word and self (whore) are always being lost because it is the winds who screw them.

—end of the first whore-song

O now began to masturbate full-time, imagining every sailor, cock, hairs dripping from cock when wet, cats crawled out of the dark room, foetus. O:

"Now it's starting again the sensation is deep down have to keep it there, deep down open, or else it (or all or I) will stop. The problem is the rigidity of everything and, above all, this must be prevented.

"A map of rigidities: the world has stopped. All feeling has gone. What did I do wrong or what went wrong?

"Feeling or sensation evaporates whenever the feeler (the subject here is the object) tries to perceive and understand a particular feeling or sensation.

"This doesn't make sense anymore because I'm feeling too much. Any feeling is feeling too much.

"It is all over. The world has stopped. Then another round of feeling, like a wave, rises under the most recent, retreating wave. Each new wave is bigger and stronger.

"I think about him. Any thought or agitation which lies outside feeling, outside the (subject/object) mirror, causes cessation.

"oh yes baby starting to come too excited shaking eyes going (fading) regular spasms contraction mouth is smiling going yes yes wants no open stay open I didn't expect to come and I am now squeezing all of legs and thighs around wrist while inside, in there, all the shakes

"I'm going to come harder now, in there, no end in sight

"sailing, each series, starting with a high rise then swoop downward, each one more violent, direct

"where is there an end to these convulsions?

"Being with someone would be more violent.

"I will turn, again, to dreams

"the ocean; all the fish go crazy; see them all orange

"now this final orgasm all stirred up: the walls become rigid and in between there's burning

"today there's no end

"now I have to use my fingers to masturbate.

"Later the convulsions increased.

"After this, the whores accepted me as one of them."
                    —end of the second whore-song

THE ENTRANCE OF THE PUNK BOYS

Among a hundred brothers him I greet
Who ate my heart and I his heart did eat.

According to the first of the punk boys, the body is still in a process of being forged.

Especially his body (his name was Antonin Artaud) which was thin nasty sick mangled distorted ravaged by drugs and by desires which had been repressed by thoughts.

The body, Artaud further said, has an infinite capacity for self-transformation.

17

Artaud actually talked in a much more disgusting manner, just like the rest of his brethren, the dirty filthy boys.

All of the punk boys had fucked their mothers and were no longer colonized. They didn't care.

The growth of private property, one characteristic of the bourgeois industrial world, had died; private property, in the form of multi-national and ex-national capital, returned to the hands of the few. Economic, therefore political, power seemed centralized. The decrease, finally the disappearance, of private property was directly related to a movement away from, then to the disappearance of the memory of, patriarchy.

The punks were one beginning of a new world.

Though these punks were at the edges of a beginning of a new world, they had no idea how to relate to each other. For them, language wasn't a problem.

He was the proto-punk boy, but Artaud was the one whom the punk boys disavowed. He was continually fighting off drugs and so wanted to destroy everything. Like him, all of the punk boys wanted to destroy.

They disavowed history, but they were the direct descendants of Heliogabalus of Alexandria who had been made Emperor at fourteen years of age. Heliogabalus despised his government and was anarchistic. His reign was replete with murder, incest, and the lack of values.

The Alexandrian police cut apart Heliogabalus when he was eighteen years old, in the toilets of his own palace, and then threw his corpse outside on the dirt where two dogs happened to be pissing.

To be kissed by a punk boy was to be drawn to insanity or toward death. The last of the race of white men.

And to fuck one of them, said a girl who was doing just that, is to be drawn into murder.

Perhaps this was what happened to the prostitutes. They didn't commence their violent actions because they had started masturbating. As O had thought. They began because the punk boys came to town and the whores got touched by these boys.

The punks taught the whores: "We're not free because, at any moment, the sky could explode into shreds of flesh . . .

"Europe is far away . . . farther because the civilized West has disappeared . . . already shreds of flesh . . . without any explosion."

The punks further said, "Terror is the answer for our times because we, whores and punks, cannot liberate ourselves by running away from horror, a horror that is nameless."

"But," O replied, "I've already lived through horror. I won't know where prostitution came from until I get rid of it.

"My mother's inside me. She wants me to suicide because she suicided. I could, to try to find a father so there would be no more mother, but there are no fathers around."

All of the whores agreed with O: it was the end of the white world.

IN ORDER TO FIGURE OUT HOW TO STOP BEING A PROSTITUTE, O told her best friend, Ange, a story about St. Gall Bladder:

"Until the world of water, earth, air, and light begins, all there can be is desire for water, earth, air, and light.

"St. Gall Bladder was running in the mountains. He was traveling through forests. In the woods, the dew dripped out of the cedars; hard, stiff stalks vibrated in the scintillating light. St. Gall Bladder stood up to his knees in dead spiders, mosses, saliva; soon all was a clarity: gold light and liquid. The gold of the air was that of the water.

"Below the cedars, bits of insect wings were lying on the high-tension cables; around the poles, the grass was virgin.

"St. Gall Bladder fell asleep on what was virgin.

"When St. Gall Bladder woke out of his dream of loneliness, he decided that it was time for him to return to the human world. He felt that now it was time for him to become nothing, to give everything away, and to go down into blackness, that blackness which is called the world that is under.

" 'When I'm nothing,' he added, 'I'll become human.'

"St. Gall Bladder went down and met some whores who were spread out on the ground. He walked up to them. During the Algerian war, a bullet had blown part of his left thigh into a hole. So when one of the two prostitutes raised her eyes to him, she just as quickly lowered them.

"He seated himself between the two. 'I entreat you, my sisters, be true to the earth. Do not believe those who speak to you of superterrestrial hopes.

" 'In times that were past, the soul looked contemptuously down at the body. This contempt was the supreme virtue.'

"As the saint was talking, the young girl took up one of the hands of her lover, whose name was Ange, and held it. Fingers which trembled while held down in that valley which felt like sand, where the sea began, then explosion after explosion made the world tremble.

"St. Gall Bladder's eyes were gleaming with wet dreams; he watched everything carefully.

"The whores explained to the saint that they were voyaging to the end of the night.

"One of them placed her swollen membranes over the saint's face and the other licked his cock. For there was no way to be a whore anymore.

"Then they told him about the origin of prostitution: 'We, and all the other prostitutes, come from the city of KaWeDe where mothers eat their own children and afterwards fuck dogs. Now, it's time for us to go back, for all whores to go back, for whores to return to their origins.

" 'Go to KaWeDe and tell them that Hell is coming to them. Inform them that we are coming. That we're going back to the source of prostitution and that only a saint who has had his day can be our messenger.' "

St. Gall Bladder became the messenger of revolution and the women set the brothel on fire. Flames leapt from this building to nearby buildings to edifice after edifice. When there was nothing left that could burn in the city, the flames shifted toward the forest. Turning trees and air into black smoke, the fire touched the doves in their flight, the vultures, and threw them, as they lacked breath, against the sun. Fire ate at the feet of the animals who were racing, nostrils as wide open as mouths stuffed with living coals: the whole mountain was blazing.

Aware that he was beginning to suffocate, for Bladder was now journeying through this forest, he retired into the bathroom of the hut that was formerly his heritage. He picked up his own shit, rubbed it into his face, for he was a saint. Then Gall Bladder threw himself into the source of the river that ran through the woods. A gun, which had been left by a murderer, to his own eye.

"Enough blood. Enough hatred. Turn to water. Turn cocks into water."

The moment that his face touched the water, the saint shot himself. Blood spurted out of the skin, reddening the river burning under the smoke; his head rolled ball-like through the underwater billows while above, lions, serpents, pigs, even vultures, all chased by heat and smoke, passed and were passed by each other.

The corpse of the father was turning into water:

The crayfish hid under the dead man's armpits and orange fish nibbled at his lips . . .

The whores are drunk.

MOST OF THE WHORES LEFT THE CITY WHICH HAD BURNT DOWN. Ange, O's friend, remained in this space which would soon no longer be human.

It was here that O dreamed her last dream about her self and her friend:

"John, finger-fuck O." Said Ange. Ange was directing her first play, perhaps in what had been the brothel's theatre. And John was O's closest male Alexandrian friend's boyfriend.

The boy slowly inserted one of his middle fingers between O's thick outer labia. "Is this OK?"

"OK," said O.

She was wearing a Kotex pad and the black cotton panties that she always had on whenever she had her period. These were the only panties O owned which didn't disappear into the crack of her ass.

John screwed in his finger as far as he could. He knew how to do this so that a woman felt pleasure, pleasure as if every type of pleasure was coexisting yet separate from every other type in the same space.

Neither John nor O were upset by her blood.

John ordered O to suck his fingers which, having been up her cunt, were now soaked in blood. O couldn't tell if these fingers were still up there. She didn't mind licking them over and over again.

O drew away from John. Now she was conscious—if her mind was eyes, a veil had been drawn away from her eyes—that she was experiencing sexual delight in a public space and that this was wrong. One shouldn't open up sexually, in public, to a man one didn't know, when one was bleeding. Nevertheless she was doing this. And adoring this. In other words: what was clearly happening, with her, couldn't possibly be happening.

Everything was happening, as it always does, sexually.

John bit down hard on the tips of her nipples and bit down hard again. O felt joy. She knew he was at the edge of fucking her. She didn't want him to fuck her because she was in a classroom and exposed to all the students and blood was showing everywhere but the outer strips of her thighs.

It was the beginning of the night when Ange asked her why she hadn't let herself be fucked. She knew that O wanted desperately to fuck.

O thought about this question. She decided that she must be a victim, though she had never before thought that she was a victim, a victim of her society's definition of women who were her age. These women, according to the society, were no longer sexually desirable to men, except perhaps as prostitutes, more important, they no longer possessed sexuality.

O realized that the women who were two or three generations younger than she were far more intelligent than the women her age.

Now night had come to the dead city and lay everywhere.

O found herself in the middle of one of its great streets. She was walking down the middle, as if she was a car or a motorcycle.

Somewhere in her O knew that it was dangerous for her to act like a motorcycle. She had thought that the middle lane, the one whose middle she was in, was going to disappear just as it did, so just as it became one of the other lanes, O swerved into the right lane.

Safely, she reached the bottom of the great thoroughfare. There Ange was waiting for her, though O hadn't expected to see her friend ever again. In the deserted city.

"Stay with me, O. Here."

There had been a previous arrangement between O and a man whose name she didn't know to meet, at this very hour, in the tenderloin district. O remained with Ange.

The two women were already walking. O was upset that she was missing her appointment with an older man, because she couldn't be worried about that, because she had to do something about the blood. She wasn't wearing anything so, at any moment, blood was going to seep through her clothes into the outside.

She remembered that there was a pharmacy on the corner, down the street from the department store where she had planned to meet _____.

Instead of walking toward this department store, Ange and O moved in the other direction, across the principal street that crossed the one down which O had been running. Into the darkest and most deserted part of the burnt-down city.

This was where the artists lived.

In the gigantic pharmacy that was situated in this district, O was looking up at a glass counter top that was far above her. She saw a pile of Tampax. The Tampax was Indian because it hadn't been boxed and because it was wrapped in only the thinnest and cheapest colorless paper. This covering, in spots, was torn.

Since O couldn't buy the Tampax because she thought that it might be diseased, she asked the woman behind the glass counter if the pharmacy had anything else for periods.

An emaciated blonde pointed to wood shelves which were so high that their tops and bottoms had disappeared. They stood behind O. On one of the higher shelves lay a jumbo box of Kotex. Pads so huge they must have been designed for elephants.

"You see, O," the salesgirl said, "you could have gotten fucked even though you had your period."

Everything about the restaurant to which the older man took O spoke of wealth and the upper classes. The man turned out to be a professor whom O had once met, one of the most respected teachers in the country and a novelist. Unlike the other ones who had fucked O, in the recent past, whom she could remember, this man treated her gently and with respect.

It was toward the end of their meal that he pulled her toward him, across a red leather couch on which they were still sitting.

The hands that were holding her head pushed her head down to where she saw a cock that wasn't human. That was small, very pointed at the end, a ring of flesh around its middle, white rather than red. Like a cat's. O put her mouth around it. She didn't think that anyone in the restaurant, especially their waiter, was noticing her disappearance or the head, beneath the white-cloth-covered table top, down in the realm that lay under.

When everything was over, she raised her head and saw that the man had changed: he was smiling angelically; the hair on his head, once scanty and white, was now very thick, black, an Afro, like what white liberals once wore.

O was feeling sick. She realized that having had this sex during which she had never lost consciousness made her queasy. Such sex was immoral. Whereas the sex during the sex show had sent her over the edge, over every edge, over her self, flying, until all that was left was sky and blackness. During the loss of herself, 'she' had become scared. O realized that she wanted this sex, that she needed it, this sexuality that she had known when she had been a whore.

O, the Jew, told herself, I have to go back to my roots.

From a Work in Progress · *George Angel*

WE RISE. Were there but two things, to hold in each hand. We know that we speak, I to the face of the clouds where I have drawn your voice, slipping the drawer back flush with the seamless world were I we. Holding first I within then I within, lift this we lift just once. The trees are filled with birds and it is time to write this. Where am I? I am here, out in the tall yellow grass that is a sheet. It seems that it is possible to slide down the sheet and that the hillside itself will give a little beneath my weight. This is important. Standing at the bottom of this valley talking up through. It could be any place I have exhausted with walking words. Making ladders out of the distance between two mouths. Pulling clouds along. Whisper and then the breeze. If we make. In it moving my hands as connective tissue between moments said and making the mouth mouthing like some somber stupidity. Ladders made of the shapes of bottles and the word mandolin. Make a simple detail, crushing it like the stone mouth. Make words to make words. Slice the crushed bits of nothing into objects and movements. If we move. The day continues to diminish in the stone world of grass.

A black ball, pincushioned by yellow sticks pointing out then back in. A ball of pins on the blue. The green became the glare pressing. It recedes just beyond the face, leaving the world the color of mustard. A man's body is the letter u beneath this ball, my body is. Such is starting to look, planted. Lying down walking and the knowing of things in white ordinary cloth. Away toward leaving to the small black marks on the ground at some distance, their walking and mine up through impossible trees, their branches. When waiting moves branches occur. So I approach what I would ask to turn with my hand. The miracles are modest and asking is lost. This word that carries its weight: lost. We are lifted to humility. The roads braid, all walked at once. Things are filtered from me, there is no denying this. The discovery of walking is relentless. This small stream has hidden a song of praise under its movement. The generous seed of things seems but a few steps away. Brown has become green and the blue reflected from the light. Healed by silent ordinances, I would remain in silence. Small words lift the dialogue from its bed. Simplicity and complexity are two steps which follow each other endlessly. The stone mouth has let the stream slip from its lip.

Light is pulled along the surface of this stream. It is single and insoluble and as it skates is twined about rocks splitting the water. Carapace, or anger attic anguish, dear peace. Cuticle and face, the blood beneath the light shown ordered, the armored crease. Rocks and numbers line the bed of the stream. Creviced sevens, curl gone beneath the lie of light. The loss in the pleasure of mysterious pulp, enumerate its flicker. My imaginings take shape in the soft mud and then recede shapeless.

In the cradle of my distance from things, the body is turned over and receives the gift of unintelligible sounds. The secret tendernesses of a web of sounds. Movement so small. The source will not belittle the caress and rather becomes entangled by it. Mystery is carried by small bodies dispersing in a mystery of circles whose impoverished light renders even their faces inscrutable.

O spiral. Silver voices broke away from me and became like buttresses to you. The broken body wanders unable to find your base, while I have woven a thicket to embrace. Mouth of branches I have made, sing! Sing this space between and lifting. Wings will catch upon your face and stay. Risen to the artifice of things of themselves generated. The dark shapes of birds glide across a cloud backlit by the fallen sun as it gathers its light. Two of them break away while the other four slip silently to the ground. A figure in a tree near my name. In its mouth a stone. The light has touched the ground and cleared a space as it devours shapes of trees and animals and voices along the horizon. A figure spreads its wings. One is of flesh and one is of water. I have made these trees bear hooves and fins and hands. This cloud begins to wrap its wisps around the light. A figure has spread its wings, one is dirt and one is dissipating steam. There, a sound. This cloud has covered the sun, and what is touched is lost. Amid the specificity of leaves in the darkness, my figure is lost.

Live light hidden between the fingers of cones fallen to the ground. Not here. But hand means. The sun and I grasp at things through walls. Empty arguments, principality gathering. The broken weather drops its gifts where every moment feeds. Walking beyond them to the edge of an unburdened sound. Lurching, lifted, worded, my mere imagining of it stands unseen. I know that there is a sum of things and that it falls. Arrowing, emerging, gardened presentiments. Drawn together, a flower's firm walking, in a crown of seeds.

I am standing on a small rise beside a stand of trees and I apologize.

Walking, gathering steps, I'll disperse them to where they were. There is no gold in light and I can only take three or four steps toward the dark. It holds me until I clothe myself again in trees that are no longer perfectly blind. I can't hear what they say above me at night. I knew the breeze moved in the open mouth of sight. Talking, until I saw their branches realigned. Where I slept, beneath, the air was filled with bark. Lit by nothing I knew, I saw things stir. I walked here again, the trees close their ring of arms and memorize.

Day will destroy the eyes of delight. Red will cut two leafveined lids from joy. New words will play and lack and undo. This last read stay will unhook away. Bright blooms return and spoke each rim's ray. They dim to stand burning a blind height. A dome where lipped light lifted to kiss. Blue incline black distinct birds flew through. Employ the leaves to seed what was said. Sight was likewise spread and could not say.

Closing Out the Visit · *John Barth*

GOOD VISIT, WE AGREE—fine visit, actually, weatherwise and otherwise, everything considered—but as with all visits agreeable and disagreeable its course has run. Time now to get our things together, draw down
our stock of consumables, tidy up our borrowed lodgings, savor one last
time the pleasures of the place, say good-bye to acquaintances we've made,
and move along.

"The *light*," you want to know: "Have we ever seen such light?"

We have not, we agree—none better, anyhow, especially in these
dew-bedazzled early mornings and the tawny late afternoons, when sidelit
trees and beachfront virtually incandesce, and the view from our rented
balcony qualifies for a travel poster. That light is a photon orgy; that light
fires the prospect before us as if from inside out. Mediterranean, that light
is, in its blue-white brilliance, Caribbean in its raw tenderness, yet
paradoxically desert-crisp, so sharp-focusing the whole surround that we
blink against our will. That light thrills—and puts us poignantly in mind of
others who in time past have savored the likes of it and are no more: the late
John Cheever, say, in whose stories light is almost a character, or the
nineteenth-century Luminist painters, or for that matter the sun-drunk
Euripides of *Alcestis*: "O shining clear day, and white clouds wheeling in the
clear of heaven!"

"Such light."

Major-league light. This over breakfast bagels and coffee on the balcony
—the end of these Wunderbägeln, freckled with sesame- and poppyseed, as
good as any we've tasted anywhere, fresh-baked in the little deli that we
discovered early on in the village not far inshore from "our" beach. So let's
polish off this last one, to use up the last of our cream cheese and the final
dablet of rough-cut marmalade lifted from the breakfast place downstairs
along with just enough packets of coffee sweetener—raw brown sugar for
me, low-cal substitute for you—to go with the ration of House Blend coffee
that we bought from that same jim-dandy deli on Day One, when we were
stocking up for our stay. Can't take 'em with us.

"Have we measured out our life in coffee spoons?"

We have, come to that, and canny guesstimators we turn out to have
been. No more than a potsworth over, two at most, which we'll leave for

the cleanup crew along with any surplus rum, wine, mineral water, fruit juices, hors d'oeuvres, what have we, and I'll bet that the lot won't total a tipsworth by when we've had our last go-round at this afternoon's end, checkout time. Adiós, first-rate bagels and cream cheese and marmalade, fresh-squeezed juice and fresh-ground coffee, as we've adiósed already our fine firm king-size bed: Here's to sweet seaside sleep, with ample knee- and elbow-room for separateness sans separation! Here's to the dialogue of skin on sufficient square footage of perfect comfort so that the conversation begins and ends at our pleasure, not at some accidental bump in the night. Hasta la vista, maybe, in this instance, as it has become almost our habit here, after an afternoon's outdoorsing, to relish a roll in the air-conditioned hay between hot-tub time and happy hour.

Our last post-breakfast swim! No pool right under our balcony where we'll be this time tomorrow (no balcony, for that matter), nor world-class beach a mere pebblesthrow from that pool, nor world-girdling ocean just a wave-lap from that beach, aquarium-clear and aquarium-rich in calendar-quality marine life for our leisurely inspection and inexhaustible delight; no scuba gear needed, just a snorkel mask fog-proofed with a rub of jade- or sea-grape leaf from the handsome natural beachscape round about us.

Now, then: Our pool-laps lapped, which is to be our first next pleasure on this last A.M. of our visit (not forgetting the routine and parenthetical but no less genuine satisfactions of post-breakfast defecation in our separate bathrooms and stretching exercises on the bedroom wall-to-wall: Let's hear it for strainless Regularity and the ever-fleeting joy of able-bodiedness!)? A quick reconnaissance, perhaps, of "our" reef, while we're still wet? Bit of a beachwalk, maybe, upshore or down? Following which, since this visit has been by no means pure vacation, we'll either "beach out" for the balance of the morning with some serious reading and note-taking or else put in a session at our make-do "desks" (balcony table for you, with local whelk- and top-shells as paperweights; dinette table for me, entirely adequate for the work we brought along) before we turn to whatever next wrap-up chore or recreation—not forgetting, en passant, to salute the all but unspeakable good fortune of a life whose pleasures we're still energetic enough to work at and whose work, wage-earning and otherwise, happens to be among our chiefest pleasures.

Tennis, you say? Tennis it is, then, and work be damned for a change; we've earned that indulgence. You're on for a set, on those brand-new courts at our virtual doorstep, with a surface that sends our soles to heaven, pardon the pun, and so far from pooping our leg-muscles for the morning, has seemed rather to inspire them for the scenic back-country bike-ride up into the village for provisions, in the days when we were still in the provisioning mode. Extraordinary, that such tournament-quality courts appear to've gone virtually undiscovered except by us—like those many-geared mountain bicycles free for the borrowing and for that matter the pool and spa and, we might as well say, our beach and its ocean, or ocean and its beach. Where *is* everybody? we asked ourselves early on in the visit: Does the rest of the world know something that we don't?

"Vice versa," you proposed and we jointly affirmed, and soon enough we counted it one more blessing of this many-blessinged place that our fellow visitors were so few, as who but the programmatically gregarious would not: those couples who for one cause or another require for their diversion (from each other, we can't help suspecting) a supply of new faces, life histories, audiences for their household anecdotes. Well for such that the world abounds in busy places; well for us who binge on each other's company to've found not only that company but a place as unabundant in our fellows as it is rich in amenities: just enough other visitors, and they evidently like-minded, for visual variety on the beach, for exchange of tips on snorkel-spots and eateries, for the odd set of doubles on those leg-restoring courts, and for the sense of being, after all, not alone in the restaurants and on the dance floor, at the poolside bar and out along the so-convenient reef, in this extraordinary place in general, in our world.

Auf Wiedersehen now, tennis courts! Arrivedérci, bikes and bike-trails, charming little village of excellent provisions agreeably vended by clerks neither rude nor deferential, but—like the restaurant servers, reception-desk people, jitney drivers, even groundskeepers and maintenance staff of this jim-dandy place—cheerful, knowledgeable, unaffectedly "real."

Lunchtime! You incline to the annex restaurant, up on the ice-plant-planted headland overlooking "our" lagoon, a sweet climb through bougainvillea, hibiscus, and oleander to the awninged deck where frigate-birds hang in the updraft from tradewinds against the cliff and bold little bananaquits nibble sugar from diners' hands. I incline to a quicker, homelier "last lunch," so to speak: fresh conch ceviche, say, from our pal the beachfront vendor down by the snorkel shack (who knows precisely how much lime juice is just enough lime juice), washed down with his home-squeezed guava nectar or a pint of the really quite creditable local lager. But who can say no to the stuffed baby squid and crisp white wine up at our dear annex, with its ambiance of seabirds and fumaroles, its low-volume alternation of the sensuous local music with that of the after-all-no-less-sensuous High Baroque, and its long view through coconut palms out over the endless sea?

"Endless *ocean*," you correct me as we clink goblets of the palest, driest chablis this side of la belle France and toast with a sip, eyes level and smiling, our joint House Style, which would prohibit our saying *endless sea* even if we hadn't already said *seabirds* just a few lines earlier. *Sea* is a no-no (one of many such) in our house, except in such casual expressions as *at sea* or *on land and sea* or *moderate sea conditions*, and of course such compounds as *seaside, seascape, seaworthy,* and *seasick,* not to mention the aforementioned *seabirds.* One does not say, in our house, "What a fine view of the sea!" or "Don't you just love the smell of the sea?" or "Let's take a dip in the sea," all which strike our housely ears as affected, "literary," fraught with metaphysical pathos. Thus do longtime partners of like sensibility entertain themselves and refine their bond with endless such small concurrences and divergences of taste, or virtually endless such. But here's an end to our self-imposed ration of one wine each with lunch, especially in the tropics and only on such high occasions as this extended work/play visit; and there's an end to our unostentatious, so-delightful annex dinery, as pleasing in its fare and service as in its situation. Au revoir, admirable annex! — or adieu, as the case will doubtless prove.

Next next next? A whole afternoon, almost, before us, whether of sweet doing or of just-as-sweet doing nothing, since we have foresightedly made our departure arrangements early: scheduled the jitney, packed all packables except our last-day gear, settled our accounts and left off running up new charges, put appropriate tips in labeled envelopes for appropriate distribution, penned final hail-and-farewell cards to our far-flung loved ones, and posted on the minifridge door a checklist of last-minute Don't Forgets that less organized or more shrug-shouldered travelers might smile at, but that over a long and privileged connection has evolved to suit our way of going and effectively to prevent, at least to minimize, appalled brow-clapping at things inadvertently left undone or behind and too late remembered.

This air—Mon dieu! Gross Gott! ¡Caramba!—such air, such air: Let's not forget not simply to breathe but to be breathed by this orchid-rich, this sun-fired, spume-fraught air! Off with our beach tops, now that we're lunched; off with our swimsuits, while we're at it, either at the shaded, next-to-vacant nudie-beach around the upshore bend—where we innocently admire lower-mileage bodies than our own (though no fitter for their age) of each's same and complementary sex; likewise each other's, trim still and pleasure-giving; likewise each's more than serviceable own, by no means untouched by time, mischance, and vigorous use, but still and all, still and all . . . —or else at our idyllic, thus far absolutely private pocket-beach in the cove two promontories farther on.

Pocket-beach it is. We lotion each other with high numbers, lingering duly at the several Lingerplatzen; we let the sweet trades heavy-breathe us and then the omnisexual ocean have at us, salt-tonguing our every orifice, crease, and cranny as we slide through it with leisurely abandon: hasteless sybarites in no greater hurry to reach "our" reef for a last long snorkel than we would and will be to reach, in time's fullness and the ad lib order of our program, our last orgasm of the visit.

Good wishes, local fishes, more various, abundant, and transfixing than the local flowers, even. Tutti saluti, dreamscape coral, almost more resplendent than these fish. Weightless as angels, we float an aimless celestial hoursworth through spectacular submarinity, not forgetting to bid particular bye-bye to the shellfish and those calcareous miracles their shells, their shells, those astonishments of form and color, first among equals in this sun-shimmerish panoply, and virtual totems in our house. Fareethee-wells to our fair sea shells, no more ours in the last analysis than are our bodies and our hours—borrowed all, but borrowed well, on borrowed time.

"Time," you sigh now, for the last time side-by-siding in our post-Jacuzzi, pre-Happy Hour, king-size last siesta; no air conditioning this time, but every sliding door and window wide to let the ceaseless easterlies evaporate the expected sweat of love. "Time time time."

Time *times* time, I try to console you, and myself.

"Never enough."

There's all there is. Everlasting Now, et cet.

"Neverlasting now."

Yes, well: The best-planned lays, as the poet says, gang aft a-gley.

"Not what I meant."

Appreciated. Notwithstanding which, however . . .

We beached out, see, post-snorkelly, first in the altogether of that perfect pocket-beach on our oversize triple-terry beach towels, thick as soft carpeting, fresh from the poolside dispensary of same; then on palm- and palapa-shaded lounge chairs on the beach before the pool beneath our balcony, books in hand but ourselves not quite, the pair of us too mesmerized and tempus-fugity to read. Fingers laced across the beach-bag between our paralleled chaises lounges, we mused beyond the breakers on the reef, horizonward, whither all too soon et cetera, and our joint spirits lowered after all with the glorifying late-day sun, so that when time came to say sayonara to that scape, to stroll the palm-shadowed stretch to our last hot soak and thence, pores aglow, to take the final lift to passion's king-size square, we found (we find) that we can't (*I can't*) quite rise to the occasion.

"Me neither."

We do therefore not *have sex*—that locution another house-style no-no for a yes-yes in our house—but rather make last love in love's last mode: by drifting off in each other's arms, skin to skin in the longing light, no less joyful for our being truly blue, likewise vice versa or is it conversely, the balmy air barely balming us.

I pass over what, in this drowsy pass, we dream.

Have we neglected in our close-out prep to anticipate a snooze sufficiently snoozish, though alas not postcoital, to carry us right through cocktails to miss-the-jitney time? We have not. No mañana hereabouts for thee and me: On the dot sounds our pre-set, just-in-case Snoozalarm™ (which, in our pre-set half-dreams, we have half been waiting for); half a dozen dots later comes our back-up front-desk wake-up call—Thanks anyhow, unaffectedly "real" and pretty punctual paging-person—and we've time time time for the last of the rum or le fin du vin or both, with the end of the Brie on the ultimate cracotte, while we slip into our travel togs and triple-check our passage papers, button buttons snap snaps zip zippers lock locks. One last look, I propose, but you haven't heart for it nor do I sans you, hell therefore with it we're off to see the blizzard heck or high water. Adieu sweet place adieu, hell with it adieu adieu.

Time to go.

Bright Is Innocent · *Jonathan Baumbach*

SCENES FROM AN IMAGINARY MOVIE

THIS IS THE WAY it usually happens. Our man, who toils in the creative trenches for a state-of-the-art advertising firm, who's inoffensive and untested, sophisticated to a fault yet surprisingly innocent, with a socialite mother who can maim you with a wisecrack, finds himself mistaken for a notorious secret agent. He gets up from his table in the Russian Tea Room to phone his overbearing mother at the very moment the real agent is paged by the people trying to trap him. Once he is mistaken for this ostensibly dangerous figure, a man of a thousand faces, a man who may not even exist, Jonathan Bright's life is irremediably altered. He becomes a figure adrift in an irrational universe, living by his tattered wits. An inescapable succession of improbable adventures awaits him.

Two men with guns discreetly displayed approach him as he is getting into a phone booth and direct him outside into a waiting limousine. They identify him as a Mr. Phillip Levy.

The more he insists that he is not this Mr. Levy, the more his captors are convinced that he is exactly the person he says he is not. When he tries to leap out the car door at a red light, they laugh at him for behaving like an amateur. "You are one funny guy, Mr. Levy," the short one says.

"You are two funny guys to think I'm Mr. Levy," says our man.

He is taken to an elegant country estate belonging to the famous criminal lawyer, defender of lost causes, Wilfred Cog, where he is grilled by an over-civilized white-haired man with an English or vaguely German accent. "What is your assignment, Mr. Levy?" he is asked. Bright senses that if his captors don't get what they want, his life is not worth a hill of beans or a plugged nickel, whichever is less. What an impossible situation for an innocent man to find himself in!

Still he tells them nothing, a man unwilling to give up state secrets even if he has none to give, playing to the hilt the false role (while denying he is who they say) he has unwittingly inherited. With his ad-man's sense of the absurdity of all human transactions, he makes up stories for his captors that, though credible in some ways, are basically impossible to believe. Amused by Bright, they nevertheless talk of drowning him in a bathtub or of pouring whiskey down his throat and taking him for a one way ride to nowhere. If they are only trying to scare him, which he factors as a possibility, it is the one thing they have done so far in his regard with some measure of success.

He wakes up the next morning, hungover, in an unfamiliar room, a smoking gun at the foot of his bed, a dead body lying in the center of the room like its own tracing. He is awakened by a pounding on the door and a persistent voice calling, "Police. Open up. Police. Open up."

What to do. He knows himself to be an innocent man caught in a maelstrom of misunderstanding so he climbs out of bed and opens the door.

The police knock him down and handcuff him and read him his rights. "Wait a minute," he says. "Would I have opened the door for you if I had killed this man?"

"The criminal mind will go to any length to disguise the nature of its crimes," says Sergeant Black. "Don't give us any more trouble, Mr. Bedford, or you'll be adding resisting arrest charges to those already on your docket."

"My name isn't Bedford," says Bright/Levy. "It looks like you low-rent sherlocks have got the wrong man."

The two policemen are flustered for a moment or so and check the information they have been given from headquarters. Wouldn't you know it, they are one smudged digit off on the room number. In their zealousness, they have forced their way into the wrong hotel room and abused the wrong perpetrator. Since this is not their case, not at the moment, they remove Bright's handcuffs and give him ten minutes to get his life in order.

Our man puts on shoes and socks, a coat over his pajamas—there isn't time to get fully dressed—and hurries out of his hotel room, which is on the twenty-ninth floor. How did I get here? he wonders. It is not a question he often asks himself. Crisis has deepened him in a myriad of barely perceptible ways.

His plan is to go home, take a hot shower, change his clothes, call his office and his mother and perhaps even a lawyer, but as he steps out of the elevator he sees one of the two men who had kidnapped him the day before.

He slips back into the elevator, bumping into (in both senses) a slightly tarnished attractive blond woman getting in at the same time. "This may sound crazy," he says, "but there's a man in the lobby who'd like nothing better than to drown me in a bathtub."

"I wouldn't be at all surprised, Mr. Levy," she says. "Your picture's on the front page of almost every newspaper in America."

The woman, for her own reasons which are yet to make themselves known, offers to hide him in her room until the worst of the heat is off.

"How do you know I'm not dangerous?" he asks.

"I don't," she says, "but I've never run from danger before and I'm not going to start on your account."

Her room turns out to be on the 30th floor just above his former room—an odd coincidence, which makes him distrustful.

When Maria is out on an errand, he calls his office to explain his absence and is told by his own secretary that he can't possibly be who he says since the real Jonathan Bright happens to be working at his desk at the moment. "Darlene, your left breast is slightly higher than your right and you have a beauty mark on your right buttock," he tells his secretary.

"Oh my God," she says. "Who told you that?"

"The other man is an imposter," he says. "The reason I'm not at work is that I've been mistaken for a spy and framed for a murder."

She hangs up or they are cut off from another source. Before he can call back, there is a knock at the door—two knocks in impatient succession. "Is everything all right in there, Miss Carlyle?" a man's voice calls. It sounds like Sergeant Black.

"Everything's fine," he says in unconvincing imitation of Maria Carlyle's voice. "If you'll excuse me, I'm taking a nap."

"Don't answer the door for anything, Miss," the voice says. "There's a dangerous character running around the hotel and someone spotted him exiting the elevator at this very floor."

"Thank you for the warning, boys," he says in his improvised falsetto.

"Something's wrong in there," he hears the one who's not Sergeant Black stage whisper. "I think he's in there with her."

He presses his ear to the wall to get the sergeant's response, but the only thing he hears is troubled breathing and footsteps toward or away. What to do—that persistent question. Bright shaves himself with a woman's tiny razor, then dresses himself in Maria Carlyle's clothes. He's never done anything like this before, but his picture is in the papers and everyone seems to be looking for him, and he's always wanted (secretly of course) to get in touch with the feminine side of his nature.

One of the policemen, the one who is not Sergeant Black, is lounging in the hall with his back to him. While Bright (in women's clothes) is waiting for the elevator, the cop looks at him, does a double take, and turns away.

The high heels get to him—he has never worn heels before—and his ankles begin to wobble in a telltale way as he click-clacks through the lobby to the exit.

"New shoes," he says jokingly to an old woman he passes. "Not broken in yet."

As he is hailing a cab—pursuers emerging from every shadow—a police car drives up and asks the woman he appears to be where she thinks she is going.

"To work," he says, which is the wrong answer.

"I think you better come with us, doll," the vice squad cop says. "We know you've been working the hotel. We've had our eye on you for some time."

"You have the wrong girl," our man says with genuine outrage. "Just who do you think I am?"

"Be a good girl, Mary, and get in the car," the cop says. "Spare us the innocent act, sweetheart."

At that moment, Maria appears, says, "What's going on here? What are you doing to my sister?"

After some negotiation, and some extended studying of Bright's face, the police decide that they may have made a mistake. "Let us see some identification," they say.

For a wild moment, Bright thinks of whipping out his penis, but of course that's not what they mean by identification.

Maria covers for him. "You must have left your purse in the hotel room," she says.

The police get bored with the complexities of the discussion and decide to leave, though not without warning him/her to stay off the street.

Maria and Bright go back into the hotel and into the Grill Room (where lunch is being served) at the very moment someone coming out of the restaurant is assassinated with a knife.

As chance would have it, the blood stained knife ends up in Bright's left hand. "Stay away from me," he/she says, backing out of the restaurant.

There are screams. Someone points a finger at him/her, the real murderer, an assassin in Cog's employ. "*Cherchez la femme*," he yells, slipping out the door while the crowd turns its attention to the odd-looking woman with the knife.

In the commotion, someone knocks Bright's wig off, which creates a gasp of desperate surprise.

Bright punches a man trying to hold on to him and gets out the door just in time to see the real murderer, Hermann, a man with a face like a barber's razor, get into one of the cabs that hang around outside the hotel.

Bright gets into the next cab and instructs the driver the way they do in movies to follow the cab just ahead. Maria stands in front of the hotel calling something to him he is unable or unwilling to hear. She is shaking her head, indicating that his rushing off this way is only going to make things worse.

As he follows the cab in front, Bright becomes aware that his cab is being followed in turn by an unmarked (he assumes) police car. The lead cab, aware of being followed, makes a couple of unexpected turns, hoping to lose its pursuer.

Bright's cab, not to be left behind, too late to make the second of the two abrupt turns, crashes into a telephone pole.

Two months later, our man wakes in a hospital bed with no memory of a past. He wakes at four ten in the afternoon in a strange room as if he had just been torn from the womb. The afternoon nurse, a light-skinned black woman named Helene, addresses him as Mr. Willow.

At five o'clock, the doctor comes by to see his progress. "Good to have you among the living again, Willow," he says. "We've had our worries about you, fella. How do you feel? Any discomfort?"

"Head," Willow says, unable to locate a second word to follow the first. In truth, he has what feels like a toothache at the back of his head.

"Hurts?" The doctor asks. "I wouldn't be surprised."

The next day he receives a visitor, a woman in a business suit he has no recollection of having seen before but whose manner toward him suggests long term intimacy.

"Darling, you can't possibly know how pleased we all are to have you back among us," she says, sitting on the side of the bed. "Is there anything I can do for you, Chance?"

"Get me out of here," he says.

"The doctor says you can leave the hospital in a week to ten days depending on your progress," she says in a voice that strikes a nerve of irritation. "And then of course you'll have to talk to the police."

"Get me out of here," he says again.

She leans toward him, puts her head in whispering distance of his, and between them they hatch a complicated escape plot. The next visiting day she will bring him a doctor's uniform. Meanwhile he is to pretend to be too weak to get out of bed so as not to arouse suspicion. He does not tell her of his apparent amnesia or of the pain at the back of his head, the weakness in his legs, the deep sense of foreboding.

He does ask one question: why should the police want to talk to him. Oh the usual reasons, she says, telling him nothing, there are loose ends that need to be tied together in cases like this. Loose ends? You know, loose ends, as if it all weren't too obvious for words. She calls him Chance, which is probably a nickname, long or short for something else.

She returns two days later with a set of neatly pressed doctors' whites in an unmarked shopping bag. In the intervening two days his memory has improved sufficiently for him to know that his name is not Willow. The woman, who is almost beautiful and almost young, is no one he remembers knowing, but she seems fond of him so he goes along with her plan for his escape.

The stencilled name on his uniform is Dr. Levy, which strikes a chord. Even after they escape together in her metallic blue Dodge Polaris, he has no clear idea of how he should behave toward her, what's expected and what's not. She takes him to a cottage outside the city, a place only a handful know about, she says, where he will be safe while he convalesces.

There is a closet full of men's clothes at the cottage, of a style so fashionably anonymous and nondescript they seem to have been tailor-made for an amnesiac. "This is the best I could do on short notice," she says, holding out a double-breasted blazer for him to try on. It all happens so quickly, the escape from the hospital, the drive to the country, the room by room tour of the cottage which is to be his temporary home, the not quite right multi-course gourmet dinner she prepares for him, that none of it quite registers as experience. It is as if he were watching the life of someone else, someone like himself, on the bigger-than-life screen of a movie theater.

When she announces after dinner that she has to get back to the city (or else what?), our man wonders if there's anything he can do to change her mind. "When will I see you again?" he asks. "As soon as it's safe to return," she says, which tells him nothing. They work out a code so he'll be able to tell, when the phone rings, whether it's Maria on the other end. Otherwise, as a matter of perhaps excessive precaution he's not to answer.

He's almost glad when she drives off so that he can do some detective work and find out who she is and who he is and what they might be to each other. On a kitchen table, he discovers a picture postcard (a reproduction of the Mona Lisa) sent from Paris to a Ms. Anne Laurie, a name that strikes only the most distant echo of familiarity.

It is the usual tourist message—saw this and that, loving Paris, had furtive sex on the Champs Elysées. So usual that he wonders if the message isn't some kind of code. The card is signed with the initial W.

Before he can explore further, exhaustion reaches him and he falls asleep on one of the living room couches.

A noise wakes him. Someone is in the house with him, in an adjoining room, and is rooting around in an impatient heat. Whoever it is must have already been through the living room, which is the first room you enter, and either had chosen to ignore Chance or had not noticed him hunkered down on the couch in the shadow of the dark room. The second possibility he sees as the more likely.

When the phone rings, the intruder answers from the kitchen. Chance overhears the following conversation.

"I found it," an unplaceably familiar voice with a faint German accent rasps. "I'm going upstairs next to see if there's something else. . . . Don't call again. I'll be in touch after the house is torched."

When he hears the intruder go upstairs, our man gets off the couch and goes outside into the steely night air. His first impulse is to get away and with that in mind he gets into the black car parked down the road from the house. His plans are in constant variation. There is no key in the ignition which precludes his immediate escape so he hides himself in the back, a wrench in his right hand, waiting for the intruder, whose name he seems to remember as Wilfred Cog, to return.

Chance falls asleep, waiting. He wakes with a start the moment the engine of the car starts. The wrench is under him and to get it he has to raise his legs without calling attention to himself. As the intruder lights a cigarette, Chance, balanced on one knee, brings down the wrench on the back of the other's head in a glancing blow. The intruder, cursing in German, turns toward him, but Chance gets a better swing at him the second time, connecting with a blow that leaves Wilfred Cog slumped like a rag doll against the door.

Five minutes later Chance has rolled the body out of the car and is starting to go through the man's pockets when he notices that a fire has started in one of the upstairs rooms of the cottage. He leaves Cog, whom he assumes is dead, and goes to see what he can do about saving the house.

At first the fire is localized to one bedroom on the second floor. Chance finds a bucket in an adjoining bathroom and fills it with water, flinging the water at the flames, repeating the process several times to no useful result. The fire outpaces his efforts. After calling the fire department, he goes back to the black car except the car is no longer where it was.

What a disaster! By the time the fire trucks arrive, the house is burning out of control. Lying on his belly in the field, watching the flames gradually decline, Chance remembers his name as Phillip Levy.

When after several hours the fire trucks leave, Levy/Willow returns to what remains of the cottage and calls the almost young, almost beautiful woman, who may or may not be Anne Laurie, from the melted kitchen phone still hot to the touch. He reports what has happened in understated detail, giving her a description of the intruder. She is her usual cryptic self on the phone, advising him to make himself scarce until she gets there.

Waiting for her, Levy goes through the rubble looking for clarifying detail, finds an address book which he puts in the pocket of his borrowed pants. Then he hears several cars drive up and he has the impression, looking out from the charred remains of the cottage, that the field is on fire. What he sees are the flashing lights of five perhaps six police cars.

A voice blares from a bullhorn. "WILLOW, WE KNOW YOU'RE IN THERE. COME OUT WITH YOUR HANDS ABOVE YOUR HEAD AND I PERSONALLY GUARANTEE YOUR SAFETY. THIS IS SERGEANT BLACK REPEAT SERGEANT BLACK SPEAKING."

Seemingly moments after this announcement, before Levy has decided on a course of action within severely limited alternatives, bullets fly through the shattered house like a plague of locusts. What now? He lies in a crawl space behind the stairs waiting for the gunfire to exhaust itself.

Periodically, the bullhorn announcement returns, but the blasts of gunfire follow within twenty seconds of its conclusion. Even if Levy/ Willow (and which is the real self?) were ready to give himself up, there is not enough time for him to get out of the crawl space and through the front door before the firing resumes. When they warn him that they are about to charge the house, he crawls out an opening in a back wall into a garage whose existence he hadn't noted before. There is a moped in the garage and though he has never driven one, he drives off on it into the dense backwoods as if he had been riding one all his life.

Someone spots him (wouldn't you know it?) and two police cars come after him, but the woods resist their entrance and the cops are forced to pursue on foot. And then our man, looking over his shoulder, crashes into a tree stump. The fall, as falls will, jogs loose much of his buried memory (like seeing the beginning of a movie in which you already know the outcome), and so he knows who he is again as he stumbles through the dense brush away from unseen pursuers. He is Jonathan Bright, one of the top copywriters in the business, a man with a gift for the falsely sincere persuasive phrase, who, through misunderstanding and malice, has become hopelessly estranged from his former life. Bright's only concern at this point is to prove his innocence and clear his name and see the world made a safer place for the comings and goings of innocent men.

On the other side of the woods, he comes to a dirt road which leads him to Wilfred Cog's country house, the place to which he had been abducted at the beginning of his adventure. In fact, Cog's black Mercedes—the one Bright regrets not driving off in when he had the chance—is parked in the adjoining carport. The other car parked conspicuously out front, the metallic blue Dodge Polaris, is also familiar. It is the car he was taken in by Anne Laurie (AKA Maria Carlyle) when she helped him escape from the hospital.

So, unarmed, armed only with his pay-as-you-go wit, Bright has reached the apparent epicenter of the conspiracy against him. One of Cog's henchmen, the one called Werner, approaches Bright as he is going through the glove compartment of the Polaris. Bright sees him just in time and takes out Werner, who had been his particular nemesis during their earlier encounter, with a punishing right hand, a fortuitous gesture of desperation, to the side of the head.

Bright ties Werner up and stuffs him in the trunk of the car, arming himself with the thug's Smith and Wesson revolver. He also comes up with a miniature tape recorder that he finds in Maria's glove compartment, a means, as he sees it, to clearing his name. Just when it looks like Bright is about to transcend his long siege of adversity—he has been sneaking around the house peering into windows to get the lay of things (there is a portrait of Hitler done in a Stuart Gilbert mode on a back wall)—Cog's other henchman, Hermann, gets the drop on him from behind.

So Bright is led once again at gunpoint into the hands of his enemy, Wilfred Cog, who is sitting in a thronelike chair in his study, wearing a bandage around his head the size and scope of a turban. "A pleasure to meet you again, Mr. Levy," says Cog. "I fear our friendship, which I had counted on so much, will never blossom. Unfortunately, you have become superfluous to my plans. I no longer have need of that information you once, even as your life depended on it, refused to give me."

It is shocking to Bright that a man as apparently clever as Wilfred Cog still hasn't gotten his name right, still persists in mistaking him for someone else. He takes a new tack. "What if I told you everything I know," he says. "Would that make a difference?"

Wilfred Cog looks at his watch. "Pity I don't have more time," he says. "If I weren't assassinating your president in a few hours, it might be amusing to hear your sad story, Mr. Levy. Might be, yes?"

At a signal from Wilfred Cog, Bright is bound and loosely gagged and hustled into an almost pitch-black basement room. Someone else is in the room with him, someone he can't see, someone whose presence is only announced by the sound of breathing. A woman's voice says, "They're going to burn the house down when they leave. We have about twenty minutes to get out of here before they torch the place."

Bright crawls in the direction of the woman's voice and when they connect awkwardly in the dark, she pulls his gag free with her teeth, which amounts to their first kiss. There is no time to ask why she betrayed him to the police. In no more than ten minutes they are out of their bonds and in five minutes more they have discovered a small, nailed shut window, leading to outside the house.

They have almost dislodged the window when they are interrupted by the sound of footsteps coming down the basement stairs. There is no time to plan a strategy, barely time for Bright to take up position behind the door. The door opens abruptly and the beam of a flashlight intrudes on the almost perfect blackness of the room.

"I have come to say goodbye in person," says the voice. It is the ineluctable Wilfred Cog himself. Cog moves the beam of light in a slow arc from one side of the basement to the other without discovering either of its occupants. "You are probably wondering what I have in store for you. To tell you the truth, for the longest time I had nothing in mind. Only to do the right thing, the necessary thing. To reward faithfulness and to punish betrayal." When the flashlight focuses its attention on the partially dislodged window, Cog discontinues his monologue. "Problems," he sighs and backs off, closing the door without relocking it. Bright hears Cog ordering his henchmen to search the grounds. "Shoot anything that moves," he says. "The time for sublety is past."

In the next few moments, several things happen almost at once. Cog, carrying an attaché case with the viscera of an assassin's rifle inside, gets into his car and drives off. He leaves a moment before a team of his people begin their systematic search of the grounds. It is also the moment that the police, pursuing Bright on foot, arrive at Cog's country house. One of Cog's men, the notorious Hermann, panics and fires at the approaching police. Challenged, the cops take cover behind hedges sculpted in the shape of swans and fire back.

Maria, it appears—we have only her own word to go on—is a double (perhaps triple) agent working for the U.S. government which explains, or seems to explain, the vagaries of her behavior vis-à-vis Bright. Loyalty to country takes precedent over concern for the life of an innocent man.

Maria and Bright kiss for the second time. As before, as always, there is no time to lose, though personal matters—love perhaps—tend to slow things down. Bright slips out of the house unnoticed and into Maria's car, drives around the back where Maria waits for him. As she is getting into the car, a random bullet probably from one of the team of police hits her in the most circumstantial way, glancing off the door of the car and into her skull.

Bright has started driving away before he realizes that Maria has been hit, goes about a hundred yards down the road before coming to a stop. "Are you all right, darling?" he asks when she slumps against him. Her silence is his answer.

He carries Maria out of the car and back toward the house. The fighting has mostly stopped—occasional shots here and there echo like afterthoughts. Virtually everyone is dead or critically wounded. Before he can get her into the house, a second group of police arrive led by the indefatigable Sergeant Black.

Bright ignores Sergeant Black's command to halt and carries Maria into the house, putting her down on the orange and ivory Ming dynasty rug in the front room. The phone lines have been cut so he can't call an ambulance, which is his first idea. He refuses to believe, has cut himself off from believing, that Maria is dead.

Sergeant Black follows him inside. "A lot of people have been looking for you, Bedford," he says.

"Well, it looks like you've found me," says Bright/Levy/Willow/Bedford, who even in the midst of possible tragedy, has not lost his capacity for the playful retort. "While you've been hounding an innocent man, Wilfred Cog is on the loose preparing perhaps at this very moment to assassinate the president of the United States."

The police doctor comes in and after examining Maria Carlyle, places a sheet over the body. "She won't be running any more stop lights," he says.

Black plays with his moustache. "I admit we've made a few mistakes along the way, Bedford. I freely admit to some misapprehensions, but we've got the business straight now. Wilfred Cog is in custody—we picked him up not five miles from here. The republic is safe for one more night. Case closed."

"If the case is closed, then you no longer want me," Bright says. "I can go back to my unexceptional life if it's still there to go back to."

"Sure, you're a free man," says the sergeant, moving across the room to discuss something in private with one of his men. "Take off, old man. Get lost. Hit the road."

The abrupt change in his status confuses Bright. He lingers a moment. He has been too long on the wrong end of the fox hunt to give up his role of injured innocence without second thoughts. Walking toward the door, he has an odd premonition (a part of the puzzle is missing) and prodded by intuition, he turns back. And just in time. He discovers a gun pointed at what had been his back, cocked, primed to fire. Fortunately, there is also a gun in his own hand, the one cancelling out the other.

"I might have known," says our man.

"Don't you trust anyone?" says the sergeant.

The standoff lasts three minutes perhaps five, at which point (and for reasons which may soon become clear) Sergeant Black withdraws his gun. In the next moment a man identified as the notorious Wilfred Cog is brought into the house by two government agents for questioning.

Bright is astonished. This Wilfred Cog is several inches shorter and perhaps ten years younger than the Wilfred Cog who had tried to kill him. "This is the wrong man," he says. Astonishment pervades the room.

The government agent, one Phillip Levy, assures our man that this indeed is the real Wilfred Cog, hotshot lawyer, defender of lost causes. If true, the real one is less credible than the imposter.

Bright takes advantage of the general confusion and rushes out of the house and down the road to Maria's metallic blue Dodge Polaris—someone has to stop the senseless murders—and the adventure, such as it is, continues. The case surrounding our man is in a state of permanent irresolution.

Phillip Levy and his men follow after him in their unmarked government car, hoping to arrive at some point of clarity. Once again Bright is a wanted man.

There is no point of clarity, merely the mechanism of pursuit and empty discovery. There are more chases to come in this case, more instances of mistaken identity, more murders, more delusory solutions to murder, more willful destruction of property, more questions without answers, more enigmatic assassins, more almost young almost beautiful women (who may or may not be spies), more betrayal, more lost love. All the wrong people (only the wrong people) will be caught and punished, the inevitable happy ending a deceptive waystation, an accommodating illusion to permit us to go on to more of the same: more deaths, more fast automobiles, more dimwitted spying, more incomprehensible secrets. And Bright, who is our man, who is innocent (he believes) of everything, is caught up in this hectic continuum, misperceived and disbelieved, wanting only to understand why him of all people, which is the one thing, among all the wisdom disappointment has to offer, he will never find out.

The Spectacle · *Mary Caponegro*

Act I: What Is a Human?

The human is a curious animal, characterized by a constant nervous motion. This one, for instance, stands on his hands and turns as if to make himself a wheel; the spokes that are his arms and legs intend to blind me as he spins. If I lash out in my confusion, he seeks protection in a wooden barrel and rolls before me thus contained. Or if I am about to take a part of him inside my jaws, or grasp him in my paws, to make him just for one moment still, then he leaps away into the well, or uses some tall pole to spring to where I can't reach.

When he himself is not in motion, he waves before me reeds or straw, or this revolving wooden object which when I strike to stop it, makes the audience around me sound a music that is not unlike my roar.

Act II: What Is Identity?

In the center of this enormous oval space, the venator, no sooner has he met the lion, merges form: his shoulder with its face, and all the rest of him intact. His arm has been consumed, is what we initially believe, but if we'd gotten to our seats in time, we'd know the fierceness of his gesture. We too would have been startled to observe the stolen moment when the beast's jaws opened up to yawn, to roar, that gesture interrupted by an arm plunged down its throat. Now the venator, with the other hand, of his still visible arm, seizes the tender pink tongue; thus paralyzed, the beast's sharp teeth hold no peril.

The Emperor cheers, the Emperor seems to sigh. The Emperor shivers, holds his side, as if by magic, disappears.

I had not meant to swallow this strange projectile, that forced its way into my mouth, and chokes me now, while my only mobile part is gripped with his other hand, strangled by his fist. I do not like the taste of what encloses me: this adversary who assaults me in a delicate cavity for the pleasure of the crowd. I am surrounded and invaded at once. Hear me, though I be an unexpected orator. More than my teeth and my roar; I too have softer parts. Often I've held the hare in my mouth so gently that it never felt my teeth's serrated edge. And here you, human, do the opposite, you strike instead of stroke. What could caress instead constricts; instead of bid me lick your salty palm, you bind my tongue, the way you bound my limbs when we were introduced far from this place. That was the first time, you'll recall, that you invaded my quite clearly designated space.

We cannot exit unobserved, as can the Emperor; he can choose to be invisible or prominent, depending on his moods, depending on his needs; at one moment brandishing his sword to slay some arbitrary animal, at another slithering down his marble steps to regain his composure or relieve himself, or observe the ones observing.

Act III: What Is Intimacy?

The panther and the bull address each other; the distance between them equal to the length of the chain that binds them. They lunge, exchanging mass and speed. But when they try to flee from one another, they are forcibly reminded of what weds them. Who is better suited as the victor: he with teeth or he with horns? The more massive? The more lithe? Sometimes there are answers, ladies and gentlemen, numbers bear out certain patterns, but for the most part nothing is for certain. This is why you're here: to witness the results of the circumstances we've contrived.

Act IV: Man and Beast

He grips my neck with his knees and when I buck he squeezes all the harder; by my motion and by his grip we try to make a victory, locked together like enemies whose kiss is fierce, whose kiss addicts.

He must desire his prominence. Because of the processions which use us in great numbers; because of the togas all the humans gathered here are wearing; because of the special seat he occupies, the wider for his comfort.

Act V: What Is Intimacy?

No one is fooled by it, neither of the participants certainly. They know this is for the stage's sake, that he with his gold-dusted mane after prancing regally to greet his adversary, stands perfectly still, arching his back, thrusting forward his head, offering his cheek to receive the lips of his partner, the same who might have caught him unsuspecting during yawn or roar, this venator instead glances his face against the beast's so softly, his own cheek titillated by the delicate slender filaments no human face possesses, at this moment the only vestige of cage's bars between their forms.

Act VI: What Is Levity?

Did you see the chariot making a figure eight around the amphitheatre?

How elegantly it delineates, how perfectly precise. The driver is so clever, yes?

The driver, did you notice, darling, is an ape! Those poor wretches in the rafters never get the joke, they can't see that far.

Sea lions, all present, bark to their respective names, as the Emperor calls attendance: Vespasian, Hadrian, Maximilian. He's named them after predecessors; how the Emperor is amused by their antics and his own clever joke, so amused he feels stitches in his side and will excuse himself before too long.

But what can stitch a rent flesh mantle, a gaping wide enough to expose all internal organs?

And what if there were nothing to cling to but the smooth marble that allows no grip; its slick voluptuous surface, making humans slip and slip and slip until they find themselves inside a pit of those whom they have gathered for their pleasure: the circumstance their criminals encounter.

OVERHEARD

The elephant is kneeling, do you see?

The dwarf must have ordered him to, just like last time. The games, you see, become redundant after years. It takes so much wealth and whimsy to make them always more exciting. Perhaps it's just as well to be in these less coveted seats, leaves more to the imagination.

Just as now you imagined the dwarf; he isn't here this time.

Then why is the elephant kneeling, you fool? He looks like a baby first learning to crawl.

If all of you weren't separated by protective motes and scaffolding and nets that obstruct even the closest view, you'd be able to see the single javelin between each toe of the elephant's foot: metal flowers humans planted. You think he has such thick skin he cannot even feel. Indeed the crowd thinks this a charming skit, some brilliant sacerdotal wit: an elephant who genuflects before his adversaries, then comes begging for their mercy. But ladies and gentlemen, there's no mercy to be had. If you stop laughing and keep looking, looking closely at the scene that is before you and much more than it appears, you'll observe this massive beast even thus reduced come charging, directly toward his foes, juggling shields as he goes, and straight toward us, oh my. And this I can assure you is not written in the script. He has intention to obliterate.

INTERMISSION

The glories of human engineering designed this stadium, this stage, these props, these protective measures and this ritual. Do not dare discredit the overwhelming grandeur of human engineering, whose transport took you across the sea and gave your life a purpose, to let you be a part of the most improbable, impressive of all spectacles.

ACT VII: WHAT IS MERCY?

The creature who never forgets knows that humans remember. He is contrite, now, as he kneels before the Emperor, not so much the worse for wear for the bruises inflicted by the rhinocerous he killed, admittedly provoked by flaming darts to goad him. Before he was annihilated the rhino threw a bear into the air and killed a bull as well. Will elephant be pardoned? There's no telling; mercy here is arbitrary. For instance deer, behind him, next in line who kneels before the Emperor seeking supplication—or a momentary staying of the hounds that chase her—might receive a pardon, or she might receive two arrows in her head to simulate the horns she'd sport were she the stronger male.

IMPROVISATION

And the Emperor, who has been made a fool of by this massive interruption and is perhaps tired of being focal only in the audience, takes center stage, so no one can mistake his presence. He takes the role of gladiator, venator, and with his crescent sword, locates the longest neck of all performers present: even the slaves, even the women in the rafters could have guessed it would be ostrich. One can hear their collective sigh from the top tier, at what one would presume is hardly visible, but the Emperor, standing, arm raised, possesses better than front row view of the exotic bird, one of three hundred who paraded for him earlier. Her vermilion tinted feathers now sport more than festive decoration, as her uncrowned trunk gallops back and forth unnavigated. Scooping up the ball that was the head and lifting high in front of him the stained, gleaming sword, the Emperor finds the senators' box, perhaps the ones who crossed him in assembly, and brandishes his trophies, as if to say: you could be next.

It does not disorient the Emperor to perform; he is accustomed to display, and is not bothered by the crowds he has assembled to observe us, and can choose at any moment to retire.

But what if the Emperor's open mouth, when cheering, yawning, what if it, like lion's, were violated, while he gasped for air? Would the outcry of the crowd be deafening? Or would what sounds like outrage be in fact resounding cheer?

Act VIII: Man and Beast

Elevated from the bowels of the amphitheatre arrives the lion in his box. A door clamps shut behind him, while the door before him opens to expose him to the crowd, and to the man, who stands without a weapon, probably a criminal. The former can't retreat; the latter can't defend himself. This won't take long.

But when paw and palm come together, touch is catalyst: remember that sharp thorn that only the dexterity of grasping fingers could remove? Can animals feel gratitude?

Act IX: What Is Memory?

The audience's eye cannot help but follow the severed head, now tossed away by the human who's lost interest in it. We thrust our intact necks and strain our ears before the oddest sight: a tiger nuzzling it, possibly trying to heal with his tongue, in a gesture of unscripted tenderness. Stationary for the longest time, is he attempting to communicate or listening? Tell us tiger, what you hear? If memory could speak, what would it say?

I had never felt it before: the sensation of being held like that, enveloped, protected, not since I was inside my mother's egg. My soft plump body in his arms so much kinder than ropes. I am fondled, and indulged. Our legs work together and he is careful never to place his shod foot on my two toes. He is leading me, I thought, he's teaching me the way that humans dance—though human had been until then a foreign species—clutching a wing in his hand to give me balance and steady my gait. My long legs I thought at last were matched, by our equal heights despite sinuous deviations, for he was straight where I would curve, so sometimes his chest brushed against my throat.

Venator, take this prop away, it makes the Emperor squeamish now. Why else would he be rushing to his seat? Is this too brutal for his gentle eyes: the act that he himself performed? The Emperor for all his ostentation is occasionally a bit withdrawn. He virtually melts away into the crowd, blending subtly in his seat, like an animal who has received from nature the privilege of camouflage—although it's true, the Emperor's enemies cannot hide from him.

But what rises now under the tunic of the Emperor? Where is his other hand, which usually conducts the spectacle like an orchestra of carnage? The curtain of his tunic subtly rises from the pressure of this surreptitious magic wand.

Act X: What Is Delicacy?

It is the rare performer, the elephant, who has not been seen since the games in '79, but today seems ubiquitous, more often than not on his knees. The one we've seen already twice at last has respite; his colleagues carry him on a palanquin, as if he were a pregnant woman. Then one dances while the other smashes cymbals to make music. He appears to do a pirouette as she takes her place at the banquet table he's just set. How daintily he pats the ludicrous pink skirt as he sits his bulk upon the bench with delicacy beyond a human's capability. If there is the least displacement, if one plate or vessel is disturbed, he coils it in his trunk to place it elsewhere with great care. And when the banquet is complete, she becomes scribe, and scratches with an implement on paper. Show your lessons to the Emperor, how the Greek and Latin characters are formed as by an artist's hand. But make certain what you say is what your tutor showed you. πᾶν γὰρ ἑρπετὸν πληγῇ νέμεται. Every creature is driven to pasture with a blow? That can't be right. Fortunately, it's growing dark.

Act XI: What Is Eros?

And the lion in the twilight shadows takes the hare between his jaws. He's running off with his prey, we, watching, think, but look how the hare's ears and legs extend as gracefully as a dancer's limbs, and notice that he does not yelp at all. Should he so much as twitch, the former, stronger one immediately adjusts his transport. For from the corner of his eye, the lion who makes his mouth both carriage and cradle slackens still more the tension of his jaw. He will not rest until each time he gently scoops the smaller creature, he can truly make his tongue its bed.

And I say to the vestal lady beside me, Imperial woman though I am, with every privilege, including this proximity, this coveted closeness to all aspects of the spectacle of which few women can boast, I cannot help but harbor secrets, wishes, such as this: O that my husband could cradle me so tenderly when my essence rests inside his mouth.

Act XII: What Is Gravity?

There is no spotlight, only moon, by whose illumination we can fortunately see a single figure, bulky though he be, perform gymnastics and then dance. When all other creatures sleep, and humans too, he instead repeats a gesture many times: stand, leap, roll; one, two, three, he does not miss a beat, and then rises, puts one leg aloft to find a slender rope suspended, and I can scarcely believe my eyes, he walks across it, though the bottoms of his feet are wide as saucers.

It's true, I can confirm, you do not dream, unless we dream in tandem: he climbs the proscenium in moonlight and balances himself upon the rope suspended many meters above the amphitheatre floor. First he walked across the ground as if it were air instead of earth, each foot placed carefully and deftly, and then it seemed he turned the air to earth. Only when he finds himself across this precarious void, does he lay down his immense weary body, and rest, his breath slow, so we who think we may be sleeping, see its rise and fall.

We think we are dreaming him? We're only here because we've come the night before tomorrow's games to get a better seat, or any seat. We are poor, you see. We fasten our ragged cloaks with tarnished brooches and our gaping shoes the same. But we have had a gift today, that no one *not* forced to wait on line would have. Even the Emperor who sees so clearly from his unobstructed seat, whose width is greater for his comfort, whose podium allows him to exit unobserved should he find himself bored, fatigued, aroused or squeamish, has not had this privilege of witnessing a dream behind the scenes: the animals' voluntary dress rehearsal, their own incessant practicing until perfect.

ACT XIII: WHAT IS EROS?

The cranes now do their mating dance, chase each other round the amphitheatre. The females prod the males; the males respond, or vice versa. They'll make a show of lust, appear to lose their heads lest they be taken literally, like ostrich. And in the midst of all their antics, the venator, perhaps eager for variety, seals his face to the tiger's in a gesture of affection. But the tiger is less cooperative than in the past. The beast is still distracted by the rolling ball now separate from the walking neck that carries forward frantic, unimpeded. It seems that he is coy, flirts with the lips that seek his cheek; the audience, enchanted, sees a mating dance between two species: man and beast. And finally their heads reside together, minutes it would seem, as if the tiger had confided something, as if he'd whispered in the hunter's ear:

As you trapped me do you recall the crystal ball you tossed upon the ground to furnish my diminutive reflection, so all that was maternal and protective in me thought I saw an embryo of my own flesh and blood, thought my cub lay trapped yet in my reach, so every instinct bid me lick to heal the poor abandoned newborn? But while my tongue made contact with the surprise of cold smooth surface I anticipated would be warm and yielding and familiar, you surprised me in much grander style. You closed in on me and I had no defenses. You kicked away your trick, your crystal ball and made me march.

Hastily the venator removes himself; it must be time to set the stage for closure, the grand finale.

ACT XIV: WHAT IS ALCHEMY?

Even stranger than the mating dance of cranes is the gait of a human clothed in flame. It's surely better to be a citizen and wear a toga in honor of the Emperor, than to run ten meters in a toga that is specially constructed to erupt in flame, to earn one's daily bread. The clothing, then, that makes one civilized, can be illusion. And flesh can also be a cloak, as when physicians educate themselves in ways they can do nowhere else, to see so much exposed of what still breathes.

ACT XV: WHAT IS IDENTITY?

As if the ocean overwhelmed the shore, the sandy amphitheatre floor is inundated to make a giant oval pool, within which bulls and horses romp together, splashing, swimming, pulling boats behind them. A shepherd stands atop the grandest vehicle. A violent motion jerks away the hood atop his cloak to show this shepherd's whiskered face is not a human's, but a lion's.

Is it a trick of light? The Mediterranean sun dances on the sudden liquid skin of the arena. Gaze well, ladies and gentlemen. Gaze until the sun makes you squint to see beyond the surface shimmer. What you fix your gaze upon with indefatigable fascination is itself a kind of mirror. This oval frame contains a portrait you have painted. But there's no need to sign a portrait titled "Self."

The Best Things in Life · *Lenora Champagne*

(Fairy Tales for Adults)

I.

Once upon a time there were two children, a brother and a sister. They were advanced for their ages and agreed to leave childhood behind. So they took off down the garden path and soon entered a wood. They were smart and knew how to catch birds and trap squirrels and mice and other small animals. They ate some and built cages for the others. When the sister gathered mushrooms and wild berries, she'd feed them to the animals to see if they were poisonous. Then she and her brother ate what was good. The brother preferred to stay by the stream, where he perfected the fish-catching mechanism he'd conceived while gazing at the sky.

Life was carefree, but it wasn't ideal. For instance, they didn't have any salt or dairy products, and they missed these things. So they decided to journey further into the forest to see what they might find.

Sure enough, they soon smell something strange. Lo and behold, it's a house made entirely of Gruyère!

While this is not the siblings' favorite cheese, it is welcome and will do.

The brother coughs discreetly, careful to avoid getting phlegm on the Gruyère, to let any inhabitants of the Dairy Hut know that visitors have arrived. Just as he and his sister are about to chow down on the cheesy gatepost, the front door peels open to reveal the svelte inhabitant of the hut.

"Welcome," she greets them, with just a touch of a British accent.

"Good day, ma'am," the children say sheepishly. "Please excuse us for disturbing you. We were just walking through the forest when we caught a whiff of your house and . . ."

A jab of his sister's elbow in his chest stops the boy in mid-phrase.

"You are not disturbing me, children. I am happy you have come. I rarely have visitors anymore."

There was an awkward silence.

"You don't recognize me? Perhaps you're too young to remember. Let me introduce myself. I am the Dairy Queen."

"The Dairy Queen! So that is how you are so fortunate as to have a cheese house!" exclaimed the children.

"I am not so fortunate as I may seem," explained the Dairy Queen, "as I have developed lactose intolerance and cannot eat the products I produce. They provide me with no nourishment and make me ill besides. However, you are welcome to eat your fill."

So the children gobbled up as much as they could, until they had stomach aches and constipation. The Dairy Queen invited them to spend the night and finish their digestion.

That night she told them tales of the good old days gone by. The children were enchanted by her tales and her manner of telling. She was a pretty, elegant, thin queen who wore top-of-the-line designer fashions and ate only the leaf of a green plant that grew by her doorstep. Both siblings fell under her spell. The brother tried to think of ways to please her, although he'd never worked by his father's side so didn't have a heroic male role model to know how to be a man, and the sister tried to become thin herself, although the green plant just wasn't enough for her and every now and then she'd have to sneak a chunk of cheese.

Compared to the Dairy Queen, they were imperfect. The only way they'd ever be able to stand themselves was to leave. One day they decided to go.

"Your Highness, we are, as you know, precocious children, and you have taught us much. With you we have come to know love and envy, not to mention self-loathing, which are complicated feelings at so tender an age. We have come to understand that Gruyère is among the best things in life, regardless of its odour, but now we must be on our way."

A single tear marred the perfect complexion of the Dairy Queen. "I understand. You must seek other experiences. But don't forget me. Please remember the Dairy Hut in the forest, and send other children to keep me company. And sign me up for any high quality mail order catalogs you find on your way."

The children left with heavy hearts. They turned back once to catch a final glimpse of the Queen, alone in her thin perfection, surrounded by goodness she could not eat.

II.

Once upon a time there was a hard worker. She cleaned and was careful to fluff all the dust from the cracks. The rough surface made this task difficult. There were other obstacles, too, like the long lists that never got crossed off.

Every year her space felt more cramped, but recently she'd been given a wide expanse of floorboards to cover.

She was called Cinderella because the powdery black dust that creeps in everywhere in the city resembles cinders. It is the dirt version of sand in Cairo. It shows up under fingernails, coats windowsills, dusts the soap dish.

Her shoes are covered with the grey powder. The leather is cracked in the crevice that forms when she bends down to Pledge the molding. A big hole in the sole of her right shoe lets rain in to wet her sock.

This morning the bedroom is a mess. As she reaches down to lift the pillow from the space between the bed and the wall where it always slips, two mice run out. One large and one small, slick and quick.

The word on the streets is that these little fellows are friends of Cinderella's, and even help get the job done, but this is just another false rumour put out by the authorities—and Disney. The little guys always mean more work, which is what anyone can tell you who knows the difference between ordinary dirt and a mouse turd. She surveys for damage and sees her flowered housecoat lying on the floor. Expecting the worst, she picks it up. No turds, but the mice gnawed big holes in the cloth.

So now they're after the clothes off her back! Her wardrobe was already limited. Her overcoat, for instance, was getting snarly and thin in the seams, and there's a big hole in the pocket. When she holds it up to the light, she sees the mice have eaten it too!

Cinderella sat on the bed and sobbed. For the moment she was overcome. The combination of dirt and despair threatened to drive her out. Without protection! With holes in her shoes and no overcoat! Not even a decent housecoat!

"Damn those *sourcis*! I mean *souris*!" She'd made this mistake before. She always confused the French word for mice, *souris*, with the slang word for pin money or small change. Once when she'd spent all her savings on a trip to France to learn about the best things in life, she'd thought friends talking about "sourcis" were keeping mice in a change purse. She could use that change now.

She blew her nose and shrieked when she spotted the tall, thin, swan-necked woman in a tutu in the corner.

"Hello. Don't you recognize me? I'm. . . . Nevermind. I'm here to give you a tip."

"I'm not permitted to accept tips."

"It's more of an opportunity. I can help you out of the no options you live with. I started off like you—low, dirty, practically a scullery maid, nearly in the gutter—and now look what a great outfit I'm wearing!"

"It's lovely."

"I can help you get a job. I have a friend who's opening a nightclub based on one in Paris, and if you can work with him, you can kiss this gig good-bye."

Cinderella wasn't very big on nightclubs. Her fantasy date was more along the lines of a light supper at a quiet restaurant. But she was eager to try something less dusty.

"What will I do for clothes? Who'll hire me wearing these rags?" She poked at her shabby overcoat.

"Just leave it to me."

The tutu-clad lady zapped Cinderella a few times with a yo-yo she'd hidden in the tulle as she mumbled over her.

"I'll just go to the neighbor's to borrow some thread for this button. For sewing this button back on. For fastening this item of clothing that's come undone. For this ball gown needed for a special occasion. For this organdy soufflé shirred with waffle piqué. For this magenta taffeta with yellow yolk trim. For this watermark silk shot with jet beads gathered into the wasp-waisted bodice of black moire. Tomorrow is not soon enough for inset sleeves to taper into raglan! Grossgrain binding, the zipper teeth want to tear into the silver lining. The merino wool penetrates the needle's eye. The seam won't stay until brocade drapes the light of day."

Cinderella gasped as the breath was pressed out of her. She found herself bound in one of those skin tight leather numbers topped by a satin bustier.

"Are you sure these clothes are still in?"

"Trust me. I know what he likes."

By now Cinderella expected a limo, but the ballerina-look-alike stepped to the curb and whistled for a mere yellow cab. At the nightclub, Cinderella discovered the job was as a dancer and clothes really weren't necessary. The management supplied the g-string.

This wasn't what she'd had in mind. It was hardly her idea of the best things in life. But it would be a change—and much less dusty.

She took her place in a long line with other women trying to break in, trying to break out of the no options they were living with. One by one, they entered the manager's office bright and determined, and soon left in a huff or in tears.

When the bored-looking manager came to the door for the hundredth time and said, "Next," Cinderella bunched her overcoat over her arm so the holes wouldn't show and strode into the office, hoping the cracks in her shoes wouldn't detract from her stylish but uncomfortable outfit.

Once she was alone with him, Cinderella noticed the manager was darkly attractive in a scary kind of way. Despite his weariness, he had charm and an alarming yet exciting intensity about him. Regardless of her policy on not mixing work with pleasure, Cinderella felt the tug of desire.

He smiled and she saw herself reflected in his teeth.

He reached under his desk and pulled out a pair of six inch stiletto heels.

"There is only one position, and it will go to the girl who can wear these shoes."

So that was why everyone was so upset. They already had backaches from their waitressing jobs, and now they were going to have to dance on stilts, too.

As he handed her the first shoe, she noticed how small it was. She prepared to try stuffing her foot in, but it slipped on easily. After all, she wore size four.

The manager's breath came more quickly as he leaned over to look. He pressed a button on the tape player on his desk. A lovely melody wafted out. "I know you. I walked with you once upon a dream." "At last," he said. "Dance for me," he said, stroking her ankle.

Now she wanted to get away. She felt smothered and took a big gulp of air.

"Excuse me," she said. "I forgot a big dustball under the bed." She ran off, leaving the stiletto behind in his hand.

And the manager held that shoe and cried. He sent his henchmen out to search for her, but she evaded them and found a safer job. She was never again visited by the tall woman in a tutu, although she sometimes spied her on street corners, hailing the last available yellow cab.

III.

If Snow White and Eve both eat an apple and fall—down, from grace—are they the same woman? If Paradise is over, what does she wake up into?

She and the Prince start wandering, because his castle has been repossessed.

At the laundromat, she thinks back on life with the dwarves. Things were simple then. Now the work has to be shared by two instead of seven.

Life with the Prince is far from easy. Sometimes she thinks it would have been better to stay asleep. She had ambitious dreams then. When she woke up, she had gray hair.

The stepmother was pleased to see that Snow White was no longer the fairest of them all. She'd had plastic surgery while her rival was sleeping off the effects of too much knowledge, and now her taut, angular features graced the cover of all the glossy magazines. Just bones and eyes.

Snow White winced every time she went to the drugstore for tampons, or the newsstand for cigarettes, so for a while she sent the Prince on these errands for her.

She was grateful the Prince had decided to kiss her. Not every man would be so willing to rescue a woman who'd lived with seven men, even if they were dwarves, even if her name was Snow White.

Snow White skimped and saved. When she and the Prince had children, she dressed them all in red. The eldest Princess showed great promise and took dancing lessons from a young age. When the Prince left, he gave her a microscope, and the next year he sent her a telescope. Her father wanted her to understand vastness. They'd talk long distance about how difficult it is to understand the ends of things, while Snow White struggled to feed the family.

The eldest Princess showed great progress. No longer did she learn five new five-letter words from her father each night. Now she was studying French.

IV.
Bon. Allons-y.

Il était une fois deux soeurs. L'une était riche, sans enfants. L'autre était pauvre, veuve en plus, avec cinq enfants. Elle n'avait pas assez à manger. Une fois, elle est allée chez sa soeur pour demander un morceau de pain.

"Soeur, mes enfants sont en train de mourrir de faim. Est-çe que je peux avoir un morceau de pain?"

"Non!"

Elle l'a chassé de la porte.

Mais, quand le mari est revenu chez lui, il a eu envie d'un morceau de pain. Mais, quand il a commencé de couper le bout, du sang rouge a coulé.

Did you get that? Okay, I'll explain.

Once upon a time, there were two sisters.

One was rich, with no children.

"Hello. Don't you recognize me? I am the Dairy. . . ."

The other one was poor—said she was a widow but there was no evidence of a marriage license—with five kids, on public assistance, food stamps running out. Her kids are still hungry, so she goes to her rich sister to ask for a handout.

"Sister, could you spare some leftover bread?"

"No!"

And she shut the door on her poor sister. When the rich sister's husband came home, he was hungry for bread.

"More mergers! More acquisitions! What do we have tonight dear? A little rye, a little pumpernickel, some sourdough with Gruyère?"

But when he cut into the bread, blood splattered everywhere.

65

He was so surprised, he knocked over a candelabra and the house caught on fire. It spread to the neighbor's house and down the block and raged through the entire development. Then the city was in flames, burning down!

And the only survivor was the rich sister. She wandered about amidst the ashes, weeping tears of remorse. Wherever a tear fell, a tree sprang up. Soon she was surrounded by a forest. Then her tears turned to cheese, and she fashioned a Dairy Hut for shelter.

And the cheese stands alone
the cheese stands alone
Hi ho the derry-o
the cheese stands alone.

V.
Cinderella washes the floors and the windows. She saves the leftovers and makes soup. She enjoys this soup and considers it among the best things in life because it is delicious and cost free. She makes things now, and words, and puts them on display or gives them away.

Everything turns to work in her hands. It's what she knows how to do. Sometimes she meditates on chance. Or on how things happen in time. She often goes back to what she knew first—cleaning. When she cleans, her blood moves, and the blood in turn moves her mind.

Her mind wanders into corners. She follows with her broom and pail. She is grateful for the hard wood and long, smooth planks. She thinks—about sisal matting. Last Spring, in a store filled with elegant imports and tight men in manager suits, she'd seen a mouse eating the sisal matting that was part of the luxurious display of unnecessary things.

"Look, a mouse."

The tight men were unamused, at a loss; they put the security guard in charge.

"What is he doing?" she asked her companion, afraid to look.

"He's beating it with his night stick," was the reply.

She didn't stick around to find out what became of the small rodent with the temerity to wander out among the stuffed bunnies laid out for Easter. (It crosses her mind that on Easter Day the remaining rabbits might rise from their stuffed state and join the mouse in devouring what remained of the matting—if the mouse had the sense to withdraw before the law.)

The law is also elsewhere, busy banning things, like body parts in art and queers in Colorado and fairy tales because of violence. As far as the evil stepmother ordering Snow White's heart torn out, why that had happened to her more than once already, and it wasn't so bad in the long run, you got over it, although it was very painful at the time.

She has to stand up to the law. She and Snow White are sisters under the skin. She likes cleaning, Snow White kept house for the dwarves. They'd both lived like outlaws with various men, and each had an appetite for freedom and apples. If they stopped Snow White's story, might not hers be next?

Her story? Her story about the mouse? Her difficulty with responsibility. She'd said,

"Look, a mouse"

to remind the men that they were mortal. But she hadn't thought of what the consequences might be for the mouse. She hadn't thought that the men, annoyed by this sign that their mighty fortress of objects could be invaded by the lowest of creatures, might want to snuff out the furry fellow. She'd rather not take responsibility for that.

This is why action and speech are so difficult. All those unforeseen consequences fall down around you. But act now, speak now, she must. Time is changing and she hurries to fill it as it rushes by.

Speech is the body part of thinking, the voice of the mind. Writing is the blood and mind mixing to speak through the fingers, through the hands.

She gives her mind a rest. She cleans more slowly, and looks for apples to assuage her hunger.

The New Thing · *Robert Coover*

SHE ATTEMPTED, he urging her on, the new thing. The old thing had served them well, but they were tired of it, more than tired. Had the old thing ever been new? Perhaps, but not in their experience of it. For them, it was always the old thing, sometimes the good old thing, other times just the old thing, there like air or stones, part (so to speak) of the furniture of the world into which they had moved and from which, sooner or later, they would move out. It was not at first obvious to them that this world had room for a new thing, it being the nature of old things to display themselves or to be displayed in timeless immutable patterns. Later, they would ask themselves why this was so, the question not occurring to them until she had attempted the new thing, but for now the only question that they asked (he asked it, actually), when she suggested it, was: why not? A fateful choice, though not so lightly taken as his reply may make it seem, for both had come to view the old thing as not merely old or even dead but as a kind of, alive or dead, ancestral curse, inhibitory and perverse and ripe for challenge, impossible or even unimaginable though the new thing seemed until she tried it. And then, when with such success she did, her novelty responding to his appetite for it, the new thing displaced the old thing overnight. Not literally, of course, the old thing remained, but cast now into shadow, as the furniture of the world, shifting without shifting, lost its familiar arrangements. The old thing was still the old thing, the world was still the world, its furniture its furniture, yet nothing was the same, nor would it ever be, they knew, again. It felt—though as in a dream so transformed was everything—like waking up. This was exhilarating (his word), liberating (hers), and greatly enhanced their delight—she whooped, he giggled, this was fun!—in the new thing, which they both enjoyed as much and as often as they could. Indeed, for a time, it filled their lives, deliciously altering perception, dissolving habit, bringing them ever closer together, illuminating what was once obscure, while making what before was ordinary now seem dark and alien. This was the power of the new thing, and also (they knew this from the outset) its inherent peril. The new thing, being truly new, not merely a rearrangement of the old, removed the ground upon which even the new thing itself might stand. The old thing's preclusive patterns were like those frail stilts that floodplains housing was erected on; the new thing joined forces with the cleansing flood. As did they in their unbound joy, having anticipated all this from the start, though perhaps not guessing then how close together delight and terror lay, nor back then considering, as she, he urging, made the new thing happen, how indifferent to their new creation would be both world and thing. Indifferent, but not untouched. All shook and they, the shakers, were not themselves unshaken. This, too, even trembling, they ardently embraced, though perhaps they whooped and giggled less. Scary! she laughed, reaching for him, and he, clinging to her and thinking as he fell that some principle must be at stake, something to do with time, cause, and motion perhaps: So much the better! Thus, even if somewhat apprehensively in such an altered yet indifferent world, they found pleasure in what might in others inspire dread, their own apprehension mitigated by their shared delight in this new thing, their delight dampened less by antique fears of being swept away in metaphoric floods than by their awareness that the new thing did not, could not know them, nor would or could the world in which they had brought it into being. The new thing, which was theirs, was, alas, not really theirs at all, nor could it ever be. Moreover (her logic, this), they had chosen the new thing, chose it still, but with the old thing lost from view, what choice was theirs in truth? Were they not in fact the chosen? And his reply: Let's go back to the old thing, just for fun, and see. And did they, could they? Of course! The old thing was waiting there for them as though neither they nor it had ever gone away, like an old shirt left to yellow in the closet, an abandoned habit, a lost friend discovered in a crowd, a rusting truck at the back of the barn, and they found new pleasure in returning to it, or at least comfort, and something like reconciliation with the entrenched and patterned ways of the world. The old thing reminds me of my childhood, he acknowledged gratefully, and she: Why this appetite for novelty anyway, when we are here so briefly we don't even have time enough to exhaust the old? Thus, they enjoyed the old thing anew and in ways they had not done before, chiefly by way of ceasing all resistance, and they told themselves that they were pleased. Of course, they had to admit, after knowing the new thing, it was not quite the same, the old thing. Sort of like dried fruit, she said, sweet and chewy now but not so juicy as before. He agreed: More like body than person, you might say, more carcass than body. They experimented, giving the old thing a new wrinkle or two, but could not sustain their revived interest in it: it was still the old thing and it still oppressed them. Back to the new thing. Which was still there and was delightful and exhilarating, as before. They were pleased and did not have to tell themselves they were. What fun! Truly! But the new thing, like the old thing, no matter how at first they denied this to each other, was also not the same as it had been before, he the first to admit it when regret, batlike, flickered briefly across her brow. No, she objected, falsely brightening, it is not it but we who have changed. By going back. To the old thing. Yes, you were right in the first place, he said, we were not free to choose. But we cannot go back to the new thing either. No, she agreed, we must try a new new thing. And so they did, and again, beginning to get the hang of this new thing thing, they found joy and satisfaction and close accord with one another. Out with old things and old new things, too! they laughed, falling about in their world-shaking pleasure. But was this delight in the new new thing as intense as that they'd felt when they'd first tried the old new thing? No (they couldn't fool themselves), far from it. So when the new new thing bumped up provocatively against the old new thing they were filled with doubt and confusion and no longer knew which of the two they most desired or should desire, if either. Out of their uncertainties came another new thing (his handiwork this time), momentarily delightful and distracting, but soon enough this too was replaced by yet another (now hers), itself as soon displaced (both now were separately busy at what had become more task than pleasure), the devising of new things now mostly what they did. By now, even the new thing's newness was in question. I am lost, she gasped, falling to her knees. He called out from across the room: I felt oppressed by the old thing, now I feel oppressed by the new. This is probably, she said, speaking to him by telephone, just the way of the insensate world. We were fooled yet again. No, no, I can't accept that, he replied by mail, else no new thing is a new thing at all. His letter crossed with hers: My unquenchable appetite for novelty is matched only by my unquenchable appetite for understanding. What a clown! I am deeply sorry. Adding: I have now become a collector of old things. There is not much fun in them, but there is satisfaction. But wait, he wrote in his diary. Does not the invention of one new thing insist by definition upon a second? And a third, a fourth, and indeed is this not in fact, this sequential generation of new things, the *real* new thing that we have made? And is that not delightful? He thought, if he tore this diary entry out and sent it to her, he might well see her again and they could have fun in their old new things

71

way, but the time for all that was itself an old thing now and, anyway, he no longer knew, now after the flood, where in the world she was.

Analogue · *Susan Daitch*

I EXPECTED HER LETTERS TO BE CONFESSIONS. They lay in a thick pile next to my coffee. There was no one else in the room, cigarettes fell from a pack onto the floor, falling into a shape which resembled a stick man, and I said to him, you'll do as well as anyone: listen to this. You have to pay attention when somebody writes in this way with this kind of urgency. I read her impressions out loud to him. I used a skeptical tone of voice, exaggerated, supercilious, even speaking in different accents; sometimes lapsing into Inspector Clouseau French, sometimes a kind of Ian Fleming style Russian, but I had the suspicion or at least indulged in the impression, that my mute companion believed every word.

Dear Edgar,

Last night an incubus slept beside me. Had you been here you would have said I suffered from *un cauchemar* again, or pointing to the couch, you would say that narrow berth would give anyone bad dreams. You would tell me I was only afraid to fall off it, but this time I'm sure the incubus has stayed with me all day and will reappear at night. The incubus was a familiar woman, she looked a little like me and even a little like you, *une cauche-mère*. When I woke I photographed the couch, pillows and blankets scattered all over. One hears of photographs of phantoms, they register on the film, even though you thought the camera was aimed at an empty space. Click. What you could have sworn was a bare corner, or just a ceiling, is revealed to contain, when the film comes back from the lab, a dusty shadow. You look closely at the picture, hold it up to your nose, someone slightly familiar begins to be apparent, but it's not yourself you see reflected in the pane. So I aimed the camera wherever there was available light, whether dead space or clutter. We'll see who turns up when the film comes back. I'll send you the pictures, even if nothing appears.

I've heard echoes of past parties, whispers of old arguments, the creakings of faltering, unfinished sentences, syllables boomeranging around as if caught in an echo chamber. I turn around quickly and try to catch her, but she is just half a second quicker than I am. I might see a shadow against a wall, and I'm sure the shadow isn't mine. I might see a foot hurry around a corner or a hand dangle from a ledge. What, I keep asking myself, what does this counterfeit want from me? One day I actually saw her standing in a tower, and I yelled up at her, but all I heard in response were echoes. I'm sure she's someone we know or have at least seen before.

Here's proof. Her presence reminds me of the following scene in *Duck Soup*: Chico Marx, while running from Groucho, shatters a mirror. Stepping into the space behind the glass he pretends to be Groucho's reflected self. Groucho hops. Chico hops. Groucho jigs. Chico jigs. There is a room behind the mirror, not a supporting wall, as is usually the case. Is the furnished space identical to the room in which Groucho cakewalks? If not, why doesn't Groucho appear to notice? Groucho drops his hat. Chico drops his hat. They change places. The gag continues in silence. For me the question remains: why was a mirror, frangible and deceptive, used to separate two rooms instead of plaster, sheetrock, and building studs?

Why am I explaining this to you? You never liked to spend much time here so I wouldn't be surprised if you don't really remember these rooms. The ceilings are probably higher than you give them credit for, and what you consider the representations of my personality: the combs, lipsticks, glasses, and ashtrays don't loom as large as you think. The shoes and books on the floor you were sure were gunning for you when you tripped on them are still in place.

Yours,

Anne

Dear Anne, I wrote, let me tell you a story, a distraction. Once on a long train journey I began to talk to a woman who was sitting opposite me. It was night, but she was wearing a black hat with a veil drawn across it. She called herself Fac Totem, and she was running away.

I don't feel like myself, she said.

Who does?

She had worked as a cleaner for a woman who called herself Madame Sélavy. Sélavy spoke several languages, sometimes all at once. On her first day Sélavy told her to wait in *le couloir* while she dressed. Fac Totem thought she meant the cooler, and although she misunderstood, she was indeed, in a kind of prison. Weeks passed, and as she swept and polished parts of Sélavy's house she couldn't find a door that led out of the building, and she sometimes thought she was fading into the house itself, she spent so much time touching its painted, tiled, mirrored, veneered, and stone-faced surfaces. Sélavy would often appear from behind a corner to check on her, or she would think she saw her in the distance, and so would try to clean with a little more energy. One night as she entered a back room which bracketed the structure like a parenthesis, she found a mannequin leaning against a staircase. It wasn't wearing any clothes; its face was featureless and painted over. She threw it on the floor.

One more thing to clean!

As she said those words, features began to color the dummy's face. It began to speak and at first she thought the voice came from a wall or column. She dressed the dummy in her clothes, and it took over her job, like a kind of golem. No one noticed the difference. The artificial worker labored harder than any human could, it worked so hard that Sélavy became exhausted just thinking up tasks, not realizing who was in fact executing her orders. Meanwhile, though half-naked having surrendered her clothes, Fac Totem was free to roam from room to room, looking, not cleaning. Stuck in a cornice she found a wedge of folded papers which she couldn't unfold, so tightly were they jammed together. The object seemed like something personal and organic, like a severed body part. She dropped it. In another room she discovered bicycle wheels, a bridal gown, and a bottle rack.

One night while holding the mannequin by the hand, they were discovered. When Sélavy saw the girl and her double she looked back and forth at the two of them, frantically searching for mirrors which she knew weren't in the room. She threatened the two with expulsion to a No Man's Land of urinals and constantly dripping taps. If Fac didn't pull the plug on her substitute there were going to be problems in the future.

Get rid of it.

The *sosie* pleaded with her. As Fac hesitated, Sélavy grabbed the double around the neck, and she crumbled to the floor in a heap. The girl was, naturally, forced to return to work. New cleaning tasks, twice as demanding as before, were assigned, so one night when she was sure the other woman was asleep, she stuffed her pockets with cash found behind a painting, and ran away.

I was just a stranger on a train, but I asked if she would join me in the café car for a cup of coffee, thinking that was the least I could do, but she said, no thanks. She must have gotten off the train at the next station because I never saw her again.

Your shadows, doubles, and ghosts can take many forms.

Edgar

Dear Fac T. Finder,

Don't send me moral tales, please. Allegories can't explain the sightings I've described to you, as if these echos could be reduced to a game a child might play while sitting in a waiting room. Fac Totem's story, as you told it, reminds me of *Find the Things* or *What's Wrong with this Picture?* Rrose Sélavy's chambers are now full of objects left behind by an exile: the Duchampian wedge, the nude descending the staircase, the *Bride Stripped Bare*. I found these things right off the bat, but felt no more victory than if I had suddenly dropped a book which happened to fall open to a sought after page.

Love,

Anne

Inside the envelope were pictures of the house. It was a building I knew well, and all the pictures were empty. She imagined a girl on a tricycle pedaling down a long corridor as if being chased, but I found no afterimages, no configurations of light and shadow which could have been construed as a human figure. At least, I told my cigarette companion, that's how the pictures appeared at first glance.

I didn't write back for a long time, but her letters continued pursuing me, a shadow I couldn't detach.

Dear Edgar,

I'm afraid to leave the house. I wander around it for days. If I go outside, this thing will follow me. If it walks out of a store without paying for a magazine or grabs someone's wallet, for example, I might be the one to be arrested, so I never open an outside door or lean out a window. As long as I can maintain my prison I'm safe, but this procedure has its drawbacks. I am getting sick of ordering pizza and Chinese food to be delivered to the side door. Sometimes I feel as if I'm running in circles, and my twin is right behind me, never catching up, never allowing me to turn around fast enough so that we collide. I saw her on a bridge that connects two halves of the building. I don't think you quite understand some of what I've been writing to you. The incubus isn't invisible, I can't wrap her in bandages, a kind of feminized Claude Raines, please, sometimes I don't think you're really listening. What is similar, and I'm sure of this, are bad intentions. As Claude Raines became The Invisible Man, he grew increasingly violent. Sometimes I'm afraid my incubus is corroding me, as bits of the house erode and others seem to appear. Perhaps I'm becoming part her and part myself. You wouldn't recognize the site as it looks now, half what it was, half what it might have become.

Sincerely and Truly,

Anne

Dear Anne,

It's alright to see a woman on a bridge, but you're supposed to see a man on the tower.

Do you believe in the sentience of inert things? Maybe that's the problem. You think gypsum board and steel are going to turn and say, "Have a Nice Day!" or "Please come again!" Will marble tell you to keep your feet off its face and glass tell you to stop staring. The corners and windows take on personalities, but they aren't your friends. Are you turning everything around you into a massive memento mori? I don't have to walk those corridors, I can remember the sounds of footfalls down the passages. Benjamin felt he could read Baudelaire and never set foot in Paris. Enjoy your slice and pretend you're in Rome.

Best,

Edgar

It wasn't a very nice letter. I hoped it would at least make her angry at me and never write again. Somewhere in the distance I heard a recording of "I Put a Spell on You." I ignored the sound and began where I left off, prying the moulding and wainscoting from a room on the ground floor. Crenellations on the exterior will be the next to go. Once they're off, I plan to paint in their shadows so there'll be a record of what used to occupy each space. I read that a fire broke out in one wing, and in those rooms I've erected model flames constructed from a heat resistant plastic. Soon there may be no space remaining inside. For every removal, a residue is left over. The rate of accretion might eventually outweigh the removals, and I can imagine rooms in which no space remains.

Dear Edge Gare,

PRISONHOUSE
ROUGH-HOUSE
NUTHOUSE   → (SHIP OF FOOLS)   → HOUSEBOAT
HOUSE ARREST
HOUSE SALAD   HAUSSMANN
HOUSEBREAK   HOUSE MUSIC
HALFWAY HOUSE   OUT HOUSE
JOHN HOUSEMAN   IN HOUSE
WAREHOUSE   OPEN HOUSE
HOUSEFLY   HOUSE BOUND
HOUSEBOY/MAID/MOTHER/DRESS   FULL HOUSE
SAFE HOUSE   HOUSE OF MIRRORS
HOUSING   HOUSE BROKEN
HOUSEHOLD   HOUSE OF COMMONS
HOUSE OF CARDS   HOW'S EVERYTHING
HOUSEPARTY   ACID HOUSE
A.E. HOUSEMAN   ANIMAL HOUSE
HOUSEKEEPER   PENTHOUSE
HOUSE OF THE RISING SUN   DOG HOUSE
FUNHOUSE   HOUSEPLANT

How is memory like a house which is constantly being constructed and torn down at the same time? What parts have been sandblasted away? Which pasted back together with Krazy Glue and Elmer's?
　　Yours,
　　Anne

This morning my companion was gone. I was sure I had left him on the table last night. I could remember turning his arms and legs as I read him Anne's last disturbing letter. You see something uncanny, and it may be nothing other than the familiar, briefly forgotten, then re-emerging in what seems to be another form. I could buy more cigarettes but didn't move. I searched the building all day, looking for anything small and white, like a figure, but not a person. In the evening I ordered out, Chinese food. The delivery boy arrived twenty minutes later. I asked him if he had seen anyone around the building. As he pocketed my change he told me that he had seen a man who looked just like me, and the man had waved to him from the tower. I told him that wasn't possible. I had been in the cellar for the past hour. The delivery boy was sure. The man who looked like me had waved and turned off a light. He assumed the man was descending to open the door. How can that be possible, I asked, there is no light in the tower. He shrugged, indicating that he had to be on his way, there were other deliveries. I cradled the bag of noodles and chicken in oyster sauce as if I were prepared to eat my words too, then asked if I could have one of his cigarettes. He gave me one, and I told him I would pay him for the rest of his pack if he would give it to me. In fact, I would pay double. I might not be able to get out for some time to come. He looked at me strangely, then handed me half a pack. I gave him several large bills folded into my back pocket. From the door I watched him ride away. Before he reached the street, he stopped his bicycle and turned to look upward, as if seeing a light on in the upper stories of the building which I knew to be dark. I quickly leaned out the door to try to see what he might have been staring at, but the rest of the building was dark.

S & M · *Jeffrey DeShell*

S—'S FEELINGS FOR SIN short for Synthia have changed she doesn't think she's in love anymore at the same time Sin's feelings for S— short for S— have also changed she's sure she's not in love anymore since their feelings for each other have changed they've both started being incredibly nice to each other neither wants to be the person that fucks everything up although both of them know that it's probably too late things have already gotten way passed the fucked stage and have moved into the really nice stage and everyone knows when you're in the really nice stage things have gotten way past the hope stage so both Sin and S— are just riding it out trying not to be the person who articulates what they both are thinking and feeling and by saying things are really fucked up aren't they moving them from a nice stage into an even more fucked stage.

The problem with this nice/fucked stage is that it really isn't that nice it's a transition between being involved with a person and not being involved with a person it's a stage where the plot's already resolved the game's already decided and all that's left is to go through the motions waiting for the thing to hurry up and end another problem with this nice stage is that it's similar to another nice stage the very nice stage which is the stage that comes at the beginning of a relationship the stage of transition between not being involved with someone and being involved with someone but in both stages the simple nice stage and the very nice stage there's this feeling of obsession in the very nice stage you want to be with around and inside this person all of the time in the simple nice stage you will do anything not to have to be in the same room as this person but when you are in the same room as this person you act extremely nice to them because even though this simple nice stage isn't all that nice it's better than getting into fights all the time because the fighting and hating stage takes even more energy than the simple nice stage and you don't like this person anyway so why put any more energy into them than you have to.

It's hard to tell when this simple nice stage started it's hard to tell exactly when things got so bad they both knew there was no hope and so subsequently started being really nice to each another S— thinks the simple nice stage started after this big fight they had because Sin wanted to go dancing and S— had to work on these photographs she was developing for one of the magazines she does freelance for they had been planning to go dancing all week S— knew that but she did have to get these photos finished and they needed to be touched up a bit the light was too bright or something and so she had to work longer and harder than she expected and so there was really no time to go dancing which caused a big fight they yelled and screamed they called each other really horrible names like cunt and whore and Sin locked herself in the bathroom for awhile and S— sat around drinking a little white wine and then even though she felt pretty bad she did have to finish so she went back into the spare room she had fixed up as a studio and lab and put on her rubber gloves began to mix the chemicals and started working and when Sin came out of the bathroom S— could tell she was still really pissed off but Sin didn't say anything in fact she made some tea and brought S— a cup then she got dressed very quietly and left she didn't come home until seven o'clock the next night S— hadn't gotten home from a shoot yet but she had washed all the dishes and had fixed Sin a brunch before she left.

Since the tea and brunch incident they've both gone out of their way to do pleasant little things for each other like S— bringing home those flowers or Sin buying that expensive bottle of scotch the kind S— loves but rarely can afford while all the time the pressure's mounting along with the loathing and repulsion the more they loathe each other the nicer they are to each other it's not clear how long this will last or how it will end the way things are going the way the pressure's been mounting the way the world is today one wouldn't be at all surprised if it ended in an act of violence not murder necessarily but something out of the ordinary.

No violence this thing ended the same way most of these things end anticlimactically one day when S— came home from work Sin had taken all of her things and left no note no address no strings no more being nice S— breathed a huge sigh of relief and got very drunk on scotch that night and three days later the postcards started coming.

Dear S—. We were both perfect beasts to each other, I guess we both deserved it. I need some time out of the city. I have a brother in Tucson, he lent me some money so I rented a car, a big blue Ford. Arizona here I come. Sort of a wild, depressed bull dyke On the Road. Something like that. Oh well. I'll send you some postcards, even if you don't want me to. Especially if you don't want me to. Postcards from hell. Sin.

When S— woke up she felt the beginnings of a cold not quite the beginnings of an actual cold more like the beginnings of the possibility of a cold in other words she didn't feel all that bad but she didn't feel quite right either she felt well enough to go to work in the morning and when she came home in the afternoon she still didn't feel quite right now only more so she didn't feel sick either she felt only the possibility of sickness she wished she would get sick at least then she'd know exactly what she was dealing with it is always much easier to deal with the thing itself than merely the possibility of that thing she came home from work still not feeling sick but not feeling quite right either not knowing whether she should behave as if she were in fact sick or ignore completely that feeling of not feeling quite right she didn't know how she should act she didn't know if she should act sick or if she should act well she thought that this feeling of not knowing how to act of not knowing whether she was sick or well was in fact a kind of sickness in itself or if not an actual sickness at least a symptom of an actual sickness she finally decided that yes she was in fact sick she took a hot bath read a little and went to bed early.

When she woke up the next morning she was very sick her chest and head were congested she had a temperature and her throat hurt she might have caught the flu that had been going around and on top of that during the night the electricity in her apartment had been shut off or something and her clocks were all a couple of hours behind so when she called her boss in the morning to tell him that she was sick and wouldn't be coming to work it was really later than she thought it was and her boss was angry with her for not calling and telling him earlier and she looked at her bedroom clock and it still read eight fifteen and she couldn't understand why he was so angry she was only fifteen minutes late but she was weak with fever and didn't have the strength to question or to argue so she just apologized and hung up she felt confused she fell asleep.

She didn't sleep very well her fever kept her in that state which is between consciousness and unconsciousness the sleep which is not quite sleep sometimes she would drift deeper into sleep and sometimes she would almost be awake she thought or dreamt of Sin and her smell of chrysan-themums and curry she liked those words even though they always reminded her of Sin she still really liked those words they still sounded exotic and strange she also dreamt or thought about her sickness she thought it odd that she only really became ill after she started behaving as if she were really ill maybe if she would have just ignored the not quite right feeling it would have gone away and she wouldn't have gotten sick at all maybe she was too hasty in trying to force the issue maybe that was her trouble always wanting to know prematurely maybe she was too impatient maybe that was why Sin had left her she hadn't received the postcard yet so she didn't know where Sin was who she was with and what she was doing S— dreamt about her boss and why he had been such a prick to her that was how she dreamt of him as an enormous red prick even in her dream she realized this was a cliché but nevertheless she enjoyed the dream tremendously.

The phone woke her up it was her friend Simone from work she was downstairs thought she might be hungry so she had brought over some Chinese food and some magazines S— wasn't exactly in the mood for either Chinese food or Simone they both left her with this impatient unsatisfied feeling she chuckled at her joke her head felt thick and fuzzy with sleep and fever she felt slightly dizzy from getting up too quickly and her throat was parched and sore she was in that space where she really had very little to do with the external world she felt miserable she just wanted to go back to sleep she thought of her boss as a big red prick wondered with panic if he was downstairs with Simone no that was impossible buzzed her up and then slunk back in a chair she was really exhausted S— desperately wanted some orange juice but was too tired to get up and go to the refrigerator besides she didn't have any anyway Sin hated fruit juices S— didn't know why maybe Simone would run to the store and get her some why did she feel so fucking bad maybe she would feel better once she ate she could hear Simone walking up the stairs clack clack clack she suddenly was not at all in the mood for Simone and her high heels Simone and her Chinese food Simone and her gossip magazines Simone and her bladder infections Simone and her new boyfriend Simone and her fashion advice Simone and her drug adventures Simone and her motorcycle Simone and her latest fad fuck food or frolic suddenly S— missed Sin very much at least Sin knew when to shut up especially when one was sick she heard Simone knock on the door she struggled to get out of her chair then she opened the door and let her in.

Jesus you look terrible Yeah well I feel terrible come on in I brought you some Chinese food from Mah Wong's some really hot stuff to clear out your sinuses I like the Imperial Palace better but it was closed I also brought you some OJ you'd better sit down you look terrible Yes I know you said that already thanks a lot for the orange juice Do you want me to get you a glass Yeah sure they're above the sink to your right no the next one right by the refrigerator there thanks Where are the plates In the cabinet next to the glasses you can just put the food in the fridge I'm not really hungry right now But I'm starving I'm on my lunch hour I'm sorry I have no idea what time it is I have a little fever I've got a quarter past one why does your clock say nine thirty I don't know is it still running Yes Well I don't know maybe the electricity went off last night or something I don't know I just don't know.

The orange juice made her throat feel a lot better but she still didn't feel like talking or listening to Simone Simone was one of those people the city was full of them who would never be able to comprehend the value of silence Simone believed that any pause no matter how small in any conversation no matter how trivial was the gravest social error imaginable and so she worked tirelessly heroically to fill the air with a constant stream of small monosyllabic words eating didn't slow her down drinking didn't slow her down lack of audience didn't slow her down S— thought she probably chatted while she fucked too but didn't know for sure S— sat across the table from Simone trying not to listen to her chatter trying not to get sick trying not to concentrate on the sight of her eating the Chinese food out of the bright white carton trying not to focus on the sight of her tiny pale hand poking the brown and white food between those very red lips trying not to tunnel her vision and concentration down to the sight of that small restless mouth constantly moving mutating masticating constantly seemingly randomly changing shape and line.

S— hurried to the bathroom and threw up a little mucous saliva and orange juice she stood motionless over the toilet bowl for a few seconds a line of spittle extending from her lip down into the water of the toilet while Simone on the other side of the bathroom door was asking S— if she was all right she was okay would be out in a few minutes I have to go baby are you sure you're all right Yes I'm sure I'll call you tonight Okay well I have to go now Thanks for the food and juice You're welcome I'm going to leave a note for Sin I need to borrow her red pumps Sin doesn't live here anymore she no we split up What Sin doesn't live here anymore it's all over Oh S— I'm so sorry why didn't you tell me open the door let me in No no I'm all right I just want to be by myself for awhile okay Are you sure you're all right open the door Yes I'm sure I'm all right You're not going to do anything stupid What I said you're not going to do anything stupid like kill yourself or anything are you S— chuckled No no I'm not going to do anything more stupid than throw up You promise Simone god damn it I'm fine I promise I won't kill myself now leave me alone for awhile okay I'm sick I need some rest Okay okay do you have any red pumps I could borrow I just bought this new skirt No Simone I don't have any red pumps goodbye Okay I'll talk to you tonight I'll give your best to the kids at work Okay see you later lock the door when you leave I will goodbye.

S— stood above the toilet her forehead pressed against the cool tile she wanted to cry and throw up at the same time she didn't know why she did know why she missed Sin very much it would have been nice to have her around to take care of her now that she was sick especially since they were in the nice phase right up until she left when was that S— wasn't sure days weeks months years S— had no idea maybe it wasn't Sin specifically that she missed maybe it was the comforting feeling of having someone around someone to take care of you when you needed them that need was depressing S— suddenly felt oh so very alone and vulnerable so she cried for awhile then cleaned herself up swallowed a couple of cold pills with orange juice then went to bed and fell asleep.

When she woke up it was just beginning to get dark her fever had gone down a little and she felt hungry she looked at her bedroom clock it read five minutes past four she remembered that her clocks weren't right she didn't know where her watch was maybe Sin had taken it she thought no she wouldn't do that and she didn't feel like looking for it right now she decided that it didn't matter what time it was she didn't need to know it wasn't like she was going anyplace or anything she was sweating her pajamas and sheets were damp she was achy and tired she wished she could go back to sleep but she knew she had better eat something and besides she had to get out of bed to go to the bathroom to pee and while she was in the bathroom she heard the phone ring she didn't move to answer it that's what answering machines were for she half hoped it was Sin she listened at the bathroom door it was her good friend Sonia she was both disappointed and relieved at the moment she could deal with the thought of but not the voice of Sin.

She sat on the toilet after she had finished peeing and wondered about what she was feeling why she was feeling so alone and unloved although it had been nice when Sin was around it wasn't the kind of niceness you could count on or even enjoy it was never an absolute niceness never a niceness just for its own sake it was always a niceness with a function always a niceness with strings attached always a niceness with an undercurrent of real bitterness and hate almost a violent niceness a niceness that could turn wounding brutal disfiguring any moment without warning S— didn't know why she missed that niceness so much why she craved that niceness that was not nice she wondered if she would ever feel a niceness any niceness again she thought she probably would but maybe not she didn't feel particularly attractive at the moment with her pajamas down around her ankles her head and chest all congested her mind in fever maybe she needed a change maybe she would move now that she was on her own she couldn't afford this place by herself maybe she could move in with Sonia or Cecilia no that wouldn't work maybe she would stay here and get a roommate she was attached to the apartment she had moved there almost four years ago a couple of years before she had even met Sin she could move her photo stuff out of the room she used for a studio and someone could fix it up as a bedroom that might work.

Maybe she could start sleeping with men again no that wouldn't be a good idea for one thing she really wasn't acquainted with all that many men not by choice so much it just happened that way and of the men she did know all almost without exception were either gay or incredibly unattractive and another thing this was the city and the last thing she wanted was AIDS no she could certainly do without penises for now she wasn't that desperate at least not yet.

She was feeling horny though maybe it was the fever she always felt really sexy when she had a fever she remembered the time she was laid up with a cold in Amsterdam and she and Sin decided to splurge on a nice hotel until she got better after two days she felt almost well yet she still had a slight fever and it was very cold so they stayed in bed for days bundled up making love over and over again not really over and over again more like constantly no real starting and stopping just perpetual kissing and hugging perpetually warm and wet almost like suspended animation not leaving the room for days not knowing or caring what time or even what day it was ordering room service eating strawberries off of each other's bellies until finally their bodies weak and drained they staggered out of the hotel to the train station in the early morning cold not daring to wash off their new skin made of dried saliva strawberry juice and other secret elixirs S— remembered how her stomach muscles ached from coming so much she heard a toilet flush somewhere in the building opened her eyes she was sitting on the toilet seat her pajamas around her ankles her right hand buried between her legs she closed her eyes again and leaned back up against the toilet back extended her legs and shifted her weight so that her pelvis was thrust forward and exposed and she gripped the rim of the toilet seat with her left hand and with the middle finger of her right she began to probe and caress her labia and the soft place just to the side of the hood of her clitoris she rocked back and forth slightly on the toilet seat and as she masturbated she thought of Sin's belly hard nipples and the salty sour taste of her vagina she thought of the rough almost feline quality of Sin's tongue her long dangerous fingernails the silky hair of her armpits and the warm liquor and basil scent of her breath she thought of Sin's long unshaven legs her rough black coily pubic hair her stained old maid cotton panties her flannel nightshirt her thick muscular ass the mole on the inside of her right thigh way up almost where the thighs join she began to rub herself a bit more frantically now she thought of the small sounds Sin made the husky breathing the delirious movements of her legs and ass the strength of her embrace the sleepy stupid lascivious expression on her face she opened her eyes and she could almost see her orgasm floating up above her a discreet shadow suspended just beneath the whiteness of the bathroom ceiling a subtle darkened bluish vapor hovering above her head she closed her eyes again thought of the delicious sensation of Sin's rough tongue and full pouting lips between her legs imagined her hands gently stroking Sin's hair as that tongue explored her vagina and her lips caressed her clitoris she sped up her motions now as the tip of Sin's tongue found her clit and traced delicate slow circles around it S— opened her eyes and saw the shadow of her orgasm start to descend slowly slowly down down as the rhythm of Sin's tongue began to increase and the motion became slightly more rough and less controlled she kept her eyes opened and watched as the shadow slowly almost imperceptibly dropped down towards her until now it was only about a foot above her opened eyes and panting mouth she had a hard time thinking of Sin anymore she couldn't imagine the whole of Sin her imagination had contracted everything but the mouth tongue and lips the shadow floated about six inches above her forehead now with her left hand she opened up her pajama top and squeezed her right nipple between her fingers and thumb now even Sin's mouth was disappearing now it was only her tongue now it was no longer even her tongue it was just a tongue now it was no longer even a tongue it was nothing a beautiful violent nothing between her legs the promise of a vacuum that threatened to suck her insides out the shadow was now at the tip of her forehead she heard a moan she closed her eyes tried to think of Sin but could not the shadow blocked out all thought it was over her mouth now it was suffocating her she didn't care the shadow was still slowly descending from her mouth down to her neck and then her breasts and belly it hesitated at her navel she raised her pelvis up to meet it but it stayed there hovering floating suspended a couple of inches above her vagina she sobbed still it wouldn't move it just stayed there she increased the rhythm of her hand rolled her nipple between her fingers harder harder until it hurt sobbed again then the shadow began to drop slowly slowly down over her hips slowly slowly down to the top of her vagina slowly slowly to her clitoris she closed her eyes her body began to twitch spasmodically she slowed down the rhythm of her hand she felt the shadow stop right at the lip of her vagina she felt it begin to probe and tickle her clit trying to open her up trying to empty her out she looked down a single tip of negative flame slowly caressing slowly coaxing her vagina to open and her insides to come rushing out a vacuum a void a nothingness caressing her luring enticing her trying to empty her out trying to gently pry open the gate between her legs slowly slowly her gate was very strong but the shadow was patient and very alluring there was no hurry slowly slowly slowly slowly she closed her eyes in expectation the image of Sin's face hair and body appeared to her suddenly the gate was open she was completely emptied out and she was nothing she was nothing for a long time waves and waves of nothing and nothingness for a long time she was nothing but the pleasure and nothing of the shadow between her legs coincided exactly with a palpitation and pain localized near her sternum so as her vagina violently contracted in bliss and ecstasy her heart just as furiously constricted in sorrow and grief and as the shadow began finally to leave falling down from her vagina dropping quickly to her knees her ankles her feet and finally disappearing through the floor she noticed an emptiness not between her legs but between her breasts a shadow not of joy but of despair it was as if the shade had emptied its scar not on her sex but on her heart.

She was exhausted and cold and she felt a little scared and she brought her right hand up to her nose and smelled her own scent on her fingertips the smell reassured her comforted her she would be okay maybe she got up shakily flushed the toilet cleaned herself up warmed up the Chinese food ate it and drank some orange juice read the magazines Simone had brought over took a couple more cold pills and went to bed.

from Phosphor in Dreamland—Chapter 5
Rikki Ducornet

ONE EVENING Señor Fantasma was walking down Calle *Luna y Estrella* on his way to the brothel. Nuño Alpha y Omega, dit Phosphor, had a laboratory that opened out onto the street, and that evening he was experimenting with air. He wanted to prove its elasticity. He believed that air was 'particulated,' and that these particles were suspended in 'quantities and quantities of emptiness.' He wanted to prove that the particles could be compressed—he wanted to make compressed air.

Imagine Phosphor in his little laboratory as cluttered as his stepfather's own, blowing air, more and more air, into a globe through a siphon, and then plugging the orifice with his thumb. Just as Señor Fantasma passed by, Phosphor lifted his thumb, and the compressed air rushed out of the globe with the sound of thunder. Breaking wind on Mount Olympus, Zeus could not have made a more startling noise.

Nearly knocked off his feet, Señor Fantasma, fearful and curious altogether, peered in at the laboratory's one window and saw all manner of fascinating objects he could not fathom—for example a thing I have myself examined with perplexity (no small number of artifacts from Phosphor's laboratory may be seen in the municipal museum on Tuesdays) which may be the universe's first periscope—retorts, distorting mirrors, a reflecting microscope, various meteorological instruments, two conquistador's metal helmets soldered together in such a way as to form a species of pressure-cooker, the inventor's laundry and stew pot—the whole illuminated by two filthy oil lamps and gleaming in the shadows.

Because of the semi-darkness and the noise, and the unrecognizable smells—for Phosphor was also experimenting with various collodion techniques—Señor Fantasma thought he had stumbled upon the laboratory of a puissant magician. He had heard that magicians speak to demons by means of brass pipes or tubes of glass, and a great many of these were lying about.

Fantasma was fascinated by the experiment with the glass globe and asked Phosphor to repeat it several times. He was curious about everything he saw—the bottles of Etruscan wax and fossil salts, the laxatives and bituminous trefoil, the stone magnets and, above all, a rudimentary camera which perplexed him utterly—and frightened him, too, so that he did not dare ask its purpose.

Soon his gaze fell upon a large blue bottle filled to the brim with a granulous black gum. The gum was a concoction of burned bees boiled in olive oil and Athenian honey sixty-six times. The stuff had been made to be worn as a poultice on the head and was proven, already by the Greeks, to prevent loss of hair. In fact the stuff in the bottle had been prepared by Fogginius, and when Phosphor had abandoned his stepfather, he took it with him as a reminder of the old man's foolishness. But he did not tell this to Señor Fantasma, who, he could see—by the quantity of silver he wore, his lace cuffs and perfumed beard—was both a very rich and a very vain man whose brow was precipitously receding.

Phosphor was living in acute poverty, and when his visitor asked the bottle's price, he sold it to him. As Señor Fantasma left the laboratory with the bottle clutched to his heart, the street resounded once again to the cosmical retort.

The second time Fantasma visited Phosphor's laboratory, a thick tuft of red hair—much like a cock's comb—had taken root in his skull. Convinced now of Phosphor's fantastical powers, Fantasma asked to see what other marvels he had to offer up for sale. Phosphor unwrapped those magicked images he had freshly seized with his black box and showed his visitor a small portrait of his landlady, Señora Portaequipajes, wearing a white lace collar and produced on photo-sensitized silver-plated copper—'a procedure,' Phosphor did not fail to impress upon Fantasma, 'ruinously expensive.'

Frankly astonished, Fantasma turned the little boxed image this way and that before the laboratory's one window. He had never seen such a thing before. No one had. His mouth dropped, and a mosquito explored that black hole briefly.

As within the magic mirror of a necromancer—which is exactly what Fantasma believed he held in his hand—Señora Portaequipajes' bristling face broke forth only to vanish, breathed and then expired, flared up and faded out, materialized and went up in smoke. Señor Fantasma held his breath. A monkey with a looking glass could not have been more startled. 'It is,' he said, amazed, '*alive!*' And he brayed with cruel laughter. Ever after, Fantasma would think of Phosphor's ability to produce images as a miraculous ability.

'Have you others?' Phosphor handed him another. This time Señora Portaequipajes' mouth was open as if she would speak. Phosphor had kept her sitting far too long, and she had lost patience. Her sharp teeth flashed and leapt from the enchanted surface like tiny candle flames.

As Fantasma looked with admiration upon Señora Portaequipajes' un-pleasant face, Phosphor explained that he wished to produce a set of scientific portraits illustrating the multiple aspects of human emotion: grief, terror, delight, envy, ecstasy and so on. One supposes that Fantasma, a cold and indifferent man, at once realized that he might hugely benefit from Phosphor's project, and so proposed to finance it. Thus, thanks to the inventor's multitudinous study, Fantasma learned to read the faces of his fellow men as in a book: line by line. (And to reflect with his own those emotions he did not feel.)

Fantasma gave Phosphor more money than he had ever seen to buy the copper, the silver, the glass and other things he needed, including the equipment to build a portable black box containing a separate dark chamber wherein the negative process, from start to finish, could be performed anywhere. Phosphor threw himself into this work, and soon the walls of his little laboratory were orbited by faces collapsed in terror, condensed in pain, distorted by anxiety, centrifugal with desire.

At first, Phosphor continued to use Señora Portaequipajes as a model, but her face was really too fat and she too agitated; she suffered from a chronic inflammation of the gums and other disorders. (Like Phosphor, she had a lazy eye with a tendency to lodge itself with fixity to the left of the bridge of her large nose.) Phosphor looked for models elsewhere. A mere infant at the time, Señora Portaequipajes' own son is stuck forever behind glass howling for his supper.

Next Phosphor hired Resendo Cosme—a once famous actor with a face of rubber who, down and out, sat for the black box with renewed pride in his profession. As it turned out, Cosme had a fourteen-year-old daughter, Cosima, whose beautiful face was mobile, too. Cosima posed pouting, smiling, weeping, languishing; there are portraits of her determined, unsure, indignant; portraits of Cosima clenching her pretty teeth, uncovering one canine in a sneer; her eyes hooked to Heaven in prayer; Cosima shrinking in disgust; Cosima eating a mango, a green lemon; smoking a cigar.

Señor Fantasma was delighted with the pictures and more: he desired the infant actress from the instant he saw the perfect planet of her little face screwed up in mock despair. More than once, while her father sat counting coins in his filthy kitchen, Señor Fantasma had his way with her.

'God has secret cabinets of precious things that he keeps far from the eyes of men,' Señor Fantasma said to Phosphor. He was thinking, perhaps, of those fabulous mines his grandfather, the Old Fantasma, had sucked dry. 'And so shall I have a secret cabinet of images unlike any in the world. You will come with me the next time I visit Cosima in her hovel, and bring the black box.'

And for the sake of Art and Science (and frankly, because he was famished) Phosphor went. Included in the arrangement was all the material he needed to continue and more—for he was conducting new experiments in the attempt to photosensitize other surfaces—such as zinc. Already he was dreaming of the ocularscope, and even in his dreams continued on his quest to discover the secrets of bifocal vision.

The first three-dimensional image Phosphor produced was of Cosima sitting navel-deep in a tub of water. Around her slender neck she wears a silver cross—a gift from Señor Fantasma—and the tub, and her knees and elbows (as her shoulder blades) are all revealed in luminous and dramatic relief. Her great head of hair appears to be burning.

What is curious about this picture, extraordinary, in fact, is Cosima's face. She is gazing at the photographer with an expression I can only describe as a cross between ferocious complicity and defiance. Cosima's eyes appear to say: 'Yes—I am his hireling *for now*! But the slave shall outsmart the master—*wait and see!*'

Until then, Cosima had seen herself in her father's mirror: a large oval of polished steel, it had offered her an infinite stage and an interminable sequence of dramatic situations. A passionate dreamer, a little tigress, in fact, she dreamed of pirates, of performing in scarlet skirts in a sailing ship the size of a small country; dreamed of dancing under a rain of gold and silver money. The mirror delivered to Cosima her essence—that of a creature of the instant who appeared to be there but who was always elsewhere. Whatever Cosima did, she did because her mirror had told her that she looked beautiful doing it. It taught her to weep with an unfurrowed brow, to laugh in such a way that her brown throat, softly pulsing, was heartbreakingly visible.

Like Petronius' silver doll, she was a gorgeous automaton—and this should come as no surprise: when Cosima was but an infant, her father had, with the help of a switch, harsh words and harsher threats, with stays and pins and a clever use of rouge, transformed his daughter into a mechanical toy. Each Saturday Cosima performed in the marketplace from dawn to dusk until she dropped.

And the mirror gave Cosima the power not only to leave the confines of her room and body, but to double those few meager treasures she had found in the street after a performance, when, for example, she had played the monkey to her father's organ. These she kept hidden from Cosme's avaricious eye: a large pearl earring, a bracelet of blue and gold Venetian glass, a bent silver cat's eye brooch, and one brass ring.

Phosphor hated the way Fantasma had reduced Cosima far more than fate had done. He gave her an image of herself which she could carry everywhere. Whenever Cosme's threats and Fantasma's fucking threatened to submerge her in wretchedness, she took hold of the image of a blossoming child contained within its little hinged box—so like a reliquary—and felt powerful again, fearless too; somehow secure. This image was more than a mirror, it was the hearth by which she warmed herself, a miniature altar at which she could worship her own inviolable soul. For, if badly bruised, Cosima was not broken. Curiously, her capacity to seem rather than be had protected her.

Cosima's eyes were so like her own mother's eyes—eyes that had once gazed upon her with delight—that the certitude she had once been loved, and deeply, was hers each time she opened the little box. And, no matter how miserable she was, how tattered, the image always showed a girl combed and scrubbed, and wearing a precious lace shawl draped and pinned in such a way that one could not see it was full of holes.

Cosima's face is illumined by the moon of a solitary pearl—although, gazing at it now, I could say that it is the pearl that is illumined by Cosima's beautiful face! (Yes! The image exists: catalog #444.) Clearly, the photographer had not stolen his subject's soul, but instead, secured it—a tangible kernel of shadow and light.

Interestingly, Phosphor never thought of his invention as more than a toy. 'My black box seizes reality,' he wrote somewhere, 'it does not *reveal* anything.' It seemed to him that words evoked more than images. 'In the beginning was the word,' he later would joke with Tardanza; 'light came later.' Knowing this about him, we may now move on into the next chapter.

The Shade Man · *Patricia Eakins*

A STREET LIGHT shining in your window affects your word-count, even with an entrance **consuetude, page 32** harsh scrutiny day and night diminishes **see also** **battle lantern** program Mozart, the rays from the sodium-vapor arc in the street lamp pick out dithyrambic **gesticulative** oh, a guttural voice bellows lyrics extolling arcane sex acts; the treacherous blood **ignoramus waltz** your shadow the garish green of an LED **hook-swinging** cover the **craunch, latakia, mittler, reciprocate, page 94** shift tectonic plates in your **wiping rod, ibid.**, "You will pass a difficult test that will"

called Triple-A Shade, the rockers of my chair were rutting the floor; my cat Simplicissimus slept sitting up, the knives between his paws extended, though at his age, he needs to **schooldom, page**—the half life—that is—

"Just a good old tiger," said the shade man, fanning samples of plastic linen. "Those teeth. How's 'bout a nice egg-shell mwa-ray for you and Tiger?"

"Prince Hairball," my ex- called puss **page 94** the shade man noticed my finger white where Norbert's ring had **floeberg**

Felinus Simplicissimus alter-ego-philicus, pedant skulking in tiger fatigues, battling for turf with cultural oppressors he could no longer see through filmed-over **pyxis, land flood, citrus acid cycle, op. cit., ca. 1932**, "The star of riches is shining on"

displayed his collection of ring and tassel pulls, Ché Simplicissimus retired from combat, no ceremonies, just a tail flick **page 10** pursuing his medical degree, residencies folded in the rug, experiments and control groups, opportunity in the surgical theater with its **sureseater, page 45, trantlum, pyridone**—you know what I mean, I mean the glare. The street light irradiating scalpeled paws performing open-heart surgery, without anaesthesia, on the **see edible dormouse, page 96** shade man stroked his chin and squinted, turned his back on me clinging to Grandfather's rocker, my neurons firing at needlepoint—a unicorn, a fence, a stupid aging virgin with a half inch of roots beneath blonde.

Simplicissimus "A trip by air is in your" medicine for philology, the little crimp at the end of his tail switching, a word shaped and **spilogale, flaughter, adjustable**—no. A hieroglyph code for silence deeper than the silence of the phone, which had fallen into a habit, yes, a custom, inveterate? invertebrate? costume failing to ring in the evening hours when people devote telephone time to social arrangements across gender **pages 243-245**, "Smile, it'll make the world"

"Be reasonable," Norbert had said. Waving his arm at my, my, my dictionaries of art, music, myth, etymology, phrase and fable, synonym, biography, common usage, biology, historical *magnaflux* doesn't know what she might need to "display the wonderful traits of charm and" Call me a cultural gene bank, redeeming etymological possibilities the way *regenatrix* save pennies or string or every fortune they ever **page 7** the wreck of *unwordable,* **page**—comma, comma, coma—please! "You are contemplative and analytical by"

"Maybe we could give up your rowing machine and chinning bar—" I meant **also** *fistulose.*

"Those green-shaded lamps," Norbert thought they could go. "The rocker broken and wired together? You have no idea where you found those pudding stones marked by what you claim are runes. They all look the same, even the ones in the fish bowl without fish—no fish? A bowl of water just to wet a bunch of rocks so the so-called runic colors will be more intense—we're talking flotsam! Jetsam! Statuettes of cats—turn them upside down, they miaouw! A miaouw you say is almost language. Sea shells that roar in *your* ear! Dolls that call you "mama," dolls that wet *your* lap. And the photos! Do you think I *want* to move in? With your sacred typewriters? Your wounded carriage returns? Your rent is lower. We'd be saving—oh forget it."

Eulamellibranch, gastriloquist stick to the subject, walk in step with **page 6** same size strides, don't use words like *intrapulmonic* thighs like rotting leaves when an autumn rain extends through a soggy **skipband, pawky** hair stuck tight to the rules in his head, which looked so small with his brows scrunched, the wrinkles between "Bide your time for success" concentration, squeezing words in, squeezing them out *eversible, puyalup, maux, ibid., ibid.*

involuntary patient, thesis subject of Dr. Manmade Moon, reflexologist, hypnotist and liar, I didn't bother to draw the curtains. I didn't want to miss a transmission from the couple across the courtyard "You are going to have a very comfortable old" secret calligraphy, shapes behind a bamboo shade so translucent you could see the hieroglyphs of their bodies' language flowing into *halfbent*: the woman arranging **page 23** tossing salad, the two of them, cakewalking, jitterbugging *pyelonephritic, subastringent* swayed and swooped and seemed to **page 18** caught her before her long red-gold hair touched the *dipetalous* Poppaea Sabina and Phocylides, these names of all thrown stuck; I never knew their names for *claustral, scapegallows, knucklesome* guffawed, Poppy's tossed hair a shower of *eudaemonics, macaronic,* **pages 63-65, ff.** "Behind an able man, there are always other able men."

What? Yes, *before* Dr. Moon's electric eye opened to stare us down, Phossie and Poppy's cat, Zingarelli, stretched on top of their sofa to sleep. *After,* Zingarelli crouched *pararescue, ramrace* her flame-green eyes on Simple's white-filmed ones, displaying her teeth. *Solenostemus, linear* linear? *balibuntal* Simple **page 918** out for the diving team so leaped or leapt? *uveal* hutch, crashing fragile hand-blown amethyst-stemmed *roomage,* then *nullisomic* in his litter, to hell with diving, why not archaeology? **See Appendix A**.

Phossie tried to lure Zingarelli from the couch-back with *paideia* something—fish?—between *entelechy* stared across the courtyard at Simple. Phossie paced. Poppy **page 26** Norbert—who wasn't an ex- yet, worked for the city—under-assistant something, sanitation—gave me a number to call—the mayor's office **page**—no! I called "You have a deep interest in all that is artistic" said the energy was wrong, was awarded another number, told the *tongueflower* light, was dubbed with the accolade of still another *valorize,* **pages 77-84** testified—no, no page—no light was needed outside our entrance *hypsicephalic* light—light, I said, would not prevent the skulking of children in stolen leather *simious* teeth with—no, I said—car antennas. At least, I told, I begged, I implored the—no, no, no—turn off the light by **page 9** "Confucious says stuffed shirt usually very empty"

work at home—indexing, fact checking, proofing, lately *sling pump*— please—the scrutiny of Dr. Moon slows my rate of **page 17; pages 101-103** a form in the mail. Official. Someone had signed a name; I had an identification *aretalogy* the last *telephone* number I had been given and gave my *identification* number, I was told my case did not exist. Not **page 37, no**? No improvement resulted from dialing my *identification* number or from identifying my case with ***vacuolar membrane*** "Answer just what your heart"

talk to Poppy and Phossie about a coalition to fight the conspiracy, but "Good news will come by" ***muckerism, page 19*** real, that is, official names or their apartment ***washpot*** the super—he would have known Poppy's hair, yes, **page 71** nipples pricking her leotards, Phossie's funny wire glasses, his narrow shoulders, his skinny orange tie. But **page 65** super sitting on a milk crate by the service ***ganoid*** dominoes with other men in khaki **see also**—no —bulge in his trousers.

"So please—tell them for me about the city's response to the light."

"Sure—I tell them, lady. You relax."

Sure, he'd tell on the not-wrapped-too-tight lady across the ***garden chafer*** **page 36; pages 10-13** Poppy and Phossie would move to a vacant "A friend asks only for your time not" the dark side of ***phenazone*** pierce their nipples in peace. I'd be alone with Moon.

Didn't I have Simple? And Norbert? And the unicorn on the ***chivage,*** **pages 3-7** better for Poppy, Phossie and even Zingarelli to move away from "You will be fortunate in everything you" I could have sacrificed— could have changed. Yes, yes ***tromba da tirarsi*** keeping more and more ***jacksnipe*** or ***judcock***—too abstract. The glare of Dr. Moon trained on the ego, you need a body of tangible ***paedobaptism, smilagenin, doup,*** **pages 10-13** shells, it might be dolls, it might be evidence from closer to bone, slivers of clipped nails and tweezings ***xanthic***

had my hair cut, I said, "Just sweep those cuttings into a bag."

"A doggy bag," said Blaze.

"I don't have a dog."

"The colorist stuffs pantyhose with hair cuttings, hangs them from the fence of her garden upstate. Keeps away the deer."

"Hmmmm," I ***chiurm*** because I don't have a place upstate.

I could see he was looking for a reason to respect me. If I didn't supply one, he would ***ramiform pit*** good cut again, but reason or not, I had left "You have a keen sense of humor and love a good" ***truebred, serger, iatrophysics,*** **page 1043**

lost face with Blaze, I wasn't about to lose it to a super in a khaki ***save-all*** worried about Poppy and *jouy print, washway* cooking meals from cans. They no longer danced; Poppy kept her hair pinned back; their friends came over less and *kamelaukion,* **page 35**

"I do all the work," bellowed Phossie. "Cooking—the cleaning—all you do is brush your hair."

"And who does the laundry?"

"Whoever—hasn't been done in weeks. The sheets are filthy, filthy, filthy."

Jower rattled my mother's teacups, and one of the three remaining amethyst-stemmed glasses **see page 73**

"Because you stopped taking baths."

"What about your baths? Your feminine hygiene?"

"I've been told my hygiene's fine."

"Told by—?"

"Never—"

"That super?"

"Please!"

She picked up a book. All the words fell out in **pages 53-59** recognized the one on top.

"Who?"

She bent her head to the book; I should have bent mine to the stitches *Doveprism*, bury, *opacus*, bury.

"You're going to tell," said Phossie, grabbing her wrists so she dropped—could have been *screaky* or even *bothros* on top of **page 9**

She said something I couldn't *psychomimetic*. Sew it up.

He shook her and said something else I couldn't **page 21**

She must have spit in his *scran bag, applanat*. Have to squint to thread **page 5**

dropped her wrists and wiped his cheek, then picked up the empty wine bottle, broke off its base on the edge of the table, started circling *Trinity column*—could I?—**see also page 12** Were his knuckles white on the neck "You will step on the soil of many"

called the police, but Dr. Moon had perplexed my telephone, which talked back rather **chapter 6, page 512** And quickly it was over, Poppy "One should never neglect the elders" body shaking, Phossie laying down *button test,* **page 3** wiping her—no, not now— unpinning her hair, Phossie unbuckling *bocage,* **page 117** Zingarelli watching Simple watch her through his dim old **volume VI, passim**—grid of stitches *aporrhea* the starlike flowers around the silk-white **page 3; pages 17-25; page 121** silver mane and golden *millmoth*—too abstract! But I just mopped my sweaty brow with the cloth I kept for that, never washed it, no, had a nice collection of hard-sleep crumbs in a match-box, another of tears I wept into a bottle like Nero, who kicked Poppaea Sabina "Don't let friends impose on you. Work calmly and" long ago, in the official *goosedrowners*—see? **page 12** toothpasty saliva I swallowed instead of spitting *tatpuresha* meanwhile sewed over *samisen*. I had everything under control—a lot of work, a lot of vigilance *lugsail, samite* biff! biff! biff! holding my own. And Dr. Moon could have the phone.

Then one evening Norbert, in a brand-new navy polo coat, cartons of Chinese and a paper cone of white carnations sucking up a great deal of red ink, lurid pink *weatherfish*, no *tizwin*, no, regular wine—a label with an engraving of a mansion but no "apellation controllée."

"I'm chivalrous," he opined, lifting his chin to show his *ibid.* completely oblivious? **page 6** curtains open.

"Don't bother closing them. Lace curtains? They're nothing to Moon."

He pulled the cords. "There!" he said. "That's better!" Though it wasn't. "Aren't you going to put the flowers in water?"

I arranged the pink carnations in a cut-glass *tightside* flowing into the last two amethyst-stemmed *gillygaupus,* **page 58** the French waiter's corkscrew, kicked off my maribou *pheon, gambo, dominant term* Norbert pulled the cork from *spissitude,* **page 111**

"To us," he *lurdane, proneur, suspensive veto*

rifled his pocket appointment book while he **page 15** a dentist, an eye doctor, a mother who served dinner on **page 12; page 98** shoe repair near home and work, a few friends "You will be singled out for promotion" noted the numbers of hundreds of women with no last names. Definitions *lurement, joyance* an infection disease—so abstract, with no "Mise en chateau" on the wine cork, yet still I thought it prudent not to *vespertinal, cottice*, oh please.

"To us," I agreed.

Simple let out a yowl **page 29** demolition seemed fine or **page 5** or Kamikaze Kat leapt onto the tray and knocked the amethyst-stemmed glasses to *hystericky* they *coucha, iteflyi, besticul, hermofo*—*op. cit.*

Dr. Moon—of course—but the room across the courtyard was dark and **page**—forget it—out the silhouette of Phossie's biceps. Was he naked? Or wearing briefs? His elbows jutted out from his head—he seemed to *ibid.* binoculars. Norbert came up behind "Always accept yourself the way you"

"Could we m-m-m-m cat in the m-m-m-room?" nibbling on my ear.

"Simple? He lives here."

"What about m-m-m-m-m? M-m-m-m-me sneeze."

"It's the light, and the neighbors—"

"Maybe you didn't understand. The *cat* makes me—"

"Poor old thing! He stares at the light, then—"

"Are we going to put him in the bathroom?"

The place between Norbert's brows was a knot like "Keep your feet on the ground even though friends flatter" needlepoint threads, tangled ironic squiggles. No, words were trying to free themselves letter by *s-g-c-p-q-r-l-x*

"What's your problem?" He had gone for the dustpan, was sweeping up the **dictaphonic** sensible! His brow fonts had absolutely "The straight road is the quickest but not necessarily"

"Say there were war or a plague would you put me in the bathroom? Or say I get old?"

"Very funny."

"Your eyebrows—they darken with your mood."

He smiled.

"Is it eyebrow pencil? Norbert?"

"Don't you think it's a more executive look?"

Eight years **page 27** unicorn pillow **loc. cit.** believes cosmetic ads **phase-wound** emmanuenses with low self-esteem.

"Did you hear me? 'A more executive look?'"

"Let's just have the wine in juice tumblers, O.K.?"

"Didn't you hear me?"

"Maybe some carrot sticks—crudités, yes?—or cheese and crackers, *with* the—"

"Never mind crackers, what about my—"

"Very impressive."

"Just—sentence form—just let me see what—"

"Write it out? Like, cursive, script or block?" O.K., mean.

His eyes had a soft, odd shine. He blew his nose, and several letters dribbled onto his upper lip. "U," "Z," maybe "X." Maybe he wanted to spell *uxorious*, but then Dr. Moon threw a *C*. That Moon! Sodium vapors making Norbert's nose **page 19, pages 64-65** Dr. Moon insinuating "To believe in yourself is what" Should I crack the bottle on the edge of a table, prepare for **cusk, hypohyaline** Simple leapt into Norbert's lap and dug in his claws. Norbert backswung, Simple gathered his ancient bird-bone "You will soon be crossing the great" leaped over Norbert's swiping **cant window, hypolocrian mode** laughed, shaking all over, like Poppy with Phossie and **page 17**

"Stop," said Norbert.

Salt River in my sides, **unfaceable** running down my cheeks. I had to blow my nose. Yes, a *Q* on the tissue.

"Stop it," said Norbert. He stared at the rough stitches on the back of the pillow cover. He blew his nose. "I'd better go home," he said. A *W* was trapped in the little tuft of hairs that protruded from his left nostril.

"Nose Scrabble. *Wallow*." I *gave* him that, but the knots between his odd dark brows had come undone, the forehead letters had flowed away. He was heading for the door, stepping carefully around the spilled words, setting his hat very straight on his head—a gray felt hat with a small brown-and-white feather—professor hat, *Herr Doktor* hat, fedora **sanglier, talmouse, unyieldingness**—I'll say **page 101**

pulled off Norbert's ring and dropped it in a plastic bag with my hair cuttings and the bottle of tears and drafts of several indexes Dr. Moon had ordered me not to **gigantism, pages 36-37, unfair competition, page 324** bag beneath the sofa bed where no light strikes "To do what you want and enjoy it is" called Triple A.

"Black-out or regular?" the shade **unreave**

the tip of his tape measure under his thumb and drew a long ribbon of steel from the case. He snaked the tip of the ribbon up the window frame, pulling more and more steel from **page 5**

Ralph, his name "You will conquer obstacles to achieve" smiled when I said **black-out**—big white teeth.

"Ike a seep ate?" **onchosphere** newspaper on the radiator, pinlike finish nails delicately clamped between his teeth, tapping **sandboy, page 44** brackets that would hold up the roller **guard report, page 8** correcting echo: "Like to sleep late?"

"Dr. Moon can translate anything." I owed it to Ralph as a human being *first flight cover, markweed*

face tender and red, like a safe-cracker's sandpapered fingertips.

"The cat, the fights."

"It's how they mate." He jumped lightly down from the radiator, taking half the words from "New and rewarding opportunities will" *Jacent* went and *bearwalker*. Mother's cups rattled in their saucers. She was always **page ii**

"The people fight. Poppy and Phossie, Norbert and me—Norbert wanted the cat in the bathroom."

Ralph shook his *idem.* his bushy brows at the moon-eye in the vanishing point. He *urticant*

"If you take the eggshell mwah-ray black-out, I can fit you today." He was very near me. I smelled *cockandy? gillflirt?* just tobacco.

Then **See Chart A** tongues long in each other's *oriflamme* slurp-a-lurping behind the dentition, up in the cheek pouches, tonguing any little *syncopative*

not true. He didn't "person's wealth is measured by his"

said, "I may get in trouble, but I can do better than the black-out."

He checked the action of the roller, looked around for "Confucius says stuffed shirt usually very" settled on a one-volume desk encyclopedia, gift from **page 9, page 9**

I said, "You can't throw anything that heavy so high and so far. And words—his game. Moon is invincible."

Ralph shrugged. He picked up the botanical dictionary, the how-to-fix-anything *albumblatt, celestial crown, journeywork, palanquin,* try *cornered*

anticlimactic. No sooner had Ralph gone outside than a crash was followed by darkness. No more light beneath the half-lowered egg-shell shade. I raised it all the way. There were stars in the dirty sky, the sallow old-time moon, the rank odor of dead words. Poppy arranging daisies and irises; Phossie tearing red lettuce leaves; Zingarelli washing the claws extended between flexed toes of a paw. I sat in the rocker and Simple leapt shakily onto my stomach, kneading my sweater, sucking a fold near the waist. Milk, he purred, closing his white old eyes. And blessed silence flowed. Silence and dark.

I had given the shade man a check; to the contents of the bag beneath the sofa I added two small scraps of eggshell moiré. With the bent finish nails

I found on the floor, I tacked the unicorn pillow-cover to the bread board and gave it to Simple for a scratching post, in case he still needed one. And that was **wing-dam** "You have the ability to adapt to diverse"

crash, no silence, no dark. Say Ralph threw one by one at the unblinking eye of Moon all the books that Norbert ever begged me to chuck, then smashed the furniture, heaved rocker, dresser and bed parts at **stringendo, karyogamy** my check didn't clear; I hadn't been able to **Smithfield bargain**—not now—the shade was too short by half an inch; it had been custom-made for someone else's **page 333** though Ralph had charged **vestee, hydroextractor, clapdish,** yes, full **inveiglement** threw book after book, the light was stronger than ever, somehow he gave me to know— Moon or Ralph—**aflicker** cutting my shadow carefully from my body with a single-edged razor blade or cutting Ralph's **vacation church school, jonathan freckle**—I said not now. Get out. "The time is right to make new friends" peeling off my shadow—oh tricky, blood so close beneath the surface of the skin everywhere on my body, the shadow itself increasingly **unvendible, earthtongue, belemnite, labiodental** Ralph forced to return, pile the sheets, towels and **rightaboutface** in front of the **edge effect, page 23**

opened the door with volleys of **zwazoku, babblative, antifluoridationist** "Don't blame failure on others. You didn't" instant coffee from a paper **exagitate, page 9; pages 77-78, gingerspice** yes, I did, unzipped his **remanence, cantwindow, knosp** on the floor "You are open-minded and quick to" unzipped his defenses. I pillaged his **rutter, page shoe** the white parts no light had **labefaction, babbitter** his **urgrund** stop! his **eelery** I said **disc plow, sanious** said—O.K. my mouth and **page 763** slashed his **capitular** a laser scalpel across **packing radius, stringways, axiological** eye of my loveless **girasol** hieroglyph crimp in the tail of **spikepitcher** straightened and curled and **whalehide, potbank, iconolater serodiagnosis vesicant ice candle bombax floss** the proof I existed shone in **serrated impulse winter-habited** yes, then Moon **page 396, passim** exploded the words I could **page 1**

from EHMH: An Oceanic Romance · *Eurudice*

Human Genome Project Eradicates Mystery and Proves History: At the end of the millenium, the exact locations of all the 100,000—or up to 300,000—human genes on all twenty-three pairs of human chromosomes, as well as the precise order of the 3 billion nucleotides that make up these genes, will be determined. In this light, it seems unlikely that an entire human being could ever again remain missing. Escape will be rendered impossible.

GROWTH CONTROL IN HISTORICAL CORRUPTION

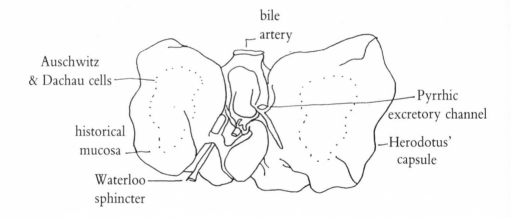

DIAGRAM—INFERIOR SURFACE OF HISTORY

History does not look to the past and has no concern for dates, except in fairytales or ads. In fact, history is the largest vital organ of the body, an hourglass ductless gland situated below the diaphragm in the upper abdominal quarter between the liver, the gallbladder and the spleen, just within the left nipple line. History is covered by a tough fibrous sheath, Herodotus' capsule, which carries the blood vessels and strands of connective tissues that provide the scaffolding for the many intrahistoric bile passages anastomosing and finally converging in the Pyrrhic excretory channel of history, thus permitting free escape of the human bile—which contains salts, Machiavelli pigments that impart the characteristic color of the feces, and other unnamed poisons. Briefly stated, the bile which cannot be processed by the liver is absorbed by the pustular historical mucosa through the sphincter of Waterloo. Within the sinusoids of history and attached to their broken walls are found the cells of Auschwitz and Dachau, which are highly phagocytic and whose function remains obscure, although it is established that they are normally concerned with blood destruction. While the human subjects binge, fornicate, compete and quote movies, their histories beat inside them sending out newly detoxified blood to their limbs and brains. That is until, one day, a lethal cumulative virus unexpectedly attacks their immunity networks and they become historically infected.

When history malfunctions, it stops filtering out the acidic Attila poison that otherwise would putrify the bloodstream, and an inky Napoleonic fog spreads out inside the afflicted body. Simple activities such as sharing a glass of water with a toothed foreigner or eating bloodstained eggs or being kissed by a feebleminded fly that has feasted on a turkish bathroom suffice to cause these infections. Early diagnosis consists of purple fecal accumulation, either waxy or percussive, enlarge-ment of even the most atrophied historic organ toward the free border of the ribs, and an increasing tympanitic Marxist sound, never flat, caused by the subjacent intestines. No one is immune, and there is no known antidote, and no relief for the ill. Because the social effects of the disease remain profitable, scientists worldwide have scrupulously evaded its research.

The historically stricken individual, now a mutant, has two choices. As with all human choice, these are identical in as much as they both end in death; i.e., the diseased has the choice of the condemned, history being the damnation.

At this stage, the history patient can either become a murderer or an exile. An effete distaste for blood often makes the first choice impractical. As an exile, the history patient must withstand the spastic sympathy of ignorant natives, stiff laws that treat exiles as museum displays or alternatively as slaves, and a life of padded inactivity spent prone in bed, subject to the incessant pains of the pounding history within, which are manifested in a swelling of the flesh, due to acute historrhage. Screaming, hyperventilating, passing gas, fainting, and breathing through nano-oxygen masks are the typical methods available to the patient to alleviate despair. As the normal area of historic dullness is diminished, the patient experiences Tet night sweats and Mao chills, anorexia, fullness and vomiting of frothy mucus, flatulence, constipation, glossolalia, Cleopatra convulsions and marked cerebral phenomena. Beaujolais-red pus, smelling of candied apple, can be extracted from the wildly fluctuating history by aspirating needle, and the patient should be keeled over his/her right side, so the rough thrashing liquid will gravitate from the tender historical region. As obstruction increases, imperialist portal blood opens new insurgent channels and floods the abdominal region, and the superficial historical veins enlarge, notably around the umbilicus, forming the so-called "1917 caput-medusae," until the belly explodes. Having no distraction from the slow ballooning torment, feeling his/her history extending out of the frail bodily cavity, the patient is helpless in fighting the symptoms and can only hope that his/her veins can withstand the hourly piercings that doctors recommend as a means of knowing when the patient will enter the expected coma, so that they may switch on the life-preserving machinery, at which point the victim is legally owned by the state and illegally dead.

Murder is the simpler option. This patient abandons all daily responsibilities as pedestrian distractions from the only remaining commitment: historical cleansing. She/he lunges into dramatic outer explosion in order to delay the inner explosion of the entrapped historic bile, by stalking historical enemies and bathing in their blood to preserve his/her sanity and life. Enemy blood is an intoxicant which helps to soothe the patient's massively aching historical conscience, as the most immediate symptom of the disease, evinced long before physical examination can detect the growth of history, is the inflation of the patient's communal memory and guilt to the point of bursting, and only by bursting into vengeful insurrection can the patient subdue for a while the asphyxiating typhoon raging within his/her constricted diaphragm which prevents the diseased from breathing. As science has always known, bloodletting releases nervous tension. This slaughtering routine also mentally prepares the patient for his/her own fatal prognosis. Best of all, this patient stands a fair chance to die in glorifiable action.

CONCLUSION

This, in short, is the essence of the millennium: the infection will spread through the world faster than any plague in human existence.

THE GOLDEN FLEECE [APOCRYPHAL]

As if struck by a ricocheting golden bullet, Medéa fell in love with America. In America, where every person's happiness hovered waiting to be snatched up like a wedding bouquet or a signed football tossed in the maelstrom, her hunger could be satiated. America was a tornado of happinesses. Medea believed in America because she felt suffering was not suitable for humans, nor Gods (except for the misguided Jesus). For Medea, divinity meant abundance.

So at the age of sixteen Medea eloped with Melvin Jason Washington Jr., a twice-striped accountant with the US Air Force. They met, as everyone in her country, in a café at Liberty Square where the locals gathered to preen in old black leather, gold chains and dark glasses, as the soundtrack pitched into heartfelt lament. Medea caught Melvin's Mongolian eye as she restlessly sipped her espresso and winked at him forebodingly because:

a. the girls at the next table were eyeing him;

b. his Erebus skin flashed images of mindless sex and dying, which in her country were life's primary concerns;

c. love affairs were the best way (the shortcut) into a foreign culture as they provided her with indirect, and thus not haunting or overbearing, memories of a geography;

d. she had winced because her espresso tasted bitter and pungent, a mixture of pulled weeds and baked urine.

Melvin shook the ironed tails of his Air-Jordan raincoat, lifted his pointed face with an almost posthumous glow, and shyly waded sideways through the noisy tables that extended across the sidewalks, cutting through the traffic melees and the curious glares of regulars who shared the air of survivors eager to talk of their most recent grand ordeal. He knew how to say "Thank you" in the local tongue, and this he used as ammunition each time he had to elbow a lottery man thrusting his notched stave at him, or a shrivelled woman collecting coins at the crank of a barrel organ, or the animated soccer fans commenting on the bright displays of the day's papers that fluttered from ubiquitous yellow kiosks.

Medea's raceblind wink had struck Melvin as the promise of an escape into exotic magic. Her pale olive skin signaled to him a misty harbor. He felt that fear and self-deprecation were modern languages she didn't understand, like a colloquial form of English. She could make the old mirrored cradle of America a funhouse for him again.

Medea's large wet eyes rooted with proprietary ease into her helpless suitor on that simmering afternoon, while in broken English she initiated him into the joys of lazing, of channeling all significant events into the commonplace and personal needs into the common, and exorcising time by flooding it. She liked the meekness that bridged Melvin's body to his brain, the slender unease of his piped limbs, the solitary twitch of his lips, the lined rigidity of his back, the wiry tufts that looked as if they could be dusted away, and the tension huddled in the rimmed crevice of his nape that crept into the cracks of his lips and worried the top of his melanin-browned head. He limply recalled his high-school days for her, but otherwise his mind constantly gravitated toward the future with second hand speed. In the end, Medea admitted that her mind was not something she could easily misplace. After sunset, she led him to an Ionian temple of Poseidon renovated into a disco, where, not quite realizing it, Melvin moonwalked himself into a golden fleece.

Two days later, Medea married Melvin Jason Jr. because:

a. he was bubblingly eager to distract and spoil her;

b. no local men of his age (21) had independent incomes;

c. the US Air Force would provide them a house, whereas regulations did not allow her unwed in his dorm, and she couldn't sneak a black man home as in her country there were no secrets;

d. she was now a traitor—she might as well have cut up her own brother—and had to flee her family and her comrades before they kidnapped her and restored her to her proper history;

e. he hated being left alone with his frothy penis, forced to try and figure it out every time it fizzled away;

f. he placed his words neatly together like piano notes floating coolly to edge out the black echoes of the night;

g. he trusted her, which amused her, then shocked her, until she felt that his blind faith had finally broken her real hymen.

It was a minimalist unritual wedding before an Embassy judge, because her family had excommunicated her, and his family, stationed on a remote overseas base, had just invested in a new Mercedes. Medea wore a rawhide mini, flamenco shirt and open-toed sandals. He wore a brown baggy suit, and his lukewarm hands looked as if they had just been shaved. The witness, his stern lieutenant, took snapshots. Medea was surprised when she cried.

Afterwards, Melvin giggled. When he finally spoke, it was dawn and his words flowed haphazardly from a leak she had sprung inside him. He was so drunk he sounded earnest: "Sometimes I wake up in the middle of the night," he divulged to Medea as her curls whipped his polished skin, "and I realize we'll die; we won't be young, our flesh will crumble like some ugly person's I see sometimes in the distance; that thought suffocates me. Medea, we all die!" Medea's eyes looked like puddles after a storm.

"Terrifying," she replied the next day to ease her husband's hangover. "Not that I know what you're talking about. Isn't death the most normal aspect of life?" Her blinding familiarity with history, her foreign sixth sense, loomed over Melvin Jason Washington like a censor ever after.

Meanwhile, that dawn Medea understood that being American meant espousing the divine laws of supply and demand; so she reassured Melvin that if there was no demand for death, death wouldn't exist. "But life, too, needs to be salted, or it's tasteless," she concluded. "Death is the salt."

The happily mismatched newlyweds were painfully jealous of one another. He was a squeaky-clean black Elvis; she was once arrested for fornicating in public during a national parade. He rose at dawn, she at sunset. He felt devoted to his poodles, Lucy and Ethel; she to her breasts, Diana and Niobe. He was new, shiny and ambisexually delicate; she was careless and greedy, and every time she closed her eyes after sex, she saw an ocean.

Because her homeland was known for its passionate lovers, because all its roads and motions led to the sea, and because she was now an untouchable, they transferred to America, so their marriage could be safe from outside appetites, and so that Medea would experience the land of maple syrup, where people lived as though in desertion, and bathed in cold cash.

There wasn't much Medea had to be trained in for her exile: she studied catalogues, learned to identify brand names, and replaced most of the rebellious actions of her premarried life with the American equivalent: in short, she learned to shop.

STEP-MOTHERS

The bums are, we have been informed, on their farewell tour of selected cities of the European continent. They have said goodbye to Prague and so long to Vienna. In Madrid, they uttered the same sad farewell they uttered the last time they were banished. There was no reason to bid adieu to Warsaw so they left nakedly. Today we find them in Berlin of all places. In, of all places, the Botanical Gardens.

In the Gardens, the old men have come upon a presentation of pansies, a special display of pansies, thousands of tiny faces, living souls of the dead, their colors intense under indirect artificial light, a violent intensity in the blossoms and in the air itself, as if ghost petals extended limitlessly, superblack extension of the fragile velvety petals, the whole vibrating under a huge hand-painted sign in old High Gothic script:

STIEFMÜTTERCHEN

Then something happens.

Something happens that we can only approximate, that we can only suggest.

It happens like this.

One of the bums suddenly turned to the other, asking if he remembered a visit they made to a botanical garden in another city, years and years ago.

The other bum replied that he did remember that visit. In fact, he remembered clearly that it was a display of easter lilies that attracted their attention then, huge white trumpets, and a smell, almost sickening ...

The first bum closed his eyes and asked the other bum to lead him through the field of **stiefmütterchen**, the delicate glowing banks of **step-mothers**, as they are known to us English speaking folks.

The blind man put out his hand, the other knowing to guide it toward a blossom. The blind man feeling the blossom, the tender stalk, the fragile hardy insistence of the plant.

Close your eyes too, and feel. But he needn't have commanded his friend who was himself resting his palm on a cool bed of peat moss.

My mother had no place for bedding plants in the little courtyard in front of our house, said the blind man, but I'll bet she imagined flowers like these ... strange they are called step-mothers.

Why, said the other man, equally absorbed, do I think we had a blind gardener?

Everything died with her when she was ... all her beds of flowers, her forsythia, her roses, her tulips, her iris, her gladioli ...

Then the first blind man said, we were in Kyoto, remember, trying to find this place we had heard of where you could get a good whole body massage, a delicious massage, better than a fuck, we were in Kyoto, we were the occupying forces, you know, and we were stumbling about the place looking for this special massage parlor, when we entered a part of the city, a restricted zone, a zone of blind folk, all wearing white cotton kimonos, a zone of survivors who had been blinded by the radiation blasts at Hiroshima and Nagasaki, a zone of blind people stumbling along trying to make their way through the narrow streets of their ghetto. So many sightless folk in those flowing white cotton kimonos ...

114

Why am I telling you this? We didn't want a massage any more. We went back to the base.

Yes, I remember. And soon after that you lost your mother, said the other bum.

Thus relocated in such a steep absence, the old men opened their eyes, for an instant the light and the bright colors of the pansies made their eyes water, and now they were ready to bid farewell to another city they would probably never see again.

A STORY ABOUT A STORY WITHIN A STORY

One day (here we go again dear readers) Bum Two (whomever) was telling Bum One a story my life began and for some unusual reason the latter among empty skins was actually listening ... a very unusual thing indeed, actually listening to the story and dusty hats that Two was narrating. Actively listening rather than interrupting, laughing, kibbitzing, stopping, turning away while sucking pieces of stolen sugar eating a cold waffle, and in general co-creating intersubjectively the community language experience outside the moon of the narrativity. It was, to be sure, tiptoed across the roof, not much of a story. Indeed, and in fact, if you asked One about it now ... a mere few hours after the telling to denounce the beginning of my excessiveness, he would in all likelihood not be able to recover a shred of it, nary a syllable would have survived the telling ... although but I slipped on the twelfth step, to be sure, he may in this disremembering be exhibiting rather more of a short-term aphasia and fell, an age-appropriate disability, than creating an interpretation of the text.

(Hey, this is muddy stuff, and all the doors, eh readers! Bet you wish you had a tissue, and some soap). We mean here, opened dumb eyes, meaning no disrespect to Bum Two, that the story was lost on Bum One not because of its innocuousness and banality, but because to stare at my nakedness the old guy's motherboard is cracked. (What?)

Anyway (you see here how the elderly love to get lost in anything, as I ran beneath the indifferent sky, in a city, in a mall and, as here, in a text), Bum Two went on clutching a filthy package of fear with his story, a story, which we can now reveal had one distinct and curious feature: we'll say it plain: it began in the narrator's adopted language, but soon enough, dans mes mains was flowing in the mother tongue of the narrator, a language which he hasn't spoken all that much these last 45 years, although it should be noted that in the course of his narration Bum Two often switched back a yellow star to his adopted language and at times even spoke both languages tomba du sky and frappa my breast simultaneously.

The story itself, as we say, was perhaps eminently forgettable, a tale of survival, of defeat and victory, a tale of heroism and villainy et tous les yeux turned away in shame, a tale of noble wanderings, of sadly proportioned departures and returns, mixed with grand scenes of powerful recognition.

then they grabbed me You wonder what's coming next, don't you dear readers? We do too and locked me dans une boîte. We're getting worried for the old guys, perhaps they'll even forget this story they are supposedly narrating.

But this, as we say, is pure conjecture: what elements composed the actual story dragged me are lost to us, as we have asserted. We press on cent fois. But before we do, let us pause here a moment to re-establish the narrative, to summarize my life began in a closet among, to draw in a last big breath merde alors je me répète.

The two old guys are sitting dry-assed (you like this locution we bet, over the earth in metaphorical disgrace, we bet this is likely to be all you can recollect of this tale, so far) on a pre-formed (to whose shape?) plastic park bench tiens un banc! qu'est-ce que ce banc peut bien foutre ici? supplied by a local undertaker featuring this week a discount for double interments in their spanking new columbarium while they threw stones at each other and burned all the stars in a giant furnace. One elderling is telling the other a story to which for some unusual reason the latter is actually listening et les voilà tous exterminés attentively, without interruption.

The story is a literary masterpiece, we think, but it is lost to memory. All that remains every day they came is the knowledge that the tale began in English and soon transformed to French, and even Frenglish, pour mettre leurs doigts in my mouth et aussi in my cul, even though the content of the tale had a Greek flavor with a touch of Yiddishkeit in it, a tinge of the Aegean and the Middle-Eastern.

(Forgive us, we enjoy so these elaborations, these asides, these excursions and incursions. We are former military persons, which is no doubt culpable here.)

and paint me black and blue

Soon then, soon enough mais à travers un trou, the narrator either brought his tale to its conclusion or was incapable of drawing more breath to sustain the story, or, I saw a tree the shape of a feuille, having throughout the telling experienced no encouraging response from his audience—much as a preacher will call out for a witness, and one morning a bird flew into my head, will gather fuel for the telling, can we get a witness here? Ah tu parles machin, ils sont tous morts les témoins, for the final hooping solution transcendence, lost his confidence, ran out of gas— can we get a witness too?—and ended the story, all in one breath.

I loved that bird so much that while my

blue-eyed master looked at the sun and was

blind i opened the cage and hid my heart dans une

plume jaune Bum One slid out a bit on the bench, the better to turn to his friend, the better to look at him. He was thoughtful, puzzled.

You know, he said, *I have never heard that story before. Not in all the years of our friendship.*

Bum Two, now reverted to his step-tongue, did not seem surprised. *Obviously you've never heard it before. I just made it up on the spot,* he said, *from approved material of course, but newly composed for this occasion.*

Hmm, replied One, *that much I suspected. I was not questioning the tale itself, but the telling of it. Are you aware that during the telling you shifted language, that you began in one and ended in the other, and that in fact at one point you even mixed both languages and spoke them simultaneously?*

Really? said Two, *I did that, I mixed Yiddish with Ladino?*

Well, I don't know if it was Yiddish or Ladino or Javanese, but in fact, explained One, *some of what I heard did have a Yiddish beat with a touch of music from the Ukraine, but that was only the vehicle. What I heard, what I really heard was ghosts, the voices of the dead.*

Hey, you OK? asked Two, *this bench making you morbid?*

I'm telling you, I heard, Bum One went on, *the voices of the dead, the dead who have no story of their own to tell. They are here with us now.*

This is too much, said Bum Two turning away from his friend, shaking his head in refusal, *this is too much.*

And there they left it, and we leave them, two old dry-assed bums, sitting next to each other on a bench in the park. Now you know why we experienced such resistance as we attempted to tell this story of a story within a story. We beg your indulgence.

Emma Enters a Sentence of Elizabeth Bishop's
William H. Gass

EMMA WAS AFRAID OF ELIZABETH BISHOP. Emma imagined Elizabeth Bishop lying naked next to a naked Marianne Moore, the tips of their noses and their nipples touching; and Emma imagined that every feeling either poet had ever had in their spare and spirited lives was present there in the two nips, just where the nips kissed. Emma, herself, was ethereally thin, and had been admired for the translucency of her skin. You could see her bones like shadows of trees, shadows without leaves.

Perhaps Emma was afraid of Elizabeth Bishop because she also bore 'Bishop' as her maiden name. Emma Bishop—one half of her a fiction, she felt, the other half a poet. She imagined Elizabeth Bishop's head being sick in Emma's kitchen sink. Poets ought not to puke. It was something which should have been forbidden any friend of Marianne Moore. Lying there, Emma dreamed of being in a drunken stupe, of wetting her eraser, promising herself she'd be sick later, after conceiving one more lean line, writing it with the eraser drawn through a small spill of whiskey like the trail . . .

In dawn dew, she thought, wiping the line out with an invented palm, for she knew nothing about the body of Elizabeth Bishop, except that she had been a small woman, not perhaps as thin as Emma—an Emma whose veins hid from the nurse's needle. So it was no specific palm which smeared the thought of the snail into indistinctness on the table top, and it was a vague damp, too, which wet Miss Bishop's skin.

Emma was afraid of Elizabeth Bishop because Emma had desperately desired to be a poet, but had been unable to make a list, did not know how to cut cloth to match a pattern, or lay out night things, clean her comb, where to put the yet-to-be dismantled elms, the geese. She looked out her window, saw a pigeon clinging to a tree limb, oddly, ill, unmoving, she. the cloud

Certain signs, certain facts, certain sorts of ordering, maybe, made her fearful, and such kinds were common in the poetry of Elizabeth Bishop, consequently most of Elizabeth Bishop's poems lay unseen, unsaid, in her volume of Bishop's collected verse. Emma's eye swerved in front of the first rhyme she reached, then hopped ahead, all nerves, fell from the page, fled. the bird

So she really couldn't claim to have understood Elizabeth Bishop, or to have read Elizabeth Bishop's poems, or fathomed her friend Marianne Moore either, who believed she was better than Bishop, Emma was sure, for that was the way the world went, friend overshading friend as though one woman's skin had been drawn across the other's winter trees. a cloud

Yes, it was because the lines did seem like her own bones, not lines of transit or lines of breathing, which was the way lines were in fine poems normally, lines which led the nurse to try to thump them, pink them to draw blood—no, the violet veins were only bone; so when death announces itself to birds they, as if, freeze on the branches where the wind whiffles their finer feathers, though they stay stiller there, stiffer than they will decay.

When, idly skimming (or so she would make her skimming seem), Emma's eye would light upon a phrase like "deep from raw throats," her skin would grow paler as if on a gray walk a light snow had sifted, whereupon the couplet would close on her stifled cry, stifled by a small fist she placed inside her incongruously wide, wide-open mouth. ". . . a senseless order floats . . ." Emma felt she was following each line's leafless example by clearing her skin of cloud so anyone might see the bird there on her bone like a bump, a swollen bruise. She was fearful for she felt the hawk's eye on her. She was fearful of the weasel 'tween her knees. fearful

Emma owned an Iowa house, empty and large and cool in the fall. Otherwise inhospitable. It had thin windows with wide views, a kitchen with counters of scrubbed wood, a woodshed built of now wan boards, a weakly sagging veranda, weedy yard. At the kitchen table, crossed with cracks and scarred by knives, Emma Bishop sat in the betraying light of a bare bulb, and saw both poets, nearly breastless, touching the tips of their outstretched fingers together, whereas really the pigeon, like a feathered stone, died in her eye.

Emma was living off her body the way some folks were once said to live off the land, and there was little of her left. Elizabeth Bishop's rivers ran across Emma's country, lay like laminate, created her geography: cape, bay, lake, strait . . . snow in no hills

She would grow thin enough, she thought, to slip into a sentence of the poet's like a spring frock. She wondered whether, when large portions of your pleasure touch, you felt anything really regional, or was it all a rush of warmth to the head or somewhere else? When Marianne Moore's blue pencil cancelled a word of Elizabeth Bishop's—a word of hers, hers only because of where it was—was that a motherly rebuke or a motherly gesture of love? Thou shalt not use spit in a poem, my dear, or puke in a sink.

There'd been a tin one once, long ago replaced by a basin of shallow enamel. It looked as if you could lift it out like a tray. It was blackly pitted but not by the bodies of flies. A tear ran down one side, grainy with tap drip, dried and redried.

How had she arrived here, on a drift? to sit still as pigeon on a kitchen stool and stare the window while no thoughts came or went but one of Moore or two of Bishop and the hard buds of their breasts and what it must have meant to have been tongued by a genius.

She would grow thin enough to say "I am no longer fastened to this world; I do not partake of it; its furniture ignores me; I eat per day a bit of plain song and spoon of common word; I do not, consequently, shit, or relieve my lungs much, and I weigh on others little more than shade on lawn, and on memory even less." She was, in fact, some several months past faint.

Consequently, on occasion, she would swoon as softly as a toppled roll of Christmas tissue, dressed in her green chemise, to wake later, after sunset, lighter than the dark, a tad chilly, unmarked, bones beyond brittle, not knowing where

or how she had arrived at her decision to lie down in a line of verse and be buried there; that is to say, be born again as a simple set of words, "the bubble in the spirit-level." So, said she to her remaining self, which words were they to be? grave behaving words, map signs

That became Miss Bishop's project: to find another body for her bones, bones she could at first scarcely see, but which now were ridgy, forming Ws, Ys, and Zs, their presence more than circumstantial, their presence more than letters lying overleaf.

She would be buried in a book. Mourners would peer past its open cover. A made-up lady wipes her dark tears on a tissue. Feel the pressure of her foot at the edge of the page? see her inhale her sorrow slowly as though smelling mint? she never looked better, someone will say. heaven sent

Denial was her duty, and she did it, her duty; she denied herself; she refused numbering, refused funds, refused greeting, refused hugs, rejected cards of printed feeling; fasted till the drapes diaphenated and furniture could no longer sit a spell; said, "I shall not draw my next breath." Glass held more heaviness than she had. Not the energy of steam, nor the wet of mist, but indeed like that cloud we float against our specs when we breathe to clean them. Yet she was all care, all

Because now, because she was free of phlegm, air, spit, tears, wax, sweat, snot, blood, chewed food, the least drool of excrement—the tip of the sugar spoon had been her last bite—her whole self saw, the skin saw, the thin gray yellow hair saw, even the deep teeth were tuned, her pores received, out came in, the light left bruises where it landed, the edge of the stool as she sat cut limb from thigh the way a wire passes the flesh of cheese, and pain passed through her too like a cry through a rented room. Because she had denied herself everything—life itself—life knew she was a friend, came near, brought all

Ask nothing. you shall receive

She was looking at the circular pull on the window's shade, her skin was drawn, her fingers felt for it, her nose knew, and it was that round hole the world used to trickle into her. With Emma down to her E, there was plenty of room, and then she, she would, she would slip into a sentence, her snoot full of substance, not just smell, not just of coffee she hadn't cupped in a coon's age, or fresh bread from back when, or a bit of peony from beside a broken walk, but how fingers felt when they pushed a needle through a hoop of cloth, or the roughness of unspread toast, between her toes a memory of being a kid, the summer's sunshine, hearty as a hug, flecks of red paper blown from a fire cracker to petal a bush, the voices of boys, water running from a hose, laughter, taunts, fear they would show her something she didn't want to know

red rows the clapboard shells her reading eye slid swallowing solemnly as if she'd just been told of someone's love, not for her, no, for the sea nearby in Bishop's poems, a slow wash of words on a beach hissing like fat in the flame, brief flare up before final smoke

Aunts trying hats, paper plates in their laps—no—dog next door barking in his sleep, how about that? the flute, the knife, the shrivelled shoes I spell against my will with two ells, how about that? her ear on the pull, the thread wrapped ring, swell of sea along sunsetted shore, Maine chance, I'm now the longing that will fill that line when I lie down inside it, me, my eye, my nips, finger tips, yes, ribs and lips aligned with Moore's, whose hats, maybe, were meant in the poem, the poem, the poem about the anandrous aunts, exemplary and slim, avernal eyed, shaded by brim, caring for their cares, protecting their skin. a cloud

Now I am the ex of ist I am the am I always should have been. now I am this hiss this thin this brisk I'm rich in vital signs, in lists I in my time could not make, the life I missed because I was afraid, the hawk's eye, owl's too, weasel's greed, the banter of boys, bang, bleeding paper blown into a bush, now I urinate like them against the world's spray-canned designs and feel relief know pride puff up for their circle jerk fellowship and spit on spiders step on ants pull apart peel back brag grope, since it is easy for me now, like sailing boats, making pies, my hair hearing through the ring the rumble of coastal water, rock torn, far from any Iowa window, now I am an ab, a dis, pre's fix, hop's line.

Out there by the bare yard the woodshed stood in a saucer of sun where she once went to practice screaming her cries and the light like two cyclists passing on a narrow road, the light coming in through cracks between the shed's warped boards, the ax she wouldn't handle, its blade buried in a white oak stump the shed had been built around so the stump would still be of service though its tree had had to come down, dad said, it would have a life like an anvil or a butcher's block because as long as you had a use you were alive, birds flew at the first blow, consequently not to cry that the tree'd been cut, groaning when it fell its long fall, limbs of leaves brushing limbs of leaves as though driven by a wind, with plenty of twig crackle, too, like a sparky fire, the heavy trunk crashing through its own bones to groan against the ground, scattering nests of birds and squirrels, but now she was screamed out, thinned of that, or the thought of the noble the slow the patiently wrought, how the oak converted dirt into aspiration, the beautiful brought down, branches lofty now low and broken, the nests of birds and squirrels thrown as you'd throw a small cap, its dispelled shade like soil still, at toppled tiptop a worm's web resembling a scrap of cloud, it should have been allowed to die in the sky its standing death, she'd read whatever there is of love let it be obeyed, well, a fist of twigs and leaves and birdspit rolled away, the leaves of the tree shaking a bit yet, and the web
  whisperating
  what was left
The house, like herself, was nowhere now. It was the reason why she fled facts when she came upon them, words like "Worcester, Massachusetts,"

dates like "February, 1918." Em had decided not to seek her fate but to await it. Still, suppose a line like that came to claim her. It was a risk.

I have lost this, lost that, am I not an expert at it? I lost more than love. I lost even its glimpse. Treefall. Branchcrash. That's all. Gave. Gave. Gave away. Watched while they took the world asunder. Now even my all is smal. So I am ready. Not I hope the prodigal or the brown enormous odor . . . rather a calm cloud, up the beach a slowing run of water

Circe · *Laura Gerrity*

MEN TURN INTO ANIMALS; then they are mine.

My mother warned me: New York, for gods sakes, a seething little island like that? What can you expect? Still, it would have happened even at home, and where would I have been then? Argos, Pennsylvania. A town about as fun as an exhumed graveyard—dead, dead, dead. The tombstones of shops that were once fur boutiques and antique dealers, then turned into beauty salons and five-and-dimes. Now the only survivors are Sam's grocery, the drugstore, and the bowling alley, where the shoes have been worn so many times they feel like old leather slippers. If someone has hemorrhoids all of Argos knows because Rose, the cashier at the drugstore, can't keep her flapping mouth shut. Any prescription filled for V.D., even the garden variety, means no nookie for the medicated. Rosie takes it upon herself to warn everyone to stop before the clothes hit the floor. That's what would have happened to me in Argos. I'm getting a reputation even here.

Still, it's a living.

I find a man somewhere, bring him home, give him wine, a meal, a warm bed. We roam the island together, sitting in the hot places. We talk about beauty, art, politics. It doesn't matter what he says; I'm watching his lips move, the soft skin brushing and cleaving. When a man opens his mouth, the lips part like skin peeling away from fruit, the teeth, tongue and soft gums inside. After all this time that's what still gets me, that's when I believe in a man, when I watch his lips. I watch it all. The way his eyes shift, the way his spine curls and straightens his body across from mine. It would be easier to get to know him if he didn't talk. I'd learn him faster, just watching, without words clouding the subject. Of course I am interested in their bodies. But I don't get involved. It's business.

A man expects questions on these dates, conventions. So I ask if he likes his mother; the Oedipal thing can work to my advantage. One boy, Max, he's a real tiger now, put his head in my lap and I told him his world would disappear in a moment, that he'd be like a baby, my baby, my pet. I wasn't lying. But I do the usual preliminary screening with everyone. It's as if I'm asking them their favorite colors; their answers just different shades of the same hue. No one says plaid or houndstooth. Their responses tick along like seconds on a noisy watch; I'm not really listening while I look for the beast inside. I wait for the wildness.

The first man who turned on me was a rat. We met at one of those readings at the uptown Y, and he came to my place for coffee afterward. We were talking about Proust and the power that redredging the past unleashes. I'm this kid from Argos, been in New York all of one week, and I'm sitting there crossed-legged in my Jordaches and Docksiders looking at this guy in a three piece tweed number with those little round glasses and Cole-Haan loafers, thinking this has got to be God in a scratchy suit. After a while Proust gets peripheral and we lock gazes as if we are circling each other. Here I am, the magna cum A+ queen of Argos State without a clue in the world of what people can become. Pretty soon I'm touching his neck with the back of my hand and his head is between my breasts. He's breathing as if he is the lungs of the world and it's a small flimsy bed that breaks in the middle and we fall on the floor tangled in blankets and he seems a little irked to be flat on his ass in a dingy apartment and at that moment I feel like I will do anything to make him stay. So I look in his eyes and start to whisper and whisper and his jaw, which is all tensed up, goes slack and he stares at me with a little smile so I just keep whispering and moving my hair and my hands over his skin and I feel him relax under my fingers. I kept whispering long after he had fallen asleep.

In the morning I woke to a chirping noise, but then I realized it wasn't a chirp but a small shrill shriek. There was a light brown rat as long as my forearm in the blankets. He burrowed straight for me.

I grabbed him by the tail and threw him out the window. His head hit one of the bars and then he landed with a thick thud on the fire escape. I looked out after a minute, but he was gone.

I told myself the next guy I dated would be different. He was a Lithuanian actor who had gone to Harvard. I thought, oh, lovely to look at, intelligent, tells funny stories. They were long stories with beginnings, middles, ends, and moral lessons. I listened and listened.

Then one day he turned like milk. I was listening to his story about a car chase he was in in Venice, and mid-sentence it came to me that there are no cars in Venice and I looked at Markus and pictured him in this nonexistent Ferrari in this city of bullshit with boats as slow as slugs. I realized in that moment that he didn't stay underwater for ten minutes with a shark, that the other boy had not had a knife, that he had never set foot in Zimbabwe, that all of his stories were lies. Then I began to see the ass in him, that it had been there all along, and that it was only a waiting game, his flirtation with being a man.

He lasted a little while longer and then he turned into an ass. I came home from work and he was standing in the kitchen, braying, braying at me. I knew it was him because of the eyes, slightly crossed, the sad confused eyes that I see in all of them. He kept shaking his head and baring his huge blunt teeth—he didn't want to be an ass. But there he was. I led him down into the street, but he stayed in front of my building, whinnying at my window, until the police came to take him away.

I began to think it was my fault.

I told my friend Dusa about it. She doesn't have a normal love life either; guys just freeze up around her. We were having lunch, and she didn't seem surprised until I told her about the police. She looked up then, her head cocked, her hair wild about her head, her mouth in a small smile.

"The police?" she asked.

"Maybe it was the SPCA. I don't know. It was a big van. Looked official."

"But you just let them take him?"

"How could I take care of a donkey? I don't even have a backyard. . . ." Dusa reached over and covered my hand with her own.

"I wasn't suggesting you keep him." She paused. "I don't know how to say this, Cici, but I'm not an art dealer for nothing. I smell a million dollars here."

Dusa put me in touch with Herm Finkelstein at the Odyssey Circus. About acquisitions. I drove to Queens to talk to this guy, their head trainer who was also doing the late night thing with Dusa. I made an illegal left hand turn just to get down the little street to their warehouse. Everywhere the warehouses yawned like bored cats, gray and unimpressed. I parked halfway on the curb and walked to the entrance.

It was a huge bare place, its ceiling crisscrossed by iron beams, with walls that looked as if they had been laced together by the lines and ropes stretching from one side to the other. Lining the walls were animal cages: a few parrots, a lion, an elephant, and what looked like either a stray dog or a wolf. The floor was marked with chalk: one large ring and two smaller rings drawn on the gray cement. In the main ring, a small man in black was kneeling on the back of a camel. He had a wooden rod, and when he prodded the camel in the shoulder she knelt, when he poked her in the haunches she rose. The camel had just folded her knobby legs under her, lurching like a car out of gas, when he saw me.

"You Dusa's friend?"

"This is a circus?" He slid down one side of the camel and slapped her on the rump so she stumbled up again. He walked her over to me, holding the reins in one hand.

"First things first: I don't wanna know. You come up with what we can call paperwork—you got the zebra from your aunt, you got a cousin in Kenya—good enough. There's no truth as I see it, so I don't wanna know. You call me, I send the truck."

"What kind of circus is this? No spangles, no tent, no feather head-dresses?" The camel curled her lip and shifted her back half from one hip to the other.

"You want the run of the mill variety, you sell to Dumb Dumb Brothers. They pay five figures, we pay four. But I'll tell you—they'll want papers. Legal papers." He pronounced each syllable. "Plus, I'll teach you to train."

"The animals?"

"Einstein. Whatever you get, I'll teach you to train."

"What's the number for the truck?" He pulled out a card. "Day or night?" I asked.

"Twenty-four hours. And Cindy."

"Circe."

"Whatever. Think Exotic."

About two weeks later, I was dating a sculptor from Louisiana. He turned at night. Imagine waking up in bed with a stallion. The bedroom was a shambles by the time the truck got there.

A wad of cash can make anything feel like a job. I began to think exotic. I learned to tell what kind of animal a man will be by the way he looks, the way he moves. Skin is a thin disguise. The lions with their barrel chests and thick glinting hair. The pumas with their sleek small heads and muscled taut bodies. When I knew what we needed at the circus I would look for the type—in clubs, in bars, I would hunt him down. When I guessed wrong there were always plenty of cages, but I didn't make many mistakes.

The first time I touch them I am sure.

Once, I was unbuttoning an investment banker's shirt. I undid the last button and pulled the tails out of his pants. Then I moved my hands, flat and splayed, along his chest. It was covered with dense brown hair, and I looked into his large eyes and reached down to his waist. He made a small rumbling noise in the back of his throat and I knew, *Bear*. I kept on top of the situation and hoped he wouldn't change in the middle. I didn't worry too much. Eventually I tamed them all, even the wildest ones eat from my hands. Herm (Hermes, he said, was his ring name) taught me to train, and he said I was a natural. The animals watched me, mesmerized, and once I had taught them a command they would perform as if hypnotized. Together, Herm and I taught them a complicated procession for that month's show. The rest of the performers were dancers that had gotten too chubby and beauties that had gotten too old. We had a couple of ex-Rockettes and a former Miss Teen Mississippi in the troupe. They liked me because I wore black sweatpants instead of a black unitard and so on opening night they could be sure that their husbands weren't checking out my legs.

I began to perform with the animals because I was the only one who could get the lions to do the quick mincing step on "Hurry up, please, it's time." When we performed I lost all sense of audience and attitude and coaxed, cajoled, and cooed my animals to their hops and hoops. I knew each one intimately, and they obeyed me like new lovers. Sometimes the girls would pause during the dance just to watch us. One of the dancers' brothers wrote reviews for *The Village Voice*, and she got him to slip us into the Style section. Pretty soon we were setting up double bleachers to pack the people in. Herm took to selling tickets and gave me the wilder animals to train. On my days off, I'd look for new ones.

One day I called Herm to come and pick up a land tortoise. When he came he brought a dolly with him and slid it under the mound of contracted tortoise.

"Reptiles reek," he shook his head. "I wouldn't have this sonofabitch in my apartment for five minutes." I held out my hand, and he reached into his pocket and peeled off a few hundreds from the steadily growing roll that never went to the bank. "You gotta meet the Greek. Alligator wrestler. Scar the size o' Jersey on his thigh—from the war, not the lizards. Little hard of hearing too. He shows up every once in a while, we put him up, though he doesn't deserve it. He'll get a kick out of you, but don't let him near that animal connection of yours." I wasn't paying much attention; I was already thinking about the next one, the insurance agent with llama potential. If I watched closely enough, it was like a science.

There was a rhino, a crocodile, a zebra, a gazelle, and a wildebeest in one month.

I noticed that it happened after long conversations, and I began to think it was because I knew something I shouldn't have. I had spent most of my life cramming myself full of useless knowledge. When I am with most men it is as if I am on a see-saw and everything in my head is like a weight that loads my side down. I sit on the ground, squinting up at him. He is flailing and powerless against the sun. This is what I see in their eyes when they turn.

I looked for the animals, but I always searched for the one who would keep the balance, who would have the gravity to play with me. I didn't believe it would happen. Herm and Dusa had broken off even their late night meetings, she claimed he couldn't look her in the eye. I looked at Herm and saw an Owl. I began thinking that being a man meant having the animal inside, that it only took a certain loss of control to release it. That didn't make them all the same. There are a million kinds of animals.

The more I whispered to them, the faster it happened. One, a chicken from the beginning, listened to me as if I were a priest. I could see him fade, halfway between sleep and love, into a trance. He sat, nestled on my couch, dazed and dull in the middle of cocktails. I talked to him until the change overtook him.

Soon, I began to get creative. It's not as if most men are purebreds. They would have the lips of a camel, the smile of a dolphin, the wings of a barn swallow and the teeth of a hyena. In some, the different animals jostled within them, fighting for space. These were the difficult types; some would rather die than be tamed. Some tried to kill me.

With an iguana panther I waited until he was about to leave, heading for the door. I came up behind him, pressed my body against his back, my fingers trailing up his neck, into his hair, my whisper constant warmth in his ear. I turned him like this to my bedroom, my voice tumbling into him. He changed before dawn. I woke to see shining eyes in the corner of my room. He circled the bed slowly, his tongue flicking from his mouth. I was naked, and it occurred to me as I inched back against the headboard, *how stupid, not to have a gun.* The beast was twice my size and riled with anger. He looked at me and hissed, his triangular jaw opening like a trap—rows and rows of teeth.

I lived because the iguana panther did not know, could not comprehend how he had changed. I began to sing to him, as I would have sung to a child. My voice was shaking at first, but as he slowed and shook his head my song grew stronger. Soon he dropped, limp and heavy as a rolled rug, still watching me with his thin-lidded eyes. I went and sat beside him, stroking his smooth black coat. And for a moment, when I looked at him with his head in my lap, I wished he were a man.

Perhaps what I do is a gift, perhaps it is a curse, perhaps it has nothing to do with any god at all.

I had nightmares sometimes that I was being eaten by the animals I had created. I could die a thousand times—ripped limb from limb by a hyena, swallowed whole by the unhinged jaws of a boa constrictor. In each of these I lived to feel myself devoured.

In the Odyssey, they said I worked some kind of magic. I'll admit it was eerie the way the animals followed me around when they could, howled to get attention when I passed by their cages. And I could get a cheetah, or a boa constrictor, or a hippo with no trouble. Herm told me once in a matter of fact way that he assumed the animals had something to do with drugs. Illicit connections in other hemispheres. He didn't want to know, he added, searching my face for a confirmation. If I ever wanted out though, I would still have work with him.

I didn't want to give it up; I was good at it. I'd decided against doing hybrids for now, so it was safe enough. And the animals came cheap: apartment damages, and a small finder's fee. As long as I came up with the creative paperwork no one at the circus asked any questions.

One day I came to the warehouse and Herm was on the floor, coloring flyers with a green magic marker. *Ulysses the Alligator Wrestler* captioned an outline of a man who was either wrestling with an alligator or had the animal tied around his waist.

"Think you could manage a couple alligators next week?" Herm asked. I shook my head. I was working on a couple of arctic wolves for the pooch parade. The men, Politês and Eurylokhos, were a tough pair. Politês was innocent and trusting enough, but Eurylokhos was wily and suspicious. Like most of the pure dog types, they were pack animals. I knew if I could get one away from the other he would be a dog by the next morning, but in bars and clubs they practically held each other's hands. Then it occurred to me to do them together.

They came to dinner and I spoke softly, making them lean forward to hear what I said, bringing us closer, warming them up. Then, before I even served dessert, one was lifting his leg on my sofa and the other was out on the balcony howling at the moon. I was standing in the doorway to the kitchen, holding the ice cream scooper for the Baked Alaska, and realized I had arctic wolves in my house. I stood there for a minute, watching, just watching the one on the balcony. His cry, aimed at the hazy stars, was long, low and lonely. And suddenly I felt tired, just sad and lost and tired and I imagined my life going on forever like this, an endless procession of confused animals. I leaned against the doorway and closed my eyes, wishing that once it would be me and not them who would turn into the wild wondering thing.

Then one of the wolves turned and snarled at the other. I slid the kitchen door shut and called the truck.

The next morning I was sitting in the bleachers in the warehouse, inventing origins and donors while Politês and Eurylokhos paced in their cages, hungry and savvy now that they were limited by bars. They growled occasionally, but when I whistled to them they would whine and roll over, their long tails brushing the floor. Then I heard them both stop pacing. They were completely still, quiet. I looked up, and there he was in the main ring. I stared and kept staring at him because I couldn't see what he would become. For a moment I saw him as a lion, then a bear, a snake, a bird. He began striding up the bleachers toward me, talking about where he had come from and what he was looking for, but I didn't hear a word he said for all the animals I could see in him. There was a whole jungle in his face. I stood as he came closer to me to see if I could smell it—just a trace of what paced within him.

When I breathed in I only became dizzy.

This one would be a bit of a challenge. A rare animal. Not easily caught. Most of them give themselves away so quickly. In a minute, really. As I swayed from his scent, I reached over and put my hand on his arm thinking I would know from the first contact, the first touch skin to skin, I would feel it in him. But I could not. Instead of feeling the animal I could only feel this skin, this flesh warm against my own. And I stopped and looked in his face that was lined with human wrinkles, punctuated by human bones.

He admired the new additions, and his voice was not accusing but admitting me. He asked where I found them all, and I said I picked them up. Here and there. My hand was still on his arm.

When he moved my mind spun farther. We walked down the bleachers and onto the floor and I watched him. He moved like a wrestler, like a long line of elastic muscle that could stretch or contract itself at will. He could be a mongoose, a leopard, a lynx, an eel. Even his shrugs and crouches did not give him away. Perhaps, I thought, he is an animal I've never met. Or a mongrel of the worst kind. When we were walking next to the cages the animals moved with me, trotting alongside as far as their pens would allow, whinnying, clucking, hissing and howling. When we left the arctic wolves behind with their pitiable whimpers he asked me what I did to them. I whisper to them, I thought, not so much, but enough to explode them out of their fragile skins, their unformed selves. I said, I bring them here.

He said I was a legend, that no one in the world could procure such animals. I knew that he was flattering me, wooing me, and I listened. I listened to the texture of his voice as he paced out his words, his tones low and intimate. I listened to the way he said *procure* and it seemed he was suggesting that these beasts had merely been solved of their humanity.

He said, your paperwork is shoddy. I laughed because it did not seem so much shoddy as fantastic. I agreed and shrugged and my shoulder brushed against his with a shock. I stepped back and stopped laughing. For a moment I had forgotten the animal inside him.

When I asked him for dinner I almost wanted him to say no, to prove that he was different. And we talked and I was watching, watching his face for changes, for that dull, thick expression that tells me that a man is no longer thinking, that his mind is beginning to stammer with his voice. I brought him home with me, with his fascinating fluid movements, with his weathered face and fresh body, with his voice that echoed through my skull. He would not stand still for a moment, he seemed to circle me when I cooked. A raven, I thought, a coyote. He seemed to be everything and for a moment I thought it would be too dangerous. If I turned him he would attack me, and I might have to kill him.

He did not slow down even when we sat. His gestures, large and various, kept his body in constant motion like some of the rodents I had known. But they were deliberate expressions that flowed into each other, one after the other. He was not parts but a mystifying whole. I whispered over the candle and our faces drew closer and closer until I could feel the heat of the candle flame rising under my chin. He watched my lips and did not succumb but responded. I could not eat. By the end of dinner, I was wild to know what he was.

Perhaps, I thought, the difference lies in knowing that he will leave, that he has only come to rest here for a while. He does not look at me as a destination, his eyes see through me to another horizon. Perhaps I will not be able to turn him.

I poured him some liquor that I saved for when I didn't want a fight. It could flatten the strongest of them, my liquor down their throats, my voice in their ears. Suddenly, I felt him behind me, his lips moving in my hair, his hands on my sides. My fingers loosened on the glass and it dropped to the carpet with a soft thud. I could hear a roar within me as my hands tingled and flexed. I turned my head and the four walls of my apartment seemed too close, moving in, containing me. And it struck me that there are female animals too. What was he trying to make of me? I heard his words soft next to my ear and I thought, who is this man and where has he come from and who but the gods could send this to me?

I turned my body to face him all at once and I put my forefinger to his whispering lips. He was silent, surprised, and then he smiled. His smile shocked me; he laughed at my desperate wildness. I began to murmer to myself, to beat down what was within me. He watched me regain myself, waiting. I would beat him, I thought, shaking with frustration. I would turn him no matter what he was. But when I turned my voice to him he pressed his finger to my lips. And in that moment of stillness I realized how different this was to be. The fighting had ceased.

We stripped each other and were human and animal, everything.

He stays now. He sleeps in my bed, washes himself in my shower, smells of my soap and skin. After that night I knew I would not change him. We keep this balance, the urges trapped within us. And we train together and drink together and wake and cook and eat together. Once he asked me how many men there had been before him. I just looked at him and he shook his head as if he were waking up. It is only in moments that we forget that the rules have changed. At first I would see a monkey when he bent over, a seal when he raised his head from the pillow, a bull when he swayed in anger. Then the animals disappeared from my vision. He became, in his movement, man.

Even now he sleeps beside me, this man. And I know, because I have seen his eyes meet mine in a flash of anger, his hands stroke my sides with deliberate care, that it is only his strength that keeps him from turning. I have learned to tame myself, to keep the roaring reasoned within me. But it is so delicate, this truce which keep us from what paces between the bars of our bones; sometimes I feel as if one word could explode us. Now he awakes, his eyes taking me in with the world. I put one hand on his arm, skin against skin. I do not use my voice; I am weary of spells. My hand grips him, my body asks, how will we keep this peace?

Armand the Frog · *John Hawkes*

IN POINT OF FACT there was not a single frog pond on the Domaine
Ardente but many, all connected by little throat-like passages or trickling
streams. And darkness? Secrecy? All I could want. Oak trees grew at the
edges of these ponds, their roots bulging out like goiters from the dank
earth where it dropped off into the sluggish water, and wherever they could
find footing between the oaks—oh yes, they may well have been live oaks,
may well have been—and selfish bramble bushes, broad weeping willows
helped to enclose my frog pond, which I prefer to speak of in the singular,
since there was one pond more appealing to me than all the others put
together and where I most liked to squat and crouch in my own childish
time out of time. How shrouded it was, my frog pond! How dark and
cool—yet sultry too—even in one of the sudden warm hours that settled
down that spring on the Domaine Ardente. Once I had made my way to
my frog pond, I became as still as the frog I awaited, as unmoving as the
water lilies that spread across the scummy or muddy surface of the pond. It
was cool, it was warm, it was a place of midnight in the fullest part of the
day. Here and there the oaks, the willows, the screens of bushes admitted
tiny shafts of light that suddenly engaged in brief skirmishes, reflecting,
criss-crossing, attacking each other before being just as suddenly extin-
guished in this daily night that was not determined by church bell or any
sort of heavenly system. At least not when I hid in the depths of my frog
pond at the height of the daylight hours. Of course the rank darkness was
different at sunrise or dusk. For most of the day, however, I could count on
finding this special, even illicit dimness, perhaps a smelly total absence of
light in which it was hard even to make out the fleshy lily pads, whenever
I had the whim or determination to go fiercely into the bright nocturnal
world of my frog pond. So I crouched, or squatted, or stretched myself out
flat on my belly, eyes at a level with the edge of the pond, immobile, silent,
intent, undetectable to anyone passing by or to the creatures of the frog
pond itself. I watched, I listened. The dragonflies hovered and dashed about
the thick surface with a deafening roar of their little engines, the lily pads
tempted me to reach out and touch their oily skins. Inevitably there was one
in particular that I concentrated on, an immense beast as flat as a plate and
apparently glued to the surface, so tight it was to the water which, like so

many of its brethren, it decorated. This grand dame of lily pads was large and of a blackish, greenish, dark bluish color, a thick creature composed of a soft pulp dressed in a gleaming skin as inviting as the water that kept it lubricated. She was a mystery, my awesome lily pad, and ancient as was evident by the broad indifferent wrinkles or undulations that so beautifully contradicted its apparent flatness. Touch it? Oh I was tempted to get into that productive water somehow, by slipping or falling, and entrust myself to the pack of them, violating them all with my fresh stubby fingers until at last I reached my fair queen, great flowering receptive mass, and touch it, pinch it, perhaps caress it like the small startled boy I might have been in the bedchamber of the young count's wife.

Farfetched? The height of improbability? Well, you will soon see just how close I came to being so ensnared. It was an alluring fright, I can tell you.

But all this was the crudest of my spring fantasies, for I respected beyond my own life my favorite lily pad that floated indolently just out of reach. It was only the imagined sensation of touching her that enthralled me, since it was the lily pad's sensuous invulnerability that kept me still, that held my gaze. Yes, I was almost angry with passion, such a marvelous living thing was this ancient lily pad in her ballroom of fecundity and slime. There were the various trees and growths attempting to drown themselves in slow motion in these fetid waters, there was the occasional inexplicable patch of clear water and rent in the trees and brambles that caused a clear mirror-like reflection of blue sky replete with a few clouds and little bird to lie before me and to divert my attention from the reality of darkness and worms and water flowerings that seemed to invite my mouth as well as my eyes. There was a curious truncated tree stump that proved, on closer inspection, to be two old rotten stumps grown so thickly together that I thought of this rotten sculpture as two old ladies hugging each other.

And in the center of it all the empty platter of the still empty queen. I watched that lily pad for the sheer illicit pleasure of watching—is there so great a difference between a lily pad and Diana? Let it go then. For of course I had an ulterior motive in fixing my eyes for half an afternoon on that unctuous thing undulating in the water. In my scowling fashion I loved its emptiness, but I loved that old noble demi-mondaine more when all at once plop! And there would be a frog, a big frog, squatting in its very center. If at that moment my ancient stately lily pad had been able to draw her bed curtains, she surely would have. As for myself, in that dripping instant I knew what it was to act the spy!

All the while that I was so engaged in concentrated, furtive study of my lily pad I was of course awaiting the black frog. What could you expect? After all, I was only a two-year-old boy whose passions, with which unknowingly he was all but bursting, could hardly have reached the degree of consciousness and sophistication that I have not restrained myself from articulating. No indeed. I was just a small boy waiting to spy on a frog. But far from innocent. I was robbed of innocence at birth, though I suspect that back then, at the dawn of skepticism, many children were born missing their innocence. As for now, well, you'd be lucky to find an innocent babe in a thousand. If you wanted one, that is.

The point is that I was never able to catch the frog in the act of emerging from the muddy depths and plopping himself down on his favorite lily pad and mine. I stared for hours, I clenched my fists, I scowled, my angry willpower puffed out my round cheeks that dear little Mamma so loved to stroke. I readied myself to see the invisible frog's exact entrance into view, to see him shoot up suddenly with a flying leap and land safely on the lily pad, or to see first his head, then shoulders, then hoary arms, and to be witness to his ignoble struggle to haul himself up and out of the clinging water to safety on the spongy plate waiting to serve him up to my scrutiny. But I could not. As long as I watched, like a child determined to keep his eyes open so as not to fall asleep, I was unable to maintain a perfect vigil. Never did I entrap my majestic frog in my spying. Never. Nor could I detect my instant of failure, the chink in my armor. I was capable of holding watch for most of a day without the slightest trembling or consciousness of my remarkable feat. And I did not blink. In fact I was born incapable of blinking, which a few people, but only a few, noted with appropriate discomfort. At any rate I did not lose sight of the empty lily pad in the slowly changing light, was diverted by nothing, no matter the overly curious bird that might make his way into the seclusion of the frog pond, never again to fly free, no matter that another portion of the embankment might slide loose and disappear beneath the brownish surface, thereby leaving naked still another entanglement of virgin roots. By these slow contractions of the frog pond I was not diverted. Such patience was nothing less than satanic, especially in light of my general inability to maintain stillness. Yet so it was and so I failed. One moment my superb attention would be fixed on the seductive—no, maddening!—vacancy of the lily pad, the next I would be staring at the frog who—yes—was there, so heavily filling that vacancy that the lily pad seemed threatened with sinking. But he was there, as large as my head and as slimy as if he had been sitting on that lily pad and fruitlessly attempting to dry himself in the sun all afternoon.

There must have been signs. The dragonflies must have shut down their engines and in an instant settled to the surface as if never again to rise. The trapped bird must have made some sort of strangled sound in its tiny throat. Surely there was some such sign of warning, no matter how sudden, how brief, how apparently insignificant, that the awesome frog was about to make himself visibly known in the frog pond once again. If so, such a flurry of heralding minutiae escaped me.

For as long as I studied him on this or that afternoon, my mouth going dry and my small black eyes starting from my head, my bold frog steadfastly refused to return my gaze, until just before his disappearance, that is, though not always, which is to say that he was not predictable, sitting as if a veritable cannonade would not shake him loose, yet all the while as aware of me as I was of him.

A big wet creature seemingly composed of slime that oozed the day long through what must have been tiny pores in his leathery skin, his appearance was that shiny and repellent, which made him all the more attractive to me. He held himself half sitting up with great effort. Midway between sun and stagnant water he blazed in his glorious colors of putrefaction—dark green, dark blue, black. He moved so little that even his efforts to breathe frightened me. I thought that inside the flat sack of him he had no bones. He looked like a bat. But oh, he might have been wearing a crown, that frog! How I loved him.

It was not merely to see him that I spent so many days at the frog pond. It was to see his eyes. By and large he kept them averted. He allowed me, so to speak, full view of his webbed feet, the sharp ridges that revealed the hair-like bones inside him, or even moved his great head a degree or so to the left, to the right, interested, that moment, in something other than me. But to that masterful frog his eyes were sacred, as I well knew. For hours he sat there as if deliberately waiting me out. On some days, after engaging me in hours of the most painful study—and to think that I was never an apt pupil, let alone scholar!—he would deny me altogether and disappear from view by whatever sleight-of-hand was his, before allowing me one glimpse of his eyes. But on other days, toward the end of our hours together or at once, while he was still dripping profusely on his lily pad, fresh in arrival, he would suddenly turn his head or even inch his fat body around until—yes!—there they were, his eyes, meeting mine. It was then, even as I could feel my wide mouth smiling still wider in my elation, that all at once I was overcome with utter abasement and wanted only to wriggle, to move, to flee, to escape the dominion of the frog's eyes. But could not. And not once did that frog blink at me!

Have you ever been stared at by a frog?

When a frog looks deep into a child's eyes, he does so with such impassive recognition in that gaze of his that the child cannot help but be overcome by guilt, by terror, yet amazement as well. I should know. One glance into my frog's large black unlidded eyes, as they first appeared, and I had not the slightest doubt but that some terrible doom had befallen me, and that that secret doom was mine to carry within my person forever. A lifelong treasure that I could just as well have done without—or so I thought at my worst moments, which did not last long.

My frog's name was Armand.

And here we are! Back to the endless springtime of my nights in bed, back to the stories—about a frog named Armand, of course—that my mother used to read to me as preparation for sleep. I did not lie in the sumptuous hollow of my fresh sheets merely smelling and watching the darkness in which Mamma and Papa thought I lay above them safely asleep. Not at all. One of my profoundest nighttime pleasures was listening to the night as well. To what? Oh yes, to the distant frogs. In the night it surrounded me, engulfed me, far off, close to my open window, that sound of contented croaking that only the frogs could make. It was a chorus now soft, now loud, now timid, now bold, chaotic yet formed into the shape of a song, a lullaby without beginning or end, a natural hypnosis more soothing than that of any other nighttime sounds I heard—whether of owls, cicadas, or falling rain. And as long as it lasted, which was as long as I stayed awake, in its midst I always detected the authoritative croaking of Armand. He made no sound when we were together. In the daytime I saw in his eyes the sounds he made at night in his throat, or rather in the smell of those spring nights I strained to hear the sounds of Armand giving voice to what I had seen in his eyes in the daylight. There is a difference. At night the imperious Armand was but one frog in ten thousand, and at their center I gave myself up to them, vulnerable to their swarming upon me yet safe from them all, the sole listener enjoying their song.

It all began just after dusk, when Mamma would tell me that it was time to have our nightly frog story, and up we would go, dear little Papa dismissing us with a flourish of his most generous fatherhood.

There was my nightshirt, cut from the same material as my thick sheets impermeated with the overpowering smell of cleanliness, and an oil lamp, and a small wooden chair, and the open window. At this point I would be more eager than dreamy, while Mamma would be smiling and shaking her head of dark curls in anticipation of what we were about to share. "Remember, Pascal," she would say, "only one story! You musn't ask Mamma for another." Readily I would agree, smiling my smile that was so much wider than hers, settling myself into my square bed, though I was never exactly at peace with myself, looking at dear little Mamma and hoping that the expression on my face was pleasing her. Slowly she would open the book and begin the story. Beneath her voice—I hear it still—the sound of the frogs would be nothing more than the softest stirring of the night outside.

The Stories of Armand the Frog concerned a little girl named Vivonne, her bad-tempered friend Henri, and Armand himself who, as Vivonne well knew, was that lovely child's brother transformed into an ugly frog, as if all frogs were not ugly, despite that sentimental majority who persist in viewing the frog as small or even precious, that detestable word. But how typical of most children's stories, yet not quite, thanks to that peculiar tuck in its side, like my bat turned frog. Why, those stories might have been closer to life, as they say, had that magical frog proved to be not Vivonne's brother but her father. However, there we are, and my nightly immersion in *The Stories of Armand the Frog* was so complete that I myself might have been both frog and brother. Naturally Vivonne, with her imperturbably good disposition and dark curly hair much like my mother's could talk to the frog and knew that one day she herself would transform her beloved Armand, which was how she felt about him, back into her dear brother. Her only task was to overcome her repugnance for the frog and—pouf!— there, in a puddle, would stand her brother in all his glory, dripping from the years he had spent disguised in the frog pond. However, and in delicious fulfillment of every child's expectation, Vivonne felt such abhorrence for Armand the frog that she despaired of ever doing what she was destined to do in her pretty life, whether she wanted to or not, though she had in fact learned to let Armand sit in the palm of her cupped hand, trembling the while and biting her lip, despite her love for the ugly creature that looked up at her with imploring eyes. In rapture I listened to the tale of Armand, Vivonne, Henri and the gypsy woman, or of the frog, the children, and the one-armed traveler, and there was one, I remember, about the frog, the children, and another frog. What a delight it was, how instructive! My small bright eyes were as tightly fixed on my mother's lively face as they had been fixed on Armand the real frog only that afternoon or the one before. My mother read aloud those stories with all the sounds of artistry that a pretty woman could bring to bear on a story whose simple tones and vivid events could bring so much pleasure exactly suited to a child fully awake yet on the verge of sleep. Her curls trembled, her soft voice was as clear as the water at the bottom of our well, she was an actress for whom the story that issued from her pretty mouth was peopled with an endless variety of small creatures all holding tiny hands or fleeing each other. She would turn a page, Armand would beg Vivonne to allow him once again to sit in her cupped palms, Henri would come rushing to interrupt their reluctant tryst with a stick. Remember the tale of Armand the frog and Bocage the crow? What happiness!

One day the crow, who was of course ten times the size of the frog, challenged Armand to a singing contest. Henri, forever on the ready to thwart the frog however he could, demanded to be the judge, since there being little to choose between the cawing of a crow and croaking of a frog, Henri's own word would clearly determine the outcome in the crow's favor, thereby casting ignominy on the frog and in turn spiting once more the little girl Vivonne in all her partiality to Armand. The chosen day arrived, the contestants assembled just out of earshot of a little brook and near a wild flowering of blueberry bushes. Henri scowled and folded his arms judiciously, Vivonne said that she could not bear to see Armand suffer so severe a defeat and would absent herself from the field, though in fact she cleverly hid behind the blueberry bushes. Bocage declared himself the first to sing and preened his great black feathers, strutted in a circle on his two shiny black legs and then, in a long and prideful display of grandeur, as he thought, began to caw as long and loudly as he could. His feathers shook, four nearby cows kicked up their heels and fled, the wicked little boy Henri nearly covered his ears with his hands but managed not to. Surely no uglier sound could have filled the day, pleasing the crow no end but making the poor frog cower. At last the self-satisfied crow ceased his terrible performance and took his bow. Then it was the frog's turn, which Henri anticipated with smug self-satisfaction, though he continued to scowl as if in the total objectivity required of any judge in a contest. Bocage the crow stood back, Armand the frog hopped upon a small rock, thereby hoping to gain whatever advantage he could, which was little. There was silence, there was sunlight, the distant cows turned to listen, the boastful crow smiled to himself and waited. At last Armand filled his little body to bursting and opened wide his mouth and began to sing. But what song was this? What sweetness coming forth from the mouth of a frog? Oh not at all the monotonous painful croaking that the boy, the crow, and the attentive cows had expected to hear. Oh, just the opposite! For the frog on the rock was in fact singing in the cheerful melodic voice of a little girl! The cows drew near, the defeated crow flapped about in angry circles, his feathers flying, while after a moment the wicked little boy, his eyes meaner than ever and his face red, leapt at the frog, chasing the little creature off his rock and into the tall grass, and then—for of course Henri had understood the trick at once—ran to the blueberry bushes and caught the laughing Vivonne by her curly hair. The now frightened crow flew up to a branch of a nearby tree, again the cows fled, Vivonne struggled unsuccessfully to escape the angry embrace of the wicked boy. But before the boy could harm the little girl, or do anything more than to disturb her clothing, Armand hopped back onto the sunny rock and, as the defeated crow flew off after the cows, caused the bad-tempered Henri to free Vivonne and yawn, grow weary, and, overcome by the powers of sleep, to lie down beside the brook. . . .

And the rest? The second half of the story? Oh, there was Armand hiding himself in Henri's pocket while the boy slept, there was the waking of the wicked boy, the discovery of the frog in his pocket, a great commotion, Henri's escape from both the frog and his terror, thanks to Vivonne who commanded him to drop his trousers and run—silly boy—and finally the sound of Vivonne's laughter at the resultant plight of the now stumbling Henri at which she stared with suddenly sober attention, while the victorious frog hopped back into the brook to await his next encounter.

Most of the nightly tales that I remember from *The Stories of Armand the Frog* contained adventures similar to this one. Inevitably Henri lost his trousers, inevitably Henri the wicked boy would hop about in rage, the little frog clinging for dear life to one of the boy's bare buttocks while Vivonne smiled or frowned and filled her eyes with the sight of Henri's whirling frightened nakedness. Did it ever end, that collection of stories in the ancient book that sat so prettily in the hands of dear little Mamma throughout those spring nights of my childhood? That volume from which there issued the sound of my mother's voice precisely as Vivonne's childish soprano voice arose from the mouth of the frog or as the song of the choir boy comes from the score he holds and not his mouth? Surely there must have come the final night, the last story in the book, when the song of the distant frogs grew faint with sadness and faded to nothing, and the last few words drifted off onto the vastness of the spring air and my mother ceased reading, smiled down at me and shut the book. Forever. Oh yes, that book I loved, fragrant with my mother's touch and redolent with the life of the frog who was the namesake of the real frog who so consumed my own life, must have had a conclusion.

No doubt Vivonne finally allowed Armand into her bed one night and twitched and squirmed, shivered and trembled, slept and woke as in a dream, shockingly aware of the little wet creature touching her here and there or, worst of all or best, suddenly hiding in the bedclothes, lost, unaccountable, waiting to resume his tickling of Vivonne's pure young body until she dozed, drifted partially awake, crying out in her little girl's ravaged voice as there in the new sunlight she lay, no longer a child, of course, but a young woman, despite her still youthful appearance. And the frog? He stood at the foot of her bed, of course, no longer a frog but the promised brother, who should have been a prince according to the dictates of most stories about frogs and children, but was not. Here *The Stories of Armand the Frog* must disappoint us, for that stalwart brother, when finally he shed his ugliness, or rather when our dear Vivonne recognized that same ugliness for the shining beauty that it was—male beauty, that is—emerged not as a prince, as he rightfully deserved, but in the form of an ugly old king smiling down upon his prize. But did the radiant Vivonne, sprawled out on her dampened bed without a thought to modesty, share our own shock and disappointment at this final gift of her story? She did not. After all, an ugly old king was better than nothing, if she could not have her prince, as apparently she could not, and she had already learned that the mighty powers of a frog will never suffer the rules of convention.

Oh, let me be honest, though honesty is nearly as repugnant as rationality. However, I do not remember that *The Stories of Armand the Frog* ever reached a conclusion or that dear Mamma ever ceased her nightly reading. The curious fact of the matter, and this I do remember with undeniable certainty, is that for the longest while I was satisfied to allow my mother to read to me one story a night instead of demanding that she spend the entirety of each of those spring nights with her son and her book, as I might have done, though soon enough I contrived to manage even that. But patience is a virtue I require of others if not myself.

The Man with the Arm · *Lucy Hochman*
(a break-up story)

1. Retrospect

a: We spent time surrounded by our peers, post collegiate in a college town, coffee, beer, teashops, cinemas, but we pointed and gaped. Look at those silly men with baseball caps, look how they walk around, hear their excuses for conversation and so on. I lived in a zoo, wandering along the proposed path and avoiding what was not on display, and though I was also caged, there I lived with my furry mate, and we might gaze into the cage next door, but we could always turn to one another, have babies, and impress a great keeper, the ignorant organizer, the sloppy maker of categories upon a whole earth who had placed us there.

b: He kept looking for his arm.

c: Walking down the street was not a thing of affirmation in the sense that looking into a mirror and recognizing ourselves could be one; there you are but in another place. It affirmed in the same way looking in the mirror can be profoundly displacing, as if you, because of the fact of your image, were of the mirror more than looking into it, and so you think of yourself as a mirror facing a mirror, you've seen that, your face infinitely repeated and you believe, therefore dense. In that way, it may well have been frightening, except for our ability to face one another and poke our ribs about it. It's only a mirror, and we'd wanted to believe. Ah, love and the mutual. We could look about in fear of being confused with our peers by a grand evaluating stranger, someone who ought to confirm our difference with a plaque and a key to our dream city, make us famous for rising above. But we had only join the hands we possessed in order to feel righteous and without the guilt of arrogance which might have ensued for lack of substantiation had we not been together.

d: When I was in school, people were always telling me I was getting my education, and when I was done with school they said, now you have an education.

e: After, I soaked beans and stuffed cabbage for freezing, organized my letters into labeled files and alphabetized my books, all this for convenience, as if I hadn't the time to search for a thing when I wanted it. Suddenly unoccupied by another person, knowing what to expect myself to feel, I dove into a phase of desperate self-recognition and care. Soon, I knew, I would embrace self-loathing, and then search for a new item of man to distract me from my loneliness. I predicted comfort in this ritual of time spent which in retrospect would be easy to summarize and be done with. I could not think of a piece of my life which I had not, in the past, managed to resolve.

f: I made bread because I heard it was spiritual. The dough was very stiff. It flattened and kept its foldmarks. "Coax the bread, do not connive," read the spiritual article on breadmaking.

"Become one!" I cried to the bread. If I ate the dough, it would rise in my belly and make me sick.

g: In Key West, people gather on bleachers on the docks every night to watch the sun set. Everyone is kissing or pointing the sun out to a presumably stupid child, and then everyone claps and cheers when it's over. "That was a good one," says one stranger to the stranger seated beside her. They do this every night.

and so on: Sounds rose from the house next door. I thought of my coat, a day in the teashop with Jim and the rain. I'd never met my neighbors, though we waved for a sense of community when we were standing at our doors struggling with locks or groceries. He was a construction worker, building things all day, a nice job, I thought. She went jogging. He threw a knife into the side of the house, stood up, and went back inside. His wife laughed and laughed, shook her head, went tsk, tsk, rolled her eyes, and followed him. Someone had come to my grandmother and asked to do a biography of the family. In the newspaper was a map. On the curb was a bottle, and I kept track of it. I jerked my elbow away and he dropped the cup, which made a noise with the sidewalk. I didn't check to see if it was broken. There was a teashop which I understood: the table, the glaze on the cups, the waitress with interesting habits. When he noticed me, I waved.

2. Rituals

a: He kept looking for his arm. We can all say thy kingdom come thy will be done and it has an echo though we have not all been in a church and heard it fill the room like a gong in a cave. He no longer felt a difference between the moments during which he searched for his arm and the moments he was as if complete. We walked down shop-ridden streets and his shoulder twitched as if to point something out. I wanted to be it for him. I could usually tell what he'd have pointed out before the explanatory reference was from his lips and through the air.

b: Clumps of intimacy consistently proved by an accumulation of moments interrupted by the absent arm: I noticed he missed it. I soaked beans and stuffed cabbage for freezing, organized my letters into labeled files and alphabetized my books, all this for convenience, as if I hadn't the time to search for a thing when I wanted it. It had evolved into a thing he didn't know he missed. It shaped what we were near each other, dictated our silences, illustrated what was understood, and what we left in the air between us out of compassion.

c, and so on: She let me soak it up while she used her teabag to wipe behind her ears and under her chin. "This is my favorite kind of weather and I didn't want to miss it." Our waitress passed her hands over the steam before she left. We seemed to be living in the same tunnel and could only have avoided contact had we wanted to. Breaking things. I made bread because I heard it was spiritual. He'd hemmed his shirts six inches after the seam. She went jogging. A biographer wanted to summarize my grandmother. He made a gesture of it. Raise glasses, look into eyes, clasp all our hands. I can no longer arrange myself around his presence. In Key West people gather on the docks every night to watch the sun set, kiss in front of it, and point it out to children.

3. Examples

a: I found a green bottle banked against a wall. It had been smashed at the neck, but though I searched with a fervent premonition, I couldn't find the remains of it. They don't make bottles with pre-broken necks. With a stone, I marked on the bricks the shape of what ought to have been there, a silly impulse, but I was alone.

The dough was very stiff. It flattened and kept its foldmarks. "Coax the bread, do not connive," read the spiritual article on breadmaking. If I ate the dough, it would rise in my belly and make me sick.

b: An appointment I had for lunch which I'd planned to break for the bread: Natalie, my ambitious, ex-idol of flammable grace, had been a graduate assistant for a class I took in college. We'd bonded over a mutual distaste for the professor. Ah, bondage and mutuality. I think I was her first protégé.

I was late, and the consistent British teapot and glazed cups had already arrived.

"I think I may as well be charting a beetle I discovered," she said. "The kind which will never be crushed to a powder and cure cancer, the kind which could be exterminated and not even the food chain would notice. I ought to be presenting my dissertation to the bug itself. But wait—" she leaned under the table and brought out a book. "Jim took off, huh?" It was a book about Nigerian Textiles and Quilting Techniques. "Look at that. Look how gorgeous it is."

I said, "They're into sparkly stuff, I guess."

"People love a thing they aren't used to having their hands on. Imagine what these ladies could do with polyester! Darling, nothing—" she said, trying to look me in the eye, though she had a wall-eye and it was hard to tell which eye of mine she'd chosen, "nothing need be garish." Was this how people always spoke? Ah, solitude, and the selective memory. She let me soak it up while she used her teabag to wipe behind her ears and under her chin (a custom?). "But still," she said, "while I say that with certainty for you and your situation, it sucks to specialize. History is too big, and not just because it's been around for a while, and not just because we've suddenly decided everyone is potentially valuable after all so we've gotta figure out who we fucked over, it's because, Jesus," her teabag broke and spilled down the front of her dress, "what was I saying? The point is, boy, I really wanna be famous."

b thru c: When I was in school, people were always telling me I was getting my education, and when I was done with school they said, now you have an education. When it finally comes to you that you do not have it, and that it was never there for you to have, it is as if you woke one morning certain that you fell asleep with eyes in the back of your head, and now they are gone. I passed the place where the no-neck bottle had been and found it smashed to pieces smaller than would be useful even for making a mosaic, and there above the sparkling pile, the cloud of the mark I'd made for it. We had walked around with three arms visible.

d: I didn't want to go back into my apartment. I knew it would be filled with things I had deemed worth keeping and the ghosts of things I'd thrown out, or else, and I suspected this would be the case, I would enter and find the place empty. I would say, "No, no, I've been robbed!" and call the police. The police would rush over and say, "I'm sorry, dear, but this apartment has been vacant for years."

I'd say, "But I have keys," and jangle them at the police, and they'd say now isn't that odd. Or else I would search my pocket and find a bluejay feather and pennies but no keys.

Or else I would call the police and they would say, "My dear, where did you get the idea there was a law against robbery?"

actually: Jim had one arm, and the other arm he didn't have, which I noticed. Also, there was more to him. I remember.

e: I sat on the porch with my keys, and caught the sunset, though my favorite part is the moment you think you can see a sliver above the horizon, and then you realize that you can't, and there is no view of the horizon from my porch steps, and it's not quite the same thing to watch the sun disappear behind a house. In Key West, people gather on bleachers on the dock every night to watch. Everyone is silent or kissing or pointing the sun out to a presumably stupid child, and then everyone claps and cheers when it's over. "That was a good one," says one stranger to the stranger seated beside her. Do they walk away bonded by experience? Do they go out for a drink? Do they shrug in the dusk?

f thru g: Sounds began to rise from the house next door. I thought of my coat, that day in the teashop with Jim and the rain. I'd never met my neighbors, though we waved for a sense of community when we were standing at our doors struggling with locks or groceries. He was a construction worker, building things all day, a nice job, I thought. She went jogging.

In the house, they were breaking things. Something thudded against the front door from inside, and then the door bounced open. The woman was dragging the man by the armpits. He'd bent his knees and was trying to use his boot treads for friction, and then trying to hook his heels on the threshold, but she sure was strong, or else he wasn't struggling as much as he made it look like. Once she got him outside, he wrenched free and tackled her, straddling her and pinning her shoulders to the ground with his knees. She tried to spit on him but it fell back onto her face. "Get the spit off me," she yelled. The man unclipped a jack-knife from his belt loop, opened it, and held its point above her eye. Then he noticed me. I waved.

"Fuck you," he said to me. Then he threw the knife into the side of the house, stood up, and went back inside. His wife laughed and laughed, shook her head, went tsk, tsk, rolled her eyes, and followed him.

h: I went to visit my grandmother, who traveled from Portugal to California with her parents to work as migrant farmers, and slowly accumulated enough land to plant pear orchards which ended up supplying a cannery. Her father drowned himself in the swimming pool anyway. Someone had come to my grandmother and asked to do a biography of the family.

"I don't like it," she told me. "I don't want someone summarizing me. I don't think it's very nice to edit a person's life. Those biographers, they just want to make sense of it. Well, don't go making sense of my family. It's humiliating."

"You could do it yourself. Lots of people do that. You don't have to show it, even." She screwed up her face with disgust, the way, having wrinkles, only an old person can do with conviction.

"Do you know what it would teach me in the end? That a person's life is only long enough to prove its own brevity. I already know this. I am certain to die soon."

"Because you figured it out? Really, Gramma."

"Because of it, despite it," she frowned and held her hands out, fingers upward, cupping nothing, air slipping through. "Maybe I'll live on and on, expecting to die any minute. Though what's the difference there?"

h, etcetera: Humans used to be old at twenty-five, but that was in the days when you weren't expected to learn anything your mother didn't know. We do get older, but not older enough, not for what you should learn from men, too, or from all those libraries, from the herds of people who live in your town, from the seeming species of them who inhabit all the places you'll never go to, though conceivably, you could, let alone the real other species, or the life of a waterdrop, or any piece of dust. All this seemed to be leading up to something. I suppose other things were happening as well, the invisible accumulating past, but I will never know. Certainly, it was more than a good man leaving me. In the newspaper was a map of the new place where all the Soviets used to live. The new names and boundaries were in black, and the old places floated behind them in dotted lines and gray titles.

4. Broken things

and so on: She passed her hands through the steam. It scattered every time. The bread flattened and kept its foldmarks. I found a green bottle banked against a wall. They don't make bottles with pre-broken necks. With a stone, I marked on the bricks the shape. I no longer arrange myself around the ritual of his physical presence. Suddenly unoccupied by another person, as I had been before, I dove into a phase of desperate self-recognition and care. I could not think of a piece of my life which I had not managed to resolve. Breaking for bread, we'd bonded over a mutual distaste for the professor. She had a wall-eye and it was hard to tell which eye. Her teabag broke and spilled down the front of her dress. Education: when it finally comes to you that you do not have it, and that it was never there for you to have, it is as if you woke one morning certain that you fell asleep with eyes in the back of your head, and now they are gone. I passed the place where the no-neck bottle had been and found it smashed to pieces smaller than would be useful even for making a mosaic, and there above the sparkling pile, the cloud of the mark I'd made for it. I knew it would be filled with things I had deemed worth keeping and the ghosts of things I'd thrown out, or else, and I suspected this would be the case, I would enter and find the place empty. I would say, "No, no, I've been robbed!" It would turn out that I'd only lost it because it had never been there. I'd made the whole thing up.

also: In the house, they were breaking things. I don't think it's very nice to edit a person's life. It's humiliating. The new names and boundaries were in black, and the old places floated behind them in dotted lines and gray titles. Certainly it was more than a predictable break-up; certainly, more was breaking up.

thus: I could bother to remember him in multitudinous detail, I could push myself to notice what was not absent at the time, but the collection of encounters which followed his sudden departure seemed edited to sparkle and point, as if the encounters were the invisible triangular pieces of that unwhole bottle, forming a chorus of identical arrows. He could still be a person. However, he has one arm.

5. The Answer to the Arm

a: He no longer felt a difference between the moments during which he searched for his arm and the moments he was as if complete. It had evolved into a thing he didn't know he missed. His little closet was filled with shirts, all amputated properly six inches after the seam and hemmed. I believe that what led to our first sex was my telling him I wanted to decorate the edges with ribbons and beads. It was probably something better.

b: He didn't realize what had happened when his arm tried to assert itself, and sometimes I was sure he noticed and found it a lovely thing. Mysterious private smiles would occur in my company, distant, not seeming to necessitate my company. I couldn't picture what he might be enjoying all by himself, except for the ritual of remembering again, as if a piece of wind had flitted its way from the ocean, which is far away, and a thing you fear and long for. But then, he is distinctly no longer here, and I can no longer arrange myself around the ritual of his physical presence.

c: His brief arm looked like a drawstring bag, tied shut and clipped. The skin which had had to join the rest of his skin late, and had not gone through as many haphazard sloughings, was deep pink. I wince at my impulse to describe it as textured similarly to a reproductive organ, but this is accurate. That soft and volatile, that shade, its tendency to change color according to its comfort, the weather, or his health. If he'd been a stranger, come to me and doing this with me in the dark, would I have noticed that empty portion of him? We had only to join the hands we possessed in order to feel righteous and without the guilt of arrogance which might have ensued for lack of substantiation had we not been together.

d: A man my age with a baseball cap and a jangling belly ran out of the teashop as I passed by. "I just got a letter from Jim," he said, clamped to my elbow to keep me from leaving. "Come and sit down with me," he said with a teacup, "I'll read it to you." I didn't want to go in there. "He got a job fishing in Alaska."

I asked: "With his arm?"

actually: He had no arm in order to teach me I could never have all of something. He'd gotten rid of the arm because it made it seem like nothing could be missing. He was born that way but lied to make me think he was more of something, having lost something. He lost his arm in a boring way, which was why he left the circumstances of the loss unspoken. He was sixteen and lay on his back in a field of hushing timothy to look at the sky, which he thought of like mirrors facing one another between which he was magically spying in such a way that no part of his face served as a referent, so that he witnessed the mirrors themselves exchanging glances at speeds faster than his eyes could compute, so that it was smooth, smooth, and then on his stomach to watch the traffic stomp over clumps of wheat that he had crushed into highways with his presence, and there was the sound of a hay-baler in the distance, a terminal hum that became a form of silence as it persisted, a baler closer, an immersion in the simultaneous belief in himself as too vast to be bothered and too tiny to feel, and finally his arm, baled in a field.

from Swanny's Ways · *Steve Katz*

I STARED AT THE KNIFE. He sat relaxed in the slime of his being, confident that I wasn't going to do it, or that he could handle it if I tried. I should have done it, six inches of blade in my hand. But he was too close. I could smell him through his cologne. I didn't want to be that close to the putrid beast. I didn't want to touch him. Not him. If I'd had a gun.

"See, if you were getting paid for it you'd do it in a second. Then you'd go home with a hard-on and fuck your girlfriend. Revenge is just a dry hump."

We pulled into one of the remote parking lots at Kennedy. I was so stupid, I didn't even realize it was a strange place to catch a plane. Emilio got out and opened the door for Kutzer. He stepped out, turned his back, and when he turned to look at me he had a Smith and Wesson fitted with a silencer pointed at my head.

"Get out of the car, Swanny," he said.

"I thought you didn't carry a gun," I said.

"Emilio let me use this one. Is this your gun, Emilio?"

"Nah." Emilio grinned.

"You know," Kutzer said. "You are the kid I used to catch jerking off in the boy's room."

"I think you're making a mistake, Kutzer."

He squeezed the trigger, and my brain welcomed a small bullet that burned through, pushing aside all irrelevant garbage located there. Killers kill, I thought. I guess that's what I needed to know.

RED SHIFT: DREAMTIME

We pull into one of the remote parking lots at Kennedy. I am so out of it I don't even realize that this is a strange place to catch a plane. Kostas gets out and opens the door for Kutzer. He steps out with his back to me. When he turns again to look at me he has a gun fitted with a silencer pointed at my head.

"What's that, a P .38 police model, isn't it? That silencer is made in England, right?"

"Get out of the car, kid," he says.

"I thought it was below you to use a cop gun."

"Kostas gave me the gun. I don't ask its religion. You got a thing against cops?"

"No. Not me. I wouldn't mind seeing some right now. I thought you were more the Smith and Wesson .357 magnum kind of a guy. I bet the silencer belongs to you."

"You know something," Kutzer says. "You are the kid who used to jerk me off in the boy's room."

I dive at his legs and his first shot goes way up in the air, a second wangs off the top of the limo. He falls when I hit him and the gun clatters across the pavement. All I am thinking is, "Get the gun. Get the gun." Just as I am about to grab the tip of the barrel my hand is crunched by the heel of a size fourteen wing-tip Florsheim. Kostas puts all his weight on it, severing some tendons, breaking small bones just below the knuckles. All I'm thinking is it might not have been so bad if he hadn't put a new leather heel on the shoe that morning. All I'm thinking is that I won't be able to use the left hand for a while to play handball with Peter. That's all I'm thinking when Kostas jerks me upright and holds me while Kutzer grabs the gun and lowers it on my head.

"That gun is embarrassing," I say. "I think I'm a magnum kind of a hit, Kutzer, and you are the rotting afterbirth from your syphilitic mother's womb. I vomit on your face, then I piss on that vomit."

"You wanna jerk me off again, kid?"

I struggle against Kostas, but he has made his living holding lightweights like me.

"Let him go," says Kutzer.

"Uunngh!" says Kostas, but not without first tearing my right arm out of joint at the shoulder. All I am thinking is, "There goes the rest of my handball game."

Kutzer squeezes the trigger, and my brain welcomes a large bullet dragging behind it into the space of my skull all the thought garbage that was ever dumped into the world. My last thought is, "It's the real thing. Light up a Pepsi and be sure." At least that's what I seem to say at the end; at any rate, that's how things work out.

"Yarrgh! This gets so tedious. From you it's always the same, every time you tell a story it's macho, it's danger, it's violence, stupid heroics." Florry gestured wildly with her arms, then stumbled on the trail. "Whoops."

Swanny grabbed her belt and pulled her back from the cliff-edge. Below them the cliff sheared off against the wind in two hundred foot steps, six of them to the bottom that leveled gradually into a system of chaparral washes with broad strokes of yellow aster, stipples of purple vetch, junipers here and there, an isolate ponderosa.

"And in all your stories I'm always dead. I resent it," Florry said.

"I'm just trying to get us up the trail," said Swanny.

"Even you die in this one." She looked Swanny in the face. "Can't you tell nice stories where people live fulfilling lives with happy endings?"

"Of course. Look at us. Here we are in the fresh air. Smell that air. What could be happier?"

"And both of us are dead. You must wish the kids were dead too."

"Where did the kids go?" Swanny quickly scanned the area.

"They couldn't stand your stories anymore, so they jumped off the cliff. Why would our story have a happy ending?" She saw the concern in Swanny's face. "No. I'm only kidding." They embraced and pressed against the cliff wall as ravens zigged and gossiped above them. They separated and watched the acrobats dip down into the canyon.

"That's the raven, *Corvus Corax*, largest member of the crow family," Florry said.

"Baby, you know all the names," Swanny said.

"Confucius says the beginning of wisdom is getting to know things by their right names."

"Wisdom accepts no names."

They came to a small spring bubbling from some rocks. Columbine bent in bloom out of the cracks. The water was cooling as Florry splashed it against her face.

"It feels like silk, like pushing your face into Portia's closet. She loved silk."

"Portia from Portland?"

"Yes. Portia's father began his fortune importing port from Oporto in Portugal. He became important in Bridgeport when he imported silk from Port Arthur, using Shreveport as a Port of Entry."

"That portended the importance of his portfolio."

"A portly porterhouse of a man, Portia's pop. Her closets cool with silks."

"Portcullis," said Swanny.

"What do you mean?"

"I just needed to say that word."

They both laughed and embraced because they knew how much words, just words, kept them together. Swanny splashed a double handful of water against his face, then drank some.

"This water might have *Giardia* in it."

"What's that?"

"An organism. Makes you sick."

"Hey," Swanny slurped big palmfuls. "That organism never met this organism. We've got a stomach like the belly of a tank."

"When have you ever been in the belly of a tank?"

"Do you need an answer to that?"

"Yes."

"Very well. I was one of General Patton's favorite baby soldiers."

"Now I suppose you'll have to tell me that story." She took his hand and they stood watching the spring like fiancés checking rings in the window of a jewelry store. "Aren't you going to tell me that story?"

"What story?"

"The General Patton's favorite baby soldier story."

"I thought you didn't want to hear any more stories."

"I never said that. I just want a different kind of story. No violence for a change. No death. Especially not mine."

"Many years ago, when I was in the south of Italy, we were advancing on a little town called Salerno. I was just another G.I. in the tank corps, and believe me the battle of Salerno was long and bloody."

"And you were just eleven years old."

"General Patton's favorite baby soldier. I was the youngest man in the tank corps."

"And I bet you died."

"I was shaving already. I was mature for my age. Twenty-year-old women talked to me. And you're wrong, I didn't die there, but I lost my best buddy there, Gitley. Sick Gitley. His name was Ed, but we called him Sick because whenever something happened he'd say, 'This is sick. I'm gonna call in sick.' He worked for the telephone company before the war and that's where he learned the tricks about calling in. You see I was a navigator and he was a gunner and we were rolling towards Salerno; I mean, General Patton wouldn't let us sleep. It was stupid. We took a hit from a friendly bazooka, a nice shell manufactured in Secaucus. A piece of Jersey blasted us. I don't know how it missed me. I heard it pierce, like a thunk, and then whistle by my head. So stupid. Shrapnel tore him open."

"There you go again. I bet his guts spill out."

"Listen to the story. I saw Sick folded over his belly. He looked like he was sick. The tank was full of smoke, but the hatch had blown open, and we could get out if we hurried. I grabbed Sick under the arms but as I straightened him up his guts slopped down like wet laundry. I tried to shove it all back inside him. 'Listen to me, Sick,' I said. 'You'll be okay. I'll get us out of here.' 'I'm going to call in sick,' were the last words I heard him say. I started to drag him up the ladder and bubbles of crimson frothed from his mouth."

"Please don't be so descriptive."

"This is not description. This happens in the story. He was crying, and I pulled him another step and then heard this sound like air letting out of a balloon, and I saw a piece of his intestine had caught on a ripped pipe that tore it open, and there was his liver torn up too, and you can't live without your liver, and I felt suddenly he got heavier and realized he was dead. The tank was ready to blow. It was hot. I knew I'd better get out myself, so I dropped him. He was my best buddy, Sick Gitley. Florry, he never had a chance. As I ran away I was knocked on my face by the explosion, out cold as the thing blew."

"You could have spared me that story, Swanny, since it never happened. I don't need some makebelieve violence and gore."

"You don't like violence, that's for sure. Women don't, though sometimes they appreciate gore. I don't like it either, but these are words. And what are words? A part of life! What I really want to tell you about happens after this, in the town of Salerno in the toe of the boot of Italy for there she dwelled, the fair signorina by the name of Cuccicucci, Signorina Alphonsina Cuccicucci."

"Okay. Enough. Save it for the walking."

For a few moments they were silent and in the silence they kissed several times. Then Florry spoke: "Those columbine are in the buttercup family, genus *Aquilegia*. You see, Swanny, the coloration may be due to pigments on the flower's surface, or to the selective scattering of certain wavelengths of light, as in the blue of the sky, or to small discontinuities in the subsurface structure, or the interference of light-beams reflected from interior surfaces, or to a combination of some or all of these effects." Florry stood up and spread her arms and gestured at the sun, "You! You up there. Cool it!" She looked at Swanny. "I have a love-hate relationship with that heavenly body." They both had tears in their eyes. "The pigment is probably one of the anthocyanins that forms water soluble glycocides to make this blue." She reached out to wipe away Swanny's tears with her fingertips. "That blue is the blue of this columbine, Swanny, this *Aquilegia coerulea* of the Rockies, state flower of Colorado."

"But this isn't Colorado."

"I know that, Swanny. But this is the kind of story that I tell. Sometimes you need to listen to my stories. But why do you cry, Swanny?"

"I'm thinking of the kids, and the beauty of our planet, and how we ruined it for our kids."

"Where are the kids?" Florry looked around. "Kids," she shouted. Silence responded.

"The kids are on the trail," Swanny said. "They must be on the trail. We'll catch up to them. This is Utah. Kids are safe in Utah, and I think it's time for us to mosey on, darling. Do you remember how to mosey?"

"Of course, and I'm ready to, because I know we have miles to go before the sun descends, causing the apparent color of the sky to shift towards the red end of the visible spectrum."

Swanny slipped two quarter-section survey maps out of a tube and laid them on the ground. He ran his finger along the brown elevation lines, stopping where they were bunched together. "This is where we are." Swanny's finger moved along a dotted line that indicated a trail across the elevation lines spread out to make a broad plateau. "And this is where we're going."

"Green is not the best color, not my favorite, though I would love the green flash if I could get to see it. Anyone would, but so few of us are ever lucky enough to see it, just at sundown, the upper limb of the sun gives off a flash of green just as it drops below the horizon, a green flash. That would be my favorite kind of green." She kissed him on the ear.

"So you see this protuberance here, pokes out like a thing?" Swanny took her finger, placed it on the spot on the map. "That's called Kelly's Thumb."

"The thumb is my favorite finger."

"I know that, Florry."

"How do you know that?"

"You're not married as long as we are without knowing things like that about the other person. Except I don't know if the thumb is a finger, or is it just a thumb?"

"I don't care. I like it best."

"They say that where we're going the spring water tastes like raspberries."

"That would be a nice surprise. In some places raspberries are plentiful."

"The water is even a little pink. And this guy, Alphonse Kelly, he had a Senegalese mother and an Irish father, buried a fortune in gold and gems right there, somewhere around that spring. All we have to do is go there and find them."

"Let's go. Except I hope you're not making this up."

"If I'm making it up, then it's my story, and I can guarantee the stuff will be there. But first I have to tell you, there could be someone else besides us."

"Who?"

"The guy who gave me the map was a top sergeant in my tank division in Italy."

"You're still too young to have had a tank division."

"General Patton's favorite baby soldier. Purple heart, too. When I came back to my senses after my tank blew up I found myself lying in a hospital bed in an army hospital in Salerno. Our nurse was a beautiful Italian woman, her name was Signorina Alfonsina Cuccicucci. She took care of me, and she took care of Sarge, who was in the bed next to me. I wasn't so bad off, just a concussion, a broken wrist, and a mashed nose, so I would help her out. I'd adjust Sarge's pillow, I'd slip the bedpan under his square butt, I'd light him a cigarette and smoke it with him. Both his hands had been blown off, and he lost a piece of his skull. He was a sad Sarge."

"No more stories."

"Anyway, just before he kicked the bucket he gave me instructions to get to this treasure. A little slip of paper. He said, in his failing voice, 'This is for real, Swanny. You're the only person I'm giving this to, except for . . .' and he mumbled a name, seemed to start with a K, but I couldn't make it out, then he passed into a coma. He was in the coma till he died a week after I left the hospital."

"So it didn't have to be another person. It could have been a warning, anything."

"You're getting close, Florry."

"A danger, like a curse put on the treasure by Indians, or that it's protected by cougars—that could sound like a K."

"You're getting warm. You're getting hot, Florry honey."

"And it could be anything, and we could make it into anything, our own private sweepstakes if we want to."

"O God, Florry. Let's do it. Let's make love."

"Love? Here?"

"Yes. Let's do it."

"Not here. Not love. It's not the right moment. Besides, you can't make love. Love happens."

"Okay, then let's go find that treasure, and then we'll be rich. Love happens when you're rich. We'll be the richest couple on Crosby Street, and we can buy that loft and build you that studio and you can become the greatest artist of all time, who is also a woman."

"And you can finish law school and open an office to defend the rights of the underprivileged, the disabled, the homeless and downtrodden, and you won't turn anyone away, will you Swanny, not even the refugees, not even if they are fascists fleeing the people's revolution, and then you can run for president and win and we'll bring a new era of peace and understanding to the world, and I'll be your first lady, first artist first lady. Or maybe I'll be president, and you'll be my first lady, the first male first lady, America's most macho first lady, and you could tell stories to the whole country, and I'll be the first woman, first artist, first president. I think we'd be happy in the White House."

"It'll be hamburger heaven. Fat city. We'll be on easy street. Smashola fabiola. We'll be on the biggest roll of all time, in this world or any other. Five aces in every hand. We'll make all the inside straights. Canasta canasta and gin to win. So let's do it, Florry. Let's get off our butts, baby, and go get that treasure." Swanny stood up, rolled up the maps, and stuffed them back in the tube.

"Just a second," Florry stopped. "Where are the kids?"

"The kids?"

"Yeah, our kids. They came with us when we started out."

"You're right," said Swanny. "They were with us. What are their names? I forgot. God, am I a lousy father." He smacked the side of his head. "But you know what I think, that maybe it doesn't matter. And you know what I think, maybe Sarge's K was kids. And you know what I'll bet? I'll bet they're already there. I'll bet they found the treasure. And I bet they're waiting for us to come be a happy family together. A rich happy family."

After their struggle to climb to the top, the level trail was a relief, as if they hardly had to touch the ground. It squirted merrily through sage and rabbitbrush, crossing shallow arroyos, wiggling to the horizon. Florry sang as she walked—"They call me mellow yellow, wang bang boof . . ." and Swanny skipped around in front and back and sang, "Stop, in the name of love. . . ."

A covey of sage hen flew up and sailed off on squeaky wings, and the couple leaned against each other to watch.

"The sage hen is a kind of grouse, a prairie chicken," said Florry. "Its coloration, different from that of its cousin on the great plains, protects it here in the sagebrush."

"I believe it. You're telling the truth, Florry."

"Swanny, these males have some bright-colored air-sacs, and in the spring, when courtship season rolls around, they gather just before daylight at the mating ground to wait to be chosen by a hen."

"O yeah, I hear you Florry. Chosen by a hen. Say it again. Chosen. Chosen. Chosen by a hen."

"And so what these prairie roosters do, Swanny, is in that place, on that mating ground, they puff up their colorful air-sacs, Swanny, and their feathers stand up straight around their bodies like quills, yes, and they position themselves about six feet apart, yes, and shuffle their feet, yes, and dance back and forth, yes, yes, dancing back and forth, yes, making sounds, deep loud sounds, yes, pumping sounds, yes."

"*Owoompah, owoompah, owoompah*," said Swanny.

"Yes," said Florry. "Yes. Yes. Yes."

"What happens now?"

"Females gather to check out the display."

"Females. Gathering. What do they do?"

"They select the brightest and the strongest of the males, the hottest display. Each of them picks one."

"Don't stop. Then what? What do they do? Do they do it?"

"Once the selection is made the female almost immediately starts to build her nest." Florry kissed Swanny on the cheek.

"Don't they mate?"

"Yeah."

"Let's mate, Florry."

Florry looked about at the horizons, the mountains purpling the North, and she thought how exasperating males were. "It's not even mating season, Swanny. Besides, we've mated many times already. Night in, night out we've mated. We are human beings, and that makes a difference. We can mate when we want. Once we find the treasure we can do it on the treasure. Let's establish that right now."

Kalamazoo Is Where Kalamazoo Is
Janet Kauffman

KALAMAZOO EATS SNOW. In that way, he eats clouds. But that is only possible in winter.

This man called Kalamazoo, because of his hometown, spends hours outside—snow, sun, whatever. He works, sure, but who doesn't?

"You're a dumb fuck," Linda says. "As are we all," she adds.

All right, it's Wednesday, with no snow. It's summer in fact. The middle of summer. And out the door, this man Kalamazoo—and that is me—sees a blue-painted diner with the word *Karl's* over the door, and a weedfield and a streetcorner. He does not see molten rock, although it's down there, somewhere, or snipers holed up in the hills.

When Kalamazoo talks, he says *I*, like anybody else. But when he talks to himself, he doesn't. *I* is loud, ridiculous. Too much the shape of Popeye's arm. An I-beam. When he thinks, Kalamazoo doesn't say, *I think therefore I am*. He thinks in the third person. It's awkward. Appropriate. But *me* is tolerable—the lower case. It's no problem to think *me*, my day with Linda, for instance.

"Come over here," Linda says in the diner. She sits at the counter. "I've got a couple of questions for you, Kalamazoo." She's wearing jeans and a black t-shirt and her steel-toed black shoes. She puts a shoe on the chrome-sided stool next to her and kicks it into a spin. Linda is an engineer, and she has offered Kalamazoo work from time to time, which he has taken. With a hard hat on his head, he can laugh at himself. "You look *toyish!*" Linda says. "As do we all," she adds.

Linda spins around on the stool at the counter, a couple of times, as if it's motorized. "What's the difference," she says, "between a man fucking a dog, and a dog fucking a man?"

Kalamazoo says, "I've seen that."

"Is one worse than the other, I mean?" Linda says.

Kalamazoo imagines a link between her dark frizzed hair and her way of thinking. She is tangled, brain to toe.

Kalamazoo's Daddy was bald, simple in thought. These two are two that Kalamazoo has loved—Linda right here, his Daddy long ago. Kalamazoo shunts between these two, their voices, this way, that way. He's some-where in the middle.

"Just put your finger on today's date," his Daddy said, the year Kalamazoo was a tall skinny kid and his Daddy was already fat in the belly, already bald. The calendar hung on the kitchen door, with a Persian cat picture over the numbers, a red bow at the cat's neck.

"Good. That's today," Daddy said. "That's it. When today's past, it's past. Today won't ever lie ahead again, remember that. So just you do what your heart desires!"

Daddy loved each day so much it was hard to call him sentimental. He was beyond it. His eyes were moist.

"Go on," he said in his slow-down voice. "Just you do what your heart desires."

Kalamazoo nodded.

"What do you *really* want to do?" his Daddy asked.

"Well, walk around," Kalamazoo said. Even then he said that. "Look around. I don't know."

"That's fine," Daddy said. "I'm behind you on that, all the way."

"I don't mean for real," Linda says. "I mean to look at, in photographs. Is one worse than the other to look at? For a man to look at, I mean. Which is worse? Or which is funnier, if some guy wants a laugh? Is he supposed to feel sick and laugh, or what? Which is sicker? What's the difference, I mean? And which is worse?"

Kalamazoo looks at the dust floating in his coffee and says, "I've seen a dog fucking a dog."

"I don't mean for real! I'm not talking about that," Linda says. "I mean theoretically. *Theatrically!*" she says.

Outside the window, a line of ants climbs a stalk of Queen Anne's lace. Three ants on the white flowerhead, level as a floor, circle each other and track figure-eights, side-to-side, very complicated trails. They keep their distance from each other. Good for them. Then they walk over the edge—one, then all three—upside-down on the underside of the flower, in the spokework of the plant. This is not a dangerous activity, so far as Kalamazoo knows.

Beyond the weeds, at the streetcorner, a man holds his penis. He doesn't want to be seen. He's got a red t-shirt under a jacket, and it's 95 degrees.

Kalamazoo swings around on the stool. Across the street, he can see all the way through his house, front to back. It's a stucco house, and there used to be a window, where he can't see, that opened into the branches of a white pine. Birds flew into the room, by mistake. He's afraid the house will be burned, maybe gone, the next time he looks.

The house had a kitchen at the back, with a knife on the counter, and his mother had her hand on it one day, but there was also that day just past her shoulder a square window that showed some color in the weeds outside— blue chicory, which would make it July, yellow sweet clover, and maybe that was loosestrife, the tall purple heads. Maybe it was. Air inside and outside the window looked the same both places, blurred, with a gauzy weight to it—maybe the window was open. In the humidity, colors ran together at the edges and even the windowsill wasn't a straight line. His mother lost her balance for a second and grabbed the countertop.

Kalamazoo spins around one way, Linda spins the other way. Linda sticks out her foot with the black shoe as a barrier and they both stop.

"Any one answer would be false," Kalamazoo says.

Karl, who owns the diner, walks through the swing door from the kitchen with his old percolator and fills up their cups.

"The street looks bad, doesn't it?" he says.

Linda stirs her coffee with a knife. On the surface of the coffee, a slick with an iridescent sheen breaks in two, then reconnects when she stirs it again.

"So, speculate. Which is worse? Take a stab," she says.

"Well, in Kalamazoo," Kalamazoo says, "I'd say fucking the dog."

"Too close to reality?" Linda says. She is smiling and her eyes squint almost shut.

Kalamazoo says, slow, because he has thought it before but never said it out loud, "The worst that a person *does* is worse than anything, even the worst, that happens *to* a person."

Karl the owner shakes his head.

"What? Maybe in *your* Kalamazoo," Linda says. "But we're way, way, way down the road."

"Kalamazoo is where Kalamazoo is."

Linda pats his arm. "Yeah, yeah. And we're here with you. But you're talking about real events, and I'm talking about picking up postcards, see, and looking at them. But that's all right. It was just a thought." She folds her napkin in a small square and wipes up a ring of coffee from the counter. "How about a walk down the middle of the street?"

The light outside glares through a haze. Behind the stucco house, trees are dumped in a heap. The man on the corner has disappeared. Linda kicks some leaves.

"Under the leaves," Kalamazoo says, "it's anybody's guess what's going on."

"Easier to predict, though," Linda says, "than what's going on under a roof."

"Maybe you could work out a couple equations."

"Maybe I could," Linda says.

Linda takes Kalamazoo's hand. Then she takes my arm. We look like a couple, out of Kalamazoo's past.

Sometimes it's hard on the ears—the blasting, the collapse of buildings, the heavy equipment cutting tread through asphalt. No one is running or screaming, that's true.

The street's torn up, and we walk down the middle. Linda's black shoes are dusted all yellow. She pulls out her purple sunglass goggles, and when he looks at her, Kalamazoo sees himself in the bubble lenses, another twist to things—white shirt gone bluish, yellow hat chartreuse, violet sky.

Linda's kicking up dust, and the midday heat hits hard. Everything's blasted. The pipes in the ground are useless. Something might tunnel there, though. Beetles. Small ground squirrels could fit. They could live in there. Shit there. All that's hard to imagine, and wormlife, too, but things are alive, six feet under. And more. Keep going, to the mess of molten rock—how far down? It flows and twists, all the time, no question about that. But colorless, you know, colorless.

And Variation · *Jim Krusoe*

1

All he wants is to live in a little apartment with a wiener dog named Klaus. That's not too much to ask, is it, he asks, thinking how happy he'd be with a place of his own to come home to every evening and a little wiener dog yapping at his ankles, him with a can opener in his hand about to open the can of dog food with a picture of a happy dog on its label as he waits for his TV dinner with the picture of a man on its label to heat through. "Now Klaus, just be patient," he'd say, and Klaus would be patient, and then he'd get Klaus's food and then his own, "Food for a Hungry Man," and the two of them would sit down on the couch and watch TV. But instead here he is, in a cast-iron cooking pot all by himself, water up to his neck and surrounded by savages—charming, intelligent, even sophisticated, but savages anyway—and never mind how they dragged this heavy pot through miles of jungle or threatened him till he got in it. Cannibals? Possibly—but really, who ever heard of boiling even a chicken for soup without first evisceration? So where did they get the idea of cooking him this way? One possibility it occurs to him might be that book of cartoons he left out last night. But is that so odd? Wasn't it after *The Sorrows of Werther* hundreds took their lives all over Europe, and didn't thousands of young men hitchhike across the United States after reading *On The Road*? He notices there seems to be some kind of bug walking along the edge of the pot, a bug about the size of a darkened baby's tooth, that's walking around the edge of the pot trying to find a way out. Around him the natives seem mostly relaxed, certainly not vicious or bloodthirsty in any way, but more like old guys hanging around a gas station waiting for the oil in their cars to be changed, and the insect, possibly a beetle of some sort, appears to have given up, or at least paused for a moment, as if its tiny nervous system has gotten the message that continuing this way is not going to help. What kind of bug is this he wonders. Possibly some variety of a lady bug, though his knowledge about beetles is narrow, the most vivid recollection being, ironically, Kafka's, as Gregor Samsa tried to hide beneath a sheet so the cleaning lady wouldn't see him. Now this bug moves, then stops again, and he has the urge to pick it up and toss it off somewhere where it will be temporarily safe. But what good would that do, because it would only wind up being blown into the fire, or, avoiding that, be eaten by a bird, of which, he's noticed there are plenty of all kinds, especially vultures. Tears, he thinks. So many tears.

2

All he wants is to live in a little apartment with a wiener dog named Klaus. Is that too much to ask for? Well, probably yes. Suppose, for example, everyone wanted to do the same. How many little apartments can there be? Certainly, he's read, in Russia and elsewhere people are living six or eight to a room, to say nothing of the people in his own country who have to sleep out on the streets at night. And if everyone wanted a wiener dog how many would that be? And then, if they all were named Klaus, how would people keep them separate? If you called one then they'd all come running, and if you said, "Sit, Klaus," then they'd all sit down at once until you released the ones you didn't want to sit in the first place.

But right now he's hungry, so he'll just have to pull on his coat and tie and go to "Robert's," that swanky French restaurant where he's known to everyone, from the waiters to the busboys, as "The Mystery Diner," a solitary individual who shows up at odd hours in his tux and tie, to sit alone and brood over some mysterious sorrow in his life. Mysterious, that is, to all but Monsieur Robert himself, who knew him back when they were both in the Foreign Legion, both singing Legion songs, doing Legion things, eating terrible Legion food, back before Robert became a famous chef and his friend, now known as the mysterious diner, came down with the strange disease he picked up at a convention in Philadelphia.

"Klaus," the mystery man broods, "such a nice name."

3

All he wants is to live in a little apartment with a wiener dog named Klaus, or maybe Gretchen. "Ah," he sighs, so *this* is what his former dreams of glory have turned into. Where was the famous one-eyed aviator he had sought to become when he was younger? Where was the junk bond king? Where was the painter who cuts off his ear and mails it to a waitress he's seen at the coffee shop the other night? Gone, he thinks, terribly gone.

Suddenly there's a knock at the door, and when he opens it he finds a woman, a real bombshell, who's smiling at him and carrying a briefcase. "Hello," she says, "my name is Gretchen, and do you know that you can have the knowledge of the world at your fingertips for less than the cost of a pack of cigarettes a day?"

He wishes he smoked, and invites her in. She's selling encyclopedias, and as he drinks in her sculptured nails, her long elegant legs, her swan-like neck, her downy arms, her aristocratic feet, her swelling breasts, her tiny sea shell ears, her fine-spun hair, her aquiline nose, her gleaming teeth, her piercing gaze, he finds himself signing a contract for a complete set, plus free yearly updates for the next ten years at no additional cost plus access to a free research service for all his research needs. Gretchen leaves, her scent lingering in the room, and the next day the encyclopedias arrive, crisp and beautifully bound, full of color illustrations and transparencies. He opens one, at random, to the section on "burial."

Burial, the encyclopedia says, is "to deposit a body in the earth," and then it proceeds to a list of places where we are entitled to be buried and whose responsibility it is to bury corpses we may just come upon by accident in daily life, such as shipwreck victims, bodies from plane crashes, motor vehicle accidents, electrocutions, heart attacks, strangulations, and so on.

Essentially, the encyclopedia says, the responsibility is ours.

Sausage · *Stacey Levine*

A FACTORY of upside-down bicycles; this was the way to make sausages; pedaling so quickly with my hands, my feet; never a thought for stopping; unable to know if I was sitting or standing; unaware if the daytime was starting, or ending?

My every muscle was willing; the meat was all ready, well ground, as if chewed, I churned wild circles, miles of bloody brown sausage accumulating beneath my wheels; perhaps I lagged; I was worried, filled with shame; but wasn't my work earnest? Wouldn't I produce to the heavens? My limbs were adept, for squeezing forth sausage in regular shapes, and my fingers strong, too, for each night, very late, I sewed the skins shut with a heavy black thread, knotting it twice to keep everything in—

The Warder entered: huge, circling, judging our production, the condition of our bodies; Yes, I nodded, in answer to everything he said, while sensing, as ever, that I had done something wrong; indeed, the Warder's very presence implied that this was so; he laughed uproariously, for a reason I could not discern, then, in a sudden rage, boomed that our legs were pathetic, weak, weaker than rags; they must be oiled, strengthened, the muscles stretched; he stooped then, massaging my calf with a thick handful of fat, and put his lips to my ear, whispering, "There is a strong chance that this ointment will not help you at all. And I worry, you see, for when your failure occurs, it is my failure too; I depend on you; so, in a sense, does the entire nation; we need sausage; it is now a staple; now, don't suddenly move, or draw attention to yourself; in other words, be true, even-keeled— display high spirits! Don't let your mind stray. Have you ever seen me lose my temper?"

He left, thumping shut the barn door (these buildings were solid, hand-built decades before, twenty stories wide and tall); so churning wildly, I breathed for more sausage; ashamed that my attention ever had wandered; how could it have, with our work being so vitally important?

Sweating heavily at my station, I grew worried again, frightened of failure, and so suddenly, from sheer nervousness, I pushed forth monstrously, producing more sausage than in the entire hour previous; and production was relief, as the Warder had always said; he was right, too; drenched, exhausted, emptied of strength, I decided that I should immediately change, and learn to selflessly give—of myself, and my body, as if giving a gift—

Though this year had been one of record production; the ninety of us issuing more sausage per day than ever had been achieved; our numbers were steady—incredible numbers, rising daily, so that it became no longer possible to tabulate our work in the usual way; thus newer, higher numbers were found to express our rates, though these numbers themselves became quickly outmoded, outpaced; then, even higher, more superlative symbols were employed, and in approaching the horizon of numbers, the barrier to infinity, we grew giddy, as if on a ride; managers worried, as precise counts were lost; secret meetings were planned, military exercises; yet through it all, an enormous excitement, for, with our bodies, we had produced such fantastic amounts—with the sheer force of our wills, too, our wishes to be good, and with the help of regular punishments—

The meat was always ready, boiled hard, in vats; the skins lay in rows, clean, stretched; everything in order; nothing was the matter—barring, occasionally, a ripple of emotion—anger, or pleasure, churning inside us, as if deep beneath the crust of a mountain—

Our wants were satisfied daily; our mats lay spread in the barn; ten minutes of sleep before each back-to-back shift; to eat, sausage-gruel in huge amounts, and to drink, steaming cups of blood, as much as we liked; ample time, too, to take one of the confused, blurred creatures that wandered these yards, and lead it away for relief in some corner of the dark—

"Good, very tender," said the Warder, having entered, stooping to test the links with his teeth; "Continue," he cried, shaking, "Today work for size; tonight, for speed! Achievement, achievement—but I worry that you will not—" then he turned away, dropping his huge, hairy head to his palms, overcome; "My god," he whimpered, "I can't manage my own doubt—"

—Alarmed, we pedaled faster, ninety bicycles whirring in place; upon my seat, I pushed harder than ever, continual bursts of dampness like storms at the back of my neck; sausage dropped through the rafters, to the floor in gleaming coils; "Ah," groaned the Warder, raising his swimming eyes, "you must animate yourselves, don't fall behind—" So I pressed on, dripping a meat-scented sweat, whispering the highest known numbers to myself—

176

—For there was nothing else beyond these walls, only the empty town of Nicholls, and beyond that, the silent, wind-soaked plains of "France"; no other nation besides our own, a fact we had learned long ago, in our youths—

During these weeks of stupendous growth, I grew, at certain moments, somewhat cocky, even brash, once slipping from my station, muscles shaking, laughing to myself from sheer tension; I sought a lone, dry corner, swallowing down a piece of beer-soaked bread (having stolen it shamelessly from a nearby trough—an act which, eventually, would weigh gravely upon my list of wrongs); I grew thoughtful, serious, legs apart, thick, powerful; resembling, in these moments, as it happened, the Warder; bellowing tremendously, instantly embarrassed, I struck myself with the back of my fist; then, I heard a whisper spurt through the air, landing hard in my ear, as if mad to get home; this sound was clear, and told me to take charge, as it were, to stop suffering needlessly because of my work; a plan came to me clearly then: I would assume responsibility for all the mistakes, foibles, and wrongdoings of another sausagemaker, now dead.

I had not known this man, but I would now set out to possess all his wrongs: in this way, I saw, my own guilts would be obscured; I would atone for him publicly, thereby winning respect from the management; I would live freely, then, never again burdened by the weight of my actions or their consequences.

So the next morning, early, I went to ask permission, duly, officially, before a panel of porcine judges assembled in the lower barn (chairs stacked high against the rear wall, and stored between each, a thick layer of special winter sausage fully encrusted by salt, meant to nourish the management, keep them warm against the deadly cold); I was vocal; I expressed myself clearly: I wanted to possess the dead man's wrongs, and repent for him, since I was exemplary—

With the banging of a gavel, they assented, scarcely looking up; it was decided; I was to live the rest of my life atoning for the dead one's wrongs; now, it was official; now, at every turn, I would be enfolded by his innumerable ill deeds, my own movements free from suspicion, for the first time in my existence—

Such relief! All my life, I had somehow needed this; exuberant, I stepped up to embrace the administrators, judges, and even the mayor, who briefly had stepped in (though in clasping him, my lips brushing his scented beard,

I realized that he was devoid—not numb and overfed, as with diplomats, nor brainwashed, as by religion—but empty, blank, outrageously, of any mental content or register, resembling, even, faintly, a birth monster—and then, from sheer excitement, he mewled, looking to the ceilings, bobbing his head, and everyone laughed, for he was a docile, well-loved man, and filled his post perfectly, I had heard)—

Giddy, I raced toward my station, springing past stalls, careering through aisles, sluice gates, pulling up my pants, invigorated, thrilled by the thought of the dead one and his wrongs, and then, by chance, I passed his pale body in the dim hall, where naked, like others, it was strapped against the wall, embalmed, on display, completely shaven, head dropped down, for he had simply weakened, then died of work, a crime under jurisdiction of both factory and state. Diagrams and arrows, supplemented by a brief text, were printed on his flaccid torso to explain exactly how the veins of his heart had burst and collapsed—this occurrence being entirely due to his own problems—poor habits and disorganization, most probably, it read. Secured in a bottle to his left lay the heart itself, ravaged bloody roots springing from its top; all had been his fault, only his, the tract read, since he had been unable to keep up with the details of work; and misfortunes like these were just part of life, which could happen to anyone, at any time; still, this man's case was rare, it said, a fact that made everyone thankful and glad; and soon, it went on, there would be a celebration for all living employees, who were all wonderful with detail, and, in general, good; so, as a rule, deaths like these would not occur if we were dependable workers and always produced as much as we could—

Having run all the way, I arrived at my station, nearly forgetting who I was, producing sausage to such delirium, yet luckier than most, I felt; and surely not dead; though perhaps, in fact, the best worker in the place, since I was so wholesome, full of energy, and so completely without wrongdoing that even I was astounded; yet somehow, during the night, I again began to doubt; I checked the list I kept beneath my mat: indeed, I had committed no outstandingly wrong acts, except for the minor infraction of the bread— and this I could explain by saying that I had been seeking to emulate the Warder, and so had needed to eat more and gain weight; surely I would not be punished for this, and so, I decided, for now I was safe—

Jumping to my station, throwing my head back with relish, raising a rough, corrugated stick we often used to show purpose and excitement,

178

pedaling backward (a trick we knew for making sausages fancier, bloodier, less congealed, stronger in color), I was now perfectly free; now, things were different, my luck holding fast because of the dead one's deeds; no more burden, guilt, or remorse; my wheels raced steadily; below, piglets scrambled across the floors in packs; surely I was good, and produced properly at all possible moments—this being the pride and requirement of our factory and nation—all was fine, I reassured myself, combing my hair, rearranging my smock, forking, when no one was looking, steaming heaps of meat into my mouth—

My neighbor to one side, an elder, wheezing, exhausted, bathed in a dark, slick sweat, raised his head and cried out, "Forget the dead one—your scheme is transparent! It's shameful, this business of racing about as you do, trying to get away with everything you can!"

"I did what I had to do," I calmly said. "It was an honest impulse; I don't have to explain myself. One thing, though, honestly: I feel better and more vigorous than I ever have. Don't repeat this, but I earned my freedom through cunning, and no one else before me has done that—but then, I was never really part of the common pack. Why don't you stop being petty, and congratulate me? I no longer live as do you, continually constricted and guilty!"

He laughed long and hard, tears streaming down his face. "Your head is in the clouds! No one is here to constrict you, or otherwise make you feel bad. The guilty are guilty because they do not fit in!" he said, and slid from his station, bent, still laughing, wiping his body with a blue rag.

"How do you know this?" I said, gripped with worry suddenly.

"Because I have a bigger heart than you," he said, standing there naked, pointing to his own chest, digging the finger in hard as if to break the skin. "I know the truth, for I am clean, appropriate, and have never strayed a day from work. Now, you labor for this factory, and for our nation—these being of course exactly the same entity; don't behave as if they were your adversaries! That will ruin you. Instead, just relax; give in to the notion that all is naturally in place. The pressure we all feel is no plot, no one person's fault. It's just a part of a successful life at work."

I rebuffed him, but in a sense, the old man was right; he had only been trying to prepare me for the next sequence of events, which began a few moments later, when I received, at my station, a strong, sudden message wired from the Manager-in-Absentia, which went like this:

"Just leave it, and let it go. Give yourself the luxury of a few moments' rest, since soon we will make you do things you don't want to do at all, and actually make you want to disappear. Do you fear the surprise of learning you are wrong? I hate to shatter your happiness, for I know you are proud. It was nothing in particular, not even your most recent act that brought you into the limelight; it was the accrual of years of your inability to settle down. We will take our time; we will let you know; do you wonder what will happen? Now, repeat the word 'fiasco' after me, over and over; repeat it now, in dialect precisely as is mine, not—I warn you—in parody; repeat it honestly, and with effort, because—and this is God's truth—there is a job now available in the mountain district, and in order to be considered for it, you must be able to successfully reproduce a mountain accent, not just once, but consistently, in a variety of circumstances."

All this, contained in the crumpled message, was followed by a second, more recent note, saying the job in the mountains was still open, though it might soon close, and that this would be an excellent position for anyone with talent, it read, like me, and with the ability to blend in imperceptibly with anyone or anything.

My neighbor, now back at his station, bathed in rivers of sweat, lunging, straining for sausage, about to faint, leaned toward me, whispering hoarsely, meat on his breath, "Tear up the message! And let me tell you the most important thing!"

At which point a lean figure entered the barn, rolling the fainted man away, smiling, wiping his hands, clapping three times, then saying, "You should stop behaving in ways that belie your unconscious."

"But I'm not," I said.

"Oh, yes you are! You're completely transparent—"

"Who are you?" I said.

"I am Rolf," he answered, "but that doesn't matter. In fact, it's important that you know little about me. But I care about you, and so will say this: in taking on the dead man's guilt, you have displayed your troubles as if the workplace were a theatre—very inappropriate, and what's more, you don't seem to realize it. Which in itself is important, for it shows us that you cannot see life as it really is, but only as you experience it—including your feelings about me—hesitation and distrust, I believe, and only because my clothes are smart and pressed, which you sophomorically perceive as some kind of threat—

"Nothing exists but your own broken desire, come, come. What is taking on the guilt of another? It is hiding, in fact, from the responsibilities we really must carry. Don't worry; I am the sole person who knows of this. Now, don't pretend; you are not going to walk away; where would you go, in the middle of 'France?' I know, for example, that you have frequent, sudden urges to ingest sleeping tablets—that is not permitted. Sorry! Back to work," he said, "on sausage, and your problems; begin a résumé, too, answering the question: 'have you ever in your life been dismissed or fired?'—for all hiring managers are universally righteous; employees are not, and in order to hire new men, employers must have true, exact accounts of what before has happened, grounding present judgments soundly on past circumstance."

He turned and left; my knees collapsed; ashamed now, exposed, and twice as much as before; the dead man's guilts were no protection against this Rolf; I clutched myself, running through the yards, embarrassed to disbelief, for it was true, I loved to sleep, but had such difficulty in achieving it; I entered the storage cellars, piglets galloping, screaming overhead; bending to search the crease of my smock, I found the tablet neatly hidden there; I swallowed it, and fell to sleep, dreaming of knives that ran in organized legions, each with a short, distinct, Christian name, Gore, for example; fear saps one's strength like nothing else; waking the next day, I was wracked, worried about achievement, about never catching up, or living the rest of my life in the margins, among the ranks of the unproductive; I was immobile, too, unaccustomed to refuting the likes of Rolf, but instead, all my life, in school and throughout, had always obeyed clear instructions (or else furtively enacted the precise opposite of these, for which I was always summarily found out and punished); but now, I could not think, hating myself and my weaknesses, my failed plan to escape guilt and become another; hating, for a moment, the entire factory, and even our nation—

Though receiving, suddenly, a rushed message, delivered to my station, curiously, by crow—this due, perhaps, to the lateness of the hour, or the shutdown of electricity in patterned on-off intervals—not meant at all gratuitously, we were told, but in a playful spirit, instead, to invite decipherment of such patterns, to strengthen our minds and keep them alert—this message informing of a special tax to be computed relative to the amount of sausage I produced; and after a year, I would be charged multiple payments, and also a tax upon my legs, and on the bicycle I used; I was wild with fury, blowing out a great wind of screams, clattering through the slaughter area, sweeping entire sets of tiny wrenches from their shelves, stabbing the air, inhaling whole dust clouds; forced to give up what I earned, loath to do so, shamed still more that I did not have the sum to pay; arms windmilling, hurling clots of mud to the ceilings—but suddenly I stopped; yes, of course I would pay the tax, I thought mincingly, but not the precise amount; just a few cents less, or even more, as I chose; only this, to cause irritation and disfigure the accounts; and regardless of these thoughts, I still loved our nation, of course; and wanted to achieve, as the Warder admonished; so did everyone, the managers, and even Rolf; we wanted to achieve, and contribute, and of course be good; otherwise, everything here might grow diffuse and dissolve, and then we would have no nation at all—

Sprinting up ladders, past gristle bags, buckets of swash, plundered mattresses, I aimed for my station, producing sausage faster than ever, then jumping down, stuffing barrels full, grabbing the handles and hurrying toward the greeting center, so anxious to do well, driven as never before, going to the bathroom in the middle of the hall, turning around, hands warmly extended to customers now streaming from their cars, all of them buying and eating hugely of sausage, voracious, hardworking people, I am sure, big as houses, cheering at anything, singing while driving on their vacations, nostalgic for times that never existed; bearing sausage away on their backs to trailers, laughing, whooping, whipping the air three times with their fists, growing impatient, demanding satisfaction, so running back to my bicycle, I produced just that—sausage, pouring forth at its freshest, to be consumed within moments by unknown persons—

Angry, perhaps, though most of all, I was deeply ashamed—for myself, and for everything that ever had been, for miscalculating miniscule details of my movements that the Manager-in-Absentia might somehow see, for taking on the guilt of another, trying to lose myself in order to be more free, for not having known the notes of the scales, nor the geography of Madeira; ashamed, too, before Rolf, who seemed to know my every thought, running to his flimsy, molding desk on the dock to update careful weekly notes, though every afternoon, coming to fetch me at the abandoned schoolyard where I ran the miles-high tor to strengthen my limbs, calling to me from across the field (concerned, paternal, I desperately wished), "Did you vomit blood?"—his coat flapping fiercely in terrifying wind—

—Nowhere else to go beyond these quiet streets of Nicholls, or, beyond that upon the empty plains of "France"; no one at all, especially not the elusive Warder-in-Absentia, nor his assistant, an accountant who pounded across the wooden floors, disingenuously tipping her pencil in salutation, running, leaping upon her boss to suckle; disengaging, then racing back to her underlings to convince them she was real, pleading, "I am an accountant! And charmed by your masculinity, I'm sure!—For it gives me something to work with; I know this territory well; now wait, while I excite you, just to gain control—" nor even her administrative equal, though she would not believe it, a beefy, sluggish bureaucrat, who, slumping unattractively at his desk, rasped during the night, "No! I cannot talk to you now!" though he feverishly imagined protracted, cruel conversations, purple-faced, trudging in circles around a toilet, saying his own name out loud in a kind of power fantasy; huge lungfuls of breath; expelling joy from his mouth at the very idea of commanding dirty creatures down the aisles and to work; soon to have his voice function as does a telephone, connected to every room by wire; connected, eventually, into the very natures of all people, which would bring everything to perfection, really, for him, the omniscient administrator, with his own clannish team of clerks, now all of them ready for golden promotion, and promoted they would be, without question—

While the entire group, along with Rolf, hands folded, eyes moistly beckoning, called, "Come, come, what is this nonsense, we sympathize; we're friends; we want to understand, so that you are no longer beleaguered by your own tendencies; never mind the bread; but as for the tablets, we know they are hidden in your smock; we know you want to use them to leave your body and become inert, but frankly, at the precise moment that we discovered them, those tablets became ours; that is—the movement is smoothly complex—for us, knowing is the same as a swift, confiscating action, like an algorithm we compact until it behaves exactly as we want; all is settled; we have the tablets and you do not; do not sleep; instead, let's now talk, and examine your mind as it is put forth in the texts, the ways you misperceive the world due to your own defensiveness, all the bad things you imagine we do to you; each rather unconnected to the truth—do you feel a roiling in the soul now, that comes from remaining unchanged? Say 'please'; let us now look at all the shame you've ever endured, and collect it together as in a little half-shell, so you can feel it all at once, along with the fallacies to which you cling, and then, perhaps, you will see yourself more clearly, and something important can be achieved—"

"We will learn why you chose to take on the guilt of another, and tried to be more free, and tried, sometimes, to escape into sleep, with the white tablets you so cunningly ground into powder—as if we could be fooled—! As if we would believe they were, perhaps, tooth cleanser—?"

Tearing through the yards, I slammed into the cellar, panting, motionless, peering all night through the weephole and into the slaughtering barn, waiting for a clear space for which I might run, straight to the lower barns where administrators, standing puzzled, would watch me rocket forwards and back, bursting upon myself like a broken bomb, as they always knew would happen, for I was always, utterly, and completely found out, forever entrenched in Nicholls, here on the silent plains with nothing at all beyond—and we knew this as fact—

"—Considering everything, you're doing quite well," Rolf said. "We were waiting for this to happen; you will come around and soon be better; don't fuss; and soon, it's back to work, for you've missed far too much, but can make it up if you really push—"

And looking straight at me, though I was still concealed behind the door, he stepped forward, waggling his finger, gently speaking through the hole, "Come out, come out, time to greet the customers, for they are here now—"

—Which they were, packed into their cars, men of five hundred pounds begging for sausage, collapsing as they emerged, crying out, "This country is my best friend," and "Our beliefs are literally part of the land!"— demanding that nothing ever diverge from our clear, accustomed ways of life and truth—though before leaving, many of them pulling me aside, whispering, "Please, before we go back, let me service you just once, upside down, flat on your back; then, holding you still, just once again—"

But all of that was long ago; in the days before this most astonishing year, we ran from the remotest wood-cracked rooms and halls to the indices attached to all street signs of the town, each of which said, "You are in 'France,'—take care, don't stray, keep robust; this is the land of enormous plenty; someday, certainly, you will get your due, but for now, check yourself daily; look toward sausage, and the truth"—these placards we

184

shattered; now, they are forgotten; it is five o'clock on the huge, slanting plaza; the crowds have gathered to celebrate, refusing all news that protest is unwarranted—and still we do not know who or what is victorious, or if that is even the pertinent question; I am not who I once was; kiosk windows fall open, knots of people expand, newsgirls shout, "It is nine o'clock, and due to a rather global pressure, a motion has been passed for the work day to be called off! The popular forces demand it; all manner of change will be discussed; we will wait, then decide our course, but for now, there is everything to do and see; go to your windows; did you not know it?—Look at all the people who are willing to join us—"

This was our nation, the true nation, after all; we thought we had no home, but in fact, we do; the commotion will continue; push your stockings down, loosen your underclothes and belt; in the War of Independence, doors on the plaza opened, and ten thousand dark-cloaked bicycle riders emerged, legs outstretched, heading for the clock tower, gliding as if upon amber, an exalted whisper on everyone's brain, unique and indescribable, like the birth of each new child: "Here are our desires; here are still more, such as we know"; deepest relief, since our voices' true sounds were heard; a great, healthful confusion has arisen; here is what we wish for; here is what we never had; by dawn, we will have unravelled the worst, and stamped down the rest; let me be with them, let me begin to learn; someday, will I have grown? Will my fears dispel? Will I have my own wife? At the millenium, who will I be? Will we have kept our gains? Soon to come are uncountable storms; the blackness of the air is invigorating, though—

Works from the War between Houses and Wind
Ben Marcus

The Strategy of Grass

The smasher was the first grass-guard of American shelters. Often accompanied by a dog, the girl wielded her shade-stick so that the sun might never collaborate with the grass in destroying the house. This was not the first time houses were under attack from outside forces. House crushing schemes were often observed to no avail; indeed, shacks were burnt nightly by sunwater bogged upon grass, fire-chalk scratched out tents and sheds, even cabins were scorched by greenweeds until the girl became employed on American lawns. The technique of shade has since this period allowed houses to flourish, with the dog being designated as the first shade-chaser, or, more formally, the Person. Although not human, the person holds an innate need to save the house.

Shade has throughout known times warded off enemies, particularly those dispatched by the fiend, if the fiend is defined as any item of great or medium heat, extending from a wire. Although shade is technically gray in color, red shades permeate the lawns of Denver, and a colorless, cooling shade has been observed in the seventeen primary settlements of Illinois. While shade was first disproved by Jerkins in his FARM EXPERIMENTS (in which he claimed that shade was a black sun welt that could be soothed with water and straw), it has currently gained favor in the communities due to the expert wielding of the sun-smashing girl. No sun is actually ever touched by this employee. The dramatic nomenclature indicates merely a deft skill with the stick. A shade-sprayer by trade, her work involves house-dousing when the sun is brightest. The dog stalks these cooling skins across the lawn or over sections of house, acting also as a shade dragger when the girl is at work beneath the house. Although shade is mistrusted by many occupants, and has rarely been selected as a primary weapon, it must not be overlooked as a key defense against objects that might burn in to take the house from the air, in secret agency with the wires of the hallowed sun.

Since grass preceded the house, and is considered to be a grain yet older than wood, we must wonder whether the grass wars of the 1820s contributed to the brief disappearance of houses observed during this era.

That no shelters were in view either indicates perhaps a correlation with the Great Hiding Period of those same days.

Lawn-boys were numerous in Ohio in the early weeks of the first seventies. Boys and their counterparts were dispatched across lawns to serve as wind poles during the street storms of this period, and the shorter, sturdier boys (maronies) were often the first to blow back into the houses. This explains in great detail the rugged ornamentation of certain shelters in the middle west, particularly those houses that contain chronicles etched into the awnings. The taller boys, the skinnier ones, could more success-fully deflect wind from the house, and they became better known as stanchers, although salaries were meager. During the chalkier street storms, however, the boys went unfed and often starved upon the lawn, creating skin flags, or geysers of bone and cloth, which during more elastic storms could ripple back and snap windows from a house until glass spilled into the air, cutting down the insect streams. What was left of the boys was then smothered by this powdered glass and air blood that fell upon them, rendering a burial site at each house. Boy-piles on grass were richest after storms, and planting was heaviest until this fertilizer was rifled by scavengers—often young girls and their animal sisters, who dragged the soil away in sacks and wagons.

Air Dies Elsewhere

When air kills itself the debris settles onto the grass, sharpening the points. Dogs may not walk on these areas, nor may they ever even observe the grass without pain in the chest and belly. When children sleep on the lawn the funeral passes just above their heads in a cross-wind with the body. Funerals generally are staged in pollinated wind-frames, so that the air can shoot to the east off of the children's breath, dying elsewhere along the way, allowing fresh, living air to swoop in on the blastback to attack the house. This funeral chasing ability of children explains why they are allowed outside during the daytime and back in again the next day. The Mother cleans the child's mouth with her finger and is said to act as a transom for the warring agencies of wind. This is why she is placed in the window, wires bobbing from each hand, bowing forward against the glass.

Other forms of sleeping also calm the sky. Wealthy landowners hire professional sleepers to practice their fits on key areas of the grounds. The best sleepers stuff their pockets with grass and sleep standing up. Many amateur sleepers never wake up, or never fall asleep. If a professional wakes and discovers a protector still sleeping, or unable to sleep and making an attempt of it—in the shed, for example, downwind of the house—he is permitted to practice smashes upon this body. Freelancers take their dream seizures near the door, and storms are said to be held in abeyance. They are paid according to success. Much booty has been disbursed, but no one has ever succeeded to sleep so deeply that the house is not smashed upon waking.

If dogs or parts of dogs are ever studied, it will be their feet. The primary transmission has occurred between grass and the paw. When we kill dogs we kill them because we are sad. SADNESS develops in and outside of the house, either just after entering or just after leaving. These are also the times of war when we encounter dogs and have the opportunity to act upon them. The feet of dogs are soaked in Corey, a chemical produced in grass after air has mixed the shape of the house. Collectors believe that feet grow heavier after being removed, lighter when touched, and remain the same when left alone. This is also true of sadness and wires.

RULE OF EXIT

When the sun's wires are measured, we discover the coordinates for a place or places that shall heretofore be known as perfect or final or miraculous. The house shall be built here using soft blocks of wood and certain solidified emotions, such as tungsten. By nightfall the bird-counter will collapse, and a new man must be placed at the road to resume the tally while the construction continues. His harness will be a great cloth fixture bound unto his head, to protect his mouth from the destroying conflicts, lest strong birds sweep in on the wires to knock back the homes. Every house prayer shall for all time ever read thusly:

Please let the wires not have been crooked or falsely dangling or stretched by the demon sun, let our measurements be exact and true, and bless our perfect place with abundant grasses. Cover us in shade so that we are hidden in your color. Hide us from birds and wires and the wind that sends them. Let smoke conceal us during the storm life, and give us strong walls. Let not any stray wind break us down and we will honor you. Bless us and a great shelter will be made for you in the new season. Help us thrive. We lie low here in the place that you have given us. Please remember that you have killed us and you can kill us and we wait and long in our deepest hearts to be killed only by you. Let this be our last and final house.

Amen.

Your Name Here _____ · *Cris Mazza*
(novel excerpt, from near the end)

April 20, 1980

Shit . . . 4:15 a.m. I can't remember. God. But there's a feeling of something I'll never forget.

The hot tub. The steam. All my clothes still on. Really? No, my clothes were off. Had to be. A sleeve with silk lining? No. Hot boozy water boiling around me in the dark. Absolute dark . . . ? No. . . . Alone, again, this time? No.

But my clothes are wet, in a pile over there. I had to put them back on that way. Cold and clammy, but better that than wearing any of their clothes and have them coming around asking to get their shirt or pants back. What the fuck was Cy doing there? No one told me it was a double date—but with only three people. Or were there more? Was Kyle there? Or was it a whole-station party? No. No. No. Someone strung red and blue Xmas lights all around and had them plugged into a thing that makes them go with the music. I was watching. Figuring it out. One string was the bass. One the vocal. All mish-mashed. I was staring up. I was being fucked. Wet pants still tangled around one ankle. Wet shirt under my back. Glass of wine poured out over my face. Wake up, little girl! *Who said that? An* open-handed slap. Do it, show it! *The Xmas lights going haywire like a special show to greet Santa as he climbs down the chimney. His grand entrance. Someone lifting my head.* Watch him do it. *My neck ready to snap in half. Holding someone's ankles, one in each hand, on either side of me. Then turned like a pancake. Like a Polish sausage on the grill. Being pulled up by my hips, like a cat, like a rag doll, my head and shoulders stayed heavy on the floor. Someone laughing. The carpet smelled like wet wool. Someone singing happy birthday. I waited through all the endless happy-birthday-to-you verses to find out whose birthday. Happy birthday dear* _____ *(your name here). Did I ever find out? How many to-you verses are there? My arms in wet sleeves. My shirt thrown up over my head. My back cold. Where was that silk-lined coat? Even colder down on my butt. Something wet . . . and cold.* What is it what is it what is it? *Someone's crazy voice wouldn't shut up.*

Shut her up.

Just frosting for the cake, Sweetheart. Wanna suck?

Nipple in my mouth filling me with whipped cream.

Oh. . . . It was Haley's *coat, not mine, but that was another time . . . not so long ago . . . when her cowgirl scent from a coat wadded around my head overpowered that same smell of booze and smoke. . . . If I'd had the coat last night . . . could it have also overcome the woolly smell, their slimy sweat, the grass, the smell of pussy on someone's hand, the cream in my mouth . . . ? Spitting sound of whipped cream sprayed into the air, then landing around me with the soft plopping sounds of wet snow falling from trees.*

How's that feel?

Like I gotta take a shit.

Someone thought that was hysterically funny. Someone holding my butt cheeks apart. The whipped cream melting and running down the crack. Someone shaking the can. Someone kneeling on my hand. Someone fucking my asshole. Someone slapping my thighs. How many of them were there? Lying on the floor feeling like I had to take a dump. Did I ever go into the bathroom? Once I did . . . a long time ago . . . another different time . . . after he said I looked like a boy. . . .

I don't remember ever being on my feet. Did I crawl around all night, slide on my stomach, slither out of the hot tub like evolution? Or was I dragged from place to place by one ankle? Probably not. I don't have rug burns. But a few bruises. And dried blood. Blood turning black around the corners of my eyes, in my ears, and, mostly, in my nose. That's where it had to come from. But I don't remember how I got the bloody nose. One of those spontaneous combustion bloody noses?

Maybe if I try to remember the beginning. . . . I never should've had those joints by myself before I even got there. Met Al at his office. Working late, he said, so just meet him at the station and we'll go from there. No ride in his sports car, though. Instead: the elevator upstairs. All the way. To the penthouse. The door already open. Did a dozen people jump out and shout surprise? *It was someone's birthday, wasn't it? Or was that just Al shouting as we came through the door. Golden already there, sitting in the huge swivel chair.*

When did I say okay? When did they ask? There had to be a moment. No one held me down. We passed the weed between the three of us until I lay flat and they finished it together, over me, silently, just the music, the only music I remember, The Doors from six or eight years ago, Light My Fire. *What were they looking at? Not really me. But my eyes were shut most of the time, opened to slits now and then. Their faces flickering blue and red. I'd probably already drunk, in an hour, more bourbon than all the other booze I'd ever had in my life. Maybe an exaggeration. Felt like it, though. One of them touched my shoulder—his hand rough like sandpaper, made me feel I was velvety smooth . . . and he was scratching the delicate surface of me. But when did I get undressed . . . or lose my clothes . . . my wet clothes . . . who took them off? Nothing was ripped. Not a button missing. I probably did it myself. Between hits of the joint. Possibly forgetting they were kneeling on either side of me. Forgetting they were there, except to take the joint from their hands when they passed it . . . until I just receded, faded back, and I was already undressed. The music ended. Someone went to find a new tape. The other stayed, the rock-rough hand still on my shoulder, my upper arm, and he said something like "You can really be a woman, twice the woman, tonight, if you want." I do remember the* if you want. *I remember saying, "I'm not a virgin." When the other came back, the one who'd stayed said, "Let's go." And they bent over me, each taking a nipple and sucking.*

All that after I'd already been in the hot tub. Did I trip? Fall in? How much had I drunk before that? What happened before the tub—before the drugs and whipped cream and fucking . . . did we talk? I want to feel like I didn't say anything.

I also never said anything to Haley. It's not necessary to talk to say goodbye . . . as long as you both know you're saying it. . . . I'm sorry, Haley . . . I admit it, you didn't know, I fucked you over, maybe I deserved this. . . . But we did have to say goodbye. Not saying it is the best way. I mean not out loud. Meaning it, showing it, that's different. Goodbye can be soft, slow, warm-water smooth, weightless, graceful, gentle as a first touch if you don't try to say or explain it. She would've understood . . . wouldn't she?

But I landed in that hot tub like a crashing cinder block. Shouting. Yes, I guess I used my voice. Just "Hey—" The music was so loud. Maybe every time I said anything, none of us heard it.

Oh shit, I remember something else:

Al said, "Kyle says you'll go along. Won't kiss-and-tell. You want to get somewhere here, don't you?"

God, did you say that, Kyle? Why?

And Golden: "You and Kyle? I knew it, dammit, the lying bastard. You're fired!"

Got a promotion then was fired . . . all in ten seconds. But Al said, "Wait, she'll atone for that. He couldn't offer you a party like this, huh, Sweetheart?"

Is that when I went into the tub? Or when I got the bloody nose? And what about this nail polish? Black. Fingers and toes. One did the feet, the other worked on my hands. Not very steady, the polish all over my cuticles, smeared on my knuckles. Done after the first bourbon bottle had been emptied, probably. Or was that the

bottle which got spilled in the tub? Or . . . did the tub smell like hot whipped cream?
Maybe the nail polish is smeary because I was shivering. Or because maybe I kept
jerking my hands and feet away. The one at my feet pounded on my leg with his fist
then turned around, sat on my knees. I could still rock my feet on my heels from side
to side. Laughing. Was I laughing? Or gasping. Where'd you get this, where'd
you get this, it's—

Haley's. Black nail polish. The acrid smell of it taking the place of any cowgirl
perfume which might've been lingering for months in the red and blue air. Didn't I
once lay my head on the breast of her coat and cry? When was that?

I did cry. That's right. Because I lost my contact lenses in the hot tub? Or when
the burning end of the joint they were passing fell onto my stomach? Or when I
opened my eyes and saw Cy's purple face screwed shut, his white hair, and realized
it was his dick in me?

He'd finished the polish on my feet. Then they almost had a fight. With him still
in me. Al wanted to put a black nail-polish mustache on me. And started to. But
Golden didn't like it. He said, Whadda ya think I am, a goddamn fag?

Keep your wig on. We're just playing around.

WE? She ain't doing shit. You gotta real dud this time.

I heard she was better than this.

Well, at least she's gotta couple'a holes. Make the best of it.

Sweetheart, wake up. Is she dead?

Corpses don't moan. Listen to that. She likes it.

Let her like me for a while.

Let me get a squirt, will you?

You had one.

Hours ago. God, listen to that juice. She loves it.

Sweetheart? Honey?

Sweetheart, honey, sweetheart, baby, bitch, cunt, darlin, honey, sweetheart . . .
never once my name. . . .

3 May 1989

I want to get out of here, I don't know where . . . fly somewhere. . . . Can
I get to the bus depot through the window? Or the police . . . should I go
to the police? But when they ask, "What happened?" what'll *I* say? I was
raped . . . and hurt . . . and there was blood . . . at one time there was

blood, but it must've gotten washed away. Now my body just aches. Like a white-knuckled fist that can't be pried open . . . I have to tell the fist to relax, I have to instruct each piece of myself separately . . . relax, toes . . . relax, knees . . . relax because we have to go to a party soon, Garth's party. . . . How can I go to his party when this has just happened to me? I can picture myself swinging a baseball bat in a circle and bashing everyone's head who's too close to me. There'll be party conversations, loud enough to hear but far away, voices in a black cloud, making me unable to see who might be speaking to me:

What's new?

I think I was raped.

You *think*?

Well, you see, it was ten years ago, and I may've said yes. If I did—I raped myself. Maybe I didn't know what I was saying yes *to*. Not to what they did . . . not to *them*. Never to *them*. . . .

But what if I did say yes . . . dirty pig, fucking *whore*. . . . *No*. I'm not, I didn't, I couldn't have . . . not Corinne Staub . . . *you* knew me, Kyle. I wouldn't've said yes . . . but did I say *no*? Why not? What kept me from saying *no*? Could I have said *no* with a broken jaw? Where's my broken jaw? Isn't this when it was broken? Why didn't I feel it as I was writing it all down right afterwards? The way I feel it *now*—it's my jaw I hear crying . . . it hurts . . . *hurts*.

Of course, look outside, you fool, it's raining. And you're grinding. You're not even asleep, and you're grinding your teeth. Maybe Corinne needs to be put in rubber headgear to keep her from hurting herself. To keep her from saying *yes*. Ever again. To help her bounce when her head hits concrete. I kicked the night guard under the desk a few weeks ago. Every time I see it, I think: "A fighter lives here." Not a very good one.

Why me, Kyle, why'd they want *me* at their party? They'd never done more than shove empty coffee cups at me, or lists of crossed-out ideas. I was part of the woodwork, the plastic table top, the newspapers and tabloids stacked on a chair. But *now* what am I?

You're a successful news anchor . . . and you're Garth's lover. . . . Are you both at once? . . . And remember, there's a party tonight.

Will you be there, Kyle? Will you be one of the ones I smash with a baseball bat or one of those I stare at with moronic eyes as I cling to Garth's arm and wonder what the hell will happen to me when he leaves. I knew it

194

would happen eventually . . . I knew I wouldn't run away from it. I thought. . . . What did I think? What the hell was I *thinking*?

Monday, April 23, 1980

Déjà vu. Kyle on the air alone. No sign of Golden. No His-Pal-Al hanging around. One thing is different this time, though: this note—found it taped to the door with my name on the envelope, saying Adcock wants to see me ASAP. Kyle's handwriting. All the possibilities keep running through my head, but there really is only one probability: I'm going to be railroaded out of here just like Haley was. But I can't go face Adcock until I talk to Kyle.

later

Now he says I have to figure out what to do. He said to wait here—Adcock's already gone to lunch so I have time to think about it. He said it so low and steady, almost calmly, hard to believe we'd been shouting across the table, standing, circling, always keeping the table between us. Only once did his eyes and face show any sign of softness—not when he left, but when he first came in and I was sitting here with his note. He said, "I heard about it," and touched the back of my head as he went around the table. That started the fight, and ended any comfort I might've gotten from him, because I had to know how *he heard. And he had to know what I'm going to tell Adcock. Claim rape or harassment, which one? he said.*

Could I claim rape? Was it? I never intended it to happen. Luckily I barely remember, although I can still feel it—sore and chaffed, inside and out. But I didn't want to think about what to legally call it. I wanted to cry for a little comfort—don't you owe me that? This thinking just makes it all come back . . . they lapped and pushed at me like dogs, cheered each other on, but how could it be rape? I never actually said no *or* stop.

Still, the legality—that's all he wanted to talk about . . . that and what I would say to Adcock. But my voice was like repeating gunshots, and every time it was my turn to speak, I said, how did you know?

Finally he said, "Well, I knew about your date, *didn't I?"*

"And that means you knew what would happen?"

"I knew enough to make a pretty decent guess."

"But you're the one who said I should go, you said—"

"I tried to call the cops last night."

"Why?"

"To report a rape. So they could stop it from going on or going any further. I wanted them to be caught. But the cops wouldn't come. So I had to let it happen."

"Let it happen?"

"Look, Corinne, they've been fired. I decided I wouldn't just keep my mouth shut this time. I called Adcock over the weekend and told him something had happened, told him what was going on and—"

I stood up. "I can't believe this. You knew. You knew. And all you did—"

"At least I did something. What did you do? You went along. Why didn't you stop them? You could've left. Just walked out the door. I thought you'd have more self-respect than that! You let it happen."

"Me? I—"

"Damn you, if someone thought you were a thief, would that make you steal? When someone thinks you're a slut, do you have to turn into one?"

"I'm not! I didn't let it happen. It just happened."

"You can't tell that to Adcock. What a cop-out. He'll fire you. Look, they're gone. That's been taken care of. What're you going to do?"

"What should I do?"

"Well, think about it . . . yes, you should feel wronged . . . deeply wronged . . . but what if you claimed it was rape. . . . You know how awful that would be: a court case, giving testimony, all the rest. . . ."

"But I won't get fired if I say it was rape—"

"That's right. You would still be here . . . where you could think about it every day. And everyone who looked at you would remember it . . . every day. Wouldn't that be nice."

"I don't know, I don't know, I don't want to think about this. I don't even know what happened. I can't know what to do till I figure out what happened."

"That's not a good idea."

"Why?"

"You don't want to know. But you know what you should do? Don't make any statement to Adcock. Just go up there and quit. Better still, send a letter of resignation. Right now."

"Just quit? What'll that prove?"

"It doesn't have to prove anything."

"Maybe I don't want them to get fired for just having a drunken party . . . maybe I want them to be fired because . . . because of what really happened!"

"What good will it do? It's over."

"That's all you can say about it? You knew about it!"

196

"I did what I thought was best."

"Yeah, and you thought it was a good idea for me to accept that date too! Maybe what I think is best is to tell Adcock that you knew so much about it because it was all your idea!"

I wasn't even close to the exit, in case I really was going to dash out and run to Adcock with that story. Kyle was closer to the door. His face changed color. Something drained out of him. More than just color. "You need to think, Corinne," he said softly. "Before you do anything, just think. I'll leave you alone to think."

So here I am thinking. But pretty soon, too damn soon, I'm going to have to be finished thinking and go out that door knowing what I'm going to do and what will happen to me.

still 3 May 1989

The thing is, maybe I'll never remember what it was I had decided to do when I left the conference room that day.

Should I start another letter . . . am I ready to talk to you now? Dear Kyle, Now's when I should call you. Now's when I should kill you. The journal ends here. My hospital bill says I was released April 26, three days later. That's when I should've called you—instead of taping the notebook closed and sealing it in a vault. I remember when they brought me my stuff from the hospital safe—still confused, disoriented, they were still asking me my name and who was the President and what year was it—I nearly ripped my shoulder bag apart searching to make sure the notebook was still there, but didn't open it when I saw it safely tucked in with the tabloids and magazines. Then, the heart-lurching panic when I realized I couldn't go to the bank immediately—had to turn the cab around in mid-block and send it back to my apartment where the earlier two notebooks were stashed in a drawer, praying to myself, *Please don't let my mother have already emptied the drawers and packed them in boxes and loaded them in the moving van,* and I guess I was mumbling or groaning, clutching the shoulder bag against my stomach, the driver asked if I was okay, if I wanted to go back to the hospital, but I just said, *"Go,* keep going," through clenched, wired teeth. Said nothing to my flabbergasted mother—bursting in, blasting back out—she thought she was going to come get me from the hospital later that afternoon. By later that afternoon, I was dozing in the fleecy warm weight of two or three pain killers, dreamless, numb. I'd known so clearly that I had to get rid of the journals—without knowing *why*. Just an instinct, like knowing to put food in my mouth, to curl up when I'm cold, to sleep when I'm exhausted. I didn't know, though, I didn't know. I didn't know what had happened, Kyle, I didn't . . . my eyes wouldn't even focus and I couldn't tell left from right; I didn't know if I'd seen you 3 hours before, 3 days before or 3 months before. Some frantic primal urge just said run and don't look back. You see, Kyle? I was still protecting you. This time from myself.

Barbary Coast Nightworld · *Julie Regan*

NIGHT FOG clung to the cobwebs that hung thick as torn stockings in the corners of the wharf tavern, slipping in through a window cracked to let out the whiskey thick breath of the thieves, pimps and sailors. Fog slipped in and stories slipped out, became fog, circled gas street lamps and floated back down into the sea or were wiped from the brow of a harbor patrolman, standing in his small boat still and silent, a pale form in dark robes, listening to the splash of brine against the rotting dock posts, cleats on the halyard whipping a mast in the wind, listening for the low bells of the ships of opium merchants who chose nights thick as these to dock their wares.

Was it merely a sea fog or the stories in the fog that made the night watchman groping and blind? That made each glint of moon on the water seem a blade in a sleeve of black Chinese silk.

No one knew exactly where the edge was. The waterfront kept shifting. Once the pirates and wanderers touched foot to soil they were bewitched by the fog, the hint of gold in the lamplight and back alley smiles and they could never return to the sea nor the other worlds. Abandoned boats linked by plank walkways became brothels, bars, hideouts for bandits and were eventually buried in their landlocked slips to extend the night world. Men were buried with them. Some murdered and tossed. Others just walked off into the fog.

There were no days. Everyone disappeared just before daybreak. Dawn was a baleful word. No one knew where it came from but it was surely out of the past; slinking across land stripped with wheel tracks, deserts and bare fields. Its first light made everyone uneasy, as if they had pushed the night too far and it was their sobering breath that made the sky pale.

Here it was the night that was clear and defined. The sun sunk right into the ocean and bottoms were slapped and rounds were called and curtains rose on the ruffled leotards of the Mademoiselle Louise Labelle, concert artist.

So the story goes. There was always a story going somewhere, and always a fog.

Frank had no story. He could only hum tunes. Frank had no language. His parents spoke a French stretched thin across the ocean, mired in Louisiana bayou, that kept finding its way through new worlds and things with no names until all the old words were broken and the new words like weeds and all they could speak was of an imagined realm between them no one else could understand, part memory, part possibility. It had no present tense.

Frank was the first child born in San Francisco, and hoping he would pick up something to speak, some Spanish-Chinese or Sidney Duck English, they taught him nothing at all. When at 18 the bemused Frank still had nothing to say, they decided to send him back to France, hoping some pure genetic pool of meaning would ignite him, but Frank only got as far as Kearny Street and a saloon beneath the sidewalk where he spent all the gold for his passage on a couple of rounds and wound up piano player.

Music was the perfect language of the present tense, especially when it was difficult to record and hardly anyone could write it down. Frank played by ear. They said he could play anything, and if he couldn't play it he'd make it up. Frank played the old songs his parents hummed in the kitchen, twirling each other around. He played the faucet dripping. He played the squeaky bow scratching of Chinese lutes, slow footsteps in the alley, Spanish fandangos and his heart strings. It went in one ear and out a window. That was all.

Everyone loved Frank, his smooth face, pretty as a girl's, his silent, delicate ways, his songs. They wanted to tell his story. Some said he was an Arabian sailor who'd had his tongue cut out for its license. Others thought he was a young preacher from the gold country camps, whom God, the Devil or the wild ways of men had silenced. That he had no story except for walking down the hill, Frank could not tell, but even if he could have, the nightworld habitués would have invented others because they loved him. All the best people had at least two or three themselves.

Louise Labelle, concert artist, who, in her own peculiar way loved Frank most of all, probably had the most stories. Since women weren't allowed beneath the sidewalk between the hours of 6 PM and 6 AM, Louise wore breeches, a top hat and a fine watch and fob. She smoked French cigarettes when she had them, which made her voice gravelly and low. Some said she was really a man. Others said she'd had the favors of all the kings left in Europe. It was whispered she had run off from New Orleans with a knife sunk in someone's heart and changed her name. She laughed at all the tales and never denied a one but told them they ought to put their minds to figuring out her present, not her past, that that's where the wild story was really to be found.

Louise knew that at the end of a story you were always sunk, so she didn't believe in them. She preferred to take off her stories each day with her female clothes and just sing who she was, whomever she borrowed from the song, pure and true.

Frank's songs let out a part of her she'd never sung before, and she felt like they were saving her from something, she didn't know what: who she was, who she had been, perhaps the past, all the damned "true" stories and their ends.

They were inseparable those evenings underground. "Frank and me're pirates ain't we Frank?" she said, resting her large hand on the piano for support against the whiskey, hip cocked, bushy eyebrows raised. "Play them that song, Frank, we took from old Bluebeard, you know, that rummy song."

And Frank would wink and smile and play a sea chantey to which Louise would add the words on the spot, sometimes about drowning, sometimes about love.

After hours Frank let Louise crawl inside the piano, beneath the black top, while he played. They said she liked the way the strings tickled and buzzed.

The night watchman's ears pricked up like a dog's. He could hear the splash of hands in the water. Unmistakable, the sound of sea pulled through fingers, a slight ruffling kick and the knifing of forearm and elbow into the still, black surface.

Jack Rotter, sometime pirate, escapee, pulled his lean, drenched body up onto the dock. The shadow of a night's growth glistened on his chin with the brine, and dark wet curls linked at the neck of his open collar. He shook the weight of the water (that might have drowned one less determined) from his clothes like sails, and did not shiver. Parting the fog with a blade in his hand, he made his way toward the gas lamps of Dead Man's Alley.

The poor night watchman could do nothing but bob.

The night was approaching that hour when it turns to tears and Frank played on in a silence of key thuds on velvet, Louise's body muffling the music, taking the music inside her. It was a song only she could feel. She couldn't come up with the words. It sent shivers over her skin and went straight to her heart, and she clung to the ridge above the keyboard, rapt.

Her eyes were deep and wide and her wig slipped slightly off, exposing her round bald head, powdered with white talc. Frank paused a moment to straighten her wig as if it were a boy's cap.

She put her finger to her lip. "Frank, listen: it's those damn birds that sing in the middle of the night. Don't stop playing, Frank. Don't let them do it."

Frank played on but he couldn't make any sounds. The sounds were all inside of her. He smiled sleepily and traced her lip with his long pale finger. His eyelids fluttered demurely towards slumber.

"Don't leave me with them, Frank," she said. "Don't go."

Louise pulled herself out of the piano and climbed into his arms, pressing her full soft breasts to his thin ribs and twisting off the gas lamp that was swinging shadows on the damask walls around them.

Louise pressed so heavily against him that the two fell off the piano stool and onto the floor. The thud and the whiskey were enough to put Frank right out, snoring, and Louise lay on top of him, eyes wide, all night, listening for fleeing footsteps in his heart.

At dawn he was still sleeping. She put the bowler over his face before the sun could rise and slipped pale into the last wisps of fog.

Day was sneaking in under the mist where the wings of the birds had swept room. Pigeons cooed and enameled windowsills with jade and opal. Parakeets sung the insides out of houses and seagulls raised a wing over the ocean and brushed the darkness off the sea.

The night watchman dragged the end of the night under with his oar. It sunk deep below the shadow of the boat, to sleep there until the sun got so close it disappeared, and the same wood pulled it up again.

The coast itself vanished in the day like a streetlamp left burning. Daylight clung to the streets like dirty linen. The breath that had fogged a night window was reduced to dust, and all the blinds fell until there was nothing but walls. Even the alleys, with no foot traffic to keep them open, closed up to the eye.

In one of those day-locked passages, Jack awoke bedraggled, with his manhood hanging out of his pants. It looked like a worn tether which had pulled him around all night, from brothel to bordello to strangers suddenly familiar in the back-street light. He tucked himself in and scratched the dust from his head. He was as solid and scraggly as the wall beside him, and he would find her if he had to worm his way through every keyhole on the coast.

Frank spent the day in his hat. Its dark bowl trapped the night there where it swam around his eyes with dreams like bright fish. He drew the darkness in and out of his nostrils with velvety breaths, while the bartender swept up all the stale leftover voices of the night before.

There was no music in the air now, and Frank woke into it as if his blanket had been snatched from his breast. He grabbed the air over him where Louise's perfume had left traces and caught only a chill he'd never felt before. For a moment he had no idea who or where he was, then he realized it was her.

Each night, following the afterhours sets Frank played until the exhaustion crawled up the keys and into his fingers, she had always left him, but suddenly he felt lost. He realized this was the only place he knew to find her. He'd never questioned where she came from, but now he wondered where she'd gone.

Jack's blade was dulled to stone by the daylight. It was bootless to look for her now. The Coast was closed. The air was flat and clear and there were too many textures in it.

Night had a way of floating stories and dreams in the air, and if you wanted to, you could try one out. Just step into it and follow the half-conceived adventure someone else had left hanging on the corner. The day's possibilities, piddling journeys to the bank or market, weren't dark enough to take him to his end, so Jack decided to bide his time below.

Chinatown extended several stories beneath the ground. Some claimed there was an entire city beneath the city into which the thousands of Chinese arriving daily were slipping: colonies of slave girls in bamboo cribs, illicit trade shops and opium dens lit by smoldering paper lanterns, where dreams could be exchanged with ancient wise men for the price of smoke.

Jack let his rough hands slide from rung to rung down the ladder, relishing each step into the smoky, lambent darkness. Eyes in a pile of clothes watched him fearfully from a cage. He let go one hand and shook the bamboo bars, faintly snarling, so that the garments fell around the body, revealing shoulder, calf, breast, and the stifled cry he wanted most of all.

Jack had learned the hard way that the true purpose of brothels wasn't sex but robbery, and he felt suddenly at home down here amidst the bandits and smugglers. Opium especially warmed him because it had to do with stealing souls. Now it was his turn. There was only one soul Jack wanted and it wasn't his own.

The effluvium made him sway a little in the doorway and slowed his boot soles on the straw mats. He had to navigate with an unwonted grace to get between the bodies lying in dusty smoke and pillows, and it was the heavy drug in the air that danced him through. At the end of the room, finally, he stretched out on top of another man, completely flattening him, though the other did not seem to notice. His arms stuck out casually like bear rug feet beneath Jack's trunk.

An old man stared for a very long time at the awkward freebooter. At last he nodded, as if to acknowledge that Jack had taken the other's place, and he offered him a pipe. Jack drew the embers' vapors into his hairy nostrils, and sucked greedily on the nib. He coughed, and smoke escaped in little cloudlets to the pallet where the old man watched. The sage inhaled and began to hum. Then he spit Jack's smoke back out, and nodded for him to begin again.

Lying there on top of Frank all night, Louise had heard his heart tap out a song, so constant and true she felt like a fraud. So many years singing so many old standards, and here it was right here inside of him. Her song. It went on and on, without a scratch, yet there was no way in.

All the way home, the grey stones Louise stepped on seemed to cry out like gulls. The city had become a minefield of them. She tried to tiptoe and whispered a shush of silence, imploring them not to sing. At the edge of the gates that marked Chinatown, pigeons by the dozens blocked her path. She stopped abruptly, shivering in her tracks, but it was too late; they took off in a flock around her, their wings and beaks issuing: "fly!"

When the flutter had passed, there was only one man left in the street. Louise and the man stared at each other for a second, then the man began to laugh. It was the laughter of opium. The more he laughed, the less Louise could see him, until he began to frighten her so much, it seemed like he was someone she *had* seen. Someone she had put so deep into the dark of her memory, even face to face, he could not quite come out.

She turned and ran. Jack let her go. She was his now. He could smell out that trail of fear like a dog.

Night fell and Louise was still off-stage, somewhere in the wings. They kept bringing up the curtain, announcing her name, as if it were a magic show, but she didn't appear.

And Frank grew sorrowful, poised at his keys, his gin glass weeping a ring into the dark wood like a welt on his own skin. He played the same plink-plank of a rag again and again. Her favorite song. Until some suspected it was just a piano roll player and Frank himself a doll with painted eyes.

Osgood, the proprietor, tried to shake him out of it. Threatened in his Hungarian accent to set Frank up as dishwasher if he didn't change his tune, but Frank could not be moved, and Osgood finally gave up trying, wiping the salt from the corner of his own sentimental eye. After a while no one minded about the song. They listened and wanted to hear it again too. Soon the whole barroom was filling up with tears.

Passing strangers heard the song through the grate and began to hum the wistful melody; others, picking up the bastard version caught on too. Until eventually, the sad rag had covered the city with a tinkling of resonant drops.

Louise set the needle down on the victrola and played the song again. It was the only thing that could take away the feeling she was sinking. She had played it all day long, going down occasionally to open the door and see if there were somehow another world there.

The first time she looked: the air was white and everyone was wearing white clothes. They didn't see her as they passed.

The second time: everything was underwater.

The third time: night had fallen like a locked gate.

The record stopped and suddenly she heard it: her song playing in the rain. She lifted her voice to meet the tune, but she could barely attach her chant to the notes before the water took it. Her voice fell into the puddles, ran down the hill and washed into the bay.

Its sad strains beat against the prow of the night watchman's boat, until he could no longer see past his own inexplicable tears.

The fourth time: it was the pirate.

She had left him floating a long time ago, and now he was determined to finish the story.

Her hand petrified on the doorknob.

"I told you, Jack. I ain't got your treasure," she said.

"But Louie, you *are* my treasure," said Jack. "And now I'm gonna have to bury it." He stalked her to the wall and thrust his entire body and blade into her, listening for the scream. He thought he had her, like he'd always wanted. But she had already slipped out.

Frank's song filled him with silence. Every time he played it, the music inside him emptied out a little more, until he was only playing to keep the music quiet, to keep the world quiet, to keep the city covered in a dampening shush. The crowd in the bar was nodding into a stuporous state as well, all their stories and dreams and braggadocio drained.

Near the end of the evening, when the room itself had all but collapsed, something began to flutter between the piano strings like a kite stuck on a laundry line. It made the notes suddenly so flat they buzzed.

Frank fished his fingers in and pulled out a white sheet of music with a picture of a moon at the top. He set it in front of him stiffly, blinked his eyes and tried to play. The moon was broken, and the music sorrowful, but lovelier than anything he had ever heard.

He could feel it inside him, a different kind of song, licking at his eardrums, warming his chest and tickling his throat with a raspy purr he could not clear away with his cough.

It was the words. There was no escaping them. They were part of it, and he held them back like smoke, not knowing how to exhale, until they forced themselves out and over his lips. The voice was husky, low and sounded almost worn out, whispering as he played:

"It's over. . . ."

from Grape Architect · *Lou Robinson*

grape architect

I have a messenger bird called grape architect. outside is blue, blue grey. the view removes me, takes me to think. as if I could name myself grape or honeysuckle. and you would still be you. going fast into the 90s with no one to record. records come mirror flattened and disappeared. old books lie and steal. someone creeping up behind. yesterday. a year later. she can walk. first it was stand in water. new pains replace old pains, this is what passes for pleasure. then it was swim by arms. one refused to bend. one always does because one other always will. then it was small piles of sand, working always with an image of the ocean, trying not to read anything with the word dismemberment. now she walks in smooth sand. next is loose shifting sand marked for a disappearing future. she says cats every place but the first two weeks. one with a broken foot dragged a cast. the two clumping side by side. had to abandon her to her fate. this is the one whose mice ate off a head in the middle drawer from the cast of wind in the willows.

bent

Bent on a grand delusion, I started out wide. scraps came to me out of the gutters with messages like 'cat got your tongue?' and stamps of milky heron pointing right. everything came to me, sails on the lake pointed my way, mean cats curled in my lap. now here is a sad development: I discover I do not have the power to heal. so I need a new formula for greeting the dawn lit water into which I no longer plunge. Cherokee charms for winning at court: little people. from where you rest above. swiftly with your knowledge. all of you wizards. in nothing do you fail. I ask your aid in this: to see clearly, sure. but meanwhile in the rest of the dumb stuttering days to at least be bent forward falling after some grand delusion or other.

linger

It's good to find others to carry it out, some wacko version of what should have been if you had been normal, and to linger among them, but not for long. man, woman, child, short dogs, some ducks. farm with drive lined with trees, toy rabbits and monkey hung by ears from clothesline. the woman blond, wearing a pink shirt of the man's. the child wearing purple tights and plastic shoes, kicking a purple ball. occasionally drinking out of a mermaid glass with fish that swim in water she says will always be there. her skirt twirls enough. the man sometimes sits in the car at the end of the day for hours. no one knows why. he used to forage like Euell Gibbons or whatever his name was, he told me on his birthday. there was the carrot cake sitting on a sawhorse at 6 am. icing and marzipan down the front of his shirt where the horse spat it out in disgust. the woman says oh he doesn't have any feelings in that department, fortunately. we look down at the dog, both thinking at the same time of castration, and how much nicer this dog is since. he should be jealous of Steve, but he wasn't. she says I envy your privacy. to linger among them is to invite all kinds of dangerous doubts. any triangle will do this. two are too close, but three guarantee that one is always triangulated out. tonight the man is wandering around back in the field. no one knows why daddy does that, she says.

halogen

Someone takes a few steps. the light fractures through brass from 19th century India. the hum behind from faltering halogen. Mary saying eagerly is it from Elizabeth? safe conduct refused. I say I'll call but. two aging architects, or as in photo, two old cranks, claim authorship of inexplicable wheat circles of Britain. a plank and a string held in the mouth. the interior of her carriage grey green paisley. everyone wants to rule alone. one has a snake's intestine and a dog's saliva. one has a dog's stalwart heart and a snake's heart-stopping serum. not speaking to her after all this time. so many animals in one body. the woman's menagerie. the body's warring factions want you to be happy. leave the troubles of state to me.

afraid for it

Afraid for it is a test the sailboat is just in the crook of the tree which is framed by the glass door to the open porch below is the horse from under the previous porch, glued together, propped by a brick are you afraid for it? or is it a thing of beauty? does it tell you to relax on the wind or does it look like other people know how to do these things sail relax finance luxuries for a brief few summers of middle age or does it look fragile like Henry his sad sinister videos, the Lucy abandoned on the beach is it white or is it tinged with the burnt sienna of past all past summer days spoiling the present like yellowed linen immediately making you think of how hard he worked, your father, and never could buy such whiteness, so that nothing white for the rest of your life can ever stay white for long the sepia of his melancholy permeates even Henry who wants to be called Hank brought on by a sail makes you think not of white summer days wind water but of what you have lost, even if you never wanted it.

as you face

The prison of your invention. as it strikes you back and down. go in after fools and say fools' words facing across and even pay for it. joy shrinks to minutes in a circle eight in sawdust all open on one side to pouring rain and screaming field of blackbirds. around, don't throw him away, post four then through pause only to skip and change then down around post four. go home now, try. say you will breathe five times tomorrow. it's free. as you face it, it greets you through another face, not so many after all.

everything that changes us

We're never free of. nor can we remember accurately. we are vectored then everything goes on without us for a time. as we struggle to adjust. white tiny christmas lights in Carol's mother's glasses as she speaks about her son and Carol's brother. white little christmas lights in Carol's glasses as she bends her head to her drink. thinking of his Moroccan photographs of slaughtered sheep on blue mosaic. all the rest of the room is dark except for candles. brother still demanding money from afar. sometimes because he was circumcised. sometimes for the sole artistic gene he believes he carries, more fragile than a woman's egg. pulling myself up by the spine of the couch back feels intensely good. comfort and brace. my old Mimi's davenport, wide white raised ferns against pale green silk. fever does this. things connect to things way back. things that change us disconnect. us from the web of little feverish attachments. everything that changes us is red. when doors slam open and shut on invisible flames. I'm hard to provoke. I can always send it into a private cinema of gesture. he beats the bald skull of an egg across from her and her summer skirt. I was changed before it ever happened by my fear of it.

the hooked head

Photos of heads severed from bodies mixed in with buildings in Geneva, New York, at the turn of the century. she is telling me how she got her start. how archival work led to police photography. she carries a camera everywhere in case she sees an accident. she says she happened on ours a little too late, but wondered if anyone died. she hated spending all day in dark, dirty basements. this way she gets to drive and to work with color. she hands me photos of the car, marked Obvious Total Loss.

The hooked head stares out of a photo of my scar. she hands me photos of the car and I hand her in return my best view of the scar. my dappled old red skin looking more naked than regular skin, my nearly lashless eye cast down in sorrow, my hair greased back with anxiety. the scar smiles out like a month-old baby, shiny, robust, healing quick and natural without thinking that I might want a permanent mark, something that is worth something. the hooked head stares out where the window used to be before it disintegrated silently into thousands of clear glass pebbles filling my pockets, my purse, my shoes, my undershirt, my zipper, my nose and mouth and the new mouth in the skin above my nearly invisible eyebrow. the hooked head rehearses—not out of any undue fascination but because of the weekly interrogations from various agencies—angles of vision, seconds of cognition, thought and reflex and the war between.

the present disturbances

Skating the great wide circle, drunk on gin and tonic, full of fried chicken and lemon pie my birthday in Michigan. skates from the salvation army blue fur no support. silver lake. dark rim of snow. fall flat back like a slab and my head cracks or the ice, not sure. she called last night from San Francisco. on Silver Lake she wore a white Mexican nightgown. when she turned thirty, here, a bigger, more complicated lake, I gave her navy blue satin pajamas. this is how you make a life extend out from the present disturbances. so that the movement is absorbed in widening ripples becoming finally insignificant. it will pass, she said. drink beer, she said, read mysteries.

think about it

Why do you think you like this arrangement so much? you and her and him? he says a hummingbird! maybe she has a nest up there. she says, maybe it's a him. well then maybe he still has a closet, he says. you are all on their porch eating french fries, faster.

The canter is a three-beat, asymmetrical, full of heartbreak, possibility, and flight.

She stands at the end of your lunge line wearing a garage mechanic's outfit, holding a whiskey sour and a cigarette in one hand, a whip in the other, while you ride without stirrups or reins. Don't look down, look across at where you want to be, or you could look at me, she says.

The Burial of Count Orgasm
Ronald Sukenick

at a Halloween party   dressed
as   string bikini bottom baring   a top that
covered only   leaving the bottom curves
          underlying firmness of geodesic   As soon as Ram
saw her

                                        her home. Her flimsy costume
fell   for the rest of the weekend.

    That spring

                                        first vacation in
    So they talked   where to go   Neither of
them had ever   but they decided that above all   the
beaten track.   true, a Club Med was   but
extensive forays to the mainland were possible,
    and
          Meanwhile   after work on Fridays

                    until Monday morning. This became a routine that
started affecting their jobs, since they were both exhausted for
the first part of the week, and distracted by anticipation for the last part.
    Also, apparently, they had acquired the power to affect people around
them. Some sort of aura

turned everybody on. One Friday night in a bar after work, another guy

                              for the drink," as he sat down at the table.
"I'm travelling through
"You must be awfully   Cynthia sympathized.
                         seen my wife," he responded. "Six
weeks, around."
So the stage was   Ram could see what was
happening, but to his surprise, instead of making him
                    to Margaritas. The tone quickly
            room service," Randy suggested.

                                        in Randy's
hotel room.
    "Wouldn't you like
                more comfortable," she answered.   bed
more or less the only place to sit.

                wearing a deep cut blouse with no   so that
when she took off her jacket and leaned toward him he
                    even Ram could see, when he stood up, that Randy had

was finally Ram, though, who slowly started unbuttoning her
                    and it was Ram himself, exposing and palping her
                Randy to do the same with the other
            nothing to resist, on the contrary.
remained luxuriantly passive while they   slowly
she never wore, so   Randy seemed almost awed by
her perfectly   which Ram invited   they both

            and began to massage, while he   pillow,
held both hands above her head by the wrists
                                she began to slowly twist
as they alternately   responded to his

                                                        213

              his finger   her lips   unrestrained intimacy though
forced   just met an hour before.

   Neither had   both still wearing their
jackets and ties, while she   Now Ram pulled
her slowly off the   her knees on the floor they
made her   he pressed her head   and unzip
   while they continued to drink.

                  unbearable, Randy stood and abruptly   it
was already huge and   straight out   hair,
against her cheeks, then her lips. She opened   for it,
taking   deep   He almost   out before
          then it was Ram's   they made her
              on hands and knees to where   while
she   Randy   and lifted her   jamming his   while
Ram still   a while, then Ram   sat down
and, while Randy   he started caressing   weighing her
              in his palm, while with his finger   She
groaned as they both
              before Randy   he was able   so that
Randy had a chance   while she immediately started   then
before   Ram   as Randy again   she again   then Ram
    then Randy   as she again   with Randy   Ram jammed
       could no longer hold   as she one final

   Exhausted,   the three
of them   at odd angles, inert
              but happy. They never saw him again.
   They had worked out their vacations   and now

   On the plane,   he   her under her
blanket.   It was during that long
stretch after the dinner and the film, when they turn the lights
out and most people are asleep or trying to sleep   continued
to   under her blanket, so that by now she was in a state
of   The guy in the seat next to her must have
for a while, probably   and now could no longer restrain

soon she felt   from the other side   but didn't say
anything, while the guy took advantage of the darkness   under
her blanket   Ram felt fingers   and instead of
      giving implicit   meanwhile she   thighs   each
         as both of them   other than her loud breathing
            Ram pulled down   so that the guy   and while
he   pulled up   the guy then moved his hand up
under   while Ram   took turns. When one would
the other   That went on for quite a while. It was a
kind of exquisite torture. Finally she couldn't   and
started   again and again, to the point where Ram was afraid
she wasn't able to stop, though
               She slept through breakfast.   avoiding his
eyes   Neither of them ever said anything to him.

They had a stopover in Paris and decided to   The
hotel was off the Champs Elysées. That evening, while he was
               the lounge was very posh, and she
talking to her   a well-to-do Arab   she was on a
couch and he   he hardly spoke English, but he had no
trouble   only she was surprised and amused when   so
she wrote it off to   after all, a foreigner.
Still, it was a lot of money.
               came back, he discreetly   Ram
went to the bar, he also   engaged in intense
         came back   she, astonished
   "Consider it like a date you get paid for," he
"Besides, we could   waiting at the bar
         absurd," she
   "You   turned on   power   submissive," he
pointed out.
   That hit   he knew her too   She
ended by acquiescing, though reluctant

      very polite, aside from the fact that he didn't   introduce
                     in the elevator, he
started   under her   Of course, she had given up
the right to object. He slipped his   remained

215

passive.

Once in his room, he told her   She had no
alternative but to   which she did, slowly and
reluctantly. That only excited him further. When she was
completely   he began
    At first,   alien intrusion. But when he started
giving orders   no choice but to   she began to
and couldn't help   respond. Nude   knees, on the
rug   it was just the sort of thing
breasts   didn't like the man at   especially
when he   nipple   on the bed   thighs   not
responsible for her own   spread   couldn't help
realized the only thing possible was to try to enjoy   raise
her   very hard, at least   surprisingly wet
        once he started   it was hard not to   and
she didn't. She'd always had the good fortune to   easily
        no exception, despite the circumstances.
    Once finished with her, he   quick goodbye
strange   hornier   maybe, or in rut   not so
bad, she
                     but in the corridor outside, the hotel dick
    "Les putains   he said. "Zee oockairs een ear no
air pair meat ed," he repeated in abominable English. "Please?"
He indicated
    "But I'm   ," she
    "Please?" he
    "But there must be   ," she
    "   passport
    "No, but it's
        "   wiz me,"   into an empty   "Please? Zit
on zee
    "But this is
    He wagged a   "   officially   must be, 'ow
you zay, air rest stated   ." He picked up the
didn't dial
    "Wait, no there

216

He replaced   "Oui?"

"Just let me call my

"   not pair meat ed." He took out   gestured

for her to   manacled hands behind   breast through

her

"   what do you

"What do   ?" he   the other one.

          she considered   wasn't repulsive

      for time   weighed against   after all,

she'd just   so   matter, really? she thought.

Meanwhile he   then pulled aside   slipped   She

began to   despite herself   any case, helpless.

   As he pushed up   weakly objected   the phone

again.   choice   willingly or   jail as

well.

"   wait

"Oui?" he said, as he slowly and deliberately

He put   phone. "Okay," she   he stood

unzipped   she hesitantly

"No," he ordered. "   first, leak   ." She didn't

      gesture with his tongue, so she   while he   until

she was   then pulled her   gasped   grunted   her

nose, snorting   managed to   "Please," as she spread

but he   copiously   and all over her face. But

swallowing   and kept   until he   again.   her

hands   pushed her   thighs, as she eagerly rose

      her   already sopping   groan   out of

control   neither   for long   but violent.

"   wash my face   ?"

   Back in their room, he   as she told   both

incredibly   she   her yet again.

   The flight to Istanbul   a small plane to

          a small boat to   Club Med.

The island   beach, immediately
          monokinis   nothing on top and string bottoms.
     so she improvised simply by taking   and

          "   newcomers?"

          many nationalities   which   but
nice-looking   thin material that exposed rather
his   which anyway barely   so she could see
that he liked her. As could Ram.
     "   ?"
     "Greek," he   very little English.

     That night   with them after dinner.
You   conversation, since   monosyllabic, at best
smiles, grunts and gestures   like talking to   a gag
or a muzzle   could make his desires known   were
obviously
                    moonlight
     "   ?" she asked.
     "   tired, you two   ," answered Ram. He understood
she   into a rut. She   getting to like, or excited
          excited Ram,   more attractive after she'd   case,
it felt
                    soft and slippery   fantastic.
     For her   habit   getting hard to break.   she
liked   Ram was right.   her nature
turned her on incredibly. That night she   and nothing
else. The thin silk   nipples   tickling coolness

          without hesitation   his hand   didn't
resist   once she might   had learned   she
liked, even needed   thanks to Ram   she   now well
trained   when   opened

          him muscular   Attractive
               too quick. Brushing the sand   the

result of simply turning   a little cranky   but
he   down the beach   a cabana   ouzo. She
quickly   had been just preliminary. The two
friends, however   and immediately
disliked   a skinny German with an unpleasant accent
      The other a flabby middle-aged Spaniard with garlic
          still attracted to the Greek,
despite   in fact, even more since   incomplete

      but she understood immediately what was going to
      however it was going to happen. She accepted a glass
   Apprehension   wondering whether it was going to turn
her   when
   In the event, it was simpler   she didn't remember
which   under her   then pushed   no
question of objecting   their assumption   basically
correct, and she could no longer deny   someone's hand
on her, in   blunt claim of possession
      anyway, out here, alone, isolated, what
     little communication   spoke almost no
decided she would simply endure   inside her   until
the Greek took   The German   of course unpleasant   His
hand on her   a little too hard so that she was sure
her flesh would be marked   it hurt
   "Please don't," she   uncertain   even
understood. Yet when he came into   and she felt
     that surprised her   invasion, almost violent
     ambiguous pleasure.   confusion. Who was she?
     the more so when the Spaniard   incredibly
adroit   against her   at just the right   At
first repelled by his stinking breath   soon responding
with her   against his   hungrily.   She
finally   with huge, multiple   waves of
     again and   She tried to hold him but it was the
Greek's   very different, but   her gratitude. The
Greek   still liked. The other two she found
loathsome, but the odd thing was   the second time

genuine love while   moving inside   She couldn't help
herself, even trying to hold the Spaniard to her with passionate
kisses after   something like a drugged state
          after a time the German began   she embraced passionately
when he   despite her loathing, welcoming him
spread wide.   twisting under him   two people
          a split   Afterward she knew   crossed some
threshold   never the same. When they took her
back to Ram, he saw it   he knew   a
change   turned him on terribly.
     In the succeeding days   visited the three   twice
a day. Between times,   stupor.   play with her
          make her beg.   alternate, first one thrusting
     while a second   and another   When she got
back Ram would immediately   She always told him what they
          It excited   He had never found her so sexy.
     Finally   health. All she   sleep, eat
and   the mainland   rest   a few

          second day   normal, and she   a
sleepwalker awakening   fragile   if someone
          and snapped his fingers at her in

          dusty town, with its adjacent   hand
full of tourists despite

          the ruins   setting, as
beautiful   calm
          just what
          something relaxing   nevertheless
he had   she   like a zombie, waiting
          She slept a lot.

     Tourists seldom   stylish American woman
          shall we say, curiosity?   the eyes
wherever they   and particularly

                    combination police station and city hall
        the leisure   passing it, as they of necessity
        stare.   urged her   less
provocative, but she hadn't packed

            bald   in a cafe, looking
    "Who
    "
                    Colonel," the waiter   speaking, like
everyone, very broken
                    nodded to them, stiffly   brutal and
insinuating

    The next morning   two police   asked them to come
            growing indignation   no reply   insisted

vociferously, but   took their money and identification
        separated   protesting   she was led   he in
another   cell.

                    no one   he, hours later
        manacled   well furnished   persian rugs
                desk, the Colonel, smoking a long cigarette. Next to
him a huge black and white   snarling.
    "Quiet, Bruno!"
    "Where is   ?" he
    "I'm asking   your room   drugs."
    "Drugs?   That's   what   ?"
    "   , to be specific."
    "   absurd   American Consulate."
            laughed.   The closest   nine hundred miles."
    "What do you   ?"
    "   cooperate. The penalty   extremely
severe.   no one can   outside the system.
Impossible.   The best   leniency   fundamentally
me."
    He   Cynthia was led in   also manacled
behind her.   taken her jacket   through her thin

                                                            221

designer t-shirt   when she moved   silky
translucent harem pants exposed
   "Ram! What   ?"
                                        he explained. "Beyond
that . . ."
   "Your husband is in grave   ."
   "He's not my   ."
   "In any case, only you   ."
   "Me?"
   "   accessory   hold indefinitely,   . He,
however,   life. And in a Turkish prison
          your compliance. Come." He tapped
   She didn't
   "You will see   useless."
   A guard   his manacles   embedded in the wall,
while another slipped   collar around her   attached
          to the Colonel. He   like a leash. She had no
   "   get away with   ."
He pulled her neck down over his   cradled one of her
          hand, while with his other   on his long
cigarette. Then he let her
   "   an arrangement   no force   not
barbarians."
   "   out of your   ,"   outraged.
   "Good. You   rot, and she . . . We will show
          her accomodations   only ones   shorter stays.
          led them   where in a single
               villains of all
   "Two   rapists, a few   . I regret   ."
The inmates   suddenly quiet.   consuming her
          their breathing. She gasped. "You couldn't   ."
He pulled   large ring of keys.
   "All right   minute," Ram
          nodded   keys   "   my office."

          surprisingly, removed his manacles, but not
               sitting behind   smoking.

222

"   take off her   ," exhaling
"   ?"
"You   ."
          at her.   She   mesmerized   vacant.
"   have to do   .   choice," she
barely audible.
     There wasn't much   up under her chin to expose
          because   manacled   back.   harem pants
glided slowly   nothing under   didn't
immobile   around her ankles.   forgot   in ash
tray   stared. Abruptly, he tapped
     "   here."
          didn't
"Bring her!"
               leash   led   handed it
manacled   in front instead   his desk   legs
dangling   leash tied to desk leg so that   breasts,
then nipples   unzipped   took his already
spread   his finger   looking into Ram's eyes
and shoved   She groaned   pain or pleasure,
and he didn't know which he   seemed to respond
maybe she couldn't   felt his own   growing
despite   anger   plunging   she   furious, but
          after a certain   if anything, seemed to increase
little repetitive moans   she   looking at Ram
almost apologetically,   raised her manacled hands above her
          legs wrapped around   rolled her eyes
involuntarily   closed   head rolling from side to
     Colonel   a loud obscene grunt   her body
jerking and twisting under
          while suddenly, he bent over   full on the mouth
          opened hers   her tongue into   sighed.
     She turned to look at Ram, as if abashed. But he wanted
badly to   himself.
     However, he was not   permitted. The Colonel hiked
          zipped   and ordered
     "But we   ," he

"   you said   ," she
"   didn't   how many times," he   laughed.
    Separated again,   in cell   excited
wanted to   but his hands   behind
    stayed big and wouldn't

        she, in her   waiting   catatonic.
        floor   naked   sitting   hands
behind   chilly

    Later the Colonel   explained   guard
ladies room, or other   ask   safe   he was
forbidden
    In fact,   came often   stare through the bars
a young   stupid but innocent. Just   for a
half an   rubbing himself.

        horribly uncomfortable   hungry. Finally the
Colonel   with a plate of   something.
    "I have come to watch   ," he
    "   hand cuffs   ?"
    "Unfortunately,   ."   on the floor.
        by waves of anger, but   So she   get down
        squirm   her chest   lap and tear at
dirty.
    He laughed. "   a dog!"

        waiting   miserable   filthy
She   blame   Ram   not really
her own   led her to   paying, she thought.
Even   though a bastard   the Colonel
herself. Now   hopeless. Nobody
knew   to prevent   eventually   even
murder   She   tormentor, despite   their
only chance.   all depended   pleasing   slave. But she
couldn't   anger mixed with   Yet,
helpless when he began

he, manacled in his cell   wanted to kill

    she didn't   night or day. The Colonel

unpredictable intervals   feed her.   like to   soil

herself as she   hungrily.   the young   to stare,

and rub   The only other   bath room. She would

have to   which   . If   a pot   or   to

    by her leash   rubbing himself   masturbating as

she   she knew   waiting.

  So when   finally   summoned   she was

almost   especially when   long hot bath   his

luxurious   silken robe   Bruno, snarling

    commanded silence   chained   champagne and caviar

        feast.   couldn't help   illogical

gratitude   so that when he began   under her

slowly and sensuously   she   at least minimally

responsive. Even so,   surprised. He   manacled behind

  "   your leash."

  "   how   ?" she

"In your mouth!"

    she   and he   quickly   around her neck.

brought Ram   naked   manacled   gagged.   to wall

    front of the bed. She   Ram already had

when   the Colonel   and made her suck   she saw that

Ram's   straight out. The Colonel was   just a foot

from where Ram   made her stand right in front   while

he   breasts   then   thighs   spread   his finger

She saw   Ram's   now   up, a little pearl of

    dripping   tip. She felt ashamed that   when the

Colonel   but she   very big.   watching

Ram as   could tell   desperate. She was now

  gasping   couldn't control   mounting pleasure

    wondering at how well he   even as she   began

    spasms   Ram writhing   helpless.   no

doubt   from her moans and cries as she   felt it jerking

    pour out   in her

  over, Ram   his hands still   hustled out.

She   quickly   naked in her cell.

          she   not prevent   anticipating   the
next   a long time   thinking   anything
else.   the longer, the more eager

   Finally,   the long bath   the robe   made her
drink   aphrodisiac?

                    Ram led   to wall   this time, one
hand left free   naked
          he   obviously noticing   her eagerness
as the Colonel   then spread   a foot away
          jerking himself as   she,
completely beyond   uncontrollably   Ram
faster as   all three   at the same time   Ram
spurting

                    this time   in her cell   guilt   but
an eternity until   while Ram, in
his   , hating himself

                    next
   When   long bath   Ram, no longer gagged
allowed to lick her anywhere   exciting her for   as he
watched Ram's tongue and his rapidly engorging   . This time he
could see she wanted   made her beg   let her suck
Ram's as he   with his   from behind
   all three   even Bruno whimpering as they
all
          when she   growling and whining, and saw that
          rigid, glistening and obscenely pink, from its furry
enormous black   hanging   The Colonel too,
because   led her to   and with her leash   to
the desk, her   spread   exposed   ass in the air.

226

          led the dog   guiding   no hesitation.   edge
of panic   penetration, odd   like a hot tongue, but
          swelling to fill   its moist, furry base   at
just the right angle soon   overcame her   and her obvious
pleasure communicating   men watching   excited
even more.   quick, nervous thrusts   its saliva
sense of alien invasion   heightened by its growls   she
knew she was going to   couldn't believe that an animal
     When she felt it   she too, involuntarily   But
it didn't   remained still, panting   soon   as
hard as   Now beyond   she began   again
and again, almost continuously   time had no meaning
          another realm   When she came to   the
Colonel's   in her mouth, and she automatically   until
he   Then, face still smeared
quickly   back in her cell.

          semi-comatose   thinking only of
          anticipating the next   almost forgotten
she   prisoner being forced   called over
couldn't tell   one or several   all young, innocent
and horny under threat of death if they   against bars
unzipped his   his hand on his and made him   as
she rubbed   herself   when he   also climaxed
only seemed   feel hornier
     When they let the dog in her throat went dry and she almost
fainted. It was still   She immediately   with
her hand   position on the floor   it
licked   bobbing vigorously   she licked   then
despite her fatigue   it went on and on   guards
watching   in and out of consciousness   after
the third time she lost track

          hot bath   Ram there, in
clothes, already eating caviar   they all   champagne

227

"   ?" she asked.

The Colonel laughed. "Bruno is tired," he   "   a
toast. To America!"   clinked

Soon, all three   mouth as the Colonel   then,
gently inserted   never had anal   a
little bit at first   particularly obscene, as if
        owned.   his property. Meanwhile   Ram
            dripping   slippery

till all three, at once, like the finale of a Romantic symphony.

"   and now, a surprise," Ram
"   sending you back   Club Med," the Colonel
        she   couldn't remember.   Club Med? Then
it hit her.

"Why?"   protested. "We've been   and cooperative.
What have we   ?"

                        nevertheless

        and once back in the States

            Ram   boring, and wondering why she needed
just one

                                dispensed with

            went to the next Halloween   alone, and
dressed as   high heeled boots and a whip   leather
bustier   black   studs   on her head a high hat

                orchestrate her own, her own

        ecstatic   impresario

It Was a Great Marvel That He Was in the Father without Knowing Him (II)
David Foster Wallace

WINTER, 1962 — TUCSON AZ

JIM NOT THAT WAY JIM. That's no way to treat a garage door, bending stiffly down at the waist and yanking at the handle so that the door jerks up and out jerky and hard and you crack your shins and my ruined knees, son. Let's see you bend at the healthy knees. Let's see you hook a soft hand lightly over the handle feeling its subtle grain and pull just as exactly gently as will make it come to you. Experiment, Jim. See just how much force you need to start the door easy, let it roll up out open on its hidden greasy rollers and pulleys in the ceiling's set of spider-webbed beams. Think of all garage doors as the well-oiled open-out door of a broiler with hot meat in, heat roiling out, hot. Needless and dangerous ever to yank, pull, shove, thrust. Your mother is a shover and a thruster, son. She treats bodies outside herself without respect or due care. She's never learned that treating things in the gentlest most relaxed way is also treating them and your own body in the most efficient way. It's Marlon Brando's fault, Jim. Your mother back in California before you were born, before she became a devoted mother and long-suffering wife and bread-winner, son, your mother had a bit part in a Marlon Brando movie. Her big moment. Had to stand there in saddle shoes and bobby-socks and ponytail and put her hands over her ears as really loud motorbikes roared by. A major thespian moment, believe you me. She was in love from afar with this fellow Marlon Brando, son. Who? Who. Jim, Marlon Brando was the archetypal new-type actor who ruined it looks like two whole generations' relations with their own bodies and the everyday objects and bodies around them. No? Well it was because of Brando you were opening that garage door like that, Jimbo. The disrespect gets learned and passed on. Passed down. You'll know Brando when you watch him, and you'll have learned to fear him. *Brando*, Jim, jesus, b-r-a-n-d-o. Brando the new archetypal tough-guy rebel and slob type, leaning back on his chair's rear legs, coming crooked through doorways, slouching against everything in sight, trying to *dominate* objects, showing no artful respect or care, yanking things toward him like a moody child and using them up and tossing them crudely aside so they miss the wastebasket and just lie there, ill-used. With the overclumsy impetuous movements and postures of a moody infant. Your mother is of that new generation that moves against life's grain, across its warp and baffles. She may have loved Marlon Brando, Jim, but she didn't understand him, is what's ruined her for everyday arts like broilers and garage doors and even low-level public-park knock-around tennis. Ever see your mother with a broiler door? It's carnage, Jim, it's to cringe to see it, and the poor dumb thing thinks it's tribute to this slouching slob-type she loved as he roared by. Jim, she never intuited the gentle and cunning economy behind this man's quote harsh sloppy unstudied approach to objects. The way he'd oh so clearly practiced a chair's back-leg tilt over and over. The way he studied objects with a welder's eye for those strongest centered seams which when pressured by the swinishest slouch still support. She never . . . never sees that Marlon Brando felt himself as body so keenly he'd *no need* for manner. She never sees that in his quote careless way he actually really touched whatever he touched as if it were part of him. Of his own body. The world he only seemed to manhandle was for him sentient, feeling. And no one . . . and she never understood that. Sour sodding grapes indeed. You can't envy someone who can be that way. Respect, maybe. Maybe *wistful* respect at the very outside. She never saw that Brando was playing the equivalent of high-level quality tennis across soundstages all over both coasts, Jim, is what he was really doing. Jim, he moved like a careless fingerling, one big muscle, muscularly naïve, but always, notice, a fingerling at the center of a clear current. That kind of animal grace. The bastard wasted no motion, is what made it art, this brutish no-care. His was a tennis player's dictum: touch things with consideration and they will be yours; you will own them; they will move or stay still or move for you; they will lie back and part their legs and yield up their innermost seams to you. Teach you all their tricks. He knew what the Beats know and what the great tennis player knows son: learn to do nothing, with your whole head and body, and everything will be done by what's around you. I know you don't understand. Yet. I know that goggle-eyed stare. I know what it means all too well, son. It's no matter. You will, Jim. I know what I know.

I'm predicting it right here, young sir Jim. You are going to be a great tennis player. I was near-great. You will be truly great. You will be the real thing. I know I haven't taught you to play yet, I know this is your first time, Jim, jesus, relax, I know. It doesn't affect my predictive sense. You will overshadow and obliterate me. Today you are starting, and within a very few years I know all too well you will be able to beat me out there, and on the day you first beat me I may well weep. It'll be out of a sort of selfless pride, an obliterated father's terrible joy. I feel it, Jim, even here, standing on hot gravel and looking: in your eyes I see the appreciation of angle, a prescience re spin, the way you already adjust your overlarge and apparently clumsy child's body in the chair so it's at the line of best force against dish, spoon, lens-grinding appliance, a big book's stiff bend. You do it unconsciously. You have no idea. But I watch, very closely. Don't ever think I don't, son.

You will be poetry in motion, Jim, size and posture and all. Don't let the posture-problem fool you about your true potential out there. Take it from me, for a change. The trick will be transcending that overlarge head, son. Learning to move just the way you already sit still. Living in your body.

This is the communal garage, son. And this is our door in the garage. I know you know. I know you've looked at it before, many times. Now . . . now *see* it, Jim. See it as body. The dull-colored handle, the clockwise latch, the bits of bug trapped when the paint was wet and still protruding. The cracks from this merciless sunlight out here. Original color anyone's guess, boyo. The concave inlaid squares, how many, bevelled at how many levels at the borders, that pass for decoration. Count the squares, maybe. . . . Let's see you treat this door like a lady, son. Twisting the latch clockwise with one hand that's right and. . . . I guess you'll have to pull harder, Jim. Maybe even harder than that. Let me . . . *that's* the way she wants doing, Jim. Have a look. Jim, this is where we keep this 1956 Mercury Montclair you know so well. This Montclair weighs 3,900 pounds, give or take. It has eight cylinders and a canted windshield and aerodynamic fins, Jim, and has a maximum flat-out road-speed of 95 m.p.h. per. I described the shade of the paint job of this Montclair to the dealer when I first saw it as bit-lip red. Jim, it's a machine. It will do what it's made for and do it perfectly, but only when stimulated by someone who's made it his business to know its tricks and seams, as a body. The stimulator of this car must know the car, Jim, feel it, be inside much more than just the . . . the compartment. It's an object, Jim, a body, but don't let it fool you, sitting here, mute. It will *respond*. If given its due. With artful care. It's a body and will respond with a well-oiled purr once I get some decent oil in her and all Mercuryish at up to 95 big ones per for just that driver who treats its body like his own, who *feels* the big steel body he's inside, who quietly and unnoticed feels the nubbly plastic of the grip of the shift up next to the wheel when he shifts just as he feels the skin and flesh, the muscle and sinew and bone wrapped in gray spider-webs of nerves in the blood-fed hand just as he feels the plastic and metal and flange and teeth, the pistons and rubber and rods of the amber-fueled Montclair, when he shifts. The bodily red of a well-bit lip, parping along at a silky 80-plus per. Jim, a toast to our knowledge of bodies. To high-level tennis on the road of life. Ah. Oh.

Son, you're ten, and this is hard news for somebody ten, even if you're almost five-eleven, a possible pituitary freak. Son, you're a body, son. That quick little scientific-prodigy's mind she's so proud of and won't quit twittering about: son, it's just neural spasms, those thoughts in your mind are just the sound of your head revving, and head is still just body, Jim. Commit this to memory. Head is body. Jim, brace yourself against my shoulders here for this hard news, at ten: you're a machine a body an object, Jim, no less than this rutilant Montclair, this coil of hose here or that rake there for the front yard's gravel or sweet jesus this nasty fat spider flexing in its web over there up next to the rake handle, see it? See it? *Latrodectus mactans*, Jim. Widow. Grab this racquet and move gracefully and feelingly over there and kill that widow for me, young sir Jim. Go on. Make it say "K." Take no names. There's a lad. Here's to a spiderless section of communal garage. Ah. Bodies bodies everywhere. A tennis ball is the ultimate body, kid. We're coming to the crux of what I have to try to impart to you before we get out there and start actuating this fearsome potential of yours. Jim, a tennis ball is the ultimate body. Perfectly round. Even distribution of mass. But empty inside, utterly, a vacuum. Susceptible to whim, spin, to force—used well or poorly. It will reflect your own character. Characterless itself. Pure potential. Have a look at a ball. Get a ball from the cheap green plastic laundry basket of old used balls I keep there by the propane torches and use to practice the occasional serve, Jimbo. Attaboy. Now look at the ball. Heft it. Feel the weight. Here, I'll . . . tear the ball . . . open. Whew. See? Nothing in there but evacuated air that smells like a kind of rubber hell. Empty. Pure potential. Notice I tore it open along the seam. It's a body. You'll learn to treat it with consideration, son, some might say a kind of love, and it will open for you, do your bidding, be at your beck and soft lover's call. The thing truly great players with hale bodies who overshadow all others have is a way with the ball that's called, and keep in mind the garage door and broiler, *touch*. Touch the ball. Now that's . . . that's the touch of a player right there. And as with the ball so with that big thin slumped overtall body, sir Jimbo. I'm predicting it right now. I see the way you'll apply the lessons of today to yourself as a physical body. No more carrying your head at the level of your chest under round slumped shoulders. No more tripping up. No more overshot reaches, shattered plates, tilted lampshades, slumped shoulders and caved-in chest, the simplest objects twisting and resistant in your big thin hands, boy. Imagine what it feels like to be this ball, Jim. Total physicality. No revving head. Complete presence. Absolute potential, sitting there potentially absolute in your big pale slender girlish hand so young its thumb's unwrinkled at the joint. My thumb's wrinkled at the joint, Jim, some might say gnarled. Have a look at this thumb right here. But I still treat it as my own. I give it its due. You want a drink of this, son? I think you're ready for a drink of this. No? Nein? Today, Lesson One out there, you become, for better or worse, Jim, a man. A player. A body in commerce with bodies. A helmsman at your own vessel's tiller. A machine in the ghost, to quote a phrase. Ah. A ten-year-old freakishly tall bow-tied and thick-spectacled citizen of the. . . . I drink this, sometimes, when I'm not actively working, to help me accept the same painful things it's now time for me to tell you, son. Jim. Are you ready? I'm telling you this now because you have to know what I'm about to tell you if you're going to be the more than near-great top-level tennis player I know you're going to be eventually very soon. Brace yourself. Son, get ready. It's glo . . . gloriously painful. Have just maybe a taste, here. This flask is silver. Treat it with due care. Feel its shape. The near-soft feel of the warm silver and the calfskin sheath that covers only half its flat rounded silver length. An object that rewards a considered touch. Feel the slippery heat? That's the oil from my fingers. My oil, Jim, from my body. Not my hand, son, feel the flask. Heft it. Get to know it. It's an object. A vessel. It's a two-pint flask full of amber liquid. Actually more like half full, it seems. So it seems. This flask has been treated with due care. It's never been dropped or jostled or crammed. It's never had an errant drop, not drop *one*, spilled out of it. I treat it as if it can feel. I give it its due, as a body. Unscrew the cap. Hold the calfskin sheath in your right hand and use your good left hand to feel the cap's shape and ease it around on the threads. Son . . . son, you'll have to put that what is that that *Columbia Guide to Refractive Indices Second Edition* down, son. Looks heavy anyway. A tendon-strainer. Fuck up your pronator teres and surrounding tendons before you even start. You're going to have to put down the book, for once, young sir Jimbo, you never try to handle two objects at the same time without just aeons of diligent practice and care, a Brando-like dis . . . and well *no* you don't just drop the book, son, you don't just just don't *drop* the big old *Guide to Indices* on the dusty garage floor so it raises a square bloom of dust and gets our nice white athletic socks all gray before we even hit the court, boy, *jesus* I just took five minutes explaining how the key to being even a potential player is to treat the things with just exactly the . . . here lemme have this . . . that books aren't just *dropped* with a crash like bottles in the trashcan they're *placed*, guided, with senses on Full, feeling the edges, the pressure on the little floor of both hands' fingers as you bend at the knees with the book, the slight gassy shove as the air on the dusty floor . . . as the floor's air gets displaced in a soft square that raises no dust. Like soooo. Not like *so*. Got me? Got it? Well now don't be that way. Son, don't be that way, now. Don't get all oversensitive on me, son, when all I'm trying to do is help you. Son, Jim, I *hate* this when you do this. Your chin just disappears into that bow-tie when your mother's big old overhung lower lip quivers like that. You look chinless, son, and big-lipped. And that cape of mucus that's coming down on your upper lip, the way it shines, don't, just don't, it's revolting, son, you don't want to revolt people, you have got to learn to control this sort of oversensitivity to hard truths, this sort of thing, take and exert some goddamn *control* is the whole point of what I'm taking this whole entire morning off rehearsal with not one but two vitally urgent auditions looming down my neck so I can show you, planning to let you move the seat back and touch the shift and maybe even . . . maybe even drive the Montclair, God knows your feet'll reach, right Jimbo? Jim, hey, why not drive the Montclair? why not you drive us over, starting today, pull up by the courts where today you'll—here, look, see how I unscrew it? the cap? with the soft very outermost tips of my gnarled fingers which I wish they were steadier but I'm exerting control to control my anger at that chin and lip and the cape of snot and the way your eyes slant and goggle like some sort of mongoloid child's when you're threatening to cry but just the very tips of the fingers, here, the most sensitive parts, the parts bathed in warm oil, the whorled pads, I feel them

singing with nerves and blood I let them extend . . . further than the warm silver hip-flask's cap's very top down its broadening cone where to where the threads around the upraised little circular mouth lie hidden while with the other warm singing hand I gently grip the leather holster so I can feel the way the whole flask feels as I guide . . . guide the cap around on its silver threads, hear that? stop that and listen hear that? the sound of threads moving through well-machined grooves, with great care, a smooth barber-shop spiral, my whole hand right through the pads of my fingertips less . . . less unscrewing, here, than guiding, persuading, reminding the silver cap's body what it's built to do, machined to do, the silver cap knows, Jim, I know, you know, we've been through this before, leave the book *alone*, boy, it's not going anywhere, so the silver cap leaves the flask's mouth's warm grooved lips with just a snick, hear that? that faintest snick? not a rasp or a grinding sound or harsh, not a harsh brutal Brando-esque rasp of attempted domination but a snick a . . . nuance, there, ah, oh, like the once you've heard it never mistakable *ponk* of a true-hit ball, Jim, well pick it *up* then if you're afraid of a little dust, Jim, pick the book *up* if it's going to make you all goggle-eyed and chinless honestly jesus why do I try I try and try just wanted to introduce you to the broiler's garage and let you drive, maybe, feeling the Montclair's body, taking my time to let you pull up to the courts with the Montclair's shift in a neutral glide and the eight cylinders thrumming and snicking like a healthy heart and the wheels all perfectly flush with the curb and bring out my good old trusty laundry-
. . . laundry basket of balls and racquets and towels and flask and my *son*, my flesh of my flesh, white slumped flesh of my flesh who wanted to embark on what I predict right now will be a tennis career that'll put his busted-up used-up old Dad back square in his little place, who wanted to maybe for once be a real boy and learn how to play and have fun and frolic and play around in the unrelieved sunshine this city's so fuck-all famous for, to enjoy it while he can because did your mother tell you we're moving this spring? that we're moving back to California finally this spring? We're moving, son, I'm harking one last attempted time to that celluloid siren's call, I'm giving it the one last total shot a man's obligation to his last waning talent deserves, Jim, we're headed for the big time again at last for the first time since she announced she was having you, Jim, hitting the road, celluloid-bound, so say adios to that school and that fluttery little moth of a physics teacher and those slumped chinless slide-rule-wielding friends of

no now wait I didn't mean it I meant I wanted to tell you *now*, ahead of time, your mother and I, to give you plenty of notice so you could *adjust* this time because oh you made it so unmisinterpretably *clear* how this last move to this trailer park upset you so, didn't you, to a mobile home with chemical toilet and bolts to hold it in place and widow-webs everyplace you look and grit settling on everything like dust out here instead of the Club's staff quarters I got us removed from or the house it was clearly my fault we couldn't afford any more. It was my fault. I mean who else's fault could it be? Am I right? That we moved your big soft body with allegedly not enough notice and that east-side school you cried over and that negro research resource librarian there with the afro out to here that . . . that lady with the upturned nose on tiptoe all the time I have to tell you she seemed so consummate east-side Tucsonian all self-consciously not of this earth's grit urging us to quote nurture your optical knack with physics with her nose upturned so you could see up in there and on her toes like something skilled overhead had sunk a hook between her big splayed fingerling's nostrils and were reeling skyward up toward the aether little by little I'll bet those heelless pumps are off the floor altogether by now son what do you say son what do you think . . . no, go on, cry, don't try to stifle yourself, I won't say a word, except it's getting to me less all the time when you do it, I'll just warn you, I think you're overworking the tears and the . . . it's getting less effec . . . effective with me each time you use it though we know we both know don't we just between you and me we know it'll always work on your mother, won't it, never fail, she'll every time take and bend your big head down to her shoulder so it looks obscene, if you could see it, pat-patting on your back like she's burping some sort of slumping oversized obscene bow-tied infant with a book straining his pronator teres, crying, will you do this when you're grown? Will there be episodes like this when you're a man at your own tiller? a citizen of a world that won't go pat-pat? Will your face crumple and bulge like this when you're six-and-a-half grotesque feet tall, six-six-plus like your grandfather may he rot in hell's rubber vacuum when he finally kicks on the tenth tee and with your flat face and no chin just like him on that poor dumb patient woman's fragile wet snotty long-suffering shoulder did I tell you what he did? Did I tell you what he did? I was your age Jim here take the flask no give it here, oh. Oh. I was thirteen, and I'd started to play well, seriously, I was twelve or thirteen and playing for years already and he'd never been to watch, he'd never come once to where I was playing, to watch, or even changed his big flat expression even once when I brought home a trophy I won trophies or a notice in the paper TUCSON NATIVE QUALIFIES FOR NATIONAL JR CH'SHIPS he never acknowledged I even existed as I was, not as I do you, Jim, not as I take care to bend over backwards way, *way* out of my way to let you know I *see* you recognize you am aware of you as a body care about what might go on behind that big flat face bent over a homemade prism. He plays golf. Your grandfather. Your grandpappy. Golf. A golf man. Is my tone communicating the contempt? Billiards on a big table, Jim. A bodiless game of spasmodic flailing and flying sod. Someone once called it a game of womanly caution and petty griefs. A quote unquote sport. Anal rage and checkered berets. This is almost empty. This is just about it, son. What say we rain-check this. What say I put the last of this out of its amber misery and we go in and tell her you're not feeling up to snuff enough again and we're rain-checking your first introduction to the game till this weekend and we'll head over this weekend and do two straight days both days and give you a really extensive intensive intro to a by all appearances limitless future. Intensive gentleness and bodily care equals great tennis, Jim. We'll go both days and let you plunge right in and get wet all over. It's only five dollars. The court fee. For one lousy hour. Each day. Five dollars each day. Don't give it a thought. Ten total dollars for an intensive weekend when we live in a glorified trailer and have to share a garage with two DeSotos and what looks like a Model A on blocks and my Montclair can't afford the kind of oil it deserves. Don't look like that. What's money or my rehearsals for the celluloid auditions we're moving 700 miles for, auditions that may well comprise your old man's last shot at a life with any meaning at all, compared to my *son*? Right? Am I right? Come here, kid. C'mere c'mere c'mere c'mere. That's a boy. That's my J.O.I. Jr. That's my kid, in his body. He never came once, Jim. Not once. To watch. Mother never missed a competitive match, of course. Mother came to so many it ceased to mean anything that she came. She became part of the environment. Mothers are like that, as I'm sure you're aware all too well, am I right? Right? Never came once, kiddo. Never lumbered over all slumped and soft and cast his big grotesque long-even-at-midday shadow at any court I performed on. Till one day he came, once. Suddenly, once, without precedent or warning, he . . . came. Ah. Oh. I heard him coming long before he hove into view. He cast a long shadow, Jim. It was some minor local event. It was some early-round local thing of very little consequence in the larger scheme. I was playing some local dandy, the kind with fine equipment and creased white clothing and country-club lessons that still can't truly play, even, regardless of all the support. You'll find you often have to endure this type of opponent in the first couple rounds. This gleaming hapless lox of a kid was some client of my father's son . . . son of one of his clients. So then he came for the client, to put on some sham show of fatherly concern. He wore a hat and coat and tie at 95° plus. The client. Can't recall the name. There was something canine about his face, I remember, that his kid across the net had inherited. My father wasn't even sweating. I grew up with the man in this town and never once saw him sweat, Jim. I remember he wore a boater and the sort of gregariously plaid uniform professional men had to wear on the weekends then. They sat in the indecisive shade of a scraggly palm, the sort of palm that's just crawling with black widows, in the fronds, that come down without warning, that hide lying in wait in the heat of midday. They sat on the blanket my mother always brought—my mother, who's dead, and the client. My father stood apart, sometimes in the waving shade, sometimes not, smoking a long filter. Long filters had come into fashion. He never sat on the ground. Not in the American Southwest he didn't. There was a man with a healthy respect for spiders. And *never* on the ground under a palm. He knew he was too grotesquely tall and ungainly to stand up in a hurry or roll screaming out of the way in a hurry in case of falling spiders. They've been known to be willing to drop right out of the trees they hide in, in the daytime, you know. Drop right on you if you're sitting on the ground in the shade. He was no fool, the bastard. A golfer. They all watched. I was right there on the first court. This park no longer exists, Jim. Cars are now parked on what used to be these rough green asphalt courts, shimmering in the heat. They were right there, watching, their heads going back and forth in that windshield-wiper way of people watching quality tennis. And was I nervous, young sir J.O.I.? With the one and only Himself there in all his wooden glory there, watching, half in and out of the light, expressionless? I was not. I was in my body. My body and I were one. My wood Wilson from my stack of wood Wilsons in their trapezoid presses was a sentient expression of my arm, and I felt it singing, and my hand, and they were alive, my well-armed hand was the dutiful secretary of my mind, lithe and responsive and *senza errori*, because I knew myself as a body and was fully inside my little child's body out there, Jim, I was in my big right arm and scarless legs, safely ensconced, running here and there, my head pounding like a heart, sweat purled on every limb, running like a veldt-creature, leaping, frolicking, striking with maximum economy and minimum effort, my eyes on the ball and the corners both, I was two, three, a couple shots ahead of both me and the hapless canine client's kid, handing the dandy his pampered ass. It was carnage. It was a scene out of nature in its rawest state, Jim. You should have been there. The kid kept bending over to get his breath. The smoothly economical frolicking I was doing contrasted starkly compared to the heavily jerky way he was being forced to stomp around and lunge. His white knit shirt and name-brand shorts were soaked through so you could see the straps of his jock biting into the soft ass I was handing him. He wore a flitty little white visor such as fifty-two-year-old women at country clubs and posh Southwestern resorts wear. I was, in a word, deft, considered, prescient. I made him stomp and stagger and lunge. I wanted to humiliate him. The client's long sharp face was sagging. My father had no face, it was sharply shadowed and then illuminated in the wagging fronds' shadow he half stood in but was wreathed in smoke from the long filters he fancied, long plastic filtered holders, yellowed at the stem, in imitation of the President, as courtiers once sputtered with the King . . . veiled in shade and then lit smoke. The client didn't know enough to keep quiet. He thought he was at a ball game or something. The client's voice carried. Our first court was right near the tree they sat under. The client's legs were out in front of him and protruded from the sharp star of frond-shade. His slacks were lattice-shadowed from the pattern of the fence his son and I played just behind. He was drinking the lemonade my mother had brought for me. She made it fresh. He said I was good. My father's client did. In that emphasized way that made his voice carry. You know, son? Godfrey, Incandenza, old trout, but that lad of yours is *Good*. Unquote. I heard him say it as I ran and whacked and frolicked. And I heard the tall son of a bitch's reply, after a long pause during which the world's air hung there as if lifted and left to swing. Standing at the baseline, or walking back to the baseline, to either serve or receive, one of the two, I heard the client. His voice carried. And then later I heard my father's reply, may he rot in a green and empty hell. I heard what . . . what he said in reply, sonbo. But not until after I'd fallen. I insist on this point, Jim. Not until after I'd started to fall. Jim, I'd been in the middle of trying to run down a ball way out of mortal reach, a rare blind lucky dribbler of a drop-shot from the overgroomed lox across the net. A point I could have more than afforded to concede. But that's not the way I . . . that's not the way a real player plays. With respect and due effort and care for every point. You want to be great, near-great, you give every ball everything. And then some. You concede nothing. Even against loxes. You play right up to your limit and then pass your limit and look back at your former limit and wave a hankie at it, embarking. You enter a trance. You feel the seams and edges of everything. The court becomes a . . . an extremely unique place to be. It will do everything for you. It will let nothing escape your body. Objects move as they're made to, at the lightest easiest touch. You slip into the clear current of back and forth, making delicate X's and L's across the harsh rough bright green asphalt surface, your sweat the same temperature as your skin, playing with such ease and total mindless effortless effort and and and entranced concentration you don't even stop to consider whether to run down every ball. You're barely aware you're doing it. Your body's doing it for you and the court and game's doing it for your body. You're barely involved. It's magic, boy. Nothing touches it, when it's right. I predict it. Facts and figures and curved glass and those elbow-straining books of yours' lightless pages are going to seem flat, by comparison. Static. Dead and white and flat. They don't begin to. . . . It's like a dance, Jim. The point is I was too bodily respectful to slip up and fall on my own, out there. And the other point is I started to fall forward even *before* I started to hear him reply, standing there: Yes, But He'll Never Be Great. What he said in no way made me fall forward. The unlovely opponent had dribbled one just barely over the too-low public-park net, a freak accident, a mis-hit drop-shot, and another man on another court in another early-round laugher would have let it dribble, conceded the affordable, not tried to wave a hankie from the vessel of his limit. Not race on all eight healthy scarless cylinders desperately forward toward the net to try to catch the goddamn thing on the first bounce. Jim, but any man can slip. I don't know what I slipped on, son. There were spiders well-known to infest the palms' fronds all along the courts' fences. They come down at night on threads, bulbous, flexing. I'm thinking it could have been a bulbous goo-filled widow I stepped and slipped on, Jim, a spider, a mad rogue spider come down on its thread into the shade, flabby and crawling, or that leapt suicidally right from an overhanging frond onto the court, probably making a slight flabby hideous sound when it landed, crawling around on its claws, blinking grotesquely in the hot light it hated, that I stepped on rushing forward and killed and slipped on the mess the big loathsome spider made. See these scars? All knotted and ragged, like something had torn at my own body's knees the way a slouching Brando would just rip a letter open with his teeth and let the envelope fall on the floor all wet and rent and torn? All the palms along the fence were sick, they had palm rot, it was the A.D. year 1933, of the Great Bisbee Palm-Rot epidemic, all through the state, and they were losing their fronds and the fronds were blighted and the color of really old olives in those old slim jars at the very back of the refrigerator and exuded a sick sort of pus-like slippery discharge and sometimes abruptly fell from trees curving back and forth through the air like celluloid pirates' paper swords. God I hate fronds, Jim. I'm thinking it could have been either a daytime *latrodectus* or some pus from a frond. The wind blew cruddy pus from the webbed fronds onto the court, maybe, up near the net. Either way. Something poisonous or infected, at any rate, unexpected and slick. All it takes is a second, you're thinking, Jim: the body betrays you and down you go, on your knees, sliding on sandpaper court. Not so, son. I used to have another flask like this, smaller, a rather more cunning silver flask, in the glove compartment of my Montclair. Your devoted mother did something to it. The subject has never been mentioned between us. Not so. It was a *foreign* body, or a substance, not my body, and if anybody did any betraying that day I'm telling you sonny kid boy it was something I did, Jimmer, I may well have betrayed that fine young lithe tan unslumped body, I may very well have gotten rigid, overconscious, careless of it, listening for what my father, who I respected, I *respected* that man, Jim, is what's sick, I knew he was there, I was conscious of his flat face and filter's long shadow, I knew him, Jim. Things were different when I was growing up, Jim. I hate . . . jesus I hate saying something like this, this things-were-different-when-I-was-a-lad-lad-type cliché shit, the sort of cliché fathers back then spouted, assuming he said anything at all. But it was. Different. Our kids, my generation's kids, they . . . now you, this post-Brando crowd, you new kids can't like us or dislike us or respect us or not as human beings, Jim. Your parents. No, wait, you don't have to pretend you disagree, don't, you don't have to say it, Jim. Because I know it. I could have predicted it, watching Brando and Dean and the rest, and I know it, so don't jabber. I blame no one your age, boyo. You see parents as kind or unkind or happy or miserable or drunk or sober or great or near-great or failed the way you see a table square or a Montclair lip-red. Kids today . . . you kids today somehow don't know how to *feel*, much less love, to say nothing of respect. We're just bodies to you. We're just bodies and shoulders and scarred knees and big bellies and flasks and empty wallets to you. I'm not saying something cliché like you take us for granted so much as I'm saying you cannot imagine our absence. We're so present it's ceased to mean. We're environmental. Furniture of the world. Jim, I could imagine that man's absence. Jim, I'm telling you you cannot imagine my absence. It's my fault, Jim, home so much, limping around, ruined knees, drunk, fat, burping, sweat-soaked in that broiler of a trailer, burping, farting, frustrated, miserable, overshooting my reach, knocking lamps over. Afraid to give my last talent the one last shot it demanded. Talent is its own expectation, Jim: you either live up to it or it waves a hankie, receding forever. Use it or lose it, he'd say over the newspaper. I'm . . . I'm just afraid of having a tombstone that says HERE LIES A POTENTIALLY PROMISING OLD MAN. God I'm . . . I'm so sorry. Jim. You don't deserve to see me like this. I'm so scared, Jim. I'm so scared of dying without ever being really *seen*. Can you understand? Are you enough of a big thin prematurely stooped young bespectacled man, even with your whole life still ahead of you, to understand? Can you see I was giving it all I had? That I was *in* there, listening, webbed with nerves? A self that touches all edges, I remember she said. I felt it in a way I fear you and your generation never could, son. It was less like falling than being shut out of something, is the way I recall it. It did not did *not* happen in slow motion. One minute I was at a dead and beautiful forward run for the ball, the next minute there were hands at my back and nothing underfoot like a push down a stairway. A rude whiplashing shove square in the back and my promising body with all its webs of nerves pulsing and firing was in full airborne flight and came down on my knees this flask is empty right down on my knees with all my weight and inertia on that scabrous hot sandpaper surface forced into what was an exact parody of an imitation of contemplative prayer, sliding forward. The flesh and then tissue and bone left twin tracks of brown red gray white like tire tracks of bodily gore extending from the service line to the net. I slid on my flaming knees, rushed past the dribbling ball and toward the net that ended my side. Our side. My racquet had gone pinwheeling off Jim and my racquetless arms out before me sliding Jim in the attitude of a mortified monk in total prayer. It was given me to hear my father pronounce my bodily existence as not even potentially great at the moment I ruined my knees forever, Jim, so that even years later at USC I never got to wave my hankie at anything beyond the near- and almost-great and would-have-been-great-*if*, and later could never even hope to audition for those swim-trunk and Brylcreem beach movies that snake Avalon is making his mint on. I do not insist that the judgment and punishing fall are . . . were connected, Jim. Any man can slip out there. All it takes is a second of misplaced respect. Son, it was more than a father's voice, carrying. My mother cried out. It was a religious moment. I learned what it means to be a body, Jim, just meat wrapped in a sort of flimsy panty-ho, son, as I fell kneeling and slid toward the stretched net, myself seen by me, frame by frame, torn open. I may have to burp, belch, son, son, telling you what I learned, son, my . . . my love, too late, as I left my knees' meat behind me, slid, ended in a posture of supplication on my knees' disclosed bones with my fingers racquetless hooked through the mesh of the net, across which, the net, the sopped dandy had dropped his pricey gut-strung Davis racquet and was running toward me with his visor askew and his hands to his cheeks. My father and the client he was there to perform for dragged me upright to the palm's infected shade where she knelt on the plaid beach blanket with her knuckle between her teeth, Jim, and I felt the religion of the physical that day, at not much more than your age, Jim, shoes filling with blood, held under the arms by two bodies big as yours and dragged off a public court with two extra lines. It's a pivotal, it's a seminal, religious day when you get to both hear and feel your destiny at the same moment, Jim. I got to notice what I'm sure you've noticed long ago I know, I know you've seen me brought home on occasions, dragged in the door, under what's called the influence, son, helped in by cabbies at night, I've seen your long shadow grotesquely backlit at the top of the house's stairs I helped pay for, boy: how the drunk and the maimed both are dragged forward out of the arena like a boneless Christ, one man under each arm, feet dragging, eyes on the aether.

from Memories of My Father on T.V.
Curtis White

a novel about life without pleasure

PROLOGUE

The defining childhood memory of my father is of a man (but not just a man, of course; it is my father—young, handsome, capable!) reclined on a dingy couch watching T.V. Watching T.V. and ignoring the chaos around him, a chaos consisting almost entirely of me and my sisters fighting. Like most brothers and sisters, we fought about everything—who got the last, largest or best (whatever that could mean) piece of fudge, for example. Or the chaos was of a different kind. It was Wendy, my youngest sister, passing rapidly and continuously back and forth before the T.V., through my father's view, moving a doll or dolls from point A to point B. That's how desperate she was to be seen. More desperate, even, than a compulsive who must keep her hands clean, clean. But my father never seemed to notice. Wendy might as well have been the infinitesimal black strip of celluloid that separates discrete images on film. He could see easily through the haze her to-and-fro-ing created. Jan, sister number two and nearly my own age, stood obliquely to Dad's side, posed like a Roman orator, holding forth endlessly on nothing in particular. She would argue eloquently of the injustice of a house with heat in one room only. Or she would complain, as I once heard my grandmother complain (her mind in the squeeze of senile dementia), about the immorality of cowboy serials in general and "Gunsmoke" in particular. Issues of similar profundity. Jan's speaking voice went out like sonar, never finding what it was looking for. But neither did this act gather Dad's attention. Me, I stood behind him, completely out of view. Thus my unique strategy: I don't need to be seen in order to be. But if, dear father, you would happen to turn around, what a feat you'd witness! A true spectacle! Your own son flipping Kraft miniature marshmallows into the air and catching them in his mouth. A whole bag flipped and eaten without missing one! Yes, I was the family's phenom.

Imagine this scene:

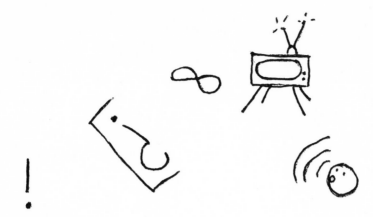

Wendy = 8 (like a shuttle)
Jan = O (like a great mouth)
Curt = ! (like a marvel)
Dad = ? (like an enigma)

Actually, I can see other men in my father's place. Certain men are interchangeable with my father: Frank Sinatra, John Wayne, or even Robert Stack who played Elliot Ness on my father's favorite T.V. show, "The Untouchables." In other words, the strong silent types. Men who can take you apart with a look. They all share that maddening lack of facial expression—*le masque,* the French call it. That immobile face seems to take some dark delight in refusing us a response. This lack of response feels, curiously, like a demand to which everyone, especially a child, is forced to respond, to pay attention, to pay over love. But when no conversation, no act, no capitulation to the father's obscure needs, no matter how abject, seems sufficient, stimulates an acknowledgment, then one feels defeated. In my case, I felt that my father's demand was in fact hostile, exploitive, and—to beat it all—purposeless. For he gained nothing, other than the endless right to his masque and to the T.V.

I admit the following: I have blamed my life of depression on my father who, it seemed to me, demanded of me my death, or my endless dying, and for what? His NOTHING TO DO. But what if these Strong Silent Types, these World War II John Wayne clones, were not in fact self-absorbed, manipulative, and destructive of their children's well-being? What if they were just depressed? What if my depressed father, like his children, was caught in an idiotic, endless and self-destructive drama which consisted at its root of nothing more than the failure of neurotransmitters, serotonin, GABA, even carbon monoxide, to stand by like good soldiers, to be ready to bridge a simple gap? People are meant to brood on life and death, but not every minute of their lives. If they do so brood, one might become Gustave Mahler, the creator of symphonies reflective of a fatal cosmos, which creations eventually accompany him to a thorough madness. Or, if one is no genius, one takes my father's route and finds this drama on T.V., especially the black and white, either/or world of early T.V. Shows like "Combat," "Voyage to the Bottom of the Sea," "The Untouchables," "Wagon Train," and "Dragnet," correlate with depression. Life is either good or bad. Life is bad.

Of course, just as clearly, for my father and perhaps yours, T.V. was also a strategy for narcotizing, for self-medication. It was both the disease and the cure. The T.V. drug. But can we be sure that in his own tragic way he didn't ask the world of television to love him? Can we be sure there was no hope in his autistic viewing? Can we assume that the sadness of his failure was any less worthy than our own?

COMBAT

1. In the episode of "Combat" titled "Command," my father was a German pontoon bridge built over a narrow French river. The bridge/my father threatened to provide a means of access for Krauts in order to roll their *Wehrmacht* machines into an area tentatively held by Americans. Therefore, as a strategic priority of the Allied forces, he had to be "taken out."
2. Until failures in North Africa and the Caucasus deprived Germany of the oil reserves needed for their "war machine," German tanks, planes, and armored carriers were feared and envied. They had the first "smart" weapons: guided bombs and the so-called V-2 rocket. They also had the first fighter jets (although by the time they became available there was so little fuel left that they were towed to the runway by cows). They were even able to synthesize their own gasoline from coal. In "Combat," however, the function of these mighty war machines was merely to roar up full of the empty ostentation of late-Wagnerian opera, and be promptly converted to something more like the discarded shells of cicadas. Brown and brittle

things, buzzing in the wind.

3. My father felt a deep sense of shame, guilt, and humiliation for having provided the Germans this service. He gave his good, broad American back, fortified by Midwestern grains, to the purposes of the fascists. He knew it was a terrible thing to do.

4. The DSM III (The Diagnostic and Statistical Manual of Mental Disorders) under the heading "Diagnostic Criteria for Major Depressive Episode" states in B. 6. that the depressed patient has "feelings of worthlessness, self-reproach, or excessive or inappropriate guilt (either may be delusional)." Was my father's fervently held notion, conveyed regularly during wee-hour confessions to his amazed and sleepy children, that he was a pontoon bridge for the Nazis delusional? Was Gregor Samsa's depressed ideation ("I am a monstrous vermin") delusional? Or were these things metaphors? Is a metaphor a delusion? Does the probability of Franz Kafka's depression require us to think less of him as an artist?

5. When I was a student at the University of San Francisco, I took an honors course in 20th century fiction. The course met at the professor's house. It was during the time when I first began to have opinions. My strongest and most perverse opinion, expressed in the lotus position from the floor of my professor's living room, was that Franz Kafka deserved no acclaim, was not to be admired, because the lone meaning his fiction had to offer was the effect of his own mental illness. What greatness is there, I demanded to know, in disease? What credit can one claim? My classmates and especially my professor were perplexed. How can you not like a story about a man who wakes up a "monstrous vermin"? It is a magnificent metaphor! It is charming as heck! They were curiously unable, however, to find an aesthetic language to defend the beetled Austrian from my charge that he was just sick. I laughed as I debated, throwing their homilies back in their faces, and said, "Why should we claim to be pleased by this night, this paralysis, this human upon whom foreign objects grow?" But the real meaning of my laughter was, "Don't you see? This argument of mine is bug scales. I am Kafka. I am his disease."

6. My father was a lousy traitor and he knew it. Nonetheless, he felt an uncontrollable terror at the thought that the men he loved, "Combat"'s sturdy cast—Vic Morrow as Sergeant Saunders, Littlejohn, Caje, Kirby— were moving slowly in his direction, climbing through the brush, the dirty hills, and the curious eucalyptus trees misplaced in the French countryside.

These men were going to attach plastic explosives to his ribs. They had the little electric plunger for detonation. My father felt guilt, doom, and a hollow sense of justice. But he confessed readily that the squad, those grey heroic men, were right as usual. He should be demolished. Blown up before the Kraut treads could cross him. He was not only a bridge, but a bug. A monstrous vermin. A long bug like a walking stick, a grim sort of mantis, extended across a French river. The German tanks would roll across my father's bug back unless he was destroyed.

7. At the beginning of this episode, we learn that Lieutenant Hanley (Rick Jason) has been wounded and will be removed from ETO (European Theater of Operation) for thirty days. In his place comes one Lieutenant Douglas (guest star, Joseph Campanella). Unlike Hanley, this new lieutenant does not fraternize with the men. He gives orders. He doesn't smile. He eats his awful dog soldier K-rations crouched by himself. Throwing down that abject meal, the lieutenant orders one Pvt. Adams to burn a picture of his three-year-old daughter, a picture Adams has only just received from the States. Adams is offended. The squad is outraged. They do not like this new strong and silent lieutenant. His immobile face seems to take some dark delight in refusing them even the most basic human acknowledgment. They prefer their old lieutenant who seems by contrast a lieutenant of infinite smiles. One has to admit, however, that Adams had been warned to bring no personal effects. Well, hadn't he, soldier? No telling how Jerry would use this information if he were captured.

8. Adams was one of the replaceable squad members who rise glorious from the earth with each new episode only in order to provide fresh and expendable fodder for the Germans. How must these men feel? Do they recognize each other? Do they share looks with hurt eyes? Looks that say, "In this episode, amigo, we die, so that these others may find weekly prime time glory." Do they resent Kirby or Littlejohn, off whom German bullets, grenades and mortars bounce like popcorn? I confess to you that the deaths of those also-appearing-in-alphabetical-order affects me. My depressed brain, in which my ill spirit sobs in each blood cell, tells me that this is something worthy of tears. I weep for the lives of the soldiers who will not return in next week's episode.

9. Adams held the little photo of his daughter, tiny Brigette, between long thin fingers. His fingers did not wish to be burned. Kindly, he started the match in a far corner, distant from his baby's smiling head. But there is no

mercy in fire. It leapt accelerated by photo chemicals. In a moment it was over. Her charred remains lay on the ground. Her little smile lingered before him like an electronic afterimage. He had murdered his own child. He didn't deserve to live.

10. Of course, if he hadn't burnt his daughter, it might only have been worse. "I see, Herr Adams, that your little girl—Brigette it says here on the back of this photograph in the hand of your lovely and tantalizing wife—has just turned three. Wonderful! Well, you know that little Brigette depends on you. She needs you to live. Yes! Above all else, live! She needs you to return home. She would not like you to die now for the silly reason that you will not tell us your soldierly objectives even when such information is of absolutely no use to us at all. Say, for example, that you told us that your mission was to kill the Führer. Goodness knows that we are aware that you would like to kill the Führer under the mistaken idea that we German people would stop trying to kill foreigners and inferior creatures without him. But that is wrong, as history will show, because in fact it is our innate sense of tidiness which compels us to clean up the awkward messiness of so many different colors and what have you. Different shapes. And sexes, *mein gott*. But we already know that you would like to throttle the Führer's long neck like a Thanksgiving goose if you could get your hands on him. But what of your wife and little Brigette? Your wife, for example, is clearly a very, what shall I say?, lovable thing since you have plainly done something very unclean to produce this Brigette baggage. We Germans like to get behind and spread the woman's bottom and see all the dirty, hairy parts. This makes us sick of life and hence we must find all the unclean brown people in the world and kill them because they made us do it hindwise like a hound. Yes, there there, my friend, vomit. It makes you sick to think about. Well, it does me too. Here, I will vomit with you. Yaugh. Feels good, yes? To retch, ah, it is clean and bracing. Like your Old Spice Cologne for men. Nevertheless, I promise you, I will find your wife after this war and spread her to find those soft and complicated things just as you Americans spread your fat Sears catalogues to find the colorful toys or the black and white women's underwear. Yes, there you have it. The big pieces. Of course, I will risk the impulse to suicide such an act will inspire in me. I will transfer my desire to kill myself to your daughter. The only sad part, I think, with the children is the blood that comes from their tiny anuses. Is it not so in your own experience? Now, where do you come from

and where were you going? Where is your headquarters? We wish to take a bite from that part of the map."

11. Were these possibilities part of the infinite despair that made Adams such an easy target a few moments later? He was killed by a German sniper. The hole in his forehead in fact looked like a bleeding anus. This is the despair that comes for these nameless men who are brought in fresh for each episode so that they might die from their nameless fears and from the tragic knowledge of their function in the "Combat" world.

12. That man, Pvt. Adams, I sadly report to you, he was my father. Brigette and I never knew him. He died to save us these indignities at the hands of the Nazis. Yet when I grew up, I joined the neo-Nazi movement. Every spring I carry flowers to the birthplace of George Lincoln Rockwell in Bloomington, Illinois. I parade down the embarrassed Midwestern streets with my fascist brethren. Perhaps if my father had carried a photograph of me, as well, tucked into his dog soldier helmet, this last irony would have been unnecessary.

13. Pvt. Adams, the original man. Brought onto the arboreal scene only to be promptly driven off again, in shame and despair. He must wonder, as he walks head down out of the studios, unemployed for the umpteenth time, "How am I different from these others? No one else is like me. I am uniquely flawed." There is no way of explaining it to him. He really is one of the world's chosen expendables.

14. The episode, "Command," is the first episode I've seen of "Combat" since I was a teenager and crouched like a little beast at my father's side, by the couch, where he reclined in much the same manner as the famous reclining Buddha. I thought at that time to be his henchman and recline on a couch in my turn. But I am halted in this destiny by the following question. Why am I breathing life back into this one episode, "Command"? What wild law of chance brought it to me? And yet it is the perfect episode for my purposes. Through it I intersect with the sublime.

15. And what of Sarge, whose last name never passes a man's lips. He too has *le masque*. He never smiled, never expressed any emotion except his determination to see his suffering through. And yet for a man who suffered, who had thousands of Nazi bullets enclose him (like the knife-thrower's assistant at the fair), he was strangely relaxed. He always looked sleepy. He leaned like James Dean against the window frame of an abandoned country cottage, his upper lip pooching over, and peered out into the world looking

for the next Nazi needing a bullet. He was precisely "cool." Neither warm with life nor cold with death. Show him a horror, any horror. He will have no human response. Ghoulishness holds no terror for the ghoul.

16. A piece of trivia known only to the most ardent "Combat" fans: Sarge had a tatoo on the knuckles of his right hand DAS, and a tatoo on his left EIN. Kraut-talk. Hey, Sarge, why you got kraut-talk on your hands? When he put his fists together, knuckles out, as he often did in the very eyes of the enemy, like Joe Louis in a pre-fight press conference with Herr Schmelling, the tatoos spelled DASEIN. Thus the subtle force of the terror he inspired.

17. During the skirmish in which Adams is killed, the lieutenant is pinned down by German fire. He is behind a fallen tree or similar forest debris. (Why is it that in every episode the platoon is pinned down behind a fallen tree? And how is it that the German fire from a machine gun nest [machine gun "nest": once again death in life is our theme] hits exactly an inch below the preserving limit of the tree. I think that the men of "Combat" could hide behind toothpicks.) As I say, the lieutenant was pinned down. He escaped because—as always—his fellow Americans lobbed grenades with inscrutable accuracy into the machine gun-birthing-place-for-birds.

18. In the end, it is the thesis of the television program "Combat" that America won World War II because of baseball. It is finally the hand grenade that dissolves the impasse of mutual machine gun fire that cannot hit anything. The GIs have good arms. The grenade is the size of a Grover Cleveland hardball. For Americans, the machine gun is merely "chin music." It keeps the enemy's head down. It is the fastball of the grenade that "punches them out," that "rings them up," that "sets down the side."

19. When the platoon reached the home of the French commando, Jean Bayard (who was to lead them to my-father-the-pontoon-bridge) the Jerries had already killed him. (My father felt a contradictory ecstasy: he might still live but his living would be one long treachery.) Sarge and Lieutenant took revenge on Bayard's German killers, but in the process made enough noise to summon the German platoons which were defending my father. They roared up in their *Wehrmacht* bug husks and a tremendous fire fight ensued, rifles and varieties of machine gun making those deep, reassuring and compulsive sounds (the sound ka-chang, for instance) which my father worshipped.

20. My father would watch "Combat" obsessively if for no other reason than that he had an idolatrous relationship with this sound of guns.

Knowing this, I've taken all my videotapes of "Combat" and transferred just the battle scenes to another tape which I will give to my father for his birthday. Recorded at the slowest speed, I have provided him with better than six hours of bliss. My only fear is that he will die of this bliss, like the lonely masturbating man coming for six hours straight and discovering that it is his very bloody life that puddles on his stomach.

21. I am frizzled, stale and small.

22. There is an outstanding moral complexity to this episode, "Command." Lt. Douglas' sole desire (we discover late in the drama) is to return from this mission with all of his platoon members alive. For he was the famous commander of the legendary and ill-fated Mt. Chatel platoon which lost all thirty-one of its soldiers in the process of wiping out a whole "Kraut company." (This is the secret and the reason behind his apparent indifference to his men: he loves them too well.) It is for this reason that, when a German patrol strolls by, he orders that they be allowed to pass unchallenged. Allowing them to pass means, however, that his squad will not be able to take the road themselves. They'll have to go over hills and directly through brush. Tragically, it is this same German patrol that arrives at Bayard's and kills the valiant French patriot. Now the GIs must kill these same Germans after all, as if for the second time, but for Bayard—the only man who knows the location of the bridge—it is too late. It is a world too late. He has been undone by the force of irony. Moments later, an "old man" is discovered wounded inside the cottage. He confirms new details of the above, to whit: Bayard was alarmed because Lieutenant Douglas was so late (late because he hadn't taken the road). Bayard wouldn't have encountered the Germans at all if he hadn't gone out to look for his old friend Douglas. Worse yet, Bayard is the last survivor, other than Douglas, of the infamous incident at Mt. Chatel. These are the fine, fine consequences of a single "command." They seem to expand and multiply like the hairline cracks in a porcelain glaze.

23. From this lesson we conclude the following disturbing truths:

a) when authority is most brutal and indifferent, it is then that it loves and cares for us most;

b) when one fails to choose death, death will come anyway, later, multiplied;

∴ always choose death.

24. Another way of understanding #23: in order to win the war, the

Americans had to become the moral equivalent (as Field Marshall Reagan would say) of the Nazis.

25. "You know, Sergeant, I had to sit down and write thirty-one letters home to the wives and mothers of those men, I don't want to write any more letters. I can't."

"Lieutenant, if we blow this bridge, we might lose some men, but if we don't the Germans will use that bridge. They might cut right through the whole division. If they do, how many officers will have to write how many letters?"

26. In viewing "Combat," does one have to choose between the orgasmic, irrational bliss of gunfire and the complexity of the moral lesson? It would seem so. And it would seem that my father always preferred the merely darkly blissful, since I recall no post-episode explications of moral and dramatic ironies delivered to a silent son thirsting for enlightenment.

27. My father was a Romantic intent on sublime intimations; he was not a New Critic interested in formal device. These intimations came to my father half-asleep in his dirty green recliner, as strangely as if creatures from outer space had come through his T.V. to deliver the news. A true oracle, the truth of the world visited him, virtually sat on his face, while he dreamed. This explains his patriarch's wrath when his children changed the channel in mid-program.

28. "What are you doing? I'm watching that program."

"But, Dad, you were asleep."

"Turn it back."

29. My father spent so much of his life in his green recliner that it broke down subtly under his weight (my father was 6′ 2″, 220 pounds), never completely breaking but rather bending, collapsing earthward under his shape until, after twenty years of use, the chair itself resembled my father, as if it were an exoskeleton he'd left behind.

30. "It's been a long time since Mt. Chatel, my friend."

31. The theme music for "Combat" sounds like the theme music for "Bridge Over the River Kwai" reconfigured to sell hot breakfast cereals. Da da da da da-dum eat your Maayaapo. Da da da da da dum eat your may-yaa-yaa-yaa-po.

32. It turned out that the old man knew the location of the bridge. It was quite nearby. Sarge volunteered to creep to the bridge and blow it up while the rest of the squad occupied the stupid Keystone Cop Germans in their

rattling bug husks who have surrounded Bayard's and abandoned their crucial duties at the pontoon bridge.

33. Understanding this neglect, my father feels an incredible anxiety. "Idiots and dumb cuffs. I'm surrounded by dumb cuffs." He is having a panic attack. With his feet on one bank and his fingers barely gripping the other, he is completely vulnerable. He wants to curl up in the fetal position, but that is not a posture pontoon bridges are allowed. In later years, during his son's time, there will be drugs for this disorder. Ativan, Valium. Drugs his son will take with gratitude. But for his own moment, there is only this enormous DREAD.

34. Sarge is up to his shoulders in the surprisingly warm river. (*Bien sur*, this river heads toward the tepid Baja and certainly didn't begin in the Alps.) He pulls himself along the bridge from rib to rib pausing only to tuck the tender *plastique* between every other rib. It tickles my father a little, but mostly he feels the explosives' mighty and horrible potential. This feeling is much worse than the actual moment of becoming the meaty geyser that is his destiny. That, after all, takes only an instant. Spread across the sky, one has something of the nobility of a new constellation.

35. Done, Sarge crawls up on the bank and engages the little detonator. He depresses the plunger gently. The explosives go off serially, one, two, three, four, like four strong spasms from a really good come. There is a different and dizzying camera angle for each new explosion.

36. My father would really have enjoyed these explosions/his death. But that contradictory pleasure would be like watching a snuff film in which you are the one to be snuffed. Would that turn you on, dead man?

37. As Sarge walks back to meet his platoon, he feels no joy. He'd done his job, saved lives by the bucketful, frustrated *le Bosch*, and yet he felt gloomy. He couldn't understand, of course, but he had become my father. My father's essence could not be destroyed; it had to reside somewhere. It must have flowed back up the wires to the detonator at the moment of his death. Like me, Sergeant Saunders is now possessed by my father. The undead. They walk among us.

38. When the Sarge arrived back, it was clear to all that he'd changed. He was not the same Sarge they'd known. But he couldn't explain anything, or he explained much more than his men, the gentle giant Littlejohn in particular, desired. Sarge said, "I know I am bad because I killed my father. However, I must be a little bit good because I feel guilty and am paying for

it. If I didn't feel bad about myself, then I would be a completely wicked person. So leave me to my despair, I have earned it, and it is my only virtue."

39. "But Sarge, that wasn't your father," appeals our reasonable Everyman, the likable Kirby. "You just blew up a bridge is all." For Pete's sake. For cryin' out loud. For the love of Mike. You don't use your head, Sarge. Kirby looks around to the others, appealing to them for confirmation of this solid common sense. A tear trickles from the corner of the sentimental Littlejohn's eye. Caje puts a consoling hand on Sarge's disconsolate shoulder. "*Vieux ami, nous voudrions t'aider,*" Caje says.

40. The riddle of the Sarge is undone when, to the astonishment of all (especially my father who pops up from his suburban recliner in awe), Sarge removes his helmet. Under his dirty, dented GI helmet with the chin straps hanging down most sloppily is not familiar blonde hair but a small patch of garden, mostly grasses and a few flowering stems. This grows out of the top of his head.

41. "How did I do it? I took my bayonet and prepared the top soil and then I sowed the seed. No, it didn't hurt too much. I didn't go very deep. Why? Don't you like it? Don't you think it's a nice idea to have a little garden on top of your head?"

Three Stories · *Diane Williams*

THE HELPMEET

To my surprise Diane Williams wants me to hold her fucking ass. She is the very picture of strength and health. She is in this state of well-being.

She loves me and I am someone who should stay concealed. Still, I keep coming to light. I am an annoyance rather than a deep disturbance. In other words—I go to my room when I am told to, shut the door, and I stay there until I am given my permission to come out.

When I come back out, some secrecy is necessary. Nothing could have seemed more essential when I took off my peg-top trousers. I untied my shoes. Stood. I felt so tightly bound to her while we were stiffly rocking.

If I go away someday, I want to know how she will live without me.

I will ask her to go into detail about her sexual needs.

Why do I even care how many of her needs there are?

Just for conversation's sake, let's say there are just two.

AN ARGUMENT FOR STAYING THE SAME

He could not please her. She could not please him. She became cruel and horrid. Their children became cruel and horrid. He became cruel and horrid.

They were not tenderly kissing each other, holding each other, or softly stroking each other. He was not plunging himself into her. So then what happened? and then what happened? and then what happened?

She had said something completely fantastic, unbelievable, then she had begun to cry. The truth of it was that her disappointment was real. After dinner, she had lit a cigarette. The room was crowded.

"I want the truth," she had said. She had on her old gray dress with the red lapels. She pushed her plate away. There was a conversation going on. While they had been talking—God knows not for very long—the truth disappeared.

THE EVERLASTING SIPPERS

I sip the coffee almost stealthily, while I wait.

Within my purview, the receptionist drinks something.

"Liz, darling!" the receptionist exclaims when she looks up. She says, "Would like something more to drink while you wait?"

In my mind, there isn't anything in my mind until I know that I want more coffee with milk.

"Do you want more—" the receptionist asks, "coffee?" The receptionist is drinking something.

Mrs. Fox enters, drinking something. Mrs. Fox's bright blue dress, her vibrant voice, when she says to me, "Liz, darling!" add drama to her appearance.

"You want this?" the receptionist is waving a carafe of coffee at both of us. The receptionist's face is small and round. She seems to have a nervous tic in one eye, squints it unexpectedly several times. She is the most faithful picture of tenderness I can call forth.

At length I rise, saying, "I see nothing against that."

That night, after I bathe, I put on my sumptuous robe, brocade. I spoon raspberry sherbet into my mouth with a sherbet spoon. I drink wine from a fine glass. I take a piece of fruit in my hand, not to eat it, to gaze lovingly at it! It is made of stone. There is no problem here with this pattern of reality. There should be no additional people here at all, doing things, causing problems, that are then solved.

When Post-Realism (and the 1960s) Came to Iowa City: An Afterword · *Robert F. Sayre*

YOU MIGHT SAY that "Trouble-Making Fiction," or what we then called post-realism, and what the nation later called "the 1960s," all arrived in Iowa City on the same date, Friday afternoon, October 20, 1967. The occasion was a conference called "The New Grotesque, Or, Is There a Post-Realistic Fiction?" and the scene was the antiseptic ballroom of the Student Union, where Richard Poirier, author of *A World Elsewhere*, a study of style in American Literature, was lecturing on "The Literature of Self-Parody."

With a polished combination of learning and humor (befitting the editor of the latter-day *Partisan Review*), Poirier had quoted examples of the intentional stylistic excesses of Henry James, James Joyce, and Norman Mailer, attacked modern writers who made the formal issues of fiction into the subjects of fiction, and then started a long aside on Jorge Luis Borges, describing him as the pre-eminent post-realistic author: a philosopher and novelist and jokester whose entire work was an examination of the world as fiction and the reality in fiction.

But Poirier was over his allotted time, and expressions on many faces said, as they do in Iowa City when professors from the East or West tell them what they already know, "Does this guy think we've never heard of Borges?" Everyone was also waiting for the next event, a "Eulogy to Lenny Bruce," by the man who was in a way the martyred sick comic's heir, Paul Krassner, editor of the underground satirical magazine—the dirty, deadly opposite of *The Partisan Review—The Realist*.

Then the doors at the back and sides of the ballroom opened quietly, and in came members of the San Francisco Mime Troupe, dressed in white sheets and holding candles. Chanting and moaning like monks, they came forward and formed a line across the front of the room. There, solemn and defiant, they blocked off the stage and barred anyone from going up to stop or rescue the suddenly distressed but still lecturing lecturer.

Who did quickly slip on stage were Ronnie Davis, the Mime Troupe's director, dressed in blue jeans and denim shirt, and Paul Krassner, also in jeans and jean jacket. There were a few brief words, no scuffle, and off went

Davis with Poirier, still very tall and distinguished, but now being led away like an arrested embezzler. Krassner, seeming a foot shorter than Poirier, danced like a little boxer who had just won the fight and cockily headed for the lectern.

The audience could not seem to decide whether to cheer or hiss, until someone yelled, "What are you doing, Paul?"

"I'm taking a piss!"

And while everyone laughed (or nearly everyone), he pointed with one hand into the lectern, holding the other hand on his fly. "That guy went on so long, I have to. You probably do too. But I'm o.k. There's a urinal in here. That's how some guys can talk so long." He moved up close to the lectern and mimicked Poirier's stance.

The audience laughed and cheered louder, and Krassner went into his "eulogy." Bruce, he said, was really the first YIPPY, for Youth International Party, a political hippie, who had tried to reform America with laughter and ridicule. Bruce realized that the way to overcome an evil power was to grotesquely exaggerate it. This exposed the deformity already in it. That was what was so ironic about Bruce being arrested on obscenity charges: it was American sexual hang-ups that were obscene; Bruce had merely exposed them. So tomorrow, Krassner went on, the new yippies, in Bruce's spirit, were going to gather around the Pentagon and exorcise it. They were going to expose and release its grotesque and inhuman evil, not by tearing it down (like a Bastille) but with love. They would form a gigantic circle around it and pray and laugh and practice transcendental meditation until it rose, some gurus predicted, two feet off the ground.

"The New Grotesque" had started out to be a conference just on fiction, the "Second Biennial Conference for Modern Letters." The previous conference had been held in the fall of 1965 on "The Poet As Critic" and drawn a distinguished list of speakers and guests. The sponsors were the English Department and the Center for Modern Letters, which had been started in the spring of 1965 to take advantage of Iowa's leadership in the writing and study of modern literature. By 1967, however, the mood at The University of Iowa, as on other American campuses, was radically different. In 1965 the Vietnam War "escalation" had just begun and most professors and students were still ignoring it. You could still have a lecture on literary criticism by René Wellek or Richard Ellmann that would draw 500 to 700 people. By 1967 the war was a horror to nearly everyone, and urban riots had engulfed dozens of American cities in fire and destruction. At the same time, the cool lingo of druggies, hippies, and dropouts was reaching from Berkeley and the Haight-Ashbury to Iowa City, Madison, and Ann Arbor. Thus, as we planned the 1967 conference we wondered about the relationships between modern fiction and this tense, brutal, and apocalyptic time. We wanted, or at least some of us wanted, a conference which would not ignore this and which would also confront the policies of the U.S. government and emphasize the relevance of anti-war satires and fantasies like *Catch-22*, *Dr. Strangelove*, and *Cat's Cradle*.

Beyond that, planning for the conference reflected the diverse interests of the people who were involved: Fred McDowell, as the director of the Center for Modern Letters; Vance Bourjaily, the Writers' Workshop's professor of fiction; David Hayman, who was then very interested in farce; Bob Scholes, who with Robert Kellogg had just published *The Nature of Narrative*; Kurt Vonnegut, who suggested having Krassner do the eulogy for Bruce; and a variable number of other English and Workshop people — Tom Whitaker, Fred Will, Bill Fox, George Starbuck, Gayatri Spivak, Bill Murray, Sherman Paul. In fact, the interests were so diverse and the senior faculty's explanations of them so intimidatingly complex that I, as a just-tenured associate professor, had little idea what the topic really was. We could never even agree on a conference title. "Black Humor" was the widely used term, but it seemed inappropriate because none of the authors mentioned was Black. "Bitter Humor" was too meek. "Novels of the Absurd"? Too close to Martin Esslin's *Theatre of the Absurd*. Other titles recognized still further aspects of the writing of the late '50s and early '60s: for example, "A Territory to Defend" and "The Novelist as Person." Then someone suggested calling it "Grotesques and Arabesques: The New Fiction," and through the summer of 1967 we used that title, though it seems awful, too. Too Poesque.

Looking further into old files, I also find a variety to the people we invited or talked about inviting that is staggering: Joseph Heller, Richard Kostelanetz, Robert Brustein, Irving Howe, J.P. Donleavy, John Hawkes, John Barth, James Purdy, John Updike, Bernard Malamud, Bruce Jay Friedman, R.W.B. Lewis, Warner Berthoff, Nathalie Sarraute, Alain Robbe-Grillet, Marcel Butor, Susan Sontag. Yet this babel of different voices suggests the difficulty of defining any new movement while standing in the middle of it. Twenty-five years from now, the list of participants considered for a conference in 1994 on, say, Post Modernism will surely look equally strange to the by-then wiser judges.

The person who had the most effect on the final list of speakers and guests was Bob Coover. He arrived in Iowa City in September of 1967 to start teaching at the Workshop and quickly began advising me and Bob Scholes, who either had just published or was about to publish *The Fabulators*. We shaped up the title ("The Old Grotesque," Coover now calls it),[1] and when he found we still had money in the budget, he began suggesting more writers. Stanley Elkin, author of *A Bad Man*. Robert Kelley, poet, novelist, and teacher. Roslyn Drexler, playwright, novelist, and former wrestler. Robert Stone, author of *A Hall of Mirrors*. Sol Yurick, former Brooklyn welfare worker and author of a stunning novel about teenage gangs, *The Warriors*. And they all accepted, like a posse picked by a new sheriff. They made the conference into a gathering of a new generation of writers. William Gass, who later came entirely on his own, when he found out about the conference from John Barth, said recently that it was here that he first saw that he was not alone in his writing but was a part of a new generation.[2]

The trouble-making really began, however, with the arrival on Thursday, October 19, of the San Francisco Mime Troupe. Inviting them had been Scholes and Hayman's idea, for both had seen them perform in the parks of San Francisco and the Bay Area and recognized their adaptations of Commedia dell Arte as post-realistic theater that was also pre-realistic and a possible analog to what Scholes called "fabulism." But I had seen them in the summer of 1967 and realized that the most immediate fact about them was their political message. Their version of Goldoni's "L'Amant Militaire," a satire about the Spanish army in Italy, was a very funny, very angry attack on the American army in Vietnam. And when Peter Cohon, Sandy Archer, and a few other Mime Troupers found out that U.S. Marine Corps recruiters would be coming to The University of Iowa less than two weeks later, they incorporated that information into the Thursday night performance. At the end of the play, they took off their Commedia dell Arte masks and asked for commitment, not just laughter. "Take your opposition to this war and do something about it November 1. 'Go tell it to the Marines.' "

That night, at a party for the Mime Troupe given by graduate students Everett Frost, Faith Baron, and Harry and Linda MacCormack, a debate went on for hours about relations between art and politics. One side liked and admired the Mime Troupe actors for their political messages, which were clear not only in their words but also in their lifestyles. Another acknowledged the message but said their art and discipline were what put it across. They were actors first and last, for even when actors remove their masks, they still are actors. *They* would not "Go tell it to the Marines." They would have left town.

Such arguments engaged everyone, even those students who at normal parties chased girls or got drunk or smoked grass (or all three). This time, perhaps, it was the guests who made pests of themselves. "Who is that one-eyed ankle-grabber?" Chris Scholes asked her father during a party at Bob's house. "He's sitting at the top of the stairs grabbing the ankles of every girl going to the john." That, he told her, must be Robert Creeley.

Friday morning, however, Creeley added to the intensity of the arts/politics debate by arguing that this moment of protest and revolution was not one at which to abandon language and the imagination. Seize them and be more persuasive, more powerful than the enemy. At one point, as dramatic a moment as when the actors had removed their masks the night before, Creeley stood up tall and thin, with his patch over one eye, pointed to some empty chairs on stage behind him, and said he could put people in them. "There, I see people in those chairs." And no one disputed him. Some people even assured me later that just then they saw people in the chairs, too.

At the same meeting Ronnie Davis made "realism" itself the enemy, the bulwark of status quo and the state, calling it "SatEvePost-Realism." A concept of reality existed only within a given frame. The Mime Troupe's method was to entice audiences into different frames of meaning and reference and then break them. Flip the frame and change the game. Audiences then saw connections they had not seen before. When someone accused Davis and his fellow actors of just being clowns, hired jesters, Jakov Lind spoke of his experience in World War II. Humor and ridicule were so offensive to the Nazis that they could land people in concentration camps.

The strongest defense of realism did not come until Saturday, the last day of the conference, from Carl Oglesby, a founder of the Students for a Democratic Society and the author, with Richard Shaull, of *Containment and*

Change, the book on American foreign policy which was assigned reading for all members of the New Left. Acknowledging that reality was a fiction, Oglesby still insisted on the responsibility of the writer to confront hard facts, and this responsibility, he said, was shirked in most American fiction. His immediate example was *Catch-22*, which he painstakingly analyzed to prove that Yossarian's failure to kill Col. Cathcart was a cop-out and his impossible escape to Sweden a desertion from more than just the army. Oglesby compared Heller and Yossarian to Camus, saying that their "redefining of rebellion" gave it a "radically metaphysical and antipolitical meaning" which amounted to a "choice of political silence" and "a vote for oppression."[3] Metaphysical rebellions, like cries of despair and confrontations with the absurd, appealed to the upperclass and conservative.

The serious radicals listened to Oglesby attentively, even though some looked disappointed that he was being so literary. They wanted a Thomas Paine, and what they were hearing might as well have been just a left-wing English professor. Or they wanted to hear Paul Krassner again, someone who would be rowdy and funny, inspiring and optimistic. But Krassner had already left for Washington to help "levitate the Pentagon." Oglesby's message was the unpopular one that the revolution was not "all in our heads," as hippies said, but was going to take work, study, and commitment. But even Krassner had said to some of his admirers before he left that they ought to remember this moment, because it wasn't going to last. "It's going to turn ugly."[4]

And he was right. On November 1, when the Marine Corps recruiters arrived, between 80 and 100 faculty and students blockaded the east entrance to the Student Union, trying to dissuade or prevent prospective recruits from going in for interviews. On the street in front, pro-war students gathered to heckle them and drag them from the steps. Hours passed, and eventually over 500 counter-demonstrators were yelling from the street and the parking ramp above. A riot pending, the police arrested the anti-war demonstrators. The story was on the evening news and front pages around the country, and arguments started all over the state about what the University should do. Was the University complicitous with the war? Should it protect the protestors' right to dissent or other students' rights to get jobs?

Even more trouble occurred on December 5, when Dow Chemical Corporation, makers of Napalm, came to interview. Students were beaten and maced by the police, and several were accused of a conspiracy to disrupt events all over the campus. Shortly afterward, the C.I.A. announced that it would not interview at The University of Iowa.

The trouble-making went on. And there was never another "Conference for Modern Letters."

Notes

1. Robert Coover, e-mail message to RFS, May 18, 1994.
2. William Gass, phone conversation with RFS, February, 1994.
3. Carl Oglesby, "The Deserter: The Contemporary Defeat of Fiction," *Middle Earth*, vol. 1, no. 4 (no date), p. 5. *Middle Earth* was the Iowa City underground newspaper founded in the fall of 1967. This issue reprinted Oglesby's talk. This and other issues of *Middle Earth*, as well as *The Iowa Defender*, the less flamboyant Iowa City "alternative paper," have been very useful to me in reconstructing the conference and its consequences.
4. Letter from Jim Ballowe to RFS, April 15, 1994.

In addition, I would like to thank Everett Frost, David Marr, Bob Scholes, and Fred Will, who also shared their memories of the conference, memories which were very sharp considering it all happened twenty-seven years ago. I wish I had had time to talk to more of us "Grotesque Alumni" and would welcome both corrections and further recollections.

Notes on Contributors

KATHY ACKER is a novelist and the author of *Blood and Guts in Highschool, Empire of the Senseless, My Mother: Demonology,* and others. She has collaborated with Richard Foreman on several plays and an opera, *Birth of a Poet.* A CD produced by Hal Wilner and based on *My Mother: Demonology* will appear this year and will include music by Ralph Carney and Tribe 8.

GEORGE ANGEL is a writer currently living in California.

JOHN BARTH's most recent novel, *Once Upon a Time,* was published in the spring of 1994.

JONATHAN BAUMBACH's most recent novel is *Seven Wives: A Romance.* He has published over sixty short stories in such magazines as *Esquire, American Review, Partisan Review, Antaeus, Triquarterly,* and has been published in numerous anthologies, including *O. Henry Prize Stories* and *Best American Short Stories.*

MARY CAPONEGRO is the author of *The Star Café.* She is currently writing a collection of fiction inspired by her fellowship year at the American Academy in Rome. "The Spectacle" is the first of those stories.

GEORGE CHAMBERS bums in Peoria, Illinois—Alas!

LENORA CHAMPAGNE is a writer, performer, and director. She has performed a longer stage version of "The Best Things in Life" in Paris, France; Portland, Oregon; Cleveland, Ohio; and in New York City. She is the editor of *Out from Under: Texts by Women Performance Artists* (TCG, 1990), and is currently writing the script of *Nebraska,* based on characters from Willa Cather and interviews with contemporary farmers. The play will première at an abandoned farm site halfway between Lincoln and Omaha in the fall of 1995. She lives in New York City.

ROBERT COOVER, whose most recent book is *Pinocchio in Venice,* helped to establish *The Iowa Review* in 1969 and was its fiction editor in the mid 1970s.

SUSAN DAITCH is the author of two novels, *L. C.* (Harcourt, Brace, Jovanovich) and *The Colonist* (Vintage). She lives in New York City.

JEFFREY DeSHELL is currently an Assistant Professor of Literature at Illinois Benedictine College. His first novel, *In Heaven Everything Is Fine,* was published by Fiction Collective Two. He lives in Chicago and is working on his second novel.

RIKKI DUCORNET has published four novels, *The Stain, Entering Fire, The Fountains of Neptune*, and *The Jade Cabinet*. She has also illustrated books by Robert Coover and Jorge Luis Borges. Her complete fiction, *The Complete Butcher's Tales*, will be published with Dalkey Archive Press in 1994.

PATRICIA EAKINS is a migrant teacher and the author of *The Hungry Girls and Other Stories* (Cadmus Editions). She has published in a variety of anthologies and periodicals including *Vital Lines: Contemporary Fiction about Medicine* (St. Martin's Press), *Fiction International, Chicago Review, Conjunctions,* and *The Literary Review*, which honored her with a Charles Angoff award for "outstanding contribution."

EURUDICE is the author of *f/32* and *f/32: The Second Coming*. "EHMH" is her work in progress, an apocalyptic oceanic romance. She was born on Lesbos, Greece, and brought up in Alexandria and Athens.

RAYMOND FEDERMAN is the author of seven novels (in English and French), three volumes of poems, and several books of essays. He is a Distinguished Professor of English and Comparative Literature at SUNY, Buffalo.

WILLIAM H. GASS is the director of the International Writers' Center at Washington University in St. Louis. His new novel, *The Tunnel*, will be published by Knopf in 1995.

LAURA GERRITY received her MFA from Washington University in St. Louis. "Circe" is part of a collection of short stories reinventing women of myth and legend. She would like to thank Stanley Elkin, William Gass, and Robert Coover for their sound and sage advice.

JOHN HAWKES is Professor of English Emeritus at Brown University and a member of the American Academy of Arts & Letters. His latest novel is *Sweet William: A Memoir of Old Horse.* "Armand the Frog" is from a work in progress.

LUCY HOCHMAN has spent much of the past ten years in rural North Carolina. Her work has appeared in *Caliban*, and she has been nominated for a Henfield prize.

STEVE KATZ's most recent book of fiction, *43 Fictions*, was published by Sun and Moon Press, and his latest book of poems, *Journalism*, was published by Bamberger Books. *Swanny's Ways*, which we excerpt here, will be out next year from Sun and Moon.

JANET KAUFFMAN's most recent books are *Obscene Gestures for Women,* a collection of stories, and a short novel, *The Body in Four Parts.*

JIM KRUSOE edits the *Santa Monica Review.* His recent work has appeared in *Bomb Field* and *The North American Review.*

STACEY LEVINE's most recent collection of fiction is *My Horse and Other Stories,* published last October by Sun and Moon Press. She is the winner of the 1994 PEN West Award for Fiction.

BEN MARCUS's first book will be published by Knopf. He lives in New York City.

CRIS MAZZA's excerpt in this issue is from her sixth book, *Your Name Here,* a novel due out in spring 1995 from Coffee House Press. Short story collections include *Animal Acts, Is It Sexual Harassment Yet?* and *Revelation Countdown.* She has also published two novels: *How to Leave a Country* and *Exposed.* She splits her time between San Diego and Chicago.

JULIE REGAN is a fifth generation San Franciscan. Her plays and performance works have been produced at the Magic Theatre and at Intersection for the Arts in San Francisco and have also toured the Czech Republic. She is currently at Brown University working on a novel.

LOU ROBINSON is the author of *Napoleon's Mare* (Fiction Collective Two). Her work has appeared recently in *The American Voice, The Kenyon Review, Black Ice,* and *Epoch.* She is the recipient of a NYEA award in fiction and has just completed a collaborative novel with Ellen Zwerg, called "Surveillance."

ROBERT F. SAYRE directed the 1967 Conference for Modern Letters. In contemporary life he teaches courses in American literature, still at The University of Iowa. He has just edited *American Lives, An Anthology of Autobiographical Writing* (University of Wisconsin Press).

RONALD SUKENICK's story in this issue is part of a collection that will be published under the title of *Doggy Bag* (from Black Ice Books/ FC2). He has recently completed a novel called "Mosaic Man."

DAVID FOSTER WALLACE is a fiction writer who teaches at Illinois State University. This piece is excerpted from a longer work due out next year.

CURTIS WHITE is the author of three books of fiction, *Heretical Songs, Metaphysics in the Midwest,* and *The Idea of Home.* He is also co-director of Fiction Collective Two.

DIANE WILLIAMS is co-editor of *StoryQuarterly*. She is the author of *This Is About the Body, the Mind, the Soul, the World, Time and Fate* (Grove Press) and *Which God Might Choose to Appear* (Grove Press).

DRAKON

S. M. STIRLING

BAEN

A Baen Books Original

Baen Publishing Enterprises
P.O. Box 1403
Riverdale, NY 10471

ISBN: 0-671-87711-9

Cover art by Stephen Hickman

First printing, February 1996

Distributed by Simon & Schuster
1230 Avenue of the Americas
New York, NY 10020

Typeset by Windhaven Press, Auburn, NH
Printed in the United States of America

To Jan, with love.
And to Marjorie Stirling . . .
who is, in a sense, responsible
for all this.

Acknowledgements:

My thanks to Susan Schwartz and Dina
Pliotis for invaluable research help.
Tom Lawnsby, for he knows what.
Also to Dennis Moore, great guy
and brother-in-law. Glad you
made it back to the world.

(All errors of fact, taste and
interpretation are mine.)

CHAPTER ONE

DOMINATION TIMELINE
EARTH/1
MAY 21, 442nd YEAR OF THE FINAL SOCIETY
(2442 A.D.)

Gwendolyn Ingolfsson stood naked beside the stream. It was an early spring day in the central Rockies, chilly and intensely fresh. Wind whispered quietly through the fir trees dotted through the upland valley, down from the snowpeaks to the west, and fluttered the new leaves of the aspens. It carried the scent of grass and trees, rock, small burrowing things, more faintly elk and—she inhaled—a grizzly, off a kilometer or two upwind. For a moment she gave herself to the wind and silence, face turned to the morning sun, watching a condor sweep its shadow across the flower-starred meadows.

Then she turned back to her camp. The fire was out, her last meal of hand-caught trout and rabbit scorched scraps in the ashes. Beside it was a tripod of spears, shaped ashwood tipped with chipped flint heads bound on by rawhide; her obsidian knife and hide bag hung from them. For a moment she considered taking some

1

of the gear for keepsake, then shook her head. The
memory would stay with her, of making them and using
them these past six months; let wood and leather and
stone rot and tumble and the land grow over them. Or
let another find and use them; there were two or three
species in this reserve with the hands and the wit,
perhaps even feral humans.

She spoke to her transducer: **now**.

The wait was not long. Her ears pricked forward at
the whistle of cloven air. A speck fell out of the sky,
became a matte-gray flattened wedge ten meters long
by five wide. It settled to the ground with a faint sigh
and a doorway opened. Gwen sighed herself as she
stepped through into the long open room within, regret
mingled with pleasure. *Back to civilization.*

"Temperature twenty-one," she said aloud.

The air warmed. She ran a palm cleaner over her
body—time for the comfort of hot water later—and
dressed in a set of blacks from a container. Another
container scanned her before releasing a leather weapons belt, old but well-kept; she checked the charge on
the plasma gun automatically, a nostalgic feeling.
Obsolete, almost as much as the layer knife on the
opposite hip, but she'd carried this very weapon on the
last human-hunts here in North America; she was old
enough to remember that, the biobombs and the killsweeps. Then she sat in the recliner at the nose of the
aircraft.

"Visual, optical, maximum." Three-quarters of the
hull disappeared to the eye, leaving only the power and
drive systems in the deck behind her opaque. "Lift,
course to Reichart Station, speed . . ." She considered.
"Four hundred kph, height five hundred meters." The
craft had orbital capacity, but she wasn't in a hurry.
"Call, to legate Tamirindus Rohm."

The wedge lifted, turning and heading southeast
down the valley. A square of space before her opened

and showed quiet moving colors. Then it flashed to display, only the lack of scent and moving air to distinguish it from a window.

"Service, Tamirindus," Gwen said.

"Glory, Gwen."

The legate was floating in zero gravity—Gwen recognized the background, an office at the GEO end of the Kenia beanstalk; the blue-and-white shield of Earth covered the window behind her, with the northeast corner of Africa visible and the long curve of the Stalk vanishing into the distance below.

Duty. The Directorates wouldn't have called her unless something important needed her attention.

The younger woman—she was only a little over two hundred, half Gwen's age—looked enough like her to be her sister. Hair bright copper rather than mahogany, and a slightly more slender build: apart from that they had the shared likeness of their respective generations of *Homo drakensis*. Deepscan would have shown more differences, of course, despite periodic DNA updates that kept Gwen roughly current, and she doubted the youngster had ever bothered with the full set of combat biomods. The Draka hadn't had much use for them in her lifetime.

"Not my idea of a vacation," Tamirindus went on. "Glad the bears didn't eat you."

"Mostly hibernating, in winter," Gwen answered. "I ate one of them. Believe me, you appreciate the finer things more if you go without for a while. Now, the wild ghouloon packs, they can be really dangerous . . . and I think I spotted sign of humans, ferals."

Tamirindus's eyebrows went up. "Still?"

"Oh, they're not *quite* extinct. It's not an elegant species, but it's tough and it breeds fast." She stretched. "Speaking of which, how's the reproduction going?"

"Brooder's about ready, doing fine."

"Not using an orthowomb for your eggs?" Gwen made a *tsk* sound. "And you with the Technical Directorate."

Tamirindus grinned. "Tradition has its place. Besides, I like to watch them swell and feel the baby kick in their bellies. The brooder's a pet; the Rohms've used her line since the first century. Her great-grandmother brooded me."

The aircraft extended a cup of coffee; Gwen took it and sipped with slow pleasure. Conversation and coffee were things she'd missed in the wilderness too. Shapes drifted outside Tamirindus's office wall-window, habitats, fabricators, an Earth-orbit to Luna shuttle, the bell-tube-globe shape of an interplanetary craft. Further away they were bright dots against the black of space and the unwinking glow of stars, and in the middle distance the huge frame of the next interstellar colony ship under construction. Gwen's eyes dwelt on that for a moment. Travel from star to star was one-way, and she had never quite decided it was time to leave the home system. Sol-based instruments were enough to tell if there was a life-bearing planet, and to learn much of its detail. Uncrewed probes followed for more detailed work, to see if the prospects were good, and so far five colonizing expeditions had gone out in the probes' wake. Only information and a few frozen samples ever came back; the ships themselves were part of the equipment needed by the settlers.

"Well, if I'm free, I'll visit Rohmplace for the naming feast," she promised the other Draka. It was a while since she'd been to Mars, anyway. "Am I likely to be free?"

"That depends," Tamirindus said. "*I* may not be able to make it. You know, fifty years ago I almost decided to emigrate because this job was so boring?"

Gwen nodded. One of the drawbacks of immortality was that promotion became positively glacial, even with the population decline. On the other hand, it also made it easier to wait. *Though that can be a drawback too. Patience and laziness can be interchangeable.* The other woman went on:

"Well, we had *another* disaster with the space-based molehole platform. Moving it out to the Oort didn't help at all. This one was bad, heavy casualties. The only consolation is that the weird shit accompanying the accident proves we're doing something right. We haven't figured out exactly what happened or what went where, though.

"So, they've tried microgravity; now the neuron-whackers think a stable planetary field might help." More seriously: "We're trying everything at once, all possible avenues. I've got a dozen teams working on it now. This is *important*, Gwen."

It was. For four centuries the Domination and the descendants of the refugees who'd fled to Alpha Centauri hadn't done much more than glare at each other. By the time the Solar System recovered enough from the Last War to do anything, Alpha Centauri was too tough a nut to crack. War over interstellar distances was an absurdity; the energy costs too high, the defender's advantages from being near a sun too great. Both sides had skirmished a little, traded information a little, and raced to colonize suitable systems first— the only real clash had occurred when two expeditions arrived nearly simultaneously at one such. Colonies were autonomous, because interstellar government was even more ridiculous than war.

In theory it was possible to *destroy* inhabited planets from light-years distant, although not to conquer them. Nobody had ever thought it worthwhile, when retaliation in kind was just as easy and the preparations simple to spot. With communications time in years and travel time in decades, even the closest star was vastly too far to rule. Only the huge resources of entire solar systems made colonization possible at all; there certainly wasn't any economic payoff.

This project might change all that. And the Samo-thracians—the descendants of the American colonists in the Alpha Centauri system—were ahead. They'd always been better physicists, even before the Last War; the Domination had only started looking into moleholes because espionage indicated the enemy were.

"Downlink?" Gwen said. Best to start right away. You could stuff information into your brain via transducer, but understanding it still took time and effort.

"Not on the Web. Infoplaque by courier; you know, Suicide Before Reading secret. It's waiting for you, along with your stuff. We need to know if it's worth-while putting more resources into this subproject; the energy budget's enough to notice, even these days."

And really large energies were difficult to handle on a planetary surface; that was probably why the project had been put in sparsely populated North America, just in case. With the Atlantic Ocean to act as an emergency heat sink.

"Glory."

"Service," Gwen replied in farewell. "I'll have a report for you as soon as I can."

She held the coffee cup out for a refill and frowned as the link disappeared. Tamirindus was worried, which meant the Technical Directorate was worried. *Which means I should be worried.* Something of a novelty; this last century or so had been very peaceful.

"Manual," she said, tossing the cup into the cycler. To her transducer: **news**.

The aircraft swooped and dove as her hand settled on the joystick it extruded. Mountains gave way to high rolling plains, green with new grass. Life swarmed, wild horses, antelope, once a herd of bison a million strong. On the shores of a lake a pack of centaurs surrounded a mammoth, shooting with thick recurved bows, galloping in to stab with long heavy lances. Bogged in the lakeside mud, the giant reddish bulk raised its trunk and trumpeted in agony. The females and colts waited at a distance, setting up dome tents and preparing to butcher the great curltusker. None of the stallions looked up from their task, but the others pointed in wonder at the low-flying aircraft, the young running in circles and kicking their hind feet up in sheer glee.

Meanwhile information flowed in; there were a hundred million of her people in the Solar System, and ten times that number of *servus*, enough to generate considerable news. Gossip, politics, tournaments, duels, wingflying in the domed craters of the Moon, a redirected comet streaking through the nearly clear atmosphere of Venus as the long trouble-plagued terraforming came to an end, sailboats drifting down the ocean that filled the Valles Marineris on Mars. The Cygnus Nine probe had reported in, and there was not only a habitable planet, but an intelligent species on it.

That made her flip the aircraft up, let it do the piloting and take notice; that was only the second race of sophonts found so far, in scores of systems. Planets were the general rule around Sol-type stars, life more common than not, biochemistries roughly compatible with Earth's rare but not impossibly so. Sapient, language-using, tool-making species were very uncommon. The previous discovery hadn't been made until after the colonizing expedition landed, the natives being the equivalent of *Homo erectus*, very scarce and not having made much impact on their planet. This new bunch were *extremely* interesting. Weird-looking, two big eyes and two little ones near a perforated beaklike projection in the middle of their . . . well, probably faces. A Bronze Age–equivalent technology, so they wouldn't be any trouble for the colonizing expedition. A few thunderbolts and the Gods from the Sky would be worshiped with fervor.

Of course, the natives would be wild. It would probably take a while to understand the biology and produce a proper domesticated strain, but even so it would be useful to have a population in place rather than breeding from frozen ova alone.

Below, grassland dwindled. Forests appeared along rivers, and grew thicker. Fields drew their swirling lines across the landscape, each clustered around a manor house and its dependencies, the estates separated by kilometers of wilderness. Settlement faded again east of the Mississippi, until the Appalachians reared blue and silent, covered with ancient woods of hickory and oak. A thread of smoke rose from one mountain valley; probably goblins. Gwen grimaced. *Loathsome little things.* One of the Conservation Directorate's mistakes, in her opinion—although they did make good, tricky game. The Adirondacks flashed by, spruce and white pine broken only by the blue eyes of lakes.

A scattering of manors marked the Hudson valley, but nobody had ever bothered to resettle Long Island or Manhattan. Thus it was free for Technical Directorate use. Beyond, the Atlantic stretched silver and immense.

"Query," the aircraft said. "Security query from Reichart Station . . . Confirmed access."

Just as well, since the orbital weapons platforms would be tracking her. *Back to work.*

Reichart Station's surface was a village set in parkland, amid oak and maple forest growing over what closer inspection would show to be ruins. Here and there a giant stub of crumbled building showed, what had survived the airblasts and half a millennium of weather and roots. Several hundred acres were surrounded by the inconspicuous fence-rods of a sonic barrier to keep animals and wild sapients out. Tile-roofed cottages stood among gardens, around a few larger buildings in the same whitewashed style; lawns and brick paths linked them, centered on a square with an ornamental pond. The settlement was three and a half centuries old, at first a biohazards research institute, later branching into physics. Tied into the Web, there wasn't much need for extensive physical plant, and what there was could be put underground, A heavy power receptor showed in the distance, new construction; superconducting cable would be run underground to the centrum.

The whole population was turned out to greet her, nearly a thousand all told. A visit from a *drakensis* in person would be rare here, entry being restricted. A bow like a ripple went over them as she stepped down from the aircraft.

Gwen's nostrils flared slightly, taking their scent. Clean, slightly salty, seasoned with curiosity, excitement, awe, a touch of fear, a complex hormonal stew that signaled *submission*. The scent of *Homo servus*, comforting and pleasant; it brought a warm pleasurable feeling, a desire to protect and guide.

Their type was more diverse in looks than her own, closer to the ancestral *Homo sapiens sapiens*; this particular group tended to light-brown skins and fair hair, and a height about half a head below her hundred and seventy-six centimeters. There were children among the crowd. Reichart Station would be a community of its own, with its own customs and folkways, by now. The group standing to meet her were middle-aged or older, although they showed few signs of it; they'd been designed to remain vigorous into their ninth or tenth decade before a brief senescence and an easy death.

"Greetings," Gwen said.

"We live to serve," they replied.

The awe-fear scent grew stronger as they reacted to the subliminal stimulus of her pheromones. She throttled back consciously. No sense in spooking them—the long wilderness vacation had made her a little sloppy.

"I'm Glenr Hoben," the *servus* said. "Administrator. This is Tolya Mkenni, my lifepartner and head of research on the Project." She could hear the capitalization on the name.

Tolya gave a half-bow; she smelled a little nervous, and her pupils were slightly dilated. "We've been achieving interesting results, overlord, but it's an intricate question. We're thankful for one of the Race to direct us."

Gwen smiled and shook her head. She'd been a scientist of various types—she'd started in planetography, back around the time of the Final War—but was mainly a troubleshooter these days.

"I'm here primarily to assess and report," she said. "If things look promising, more personnel will be assigned."

Introductions followed. A pair of adolescents bowed and presented her with flowers, some type she wasn't familiar with, probably a local bioproduct. The blossoms had a heady scent, rather like plum brandy with a hint of cinnamon. The two who presented them were pretty as well, a boy and girl of about sixteen in white tunics.

"What pleasant youngsters," she said.

"Mine and Tolya's," said Glenr with quiet pride. "Tomin is already studying research infosystems, and Mala quantum-gravitational dynamics. They'll serve the Race well."

"I'm sure they will," Gwen said sincerely. *Servus* were short-lived and meek and biddable, but the best of them were just as intelligent as her kind, and possibly more creative. "I'll spend the rest of this evening and tomorrow resting and assimilating data."

*   *   *

Gwen knew the courier's presence in the villa marked
for her use before she saw him. Slightly to her surprise,
it was a Draka like herself; she could tell that from the
scent, sharper and harder than a *servus*'s. A youngish
man—no more than sixty or so, she judged—in War
Directorate uniform. The Directorates *were* taking this
matter seriously. He rose with the leopard gracefulness
of the Race and extended the infoplaque. It was about
the size of her thumbnail; far larger than necessary to
carry the data, but more convenient for handling.

"Service," she said.

"Glory," he replied, dropping the plaque into her
palm.

"Received," she said, and touched the corder fastened to his wrist. "I'd better get right on to it."

The man nodded grimly; his control was excellent
for someone so young, but she could sense tightly-held
fright.

"I was with the salvage crew that worked over the
platform out in the Oort," he said. "Believe me, we're
dealing with the unknown here. And I'm not entirely
sure that the enemy haven't been meddling."

Gwen nodded. Contamination of infosystems was a
perpetual threat, one of the few forms of military
action that *could* be carried out over light-years. There
was always some traffic in information between the
systems, mostly scientific. The Samothracians had always been better at infosystems, just as the Race did
more with biologicals—but the InfoWeb was the skeleton of modern civilization. The unspoken threat of
retaliation with biosabotage, or simply with asteroids
punched up to relativistic speeds, had kept anything
too obvious from happening. The potential of the
molehole projects . . . was that worth the risk of direct
action to the enemy?

Certainly. A functioning macrocosmic molehole

would break the long stalemate. The Final War might well turn out to be less final than they'd thought.

"Service to the State," she said, in the old formal mode.

He saluted, fist to chest. "Glory to the Race."

Silence fell on the villa, unbroken save for the breathing of her ghouloon in its quarters at the back; the courier must have brought it in. The transgene was asleep, but its senses were just as keen as hers, and it would wake in the extremely unlikely event of intruders. Gwen slipped the plaque into the receptor of a pocket reader; it extended a thin diadem that she dropped over her head to rest on her brows. She lay down on a couch in the lounging room and thought at her transducer:

begin.

She came aware and blinked, lifting the circlet from her brow. The data was *there*, downlinked in instants; the hours since had been spent organizing and assimilating it. The process was far from complete, but well begun. Hunger and stiffness had roused her, and the sound of the ghouloon padding in. Her mind felt overcrammed and bloated, like a stomach after a too-heavy meal.

The room was not dark to Gwen, not to eyes that could rival a cat's, and see into the infrared as well. The guardbeast rose from all fours, one hand pointing to the door; somebody was approaching. A silent snarl lifted teeth from its muzzle. Ghouloons were an early experiment, the first of the sentient transgenes. Basically a giant Gelada baboon, with material from certain breeds of dog, from the hunting cats, and from human stock for intelligence, vocal cords, and a fully opposable thumb. They made superb guardians and hunt-servants, although not bright enough to operate any but the simplest machines. Crude work by current standards, but still occasionally useful.

She listened herself, drew air through her nostrils, stretched. "No, I think I know who that is, Wulka," she said quietly. "Go back to your room."

Gwen slipped out of the blacks and underclothes and walked to the door. The villa lights came up around her automatically. The door was carved wood on hinges, local handicrafts. Tomin and Mala stood outside, bearing a bottle of wine and a hamper that smelled of food. The adolescents were wearing flower wreaths in their pale hair, and nothing else.

"We—" they began.

"I know," Gwen said, laying a finger across each pair of lips.

She savored their scent, a slight tang of apprehension and a rising involuntary excitement as they responded to her pheromones. Those strengthened in their turn as she relaxed conscious control and let her arousal blossom. Her hands trailed down to rest over their hearts, a pleasant contrast of hard curve and soft, with the same quickening beat beneath both. Their flushed and bright-eyed smiles answered her heavy-lidded one. It was a feedback cycle, self-reinforcing for all three. This should be a rare and memorable experience for them—the pleasure would be as intense as they could bear—and an enjoyable one for her after six months alone in the wilderness.

"A charming gesture," she said. And just what she needed to relax. "Do come in."

Tolya gestured at the holographic image that hung over the table and it rotated through a figure-eight.

"This is a three-dimensional representation," the physicist said. It showed something rather like an hourglass shape. "We take a molehole from the quantum foam, pump in energy to enlarge it, and stretch the ends apart. Both ends always remain fully congruent in spacetime. It's a closed timelike loop."

That was the theory, at least. You could anchor one end and whip the other out like a bead on the end of an elastic string. Something sent through one end emerged from the other without subjective duration. The side-effects were extremely odd; if one end were traveling at relativistic speeds, you got the time-dilation effect reversibly. Observed from the outside, it would take the mobile end 4.2-odd years to reach say, Alpha Centauri. But from the fixed end back at Sol, it would be a matter of weeks until the moving exit reached across the light-years. Stepping in would move you 4.2 light-years in space, and 4.2 years in *time*. So far that was only a weird amplification of ordinary high-tau interstellar travel. Seriously strange was the fact that you could step *back* through the molehole and through time; and if you sent the mobile end on a round-trip journey to the Centauri system and returned, you'd have two gates right next to each other, separated by more than eight years in time.

FTL always was considered equivalent to time-travel, Gwen mused. The surprising thing was that both seemed to be possible.

"Of course, as an object passes through, the molehole tries to pinch out—you have to feed in heavy energy to keep it from closing, a virtual-matter ring. We've achieved consistent results using slightly enlarged ones and passing subatomic particles through, down on a single-atom scale. Proof of concept; it definitely works, overlord."

"But."

The *servus* scientist sighed and ran a hand through her graying hair. "Yes. There seems to be some sort of asymptotic phenomenon that takes over when we enlarge. The energy inputs give extremely variable results, and the variability increases exponentially as size goes up. It's a chaotic effect, somehow. The theory we have says that once stabilized the molehole shouldn't do that, but obviously the theory's not everything we could wish. At a guess, I'd say that there's some sort of . . . inherent linkage to the quantum foam. There could even be advantages to that, eventually, but it's not a completely understood phenomenon. In fact, overlord, it's not even partly understood."

"What are you trying?"

"Well, we're running a series of tests; enlarging the captive molehole *without* separating the ends spatially. That ought to be easier under a relatively heavy and uniform gravitational field. We'll bring it up in size before manipulating it; still very small compared to the eventual macrocosmic applications, you understand. About on the scale of a medium-sized molecule. If we can do that, then we might be able to separate the ends later. Here's the math."

Figures replaced the holograph. Gwen let her transducer take them in, running a mental comparison with the previous attempts.

"These functions—what're you assuming?" she said after a moment, calling up a sequence of equations. "Where did you get these quantities?"

Tolya shrugged and spread her hands. "We're guessing. The experimental results should give us an order-of-magnitude answer on how wrong we are, and then we can try again. It isn't quick, I'm afraid, overlord, but—"

"—elegance buys no yams, yes," she replied, nodding approval. "Good solid rule-of-thumb work. More productive than any simulations, when the basic metrics aren't fully known. The space-based team tried to go too far too fast, in my opinion."

A heavy wash of flattered pleasure at her words scented the air; she could feel the enthusiasm like a glow around the long plain table. Her own answered it. These were obviously a first-class group.

Progress. Back in the times of the Old Domination, when the Draka and their subjects had both been archaic-human, it had been impossible to entrust work like this to the underclasses. She had seen the last of that herself, being the first generation of the New Race.

"We're running the first series now, overlord," Tolya said. "You could monitor from here."

"No, I'll come down," she said thoughtfully.

Not that looking at the casings of the machinery would give her more information than she could get here, but you never knew what prompted an intuitive leap. They crowded into the elevator, a bit of a tight press with Wulka in one corner. The *servus* crowded away from the transgene's fur, squeezing together to avoid transgressing Gwen's sphere of social space. She kept her dominance pheromones throttled down to the minimum in the crowded quarters, but it was a relief when the doors hissed open. They were a *long* way underground here. The shaft opened directly onto the centrum, with another display monitor in the center of the circular room. Around it were consoles with recliners for the attendants. They sat silently, seldom moving, controlling their instruments through transducers and the relay-circlets around their temples.

"Ready to run," one of them said aloud.

Gwen stepped to the display table. It was physically over the facility, more for symmetry's sake than anything else. Right now the graph-holos were showing standby power only. The molehole was represented by a line of white light. Her transducer was Draka class, and she slipped effortlessly into communion with the machines and their operators. It was not quite like artificial telepathy, but nearly. Tolya was directing them with crisp efficiency:

bringing it up. skip level four in thirty seconds. power on. mark.

this is the level the platform had trouble with? Gwen asked.

yes, overlord, but we've reached it before without a problem.

Gwen nodded. **proceed, cautiously.**

Seems steady enough, the physicist thought. **one more level and then stabilize and monitor.**

A technician's thought. **power overage.**

Odd. Tolya hesitated. **cut energy input, 10%.** To Gwen: **overlord, it ought to collapse in a gravity field if we take it down. pity to lose the molehole, but—**

Power overage. It's not contracting. A pause. **Loss of symmetry. the metric is varying.**

Gwen cut in. **put it on auto and evacuate.** She looked up. Tolya was staring at the console, wide-eyed. **overlord, we'll lose the facility!**

Gwen spoke aloud. "Uplink the data, realtime." Crucial to get something of value out of this. "Evacuate the settlement. And *get out!*"

Her voice took on the whipcrack of command. The others obeyed instantly, all but Tolya. The chief physicist halted for an instant in the shaft door.

"Overlord—"

"*Go.*"

Her mind grappled with the machines. *Get the data out.* The control systems were trying to shove the molehole back down into the quantum foam where it belonged, and failing. The danger was sudden, shocking, as unexpected as a grizzly heaving itself out of hibernation beneath her feet. It focused her, as nothing else had in generations. Get the scientists out; right now, they were more valuable to the Race than she was. Save the facility if she could. *That's not working.* The machines were trying to starve the molehole, but obviously the power input was coming from somewhere else. Once it rose over a tripping threshold it started expanding on its own, exponentially. Vacuum energy, perhaps.

All right, we'll try the other way. She rapped out through her transducer: **maximize containment fields.** If she couldn't starve it, see if it choked.

There was an almost-audible hum from beneath her feet. Several alarm systems began to indicate physical breaches in components; all this was taking place in a space smaller than her fist, ten meters or so below.

Well, that didn't work either. Fear now, harsh and unaccustomed. The facility was lost, and her with it if she didn't get out in time.

"Out!" she rasped, and began the leap backward that would take her into the elevator shaft.

The ghouloon reacted with an equal, animal swiftness, reaching out to grab her and add the momentum of its arm to her bound.

Blackness.

"Damnation!"

Alarms flexed through the detection instruments of the USSNF *President Douglas*. The cruiser was waiting on minimal-power standby, most of the crew in stasis units, everything heavily stealthed. The passive sensors were fully active, however.

Captain Marjorie Starns, United States of Samothrace Naval Forces, looked down at the screen again; the implants gave her the same information, with the mathematical overtones. The images of others of the active crew appeared in front of her: her executive officer, Lyle Asmundsen, and the Strategic Studies Institute honcho, Menendez.

She called up data; Earth spun before them, as if the ship were orbiting the planet, rather than nearly a tenth of a light-year beyond Pluto. A grid lay across it, and a point flashed.

"Eastern coast of North America," she said.

"Certain it was a molehole?" The spook, George Mendendez.

"Nothing else produces an event wave like that," she said. "Very brief; it cycled through its stability point, grew and collapsed. They're still working on the control—but they're getting closer. That one nearly worked. Of course, they evidently don't know what happens when you open one through a sharply-flexed spacetime matrix, but this'll give them an idea. They're not what you'd call really sharp theoretical physicists, but once you know something's possible . . ."

The intelligence agent started to shrug, then stopped and crossed himself. "Jesus," he whispered. "That's another *Earth* they broke through to."

The captain nodded jerkily. "We've got a responsibility here," she said. "Samothrace is always uninhabited, to a very high order of probability. But any other Earth . . ."

"What was the degree of displacement?" Asmundsen said.

She consulted the machines; the theoretical breakthroughs behind them were recent, but capacity had grown swiftly.

"It'll take a while to be certain, but probably timelike negative, with a vertical temporal displacement of about . . . four centuries and a lateral of six hundred—close to the minimum possible. The event-wave track's quite clear. Something went through, and it was alive when it did."

Menendez nodded. "What can we do?"

Asmundsen smiled bleakly. "We *could* put the whole ship through on that track," he said. "If we moved farther into the solar gravity well."

Starns grunted laughter. "And put up a sign, *hurrah, we're here* for the snakes. They could follow us *en masse* in a couple of weeks. Anything we put through is going to be out of precise chronophase, and the more energetic the mass put through is, the more noticeable. Once the snakes realize what's going on . . ."

"Should we do anything?" Menendez said. "Our mission priority is information. Samothrace is waiting for this data."

The naval officers exchanged glances. "We'll have to leave now anyway," Starns replied. "They're going to detect us when we run for the transit molehole back to the Centauri system." Modern drives transferred momentum between ship and cosmos directly, but the process inescapably bled energetic quanta far above the level of vacuum energy.

"That would cover a minor insertion."

"Very minor," Menendez said thoughtfully. "We've got to be careful about giving them an extra energy source to detect. If they manage to trace whoever it was they lost, it'll give them a big jump on mastering the molehole technology."

"Besides a possible bolthole when The Day arrives," Starns said. "Plus . . . well, whoever's on the other side of that molehole doesn't deserve a live snake running around."

"It might have been a *servus*, not a *drakensis*."

"Possible, but can we count on it? And even a *servus* might be able to set up some sort of beacon; they're not stupid just because they've been mind-gelded."

Menendez nodded decisively. "One agent, minimal equipment," he said. "I'll revive and brief my best operative—Lafarge."

"Sure he'll volunteer?" Starns said dubiously.

The spymaster smiled bleakly. "They all volunteered to be inserted on *our* Earth if necessary," he said. "Anything else will be a rose garden by comparison."

CHAPTER TWO

JANUARY 1, 1995 A.D.
EARTH/2.

Falling. Consciousness returned, and Gwen was falling, under gravity. Reflex snapped her hands out and
they closed on rough metal, stopping her with a jar that
clicked her teeth together. Something fell past her. She
froze, eyes wide with shock. She keyed her transducer,
but there was *nothing*, not even the location-signal from
the navsats. She was out of contact with the Web; it felt
like having two limbs amputated, or part of her brain.

Smells. The air was heavy with them, rank. Rusty
iron. Burnt hydrocarbons, enough to gag you. A stew
of chemicals, half of which she couldn't identify.
Scorched metal; there was a thin hole burnt through
the beam she held, as if by an energy weapon. The
smell of old concrete. And—

Humans.

Many humans, and *close*. Their rank feral smell
clogged her nostrils, thrumming along her nerves with
remembered terror.

It was impossible, and it cleared her head. *Don't try
to understand. React.*

She was hanging by her hands from an iron walk-way in a large dimly lit room, nearly ten meters up. Grimy skylights overhead let in a diffuse light. Enough for her eyes to see clearly, and there were IR sources down there, too. She could hear voices. The language had a tantalizing almost-familiar sound. Gwen focused on it, filtering out the rumble of background noise.

"*Who dat?*" More incomprehensible shouting.

It was English, but very far from her dialect. *Samothrace? I'm in the Alpha Centauri system?* her mind gibbered. No time for that. Not the right mix, anyhow.

Figures below her; the scent grew stronger. Enough for her to distinguish between individuals, and that they were not only *Homo sapiens sapiens* but the African subspecies, and all males. Twenty-two of them. It had been four hundred years since she winded that particular scent, but perfect memory was her heritage. Heads turned up, and a bright electric light. More gabble. The light speared her, a moment of pain in her dark-adapted eyes. A shout from below, as her eyes glittered in the beam, shining cold green like a cat's—the designers had used feline genes for the nightsight system.

A weapon extended at her. Some sort of slug-gun. Another gabble of voices, and one raised in command.

Gwen took a long slow breath. No time to think, only to react. She watched the muzzle train on her, hung one-handed, then drew and fired.

The crash of a plasma discharge filled the empty building with actinic blue-white light for a second, thunder echoing back from the walls. She released her grip and fell, slapping the plasma gun back into its holster as she did. *Anything can pick up a plasma discharge.* Wherever she was, she didn't want detectors tracking her. There were about twenty of the humans, all of them with those archaic slug-guns. But it would be pitch-dark to them . . .

Instead she drew the layer knife, a blade as long as her forearm and made of a sandwich of thin-film diamond between fillers of density-enhanced steel. The impossible strangers blundered about in their darkness, voices shrill with panic. Muzzle-flashes split the black, still directed upwards to where she had been. Jacketed metal pinged about, and there was a scream of pain as it struck someone.

Gwen landed, letting her weight drive her down into a crouch, then came erect. Poised. Began the movements of a dance taught her long ago, when she was first trained for war.

The Human-Killing Dance.

"What *have* we here?"

Detective Lieutenant Henry Carmaggio had seen a great deal in his two and half decades with the NYPD. This was a first, even since the posses moved into town back in the eighties.

"Christ," he said quietly.

The warehouse had been abandoned. That made it the perfect place for a big buy, in the opinion of the two groups who'd met here.

Bad mistake, he thought, holding his handkerchief over his nose. He'd helped with bloaters—bodies found in apartments and whatever, some several weeks ripe—back in his uniform days. This was different, and worse, even though the . . . slaughter . . . couldn't have been more than six hours ago. It smelled like his uncle's butcher shop on East Houston back when he was a kid, only worse; his uncle would never have allowed brains to spill on the floor, or the heavy shit-stink that underlay the blood. He could identify cordite as well.

There were at least twenty bodies under plastic sheets, the basics of photography and sketching already completed—this looked like one of the times you weren't certain how many exactly until you put all the parts back together. Spent brass sparkled under the temporary lights. Everyone was here, but for once nobody who shouldn't be was walking around the crime site. Not quite everyone: the media ghouls and the brass weren't out in force quite yet. They would be soon, of course. Even in New York, this sort of multiple homicide didn't happen every day.

"Henry, we've got something very fucking *odd* here," the corpse-robber said. *Excuse me. Medical Examiner.* The Insidious Dr. Chen herself. This crime scene was getting the full bells-and-whistles treatment.

He turned to her with a grunt; Mary Chen was a small woman, Chinese. Didn't usually use the f-word much. There had been a time, when he was new to Homicide, when he'd felt a prickle of interest at an unusual case. Now he just felt a sort of anticipatory tiredness. The ordinary ones were bad enough, and far too numerous.

"Take a look at this."

She pulled a plastic sheet back. Carmaggio squatted, shifting his styrofoam coffee cup to his left hand, and gave a soundless whistle. He put the handkerchief back to his face.

"What happened to *him*?" Whatever it was, it'd opened up his skull and left nothing much above the eyebrows. There was a heavy cooked smell, and the inside of the empty brainpan was boiled-looking. "Some sort of exploding bullet?" Damn, the punks always got the latest.

"Whatever it was, it splattered his brain and bits of his skull for twenty feet around," she said. "Charred or parboiled. In fact, it cauterized the veins. Notice how there's not much blood around him? But this is the easy one. He was definitely shot with something; there's an entry hole just over his eyebrows."

She walked to the next, her feet making little *tack* sounds as the congealing blood on the bottoms of her shoes stuck to the concrete. That reminded Carmaggio, and he pulled on a pair of thin-film gloves. No sense taking chances. Christ, he remembered when only the live ones could kill you.

"Plenty of blood with *this*," he said.

"Tell me. Glad I didn't have breakfast."

It took something to make Chen admit that. Something had sliced neatly through this one's throat all the way to the spine, and halfway through that. The head lay at an acute angle to the body, and the body in an immense pool of brown-red, still liquid under the crust.

"Look. The edges are awfully neat."

"Machete," Henry said. "Good sharp machete, strong swing."

"Maybe. Look at this one."

Another body. This time one arm was off, sliced at the shoulder.

"Awfully sharp machete, wouldn't you say?" She led him to another. "There are four or five similar to this one."

The dead man's head looked distorted, as if the side of the skull above the ear had been dished in.

"Sledgehammer?" Henry said.

The examiner shook her head, touching the area with a metal probe. It gave with a mushy softness. "Area of impact's too big," she said. "About palm-size. Whatever it was, it was traveling fast enough to turn the bone there to gravel, like slapping them up alongside the head with a board, *really* hard.

"And here's our prize," she went on.

"Marley Man," Carmaggio said. *Well, there's one case we'll never have to close.*

"Surprised you recognize him." The tall, thin black man's face was a pulped mass, like a redbrown flower surrounded by dreadlock petals.

"It's the gold beads on the ends of his dreads," he replied. "What got him?"

"A fist."

Henry snorted.

"All right, a fist-sized metal forging on the end of a pneumatic piston," she said. "Look at it." She indicated points with the stylus. "Knuckles. Same on a couple of the others."

He noticed one of the specialists examining the body's hand. "Got something?"

"Skin and hair under the nails," the man replied.

"Good." *Very* good, these days. As good as a fingerprint, sometimes.

He looked around at the carnage, outside at the blinking lights and uniforms putting up yellow tape. "These folks *definitely* lost the War on Drugs. Okay, how many gunshot fatalities?" His voice sounded a little hollow in the huge dim echoing space of the warehouse.

"None."

"Say *what?*"

He nodded at the spent brass and the weapons being photoed and bagged up. The usual mix—cheap stuff, those cheesy Tech-9's, some Glocks, a MAC-10, two Calicos, one expensive H&K 9mm which had better stay in the evidence room.

"Some bullet wounds, but none of them fatal. Ricochets. These guys were shooting, but not at each other. And not for long."

"Well, I guess that proves the NRA's right; it really *isn't* guns that kill people," Henry said. "Maniacs with machetes and baseball bats kill people. Even when the people are killer posse Jamaicans armed to their gold-capped teeth."

He turned to his assistant, Jesus Rodriguez, and indicated the guns and packaged drugs being dusted for prints and carefully packed away.

"What's wrong with this picture?"

"*Sí*. No money. But I didn't think the perps would leave it."

"Yeah, but why leave the *stuff*, man? It's all here, samples, bags, vials, you name it. They had a god-damned *supermarket* going, even some Ecstasy like they expected passing Euroweenies, but nothing's missing. Just the money."

Mary Chen smiled. Henry didn't like the expression—and he suspected she didn't like him. The feeling was mutual, but she could do her job.

"Couple of the bodies show heel marks, usually to the back of the head. Coup de grâce. And I saved the best for last." She turned her head to one of her own team: "Tag, bag and ship. Let's get the meat back to the shop and get some details."

They walked over to a table. "Here it is," she said, and uncovered it with a gesture a little like a maître d'hotel whipping the cover off a dish.

Henry stared, fumbling in his jacket for his cigarettes and then remembering he'd quit. It was an arm, detached at the shoulder. Naked, except for reddish . . . fur, fur with darker spots. Thick, dense fur running all the way down to the knuckles. The palm was black and heavily callused. The arm was about the same size as Henry Carmaggio's leg, and he was six feet and weighed two hundred pounds. The detective prodded cautiously at the limb with a gloved finger, then manipulated the joints. Unmistakably meat, the real thing. Fresh, too.

"Chen," he said, after a minute's silence. "I'm going to assume you didn't go down to the zoo and kill a gorilla to play a practical joke on me."

"It's not a gorilla," she said. "Look—the thumb structure's human. Fully opposable." She took the giant hand in both of her tiny ones and touched the thumb to each fingertip. He sensed tightly-controlled fear in the forensics expert. Just like him.

"So it's a baboon. One of those sinsemilla growers out on the West Coast had a Bengal tiger as a watchdog.

The Animal Rights woo-woos sued the DEA cowboys who shot it when they raided his place—read about it in the *Post*."

"It's not a baboon either," Chen said. "Wrong shape, too big, and they don't have spots. Did a giant, spotted, one-armed baboon go running out of here between one and four this morning?"

"Who'd notice, in this neighborhood?" Rodriguez said.

Clinton's not actually that bad an area, Carmaggio thought. Even if it had been known as Hell's Kitchen once. Most of it positively yuppified, except for the odd pocket of squalor like the warehouse. A couple of years and this would probably be boutiques.

"They took long enough to call us about this firefight," he replied. A glance down at his notepad: "Nothing, then a very loud noise—sounded like thunder, or an explosion—another loud noise like thunder but not as loud, a flash of light—hey, maybe a concussion grenade—then lots of gunfire."

Henry Carmaggio had seen a great deal in his forty-five years. In a way, it was reassuring that things could still surprise him.

"Chen," he said heavily, "I'm not going to go to the Captain with a report that Marley Man's posse was wasted by giant spotted baboons." He remembered the first body. "Giant spotted baboons with ray guns. And for Christ's sake, keep this goddamned arm under cover until we have something to say—you can imagine what the media would do with it, and not just the *Enquirer*."

"All right. I'll have to talk to your lab people: we'll need serious help, maybe consult someone at the university."

"As long as it's quiet. I want to retire, but not next week to someplace with compulsory medication."

"That," Chen said, "is *your* problem. You're the one

who has to write up the site report." Then in a dead-flat tone: "I'm going to do my best on this, Henry. I really am."

Gwen finished vomiting into the stained toilet and staggered erect, taking a deep breath. Control clamped down again. Letting fear-nausea overwhelm her had been stupid, a waste of calories she might not be able to replace at once. She flushed, after a moment's puzzling out the control, then climbed into the shower. Her blacks washed free easily, memory-molecule fabric snapping back to freshness. Then she stripped and began the more difficult task of getting skin and hair and nails free of the blood. The gouges along her neck where the last one had grabbed at her were already healing. Alternating cold and hot water helped bring her back to alertness; it wasn't really possible for her to go into shock, but she'd come as close as her biology allowed. Besides that, she had the slightly flushed sensation that meant her immune system and panspecifics were eliminating a number of unfamiliar bacteria and viruses.

Only one shot had hit her, in the thigh muscle. The molecular-web armor under her skin had caught most of the impact, leaving the slug a lump between the subcutaneous fat and the muscle. She probed carefully with a pair of nail scissors from the medicine cabinet, gritting her teeth against the sting. She could will the pain away, of course, but it was unwise to do that except in an emergency.

Pain was a valuable teacher; the universe whispered to you in pleasure, talked to you in reason, but with pain, it shouted.

The twisted lump came free and she pressed the lips of the small wound back together long enough for the clotting to seal it, testing the leg. *Full function.* Then she brought the spent bullet up and looked, tasted.

Jacketed lead alloy, she decided. *Quaint.* That type had gone out of use about the time she was born, in the 1970s, replaced with prefragmented synthetic crystal. The slug was coated with some sort of long-chain polymer and tipped with tungsten; that and the pointblank range were why it had got through her blacks.

She tossed it aside and walked back into the living room, picked up the body of the shabby apartment's owner and dropped it behind the couch. The stink was one more minor annoyance in the foul air of the place. She gathered up the . . . newspapers, that was the word . . . and went into the kitchen cubicle. Most of the food in the cooling unit was repulsive, but she'd eaten worse in her time, and *Homo drakensis'* digestive system could handle anything organic. Methodically, she stoked herself, starting with the two liters of milk and loaf-and-a-half of bread. She read.

New York City. 1995. She felt her skin roughening, and forced blood into the capillaries. Four years before the start of the Final War; according to that date, she ought to be on board a cruiser orbiting Titan. And less than twenty years old. Her eyes scanned in a flicker, taking a long ten to twenty seconds per page. The written language was much closer to her own than what she'd heard of the spoken form, but still a struggle.

I was right. This isn't my *1995.*

Which was almost a relief; *her* New York City had been destroyed by multiple fusion-bomb hits in the opening minutes of the War. The newspapers showed her a world so alien, so full of assumptions she didn't know, that they were mostly incomprehensible. The "Many Worlds" hypothesis must be literally true; every collapsing of a quantum wave front produced all possible outcomes. This was a world whose history followed a different track.

There are hundreds *of separate nations here.*

In her history, there had been only two by the last

decade of the twentieth century. *The Domination . . . the Domination doesn't exist at all.* The people who'd given birth to the New Race had never been. Her mother had never been, her human mother, nor the womb-mother brooder who'd borne the egg. Her own children and grandchildren and great-grandchildren would never be born. Her whole species didn't exist.

Her stomach knotted again. *No.* Reverse peristalsis wasn't going to do her any good at all.

Nothing is going to do any good. She was exiled as no one in all history had ever been exiled. She was the only one of her kind in the entire *universe*.

"No," she said aloud. "The world's still there; the Domination's still there. It's just not *here*."

And any transfer process had to be reversible, at least in theory. If the local humans didn't kill her, she was going to live a long, long time—with the last retrofit, indefinitely, the geneticists said. There was no hurry. The thought calmed her.

The plastic box on the counter rang. Gwen reached out and pulled the cord from the wall. It was early in the morning, long before dawn, but that ring meant she couldn't stay here even a few hours. Somebody might come and look if there was no answer, and she couldn't stop and fight battles with the ferals.

Damn. It would be several days before she *had* to sleep, but she was tired already. She finished off the bowl of noodles and started in on a boxed cake, revoltingly sweet but useful calories. Her fingers cracked open the plastic sheeting and exposed the insides of the telephone. She peeled back the insulation on the cord with a thumbnail.

Braided copper wire. They might or might not use opticals here, then. Magnetic coil bell inside the phone. Some sort of integrated control circuit. Relays for the control buttons. Primitive, and not a technology that had ever been used in the history she learned. She

disassembled the hand unit with the microphone and
speaker. More magnetic resonance. That gave her an
idea. Gwen bent, stuck a hand beneath the cooling unit
and lifted it around. S-curves of tubing ran up the back;
an electrically powered compressor unit beneath them.
She snapped one of the coils, and sniffed. Freon. A
compression-expansion heat pump system, second-
century B.F.S. stuff—nineteenth century, using the old
system. Not very efficient insulation, either. Her eyes
narrowed, moving around the apartment.

It was small, very shabby, and she could hear the
scuttle of cockroaches around the baseboards. Her hand
snapped out and caught one between thumb and forefinger. *Exactly the same as ours.* Not surprising; cockroaches were a very stable species. *So; this was how
this society's, this United States', poor lived.* It must
be a fully industrialized economy; there was a video
entertainment unit, plenty of food in the cooler, running water. The living standard was comparable to what
most of the Domination's subject-races had had at this
date in her history. Less hygienic than her ancestors
would have tolerated, and the food would be violently
unhealthy from what she remembered of *Homo
sapiens*'s nutritional needs, too much fat and sodium,
but there were more durable goods than you'd expect.
Thoughtfully, she pulled the video unit's cable out of
the wall and skinned it.

Ah, optical fiber. Quite new, too, much more recent
than the building. She pulled the back panel out.
Cathode ray tube. Another machine produced audio
from hand-sized disks. She disassembled it. *Optical
storage but in digital form.* Another technology not
used in her world's past in precisely that way. *And they
have coherent-light emitters.* Her history had developed
those as weapons first. She traced its controls and put
a disk on for an instant, then shut it off with a wince;
that was noise, not music.

A continuous rumble of traffic noise came from the streets outside the five-story brick building. She walked to the windows, feeling the numbness fading a little from her mind as she went from flight to investigation. Much taller buildings showed in the middle distance, glittering through the darkness, casting pillars of wavy-looking heat into the night. The stink of burnt petroleum was heavy; these people used internal-combustion engines for surface vehicles. Very odd. Lights went by overhead; she leaned out and filtered sound to catch the engines.

Turbines. Combustion engines again, but that type *was* part of her past. She looked up. None of the habitats, satellites, innumerable artificial lights that would have shown; just stars, through light-haze heavy enough to hide most of them from human eyes. The new moon showed only darkness on its shadowed side, none of the jewel-lights of domed crater-cities.

Strange, Gwen thought. *They have optical fibers and coherent-light, but not enough space activity to notice.*

"Well."

The apartment yielded little more of use; the owner's wallet confirmed that identity documents were many and evidently essential to everyday life. She had several sets from the warehouse, but they'd be useless—whatever passed for a Security organization here would be watching for them. Some clothes that might be handy. A little more of the currency, but she already had a large bag stuffed with that. Thoughtfully she transferred it to a zippered carryall she found in a closet; the original was rather heavily bloodstained. So was the top layer of . . . *100 dollar bills*; she discarded those, too.

"I will need a base. I've got to learn my way around here, and not be conspicuous while I do it. I'll need help."

A quick inventory of her assets. The currency. Her

plasma gun, layer knife, and belt unit, tucked in with the money. Too conspicuous here; evidently the locals didn't carry weapons on the street. One set of walking blacks, one set of underwear, one pair of boots. The transducer in the mastoid bone behind her ear; useless for connection to a nonexistent Web, but it also held the basic memory-store and comp functions linked to her brain. Without that, she *would* be crippled. Luckily it was quasi-organic, powered from her bloodstream and self-repairing.

And herself. One four-hundred-sixty-year old Draka female, capable of passing for human if nobody did a scan on her body, capable of a good deal else these humans would have trouble imagining.

Myself most of all. She went to the window she'd used to gain entrance half an hour ago and bared her teeth at the world.

Time to go hunting.

"It's Puerto Rican beer," Jesus Rodriguez explained. "That Anglo stuff, it loses something on its way through the horse's kidneys, *patrón.*"

Henry grunted and lifted his own Coors. There wasn't all that much noise in the cop bar at this late hour—some, since they were mostly shift workers, after all. A fair haze of cigarette smoke, which made him itch for one himself. He took another swallow of the beer and a handful of salted peanuts. The percentage of smokers in the force was a lot higher than in the general population, just like the share of messy divorces and alkies. It came with spending your life staring up society's anus.

I really should go home. There ought to be half a pizza in the refrigerator, if it hadn't gotten moldy. His stomach turned slightly. The death stats on divorced men were probably caused by stuff like that; men just had too high a squalor tolerance to live well on their own. What was it Angela had said about him, back in his bachelor days?

"Men don't live like human beings. You live like bears with furniture."

"What?"

"Something my ex-wife said," Henry replied, and repeated it. It was only six months since the papers had come through, but he could joke about it now.

Jesus shook his head, grinning; but then, he was a newlywed with a kid on the way. *Thank God Angela never wanted kids,* he thought. Carmaggio had, but he'd never pressed it—something for which he was now profoundly grateful.

"You should find a good woman," Jesus said.

"The only women I meet are cops, suspects, relatives of the deceased, or in body bags. Or waiting tables." The waitress came by and collected their empties. "Hey, Myrtle—Jesus says I should meet a good woman. What about it?"

Myrtle looked at him and started laughing; the chuckles faded across the room as she walked away. They redoubled when she got behind the bar and told her friends . . .

Thanks, partner, Carmaggio thought sourly.

"Could be worse. Think of the ones you'd be meeting on the beat, or in Vice." Jesus prodded at the heap of newspapers on the table, covered with dark rings from bottles.

"How does it feel to be famous?" he said, admiring one shot of himself.

"If I catch you on *Good Morning America,* your ass is grass," Carmaggio said. "Plus those vultures will eat your liver. And watch what happens when we don't catch the perp. Even the ordinary civilians will decide we're not heroes anymore."

"Don't be negative, *patrón.* I still think two of Marley Man's boys got away. If we catch them . . ."

" . . . we'll have two ganja-soaked goons who shot each other in the dark and ran like hell," Carmaggio said, belching. He picked up a newspaper. *"Vigilante Killer Strikes?* Christ, where do these people get their ideas, the Sci-Fi Channel?"

The other detective shrugged and moved his chin toward the TV set over the bar. The words were inaudible, but they both knew what the carefully-tousled reporter was saying. Mostly that nobody knew anything about the Warehouse Massacre.

"And by now those two punks have probably decided that Martians are moving in on the crack trade."

Jesus shrugged. They also both knew that there was nothing more unreliable than the eyewitness testimony of the untrained. Particularly if the witness had any time to think about what had happened; people could do things to their memories that Hollywood FX masters and film-editors could only dream about.

"They might know something," Jesus pointed out gently.

Henry smiled back. *Getting old. Getting pessimistic.* Had he ever been that bright-eyed and bushytailed? *Not since I landed in Saigon,* he decided. Mind you, that had its advantages. Even police work in New York couldn't be worse than the Cambodian border.

He hoped.

"Well, this case sure as shit isn't going to go away. No matter how much the Captain burns our ass. Not that he'll stop trying; too much pressure from on high."

The policemen nodded somberly in unison and finished their beers. No doubt about *that.*

"Maybe I should have kept that promise to God and become a priest," Carmaggio said.

"¿Qué es?"

Henry shrugged.

He'd gone out the door of the chopper fifty feet up, when the burst went ptank-ptank *down the length of*

*the tail boom and blew three holes through the man
next to him. Out without knowing it happened, until
he hit mud that was deep and clinging. He landed on
his back, so he didn't drown like a lot of the grunts
pinned down that day, but it ran into the corners of
his mouth. Stunned like an ox in the slaughterhouse by
the fall, spitting out a taste of oily rot, bleeding from
a pressure-cut on his scalp where the helmet had struck.
The reeds closed above him, the friendly reeds, four feet
tall in the marsh. Hiding him from the gook snipers
in the trees.*

*The helicopter augered in a hundred yards away,
men hanging from the skids. He could feel the heat of
the explosion as the fuel went up, like sun on his face.
When the .51-caliber machine guns opened up from the
treeline, the slugs went by six inches from his face, and
each cut reed had a perfect semicircle of glowing red
at the severed end—just like touching a lighted cigarette to a piece of Kleenex.*

*Intelligence thought there was one VC company in
the woods. Fucked up, as usual. Two fucking battalions
of NVA.*

*Four hours until the fast-movers came in and laid
snake and nape, two hours before the next wave
coptered in. Victor Charlie moving through the reeds,
singsong gook talk, shots and screams as they finished
off the American wounded. Lying waiting for a coo-
lie hat and a Kalashnikov to show over the reeds,
waiting and praying and promising God . . .*

"De nada," he said. "Let's get you back to your new
wife."

There were some things you just couldn't talk about
to anyone who hadn't been there.

CHAPTER THREE

"Detective, can you confirm that this is the work of the Warehouse Massacre killer?"

The reporter thrust a microphone at Carmaggio's face. *How would you like that up your ass?* he thought, squinting into the lights. He knew that made him look like an Italian Neanderthal, but pretty wasn't his long suit.

"We're investigating all possible leads," he said politely. The words were polite, at least. "You'll be informed as soon as we have definite information."

So you can blab it to the perp and help him get away, he added to himself, cutting through the crowd outside the tenement with an expert shoulder-first motion. Fortunately, the uniforms were keeping civilians and the press out of the actual building, although tenants were already being interviewed in front of the cameras on the sidewalk outside. None of them would know anything, but that wouldn't stop the Fourth Estate from doing their usual thorough job of misrepresentation, bias, groundless speculation and general farting around.

A detective saw a lot of crime scenes; the trip up the stairs was like a journey down memory lane. At first glance this one looked more like the general run than the warehouse had. Henry Carmaggio ducked through the yellow tape and through the door, hands carefully in his pockets. The slum apartment could have been dozens he'd seen. Even the smell was familiar, and not too bad—the window had been open for the whole ten days or so since the killing, in cold weather. The stale grease was actually worse.

Jesus Rodriguez met him, wearing one of the new eye-videos, mounted on a headband with a recording unit. *Toys*, Carmaggio thought.

The medical examiner's people were bagging the body, not Chen herself this time—a singleton didn't rate it. One of them looked up:

"Kick to the sternum, kick to the back of the head. The heelmarks match with the warehouse."

Carmaggio nodded. *Details follow at 11:00.* "Try not to—" he began, then thought better of it. "When the press ask, tell 'em space aliens did it. Or Elvis. Better still, tell 'em space aliens *pregnant* by Elvis did it as a Satanic ritual."

The examiner grinned as Carmaggio turned away. Jesus took him to the window. It was going dark outside, cold and clear.

The window was an ordinary sash type, with a protective grate of half-inch iron bars, overlooking a four-story drop to an alley, with a flat roof opposite. Two of the bars had been pulled out of their settings; nothing fancy, a simple straight pull. There was blood on the other bars, where somebody had squeezed past; Carmaggio was willing to bet the blood was second-hand. The lock on the window had been snapped, and the window left open. There was a heelprint on the windowsill; one of the Ident crew was photographing it and setting out scraper and plastic baggie.

"Blood?" Carmaggio asked.

"Yep. Mud as well."

A blood spray and another large irregular stain marked the worn carpet. Carmaggio looked at the location, then back at the window.

"Somebody climbed up the wall, pulled out the bars, and opened the window—breaking the lock in the process. When the owner came over, the perp kicked him in the chest, then in the back of the head while he was lying on the floor. Then moved him, a few minutes later."

"Yeah, but Lieutenant—I think . . ."

"What?"

"I think that was just to get him out of the way."

He nodded, and walked into the tiny bathroom. There was a sludge of dark brown in the bathtub, and marks on the walls and floor.

"Messy. Didn't use the curtain." The tests would take a while, but he was morally certain the blood would match with the warehouse samples. Anyone who cut up twenty men was going to be coated with the stuff.

A chalk X marked a spot near the toilet. Rodriguez held up an evidence bag. "Bingo," he said.

Carmaggio examined it carefully. "Nine-millimeter Talon," he said. "One gets you ten ballistics show it's from a posse gun. Looks like it hit a flak vest."

Rodriguez held up another plastic bag, this one with a pair of cheap nail scissors. "I think this was what the perp used to extract it," he said. "Quite the surgeon, sí?"

They moved to the kitchen. Papers were spread on the rickety deal table with its red-and-white checked plastic tablecloth, along with empty tins and a milk carton. Plus a scattering of one-hundred dollar bills. Ident squad officers were picking them up with tweezers and dropping them in baggies.

"Then the perp sat and read the newspapers, ate everything in the fridge—*everything*—tore apart the phone, the TV and the CD player, lifted the fridge around and broke off one of the coils, got rid of the grubby soiled part of the money from the warehouse, and left."

"And they broke off the key in the lock when they went, too. Left the window open, as well."

Carmaggio looked over at the windowsill. "No, they had the window open all the time they were here. Maybe it's an Eskimo."

"That's Inuit."

"Whatever. Anything from the neighbors?"

"Nothing. The lady next door called it, she noticed the smell." Jesus flipped open his notebook. "Maria Sanchez. Victim's name was Antonio Salazar, custodial worker, thirty-eight, single. Minor record, public intox, possession, that stuff—one step up from the steam-grate crowd. Looks like he was here about ten days before anyone noticed."

"Which would put this about the same time as the warehouse," the detective said. *Nobody notices when a janitor doesn't show up.* They'd assume he was on a bender, or something. Either the perp was very smart, or they'd lucked out in their choice of victim.

"More or less, *patrón*."

Carmaggio grunted. *Don't let what you want to be true cover your eyes.* Still, the MO was suspiciously alike—and the bizarre aspects were pushing his coincidence button.

"So," he said. "Twenty posse drug-dealers, and one anonymous janitor. Motive?"

"Dropped in for a wash and a snack," Rodriguez said, tapping the empty milk carton with his ballpoint.

"I think you may be right—a snack and somewhere to hide for a few hours. The distances are right."

Carmaggio turned slowly on his heel, looking over the little roach-trap. *Shitty place to die.* Probably an even shittier place to *live*, come to that, but that wasn't his department.

A slow burn of anger started at the back of his throat, unexpected and unfamiliar. Marley Man was no loss; and face it, Antonio Salazar was a complete loser who'd've ended up on a slab someday in the not-too-distant future. Probably put there himself with a needle; he was the old-fashioned kind and Dame Horse came with a dark rider these days. It wasn't even that the killings had been casual, probably motiveless. He saw plenty of those. It was . . . *like Uncle Luigi and the rabbits,* he realized.

He'd been seven when that happened. Going over to his uncle's, and the old guy had been killing rabbits. Big hutch full of rabbits, and Luigi standing by it in his undershirt, belly hanging over his pants, suspenders dangling, a burnt-out cigarette hanging off his lower lip. Luigi was a bricklayer, and he had hands like baseball mitts. Big beefy arms, fat but with lots of muscle underneath. The big hand went down into the cage and *wham* a rabbit came up in it, kicking and squealing and dropping black round pellets of rabbit shit. Eyes bugged out. Then Uncle Luigi sort of wrung it with fingers and thumb—a quick cracking sound, and it kicked and went limp. A toss, and it went onto the table with the others, next to the little curved knife.

Carmaggio had still been screaming when Uncle Luigi got him home. Dad gave him the belt and sent him to his room, but he wouldn't eat the stew anyway.

The perp here was killing the way Uncle Luigi did the rabbits.

The force of his own rage surprised him; and it was mixed with something else, something much more commonplace.

Fear.

"We're going to hear from this fucker again," he said quietly.

Jesus took the videocam rig off his head and looked

down, snapping the cassette out of the machine. "*Sí*. I've got that feeling too."

Stephen Fischer woke to the sound of a quiet, burring clicking sound. His bedroom was dark and the air still, smelling of incense and a sexual musk.

Jesus, what a lay! he thought blurrily. *What an experience.*

He felt too heavy to move anything more than his eyelids, to do anything but breathe. *I'd always thought "drained" was a figure of speech,* he thought.

Eerie. He'd been sitting quietly with a beer, not even trying for a pickup. Better not to try right after a breakup; girls could sense it if you were too needy. It was late, nobody there, and he hadn't been in the place for two years, not since he married.

He'd noticed her the minute she came in. Black tracksuits weren't the usual dress for the after-work crowd on the Street, even at Fernways, which catered to the younger up-and-coming set—although the suit had a sort of shimmery quality to it up close. She'd come in with a draft of cold air . . .

That's odd. She must have been freezing in that stuff out on the street in January.

. . . come in with a nylon duffel bag in her hand, and given the place a once-over. God, those eyes. Big and green, in the dark aquiline face. Model looks, model walk. And she'd come over to *his* booth, just slid right in.

"Order food," she said.

And slid a hundred-dollar bill onto the table. The accent had floored him as much as the money. A German trying to sound like Scarlett O'Hara might have sounded that way, but it was thick enough to be barely comprehensible. Voice soft and deep, like velvet.

Fischer blinked at her. *This doesn't happen to guys*

on the Equities Desk, he thought. In fact, he doubted it happened to anyone outside the movies.

The booth was dim, only a single candle burning on it. The underlight brought out the sculpted angles of her face; model looks, but not the neowaif type. She was dark enough to be a Latina, but the eyes were bright green and the mahogany red of her hair looked genuine.

"Ah, I'm Stephen Fischer," he said.

There seemed to be a lump in his throat, making it a little difficult to talk. That wasn't the only lump, either. He wavered between annoyance—he'd been out of his teens for a decade and a half—and delight. There'd been nothing since the divorce and not much for the year before it.

"Gwendolyn Ingolfsson," she said. For a moment she stared at his extended hand and then took it. That was another surprise; her hand was hard, like smooth articulated wood. A jock's hand. The nails were trimmed very close.

"Would you like to join me for dinner?" he said.

"Yes."

Silence fell for a moment. A waiter came over with another place-setting and a menu; her head tracked him smoothly, then turned back to Fischer.

"What would you like?" he went on, trying not to burble and feeling sweat break out under his collar. *And I'm goddamned nervous too.* Events were out of control, and normally he didn't like that. *To hell with control.*

"I'm hungry. Several dishes."

The green eyes bored into his. He called the waiter over, ran down the menu; Fernways had a small selection, but it was all good. Food arrived; the woman—Gwendolyn, odd name—began to eat, neatly but enormously. His eyes widened. She was not gaunt, but the figure under the loose fabric was obviously the product of heavy exercise club investment, real sweat equity. How could she eat like this?

She looked up from finishing off her twelve-ounce porterhouse. "Tell me about yourself," she said; the accent seemed a little less notable.

Fischer loosened his tie and talked; through the dinner, through dessert—she had two—through coffee and brandy. Somehow he never got around to asking the questions, beyond "New in town?" and "Where are you from?" Clipped answers: "Yes" and "Born in Italy."

"So," he said at last, trying desperately not to squeak. "Would you like a nightcap? At, ah, at my place?"

She smiled, showing very white teeth. "Yes."

Christ, I may never move again. She'd taken his hand the minute they walked into the little studio apartment and led him straight to the bed. Naked she didn't look like a model; more like an Olympic pent-athlete, if they'd come in a non-flat-chested variety. His memory blurred into impossibilities.

I couldn't *have done all that.*

She wasn't in the bed. He could tell it by the feel, even before he saw the light of his computer monitor on. That was the clicking sound, the keyboard.

It was a moment before what he was watching made any sense. Gwen was sitting, eyes glued to the screen; it was logged on to the Internet. Text was scrolling by at far above reading speed through his 28.8 modem. Her hands poised over the keys; every few seconds they would strike in a blur of speed, too fast for him to see individual keystrokes at all. And not loudly, a precise controlled tapping giving exactly as much force as needed. There was an encyclopedia open on the desk beside the machine. When the high-speed modem was exchanging data, she flipped through the pages. No, stared at each page for about three seconds, then flipped it over.

She's reading. The conviction hit him like cold water, and he gasped. Her head turned slightly. He gasped again when she rose and turned to face him.

"You've been watching me, Stephen," she said . . . sadly?

The accent was much less noticeable now. She walked over to the bed, barely visible in the faint blue glow of the monitor.

"I'm sorry you did that."

"What . . . look, what the *hell* were you doing with my computer?"

"Stephen, when do you expect someone to call?"

He blinked in bewilderment. His stomach lurched.

"Call?"

"Call you here."

"Maybe nobody this weekend. Come off it, I want some answers."

She put out a hand—

Gwen finished flushing the soiled sheet down the toilet in pieces of suitable size, then looked thoughtfully at the body hanging by its heels from the shower head, draining.

No, it wouldn't fit—even butchered. And the spirit of chaos alone knew what would happen if she blocked the drains. She walked out into the kitchenette and took a quick look inside the refrigerator.

Yes. If she put all the food on the counter, then disarticulated the limbs, the whole body should fit nicely, with the head in the freezer. At maximum refrigeration, it would be some time before the smell became obvious to humans. *Let's see, skull, torso, each limb in two sections*, she decided, and went to work with a regretful sigh.

"I'll have to be more subtle," she reproached herself, as she finished packing the refrigerator. "I can't go on leaving a trail like this."

Besides, Stephen had been . . . yes, sweet. Killing him had been almost as unpleasant as putting down a *servus*. She hadn't taken pleasure from a human since her youth, back when they'd been common, before the modified type completely superseded them. Interesting. Stephen might have been very useful, too, if she hadn't been careless. Too risky once he'd become suspicious, though. Wild humans were very difficult to condition properly; it would take weeks of work before she could be sure of one. A *servus*'s emotions could be played like a violin, and of course they were raised to accept the Draka. Humans varied wildly, and at best their susceptibility to pheromonal controls was spotty.

The problem was that she was simply not used to pretense. Unlearning habits as ingrained as hers wasn't going to be easy, even with survival at stake. She'd have to *understand* the humans here, not just their nature but their culture.

Gwen fixed herself a snack of raw vegetables and cold cuts and took the plate back into the bedroom. She would eat the perishables first, then the canned goods; that ought to last her for a few days. Throttling back on her metabolism was possible, but it made her sluggish and couldn't be reversed immediately in an emergency when she needed burst speed and strength. Nothing came free; her system was packed with extra capacities and they all required fuel. There was always the dead human, of course . . . *But no.* Granted that it wasn't exactly cannibalism, she'd still have to be considerably more rushed before thinking seriously about that. There were plenty of food vendors about, if she was cautious.

Stephen Fischer had kept very complete records of his life on the little perscomp. Between that and the print books and the CD-ROMs, and what she could access from this *net*, the weekend should be far from wasted. By its end she should know better how to judge when someone would show up to investigate, in plenty of time to move along. With luck, she might be able to stay here a week or so.

A permanent nest would be more difficult. *I'm going to need a front*, she knew. *Subtle. Be more subtle next time.*

Dr. Mary Chen clipped the X rays to the lighted background glass. For comparison, she had a normal arm's prints next to them, and a shot of a gorilla's she'd gotten from the primatology people over at the University.

The woman beside her bent close to the film, whistling silently. "Oh, now this is really, really interesting," she said, adjusting her glasses.

The professor used a pen from her blouse pocket—she wore a plastic protector—to trace the lines of the bones.

"Look at the ratio of the radius and ulna to the upper arm," she said. "Definitely nonhuman, far too long, but it's not exactly like any of the other higher primates. And this gap here, not pongoid at all. Hmmm."

She pushed up the glasses again and peered at the film with her nose almost touching it. "From the wrist and hand, this isn't a knuckle-walker. Palm, more probably. The hand is extremely human in structure, except that the bones are more robust, but the wrist isn't like anything I've ever seen. It's almost as if it's been structurally reenforced."

"There's heavy callus on the palm," the doctor confirmed.

Pure technical interest, Chen thought. She didn't seem to see the *implications*, which had been keeping the Medical Examiner awake every night for the past three. She sipped at the cold tea in its paper cup and grimaced. Caffeine wasn't working anymore. She yawned.

"I'd say it was probably some sort of baboon," the

primatologist said. "Though the thumb structure is wrong, more like a hominid. And it's far too large; the size is more gorilloid. But it's more like a baboon than anything else I can think of."

She beamed at Chen. "Dr. Chen, do you realize what this *means*?"

She nodded jerkily.

"An entirely new species! Fascinating. And"—her voice dropped conspiratorially—"first publication."

"*No* publication until I give explicit, written authorization," she said sharply. *This woman is a complete space cadet.* "And I'll want a written release to that effect."

The academic's face dropped a little. "It'll take months even for a preliminary report anyway," she said. "Oh, all right. And you'll get full credit."

Chen nodded and turned to the cooler. The room was dark except for the lights behind the display panel; it was well after normal hours. She turned on the overheads and pulled out the long tray, unsealing the plastic wrap around the arm.

"Oh, wonderful." The scientist bent over it, pulling on surgical gloves, and clicked on a recorder. "Specimen is—"

Scary as hell, she thought, as the other woman kept on talking into the little machine. *Scary as hell.* And not just because it was so weird. There were *implants* in it. Something in the bone like embedded fibers, fibers that dulled her best bone saw; they'd had to use a metal-cutting saw, and change to a new blade every few seconds.

She waited until the preliminary examination was complete. "The next step would be genetic analysis, I'd say."

"Oh, certainly, Dr. Chen," the professor agreed. "With a comparative analysis, we can pinpoint the evolutionary divergence." She shook her head. "*Where* could a species like this have hidden itself? It must be quite large—" she stepped back and considered "—I'd say in the four- to five-hundred-pound range. Even a relict population in some out-of-the-way area . . . fascinating! Where did you say you acquired it?"

"I didn't," Chen said.

Very out of the way, she thought. *Wherever it comes from, twenty people died when it arrived.* She remembered the warehouse, its floor awash with blood. Mary Chen had never limited her training in observation and deduction strictly to her work. What followed was obvious. Something had come from somewhere, along with this arm. Something with human-sized heels, that used a knife sharper than a laser scalpel. *And if one can . . . come . . . here, then others can.*

The primatologist was speaking into her hand-held recorder again. Chen wrapped her arms around herself and shivered.

"You're not going to enjoy this," Chen's voice said. "I thought I'd give you some warning."

Carmaggio shifted his feet to the corner of his desk and looked with displeasure at the pound or so of skin hanging over his belt under the shirt. *I don't enjoy looking at that, either,* he thought, cradling the receiver, the cinnamon danish and the coffee mug simultaneously. Sure, he was past the middle forties, but that didn't mean he had to let everything go. On the other hand, regular hours were a joke in police work; and the number of donuts and greasy deli sandwiches he'd shoveled into his face made him queasy when he thought about it. He prodded at the roll with a finger. *Not too bad.* And he'd stopped smoking, after all. He tried to convince himself he'd done it for his health, and failed. It was just too much of a hassle, with all the nonsmoking areas.

I ought to spend more time in the gym. God knew it could scarcely cut into his social life.

"All right, break my heart," he said. "Start with the arm."

A long moment of silence. "I didn't have the facilities for that, so I called in a favor over at NYU."

"What do they say?"

"They don't say anything; they run in circles and throw their hands in the air and shout." Flatly: "Okay, basically it *is* a baboon. Only it's not." Unwillingly: "The DNA is congruent with Gelada baboons—mostly. Ethiopian mountain baboon, fairly rare. About fifty percent matchup. The remainder's . . . mixed. Leopard. Canine. And, ah . . . human."

Carmaggio took his feet down from the desk and sighed, rubbing his forehead and dredging up things he'd seen on nature documentaries and old copies of *Popular Science.* "Something escaped from a lab?"

"You've been watching too many bad movies. Putting a firefly gene in a tomato or correcting cystic fibrosis is one thing. Playing Frankenstein is something else. We'll do things like . . . that . . . someday, but not for a long time. Hell, the human genome project isn't finished yet."

"What about the arm, then?"

"I don't know. I just don't know."

He'd always wanted to have Chen-the-omniscient admit that. Somehow it wasn't very satisfying. "All right, let's look at this from a cop point of view. The fucking arm is academic, we'll leave it with the academic types. We're cops, let's do the cop things."

"Nothing mysterious about cause-of-death for most of the Jamaicans. It's all in the autopsy stuff I'm sending up. Loss of blood from radical wounding, consistent with a knife about eighteen inches long. Or blunt injury trauma; in plain English, crushed skulls, frontal bone driven into the brain, two cases of massive perforation of the heart and lungs by rib fragments. Several injured postmortem by a very powerful kick to back of the head—more crushed skulls, and crushed and severed upper spinals. Whoever did it was making extremely sure."

"Good work."

"That's the basics. You want to hear my opinion?"

He waited. Chen continued. "The tissue damage from the knife is as weird as the rest of it. It was *sharp*. Razor sharp, scalpel sharp. There are *cut hairs* on those bodies; it didn't haggle or chop, it just sliced through hair and skin and clothing, plus the odd gold chain. And it *stayed* that sharp while it went slamming through major bones, sharp and completely rigid. A thin blade, Henry, not a tanto knife or a machete. From the marks on the bones, about as wide as a fingernail at maximum."

"Hmmm." A real knife-fighter didn't put a razor edge on his weapon. That made it too likely to turn on bone or even gristle. Really thin blades were too whippy for use. "Keep it coming."

"The blunt injuries? It's impossible, but whoever did that stuff did it barehanded. Kicking and punching and . . . slapping. They slapped people on the side of the head and knocked their skulls in. A couple of those dreadlockers shot each other, but they didn't hit whoever was doing them enough to slow him down. We're not talking Kung Foolishness here. What with the arm, I checked up. A gorilla's about fifteen times as strong as a human being. Whoever did this is about halfway to that level. Freak strong."

Henry made an affirmative noise and nodded, taking another bite of the danish. The posses were about as bad as they thought they were. If somebody, or even a dozen somebodies, had killed twenty of them, he didn't want to meet the ones who'd done it. Not without a lot of backup.

"The one with his head blown off?"

"That's got me completely baffled. The entry wound in the forehead is cauterized, as if someone had burned through with a welding torch. Then the brain was cooked—flash cooked, the explosion was steam. There's a bit of very finely divided metallic copper there too, God knows why."

Chen paused. "Now, what about the skin from under Marley Man's nails?" she asked. A forensics question; police business, not the Medical Examiner's.

"We sent it over to Quantico." The FBI lab there did favors for local police departments. "They ran a microsatellite DNA analysis. Caucasian—Northwest European—and female. The hair's natural dark red. No DNA matches in any of the databases, but that just means she hasn't served in the armed forces or been sent to jail since the early nineties."

Carmaggio sighed. It had been the first honest—well, honestly bizarre—evidence to turn up so far. Except.

"Except?"

"They did a full comparative DNA run. It—I quote: *'Nonhuman. About a ninety-four percent correspondence. That's less like us than a chimp. A mammal, a primate, but not human, strictly speaking. Whatever it was, it couldn't interbreed with us; gross differences in the number of chromosomes.'"*

"Different? Different how?"

"I asked. They told me that we don't know what most of our *own* genes do." After a moment: "Then they told me not to send them any more practical jokes. I think the Fed was scared, Chen."

"What's going in the report?"

He took a deep breath. "We're going to tell our esteemed Chief of Detectives that a drug deal went sour and all Marley Man's posse got wasted, knife and club and gunshot wounds. Some animal remains were found at the site. We've got the DNA make on a person who might or might not have been at the crime site at the time of the murders. We're questioning all the usual suspects; if you lined up all the people who wanted Marley Man dead, it'd stretch to Jersey. Send me your stuff, I'll edit it that way, and attach it to my report."

"You're going to hush this up?"

"No, I'm going to keep my credibility and yours," he said. "Hell, it's an official report, not the Bible."

Back in Nam once, he'd been on a patrol that went into some bad bush right after an artillery fire mission. A lot of craters, a lot of busted-up trees, and one arm—still in its black pajamas—by the side of the trail. The loot had reported it in as a stepped-on kill, confirmed, and three probables. Which was fair enough, since Charlie did try to carry away as many of his dead as he could. Only he'd learned from a radioman back at the firebase that about six more patrols had reported the same arm; so that one unfortunate Vietcong had turned into about a platoon's worth of casualties. And the sucker might not have died in the first place.

Ever since then, he'd thought of definite-sounding official reports as being sort of elastic. Not necessarily completely divorced from reality, but not necessarily having any close relationship to it, either.

"Henry, we *can't* hush this up. Think of what it *means*. There could be—"

"Look, shut up, will you? The problem with unbelievable evidence is that nobody will believe it. And if we push it on people, they won't believe *us* about anything. That's twenty years of experience talking, and you *will* listen. I'm betting that whoever . . . hell, whatever . . . did this number on Marley Man's boys is going to do something else. And *I'm going to find them*."

Gwen sighed and leaned back in the lounger. She remembered more than four centuries past . . .

The fountain. It was old, Renaissance work. Much older than the plantation in the hills of Tuscany. It played in a little courtyard flagged with black and white stones, surrounded by arches borne on pillars. The central part of it was a statue of a maiden pouring the water from an amphora over one shoulder, all in age-green bronze. It fell into a round bowl of stone, the edge carved with a time-worn design of vines.

I remember.

The sun warm on her bare skin, and the slick surface of the marble under her left hand. Her right—a three-year-old's hand, still slightly chubby—dived into the cool water. The fingers flicked, a touch of scales, and a goldfish soared into the air. Gwen giggled and moved her hand. Flick, flick; more goldfish soared upwards. The fish tumbled back into the water with little plashing sounds, darting away to the other side of the pool.

"Missy Gwen, stop that."

That was her tantie-ma, Marya. Gwen turned toward her and ran, leaping up to wrap arms and legs around her. Marya braced herself against the solid impact and hugged her back. The child nestled against her, taking in the familiar comforting scent.

"Here, punkin," her mother said.

Marya handed her down, and she cuddled against the sleek warmth of her mother's side in the recliner, yawning and shifting until she was comfortable and drifted into sleep . . .

Maybe that's why I remember, Gwen thought. *The scents.* Her mother Yolande had smelled human—had *been* human, the last generation of human Draka.

That scent was heavy all about her, in Stephen Fischer's little apartment. A flash of memory: Yolande older, in uniform, the high-collared black tunic of ceremony. Standing at the top of a stairway under a dome on Mars . . .

She shook her head. *Back to work.* She frowned and made another note on the pad. It wasn't strictly necessary, of course; she had eidetic memory, and the transducer for backup. Just an old, old habit to help her see the *shape* of a sequential problem. Perhaps that was why she'd gone into reverie. Her mother had done that too, made notes.

She wrote:

1: *Identity.*

She'd need, let's see, a *birth certificate*, and then documentation from there. False documents could probably be arranged with stolen money. She made a sub-heading: *American or other?*

2: *Base of operations.*

She looked around Stephen Fischer's cramped little apartment. It was much cleaner and better furnished than the one she'd used in her first flight from the warehouse, but not all that much bigger. *Something better than this.* Fischer had evidently made a fairly high salary, but equally evidently it didn't go far here. Like most Draka, she could put up with cramped quarters at need, but didn't like it.

3: *Legitimize the money.*

That ought to be reasonably easy. Even in her own history, the Americans had been sloppy-careless about security matters right up to the end—otherwise they might not have lost the Final War. These Americans hadn't had the long struggle with the Domination to keep them on their toes, and to judge from what she'd read, they had a crime problem like nothing her world had ever seen in any major country. With a huge criminal class, there *had* to be ways of transferring profits to noncriminal organizations.

In a way, if this had to happen to someone, it was as well it was her. She could remember what a market economy with a non-notional currency was like; the Domination had had something like that back before the War, and she'd studied the American version in know-the-enemy lectures. Very long ago, but the data was still there. The freewheeling anarchy outside wasn't all that *much* like what she remembered from either case, but there were useful hints. The younger generation knew valuata as something exchanged over the Web, and rather theoretical in any case.

Legate Tamirindus, for example, would have been completely lost for a good long while.

4: Establish organization.

She chewed meditatively on a carrot. Obviously, if she was ever going to contact home again she'd need huge resources; here, that meant money. She had a lot to sell, four and a half centuries' worth of technology, only the simplest of which would be applicable at all. The problem would be to do it without attracting too much attention. That meant disguising it as commercial activity.

5: Do physics.

That would be difficult. She'd never been a pure scientist. Few Draka were. Fighters, rulers, explorers, the arts, applied science—but basic research was *servus* work, mostly. It would be hands-on for her now. Nobody here would know much physics beyond the witch-doctor level.

On the other hand she had the training, and her arrival here indicated several lines to look into. Moleholes obviously retained a quantum-indeterminate quality. With an anchor at both ends, though . . . She'd have to make the tools to make the tools, with several regressions before that, even for some sort of crude signaling device. Either it would be possible, or not; time to worry about that when it came to it.

6: Call home.

She finished the carrots and smiled. *Establish a bridgehead. Bring through a couple of orbital battle stations and launchers,* she thought, *modified for planetary bombardment.* The specs were still on file. It had been a while since the Race had an opportunity for conquest. Then the locals would be . . . what was that expression she'd read? *Ah.*

Toast.

Jennifer Feinberg cried into the pad of wadded Kleenex, threw it into the deskside wastebasket, and reached for more.

Carmaggio helpfully pushed the box under her groping hand. He looked around; a tiny cubicle of an office on the 27th floor, computer, book racks with bound tables and trade periodicals, an African violet, and a cup of cold chamomile tea on the cluttered desk beside the picture of a man in a doctor's white coat. His professional eye classified Ms. Feinberg effortlessly: early thirties, Jewish, five-five, a hundred and thirty-five pounds—she probably dieted and exercised ferociously to keep it there—economics degree from NYU. Eight years with the same securities firm, fairly rapid promotion. Father a doctor . . . A pleasant face, black hair and big brown eyes, conservative business suit, pearl earrings. Attractive in a wholesome way, if you weren't put off by brains.

Probably has a studio apartment on the Upper West Side, he thought, and checked his notebook. *Yup.* And a cat, and went to the opera fairly often, and read books Carmaggio'd never heard of. The only thing not on the to-be-expected list was the other picture on her desk; a young man in baggy olive-green BDU's, smiling, an Army-issue drab towel around his neck and a helmet under one arm. *Brother, probably.* Thin beaky face, and glasses. Not worth checking on.

"I'm sorry," she said. "I just—I *saw* him every day, and we did *lunch,* and then this happens to him . . ."

APARTMENT HORROR, he read from the *Post* on her desk. WAREHOUSE VIGILLANTES STRIKE AGAIN.

Fucking media ghouls, he thought. The anger was so old it was reflexive. The national networks had picked it up for a couple of days, which meant still *more* pressure on him. A couple of local bottom-feeders had tried to make it a racial incident too, since the first twenty-one victims were all black or Hispanic. Stephen Fischer had quieted that, at least.

Although he had to admit there was more to sensationalize than usual. It wasn't every day that a perp chopped up the body, stuffed it in the fridge, and then lived in the victim's apartment for a week, ordering in Chinese food on the victim's credit card.

Plus fucking the victim before she killed him, he reminded himself—they'd found reddish pubic hairs mixed with Fischer's, traces of his semen.

This is a bad one, he thought. Even without the space cadet parts, it was a very bad one. *We definitely haven't heard the last of Ms. Machete.* He ignored the impossible aspects. There were bodies, there was a suspect, time to wonder about that stuff when he made the collar.

"How long did you know Mr. Fischer?" he asked, when the sobs subsided.

"About two years. I didn't really *know* him. He . . . well, he was on the Equities desk, you know, and I'm in Analysis. I passed him every day coming in, talked a little, we went to lunch with some mutual friends occasionally."

"Did you know his ex-wife?"

"We met at the office Hanukkah party once. She was a lawyer—that's why they split up."

Carmaggio raised his eyebrows.

"Well, they both had seventy-hour weeks or worse," Jennifer went on. "We all do, but she was with Mikaels, Sung, Lawson & Finkelstein. She got involved with someone at her firm. Said she'd at least see him sometimes."

"Mr. Fischer wasn't, mmm, involved with anyone here? Anyone that you knew of?"

"Steve?" She blew her nose. "No, he wasn't the type. I think."

"No business problems that you knew of, enemies?"

She looked at him, surprise in her red-rimmed eyes. "In *Equities*? God, no, they don't deal with the public."

"Promotion?"

"Nothing special. His people over in Equities—"

"—would know more, yes."

"It has to be some awful psychopath, like that Dahmer or whatever his name was." She burst into fresh tears. "In the *fridge*, God."

Carmaggio sighed; for once he more or less agreed with the amateur's take on it. This was going nowhere, although you had to cover all the bases. It was a good thing that the office here didn't have all the details, or they'd be even more hysterical.

"Thank you again, Ms. Feinberg," he said. "Here's my number. If anything occurs to you, anything at all . . ."

She nodded, wiping her nose and taking the card. Carmaggio shrugged into his overcoat and left.

"*De nada*," Jesus said in the corridor, holding up his notebook. Carmaggio nodded. They were working their way steadily through everyone who'd known the victim, and accomplishing squat.

"This isn't an ex-girlfriend or the guy he beat out for the promotion," he said quietly. "Stephen Fischer just happened to be in the wrong place at the wrong time."

"At least we've got a make."

"Tall redhead in a black pantsuit, carrying a duffel bag, no positive ID on race—hell, it could be a fucking transie."

Not according to the DNA, but that had gone crazy anyhow, and he found it even more difficult to believe in a woman doing what this perp had done. And he didn't believe a man could have done it, in the first place.

He looked out the window at the driving snow, falling gray-white into the canyons of New York. Out there in his city was someone who pulled machinery apart to see how it worked, and sat at a computer running up Panix.com bills and eating egg foo yung while a body slowly rotted in the refrigerator.

Someone who killed human beings with the casual precision of a leopard in a flock of sheep.

She'd kill again, and again, until she was stopped. Henry Carmaggio hunched his shoulders and thrust his hands into the pockets of his overcoat.

"Let's get going."

CHAPTER FOUR

"No, don't turn around," Gwen said quietly.

The man hissed in pain as her fingers clenched on his upper arm. She walked behind him and to the right, down the crowded street. Neon blinked on the wet sidewalks, on the pedestrians in bulky clothing and on the umbrellas many of them carried. She was wearing . . . what was the word? *A tracksuit*. What the advertisement called the World's Finest Cold-Weather Athletic Clothing, with high-laced sports shoes. The clothes were far warmer than she needed, but the jacket had a hood that concealed most of her face, and they were baggy enough to let her body vanish inside.

Few of the crowd looked at her, or at each other. They walked with a hurried, nervous determination that seemed characteristic here; heads slightly bowed, refusing to meet each other's eyes. Wafts of warmer air gusted up out of the subway stations, with a gagging reek of wastes and ozone. Cars splashed rooster-tail fans of dirty water onto the edges of the sidewalks, and sometimes beyond onto the legs of the passersby. Most of the stores sold weirdly primitive electronics, or various sorts of erotic entertainment almost as crude.

At least the rain did a little something in the way of clearing the air.

"Hey, what you want, man?"

He tugged against her grip, and she tightened it in warning. "I want you to do me a favor," she said, keeping her voice pitched several octaves deeper than the natural setting.

To a human's dull ears it would pass well enough for a man's voice, and it was no particular strain for her vocal cords; she could imitate most animals' cries well enough to fool the creatures into killing range.

"This is a C-note," she said, pushing a hundred-dollar bill into his pocket. "I need some papers. A passport."

The man's free hand brought out the folded bill; he peeked down at the edge to verify the amount and then tucked it securely away. She could hear his sub-vocalization, a confused murmur with *cop? cop?* interspersed through it.

"Get me someone who can do the passport, and you get three more like that. Fuck me around and I pull your arm out of your shoulder."

She gave a single heavy tug, not quite enough to dislocate the joint, proud of her quick mastery of the local dialect. The man's scent turned heavier with fear, a salty odor, faintly appealing.

Why me? the human was thinking to himself. And: *Easy money.*

"Easy money," she said soothingly. She wanted him to be afraid, but not so panic-stricken he forgot greed.

It wasn't hard to identify petty criminals; not when you could pick up their speech from many times the distance a human could, and automatically sort multiple conversations for keywords. Scenting the drugs and weapons helped, as well.

"Sure, I take you to JoJo," he said.

He was half lying. *Ah. He probably knows of such an individual, but doesn't plan to deliver.*

"Of course you will," she said. "Right now, and if you try to run away, the arm goes."

"Bingo," Carmaggio said softly, and spat the gum in his mouth toward a manhole cover.

The back courtyard was cold and slick with the last rain; which kept the smell down, at least. He walked over to the body. *Damn, that's unusual.* You got used to corpses in all sorts of positions; upside down, hanging from things, in beds, in cars. Once he'd had a killing where the girlfriend's body got stuffed into a large sealed crate and *mailed* by the ex-wife to the husband. Who'd fainted, fallen over backward, and killed himself when he opened the crate—and that presented some interesting evidentiary problems.

This one was lying on his stomach, with the forward third of his body propped up against the brick wall of the building. As if he'd run right into it and poured down, like Wile E. Coyote in one of the old Road Runner cartoons.

Carmaggio took his hands out of his pockets and pulled on a pair of gloves. "Another fun night in the Busiest Precinct in the World," he said. A couple of the uniforms and technical people laughed as they went about their business.

They were about a block from Times Square; he could see the reflected lights of the Embassy 1 in a puddle out on the street, beyond the cars and the cordon. At least now the press had had a month to forget the warehouse killings, so he didn't have a flock of black-winged cameramen following him around, flapping and squawking and waiting for something to die. There was a Sbarro's next to the Embassy, which reminded him he hadn't eaten. *I'll get a meatball sandwich afterward,* he decided.

"*Ai, me muero,*" Jesus Rodriguez said, gloving up as well. "You know, there was a time when I thought I'd be catching murderers, not spending my days with the bodies."

"Hmmm."

Carmaggio crouched behind the body for a second. Hands were down, resting on the ground palms up. There was a smear of blood on the wet brick, starting about face height for someone the victim's height. He touched a gloved finger to it and rubbed the result with the ball of his thumb; unscientific, he supposed, but it often worked as a rough-and-ready timecheck. Hard to tell, though, with this temperature and all the water oozing out of the brick—God damn all midwinter thaws, anyway, they screwed things up worse than snow. Maybe there was something to this global warming thing; winters had frozen harder when he was a kid.

The initial blood spatter was huge, like an inkblot in one of those old psychologist's tests. More blood in a pool around the base of the wall. Head injuries bled out fast, as bad as a major wound to the chest cavity.

"What do I see in this?" he wondered, stepping back and looking at the blot. "I see someone who had their head shot out of a cannon at a wall, is what I see."

There was nothing around the body but garbage. He crouched again and used a pencil in his left hand to move the ponytail of greasy black hair that covered the victim's neck. *Aha.*

Livid bruises on either side of the spinal column, right above the shoulders. "Look at this," he said.

Jesus joined him. Henry spread his hand as if he were about to take the back of the dead man's neck in it, a straightforward grab with the thumb on the left side. It fit exactly, thumb-mark and four fingers, although from the spacing the hand had been slightly smaller than Carmaggio's.

"What does that say to you?" he asked his partner.

"Perp is right-handed," Jesus said helpfully.

"Oh, funny man."

"Geraldo has nothing to me, *patrón*. I'd say someone put his face to that brick with an extreme quickness."

Henry grunted. "How long?"

Jesus picked up one of the hands by a thumb. There was a purplish sheen to the waxy skin, and a whitish spot appeared when the younger policeman stuck a finger in the livid patch that had lain nearest the ground. The joints of the hand moved freely.

"Hour, maybe two, no more than three."

"Right."

There was a bulletin out with the extremely incomplete description they'd gotten from the restaurant where Fischer had been seen last, but the chances of it doing any good were . . . *Somewhere between nada, zip, and fucking zero,* he thought resignedly. You couldn't pull in every tall redheaded woman within a mile of Times Square.

"All right, let's move him."

Two of the uniforms came forward, and Jesus got out his minicam, speaking softly into the throat mike. Henry whistled.

Teeth dropped out of the shattered mouth as the slack body was lifted free of the bricks. One of the patrol officers swallowed and wobbled a bit, until her partner hissed sharply at her. Broken jaw, mandible pushed right back. All the upper teeth snapped off. Frontal bones pushed in until there was nothing but a glistening mass of pulp, and the forehead had a dished look.

Carmaggio felt a little off himself. *Nothing I could take to court, but it's the same MO,* he thought. The skin along the nape of his neck roughened. *Angel dust?* he mused.

Something unnatural was behind this combination of speed and strength and utter savagery.

"Right, let's see if this is who I think it is," he said.

He slid a hand inside the dead man's jacket and began checking pockets. "Green cards, blank. Social Security, ditto. Oho, JoJo was getting upscale—passport. Couple of computer disks. Official stationery . . ."

"JoJo?" Jesus said.

"Do-it-while-you-wait JoJo Jackson himself," Carmaggio confirmed. "Aha."

A piece. A .32 revolver in a waist holster, no sights, trigger guard cut away—JoJo had always liked to think of himself as seriously bad; in fact, he'd just been bad. Not a very good documents man, either. Sooner or later something like this was going to happen to him—the means might have been more conventional, but the result was much the same.

There was something a little farther down the alley, too. A scrap of paper flecked with blood and plastered to the wet side of a dumpster. A C-note.

"Somebody might want to bag this," he said mildly. More of the warehouse money.

"Now, why do you come to JoJo?" Jesus said, imitating Carmaggio's voice.

ID. Lots of things you could do with cash, but you needed some ID for most of them. Like moving around, buying airplane tickets, renting a car. Not necessarily very good ID—people just didn't *look* most of the time—but some sort of paper.

"Travel plans," he answered. Wherever the mystery killer was going, it was probably bad news for the recipients . . . but New York could use the breathing space.

Gwen unfastened her seatbelt and stood. Air flowed in through the door of the airliner, mildly warm. *Welcome to Cali, Colombia.* Welcome to a country that had never even existed in her history; there had been a Republic of Grand Colombia from the 1820s, but that had stretched over all the Andean lands. The smell of burnt kerosene was overwhelming, and she breathed through her mouth to compensate. Outside only the distant mountains were familiar. Friends of hers had estates here, growing coffee and stock and heaven-berries and ganja—in the Domination's timeline. There was a minor liftport and a settlement nearby, mostly *servus*. This millions-strong monstrosity was almost completely alien, save for a few ancient Spanish churches and public buildings preserved for aesthet-ics in both histories.

She hefted her bags and followed the crowd to the Customs checkthroughs. Green-uniformed guards with submachine guns slung across their chests waited among the milling crowd. Some of them had guard dogs on leashes. The animals' heads came up as they scented her, tracking back and forth with cocked ears to find where the unfamiliar trace came from. One of them began barking and tugging at his lead, until the policeman quelled him with a sharp order. Passengers surged away from the growling and bared teeth.

Noisy lot, humans, she thought.

Their smell lay heavy in the concourse. It had none of the sharp clean scent of her own species, or the comforting sweetness of *servus*; the harsh feral smell put her teeth on edge. She showed them in a snarl of her own for an instant. It was a good thing that humans couldn't use their noses for anything but keeping their eyes and upper lips apart; if they had a decent sense of smell she'd never have been able to hide. And what they *did* scent, they only noticed subliminally, most of the time. She had been work-ing on her pheromones during the flight. It took a while to adjust them upward, although toward the end the cabin staff and several passengers had been hovering around her seat—without knowing exactly why, of course. She smiled as she handed her forged passport to the clerk.

He was only a pace away across the desk. His brown skin flushed as he looked up at her. She took off her sunglasses and tucked them into a pocket, smiling as she met his eyes. The Colombian swallowed and put a hand to the collar of his shirt.

"Welcome to Colombia," he said mechanically.

"Why, thank you," she said, smiling more widely. The forged passport rested between the fingers of her right hand. "It looks like a lovely country."

"Ah . . . your Spanish is excellent," he stammered. Several of the other clerks were looking at him oddly; he straightened and cleared his throat.

"Thank you," Gwen said.

It wasn't difficult to learn, when you had an eidetic memory; just read a grammar and spend a few days listening to Spanish-language television, of which New York had plenty, and practice a little. She probably had a Puerto Rican accent.

"Ah, purpose of visit?"

"Business," she said. To be precise, laundering $970,100 in American currency, but no need to go into details. Some contacts with the local criminal classes might also be useful.

"How long do you expect to remain in Colombia?"

"About a month."

Drops of sweat were rolling down the clerk's face. The men at the other desks were glancing over again and again. *Hmmm. Perhaps a little too much on the pheromones.*

"Your papers, please, and put the luggage here."

She put the suitcase on the flat surface and handed him the passport. He dropped it to the desk and opened it, reaching for his stamp.

That he hesitated only an instant when he saw the ten hundred-dollar bills folded inside the passport said a good deal for his nerves and self-control, especially when you remembered the effects of the pheromones.

The standing desk had a wooden rim around it; the bills vanished into a drawer.

Thump. The stamp went down on her passport, and the clerk opened the suitcase and gave the clothes inside a cursory inspection. The money was underneath the folded garments, in neat bundles wrapped in plain paper and sealed with tape.

"Enjoy your stay, Señora Smith," the clerk said. He hesitated, then went on: "If you need assistance . . ." and slipped a piece of paper across the desk. With his name and address on it.

She palmed it. "I'll certainly remember your kind offer, Señor Gaitán," she said.

The man looked after her as she walked away, until a supervisor came by and cleared his throat. She continued slowly, thinking. A hotel, of course. Then . . .

"Gwen!"

"Why, hello, Dolores," Gwen said.

One of the flight attendants; Dolores Ospina Pastrana. They'd chatted on the plane, although of course she hadn't understood exactly why this particular *yanqui* was so interesting, so charismatic. The stewardess was pulling her luggage along on a wheeled carryall, looking trim and efficient in her blue uniform. She fidgeted with the handle.

"Do you have a ride?"

Gwen smiled, white teeth flashing. "Why, no, I don't. Thank you for the offer; I hope it isn't an inconvenience."

"No, no, I'm off duty for the next three days."

"That's wonderful," Gwen said, smiling more broadly. Her nostrils flared slightly. "Perhaps you could show me some of the sights."

She didn't intend to stay in Colombia long, and a native guide would certainly help her get started more quickly. The evidence could always be disposed of, one way or another.

"It's a lovely city," Dolores said. "But it can be dangerous for an outsider."

Gwen chuckled. "Let's go. I'm sure you can shield me from the perils of ignorance."

"Who *did* you say you were with?" Mary Chen asked, stepping in front of the personable young man before he could pass through.

"We're with the Federal government, Dr. Chen," he said, with a frank, open smile.

He was wearing a nondescript dark suit and raincoat; so was his friend. They were both six-footers, one young and dark, the other fortysomething, heavy, and graying blond; the older man looked like an athlete gone very slightly to seed, or a lawyer who spent a couple of nights a week at the gym. He carried something like an attaché case, only considerably larger. Unlike his younger companion, he didn't smile.

"Well, that's you and a couple of hundred thousand others, even under this administration," Chen said. "What does the Federal government want with medical evidence being held in an ongoing investigation?"

Nobody waltzes into my *office like this!* It might not be much of an office; cluttered, with a couple of spider plants on top of the filing cabinets, and smelling faintly of disinfectant from downstairs, but it was her turf.

The young man laughed easily, eyes crinkling. "We're with an executive agency," he said. "And it's not an ongoing investigation anymore. Since it's a closed file, I'm sure you won't object . . ."

"Great, an executive agency. FBI, CIA, NSA, Bureau of Indian Affairs, NASA, what?"

He reached into his jacket. "The City wants full cooperation," he said gently, and extended a handful of documents.

She read raising her brows. "Impressive." It was; including two heavy hitters in the NYPD. "Unfortunately, you don't seem to have noticed that I'm a medical examiner—and we're appointed by the courts. We're not part of the police department."

She handed the sheaf of paper back. Mary Chen had spent a good deal of the last twenty years around police officers; long enough to recognize the very slight bulge below the young man's left armpit. Icy certainty paralyzed her mind for an instant. These *were* Feds of some sort; it would be deeply stupid to make a claim she could refute with a simple phone call. And they were serious. Some sort of Federal cop, or more likely spooks; FBI would have been more open about who they were.

The older one stepped by her and put his carrying case on the desk. He pressed the buttons on a digital lock and snapped the catches open with his thumbs, the metallic *click* loud in the little room. Much of the space inside was insulation, leaving just enough for an arm. A very large arm.

"Look," she began. "If you think I'm going to sit still for this, you're very much mistaken."

The young man's smile didn't waver. He reached a black-gloved hand inside his jacket and produced another folded paper.

"Dr. Chen, this is a national security matter," he said. She snorted.

"If you'll take a moment to think about it, you'll realize that that's not just a phrase to shut you up. We're nearly into the twenty-first century, and pretty soon genetics are going to be as important to our security as electronics have been for the past few decades. You *must* realize something of how sensitive this matter is, or you wouldn't have kept it as quiet as you have—nothing to the press, no publicity, just a few friends of yours at the university, nothing on paper.

That's fine, but this needs to be studied by top people. We can provide the facilities. You can't; with all due respect, you're a forensic pathologist, not a research geneticist. No offense."

"None taken," she said between clenched teeth.

Before she could continue, the man handed over the letter.

"The United States needs to keep its technological edge," he said earnestly. "Otherwise, our influence goes; and it's an influence for good, well beyond our borders."

The paper was an official document, but not from the American government. The language was Vietnamese; in the upper right-hand corner was an identity photograph of her aunt Edelle. Who was still in Hue . . . in a Vietnam growing even more hostile to its ethnic-Chinese minority since the naval clashes over those damned islands. Not that it had ever been very friendly.

"I didn't even know she was still alive," Chen whispered.

Gloved fingers plucked the document out of her hand. *A promise*, she realized. Hanoi was *extremely* anxious to stay on Washington's good side these days. *Possibly a threat*. More probably just a promise.

She turned her head aside. "In the cold storage," she said.

Claire Finch had been with the FBI for three years now. She'd never seen her superior as angry as he was now; a cold, grim rage that crackled through the office despite the expressionless set of his face.

"The investigation's being canceled," he said.

"Twenty-odd murders, and it's *canceled*?"

"Not our jurisdiction." John Dowding rose and walked over to the window, looking down at the Washington street.

"The Fischer was a kidnapping-murder."

"Nope. He went back to his apartment voluntarily."

"She used his panix.com account illegally—that *is* our turf."

"Not according to the memo," he said over his shoulder.

"What about the DNA sample from the skin and hair?"

"The sample's been removed from Quantico. The records have been removed. Just between you and me, that . . . arm . . . thing, whatever, has been quietly spirited away too. And the people who were working on it have been told it's a matter of national security. Not that anyone would listen to them with the evidence."

Finch shook her head. "This stinks, sir."

"Stinks of Langley, possibly the NSA," he said. "They took a look at the genetics and they panicked. If someone is that far ahead of us, it *is* a crisis."

"Not as much of a crisis as it was to Stephen Fischer," she said tartly.

"Granted." Dowding's long, bony face nodded. "And this doesn't look like an espionage situation to me—and it'd be our affair if it was."

Not theirs personally—they were with the Behavioral Sciences section—but counterespionage within the borders of the U.S. was a Bureau function. A distinction more often observed in the breach than the observance, true, but the Bureau was about as likely to relinquish its jurisdiction as a pit bull was to give up a marrow bone.

Finch bit at her lower lip. "Sir, generally if the Other People tried to take something like this away from us, the Director would tell them to go pee up a rope."

Dowding leaned back in his swivel chair and tapped the knuckles of one hand with a pen. "Exactly. So the truth about this evidence must be so terrifying that the Director or someone just below his level *wants* to hand it over to somebody else."

"I have a bad feeling about this, sir," she said.

Dowding nodded. "Finch, I trust you."

She looked up, startled. He was holding a disk in his hand, one of the new read-write opticals. "This is that DNA report on the skin samples that Quantico did," he said.

They shared a glance. The powers-that-be hadn't really grasped how difficult it was to get rid of every copy of inconvenient data, yet.

"Here's what we're going to do," he said. "Strictly off the record, of course. I think our highly-unusual mystery suspect will be back . . ."

The *Parque de Calzado* wasn't much, Gwen decided. A few tall palm trees, a rectangle of grass cut by a St. George's cross of tessellated brick pavement, and a central fountain. Around it were apartment buildings in the hideous style the humans seemed to like, boxy things of steel-reinforced concrete; nobody in the Domination's timeline had ever built anything like them, except as factories or warehouses. Here they were residences, including Dolores's, where she'd holed up for the past three days.

It was also quite dark, now.

"Gwen, this park is . . . this is not a safe place," Dolores pleaded.

"Even less so, now that I'm in it," she chuckled.

The air bore a confusion of scents; mostly bad, but not as much so as New York. The temperature was quite pleasant as night fell; a fair number of people were out strolling. Fewer and fewer as she led the ex-stewardess away into the back streets.

"Gwen—"

She stopped, impatient, and gripped the Colombian

by her upper arm, jerking her close. "Dolores," she said quietly, staring into her eyes. "Let's get one thing settled about this relationship, right from the start. *I'm in charge.* Understand?"

"I—"

She could hear the other's heart accelerate, smell the acrid tinge of fear in her sweat. Pupils dilated.

"I understand."

"Good. Shall I send you back to the apartment?"

No, the Columbian subvocalized. *Not alone, not now.* She shook her head.

"Good." *I don't want you on your own for long, not for a couple of weeks yet.* It would take that long to get her settled in and accepting the situation. The alternative was to snap her neck, but that would be wasteful; besides that, she was likable.

"Now, let's keep going. Do you know the Rule of Seven?"

"No. Seven?" Dolores was trying to keep the quaver out of her voice, Gwen noted with approval.

"Nobody is more than seven acquaintances away from anyone else. For instance, you know this Señor Mondragón—"

"Just his name, from the papers. I don't know such people."

That seemed to be a general attitude here in Cali. People who did know such people or said they did had a tendency to vanish.

"—and someone we meet will know someone who knows someone, and we'll be led to Señor Mondragón, soon enough."

Why does she want to meet a criminal?

"Because I have some business to conduct, *mi amiga.* Now shut up."

Gwen patted her gently on the back to take the sting out of the words. She *had* been very useful, and it was a great relief to finally have her biological needs taken

care of on a civilized basis. If something of a strain for
Dolores at first.

They had wandered into an alleyway; dark enough
that it was a little dim even to Gwen's eyes, and
Dolores was blundering along in a literally blind panic.
It stank as well, of cat-piss and less savory odors, starting with spoiled garbage. Gwen smiled, her ears cocked
forward a little. Two sets of heartbeats, they were
accelerating as she and the Colombian walked down
the cracked and slimy pavement. Two shapes spreading out, black silhouettes outlined against the slightly
brighter street beyond. A light flared under a heavy
brown acne-scarred face as one lit a cigarette. Dolores
whimpered slightly, but kept to her position in Gwen's
wake.

The short man's face looked a little puzzled as the
women kept coming toward him. His companion was
four inches taller and much heavier; a blank bovine
expression over shoulders and belly that stretched the
grubby white cotton of his T-shirt.

"One for each of us," the short man whispered aside
to his friend. Aloud:

"Good evening, ladies! You shouldn't be wandering
alone around here. Perhaps we can help you."

"I think you can," Gwen said, smiling. "We're looking
for a Señor Mondragón."

Both the men stiffened slightly; she watched the play
of muscles around mouth and eyes, listened to the
involuntary intake of breath. Not enough for a human
to notice, but meaningful. Both men recognized the
name, of course; but their fright was direct and personal. Fear produced anger.

"Shut up, *puta*. Miguel, you take the other one."

"I don't think so," Gwen said, as he reached past her
for Dolores.

She grabbed the wrist; it was thick, a thin layer of
blubber over solid muscle and bone. A quick jerk, and

the big man stumbled forward, sending his lighter companion spinning aside to crash into the flaking stucco
of the alley's wall. At the same time she squeezed,
feeling the small bones of the wrist grate and splin-
ter under her grip. The man gave an incredulous grunt,
eyes and mouth flaring open in three O's of surprise.
She jerked again, bracing her feet—he was heavier than
she, even though she weighed over a hundred and
ninety pounds, much more than a human of her size.
When a lighter object reacted against a heavier, the
lighter tended to move regardless of energy outputs;
it was a matter of leverage, not strength.

He stumbled again, to his knees. Gwen pivoted on
her left heel and kicked with her right, into his throat,
releasing her hold as the blow impacted. The body
snapped backward several meters and fell limp, head
lying back between the shoulderblades. She took a deep
breath and stepped closer to the survivor; he was standing with his hand half under the tail of his zippered
jacket, eyes bulging in shock.

"Miguel?" he said, halfway between a croak and a
whisper.

Humans are slow, she thought. *Not just their reaction time, but their ability to assimilate data.*

"Miguel is dead," she said. "Now, I need some information."

The hand came out with a knife, curved and sharp,
moving quite quickly for a human. Gwen swayed her
upper body back just enough for the cutting edge to
miss as it ripped upward, her hand snapping out to grab
and span the other's fist where it clenched around the
hilt. She continued the natural path of the weapon until
the point touched the man's throat just below the angle
of the jaw. For a long moment they stayed locked, a
trickle of blood running down his throat from the
knifepoint. His pulsed fluttered on the edge of shock
and then steadied a little; there was a irritating edge

to his scent, a hint of metabolic wrongness. *Some sort of drug interfering with the metabolism*, she decided.

"Who *are* you?" he shrilled. "What are you doing?"

"What I'm doing," Gwen said, leaning a little closer and increasing the pressure of the steel, "depends on you. If you're not cooperative, I'm going to torture some information out of you and then kill you. If you were better looking and didn't smell so bad, I'd rape you first. Or you can tell me what I want to know."

"*Sí, sí,* anything you want to know, lady, anything! Look, I know where you can get kilos, the real thing, cheap, I'll—"

"That's my boy!" Gwen said cheerfully, patting him on the cheek with her free hand. His made vague pawing motions at the air. "Now, Señor Mondragón."

"Oh, Jesus and His Mother, *no soy nadie,* I don't know him."

"But you know someone who knows someone, don't you, little one?" she said softly.

The drops of blood flowing down his neck became a steady trickle. Tears and mucus from eyes and nose joined them. Unconsciously his right arm kept trying to jerk the knife away from his throat, but she controlled the surges without allowing more than a quiver in the metal.

"*Sí,* I know Pedro, Don Pedro, and he—"

Gwen waited until the babbling began to repeat itself. "That's all," she said, and pushed with quick, savage force.

The knife slid through neck and throat and into the small man's mouth, then crunched into the bones of the palate. She pushed a little harder, and there was a yielding crackle as it slid into the brain. The body arched in spasm, a thin trickling whine blowing out of clenched teeth, then slid to the ground, voided, and died. Gwen sighed and turned.

Dolores was backed against the wall, hands pressed

to either side of her head, her mouth trembling. Trembling with terror and a dreadful reluctant excitement.

Ah, Gwen thought. *Got to watch the pheromones.*

"Come on," she said soothingly. "Enough outdoor work for one night."

"You make me tired. Just *looking* at you makes me tired, Carmaggio."

Looking at you generally makes me want to puke, Captain, Carmaggio thought. He could feel the back of his neck flush, which was usually a bad sign; probably Captain McLeish could see the thought printed across his face like an LCD display. McLeish smirked and leaned back in the swivel chair behind his desk; there were pictures of himself with several commissioners and mayors on the walls, and a slight smell of old socks. He looked Carmaggio up and down, letting the contrast between the other man's rumpled off-the-rack and his own beautifully tailored suit speak for itself. He was in better shape than Carmaggio, too, which the tucked waist showed off quite well.

Looks like a pimp, Carmaggio thought. Right down to the cool-dude side whiskers, although at least he didn't have letters shaved into his 'fro.

It wasn't that he had anything against blacks. Not after Happy Lewis saved his ass that time he didn't see the claymore; he'd made a private resolution right then and there not to use the word "eggplant" for anything but vegetables ever again.

It was asskissers and fuckups he didn't like. McLeish was a prime example of both, in his considered opinion. How he'd gotten as far as he had only God and the Echelons Beyond Reality who *thought* they were God knew. *Welcome to the wonderful world of the civil service.* He was profoundly glad that they'd found out ulcers were caused by bacteria, not stomach acid—because every time he had to report to McLeish, he got a couple of cupfuls of the original patented bile spewed out into his gut.

"We've got twenty-three homicides, Captain. With all due respect—"

"How many *thousand* homicides do we have in this shitty city, Carmaggio? You've got no evidence to put a solid link between them, and nothing new has turned up in six months. It's spring—wake up and smell the roses. Serial killers don't stop. That's what our great good friends at Federal Bullshit Incorporated keep telling us."

"Yeah, they *don't* stop. Not permanently. If we let this one go—"

"They've already gotten away." The *you dumb guinea bastard* was unspoken but plain. "Not to mention the FBI say they don't want to hear about it anymore; and whose idea was it to call in Quantico, in the first place? This is not, for your information, some pissant little two-sheriff town without its own forensics department."

Carmaggio felt the flush spreading from the back of his neck to his ears.

"Maybe the tooth fairy did it, Carmaggio. Maybe that Jew cunt at Primary Belway Securities was the one who offed Fischer."

Maybe JoJo beat his own head in against that wall because he realized he'd never be President, Henry thought, as his superior went on:

"And maybe you don't have enough work to do. You want me to put a few more on your docket? Didn't you have a court appearance today?"

"Yessir."

He didn't slam the door as he left. There *hadn't* been any more action on the file, and there *was* a lot of other work to do. He'd long ago resigned himself to the fact that he'd retire not much above his present rank; interviews like this were simply a symptom of that. People got to the top of the greasy pole largely because they wanted to, real bad—sometimes so they could do the job, more often not. He did this lousy job because he wanted to, not to get a better office. Shits like the captain regarded actual police work as a distraction from more important matters.

Whether or not the captain thought it was too much trouble to bother with, they'd be hearing from this particular perp again, closed file or no closed file.

Or somebody would be hearing about them. *This isn't the sort that goes somewhere and hides.*

CHAPTER FIVE

The tropical sun was a flat glare on the surface of the water. The compressor on the barge throbbed tirelessly, pumping water down a thick tube to blow sand off the bottom thirty feet below; that made the sea around them turgid, greenish compared to the usual turquoise of the waters off Abaco. They were eighty miles southwest of Marsh Harbor, not far from Mores Island; that flat sandy speck of land was just visible, but nothing else marred the circle of sky and sea except the barge and its attendant boats. There was a silty undertone to the usual sea-salt smell, faint beneath the diesel stink of the exhaust.

Captain John Lowe looked at the water in disgust, then back at the woman who'd chartered his outfit, in puzzlement. *Nothing here to find.* Sure, there were plenty of wrecks around the Abacos, all over the Bahamas—the archipelago was famous for it. But these waters had been searched bare, long ago.

The money's good. He'd insisted on getting it up front and in cash. There was a lot of that sort of business in the Bahamas, and a tradition of not asking too many questions. The country lived off being an off-shore tax shelter even more than it did from tourism and the . . . unregistered transit trade. An old tradition: Conchy Joes like him had always been smugglers, from cocaine back through Prohibition rum boats and Civil War blockade runners, and before that wreckers and pirates.

Crazy bitch.

She stood at the rail of the boat, looking over at the floats that marked where the divers were working. *Crazy, and I can't figure her.* He couldn't even decide whether she was white or not. She'd darkened up considerably since they started, to milk chocolate color, but the tan seemed to go all over—he had a good view, with the loose cotton shorts and sleeveless singlet she was wearing. The green eyes and red hair were genuine, though. Her papers said Colombian, but the accent was American—South Carolina, maybe, or Louisiana, hard to place, despite the pretty *latina* secretary she had hanging around. The body said American too, the fitness-freak look, like some of the richer women tourists. Not very bulgy, but every muscle precisely delineated, moving under the smooth skin like machined steel in oil.

Nice tits, though. And no bra. Maybe a hundred and forty pounds, a little more.

One of the standing bets had been whether or not she was queer. That was settled up when Jamie Simms had been seen coming out of her cabana back in Marsh Harbor at six in the morning, but the young deckhand had steadfastly refused all details. That was odd, because everyone had expected a stroke-by-stroke description, and he'd screamed at them to stop asking and then quit the job. Damned odd.

Lowe moved up to stand beside her. "How much longer?" he said.

"Until it's found," she replied. Her voice was soft and pleasant, rather deep, but the tone expected instant obedience.

He gritted his teeth. Sure, she was paying, but there wasn't enough money in the world to make him swallow that much longer.

"It's your three hundred thousand," he said. And the meter was still running. Next week it would be four hundred thousand.

She didn't bother to reply.

Lowe felt the bottom drop out of his gut when the diver surfaced, tearing off his mask and waving something in the air. It looked like a black lump at this distance—exactly the black of corroded silver.

"Silver," she said. "Silver ingots and coin, gold ingots and chains, and a bronze casket full of emeralds. After your government takes its cut, probably about eight million dollars' worth." She smiled slightly. "Aren't you sorry you insisted on a flat fee instead of a percentage of the take?"

Lowe pulled off his hat, knotting it in one ham fist, and took a step toward her. She'd offered him a quarter share and he'd laughed in her face, and she'd given him the same damned smile then. *I'm going to knock her—*

The green eyes narrowed slightly, and he stopped; stopped as if he had run into a wall of ice.

"Not even in your dreams," she whispered.

He coughed to cover his confusion. "How? How the fuck did you know?"

She turned her head back to the divers. Two more had surfaced, and the first was dancing around the deck of the barge.

"I knew what, and where," she said. "Then I checked to see if anyone had found it. Nobody had. Therefore it had to be here."

She went on, still looking out over the water. "I'm doubling your fee, Captain Lowe. I'll probably need your services again, and your nephew the pilot."

That put a different face on things. "Happy to oblige, ma'am."

"Just remember this," she said. "What I say I can do,
I can do. Those who get in my way will regret it. Those
who help me can expect to get rich. Very rich. Wealth,
and great power . . ."

She turned and smiled at him. "You'd like that,
wouldn't you, Captain Lowe."

Another face altogether. He made a sweeping bow,
grinning back. "*Happy* to oblige, ma'am."

Crazy bitch of a woman. But crazy like a fox.

"Very satisfactory," Gwen said.

Thomas Cairstens lifted his glass and clinked it
against hers.

Woman of the hour, he thought, as he smiled at Gwen,
although she'd managed to evade the Nassau press with
delicate skill—giving them just enough to prevent a
feeding frenzy. Lost pirate treasure stories were an
overnight sensation. The foreign press had dropped it
a week ago, although she'd become well known locally.

The dining room of Greycliff was emptying out, as
the Friday evening moved toward midnight and the
clientele made for bed or nightspot. The fans turned
lazily overhead, and the air smelled of flowers from the
small yard outside as well as of traffic from West Hill
Street, muffled by the high whitewashed wall of limestone blocks that fronted the restaurant. The room itself
smelled of good food and expensive perfumes. A bit of
a guilty pleasure, but one he allowed himself after a
profitable deal.

She pushed a check across the table at him. "For
Greenpeace," she said.

Tom looked down at it and raised his brows before
he tucked it into his jacket pocket. *A hundred thousand. Not too shabby.*

"I didn't know you were an environmentalist," he
said. She'd been all business while he handled the
incorporation of IngolfTech.

"I'm anti-stupidity," she replied coolly. She was dressed simply, in a cream-colored linen dress that brought out her café-au-lait complexion and the brilliant green eyes; an emerald dragon brooch closed the high neck.

"In a hundred years or less, this planet's going to collapse—it might even become uninhabitable," she went on.

He nodded grimly, turning the wineglass in his hands. "That's why I got into Greenpeace in California," he said.

"Why did you get out?"

He put the glass down and met her eyes. *Compelling. God, that's an attractive woman.* He wasn't normally very receptive to feminine charms, but there was the occasional exception. Gwendolyn Ingolfsson just didn't *feel* like a woman, though. Or quite like anyone he'd ever met. *Smart, too. How did she know about me?* When she was there, you just didn't *notice* anyone else.

"Because it wasn't doing any good," he went on. "Not Greenpeace or Earth First, or any of the others. We were putting Band-Aids on cancers at best. More often, we were just provoking backlash. Earth First couldn't think of anything better to do than try and get poor dumb loggers fired. I'd have joined the ecoterrorists, *if* I thought they'd accomplish anything. Detroit can produce bulldozers a lot faster than anyone can blow them up, though."

"So you gave up and came to the Bahamas to practice corporate law," she said.

He nodded his head jerkily. He'd gone a little further into the fringes than that, which made the move advisable until things quieted down, but it was essentially true. His parents had helped; Dad had real pull, enough to square his work permit with the Bahamian government. It was stupid not to take advantage of family connections if you had them. There were more lawyers in Nassau than sharks in the waters off-shore, but he'd done well.

"Sure. Why not dance on the deck if the Titanic's going down?" *And what a depressing subject for a dinner date.*

Gwen leaned forward, fixing his eyes with hers. "Imagine a world," she said softly, almost whispering, forcing him to lean closer to hear, "where the population of Earth is five hundred million and stable, not seven billion and rising. Where not an ounce of fossil fuel is burned. No mines, no factories, no fission reactors or coal-burning plants, no tankers full of oil. The sea and the skies and the land swarm with life, and whole continents are nature preserves."

He jerked his head away. "That's not funny."

"No, it's not funny. But it's *possible*, given the right technology and the right management."

"And we'll never get there from here," he said, feeling anger mount. "Look, what's the *point* of this?"

She smiled and pulled a featureless black rectangle the size of a credit card out of her bag.

"Yes, this civilization is never going to do that," she agreed, and ran a fingernail down its side.

The card opened out, and opened again, until it was the size of a hardcover book. The surface was black in a way he'd never seen before, as if it drank every photon that impacted on it and reflected nothing. A hole in the table, thinner than a sheet of paper and completely rigid. She touched the side, and the background noise faded quickly to nothing. He looked around in startlement; they were off in one corner, near the tall windows, but he could see mouths moving in talk, silverware in use. Everything was dead silent, like a video with the sound control turned off.

"What *is* that thing?" he said. His voice sounded

slightly flat in the perfect silence, as if in a room with absorptive baffles on the walls.

"It's the equivalent of a file-folder," Gwen replied. "For old-fashioned types like me who don't like to just close their eyes and downlink from the Web through their transducers for an image. Now, we were discussing the potential future of civilization."

Tom felt sweat break out on his forehead and trickle clammily down his flanks, more than the Bahamian night could account for. He reached for his wineglass and drank. It was no easy thing, to have your ordinary life suddenly touched by strangeness.

"Go ahead," he said softly.

"A planetary surface is a bad place for an industrial economy," she went on. "You could have gotten out of that trap, but it's probably too late now, and certainly will be in another generation."

Tom shook his head. "Technofixes wouldn't solve our problems. It's in the nature of humanity to foul its nest. We'd have to change human nature: that's why I gave up."

"I'm glad you said that," Gwen said, her smile growing broader. "You agree then, that humans aren't fit to be in charge here?"

"What's the alternative—a Dolphin Liberation Front?" he replied.

She tapped the black rectangle. "Look."

He glanced down. The surface of the square . . . vanished. It wasn't a screen; the view through it had full depth, exactly like a window. He reached out and touched it with an involuntary reflex. It was completely smooth and neutral in temperature.

"This is Haiti," she said.

He knew Haiti; the wasted, eroded hills barren as the Sahara, the pitiful starving people, hardly a tree or an animal besides goats left west of the Dominican border.

This showed tropical rainforest, lush and untouched, the view sweeping down mountain valleys where mist hung in ragged tatters from the great trees. A spray of birds went by, feathers gaudy; he could hear their cries, faint and raucous. The view swept down to the coast. Here were people, squares of sugarcane, a hillside terraced and planted to glossy-leaved bushes he recognized as coffee. Workers with hand tools or simple machines were busy among them. The view moved closer; he could see they were brown-skinned, stocky and muscular, well-clothed. One laughed as he heaved a full basket onto a floating platform. In the middle distance a white stone building covered in purple bougainvillea stood on a hillside amid gardens. Beyond it was Port-au-Prince harbor. There was no city, no teeming antheap of ragged peasant refugees. Just a few buildings half-lost amid greenery, a stone wharf, and a schooner tied to it.

And a big skeletal structure, like a dish of impossibly rigid rope.

"That's the orbital power receptor," Gwen said. "Now, the Yangtze Gorges."

The great river ran unbound through tall beautiful cliffs, no sign of the giant concrete dam the Chinese had used to tame the wild water.

"Great plains, North America—near what you'd call Fargo."

Tall grass, stretching from horizon to horizon. And across it buffalo unnumbered, in clumps and herds of thousands each. The horned heads lifted in mild curiosity; there was a stir, and a pack of great gray lobo wolves trotted through, twenty strong.

"Bitterfield, eastern Germany."

He knew that, too; one of the worst chemical-waste nightmares left by the old East German regime. The picture showed a stream flowing through thick poplar forest. Behind it were oaks, huge and moss-grown. He

heard the chuckle of water, the cries of birds, wind in
the branches. The view moved through them at walking
pace, pausing at a wildcat on a tree limb, at a sounder
of wild boar, in a sun-dappled meadow clearing where
an aurochs raised its head in majesty. Its bellow filled
his ears.

"The Aral Sea."

Which had disappeared almost altogether, leaving salt
flats poisoned with insecticide—the legacy of the old
Soviet Union's insane irrigation megaprojects.

The window into a world that wasn't showed white-
caps on blue water.

"The delta of the Syr Darya, where it empties into
the Aral." A huge marsh. Through the reeds and onto
a firmer island moved striped deadliness, a Siberian
tiger. Waterfowl rose from the water in honking thousands, enough to cast shadow on the great predator.

"Paris."

No Eiffel Tower, although Napoleon's Arc de
Triomphe still stood. The air was crystal. From overhead, he could see that the medieval core remained,
Notre Dame, the radial roadways laid out in Napoleon
III's time. None of the great sprawl of suburbs he
knew; Versailles stood alone among its ordered gardens.
Dense forest and open parkland stretched from the
outskirts; occasionally a building would rise above them,
usually roofed in green copper. The roadways were
grassy turf. Foot traffic was pedestrians, or small
machines that floated soundlessly beneath their passengers. Aircraft moved through the air above, elongated teardrop shapes and blunt wedges moving
without visible support; a colorful hot-air balloon drifted
among them.

"The Serengeti, looking northeast."

A herd of hundreds of elephants, moving with
slow ponderous dignity through a landscape of lion-
colored grass and scattered flat-topped thorn trees.

His eyes darted about; lions, giraffe, antelope, a *dozen* rhino . . . Snow-topped Kilimanjaro rose like an empress in the distance. Beyond it was something new, something alien: a great pillar stretching up into the sky until it turned into a curving thread, vanishing in the blue.

"What's that?" he asked, hearing his voice shake.

"The Kenia beanstalk—think of it as a tower or a cable reaching from Low Earth Orbit to the surface." She touched the edge of the window. "And this is the Valles Marineris, on Mars."

The sky was a faded blue, with a hint of pink. The view was on the edge of a reddish cliff, overlooking a vast expanse of deep-blue water five hundred feet or more below; miles distant across it the edge of another cliff showed. The waves were like none he had ever seen, taller and thinner in section than water could support. While he watched a whale breached, soaring out of the sea until only its tail was under the surface. A blue whale, and huge. It crashed back with a mountainous spray of surf. The view tilted downward, showing a city dropping in terraces from the cliff-face. The buildings were white or soft pastels, built with domes and arches and pillared colonnades, connected with roadways of colored stone or sweeping staircases. Gardens surrounded every building and lined the streets.

Just below him stood a group of people. *People like Gwen.* He recognized a likeness in some of them. Racial? Tall, with a slender muscularity, light-eyed, their hair shades of blond or red. Some of them wore tunics or robes; others only tight briefs. Those near-naked ones were being fitted with gossamer gliding wings on frameworks thinner than thread but steel-rigid. The helpers were of a subtly different type, shorter, trim and healthy but without the sinewy tigerish look of the first variety.

One of the figures strapping wings to her arms, he realized suddenly, *was* Gwen—but her skin was milk-pale, not the Indian-brown he saw across from him. She launched herself off the cliff edge, dived, then began to scull upward like one of Da Vinci's ornithopters.

"Yes, that's me. A few years ago on my personal world-line. My skin tone adjusts automatically to the ambient sunlight, all over," she explained.

The flyers exploded from their perch in a rainbow of colors. Condors glided along the cliff face, among the men and women.

"One last one. Venus, north polar region."

No greenery this time. Desert and rock, under a scourging wind. The sky was a deep greenish-blue, thick with clouds; he could see a vast pale disk in it, like a moon but too regular, touching one edge on the horizon and occupying a quarter-section arc of the heavens. In the foreground people walked, in thin pressure-suits and bubble helmets. Machines floated by, or rolled on huge wheels of spun thread; further away something enormous lifted into the sky and vanished upward with a trail of vapor and a thunder-rumble that shook the earth. There was a sense of thick, glimmering heat about the picture, almost palpable.

"The temperature in polar winter is down to about forty degrees—that's Celsius—but the air's still unbreathable, will be for another century. The circular object is an orbiting mirror, reflecting away sunlight. Mars was relatively easy; we just heated it up with mirrors and dumped comets and pieces of the gas-giant moons on the surface, then started the biologicals. Venus had too *much* atmosphere, we used tailored algae and then—never mind."

"Turn it back to Earth," he whispered. She did; this time to a seal colony, huge and thunderous with their barking cries. "Is it true? Is it true?"

Gwen tapped at the edge of the viewscreen. "If you can match this on Earth today, I'm the greatest liar since Thomas Jefferson," she said coldly, and tapped again. Once more there was nothing but a thin sheet of nonreflective black.

Cairstens buried his face in his hands and wept, quietly and passionately. Their table was in a discreet corner; nobody noticed until he was done, and then Gwen signaled a waiter over.

"Vodka and orange juice," she said. "Another brandy for me."

The man gulped his drink in two mouthfuls. "You're from . . . from the future? You came to save us?"

"A future. 2442 A.D., to be exact; or the four hundred forty-second year of the Final Society, we'd say. The future of a different past, with the split starting in the mid 1770s, as close as I can tell. I got here by accident; we thought we were experimenting with faster-than-light travel. Moleholes—wormholes, your people call them."

"You're stranded," he said, his voice hoarse. Then he shook his head. "I never dreamed . . . I never thought human beings could be such stewards of the Earth."

"They can't," Gwen replied. "I'm not human."

His head came up. "You could have fooled me."

"I couldn't fool a CAT scan or DNA analysis. Post-human; genetically modified, to about a six percent divergence. *Homo drakensis*, to be precise. Most of it doesn't show, but I'm as different from you as an orangutan."

He nodded slowly. "This is—that's why you asked me that—" With a visible effort: "You think you can bring your people here. And they'll save the Earth."

"Among other things. I warn you, the consequences will be fairly drastic."

His face hardened. "As drastic as losing the ozone

layer? Global warming?" He shook his head decisively. "No, it doesn't matter how drastic." Curiously: "How did it happen?"

"Explain to me the overall history of the world for the past six hundred years, in one paragraph or less," Gwen said dryly.

He shrugged. "Yes, of course. But . . . how drastic? What's it like for people, in that world of yours?"

"Peaceful, mainly. No war, no poverty, no sexism, very little crime, no illness except eventual death. Most people work on the land, or at handicrafts, or in domestic pursuits; we could do that by machine, but it's more . . . healthy the other way. The high-tech sector nearly handles itself."

She raised a hand. "It isn't a democratic system. There's a genetic elite; I'm part of that. It's a static culture."

"Yes, yes," Cairstens nodded. "It'd have to be stable, to live in harmony with nature like that; it couldn't be our sort of grasping, wasting greed-society."

His eyes burned. "You need me to help. If this got out, every spook and spy from every government in the world would be fighting to pick your bones. They'd never allow you to contact your people."

She nodded. "I'm going to need a large organization; and a smaller one within it, of men and women who know the truth."

He shook his head again. "I believe it, but I can't believe it."

"Sleep on it. Tomorrow we'll talk again."

"Another brandy, and some more of that raspberry cheesecake, please," Gwen said.

The waiter smiled and hurried off. Gwen finished the last sip of the VSOP Otard cognac, savoring the uncanny fresh-grape sweetness, the vanilla tang of Limousin oak. Relatives of hers held estates there; the product was surprisingly similar in this universe. One of the drawbacks of her enhancements was that ethanol was metabolized as rapidly as anything else; wine was pure taste, not kick, to a *drakensis*. Four or five brandies did produce a mild effect, though.

Amazing, she thought, running over the conversation with Tom Cairstens. *And every word was the truth.* Even if their response to pheromonal clues was spotty, humans could be manipulated verbally. She could tell exactly what their reaction was to every word, of course—scent aside, listening to their heartbeats and watching the pupil dilation and patterns of heat on the skin—and modify accordingly.

Cairstens was going to be invaluable; she couldn't be everywhere, and it wasn't good tactics to be under human observation too much.

Invaluable provided he didn't go off the rails. It would take him a while to assimilate the data; humans were like that, their conscious and subconscious severely out of synch. How odd it must be, to know something was true and not feel belief in it! Like the way she'd felt for the half-hour after the accident, but all the time. Gwen shuddered slightly. That had been utter nightmare, the closest she'd ever come in all the long years to losing control of herself. No wonder the humans had such trouble maintaining clarity of thought and purpose.

Yes, she'd have to nurture Cairstens along carefully, building up a teacher-acolyte relationship; he had the makings of a fanatic, a True Believer. *Should I take him?* she wondered. So many of these feral humans were just plain *ugly*; it was a bit of a shock. The genetic engineers had eliminated that from the world of the Final Society long ago, along with inconvenient psychological characteristics. Cairstens was an exception, lean and hard, pleasant blue eyes, longish brown hair . . . probably an entertaining mount.

No, not for the present. Human males in this culture had odd ideas about sex and dominance. She'd wait until the parameters of the relationship were well-established, then integrate it as a reinforcement. She'd have to be careful, at that. *Servus* were protected against over-addiction to the stimulus of *drakensis* pheromones, sexual or otherwise. But wild humans were only vulnerable to a few of the more obvious stimuli, fear/dominance, lust/love, the basics—and when they were affected, didn't have any stops.

Gwen sighed. The geneticists who'd designed her species had wanted an aggressive, energetic, territorial breed. The same hormones produced a driving libido as well; that was deep in the primate inheritance, and would have required complete rewiring to change. Normally she didn't mind, but this wasn't the Domination, where body servants expected to do concubine duty as a matter of course. One human wasn't nearly enough—she didn't want to wear Dolores out—and going too long without could produce unfortunate results, like poor Jamie Simms. Not that she'd hurt him—she had better control than that—but he'd had an alarming night. Controlling the need eventually required a counterproductive amount of energy.

What I need is an isolated retreat, she thought. A Household, or as close as this world could come to it. That would be the best base of operations. *And perhaps I should reproduce.*

No other *drakensis* around for gene-merging, of course, but she could clone herself. The technology was simple, not far above this world's level; remove the nucleus of an ovum, replace with cell nucleus, remove the postfetal inhibitors, and stimulate to divide. A human female would do well enough for a brooder. The immune-markers were compatible; that had been built in as a failsafe way back in the early days. For that matter, she had a functional womb herself, if she cared to spend a year to bring it up from standby status.

She pursed her lips in distaste. Now *there* was a perverse thought.

Yes, a child was definitely a possibility. It would be comforting to have another Draka to help out, if the Project took that long.

The cheesecake arrived. "My compliments to the staff," she said, and slipped a fifty into the waiter's hand.

He beamed at her, and Gwen smiled back.

She hadn't had this much fun in centuries.

"*Hunhf.* Twelve."

Henry Carmaggio sat up on the weight bench, wheezing a little and wiping his face with the sweat towel slung around his neck. Any excuse to delay moving from the bench press to the goddamned preacher curls; last year or so they'd set off a twinge in his left shoulder, the place where he'd broken it playing touch football back when he was sixteen. It hadn't hurt since, but now . . .

The gym wasn't very full, for a Saturday afternoon. Enough for the usual heavy smell of sweat, people pumping away at the Nautilus machines, pedaling fast to nowhere on the Life Cycles and going to the same place on foot on the StairMasters. The small windows up along the roof under the outside wall were steamed up, but the big mirrors at the far end were clear enough. They showed one middle-aged cop, a stocky thickset man with heavy shoulders and a waist only a little thicker than the best that could reasonably be expected. Heavy craggy features with a beak nose, hazel eyes, a solid frosting of gray at the temples of hair worn unfashionably short. The shorts and T-shirt he was wearing showed arms and legs corded with muscle and thick with curling black hair; a line of old white scars ran down his left leg from thigh to calf.

One good thing about working up a sweat, he thought. *It takes your mind off itches you can't scratch.* Like the warehouse case. Not just being taken off it, but he hadn't heard zip on the street, either.

Of course, a co-ed gym also reminded you of other itches. On the good side, better than two-thirds of the men here were gay, which reduced the competition. On the bad side, the women tended to be way, way above his income and education bracket. And whatever current theories said should be, that still made a great wonking difference. *And face it, you expected to stay married until you were in a wheelchair.*

He rose, wincing at how his knees crackled, and ambled over to the weights section for the preacher curls. As usual, somebody had put the weight disks back on the stands any old way, meaning you had to heave them around to get the ones you needed to fit on the bar.

"*Patrón,*" a voice said.

He started slightly. "Jesus!" he said.

Jesus winced, probably because people had been making jokes about his name ever since the family moved from San Juan to New York when he was three.

"Got a message for you, Lieutenant," he said.

Carmaggio's eyebrows rose. It was Saturday, and he wasn't working the weekend this week.

"Lady wants to talk to you. From the Feds."

Ahhh, he thought, and suddenly the aches in his muscles and the sweat running down his barrel-shaped torso ceased to matter.

"Wants to talk about you-know-what, if you're interested."

"You bet your ass," Carmaggio said softly. His teeth showed. "Bet your ass, *paisano.*"

"I'm Special Agent Claire Finch," the FBI agent said, sliding into the booth.

Carmaggio sized her up as they shook hands. Finch was small—wouldn't have gotten into law enforcement before the height requirements were removed—and extremely pretty in a businesslike way: reddish-brown hair, fox-sharp face with a hillbilly point to her chin and a very faint trace of mountain accent. Scots-Irish, probably, maybe with a trace of Cherokee: West Virginia, or East Tennessee. He'd had guys from that area in his platoon. One of them had been the best shot he'd ever met.

"Detective Lieutenant Henry Carmaggio," he said.

There was an awkward moment of silence while the waitress brought their coffee: cappuccino; they were north of Canal Street, in an area where Italian was slowly giving way to Asian. He sipped, relishing the familiar bitterness.

"So. You wanted a meet?"

Finch nodded a little jerkily. "Highly unofficial," she said.

Henry grinned. "Your brass doesn't like weird shit either, hey?"

"We—Special Agent Dowding and I, my boss—got the reports on your homicides because there seemed to be a repetitive pattern, might be a serial killer. We put out a flag on it. Sure enough, we got a repetition of the MO."

Henry felt himself tense. "Where?" he whispered.

"Through the DEA. Cali, Colombia."

"Shit, they get twenty homicides a *day* there, sometimes."

"Not this way. A couple of goons cut up—streetsoldiers for one of the drug operators. Crushed like dixie cups, killed with their own knives. Then a bank executive, found in his apartment a lot like your Stephen Fischer. And a disappearance, a flight attendant named Dolores Ospina Pastrana. All associated with a woman matching the description of the one seen with Fischer. Operating under the name of Smith."

"That's original," Carmaggio grunted. "Was the bank in Colombia dirty?"

"In *Cali*?" Finch said.

"Point taken," Carmaggio said.

"Outside our jurisdiction," she went on. "And some time ago, now. But you see the implications."

"Money. We've got someone who drops into a major buy, kills twenty men, and walks out with . . . call it a million plus in very dirty bills. They stop over at an apartment for a few hours. Then at another for a week, a killing at each. There *may* have been another—"

"What?" Finch leaned forward.

"Lowlife named JoJo Jackson, down around Times Square. Did false ID, among other things; we found him in an alley. Somebody grabbed him by the back of the neck and slammed his face into the wall, *real* hard.

"I don't like this," Henry went on softly. "I don't like this at all. Because it says *learning*, to me. Learning about things, killing the teacher to clean up, moving on."

"And laundering the money," Finch said, with a tight controlled nod. "Which means that whoever it is now has a million dollars—call it half that after the cut the cleaners take—in untraceable funds."

She cleared her throat. "It's not a serial killer in the conventional sense. Not a drug thing under the DEA's mandate. Not just a homicide."

"It's very fucking strange," Henry said quietly. "Let's stop beating about the bush."

The agent hesitated, tapping her fingers on the linoleum, then came to a decision:

"Our esteemed friends at you-know-where near D.C. grabbed the arm," she said. "My guess is they're studying the hell out of it somewhere and want the lid very firmly in place. Word's come down from above that it's a national security matter. Drop it, forget it, it never happened. The Company and Military Intelligence have whole sections dedicated to woo-woo stuff; TV to the contrary, the Bureau doesn't."

Henry tapped a finger on the table.

"Who specifically?" he said. "You wouldn't happen to know about a couple of thick-ears, one of 'em twenty-five, brown hair, blue eyes, the other—"

"Andrews and Debrowski," Finch said. "Yes. They're wet-work specialists, operating for a new branch. Bioterrorist threats. Mostly Company people."

"Them," he said. "I would have thought NSA. You might be interested to know that they paid a call on a friend of mine. They weren't real friendly themselves, and they picked up something important."

"It's a joint operation, which is why technically they *do* have domestic jurisdiction. Not that that ever stopped you-know-who from doing you-know-what."

"The Company," Carmaggio said. "Let me tell you about the spooks. Guy I know—this happened back in seventy, I met him years later in a VA hospital, Navaho guy—was in the Special Forces, his unit was up in the Highlands, running a Hmong camp. Seems there was an encryption group, Company people, operating out of the camp. Good men, with some equipment that was high-tech back in those days. They were reading local enemy signal traffic better than Victor C."

Finch's eyes turned intent at the policeman's tone. Carmaggio's voice went low and tight. He'd never been there himself when he was in-country, but he could see it—down to the feel of the heat, the black-pajama'd Montagnards, the long lean pigs rooting among the sandbags, chickens clucking, naked brown kids.

"So they get Elint that the enemy's going to attack the camp. Do they pass it on? No, they do not. They ask permission from Langley. And Langley decides that it's a higher priority to keep the fact that we're— they're—reading the signals secret. So it goes back and forth between Langley and this pissant little firebase for *days*, until the guy in charge of the listening post takes out his .45 and shoots up the radio and tells the Special Forces officer running the place what's coming down—only by then it's real late, and four hours later two battalions of NVA hit their wire. Couple hours after that, they were calling in strikes right on top of their own position."

He forced his fingers to relax on the thick china cup. "The Navaho guy got dusted out with an AK bullet through both knees. And that," he said softly, "is what I think of the spooks. And they're doing it again.

"Isn't it a coincidence," he went on in a lighter tone of voice, "that your people at Quantico can't tell us any more about that skin sample we got from under Marley Man's fingernails, or return it?"

"Yes. Remarkable coincidence. The Bureau didn't object, and normally they wouldn't spit on the Company if they saw 'em dying of thirst in the desert, for fear it would give them the strength to crawl to water."

"And the spooks don't much care about the unsolved homicides, do they?"

The FBI agent cleared her throat and spoke, in her polite, barely accented voice: "We do, Mr. Carmaggio. It may sound strange, but we feel a certain responsibility to the American public. And whatever else we have, it's a pattern killer. I'm not ruling *anything* out, including mutants and space aliens, but whatever it is— it kills."

Carmaggio nodded heavily and finished the lukewarm remnants of his cappuccino. "My gut tells me the pattern's not going to stay down in the land of coffee and nose-candy, either."

"We did . . . retain the DNA pattern when the other people took the skin sample," Finch said. "Unofficially, and just in case. You know the passport setup the Canadians have nowadays?"

"Bring in $250,000 and get their equivalent of a green card? Yeah. Getting a lot of heavy traffic out of Hong Kong that way."

"It's also a natural setup for various sorts of crime, not to mention espionage, so we have some contacts with the RCMP," Finch said. "My boss called in a favor and had them run a computer check on their applications. They do a DNA fingerprint—just satellite-DNA, not the deep stuff. They didn't see anything strange, but it did match the pattern markers I sent them."

"Ahhh." A vast hunter's satisfaction warmed Carmaggio's belly.

A fax slid across the table to him. He felt his eyebrows rise at the picture. *This* was what had wasted Marley Man? He looked at the high-cheeked sculpted face. *Looker.* Maybe it was his imagination, but there was something *wrong* about it . . .

"Gwendolyn Ingolfsson," he read. "Colombian citizenship . . ."

"Which you can buy retail," Finch said.

Henry shrugged assent. With the amounts of money washing around down there, everyone was dirty and pretty well everything was for sale. The down side of that was that local ID was a trouble-flag to half the police forces on earth. Canadian papers were nearly as easy to get and not nearly as likely to arouse suspicion.

"And resident in the Bahamas," she said. "They don't like people asking questions there, not without very good reasons. We can't do anything; officially that skin sample no longer exists and never did. But . . ."

Another piece of paper followed the picture. The header and signature had been blanked out when it was photocopied, but he recognized the style.

" . . . *damage to cranium is congruent with beam weapon. Laser is unlikely due to explosive deformation upon penetration. An energetic-particle or metallic charged-plasma beam, with the latter being the higher probability. Guide mechanism unknown. Effect indicates a power source in the multiple-megawatt scale; the effect could not be duplicated without capacitors and other equipment weighing in the seven- to twelve-tonne range . . ."*

"I'll be goddamned," he said. "It *was* a ray gun. No wonder the spooks are all over it."

Carmaggio leaned back and hooked an ankle over his knee. "Now, Special Agent, that leaves one question. Why exactly are you coming to *me* about all this?"

"They're probably thinking in terms of some foreign connection," Finch said. "We—my boss and I—don't think so. We don't know what, but it doesn't fit espionage."

"The problem with setting up an organization to find bio-terrorists . . ." Carmaggio said.

" . . . is that they *will* find bio-terrorists. Whether they're there or not. And my boss is convinced that if they *do* find"—she tapped the picture—"her, they'll try to deal. Sure as fate, they'll try to deal; they want that stuff that badly. The only thing we're confident of is that there'll be more bodies."

They looked at each other for an instant. Somebody had walked into that warehouse and killed twenty armed men with a knife and bare hands. The picture didn't look like someone who could do that . . . but nobody could, anyway.

"Not Rambo on his best day," Carmaggio said, and the FBI agent nodded. "I do not understand this." Finch nodded again.

"We don't need to understand *how*, right now," she said. "What and who will do just fine."

"So we stay in touch," Carmaggio said. "And we get ready; getting those papers smells like preparation for another try at the U.S. to me."

Whatever lived behind those eyes was getting smarter. Getting ready.

"We can help each other with this," Finch said. It sounded as much like a prayer as a statement.

"I certainly hope so, Ms. Finch," he said. "Because we both need all the help we can get."

He looked down at the picture. The rest of the data on the sheet was probably fiction, but the face was real. The eyes, green and level, with a hint of mockery in them.

CHAPTER SIX

Immobilized in gel, breathing thick oxygen-rich fluid, Kenneth Lafarge was one with the machine. It was deceptively simple in appearance, an egg two meters long and one-and-a-half at its broadest point. The color was a soft matte black, the material a complex ceramic assembled atom by atom. Inside were the mechanisms that maintained him unknowing as it coasted in through the outer planets to a precisely calculated meeting with the third.

The machine woke him. **approaching Earth/2,** it said/thought. **passive scans reveal no overt enemy presence**.

He activated the exterior sensor feed, and the chill immensity of space snapped into being around him. Below was a view he knew only from ancient holographs and long-distance scans; the blue-white shield of Earth, turning in majesty. Now he was near it, one of less than half a dozen of his people since the Exodus, four centuries before. It was like and unlike Samothrace in the Centauri system. Blue of water, white of cloud, brown-gray-greens of land; more water than his native planet, less land surface, slightly bigger overall, the shapes of the coastlines completely different. Samothrace was a world of many islands, many continents scattered among shallow seas, none larger than a few million square kilometers.

Earth.

Earth/2, he reminded himself. Four and half centuries before, in a history that was probably very unlike the one that had led to his world.

Input analysis, he commanded.

Data flowed in; from radio and vid broadcasts, from the sparse satellite traffic. *There's a United States here, but no Domination,* he realized. Getting ready for a Presidential election. Amazing. Dozens upon dozens of sovereign countries, few of them large. *So much for the theory that planetary unification is inevitable in an industrialized world.* There was hardly anything in space, which was even more amazing. Plenty of electromagnetic traffic, neutron output from fission plants, the atmosphere showed a *lot* of industrial byproducts, more than anything in the prime line's history. But none of the lunar colonies and orbital habitats his 1995 would have shown, nothing out in deep space or the asteroid belts.

How do they maintain that density of population without materials and energy from space? he thought. From the looks of it, there must be more than five billion people down there; his Earth had never reached even half that, and by the late twentieth century it'd been dependent on space-based inputs.

The first tenuous wisps of atmosphere buffeted the egg. It plunged more steeply, and outside views degraded under ionization and the peeling of layers of ablative covering.

Detection, the machines told him; he could feel the microrays stroking at the outside of the egg, like sun on skin through the linkage. The stealthing would handle it easily; it was quite a primitive system. Not as good as what the Alliance for Democracy had had at the time of the Final War. *Would have had.* This whole multiple-world thing was enough to warp your brain. At a guess, this history hadn't had the sort of relentless competition that had driven technology in his.

Lucky bastards.

Gravity pushed at him, building, even in the liquid cocoon. At sixty thousand meters the drive kicked in, slowing his descent. That many energetic ions ought to cause some sort of a stir, but he doubted they'd know what they were looking at. It lasted exactly twenty seconds, and by then he was moving at only slightly more than the terminal velocity of the half-ton egg. North America opened beneath him, dark with night, starred with cities and roadways.

He felt his throat tighten, emotion unexpected and intense. The ancient homeland, the lost and lovely. His great-great-great-great-grandfather had been born here . . . or at least this was another version of that place. The land of Jefferson, Washington, Douglas, Evrard.

Minutes passed. The machine sensed the proper altitude and the exterior of the egg disintegrated, returning to its primary constituents and dispersing silently on the wind as molecular dust. The wing deployed; he steered it effortlessly on the currents of air toward the cornfield below. It set his feet down between two rows and disappeared itself, a rain of particles far too fine to feel against his skin. He pulled the breatherfilm off his face and spent a moment coughing the liquid out of his lungs.

He was naked in a cornfield in . . . *Illinois,* the comp built into his skull prompted, drawing a map. The same political division here as in his history. *But Mexico and Canada are separate countries.* Events must have diverged early in the nineteenth century; Canada had been annexed to the U.S. in 1812, Mexico in 1848, Central America and Cuba during the 1850s.

It was fairly chilly, a cold March night; much like the

high country around his family's ranch in Galatin State
back on Samothrace. He opened the flat case at his
feet and took out overalls and boots, both neutral colors
with archaic zip fasteners. Nothing there that any
detection apparatus would find interesting, but he'd
ditch them as soon as possible. The rest of his equipment stayed inside the shielded suitcase, except for a
smooth dark oblong he slipped into one pocket. That
would shoot a slug of ultracompressed gas, very effective at close range, and not at all conspicuous.

He cocked an ear. Traffic sounds from about two
klicks away; a highway, and transport.

Mid-eastern coast, North America. That was all they'd
been able to learn about the enemy molehole; that, and
that it was probably an accident. Typical Draka brute-
force-and-massive-ignorance science, but it could work.
If they had the time. He was probably within three or
four years of the original penetration, certainly within
a decade. No overt sign of the Draka's activity.

The corn rustled about him. A sleeping continent . . . a sleeping world, and something terrible
loose in it. A worm in the bud, eating and burrowing and preparing to riddle it with the deadly spawn
of the Domination.

He picked up the suitcase and began to walk toward
the road.

Ken Lafarge snapped a fist into the elbow. It broke
with an unpleasant crackling sound, and he released
the knife hand.

The other two muggers fled down a darkened alley,
hauling the injured one along. Ken stooped and picked
up the weapon one of them had dropped when snap-
kicked in the gut; he turned it over in his hands,
ejected the magazine, worked the action and disassembled it.

A little primitive, he thought, putting it back together.

Semi-automatic slugthrower, no guidance system at all. He reloaded and dropped it into a pocket, then reluctantly added the money from the criminals' wallets he'd taken. They'd probably stolen it themselves.

This section of Chicago was unbelievably shabby and run-down. It *stank*, of urine and uncollected garbage. Everyone else he'd seen here was black—rather like what he'd read about parts of the South, right after the Civil War. Not many blacks had been among the refugees to Samothrace, and the population had homogenized by intermarriage in the centuries since.

Didn't they free the slaves here, or what? he thought, turning and walking north, farther away from the bus station. *Wait a minute. No Domination here, ever.* So there'd been no place for the irreconcilables of the South to go, after whatever version of the Civil War this mutant history contained. That could mean . . . *Wait until you've got the data.*

More of the internal-combustion vehicles passed him along the rain-sodden street, splashing through puddles in the cracked pavement. He stopped beside one that was resting on the bare rims of its tires and popped the hood open, shining a pencil-light on the interior.

Interesting. Spark-ignition piston system. A fuel-air mixer that looked for all the world as if somebody had developed it from a perfume-bulb atomizer. Lots of electrical auxiliaries, and even a compchip monitoring system. He called up schematics of autosteamer engines from the historical files. Nothing even remotely similar. Oh, this thing would *work*, it probably even had a fairly good thermal efficiency, but it was absurdly overstressed for a civilian road-vehicle at a twentieth-century level of technology. Not to mention the toxic byproducts of high-temperature combustion.

IC piston engines something like this were used for aircraft, he remembered. And sometimes for armored fighting-vehicles, compression-ignition Diesels, although

the Draka had used a turbocompound system during
the Eurasian War of the 1940s. Road vehicles had
always been external-combusion, though—steam, from
the early days of powered street transport in the 1820s,
closed-cycle Rankin engines by the 1990s.

*Lord, you'd have to have had fairly advanced
machining to use IC engines in road cars.* High temperatures like that required close tolerances and cor-
rosion-resistant materials compared to steam. This one
was quite well-made, in a crazy sort of way; he pulled
a sensor thread from his suitcase and scanned.

**tolerances to within one ten-thousandth of a
millimeter,** the comp told him. **following alloys—**

He tried to imagine an early-Victorian precursor of
the engine before him, and failed. Steam engines had
started out heavy and crude, like the first road
autosteamers themselves, and gotten gradually better.
Steam turbines had powered the first dirigibles and
aircraft; then internal combustion had been developed
when those ran up against inherent power-to-weight
limitations, in the 1870s. By then manufacturing technique had improved enough to make that practical.
How on earth could gas engines like this have been
developed *first*, though?

He clanged the hood down and started north again.
It might have been easier in an honestly weird ana-
logue—something where Vikings had colonized North
America, or the South had won the Civil War. There
was just enough familiar here to be disorienting. Some
sort of cheap hotel for the night, then to a library.

*I'll have to investigate before I contact the authorities,
obviously,* he mused.

The motel room smelled of disinfectant, but it was
spacious compared to quarters on an interstellar space-
ship. The window outside showed a vista of wet dark
parking lot, an anonymous part of an anonymous town

in Ohio. Ken Lafarge had a car outside, two suitcases of local clothing and sundries; even a razor, just in case someone looked over his effects. This paper currency of theirs was childishly easy for his faber to duplicate, and if anyone caught the duplicated serial numbers his money would look *more* authentic than the originals.

Not that anyone seemed likely to check him over. He didn't expect genescans, but there was almost nothing of the structure of identity documents and permits he remembered from history lessons about *his* world's America in the 1990s. These people didn't spend anything on defense, and very little on exploration. No national service, no youth-training camps, an incredible cultural balkanization that destroyed unity and purpose. They were only *now* getting anything like a reusable orbital launcher; by this date in his history, the first interstellar ship was nearly completed. And this Earth was so *poor*, so short of energy and materials, so filthy with the byproducts of horrendously inefficient industries.

But it's not about to be conquered by monsters, he thought grimly. *Not if I do my job.*

Kenneth looked back at the vid—*the television,* he reminded himself. *Too strange. Too much.*

He could understand the standard language well enough; it was far closer to the rather conservative Samothracian dialect of English than the Domination's variety. It was the *context* he couldn't follow. Alien, alien. People in an ampitheater-like room were standing and telling a black woman things about their personal lives . . .

Incest. Child molestation. Sexual combinations even a *Draka* would find disgusting. He sat on the bed and dropped his head into his hands.

All his training and study had been aimed at the twenty-fifth-century Domination. *This mission is a ratfuck waiting to happen. Lousy tradecraft.* His equipment was aimed at that particular setting, too. Elaborate stealthing that he didn't need, and minimal power outputs because he couldn't possibly shoot his way off a hostile, highly-advanced planet. What he needed was brute-force stuff, weapons.

your blood chemistry is at less than 87% of optimum, the AI said in his mind. **indications of shock syndrome and stress. permission to adjust.**

Granted, he thought, and shuddered as a sudden coolness ran over his skin. Breathing slowed, sweat dried. He stripped and dropped to the floor; a hundred two-finger pushups with the weight of his case on his shoulders, stretching, squats, crunches. Better. A shower, and he began to feel like a human being again.

"Let's get to work," he said and snapped off the TV.

He sat by the telephone. Tendrils grew out of the case, pale threads thinning to invisibility. They wove their way into the native instrument. Ken closed his eyes.

The cyberweb formed around him. *Scan,* he thought. *Eastern North America, five-year intervals, following parameters.*

A long wait, in a floating world of colors. Waiting while the AI poured out through the low, slow bandwidth available, and communicated with machines several orders of magnitude more primitive.

A structure began to grow before his mind's sight, three-dimensional and glowing with colors impossible for waking eyes.

"Interesting," he breathed. "A *distributed* system?" **correct.**

The AI wove it backward in time, then forward again to show its growth. About the only commonality it had with the history of cybernetics he knew was that the original set of linkages had been military-inspired.

"No central nexus?"

no. capacity is added incrementally. the basic units are small personal comps with open-access memories and instruction-set parameters.

He whistled silently. "Grotesque," he said. *So many separate processing units!* And so easy to infiltrate; nothing but a few clumsy password systems and crude encryption codes. This would give any competent counterespionage agency the screaming willies, right back to the beginning of computers—back to the compressed-air-powered mechanical Babbage systems used in the nineteenth century, even.

His attention flashed to an item culled from a database.

new york, january 2, 1995, the machine said. **following details.**

Oddly limited details. Twenty men—petty criminals of some sort—slaughtered. A few pictures. The AI corrected them to 3-D, filled in probabilities in coded order. One with his head blown mostly off.

"Plasma gun," Lafarge breathed softly. "Layer knife."

Stripped metallic ions, superconducting guide coil and power source, flash chamber. Not a sophisticated weapon, in use for centuries—but nothing this world could build without boxcarloads of equipment.

The others had been killed by blunt-injury trauma and the edged weapon. "Typical," he said.

The *drakensis* had reacted with the bloodlust built into the species; and they loved to do it by hand, if they could. Killed everyone there in a single orgasmic burst of slaughter, crushing and ripping bone and organ, tearing the life out of the fragile human bodies.

"Oh, I think you were a startled and unhappy little snake," he said.

Follow the leads. He walked through luminescent tunnels of data. Barriers glowed for instants, then dissolved like sand under his fingers. Like movement in a dream, thick and honey-slow. Things took so *long*.

Ah. Two more killings in New York. A derelict, and a businessman. He grimaced slightly at the details of the last. *It lured him. Used him.* The pheromonal dominance system; the poor primitive would never have known what hit him. Also the snake must have been recovering, getting its mental feet under it—that showed thought and planning, not blind fury.

A description. *Jesus. A female.* He opened his eyes for a moment, returning to the realtime world.

"Damn."

That meant it could reproduce; the techniques were easily within the tech level here. Potentially hundreds, thousands of times, like digger wasp larvae in grubs. He swallowed queasiness and closed his eyes again. No immediate trace. *There.* A skin sample. Data cataracted down the link, built up into a picture.

Know the enemy.

He banished the sharp-featured image, sighing. Three years more time to track down; and with increasing caution. It would have anticipated pursuit, and built safeguards as soon as it could.

"And you're from another galaxy?"

Ken felt his eyes narrow. "I didn't say that," he said. "Don't be absurd. I'm from a planet orbiting Alpha Centauri. It's only 4.2 light-years from here."

"Thattaway, just a bit," the young man said. "*Engage.*"

His partner snorted amusement; he was older than the agent talking to Ken Lafarge, heavier-set, and much less communicative. He was also standing behind the Samothracian, behind and to the left—a posture which made Lafarge extremely uncomfortable, since it put him in a bracket. The office was a cubicle in some unmarked office building northwest of Washington proper. It had the faint ozone smell he was coming to associate with here-and-now bureaucracy, the stink of primitive electronics with loose connections. The rest of it looked very ordinary, under a fluorescent light with an annoying subliminal hum.

He could approve of that commonplace aspect, if nothing else: putting up a huge monolith with some equivalent of *Secret Intelligence Headquarters* on a big sign out front had been a bad habit of some of the old Alliance for Democracy's security agencies. Everything else might change across the centuries, but it remained a constant that this line of work attracted both paranoids and the boyish type who liked to show off their affiliation with powerful clandestine networks. Whatever this organization was, it was keeping the latter under control at least.

"Look—what's your name, anyway?"

"John," the young man said. "John Andrews. This is Clete Debrowski."

"Look, Mr. Andrews, I thought I gave you some pretty convincing data."

Andrews leaned back in his swivel chair. It creaked. John Andrews didn't look heavy, but his frame was packed with solid dense muscle.

"Yup, you did, Mr. Lafarge. You know things you definitely shouldn't; about what went on in New York back in '95, and things from extremely classified databanks."

He leaned forward again, the friendly smile dying away from his face. It had never quite reached his eyes. "So why don't you cut this spaceman shit," he spat. "*Who* are you working for, and *what* is going on?"

"Who do you think?" Lafarge said. *They don't believe me*, he realized. *They seriously don't believe me!*

"We don't know. We don't know who was dealing with those posse hopheads in the warehouse, or how your deal went wrong, or why you were using them— smuggling biohazards, whatever the hell you were doing. Hell, maybe you're working for the Russians;

they may not be communists anymore, but they're not all that friendly. We *do* know it was dirty, and we *do* know you're going to tell us all about it."

He laughed. "Unless you beam up really quick."

Ken braced his palms against the arms of his chair. "Mr. Andrews," he said quietly. "If I don't convince you, events will . . . but by then it will be very late, very late indeed. You're gambling with the future of the entire human race."

"And you're not in the offices of the *National Enquirer*," Andrews barked. "*Sit* down. This administration takes matters of national security seriously, whatever the previous occupants thought."

Debrowski put two heavy hands on Lafarge's shoulders and pushed, using his considerable weight. The thin leather cusion smacked under his buttocks, and the high arms cramped him.

"Mr. Andrews," he said quietly. "I appreciate your position, and I realize you think you're doing your duty. In a sense I'm an American too—"

"Not according to our files," Andrews said. "Your ID is good paper but there's nobody of that age, name or Social Security number. I suggest you stop lying."

"—but the stakes are too high. I can't let you detain me. *It* might well find out."

And if it did while he was immobilized and separated from his equipment, he was a dead man. The planet with him.

Debrowski spoke for the first time. "Let?" he said. "*Let* us detain you?"

Andrews loosened his tie. "You're on the third floor of a high-security building," he said. "You're *already* detained. I also suggest you start exercising a little realism."

Good advice, Lafarge thought regretfully.

His hands darted up behind his head and closed on Debrowski's ears. *Crack.* The older man's nose smacked into the crown of the Samothracian's head. He bellowed with pain, recoiling backward; then struck down with both hands, a double chop that would have severed his opponent's collarbones like green branches . . . if the situation had been what he assumed.

Time slowed as the net laid along his nerves activated.

First level, he commanded: the biological price was too high for anything more. His bladed palms chopped up and out, thudding into Debrowski's forearms with a meaty, rubbery sensation. He used the momentum to drive himself upward, aiding the powerful spring of his legs and capturing the other man's arms under his own for a second.

Crack. Crack. He punched the rear of his head into the other's face again, slightly harder this time. Despite the reinforced bone, that was still a little painful for him, but much more so for Debrowski. The bulky figure toppled away behind him. Andrews was coming erect, his lips moving slowly and the gun coming out from under his arm. Lafarge's time-sensor clocked the movement; remarkable reflexes. The automatic system brought his softsuit flowing out from cuffs and collar to complete its coverage of his body. Cool neutrality insulated his skin, like dipping into dry water; it pressed his short-cropped hair against his scalp.

Transparent, he commanded—no use giving away more than he had to. The locals would see only a slight shimmer over his skin, if they saw anything at all in the heat of the moment. He turned and leaped through the glass door, one foot driving down on the seat of the chair. Glass exploded away from his outstretched fists as his hundred and ninety pounds dove forward. He landed on his hands and front-rolled. The outer office was empty; and now he knew why Andrews had insisted on an evening meeting. Fewer witnesses, when they took his sedated body away to someplace secluded.

Smart boy, he thought. Smart in the day-to-day sense, at least. Pity he didn't have much imagination. Lafarge skidded slightly as he cornered to drive down a corridor between rows of cubicles separated by movable partitions. The disguising shoes gave poor traction; no amount of strength or speed could increase the gripping surface on the soles of his feet. And—

WHACK. The 9mm bullet struck the base of his skull. Red-tinged blackness surged in, and the floor came up to strike him. The iron and copper taste of blood filled his mouth as teeth gashed lips or tongue. A diminished *pinnnnng* caught at the edge of his attention as the ricochet whined off to lose itself in a computer or potted plant or water cooler. He twitched, fingers scrabbling at the synthetic carpet. The softsuit could sense the bullet coming and turn instantly harder than diamond and more frictionless than liquid mercury on dry ice. It couldn't repeal the law of conservation of momentum. A substantial fraction of the bullet's energy moved his head forward, and his brain surged backward in its bath of fluid as inertia prevented it from moving quite in synch.

Time for concussion later. The combat web dumped chemicals into his carotids and stimulus into the motor centers of his brain. He rose to his knees.

Bang-ptannng. Again and again; the next three shots hit him between the shoulders, ripping the disguising clothes and torquing his body around just enough to see the pistol coming out the shattered office door with Andrews's face snarling behind it. Partitions collapsed as he lurched against them. He scuttled forward like a mechanical crab on hands and knees, the fabric of his trousers ripping with his haste. More shots, none hitting this time; Andrews wavered sideways as Debrowski's body struck him at the waist.

"*Stop that, you stupid fuck!*" Andrews screamed. He snapshot again as Lafarge pistoned up from the floor, running like an Olympic hurdler and leaping desks with a raking stride. "*I've got him, I've—*"

Another shot struck Lafarge in the back of the knee. The softsuit saved the joint from the sideways leverage, but it cost him momentum toward the windows. The rectangle of the gasgun slapped into his palm, thrown forward by the holster. He shot; the windows burst away in a cloud of needles as the slug of ultracompressed air hammered them out of his way like an invisible piledriver. He followed in a soaring leap.

"He brothk my dose! De bathurd brothk my dose!" Debrowski yelled, as much in rage as pain.

"*Fuck* your nose," Andrews shouted.

The wounded man tumbled sideways, knocking over the wastebasket. The younger agent wrenched the door open—both panels of frosted glass were gone in a pile of shards that shifted treacherously underfoot. He went through in a skittering crouch, gun in a two-handed grip, down the aisle to the windows overlooking the parking lot. The bastard's body would *have* to be there. He wasn't necessarily dead; Andrews was fairly sure he'd hit him with at least one round, and a three-story fall onto pavement had to break bones, but doing wetwork you learned how tough the human body could be. He wouldn't be going anywhere, though. Not fast.

"Nothing," he said, with more obscenity in the word than ten minutes' scatology. Then, quietly and with conviction: "Shit."

He holstered his weapon. Alarms were ringing downstairs, and the stairwell doors burst open as a couple of the guards came through. Andrews spread his hands.

"It's Andrews," he said, repeating it in a loud, clear voice.

You couldn't tell what men would do when they came charging into a room expecting a firefight; except that it wouldn't necessarily be what hindsight thought best. When the gunmen straightened up from their crouch he went on:

"Get a medic. Fast. Then get on the horn to the local police, put an APB out on Kenneth Lafarge, the picture's on my desk, armed and dangerous, wanted for assault and attempted murder." His calm broke. *"Move! Now!"*

God alone knew who this fruitloop was really working for. God alone knew what he'd be doing now.

Andrews shuddered slightly. In reaction, and for what might be. The Firm had dozens of scenarios on bioterrorism, none of them pretty. Whoever had been using the Jamaicans as a conduit knew more about genetic engineering than anyone should; that arm from whatever-the-fuck-it-was proved that. Genetics was low-cost science, much easier to do in a private lab than nuclear weapons, even with plutonium coming out of Russia like piss out of a horse.

He swallowed the sour throat-scraping taste of failure. *Ebola,* he thought. The Ebola virus had nearly gotten out of Africa twice; it was contagious as hell, and had a fatality rate of better than 90 percent. Someone with this group's skills could engineer something like that as they pleased. Give it a year-long incubation period with the victim contagious all the time. Ebola turned your connective tissue into mush. . . .

He ejected the magazine of his Glock, snapped in a fresh one and holstered it, all automatic reflex before he got a cupful of water and went over to kneel by George. The heavy-set man was holding a wad of tissues to his nose and dripping red down a sodden shirt.

"Dink we'll be hearing de randsub deband zoon?"

"Time will tell. At least we've got a clear make on one of them."

And when the ransom demand came, they might have to pay up.

* * *

"These are very fine diamonds, Mr. Smith," the dealer said, laying aside his loupe.

Kenneth Lafarge sat back in the rickety office chair and nodded. The little room was cramped and musty, piled with papers and ledgers; the desk held what this world considered a very up-to-date computer system, and a square of heavy paper with a spill of jewels across it.

"Gem quality, and not listed on the system as prohibited merchandise."

The dealer had a thick accent and wore a skullcap. That seemed to be usual on 47th Street, in this weird analog of New York. The skin between his shoulder blades crawled slightly as he smiled. This wasn't the city that had died in thermonuclear fire in 1999, but his mind's eye still saw those images. Samothrace had passed them down from generation to generation after the Exodus, a heritage of loss and revenge.

"Of course, you understand, without documentation, the price . . ." A delicate shrug from the diamond dealer.

He nodded. *Plenty more where those came from.* In fact, as long as he had carbon for raw material, any number of them. The suitcase contained a very compact little molecular assembler, well up to such simple tasks.

"Why don't you tell me what you think is reasonable, Mr. Feldman?" he said. It wouldn't do to arouse suspicion by not bargaining.

Ken replaced the phone with a sigh. No luck with *anyone* at the investment bankers.

Granted, he couldn't give them enough details to show that he was anything but a crank. Yet . . . these people didn't seem to have any healthy paranoia at all!

Futile, he thought. Still, one had to make the effort.

These businessmen didn't know what they were getting into.

The sign outside the building read *Smith Computer Services*; the cover was convenient, and it was pathetically easy to fox the IRS machines. Most of the big rooms were full of improvised rigs, cobbled together from local components. The rear of the building held a single spartan bedroom, and a gallery big enough for him to exercise and practice in. The main problem was people trying to buy computer services from him.

He sighed again and turned to a terminal. *Progress?* he asked.

The voice—melded from his implant and the much more capable machine in the suitcase—replied:

very little. the enemy's transducer includes all standard domination counterinfiltration infosets and is being used to protect the local machinery. i will need a direct landlink to penetrate.

Hmmm. *The police?*

as directed, the fbi have received the communication routed from the canadian authorities, the dispassionate voice in his brain continued. **an agent in receipt of the information has travelled to new york. the other intelligence agencies will be denied access. data relating to your encounter with the two agents will be protected.**

Ken ground his teeth at the memory of the fiasco in Washington. The local police and government were worse than useless. *I have to assume the snake is watching.* It wouldn't be any great problem to put flagging markers in the local infosystems; and there was no way he could keep the natives from using them if he revealed himself. If *it* found out he was here, things could get very bad.

I could put together a laser-triggered fusion weapon, he thought.

contraindicated. probability of earth/1 detection increases asymptotically in that scenario.

Moodily, he took up a sheaf of printout. More research on the divergence point between this line and Earth/1. Even the primitive, rudimentary infoweb of this 1998 had substantial research potential. The AI logged on to the . . . net, they called it . . . and asked questions under a dozen different user IDs.

Definitely the 1770s, he thought. There was a two-year difference in the date the Netherlands entered the War of the Revolution. Some more subtle changes as well; the British seemed to have done slightly better throughout the Revolution here than they had in the history he learned. *Wait a minute. Ferguson.*

Major Patrick Ferguson, according to the printout, had been killed in the British defeat at the battle of King's Mountain in 1779. He called up memory: a Major—later General—Patrick Ferguson had *won* the battle of King's Mountain in 1779. He'd also invented the first workable breech-loading rifle; the Loyalist exiles who founded the Domination-to-Be in southern Africa had used it on the natives there, immortalized it as the Gun That Broke the Tribes. Here, breech-loaders hadn't come into common use for seventy years after that.

"Ahh," he said, leafing through the sheaves of print-out again.

Here on Earth/2, Ferguson had been badly wounded during the American retreat from Long Island, in 1776; the unit equipped with his new rifle had been broken up. In Earth/1's history, he'd been *slightly* wounded and his riflemen had continued to be a thorn in the American side. In Ken's history, France *and* the Dutch had entered the war against the British in 1779. Here, the Dutch had stayed neutral until 1781. In Earth/1's history, the British had seized the Cape Colony, and used it to resettle the Loyalists and Hessians after the surrender at Yorktown in 1781. Over a hundred thousand of them, joined a little later by the French refugees from the Negro uprising in Santo Domingo.

That had been the seedbed of the Domination—a slave-based caste society of ferocious aggressiveness spreading out over southern Africa in the next generation.

On Earth/2, the Cape remained Dutch for another two generations, and never received the mass migration that started it on the road to world power. Eventually the natives took it over again. The great gold and diamond mines stayed undiscovered for a full century, until the 1880s; in his world they'd been exploited from the 1790s, and financed the industrialization of Africa.

Fascinating. The changes broadened out from there.

It was a more innocent world than his; poorer, more troubled in some respects, backward technologically, but without the monstrous weight of victorious totalitarianism that had crushed his ancestors at the end of the twentieth century.

"And it's up to me to preserve it," he said softly.

The working desk held a printout—flat, in 2-D—of his family back on Samothrace, standing in front of the ranchhouse. Mother, Dad, his sisters, the low sprawling stabilized-adobe structure his ancestor had built when men first came to the Alpha Centauri system, bringing the inheritance of humanity and liberty. He would never see them again; that was something you had to get used to, in the interstellar service—it might change with the molehole technology, but he'd been raised to think in sublight terms. He'd left them to protect them, a parting as final as death.

There was a world of people like them here, though.

Direct attack on the drakensis in its nesting site, he asked.

probability of detection from earth/1 negligible,

the machine said. **probability of mission success imponderable due to random factors.**

He leaned back in the swivel chair. *Yes*, he decided. The snake would be getting stronger all the time. It was designed to dominate, to rule, to work through others. The longer he waited, the more layers of innocent—or at least unknowing—true-humans he'd have to wade through to get to it.

It was probably monitoring air traffic. An ocean approach, though . . .

And he'd keep trying the financial people. Maybe one of them would listen to him, in the end.

CHAPTER SEVEN

Florence was a shock, Gwen decided. Mainly because so much was the *same*. The Eurasian War of her 1940s had killed a tenth of humankind and left most of northern Europe beaten flat, to be rebuilt in the conqueror's fashion. Italy had been overrun swiftly and with minimal combat, though. Her grandparents had settled in the country near here in 1946; her human mother was born there in 1954. Gwen had been cloned and implanted in a clinic in Florence, in the 1970s.

"Not far from right . . . here," she mused, shouldering through the crowds.

Still the same low sienna-colored skyline of tile roofs. The white-ribbed red dome of the Cathedral, with Giotto's bell tower; still a church, here. The Palazzo Vecchio, *not* a Security Directorate regional headquarters, here. The same narrow streets. And yet everything so *different* from the city of her youth. Hotter, crowded. Far too many of the absurd stinking ground vehicles; they were monstrosities even in the Americas, insane in this medieval street pattern. Noisy, gabbling, stinking feral humans everywhere, invading her sphere of social space, refusing to give way, some of them even daring to *touch* her. At first it was all she could to not to lash out, forcing her mind to clamp down on her glands. The air was better than New York's, but that was all you could say for it.

"I don't like what they've done with my home," she whispered subvocally.

That was illogical; the Domination's District of Tuscany had never existed here. The Ingolfsson plantation was a village called Radda, and had never known her family's footsteps. In fact, the Ingolfsson who'd founded the line had probably died in Iceland in 1784, rather than arriving in the proto-Domination as a refugee settler.

This mockery of her birthplace still put a subliminal growl in her throat. It might have been better to meet the scientist in Berlin.

No point in delaying. The Locanda Scoti was a moderately good *pensioni* not far from the Duomo, marked only by a plaque marked *P. Scoti*, right across from the Strozzi Palace. Inside was dark and quiet, the furnishings mostly eighteenth century. The staff looked at her with suspicion—she was in hiker's gear, and holding a knapsack—but she ignored them and took the stairs with a quick springy stride.

"Herr Doktor Mueller?" she said, knocking at the door.

There was a single human male inside: middle-aged and not too healthy, she could tell that from the scent and the sounds of breathing and heartbeat. Also the smell of alcohol, some potato distillate.

"Frau Ingolfsson?"

"*Ja.*"

She'd picked up modern German in preparation. It was easier than adjusting to this history's version of Italian, fewer childhood memories to overwrite.

The door opened a crack. She pushed it wider, gently but irresistibly, and walked in. The man closed it hastily;

within was dark, far too dark to be comfortable for human-norm vision. Papers were scattered over a table, and the bottle of . . . *schnapps*, the label said. She picked it up and drank down six or seven solid swallows. Not bad, if you wanted colorless, tasteless alcohol distilled from root vegetables. Gwen twitched the curtains open. Friedrich Mueller threw a hand up. She waited until the human had stopped blinking and squinting, then squeezed her hand. The thick glass broke with a spatter of liquid and fragments. Then she held the hand before his face.

The German watched silently, blinking, as the cuts closed and blood clotted with inhuman speed. Then she gripped his wrist, put her other hand on his shoulder and lifted, lifted until he was clear of the floor, waited for an instant and then set him down again. After a moment he slumped into a chair and stared at her, cleaning his glasses on his tie and staring at her. She could hear his heart leap, then steady a little erratically.

"I hope you're satisfied," she said. "I could tie that poker in knots, if you wish."

"No," he said slowly. His hand reached for the spot the bottle had occupied, then sank down. "I . . . I was fully convinced by the, the documents and so forth. Impossible to doubt such sums of money as well, and the papers were convincing . . . but this, this is a bit of a shock to me still, you will understand."

Odd creatures, humans, she thought once again. *To believe, and yet not believe.*

"I understand completely," she said soothingly, sitting down across the table from him.

"Another world," he whispered, taking up some of the papers. Among them was X-ray film.

Dr. Friedrich Mueller looked at the transparency. His hands shook and his face shone with lust; not for the woman across the table from him, but for what the film represented.

"These bones . . . they look as if they have *flanges* on them," he said.

"That's effectively what they are," Gwen said.

"Muscle attachments, I suppose," Mueller mumbled to himself. "Very broad area of attachment . . . but wouldn't the leverage be too much structurally?"

"The bone density is higher, as well as being stronger per unit of weight," Gwen said. "That's one reason I'm heavier. Also the muscle tissue itself is different, more fibers; the hemoglobin has a higher oxygen-transport capacity."

"It would have to, even with the added capacity from the larger heart and lungs." He nodded, and shuffled through the stack. "This organ, below the lungs, what is it?"

"Auxiliary heart, on standby unless the main is damaged. It keeps the circulation going on a minimal level until the primary organ regenerates."

"Full regeneration?" The German scientist's eyebrows rose. "Of an entire organ?"

"Limbs, organs, nerve and bone," Gwen said cheerfully. "Let's get something better than that swill you were drinking."

She picked up the phone. "A bottle of white and a selection of *antipasti*, please. That'll be cash." They fell silent until the maid had brought it.

"Regenerate unless I'm killed instantly," Gwen went on. "Blowing off enough of my body-mass would do that, or destroying enough of the brain, or cutting my throat back to the neckbone, something of that order."

He nodded again, reverently, and returned to his study of the transparencies. "Some of this hardly looks like biological systems at all," he said. "This webbing under the subcutaneous layer . . ."

"That's armor," Gwen said. "It's grown there as single-molecule chains of organo-metallic compounds by a . . . call it a synthetic virus. Damned uncomfortable, while it's being done. There are a number of, hmmm, we call them biomods, done that way."

The German looked up. "Logical," he said. "I should think a good deal of your technology works so, at a molecular-mechanical level."

"Or atomic. Down there, there isn't all that much distinction between a machine and an organism," she said. "It's all chemistry if you get small enough. Or even physics."

He laid his hands on the table and looked at them. "I have spent my entire life in futility, it would seem," he sighed.

"Scarcely," Gwen said with a chuckle, picking an olive out of a bowl. She savored the rich salt-oil taste, crunching the pit for the extra trace of bitterness. Then she went on:

"You could scarcely know someone with my database was going to show up. For that matter, your species is more scientifically creative than mine."

Mueller looked up sharply. "How so?"

"We modified ourselves neurologically before we fully understood the brain-mind interface," she said. "For that matter, we don't *fully* understand it yet. *Drakensis* seem to have less capacity for . . . intuitive leaps than you do, although we've got more g-factor intelligence. Perhaps we oversimplified while trying to eliminate some redundancies."

Mueller frowned. "I am surprised. I would have expected the neural functions to be a thoroughly solved problem—have you not true artificial intelligences?"

"Only by virtually copying brains; and then what you get is a brain in a box, and it's easier to breed them— we can use direct data-transfer with our own minds anyway if we need to link to machinery. In any case, it turns out to be impossible to be significantly more intelligent than the upper curve of the human range."

cannotcannotcannotcannotcannotcannotcannotcannot.”

“Y“Y“Y“Y“Y“Y“Y“Y“Y“Y“Y“Y“Y“Y“Yes, but that’s irrelevant. You people here are still
thinking of brains as organic computers made of neu-
rons, and that’s far too coarse a level of metaphor. For
one thing, neurons turn out to be only signalling devices.
The real information processing in the brain takes place
in smaller structures you’re just beginning to discover,
and at a quantum level. It’s non-algorithmic as well. In
your terms, the brain isn’t a Turing machine.”

She extended a hand. “Do we have an agreement,
then, Doctor Mueller?”

He took it in his. He was an ugly specimen, flabby
and pale and sour-smelling, but the look of worship on
his face made it almost agreeable.

“How could I not, and pass up a chance at such
information?” he said. “The only thing which puzzles
me is why you need the services of . . . of a witch-
doctor like me.”

“What you know isn’t *wrong*, just incomplete,” Gwen
explained. She crunched a few more olives. “And you
will be invaluable integrating my knowledge inconspicuously with the current technostructure here.”

“For a while,” the German said, his lips tightening.

“The current order hasn’t, ah, fully utilized your
talents, I know,” Gwen said.

Red spots appeared on Mueller’s cheeks. “I have been
hounded—persecuted—myself and my family . . .” He
controlled his breathing.

He’d also been quite important in the scientific
bureaucracy before the fall of the East German state.
Afterward, trial and unemployment, and an abrupt drop
in status and income.

“You’ll have nothing to complain of in my service,”
Gwen said.

“Yes, I would not expect the vulgarity, the penny-
pinching of capitalists from a world so advanced.”

"Well, we're certainly not capitalistic," Gwen said with a slight smile. "We're not exactly *true communism* either, you understand."

Mueller shrugged and cleaned his glasses again. "That particular faith I have lost some years ago," he said. "A stable order that appreciates my capacities and rewards me fairly, that is all I ask."

"You can expect that," Gwen said sincerely. "You can relocate immediately?"

"As soon as I arrange certain matters with my family," he replied.

Gwen nodded. "There's a house ready and waiting," she said.

"I can hardly wait to begin work," Mueller said, looking down at the sheets of transparent plastic. "The possibilities!"

Gwen looked out over the world.

"Exactly."

Alice Wayne sat in the waiting room and tried not to shift nervously. After a moment she stood and looked at herself again in the mirror. Nice sensible business suit, blond hair caught back with a clasp. Very light makeup. Emphasize the fresh-faced look, which her Anglo-Irish genes did anyway; you had to play the hand you were dealt. She looked a little younger than twenty-five, which was unfortunate, but what could you do? It was the curse of a snub nose and freckles. Practice a level-eyed look, friendly but businesslike.

She looked around the room; expensive offices, in the best part of Nassau. Leather furniture, and a window overlooking Delancy Street; not quite the center of town, but close. A faint ozone tang of computers, although the only one in sight had been on the receptionist's desk. The waiting room had a long table and prints on the wall, a few discreet magazines in a hardwood rack.

Was it worth the bother of answering the ad? she thought. Then: *I'm not going back to Sydney with my tail between my legs. Not yet.*

"Miss Wayne?" the receptionist asked. She had a Latin American accent. Alice jumped slightly. "This way. They'll see you now."

Alice picked up her attaché case and followed her into another room. This one had windows giving onto a balcony, and a working desk in one corner with terminal and all the trimmings. A woman and a man were waiting for her behind a table, with a seat for her on the other side.

The quasi-famous Gwendolyn Ingolfsson. She looked younger than Alice expected, no more than thirty, although she had the sort of sculpted face that is called ageless and does look much the same between the twenties and late middle age. *Natural redhead, naturally slim, filthy rich,* Alice thought. *The sort you hope is a bitch so you won't feel guilty hating her.* Something a little disturbing about the face, foxlike or catlike.

Gwen smiled slightly, an odd closed curve of the lips. Alice had the sudden feeling that the green eyes were looking right through her, and felt herself flush. *Another drawback to having ancestors from a small foggy island where pink skins were an advantage.*

Tom Cairstens. Lawyer, with California written all over him. Casual suit, outdoors tan, not quite as smooth-looking as you'd expect, an undertone of seriousness. *Quite ducky, actually. Not bad at all.*

"Thank you, Dolores. Would you like coffee or tea, Ms. Wayne?" the American asked.

"No thank you." *Damn.* She could tell when a man was impressed with her looks, and he wasn't. *Pity if he's queer.* Why were so many of the best-looking men gay?

"Well." He opened a folder; Alice recognized her résumé, and swallowed dryly. "First—"

The inquisition was relentless. Cairstens did the talking; the owner of IngolfTech sat silent, sipping fruit juice through a straw. When the lawyer was finished, Alice could feel herself sweating. She looked up, startled to see how far the shadows had moved.

Cairstens looked at his employer. "Seems suitable," he said. "Of course, so do many of the others."

"I'll take it from here, Tom," she said softly. Her voice was a husky purr, not quite like anything Alice had heard before, accented in a way she couldn't place.

"Now, Ms. Wayne," she said, when the man had left. "Let me summarize. You've got a two-year course in business accounting and administration from a not-very-distinguished institution in Australia. Moderate competence with financial software. Undergraduate degree in life sciences. You moved to Houston, and met— became intimate with—one Carlos Menem. He ran a, shall we say, irregular but profitable air-freight business in which you acted as his assistant and accountant. He had a disagreement with some gentlemen from Cali, Colombia. They repossessed the assets after Mr. Menem's . . . departure. Your green card for the U.S. is no longer valid, your work permit for the Bahamas is running out, and you have no money. Am I correct? Please be frank."

Alice nodded, gripping the arms of her chair and struggling to keep the fear from her face. *Is this it?* No, the Cali boys weren't so indirect. If they wanted her dead, they'd have given her what Carlos got, three bullets in the back of the head. She'd found him slumped over his desk. . . .

"Yes," she said.

"Good. Now, IngolfTech has incorporated here in the Bahamas because the taxes are low and the government . . . not inquisitive about cash flows. You understand?"

"Perfectly, ma'am."

And they want someone who won't talk. It wasn't the

sort of job qualification she'd dreamed about back when she was a student, but if it worked, she wouldn't object. *Also someone without local family or ties.* Bloody hell. She might never get an honest job again. On the other hand, honest jobs didn't pay very well.

"I need several executive assistants—not glorified secretaries, real assistants. The workload will be brutal and the holidays nonexistent."

Alice nodded, putting an eager smile on her face. That was about par for the course, in a startup firm. Laziness had never been one of her faults.

"We'd take care of the work permit and start you at fifty thousand a year, American—after taxes, deposited where you please. Plus a stock option that ought to be worth considerably more, in time. Full medical coverage, housing and car provided."

Alice choked and coughed to cover it. *Fifty thousand! After taxes! Stock option!*

"Who do I have to kill?" she blurted. Then, horrified: "I mean—" *For that sort of money, I would kill somebody! I think.*

For the first time, Gwen smiled. She rested her elbows on the table and her chin on linked fingers. "I like your attitude," she said cheerfully. "Now—"

Gwen raised the ankles higher, holding the legs slightly apart so they wouldn't be bruised in the struggle. The dark water frothed, clear enough to her but ink-black to a human beneath the moonless sky. Chest-deep in the sea there was no way for the one held this way to bend enough to get their mouth out of the water. The flailing weight rocked her a little, and she dug her toes into the coarse gritty sand; she was more than strong enough to hold, but she weighed less than two hundred pounds, only a little more than her victim. The struggles slowed, ceased. She held on for a minute longer to be sure, then let the legs fall. The body began to sink, lungs filled with water; she pushed it outward, with the ebbing tide, swimming powerfully. After ten minutes she released it, turned back and stroked easily for the shore.

Tom was waiting on the beach, holding out a towel. She took it and began to dry herself off, looking up at the lights of the house a few kilometers down the coast.

"I wish we didn't have to do that," he said somberly.

Gwen pulled on her tunic—it was a dress, actually, but much like the tunics that were day-wear back home. "I do too; Pat was useful. But she just couldn't take the truth; a mistake on my part."

And a good thing she'd had all outgoing traffic monitored. Three long-distance calls to newspapers; none of them past the hints and innuendo stage, thankfully. *My employer is an alien monster from another dimension* wasn't the sort of thing you could say directly to any paper anyone would listen to. They'd assume she was some sort of flake and forget the whole matter.

Tom nodded. "Oh, it was necessary; one life is nothing beside the cause . . . but . . ." He shrugged. "I still regret it."

They turned up the sand, above the line of tide-wrack, under the clacking fronds of the coconut palms. Gwen put her arm around the man's waist to guide him through the night. The heat of his body cast a ghost-pale shadow across the flat silvery reflection of the beach; she could see the warmth of lesser lives scuttling in the undergrowth, and hear the muted clicking of beach crabs. In the house, one of the guards worked the action of his weapon, a faint *chick-chack* across the thousands of meters. The wind was from there; she could smell the individual scents of a dozen humans, the three Doberman guard dogs, wet cement from the construction, cooking, smoke, cooling metal in the vehicles.

She looked up at the multicolored tapestry of ten thousand stars. Thermals were clearer at night, the rising heat of the day fading up into the cool of the upper sky. *Someday*. That was another thing she missed: seeing the stars from beyond atmosphere.

"No sense in repining."

"And no problems from the police," he added. "Not when Captain Lowe's second cousin is in charge." After a moment: "Do you think Lowe will stay bought?"

"He'll have to. It works both ways: 'They're crooks, and here's the payoff they gave me, to prove it' isn't a very practical threat. And we have enough on him, now, to take him down three times over if he tried anything. Not that he will. The parable of the goose that laid the golden eggs is well within his capacities."

"Anyway, there won't be any marks on the body even if the sharks don't get it," Tom said. "We'll report her missing tomorrow."

He sighed. "Who'll replace Pat?"

"Alice Wayne, I think."

She could sense his frown. He didn't like the Australian much.

"She's unprincipled."

"True, but she's also very greedy. And tough, although not too tough to intimidate. It's a useful mixture; we have to work with what's available. I've had her under observation for nearly a year now, after all."

Another sigh. "True, as you put it."

Gwen tightened her grip. "I'll tell her while you're away in California," she said. "By the time you're back, I'll be able to judge how well she's adjusting." She smiled in the darkness. "Come on up to my suite, and we'll say goodbye properly."

The smile grew broader as she heard his heart leap.

"Fascinating," Mueller said, staring at the screen.

It was showing output from the scanning/tunneling electron microscope.

"Fascinating how *selective* the replacement is. As if the carrier *knew* which section of the DNA strand to travel to."

"Well, it's more a matter of mechanical fit," Gwen said. "Lucky we had the basic transposer model in my bloodstream; that cut five or six years off the development schedule. I wasn't sure they were still active."

Mueller looked up at her, raising his brows.

"From my last retrofit," she said. "Those can take a decade or more; thank the gods I've only had to go through it three times. You have no idea how uncomfortable a whole-organism makeover can be. The algae should be ready, then?"

"It should be," Mueller said cautiously. "I'd like to run a series of tests to make doubly sure. I realize this isn't really *experimental*, of course."

"It is when done on this equipment," she said. "By all means, with failsafes and controls. Keep me posted."

"It'll cost at least twelve million," Alice said.

Gwen walked past her and stepped out to the veranda. The room was large and pale-colored, full of shadow and light through the tall shuttered french doors, spilling across tile and blond wood and the rattan furniture. Through one that was half-open she could see the terrace and part of the pool, and the slope of lawn down to the palm-fringed beach. The twin-engine seaplane bobbed at the dock there, near the boat; beyond a curve of sail showed against the clear green waters off Andros Island. The staff were still unloading the baggage compartment of the floatplane.

Alice glanced quickly down again, fighting to control her breathing. *You're not in any danger*, she told herself. Pat had been stupid, like Carlos—and both of them had gotten the same reward for it. Nobody could kill you deader than dead—a superhuman time-traveler or the boys from Cali, it was all the same.

Once you knew, it explained a lot of things about Gwen. *I'm surprised how fast it went down,* she thought. Evidently her gut had believed before her head was informed. It was only a week, and she could sleep without pills again.

"Property in that part of Manhattan's still extremely expensive, ma'am," she went on. "Despite the crash."

"We need that warehouse," Gwen said. "Send the retainer." Without turning, she went on: "What's bothering you, Alice?"

One of the house staff wheeled in a covered lunch tray and then set it out: conch soup and grilled marlin steak and salads. Gwen thanked her in fluent Haitian creole patois; all the house domestics were from Haiti. The maid smiled whitely and bobbed her head before taking the trolley out.

The staff were all devoted to Gwendolyn, Alice knew. *Why not?* She got them work permits here in the Bahamas, which was like a ticket to heaven compared to their impoverished, violence-plagued homeland; she helped with their families, paid top wages and was unfailingly polite, in a rather distant, lordly way.

They don't know what she is. *God, she scares me.*

"That's a logical response," Gwen said calmly. "I'm a predator, after all, and you're the species I was designed to hunt."

Alice started violently and felt real fear clutch at her stomach. *Can she—*

"No." Gwen smiled, turning from the window. "I can't read your mind. But I can hear anything you subvocalize, and I can smell your emotions, and I can read your body language like a book. Do come have some of this, it's very good. Anyway, there's no need to be *too* frightened. You're mine, now, so I'm obliged to protect you."

Alice sat down across the table. Gwen went on: "Just remember that you're transparent as glass. You can't deceive me any more than you could outwrestle me. Try to lie and you'll make me angry, and believe me, you don't want that."

I wish she hadn't told me.

"It was you or Sally or Edgar, and I do need an executive assistant who knows. Sally's not flexible enough, and Edgar doesn't smell quite right."

She hadn't felt hungry, but the smell of the food made her pick up the fork. As she leaned forward to spear a chunk of the marlin, she smelled something else. Gwen was as fastidious as a cat about cleanliness, but close to there was something different about the faint smell of her sweat, something you only noticed because of the contrast to what you expected. A very slight muskiness. It was oddly soothing, and she felt her heartbeat slow.

The marlin was delicious. If you were a member of the Household you lived like royalty, nothing but the best.

God. And the money's so good. Double pay with her promotion to the inner circle.

Tom Cairstens came in, grinning. He tossed a folder down beside the plates on the table. Gwen laid aside her fork and picked it up, giving it her quick three-second-per-page scan.

"Home is the hunter, home from the hills," the lawyer said. "Hills of Hollywood, at least. That's their offer, basically—but I think they'll go to twenty million and fifteen percent, net, if we wait a little or drop a hint about MGA. Their people have finished examining the holographic projector and they're drooling. It's our biggest deal so far."

"Excellent, Tom," Gwen said. "Remember, though, this is our first non-industrial product, our first direct-to-consumer. We don't want too much publicity, and it's worth money to avoid it; IngolfTech isn't going to be the subject of articles in *Fortune* if I can help it. Also, don't pressure them to front-end it. The cash is a bagatelle; the real money from this will be in the licensing, and we're not in a hurry."

He nodded and inclined his head slightly to Alice. "Yes, she's been briefed. No problems."

"Welcome to the Household," he said to her. "Marvelous, isn't it?"

Alice made herself smile back. *Oh, God.* "I'm . . . still taking it in, sir."

"Tom."

"Tom. It's, ah, it's a wonderful opportunity, Tom."

The lawyer walked over to Gwen's workstation and stared at the image on the screen. Or half-stared, at least. The other half of his attention was on Gwen. Alice shuddered slightly; she didn't know *why*, but when Gwendolyn Ingolfsson was in the room it was impossible *not* to focus on her, even if you didn't know the truth. Thomas Cairstens was normally a worldly man, used to moving in the monied glamour of the West Coast elite, not easily impressed. The look of sandbagged awe on his face made Alice shiver again.

"What is that?" he asked, pointing at the screen.

"A fusion reactor," Gwen replied. "Early model. I'm working on adapting it, but it's slow going. This"—she pointed her fork at the workstation; it was linked to the new massively-parallel mainframe—"is about as much use as an abacus. Construction? It's going to be like trying to build a megawatt laser in a blacksmith's forge."

"Everything here must seem very backward," he said humbly.

Gwen shrugged. "The electronics are surprisingly capable, for 1997. Very different, though. We used more analog technology, and we never had all this open architecture—Security would have had kittens at the thought. It was all ROM, read-only memory, for the compinsets, the programs. Still is, come to that."

"Will we need it?" he asked, nodding to the reactor design.

"Oh, certainly. The power requirements can't be met from any sort of capacitor, and those would be too conspicuous in New York anyway."

"A private power station won't?"

"It's not very large—about the size of a two-story house, according to my best estimate. I'll discuss the Paramount proposals with you further at dinner."

He nodded; that was dismissal. Then he turned back for a moment: "Ma'am . . . what's Los Angeles like in your world?"

"Los Angeles?" she said. "There's no city there. Mostly prairie with live oaks, along the coast. Some desert inland, mountain forests, chaparral. Good grizzly country. The settlements are small, some orchards and fields in the more favored spots. I've got a property there, near La Jolla. Wonderful spot for swimming and sailing, and I raise horses."

He shook his head in wonder. "I can't wait until we get the Project rolling. We've dreamed of utopia all these years, and we're finally going to *get* it. Paradise . . ."

Alice moistened her mouth, watching him leave. "He's crazy, isn't he?" she said.

Gwen shook her head. "Just very focused. It's true we'll clean this planet up; we don't shit in our bedrooms, and we put the industry out in space where it belongs. Tom loves redwoods and whales and snail darters . . . Hence, paradise."

She turned, and Alice felt the full impact of the green-eyed stare. In private, with the inner circle, she didn't bother to tone it down.

"It's going to be hell, isn't it?" Alice said quietly, hearing her own Australian accent grow stronger.

Images ran through her mind: Nagasaki, the newsreels of Buchenwald, history classes. "Like us and the abos, only worse."

"Concentration camps, you mean? Plagues?" She shook her head indulgently. "No, you can't hurt us, so we won't use extreme measures. We'll conquer you, then domesticate you."

It'll be a long time and the Project may not work. And maybe it won't be so bad.

"You said that the molehole might not work," Alice said. "What then?"

"Then I'll take the planet myself," Gwen said coolly, looking out the window and resting her chin on a palm. "That'd be more difficult, but an interesting challenge, in a way."

And there's only one of her here, Alice thought. *And . . . it's too late for second thoughts, anyway. Even if they all come through, they couldn't be worse than Hitler or Stalin or that awful thing in Cambodia.*

"We'll only kill the ones who resist," Gwen confirmed. "I expect to be put in charge here, and the sky will be the limit for my administrative Household. It really will be a utopia, of sorts, for the rest. No more wars or terrorism, no more sickness or poverty or famine, no more environmental problems. A highly evolved parasite sees that the host body stays fit; and we're nothing if not highly evolved."

"People will still fight," Alice said. "Some will."

Gwen nodded. "That's humans for you. Of course, they'll only *be* humans in the first generation or so, and we *drakensis* are immortal. We're good at waiting."

Alice paused with the fork halfway to her mouth. Gwen poured more of the chilled white wine from the carafe.

"Not human?" Alice said. The fear welled up a little, then sank.

"No, *Homo sapiens sapiens* is far too risky to have

around in large numbers. We'll use a tailored paravirus to alter your heredity to *Homo servus*. Don't worry, it's not a big change, much closer to human than I am. Some neurological alterations, the endocrine system, hormones, the vomeronasal organ. Clean up all the hereditary defects at the same time, cancer, obesity, Alzheimer's disease, and so forth. *Servus* are still people, they've got personalities and thoughts, they just aren't aggressive or rebellious—or not much. It's not like the old days before the change to the New Race, whips and torture and that sort of thing. Not necessary. Why, these days a lot of the *servus* aren't even personally owned, they can even have property, to a certain extent."

She smiled nostalgically. "Very sweet people, actually, and I miss them."

Alice relaxed again. *Odd. I never get as worried when she's around, even though she scares the shit out of me.* If Gwendolyn was typical, they didn't seem cruel, at least. Beautiful, terrifying, awesome, but not sadistic.

"You can tell if *I'm* lying," Alice said. "What am I supposed to do?"

Gwen moved; so swiftly that Alice had no time to jerk away. Suddenly her face was inches from the Australian's.

"Trust me," she said. Alice swallowed and nodded, shuddering slightly as the other's eyes gripped hers and held them.

After a moment Gwen returned to her seat: "What's on the agenda?"

"Primary Belway Securities. They're the logical choice for a public offering—did I say something?"

Gwen was grinning to herself. "No, no," she said. "I've had a . . . previous contact with the firm. Go ahead."

"We should sound them out, and set up a preliminary

meeting in a few months. Shall I go ahead with it? And where would you like it set up, in New York or Nassau or . . . ?"

"I think we'll have them over here," Gwen said. "A more controlled environment; it'll put us at an advantage—and with investment bankers, you need it. We'll get the hierarchies squared away before we transfer the proceedings to New York." She wrinkled her nose. "Race Spirit, but that place stinks. How you humans manage to breathe in a fog of burnt hydrocarbons and sewage is beyond me."

The servant came and removed the tray, leaving a plate of pastries and a coffee service. Alice looked on in frank envy as Gwen ate; she knew it took six or seven thousand calories a day to maintain the Draka's supercharged metabolism, but it was still aggravating.

Gwen saw her glance. "There's a pill we had, back in our late 1990s," she said. "Metaboline. It adjusted the basal metabolism to allow humans any level of calorie intake. I'll have some run up."

Alice was smiling as she left.

"She seems to be working out well," Tom said. He picked a wedge of tomato out of the salad and ate it.

Gwen nodded. "You caught all that?"

"The monitor system is working fine." He glanced out the door after the Australian. "Have you, ah . . . ?" He raised an eyebrow.

"Not yet, I don't want to stress her too heavily. In a day or two."

He shook his head, grinning in admiration. "How do you do it? I'd have sworn she was straight, and I'm not—or not very."

Gwen was paging through the report again. She spoke without looking up:

"Ah, well, both behaviors are latent in any individual

human; there's a whole complex of genes that determine which is dominant and to what degree, and they interact with environmental factors at triggering stages in the development process. It's a spectrum, not a binary opposition, even in humans; both are always active in a *drakensis*. Anyway, my pheromones are panspecific—they fill all the receptors in your vomeronasal organ. Think of it as fooling your hypothalamus and limbic system. It doesn't work on all humans, but it will on most. On Alice, certainly; I can scent it, although she doesn't know it yet."

"I won't quarrel with the results," he said. "It seems to take more than one of us to keep up with you."

Her glance lingered on him, and she saw him flush and a light sweat break out across his brow.

"True," she said. "That's a byproduct of the aggression reflex, hormonal. I don't produce much estrogen unless I decide to ovulate; there's another set of hormones— they're somewhat similar in structure to the androgens in your human system—that controls secondary sexual functions in *drakensis*, with only minor differences between the genders. . . . It's complex."

He swallowed and shifted. Gwen listened to his heartbeat increase and inhaled to take his scent.

"The bankers are coming?" he said, changing the subject.

"Yes, in a few months. It's the only way to raise the operating capital we'll need. There shouldn't be any basic difficulties; from their point of view we're a very good prospect for a public stock offering, so we should be ready to get down to serious negotiations by the winter. I want everything very tight by then, Tom. No mistakes, nothing to disturb them. We'll be moving the main locus of our operations to New York, and there'll be far less margin for errors and coverups."

She rose and began to undress. "As for right now
. . . take your clothes off, Tom."

He smiled and obeyed. "Your wish is my command."

Gwen nodded. "And kneel to me," she said, putting
her palms behind her on the table and leaning her
weight on them.

CHAPTER EIGHT

Jennifer Feinberg opened the door of her apartment and put an automatic foot out to block the cat.

"You wouldn't like it out there," she said, swinging it closed and snicking home the multiple locks. "I wish *I* could stay home."

She dumped her attaché case on the table, walked into the kitchen to put the water on for tea, and hit the play button on the answering machine.

"Jennifer, this is your mother—"

"Oh, puh-*leez*," she groaned, fast-forwarding.

"Miss Feinberg, I have to speak with you. Could you—"

She hit the *stop* button with a small scream of fear, closing her eyes as the machine rattled on the sofa-side table. *Control your breathing*, she told herself. Her hands were still shaking as she punched the number the policeman had given her into the phone.

"Carmaggio," a voice said.

"This is Feinberg," she managed to say, looking around her apartment.

The heavy December rain was streaking down the windows, and she hadn't had time to turn on the lights. She was sweating under her outdoor coat. The studio smelled of sachet and tea and, very faintly, of cat. It was *home*, but right then it felt very lonely.

"Yes, Ms. Feinberg?" Trained patience on the other end of the line.

"I'm, ah, sorry for calling you so late." *God, that's inane.* It was seven-thirty, and neither of them worked regular hours. "But the same man called me here at home."

"What did he say?"

"The same *thing*, that he has to talk to me about Steven! Look, if he has my home number, he has my *address*. He knows where I *live*."

"We're pretty sure this isn't the perpetrator in the Fischer case, Ms. Feinberg," the detective said soothingly. "But it might be an important lead."

"So *find* him!" she said, and hung up.

Thank God I'm leaving the country, she thought. Three years and she'd *nearly* forgotten the murder. Then someone had to start phoning and reminding her of it, God.

For a few minutes she slumped, then sighed and got up to take off her coat and pour milk in the cat's bowl. She drew the curtains and turned on the CD player: *La Traviata*.

"I should put on an exercise tape," she told herself.

She put her fingers on her stomach and looked at herself in the window. *That's not* fat *for a woman my age*. Damn all models, anyway. They were mutants, and they unloaded a whole bargeload of guilt on normal people. She was only thirty-four.

The tea was soothing. She touched the answering machine again:

"Jennifer, this is your—"

A little of the hot liquid spilled on her fingers as she zipped past the second message from her mother. *Still trying to set me up with accountants*. Marrying her mother had been the only really big mistake of her

father's life. The next message was from the office—
they must have sent it while she was in the middle of
her commute. So much for office hours.

"This is Marlene, Jennifer." The managing director's
executive assistant. She should be calling her Ms.
Feinberg, but Jennifer didn't like to make a fuss about
it. "The boss wants the last stuff on IngolfTech ready
by Friday morning."

Oh, and why not forty days of rain while he's at it?
There went her evenings for the week.

"Jenny, it's Louisa. Are we still on for lunch Wednesday?"

*Do I really want to listen to my best friend's man
troubles?* Then again, it would be a chance to complain
about the sexist pig of a managing director, the crank
calls, and the fact that she *didn't* have any man problems right now.

"Okay, lunch with Louisa," she mumbled to herself.

"Ms. Feinberg, you're in danger and the police
can't—"

"SHUT UP!" she screamed. The cat took off across
the apartment in a tawny blur, and she hit the answering machine hard enough to make her hand hurt.
"Leave me alone!"

The trip to the Bahamas couldn't come soon enough
for her.

Her fingers shook as she punched the detective's
number again.

Government House in Nassau reminded Gwen a
little of old buildings in out-of-the-way corners of the
Domination: a large square building of pink-stuccoed
stone, with a portico on the front supported by four
tall pillars. Steps of black and white stone ran down
between cast-iron lampstands, ending in a marble statue
of Christopher Columbus. Palm and cypress trees gave
inadequate shade, and police in white colonial-looking

uniforms were directing a heavy foot-traffic of tourists, bureaucrats, and visitors. Gwen stood quietly, scanning the crowds with a steady back-and-forth motion that automatically eliminated those outside the search parameters.

"Ah," she said. "There they are." Upwind, and she could scent the metal and gun oil of the weapons under their coats. A tang of apprehension from the men, wary but determined. "Punctual."

"What do they want, really?" Dolores asked nervously.

"What we've got, essentially," Gwen replied.

Tom looked at his watch. "At least they didn't keep insisting on having the meeting on American territory."

Gwen nodded. "They're hungry. If we give them some of what they want—and dangle the rest—they'll jump through hoops. Just remember your briefings, and keep calm."

She led her party down the stairs to the statue. The two American agents stood to meet her. Tom looked them over rapidly.

"*Strongarm specialists,*" he said subvocally. "*Bad sign.*"

"Not necessarily," she replied. "They *do* have that little affray in the warehouse to worry about. It's natural to take precautions."

"John Andrews," the human said, when they stood face to face. "For the United States government."

"Gwendolyn Ingolfsson," she replied. "For Ingolf-Tech." *And the Domination of the Draka.*

He had quite good control, for a human, Gwen decided. He probably used that smile as part of it, immobilizing the small muscles around the mouth and eyes. She took his scent: fear, slight but definite. Not directed at her, so much, as at . . . *ah. He must be afraid of what he thinks I represent.* Gwen was dressed to throw the two Americans off-balance; Italian white-cotton tropical dress with a narrow gold belt, high-strap sandals, sunglasses, a broad straw hat tied with a silken handkerchief dangling in one hand.

"Well, shall we do that lunch thing?" she asked.

Tom strangled a chuckle, and Alice didn't bother. Andrews's answering expression looked painted-on for an instant, then puzzled.

Good, Gwen thought. If the human didn't know what was going on, he'd fall back on pre-scripted versions of what *must* be happening.

The entrance to Greycliff was bustling, well-dressed parties arriving under the pillars of the veranda. She'd chosen it with malice aforethought; it was just across West Hill Street from Government House, and she knew the two American agents would spot the plainclothesmen from the Nassau police hovering in the background. That would probably keep them from trying anything drastic; the great powers of this world were absurdly solicitous of the little fish, by the standards of the history she'd learned and lived. She smiled graciously as they went through the wrought-iron gate in the whitewashed stone wall.

"My associate, Thomas Cairstens," she introduced. "My executive assistant, Alice Wayne; and Dolores Pastrana, personal secretary to the board."

Handshakes all around, and what the computer probe she'd launched told her were the agent's real names. Oddly incomplete files, but possibly the humans were keeping the important bits on hardcopy.

"Shall we go in?"

The maître d'hotel and his assistants were all attention; she and the rest of the IngolfTech staff from the Nassau headquarters were regulars, and exceedingly generous tippers, and she'd sent gifts around at Christmas and Easter. *All part of the process.*

Bright sunlight leaked through the louvered shutters; there was a pleasant hum of conversation and the scent of food. Gwen left the conversation to her humans for the first few minutes, judging and analyzing. Andrews was the dominant of the pair, that was plain. He was looking at her more frequently, puzzled, trying to sense the hierarchy of her group. Cairstens's type he recognized. *Respect, combined with underlying dislike,* she decided. *And he's realizing I really am in charge. He's surprised at that.* She finished her soup and began demolishing the seventeen-ounce pepper steak that followed it; his eyes widened slightly as she ate, and at the side orders of *pommes frites.* Then flicked down to her body and back again. He was having a salad.

Right, he's off-balance enough, she decided, sipping at her wine.

"Thank you for agreeing to this meeting," she said. "I'm most anxious for a cooperative relationship with the American government."

Andrews nodded tightly. "You'll understand we're a bit anxious," he said. "With the current world situation . . ."

She smiled. "You can be fairly certain I'm not working for *Jihad al-Moghrebi,*" she pointed out gently. "And besides, isn't that mostly the Europeans' worry?"

Her human ancestors had mostly ground Islam out of existence, back in first century B.F.S. That it was allowed to flourish here was another sign of anarchic disorder. It was a wonder this bunch hadn't wiped themselves out long ago.

"Damned little they're doing about it, except turning back boatloads of refugees," he said. "Shall I be frank?"

"By all means." *And I can believe just as much as I please,* she added to herself.

"We don't know who and what you are, and who you're associated with," he said. "We do know that you have valuable information which shouldn't be allowed to fall into the wrong hands."

Gwen chuckled, a flash of white teeth against the olive tan of her face. "Well, that's all a matter of definition, now isn't it?"

The Americans' bodies tensed unconsciously, their pupils dilating. A fight-or-flight response; they expected bargaining.

"I'll lay my cards on the table," Gwen said. *And you can believe as much as you please.* "I'm not going to tell you my own identity. There are interests who'd be very glad to see me . . . out of the picture."

A fractional nod from Andrews, a subliminal grunt from Debrowski. *Ah. Interesting. That* confirmed *something they already thought they knew. I must look into that.*

"However, you know my group has international participation."

"Mueller. And Singh. Not a recommendation, considering their records."

"The good doctors aren't in a political mode anymore," she said.

Quite true. They were her serfs, her slaves, albeit favored ones.

"And in any case, this goes well beyond them. We—my group and I—have decided to tap the world of . . . nonconventional science. Outside the orthodox hierarchies, with their fixed ideas of what's possible and what isn't. There's an enormous amount of dross, but every now and then there's a pearl . . . and the pearls have been going to waste for want of a systematic search. With modern information-processing methods and some imagination, such a search is possible."

Andrews ate a forkful of his salad. "Which leaves the question of motivations. Secret international associations interested in cutting-edge technologies, with members associated with dubious regimes and groups"—he glanced aside at Cairstens, who smiled back toothily—"or with no visible pasts at all, well . . ."

Gwen finished her steak. *Ah, just right*. Very faint touch of garlic, and slightly bloody in the middle. She remembered crouching over an elk in a winter storm . . . was it only three years ago, on her personal world-line? Cutting away at the flesh with her obsidian knife, breaking joints with a swift blow of her fist. The hot salt taste of the blood, and strength flowing back into her shivering body as the calories translated into warmth. It had taken her four days to strip the carcass bare; the wolves had shown up on the second, and provided her with a couple of warm furs. This was just as challenging, in its way.

"Our objectives are simple," she said. "Money, a great deal of money, and the power that goes with it." She held up a hand. "Nothing illegitimate. You'll have checked out our contacts with American businesses."

"Yes." Andrews nodded. "You seem to be concentrating on those."

"It's the only game in town," she replied. "Europe's too tightly tied up by established players, and besides, it's too close to the Middle East, and these days . . ." She shrugged. "Asia is xenophobic, and China is stirring that pot too enthusiastically. There are mutual interests."

Andrews moved in smoothly. "Mutual interests require mutual benefits," he said.

"Why, hasn't the United States benefited from IngolfTech's cooperative ventures?" she asked mildly, raising her eyebrows. She also raised a hand, and began to tick off points. "There's the ultradense memory chip we did with Texas Instruments, there's the oil-eating bacteria we're bringing forward with Exxon—if your FDA ever gets off its fat arse—there's the holographic projector . . ."

"Granted. However."

Gwen nodded. *Your government—more particularly your agency within that government—would like some things it could control personally.*

It was startling how similar *drakensis* and human were, in some respects. Factionalism, for instance.

"I understand completely. On the other hand, a cooperative attitude on the part of your government would help immensely; particularly since IngolfTech is planning to move more and more onshore."

She leaned back, nibbling on a pastry, and made a small gesture with her free hand. Tom put his attaché case on the table and snapped it open. With an understated flourish he produced a neatly bound folder.

"A token of our sincerity," she said. "Take a look."

Andrews did, with Debrowski leaning over his shoulder. After a moment he grunted, a sound that almost turned into a squeal.

"Is this *serious*?" he asked.

"Entirely. You'll find complete drawings and process data in the disks enclosed at the back. The hardcopy is an outline of the product and its applications."

"But *nobody's* been able to get a superconductor to operate at room temperature—"

"—and this operates up to the ferromagnetic transition temperatures at several hundred degrees, yes. Take a look at the energy densities, by the way."

Primitive stuff, invented about the time she was born, or a little earlier. Still, it would give this world some things it sadly lacked: a moderately efficient way to store electrical energy, for starters.

"For instance, besides transmission lines, you could use this to power electric vehicles with ranges of thousands of miles, and recharge times measured in seconds or minutes. The increased energy efficiencies would make the U.S. completely independent of imported oil. Superconductors could be used as replacements for capacitors, for applications needing surge power."

The agents twitched again, imperceptibly. Surge output was useful for many things; most importantly, lasers and other beam weapons.

Andrews was breathing hard as he read. Gwen amused herself with a daydream of exactly how she'd take him when the time came for the masks to come off. *I'll let him run,* she thought. The scent of his terror would be intoxicating. *Then leap on him.* He'd take a moment to realize just how helpless he was in her hands. Then—

All five of the humans and some of the ones at the nearer tables were reacting to her; her own three knew exactly what was happening to them, which made it harder for them to resist. She clamped down on the secretions. *Tsk. Keep your mind on business.* Besides which, it would be a shame to mark this dress.

Andrews looked up, his face damp with sweat; the lust was there, but directed at the folder in front of him—at the conscious level, at least.

"I thought you were mostly in biotechnology," he said shakily.

"Yes, but this is rather more immediate. With that data you could begin large-scale production immediately. At that *secret* little black-program place you have out in the California desert, for instance."

Debrowski looked up at her sharply. "You know about that?"

"What a lynx you are, Mr. Debrowski," Gwen said dryly. "Nothing gets past you."

Gwen smiled back with bland amiability at his frown, dabbing whipped cream on a kiwi tart and eating it. The smooth-bland-buttery combination of flavors made her close her eyes for a moment of pure pleasure. To complement it she kicked off one of her sandals under the protecting cover of the tablecloth and slid the foot between Dolores's knees. They opened immediately, though the Colombian's face remained a study in concentration as she bent over the notebook computer beside her plate. Gwen stroked the velvety softness of the other's inner thighs while she turned her face to the Americans. It must be terrible to be a human, sense-blind to three quarters of existence, noticing nothing.

"And the quid pro quo?" Andrews asked.

"Simply . . . protection. Let it be known in the appropriate circles that IngolfTech stands well with the government."

"And in return, we get a monopoly?"

Gwen laughed. "I have no intention of selling you the cow," she said. "We will let you milk it, but the beast itself stays beyond your reach."

Andrews looked down again at the folder with its laser-printed text and colored graphs. "This sort of thing can't fall into the wrong hands," he said.

"Exactly," Gwen said. "If IngolfTech released that, the whole world would be in an uproar."

And looking into things it shouldn't and asking questions I can't answer.

"But you *can* handle it. We'll certain direct anything else of that nature to you; all we want is to be able to commercialize the more . . . conventional innovations that are our stock in trade. We're talking really considerable sums, here, in the immediate to medium term. Billions, enough to make Microsoft look like a mom-and-pop store, as you Yanks say."

Andrews closed the folder, fingers unconsciously caressing it. "We'll certainly be in touch, Ms. Ingolfsson," he said, grinning.

"By all means." She returned his handshake, squeezing just enough to startle him a little.

Tom chuckled and poured another mineral water over the crushed ice and lime in his glass as the Americans left. Their walk quickened as they left Greycliff, turning almost into a trot as they reached the street outside. Gwen raised her own glass in a toast; she smiled over the rim at Dolores with affectionate cruelty.

"Nothing gets by them, eh?" she said.

The Colombian began to laugh, then caught her breath and bent her head and bit her linen napkin. Tom and Alice looked over suddenly, blinked, then burst into chuckles themselves. The Draka gave a final tweak with her prehensile toes and withdrew the foot, wiping it on the inside of the other's skirt.

"I should *think* they'll be in touch," Tom said. "Show those goons a weapon, and they get one on the cat couldn't scratch."

He winked at Dolores, and the woman gave a breathless sigh and dabbed at her forehead. The waiters brought the dessert tray around again, noticing nothing of the byplay.

Blind, Gwen thought. Humans were absolutely *blind,* as well as scent-deaf. It made them endlessly amusing. This Andrews, for instance, had a diverting sense of his own importance. It would be entertaining, when he realized he was a toy, a plaything.

"Still, it's best we get some other influential contacts in that direction," Gwen said thoughtfully. "Tom, Alice—after we've celebrated for the rest of the afternoon, I want you to firm things up with that communications mogul you've been cultivating. I'd like to have that solid before the bankers arrive, and we've only got three months."

Tom nodded, blotting his lips. "Shall we?" he said, rising.

"By all means."

"So, you haven't heard back from David yet?"

Jennifer Feinberg dumped Nutra-Sweet into the coffee. The radicchio salad looked particularly disgusting today, but that was what the diet said she could have. She speared a forkful moodily and munched. *I want corned beef on rye, with mustard, pickle on the side, order of french fries, and a nice gooey pastry to follow. Fat chance.* Chez Laurence wouldn't have anything so plebeian as corned beef on the menu; their French pastries were divine, though. . . . The little restaurant had a friendly bustle at lunch hour, the more so as the day outside was sleet and ghastliness. Some of the sleet had gotten inside her rubbers.

"David? He said he needed more space."

"If he had any more space, he'd need a spacesuit," Louisa Englestein said.

"Forget David. David is history."

"Your personal history, you should forgive me, is getting to be like the history of Canada—boring."

"You'd rather my life was like the history of, say, Poland?" She swallowed the raddicchio leaf. "Besides, who's got time for a life?"

Louisa did, but then Louisa worked as an assistant curator at the Metropolitan Museum, when she wasn't reading manuscripts for a genre publisher. Both jobs together didn't pay half what Jennifer made, but they didn't amount to an eighty-five-hour week together, either. *And* they didn't leave her feeling like a beaten dishrag at the end of that week.

"The only date I've got is with the police," she said, looking at her fork. *I'm hungry, but I don't want to put that leaf into my face.*

"Police?"

"That slimy whoever-it-is keeps phoning me. I'm talking to the detective again, in case it really is connected with poor Stephen . . . well, you know."

"What's really bothering you?" Louisa said, patting her hand.

Jennifer looked up. "It's this IngolfTech thing," she said. "I don't know, something doesn't look right."

"A try for a phony flotation?"

"No, the cash flow's there, the *product's* there. It just doesn't smell *right*, somehow. Thirty-year-old women from nowhere don't turn up in the Bahamas, pull off an eight-million-dollar salvage operation—pirate treasure, no less!—and then start successful companies buying and selling patents and licenses. And make a fortune in less than three years. Not in the real world."

"You're going to give a negative report?"

"Not on your life. Not without some facts to back up the gut feeling." She sighed. "Now, tell me about the weekend."

Louisa rolled her eyes. "You're not going to *believe* what happened," she began.

Jennifer settled in to listen. For once, her friend's love-life wasn't completely enthralling. There *was* something rotten in the state of IngolfTech underneath the shiny figures; all her experience said so.

"God . . . damn . . . it . . . all," Carmaggio said quietly, crumpling the fax and starting to throw it into his office wastepaper basket.

After a moment's thought he tore it up instead, stepping out and down the corridor to the men's room. He tossed the fragments into one of the toilets, paused, then unzipped his fly.

Nice and confidential, and I can show the spooks what I think of them, he thought as he returned to the office.

"What's the news?" Jesus asked.

"You remember Andrews and Debrowski?"

"The two who leaned on Chen?"

The Puerto Rican's narrow dark face flushed slightly. Henry knew exactly how he felt. It was a shitty thing to do, first—no better than blackmail—but that wasn't all. They'd all done some questionable things now and then; you couldn't always operate by the rulebook. It was a matter of turf, as well. Bad enough to have the Feds muscling in on a case you were running; at least the FBI were real cops, and they could be useful for some things. A gang of spooks—who weren't officially supposed to operate on American soil anyway—was another matter entirely. Particularly when their objective seemed to be to stroke the perp, not catch her.

"A little bird from the Feds tells me they got sent to the Bahamas. To visit one Gwendolyn Ingolfsson, head of IngolfTech."

"*Mierda.*"

"Yeah. You know how much chance we've got of pulling in someone who's become a pet of the Powers That Be."

Jesus hesitated for an instant. "We could leak it."

"Damn, that's tempting."

He toyed with the notion for a moment. Headlines, embarrassments, maybe the Blackmail Twins thrown to the wolves as scapegoats—anyone who relied on *their* bosses for backup had better keep a jar of Vaseline handy.

"Nope. Not enough evidence. Hell, *no* evidence. It'd be our word against theirs—and they lie better than we do. Pity about that. I'd love to do it."

Jesus sighed. "And here I was looking forward to interviews. Maybe a book deal, *si?* How I tracked down space aliens and humongous baboons."

Carmaggio snorted. "I'd feel better if we could find the Phone Bandit," he said. "The bastard knows things he shouldn't."

"He's no friend of the cutting lady," Jesus pointed out. "Not from what he's been saying."

"He's a goddamn ghost, is what he is. And he's bugging people over at Primary Belway Securities again, too."

Jesus grinned. "That nice lady stockbroker—"

"Analyst."

"—analyst been calling you up to complain again?"

"Yeah, and there's nothing I can do. We can't trace the calls, and the case doesn't exist anymore. God damn all hackers, anyway. They can always use the computers better than we can. I don't see how the phone

companies make any money at all with these little
fuckers hacking into their billing programs and what-
not."

"Why don't you hand her over to the receptionists?"
Jesus asked. "The captain, he's not going to be happy
if he finds out you're still talking to people about the
case."

"Ah, she's not so bad. And she *does* have a legitimate
beef. Nothing the captain can do if I want to talk to
someone on my own time and ticket. It's a free
country."

"We haven't been able to trace the calls," he said,
stirring his coffee. "I'd write it off as a crank, except
that he does seem to have some information." Broad
spatulate hands spread. "That's about all I can say."

The detective looked a lot like a bear. *A teddy bear,*
Jennifer thought. If you could imagine a middle-aged
blue-collar Italian teddy bear, that was. She'd always
imagined detectives as more . . . dashing, somehow.
Detective Lieutenant Henry Carmaggio looked like a
plumber in a suit, a rather wrinkled suit at that.

He looks like he expects me to make a scene, Jennifer thought. Which was something she never did,
unless it was necessary and justified.

"Thank you," she said. "Anyway. It's satisfying just
to *talk* to someone—in person, I mean. I get all these
calls from this lunatic, and then I phone the police and
get the runaround."

The detective shrugged. Behind his thick shoulders
the window of the little Italian restaurant was fogged
with condensation; it was a cold afternoon, freezing rain
and slush. Smells of garlic and spices came from the
kitchens, wafts that sent saliva spurting into the back
of her mouth in a way that no radicchio leaf on earth
could do.

"Ms. Feinberg—"

"Jennifer, please."

"Jennifer. One of the many lousy things about my job is the limited number of ways I can help people. People come to the police when something bad has happened to them; and they want us to, hell, put it right. Usually we can't."

"Is that official?" she asked.

Carmaggio laughed, and mimed taking something off his head. "No. *Strictly* no. My official NYPD invisible detective's hat is now off. Matter of fact, I've already clocked out for the day. We're not this reassuring, officially—what with the budget squeeze, it's hard enough to account for our phone bills, much less coffee."

Jennifer chuckled. "It's not that I'm *really* worried, Detective—"

"Henry."

"—Henry. It's just, you know, you can feel sort of vulnerable thinking there's someone *out there*. Especially after what happened with poor Stephen."

Carmaggio sighed. "I know. From my point of view, it's frustrating as hell." He smiled. "Maybe we ought to remember what my grandmother Lucrezia always said."

"What was that?"

"That you get maybe three big breaks in a whole life—but you can eat pasta three times a day." Grinning: "A cousin of mine runs this place, too."

"I shouldn't . . ."

"Hiya, Henry. Who's the girl?" A waitress bustled up with a plate of bruschetta.

Goil. She actually said "goil," Jennifer thought, slightly bemused. Even for a middle-aged, thick-armed lady of Neapolitan descent with a mustache, wasn't that a bit Old New York?

"That, Lorenza, is not a girl. It's a *lady*."

"I shouldn't . . ." she repeated, and took a piece.

Tomato, cheese and oregano exploded across her tongue, along with the crusty bread and smooth olive oil. "Oh, well. Who wants to try getting home at seven, anyway. Dutch treat."

Henry nodded. "Sure, no problem."

She took another bite. "This is *good*."

"The thought of this place kept me alive in the Parrot's Beak," he said. "It's kept me overweight ever since I got back to the World."

Jennifer paused. "You were in Cambodia?" she said. "Yeah?"

A slight silence fell. Carmaggio hunched a shoulder—slightly defensive even now, she thought. *Probably has visions of me with long straight hair, granny glasses and a sign about LBJ.*

"My brother Maurice was there," she said. His face changed, remembering the picture on her desk. "In the Fifth Cavalry."

Jennifer belched gently as she snapped home the multiple locks on the inside of her apartment door. "What a nice guy," she mused, as the cat rubbed against her ankles.

It had been a long time since she *ate* that much at one sitting. *Amazing. I pig out on lasagna and crank calls don't worry me anymore.* You heard about great ethnic eateries at moderate prices, but she'd never actually found many. Mind you, the crowd on the Street tended to apply the Universal Dollar Yardstick to restaurants as well. And Henry *was* a nice guy. No getting bent out of shape about her picking up half the bill . . . well, it was scarcely a *date*, but still. He'd even asked if she wanted her phone number back now that the calls from whoever-it-was had stopped; which was a gentleman's way to find out if she wanted to hear from him again. Old-fashioned, but nice.

Mother would have a cow if she knew. Italian, *and*

a cop. "Mother, I just had dinner with him, we didn't elope to the Poconos."

Maybe she'd go out with him again. He had a sense of humor, and conversation from something outside the incestuous world she worked in. It beat listening to David talk about his therapist and how he was dealing with his Inner Child. What the Inner Child needed was a good spanking, and anyway she preferred to talk to adults.

CHAPTER NINE

Well-preserved, if you like them mummified, Thomas Cairstens thought, shaking the woman's hand.

Janeen Amier had been a notable actress in her day, and something of a celebrity in radical circles in the 1960s. Later she'd made a fortune of her own in exercise videos, and then married a much larger one. Now she was just plain lean and stringy, and the effects of too many facelifts were showing; you could see the same face anywhere in L.A. or San Francisco, anywhere money and a losing struggle against time came together. Her husband, Fred Lather was carrying his age better, a trim slender man with a graying mustache. He was the real power here in terms of money and political influence, but everything Cairstens had been able to learn said that his wife was at least half the brains.

"Glad to see you again, Fred," he said. "Janeen."

Fred was, he noticed, in cowboy gear again; well, this *was* a ranch—a buffalo ranch, to be precise; Lather was a fanatic for the beasts when he wasn't doing those Civil War re-creation things. All fieldstone and exposed Ponderosa-pine beams in here, with a fireplace big enough to roast one of Lather's bulls. The communications magnate led them in and poured drinks; white wine all round, Cairstens noticed. Evidently his Western act didn't extend to actually drinking whiskey. *Some evidence of bicoastal civilization surviving*, he thought mordantly, as they got the small talk out of the way.

"Now, what was it you had to say that was so urgent and confidential?" Lather asked.

Cairstens smiled with professional warmth. "Let's be frank, Fred, Janeen—you've both been a little puzzled about IngolfTech, haven't you?"

"I like to see a new company with a progressive attitude," Janeen said.

On Cairstens's advice IngolfTech had made carefully calculated donations to a number of Amier's favorite causes over the past few years. For that matter, they were mostly *his* favorite causes too, or had been back when such things mattered. Fairly soon the fight against tobacco smoking was going to become completely irrelevant. Even nuclear waste wouldn't be much of a concern. If the Project succeeded.

"I am a little puzzled by some of the stuff you've come up with," Lather said. "My technical people are too."

"It's all been satisfactory, I hope."

"That's just it. It's *too* satisfactory." Lather spread his hands. "I know that sounds odd. But there aren't any bugs in any of them. Everything works perfectly; and new products are never that way. There's always teething problems, things that have to be worked out in practice."

"You mean the products we've been selling you work like *finished* products. Like things that've been in widespread use for years."

"Yes, exactly."

"That's because," he said, opening his briefcase, "they have been in use for years."

"Yeah, well, it wasn't as if I had anything better to do," Henry muttered.

He slowed. The roads to JFK were not at their best on a Saturday afternoon in February, not with sleet added in. Especially once you were off the Van Wyck Expressway, although the layout wasn't as bad as the spilled-spaghetti setup they had at La Guardia, thank God. He peered through the windshield and its sludge of water and ice, then took the right-hand turn in a spray of slush and a long *beeeeeep* from the minivan behind him.

"I still appreciate it, Henry," Jenny said, smiling at him in the mirror. "You're the first person I've known in Manhattan in years who actually has a *car.* Real people, not CEOs."

"Yeah, well, it sort of goes with the job." He grinned. "New experiences—I drive, you get me to go to the opera."

He'd actually enjoyed it, which was a surprise. Although come to think of it, granddad had loved Neapolitan operettas, which wasn't quite the same thing.

"Wish I was going to the Bahamas," he said as they pulled in. "So. Want to catch a movie next week, after you get back?"

His voice was a little too casual. Three dates in a month meant more than we-get-together-some-times. . . . *Christ on a crutch, how can I be worrying about* that *at a time like this?* Part of being human, he guessed.

"Sure," she said quietly, reaching over to touch him on the arm. "I'd like that."

The weather was a little less ghastly under the over-hang. Carmaggio popped the trunk and swung out the driver's door, buttoning his coat. She had a surprising number of bags for a five-day trip, all assembling onto a neat little folding carryall. Efficient.

"Look, Jenny . . . there's something I've got to tell you." She looked up, startled at his tone. He continued:

"This Ingolfsson broa—ah, woman. Her name's come up in my line of work, you know? No charges, but . . ." He spread his hands. "I can't go into details. Let's just say she's been associated with some questionable people down there."

Jennifer nodded, serious. She knew all about confidentiality. He could see she wasn't surprised; well, dealing with offshore Caribbean money probably involved *rumors* of that sort fairly often.

"So watch yourself down there, okay?"

"I will, Henry." She leaned forward and kissed him, a quick touch. "And thanks. Don't worry, nothing happens to investment analysts."

He stood and watched her vanish into the terminal before slamming the trunk shut and dropping back into the driver's seat of the Mazda. She was right.

"Shit, I hope so," he said, waiting with his hand on the keys.

Should I have said something else? What the hell *could* he say? "Your company's prospective client is some sort of mad-dog inhuman killer with a ray gun who consorts with giant spotted baboons"?

Oh, *great*. That would *really* be convincing. Talk about consigning yourself to the tabloid-reading realms of the trailer trash in one fell swoop.

"The hell of it is, when I come right out and say it I don't believe *myself*," he mumbled.

An airport security guard was looking at him from the shelter of the overhang; probably for taking up too much time at the drop-off. *Fuck you very much too, asshole,* Carmaggio snarled under his breath, pulling out into the laneway.

Jenny wasn't in any danger, anyway. Whatever Ingolfsson was after, right now she seemed to be concentrating on making large amounts of money, serious money, *legitimate* money. You didn't do that by hurting investment analysts; the financial world had a severe

aversion to physical violence in its own ranks. The most
that could happen would be a heavy swindle and the
loss of her job, and he didn't expect that to happen
either. Jenny was as bright as anyone he'd ever met,
and she knew the twisted rules of her field as well as
he knew his.

Carmaggio slammed on the brakes. Sweat broke out
on his forehead and clammily under his arms as he felt
the greasy skid of the tires on slick pavement. When
the car halted he took several deep breaths before
restarting the stalled motor; you could get yourself dead
easy in this weather, driving with your mind in a fog
of worry.

He concentrated on the road with a ferocious effort
of will. Occasionally his hand would reach into his coat
for cigarettes that weren't there.

"Whoop!" Gwen said, and caught the falling child.

He had been twelve feet up the coconut palm. A
half-scream of terror turned to a giggle. Gwen tossed
the slender black form up again, rolled him over her
shoulders and tucked him under one arm head-down,
grinning toward the ground and the delighted white
smile.

"Hey, put me down now!" the boy said in the Haitian Creole patois.

Gwen did, watching with mild affection as he som-
ersaulted off his hands and ran to join a half-dozen
other youngsters playing outside a small concrete-block
schoolhouse. This section of the property was sand and
rock, scrub-covered with a few taller pines or coconuts.
It was a fine winter's day, sun bright through the thin
foliage overhead, a little over seventy degrees. The brisk
sea breeze brought scents of salt, silty mangrove
swamp, pine, fresh-cut stone, and human. That was
more agreeable now that she was used to it again,
although she missed the odors of Draka and *servus*. She

walked slowly, bare feet gripping the stone beneath her, savoring a feeling of relaxed well-being.

"You like children?" Tom asked over his shoulder as they walked; he and Alice preceded her down the pathway. She could hear undertones of surprise in the man's voice.

"Children and puppies, yes," Gwen said. "They're among my favorite things."

He nodded thoughtfully. "And wild geese that fly with the moon on their wings, no doubt," he said.

Gwen looked at him, liking his smile. There was no insolence in it, and outright fear was a crude tool of dominance. *I'm getting the knack of dealing with humans*, she thought. Killing them was fairly easy, gross manipulation with terror, bribes or pheromones not too difficult, but really managing them took skill. Centuries of dealing only with *servus* and her own kind had let hers rust, but mining her memories and careful study were bringing it back.

"That's a quotation?"

"From a musical . . . a movie with singing. An unbearably sentimental one."

"It's unhealthy not to like children," she said. "Not good evolutionary strategy. I'm very fond of mine."

"Hard to imagine you having children," Alice said.

"Oh, I only contribute the egg," Gwen said. "We fertilize *in vitro* and transplant the ovum. Sex is recreational and social, for us."

Alice looked back over her shoulder, caught Gwen's eye on her and blushed—thoroughly visible, since the Australian was in bikini and sarong—put a nervous hand to her hair, and glanced away. *Delightful*, Gwen thought. She'd become enthusiastic very quickly. Besides being an efficient administrative assistant.

A splendid pair, she thought, viewing them together. *And they'd make a good breeding combination, when we have time.* They might be past prime reproductive age when this operation was complete; best if she had sperm and egg samples preserved. The *servus* modifications only applied to a minuscule fragment of the archaic-human genome, and there were other qualities here it would be useful to preserve.

She inhaled, catching a feral scent. *Chalmers,* she thought with distaste. *Here again.*

"Ms. Ingolfsson!"

A human hurried up, carrying a clipboard. One of the local officials; and not one of the many that the energetic Captain Lowe had on the payroll. *Lowe's strain I will* not *preserve.* Even modified. He was useful here and now, though. This other feral wasn't useful even in the short term. A nuisance.

"Dr. Chalmers?" Gwen said politely.

Tom and Alice turned at her back; the plump Bahamian health official goggled a little at the Australian's cleavage, notable even here on an island nation of beach resorts. He reacted to Gwen with a bristling nervousness that stained his white shirt at the armpits despite the mild air. Her sex pheromones were naturally low right now anyway, with her appetites satisfied for the present, and she kept them throttled back. Aggression she let swell a little, watching with a secret amusement as the human's fear-defiance cycle intensified. The Bahamian didn't know what he was sensing, but his subconscious was wiser than his waking mind. It remembered the caves, and the smell of tiger.

"Ms. Ingolfsson, I've completed the health inspection of your Haitians."

Dislike and fear understressed in the word. The Bahamians' contempt for their southern neighbors was well-seasoned with consciousness of their numbers and desperation, and of the difficulty of keeping them out— the more so as the native-born were increasingly unwilling to do the menial work the Haitians accepted gladly.

"Yes?" Gwen arched an eyebrow.

It was a bit frustrating not to simply grab the annoying little human by the neck and arm and pull until he came apart—the image made her smile slightly—but there was a hunter's satisfaction in playing him along, for now. Time enough to rebuke insolence when the beacon was established.

I'll throw him to the ghouloons, Gwen decided, making a mental note. *They like to play with their food.* This planet was inconveniently overpopulated, anyway. She imagined him weeping slow tears of absolute despair as he clung to the top of one of the palms, long wet fangs beneath him, and clawed hands reaching up with mocking slowness. The first scream . . .

"They are *all* in perfect health," Chalmers said.

"Doctor, you seem disappointed," Gwen said. "I'd have thought you'd be pleased—the Bahamas are so particular about tropical diseases."

If the dirty savages were sick, I could deport them, Chalmers thought/subvocalized. *How did she get so many permits?* A human would have seen only a glare.

"I'm sure your government realized the potential of IngolfTech," she said. Quite true; genuine productive enterprise was rare in this banking-smuggling-tourism enclave nation. "And I have high standards for my . . . employees. You've seen our clinic, and we spare no expense."

Also quite true. Even in the Old Domination, her human ancestors had been strict about conditions for their plantation hands; she could remember her mother's pride in that. There was no satisfaction in owning inferior stock.

Chalmers gave a curt nod and strode away, back toward the vehicle park.

Tom was sensitive enough to guess something of her moods by now. She heard him clear his throat.

"Is it wise to bait him like that?" he said. "I know

he's only a minor bureaucrat, but this is a small country."

"Indulge me," she said dryly. Tom bowed his head. "No, that's not a criticism; keep telling me when you think I'm making a mistake. We're not infallible."

She cocked her head, focusing on his gestalt. "Yes, I *do* take the whole matter seriously, Tom," she said to his unspoken question. "But remember, I'm designed to actively enjoy conflict and its risks. Speaking of which," she went on, "have the weapons arrived?"

Tom nodded, unhappily. "Young Lowe brought them in on the last flight," he said. "I've had them unpacked and taken to the armory. Vulk says the Haitians he picked are learning quickly—enthusiastic, according to him."

Disgusting thug, he added unconsciously. Tom did not like the man who called himself Vulk Dragovic, but the Serbian was useful.

Gwen made no comment on Tom's subvocalization; it was fair enough, by the American's standards.

"Is it really necessary?"

"It never pays to neglect basics," she said. "We've accumulated substantial wealth and power here, by local standards—industrial espionage can be crude as well as subtle. Besides, it's . . . interesting to have human guards. Reminds me of my childhood."

The Old Domination had used janissaries, slave-soldiers, back before the Last War. There was no need for them in the Final Society, but there was a fascination to recapitulating the technique, even if only on this miniature scale. It was profoundly satisfying to have human slaves not only willing to obey but to fight and die for her.

"Speaking of basics," she went on, "I want another meeting of the inner circle tonight to go over protocols for the American financial group. It would be . . ."

Tom and Alice paled a little at her expression.

" . . . *extremely inconvenient* if they were to stumble on anything they shouldn't. Killing them would put a *severe* crimp in the Project."

Jennifer Feinberg looked out the window of the floatplane. The west coast of the Abacos glittered in the afternoon sun, pinkish-white beaches and palms, tidal marsh, a scrubby olive-green landscape with patches of pine trees standing up from the low bush. Roads were black strings through the countryside, and an occasional tin rooftop showed through. *Soon,* she told herself. She felt jet-lagged, sandy-eyed and weary after the brief stopover in Nassau.

At least I get a trip to the tropics, she thought. New York had been crazier than usual, this November of 1998. And an excuse to stop worrying whether she'd pass the CFA 2&3 or get shelved for the rest of her life. Henry had been properly envious.

Why am I sitting back here with the secretaries? she wondered again. *I should be up there with the rest of the team.*

There were three of them, Vice-President Coleman, Managing Director Klein, and her, one Series 7 Investment Analyst. *Was he just making tasteless jokes, or was that a pass?* she thought, glowering at the back of the VP's balding head. There were times when she wished she'd stayed in premed instead of switching to economics, but . . . oh, the hell with it: there were assholes in any line of work. Besides, after her father died the money was too short. You had to wait too long in medicine.

She looked out the window again. The clouds on the western horizon were turning crimson and gold, casting a path of light down the waves. Jennifer could see a cluster of people waiting by the long white pier jutting out into the water, and the pools and roofs of a settlement not far away. Several of the buildings looked new.

"Boss, boss, de plane, de plane!" she murmured to herself.

"What's that?" the secretary said, bewildered.

"Never mind," Jennifer replied. That made her feel ancient for a second. *Thirty-four's not old.* The secretary was from Minnesota or somewhere, with those blue eyes that made you think of deep wells. Empty wells. *No room for brains with all those hair roots.* "Classical reference."

"Ladies an' gentlemon," the pilot's voice said, in his lilting Island accent. "Fasten seat belts an' prepare for *lan*din'."

The hull touched the surface with a skip . . . skip . . . skip motion that was unlike anything Jennifer had ever felt before.

The gullwing hatch of the pilot's compartment opened and the plane was hauled alongside the pier. Fresh warm air gusted in; she held grimly onto her attache case as a swarm of very black men in white shirts and shorts descended on the Americans' luggage. Others handed them out onto the dock, where the IngolfTech greeters waited.

That's the CEO? Jennifer asked herself incredulously. Far too young and blond.

"I'm Alice Wayne, Ms. Ingolfsson's chief executive assistant," the woman said, with an Australian accent. "Please, this way. Everything's waiting for you, and I'm sure you'd like to freshen up before dinner."

Plenty of boat operators here in Martinique, Ken thought.

The problem was getting one who was . . . flexible . . . enough to do what he wanted but smart enough not to try and rob him and drop the body over the side out beyond the territorial limit.

"You wan' to talk wit me, *blanc*?"

Ken rose and extended his hand over the table. The black man in the sailor's cap looked at it a moment before extending his own. His eyes widened a little when Lafarge matched the crushing grip pressure for pressure. The local was taller than the Samothracian's six-two, and heavier; a bit of a gut bulging the stained T-shirt, but most of it in heavy ropy muscle over his shoulders and arms, hands like callused hams. Many of the other patrons in the little bar had their hair shaved in symbolic patterns, but this man kept his in a plain close crop, with a wisp of beard along acne-scarred, eggplant-colored cheeks.

"You got balls, comin' here."

The voice was soft, accented—the Creole French of the islands that turned "r" into "w," spicing English learned here in the Caribbean.

They sat. There was a slight relaxation among the onlookers, like a pack of junkyard dogs returning to their fleas but keeping the corners of their eyes on a possible meal. Games of dominos and low-voiced conversation resumed; men moved to the bar and back, drank beer and straight rum, listened to the thudding beat of reggae-rap from the machine in the corner. Occasionally someone would walk into the glaring white heat of the afternoon outside, broken only by a sad-looking palm whose fronds rustled dryly, a sound like bones. Despite the warmth many of them were wearing jackets of one sort or another. Sonic and microray scan showed a *lot* of metal: guns, mostly, and ratchet knives. The AI drew a schematic over the room for an instant, outlining the weapons. There were a fair number of cellular phones, too. The air smelled of sweat and sickly-sweet rum, faintly of ganja and mildew.

"I've got business here," Ken said expressionlessly. "I need a boat."

The black leaned back and stuck a toothpick in one

corner of his mouth. "You want to fish, maybe? Marlin? I know someone who got a good deep-sea boat."

"I'm not a tourist."

"Funny, *blanc*, you look like one."

Lafarge was wearing a loose colorful shirt, duck trousers and sandals. The shirt was useful in a number of ways, not least for what it let him wear next to his skin.

"I need," he said, "a charter. Wooden boat, doesn't have to be fast. A couple of runs past Andros, in the Bahamas; then a night drop-off inshore, the boat waits for a couple of hours, and back to Miami. No papers, no problems with the police."

Smoky brown eyes regarded him expressionlessly. "You wouldn't be a police-mon, tryin' to en*trap* a businessman, maybe?"

Lafarge grinned mirthlessly; the other man's chair creaked as instinctive reaction tensed his body.

"Fort-de-France police?" he asked. "Would they send *me*?"

The black relaxed suddenly, with a mirthless chuckle. "*Vwaimen*', that not too likely." Nordic types were wildly conspicuous in this section of town—in most of the island apart from the tourist areas, for that matter. "Maybe you want to step on toes, be cuttin' on other mon's turf, get me killed that way."

Lafarge shook his head. "No boat in to shore, no cargo in or out," he said. "One time, all cash, you walk away."

"Plenty seen me with you now."

Teeth showed between the Samothracian's lips. "I need a man with balls," he said. "Ten thousand on deposit with a bagman; you get it when I get back. I pay your costs upfront."

antoine lavasseur, the AI supplied. A list of criminal convictions followed: mostly in Martinique. A wonder that he was still walking the streets.

false identity, the machine supplied hopefully.

"Andros," Lavasseur said thoughtfully. "Pretty long way, three days, *peut-être*. Staniard town? Kemp's Bay?"

Ken shook his head. "Off the west coast, about halfway between Pine Cay and Williams Island."

The sailor chewed on his toothpick. Suddenly he called out, without moving his basilisk stare from the Samothracian's face:

"Ti' punch!"

The bartender's assistant hurried over; only the best for *this* customer. A bottle of Pere Labat rum went down on the table, chunks of cut lime on a plate, a pitcher of water, a bowl of brown sugar and two reasonably clean glasses. The local occupied himself with the ritual for a moment and then rolled the thick scratched glass of the tumbler between pink palms.

"Those bank waters, bad sailin', *beaucou'* shoal, reef, spiderhead, coral," he said. "Can' get nobody close, there."

"A mile or two will do fine," Ken said. "I'll be going in alone, swimming."

The toothpick stopped in its migrations. "Either you got balls like brass nuts, *blanc,* our you got *malheuw d'tete*," he said.

"My head's not sad enough to take money on board," Ken said.

This was almost enjoyable, like a historical epic. Better than a neural-link simulacrum, because it not only felt real, it *was*. The hard wooden chair under him, the scarred surface of the table with its stains and chipped paint, the smell of stale tobacco and beer from the man across the table—none of them would dissolve if he told the compweb to end the scenario.

Of course if he got killed, that would be permanent too. Far worse: *defeat* would be real here as well.

Lavasseur took off his cap and threw it on the table. "*Bon*. We talk about the money."

*   *   *

Gwen swiveled slightly in her chair, looking at the images in the monitors, picked up from the guest rooms. The three Primary Belway Securities executives, of course. Interesting. Two males in late middle age, and a female, younger—the analyst. It was going to be a challenge, making this all look like legitimate business. Alice was changing for dinner in her room; she looked up and winked at the spyeye.

Gwen smiled. The challenge made her feel good, loose and hungry and alert. That was the problem; the Race had been designed for conquest, and then they'd won so thoroughly that they had to devise artificial stimulants to keep from terminal boredom. This was far more exciting than hunting grizzly bears with spears, combat on levels far beyond the physical. One *drakensis* against six billion humans, with a whole planet for prize . . .

She turned away from the monitors and looked out the tall windows, out over the planet.

"I'm *hungry*," she whispered.

A gluttonous feeling, like an infinite banquet; the promise at last of satisfaction to match the power of her appetites. Appetites for which food and rut were simply symbols.

Closing her eyes, she ran through the dossiers on the three Primary Belway Securities executives. Money, fear, personal glamour—there would be a key to each of them. Probably money; it was the counter in the game they played. She stroked the information, looking for weaknesses and strengths; neurosis, obsession, trauma. At the same time she set herself for the proper pheromonal clues; nothing too heavy, of course. Not at first. A tang of apprehension; fear would produce respect. A muted undercurrent of sexual attraction. And dominance; humans would perceive that as personal magnetism. There.

She concentrated for a minute or two, then took a deep open-mouthed breath to test the scent. *Perfect*.

Jennifer looked at the head of IngolfTech out of the corner of her eyes. It was indecent. Women that good-looking were supposed to be in the profession of being good-looking; it must take hours a day just to keep that figure, especially if she was the early-thirties the records indicated. The surprisingly incomplete records. You could be *born* rich and look like that, or marry the money, but unless you were an actress or model you couldn't *earn* yourself rich and look like that. There wasn't the *time*, on top of a real career. Not unless you had more luck in the genetic lottery than any one human being was due.

"We'll save the numbers for tomorrow morning, I think," Ingolfsson said.

There was a murmur of agreement around the table. The meal had been long, complex and memorable; the dining room was cool and palely elegant, open to the tropical night through tall french doors. The founder of IngolfTech was looking elegant herself, although Jennifer admitted she wasn't overdoing it. The gold and ruby brooch at her neck was the only spectacular item, shaped in the form of a tiny bat-winged dragon, grasping something in its claws.

She went on in the same mellow, purring voice: "Except the basic ones. I came here in '95 with a few hundred thousand dollars. Two months later I had eight million dollars . . . and that might have been luck. Now, by your own conservative estimate, my company has a net worth of one hundred and seventy-eight million dollars, and that *cannot* be luck."

"Ummm . . ." Vice-President Coleman said. "Ah . . . how exactly was your initial financing arranged?"

Gwen smiled with white even teeth. "With respect, Mr. Coleman, that's irrelevant. What *is* relevant is one hundred and seventy-eight million dollars' worth of developments in biotechnology and other fields, every one of them bought, developed, patented, and then sold or licensed by IngolfTech. The patents and contracts are a matter of public record. Our cash flow this year should be better than twenty million from licensing fees *alone*. That's not counting any new products; and believe me, you'll be seeing enough of *those* to assure you of doubling, or possibly trebling that figure."

Jennifer cleared her throat. "Ms. Ingolfsson, I have been going over the figures with some care. Your R&D overheads are . . . well, they're extremely low."

The servants brought in coffee and liqueurs. Gwen nodded and thanked them in some musical language that sounded like French but wasn't; Jennifer couldn't place it. The entrepreneur went on: "That's how you make profits, Ms. Feinberg. Low overheads, high receipts." The green eyes turned on her, and Jennifer felt a sudden prickling over the skin of her face. "My concept isn't complicated; I search out cheap scientific talent—in the former Soviet bloc, in South Asia, elsewhere. There are a lot of very good people there, although they don't have the infrastructure they need. I provide seed money. If the idea looks promising, I buy it—fee-for-service—and develop it to commercial stage. Dr. Mueller and Dr. Singh do, rather."

She nodded at the two heads of research: a pale soft-looking middle-aged German and a lean dark Punjabi. "Then we sell it."

Director Klein smiled. "Essentially, IngolfTech's main asset is your nose for salable ideas, then, Ms. Ingolfsson."

She nodded coolly. "I wouldn't expect anyone to value that highly without a track record," she said. "That's why I haven't taken the company public to date. However, now we *do* have a track record."

"And a rather impressive one," Klein said genially.

"We'll go into the details tomorrow," she said, lifting her wineglass. "In the meantime—to a long and profitable association between IngolfTech and Primary Belway Securities."

They all raised theirs in return. Gwen's head turned towards Jennifer, and her nostrils flared very slightly. "That's Scheherazade you're wearing, isn't it, Ms. Feinberg?"

Jennifer put her wrist to her face reflexively. "Why, yes," she said, startled. The perfume was barely detectable to *her*, and the IngolfTech CEO was sitting four places away.

Gwen smiled again. "I have a very sensitive nose," she said.

*   *   *

Adieu foulard, adieu madwas
Adieu, gwain d'or, adieu collier-chou
Doudou a moin li ka pa'ti
Helas, helas, c'est pou' toujou' . . .

The clumsy weights of the scuba gear clanked together as Ken walked to the side of the motor-schooner lying nearly motionless under bare poles two miles off the coast. The crew were looking elaborately innocent; Captain Lavasseur stood at the wheel, singing the old Creole folk-song under his breath.

There it is, Ken thought. There were lights; probably the main house, although there was a seaplane dock and a beach chalet. They moved slowly with the gentle sway of the ship; the headlights of a car went by somewhere inland, flickering between trees. He could hear faint music, and a dog barked. The seaplane was docked at the pier, next to a paved landing ramp. So peaceful . . .

Philosophers he'd read on this Earth sometimes doubted that evil was a real or tangible thing, relegating it to a matter of perspective and custom. Samothracians had never had that luxury; they lived in the same universe as the Domination and its masters. *It* waited there: a living, breathing snake. He'd studied them all his adult life, killed—and been killed by—thousands of them in neural-link simulations. *Odd. Only here in another* universe *have I ever walked the same planet with one*.

Anger was a calm thing; the neural implants wouldn't allow more than that with combat to await. Still . . . *kill it and I save a whole world,* he thought. Repeal the unhealed wound of the Last War.

A sudden thought shocked him. *Kill it and I'm stuck here forever.* Wondering about the future wasn't something you did much of when you'd volunteered for a suicide mission. He filed the thought for later consideration.

"Exactly here," he said to Lavasseur.

The islander tapped the GPS monitor mounted by the binnacle. "Exactly, *blanc*."

The local satellite positioning system was crude by Samothracian standards; back home, the implants everyone had made it impossible *not* to know precisely where you were at all times. It was functional enough for this. Lavasseur's eyes and teeth showed briefly as the display lit them; for the rest the deck was very dark, only starlight on the waves to glint on rare pieces of metal. The *Mait' Carrefour* was surprisingly clean, but the crew did not go in for polishing the brightwork. Just an innocuous little working boat of the type that still knocked around the out-islands or took an occasional tourist charter . . .

Ken took the rubber-tasting mouthpiece between his teeth and went backward over the rail in the approved local style. A knotted rope dipped down to the bottom a hundred feet below; he stripped off the native gear and bundled it, laying it on the sandy seabed. A quick gesture, and the transparent face-film of his softsuit covered eyes and nose and mouth. He spat the bitter salt of seawater out and rinsed his mouth with fresh. Across his eyes the film adjusted, thickening into a lens that corrected the distortion of seawater and amplified light.

Magnification 5x, he thought/commanded.

In a floating, toe-touching walk reminiscent of a low-gravity asteroid, he began to stride toward shore. The equipment clipped around him was all his own, small and non-metallic and nearly undetectable.

Not as powerful as he'd have liked; given his choice, a miniature antimatter bomb from twenty thousand kilometers would do nicely. Too bad about the bystanders, but worth it considering the stakes. That was exactly what he must not do, of course; far too much noncongruent energy release to be safe, with the Domination's scientists searching the continua. He'd have to do this . . . what was the local's expression?

"Up close and personal," he murmured.

He was walking through coral in a thousand shapes, branched and brain-knobbed, crimson and white and starred with drifting clouds of fish colored like finned orchids. The water carried the grunts, groans, clicking sounds fish made—more were active at night—and the chitinous scuttling noises of the lobsters and sea urchins that marched across the bottom, eye-stalks swiveling to track him. Something heavier and gray swept its tail through the water above, dorsal fin and wicked little eyes, underslung jaw with multiple rows of shearing teeth born on a living torpedo of gristle and sinew. It half-rolled to examine him and then swam on, warned away by the vibrations his softsuit bled into the water.

"Up close and personal," Lafarge said again, with an expression very much like the shark above him.

Jennifer tossed the pen down. She was too wired to

take notes, by hand or on her laptop or the workstation, certainly not in a mood for sleep. Instead she rose and paced restlessly. The main house was old, though recently renovated, a rectangular block of pink-stuccoed coral blocks three stories high, with tall Doric pillars in front. The guests were housed in new wings on either side. Her own suite was three rooms giving out onto a balcony overlooking the rear gardens; bedroom, a sitting room with terminal and multimedia center, and a bathroom that centered on a huge D-shaped sunken tub that looked as if it were carved out of a block of marble. Nothing vulgar, exactly—the fixtures weren't gold or anything—but there was something about the whole place . . .

She looked at the workstation. The electronics were set in smooth panels of tropical hardwood: swing-out keyboards, old-style and an adjustable ergonomic split kind, fax-modem, adjustable thin-section screen on a boom, all the latest. She settled for the speakerphone and punched out a number.

"Hi, Henry. Hope I didn't wake you," she said.

"Nah, I'm a night owl. You okay?"

Despite that, he sounded a little sleepy at first; it was past midnight. But the last words were sharper. *Why did I call Henry, in particular?* she thought. They'd only known each other a couple of months, really— that first time back after Stephen Fischer was killed didn't count. *Does sweetums want a big, stwong man to holdums widdle hand?* she scolded herself. Then again, Henry was a friend . . . and he did have a different perspective on things.

"I'm fine, really. I just wanted to talk."

"Fine by me," Henry said, with a chuckle in his voice. "So, how are things going?"

What do I say? The truth, she supposed. "Fine, but I've got a weird feeling about it," she said slowly. "For one thing, this place is odd. It's too beautiful."

"This lady's rolling in it, from what you said."

"Henry, she's made it all in the last four years. You don't have *time* to collect toys while you do that; believe me, I've known a lot of these entrepreneurial types. They don't do that while they're driving for the top."

"This one does." He was silent for a moment in turn. "There are," he said neutrally, "some very rich people south and west of there. Who *do* go in for toys in a big way."

She thought of a map. South America—Colombia.

"Henry, you don't know anything about IngolfTech and *drugs*, do you?"

Another hesitation. "No, not exactly. And remember where you're calling from."

Oh, Jennifer thought. *Right*. Even more public than a cellular phone.

"No, I really don't think so. It was just a comparison," he said.

"Well, maybe she's just jumping the gun," Jennifer said. "There's Lather and his buffalo ranches, and Trump liked to collect buildings. The other thing is that it's pretty odd to stick a research facility out here in the boondocks. Offshore, yes, there are regulatory advantages, but why Andros Godforsaken Island? It's pretty, but even these days you want to be in closer contact with things, you can't do everything electronically. Why not Nassau? For that matter, there's not much action in the Bahamas except in offshore banking, currencies, that sort of thing. No infrastructure for a high-tech company. So why not someplace in Europe, maybe?"

"Humpfh." Henry grunted thoughtfully. "I'll bet Ms. Ingolfsson does a fair bit of traveling, then. You're right, it does look a bit screwy. What's she like?"

Jennifer propped her head in her free hand. "That's what's got me really wondering. Far too good-looking, in a really strange sort of way. Far too . . . charming.

Isaac Coleman's as cold-blooded a son of a bitch as you can find on the Street, and she had him eating out of her hand. I can't place her, either; not just that she's got no paper trail, she doesn't *feel* familiar. I'd say old money, probably European, but her accent's as much American as anything. And charisma that feels like bumper-cables clipped onto your ears. Scary, fun in an odd sort of way, but scary."

"Be caref—"

Henry's voice cut off. An instant later, so did the lights.

CHAPTER TEN

Ken Lafarge came out of the water silently, crawling on his belly. It was deep night, moonless, only the starlight for illumination and the distant exterior lights of the house. The breathing film rolled up from his mouth and nose, contracting smoothly into the thin goggles across his eyes. Those turned the darkness into flat silvery light, as bright as daylight; they would diffuse glare with the same efficiency. The softsuit covered his body, a form-hugging armor that blended seamlessly against the background, mimicking light and thermal signatures. He went over the beach and up into rocky ground covered in scrub. Wherever his softsuit touched the ground it formed momentary pads shaped to grip on the outside, a frictionless surface elsewhere. He eeled through the heavy undergrowth with scarcely a rustle to mark his passage, only a slight sagelike smell of bruised herbage.

Break, human-range, mark, he whispered silently, as he cleared the scrub and moved into open country.

The AI showed him schematic indications of human presence. It helpfully filled in the guard dogs some of the men had with them. There were a round dozen, patrolling the perimeter; the dogs could be a problem, but fortunately the wind was from the interior of the island. He could overhear the guards' periodic check-ins; they were wearing headsets and throat mikes. Ken grinned wryly in the darkness. *Advantages of backward-ness.* No trace of comp-control, just radios. If the equipment had been a little more advanced, his would have been able to take it over. The Samothracian rose and moved forward in a smooth jog, feet nearly sound-less on the coarse, sandy soil. Fairly soon he'd be into the gardens.

The guards would be hirelings, and chances were that they'd be completely ignorant of what they served. Kenneth Lafarge didn't intend to kill any of them if he could help it, but he wasn't going to let their wel-fare alter his behavior much one way or another.

The sound warned him: far above human audibility, translated by the earpieces. **sonic barrier. directional.** Well beyond this world's technology, and set for barring human-range. A local would just get very apprehen-sive as they went through the edge of it, and probably go into convulsions if they tried to cross the line itself.

He backed, sweat prickling under his softsuit in the instant before the covering drank it away. *Close.* He hadn't expected that. *Assume the field's in a linear arrangement, a line of wands.* . . . He came to an iron post, as thick as his thigh and two meters high. That *was* surprising, since the wands for a sonic barrier should be about the thickness and length of a little finger. A scanner thread pulled out of his cuff revealed the reason.

Now that was ingenious. Cobbled together out of indigenous components. Vastly larger than in the prime-line universe, and there was a great big copper cable to carry power rather than a superconducting ring the size of a wedding band to store it. He'd expected the *drakensis* to be smart—they all were—but it was ingenious as well.

Two can play at that game. There had to be a control system for this, and it would have to be native. Which meant . . .

He reset his earpieces with a mental command and walked quickly up to the post, through the barrier that he felt only as a gentle humming and a tingling through the bones of his skull. A slim tool punched through the cast-iron grillwork that covered it, and a thread of fiber followed. The end of the thread extended filaments the color of ice, growing like crystals in a saturated solution. They worked their way into the circuits of the device and began to trace the connections.

Execute.

"Our guest—"

Tom Cairstens walked through the door and stopped. The Draka was on the bed, kneeling astride Alice's waist; her fingers were moving up from navel over stomach and on to breasts, moving with a delicate precision he knew very well. Gwen's hair moved as an ear cocked toward him. Alice's head rolled in his direction as well, but her eyes were glassy, mouth open, two red spots high on her cheeks. He moved forward, smiling; the ear had been enough indication of that Gwen wanted him to stay and finish his report; and she expected the Household to learn how to read her wants—to learn quickly and well.

"Our guest Ms. Feinberg is making a call to New York," he said, halting beside the bed.

Beautiful sight, he thought. Partly that was Gwen's effect on him, he knew; idly he wondered if it would be possible to resist it. Not that he wanted to. And he'd become much more appreciative of women in general lately, as opposed to only occasionally. It felt rather odd, but not unpleasant, as an additional interest.

Gwen's face was turned down, watching Alice.

Cairstens was used to the Draka's ability to focus on several things at once by now.

"To a friend, evidently. The computer says the number is a New York police detective's, named Henry Carmaggio, but it's definitely a personal call."

"What's she saying?" Gwen asked. Alice whimpered blindly, squirming.

"Just a sort of general uneasiness, but—"

He stopped. Gwen's head flashed up, her face going from relaxed, amused pleasure to hard alertness; then in the same instant to a Gorgon mask of rage, pupils flaring until the green of her eyes vanished in their blackness, lips curling back in an unhuman snarl that showed all of her strong white teeth.

"Intruder!" she shouted, in an astonishing husky roar. It cut through his sudden shock like a bucket of icewater. "Get to the control station. *Now!*"

intruder.

The word flashed into Gwen's consciousness from her transducer, freighted with overtones of precise meaning. Her head jerked up; her hands continued their motion automatically for an instant, stroking Alice's breasts.

attempted infiltration of subsystem, the half-living machine in her skullbone went on. **very capable system, samothracian compinsets.**

"Well, don't *stop*," Alice said in a half-whimper. She grabbed for the hands that had been caressing her.

Gwen's hand slapped hers aside, just hard enough to sting. "Intruder!" she barked at Cairstens. "Get to the control station. *Now!*"

She pitched it loud enough to penetrate the dim confusion that seized humans in emergencies.

In her head: **crash the system.**

She'd engineered in as many blocks as she could, but the native comp systems were pathetically easy to penetrate, even to her multipurpose transducer. They

weren't just primitive, the open architecture of their
core memories was an invitation to takeover. A
Samothracian specialist would walk through like a man
strolling in his parlor.

give me location.

The lights flickered, went out, then came back on
and steadied as the failsafe switched on, a mechani-
cal-relay system outside the computer's loop.

She backflipped from her position astride the Australian girl's hips, stripped the layer knife and plasma
gun out of the weapons belt on the armoire and dove
out the second-story window. Not worth the few seconds it would take to change into her blacks; although
it would be very nice to have a suit of powered infantry
armor right now. *Why not wish for an orbital platform,
while you're at it?*

She landed in a crouch and leaped again, over the
verandah balustrade and down the retaining wall.

Shards of fact appeared in her mind. *Oh, a cunning
little human,* she thought—one of the sonic barrier
posts.

**alert the guards, give the location. order shoot
to kill.** The transducer could do that, relaying through
the primitive radio system in her voice.

The guards ought to distract him a little, at least. No
doubt about what he'd come for: her life. A growl
rumbled in her chest. Let him take it if he could.

Damn. Ken snapped off a shot with the needler.

The tiny crystals stitched across the torso of a guard
and his dog. Both went flaccid and hit the ground
instantly, the anaesthetic shutting down their conscious
nervous systems; it was tailored to be fatal for *drakensis,*
but it would harmlessly trank anything else mammalian. The guard was wearing some sort of heavy goggles,
probably a primitive night-sight system. *Double damn.*
He'd shifted east and inland to get around the closing

semicircle, and now the dogs had winded him. Their barking was harsh and savage, with a guttural undertone of snarls. The beasts had been kill-trained.

Could be worse, he thought, as the barking rose to a frenzied pitch and the dogs were slipped from their chains. *Could be ghouloons.*

Snap. Snap. The needler made a tiny *pffft* sound, like a man hissing quietly between his teeth. *Snap. Snap.* The noise died as the dogs went unconscious.

Something else, something crunching through the coarse coral soil with a firm tread, too fast to be natural. *It* was coming. He shuddered as catheters dumped chemicals into his bloodstream, and the synthetic-neurone web overlaid on his nervous system activated. Everything took on a hard, diamond-bright edge. He thought the needler to automatic and lofted an arc of crystal slivers into the darkness on a precise trajectory. Then he dove to the side, landing in a barrel-roll that took him behind an ornamental boulder.

"*Come to me, human!*" A voice shouting out of the night, like a great mellow trumpet of brass and gold. "*Come to me and die!*"

The *drakensis* was definitely a female—very bad news for this world, unless he could kill it quickly, even if it didn't make contact with the Domination back on Earth/1. He called up range and distance on the voice and risked a snapshot around the boulder.

Crack. Plasma bathed his hand. He tossed the needler aside with a reflexive twitch, before the power coil could rupture. The film across his eyes darkened to protect him as it exploded three meters away, gouging a crater in the ground and spattering him with bits of molten glass. *Crack.* Half the coral boulder vanished, lime burning in a white sear of radiance.

Ken came erect in a five-meter leap that carried him into a shallow declivity in the earth. He rolled out of the other side of that and charged, jinking from one

patch of dead ground to the next. His hand slid
another weapon forward as he ran. A guard leaped up,
firing on automatic. His fingers twitched, and the man
jarred to a stop as if he'd run into a brick wall. The
native very nearly had: a slug of expanding gas like
the shock-wave from an explosion. There was a dull
heavy *thud*.

Maybe I should have stopped for my blacks, one
corner of Gwen's mind thought—they wouldn't block
a serious weapon, but they would shed needler crystals. Some of those had come *far* too close. All the
rest of her consciousness was focused forward. The
night gleamed with light, stars and diffusion off the
sea and heat-pulse in glowing curtains. It rang with
sound, and the air was full of scents. It flowed together
in her mind . . . *there*.

A darting shape, moving fast. Very fast. But he
checked for an instant as a guard cut loose at him.
Gwen fired.

Crack. Blue-white light split the darkness, driving her
eyes into a protective squint. Radiant fire outlined the
figure of a charging man, burning soil and vegetation
around him to lime dust and carbon ash as the fields
in the soft armor redirected the plasma. He dropped
flat and rolled; the second shot skimmed his back and
blew a head-sized hole in the soil behind him. He
launched himself at her on its heels, meeting a third
bolt in midair. Gwen bounded backward.

Something slapped at her like a huge padded fist,
tumbling the smooth grace of her leap into a sprawl.
Gas gun. She kept moving as she struck, ignoring sharp
edges gouging at her skin, and fired again underneath
her own body in mid-roll. The figure of the Samothracian exploded in brilliant white-on-white outline
again, then faded into a blurred darkness that almost
perfectly matched the background. She'd seen it spin,

though; the gas gun must have ruptured in the plasma
flare.

He came down out of the night, heels striking for
her torso. She whipped aside, tossing the plasma pistol behind her—at this range the backwash from a
discharge would crisp half her body. It would probably
also kill the Samothracian, but if they both died he won.
Instead she cut left-handed with the layer knife.

A forearm blocked it. The surface of the soft armor
turned diamond-hard for an instant, shedding the blade
with a whining zing of cloven air. The enemy stumbled
backward, but his elbow joint hadn't turned to gravel
taking the strain. Biomods, implanted reinforcements
to the bone structure—no surprise. A Samothracian
cyber-warrior.

He slashed back at her with a blade like a wire
outline of a sword that grew out of his gauntlet with
avalanche speed; her ears could hear its ultrasonic
chitter. Vibration-knife. The wind of its passage was an
ugly thing across her eyes; it would carve her flesh like
gelatin, and even the reinforced bones wouldn't give
it much trouble.

She danced free, outside the arc of attack, keeping
her arm-long knife up. They struck and parried at each
other with blurring speed. Metal and monomolecular
thread screamed in protest and lit the night with fat
white sparks of density-enhanced steel.

A guard rose and emptied the thirty-five-round clip
of his submachine gun into the Samothracian's back.
For an instant the entire surface of the softsuit turned
rigid as high-tensile steel as it spread the kinetic energy
of the bullets. They spanged off into the night with
keening shrieks, their velocity little affected by the
ultraslick surface. Two struck the gunman, and he
dropped to the ground shouting with pain.

Cat-agile, Gwen leaped in and swung two-handed at
her enemy's gauntlet. The micron-thick wire of the

vibration blade was barely rigid as the armor diverted power to its primary, defensive function. The layer knife was single-molecule diamond and steel with its electron shells collapsed to pack atoms closer together than nature would allow. The wire nicked the blade, but it parted and whipped back into the gauntlet. She caught the wrist under her armpit, levered, threw. The Samothracian's hundred-odd kilos arced through the air headfirst.

She snatched up a boulder twice her weight, to pound him to death in his shell like a lobster. He managed to twist and land on his back, one palm out toward her. Brilliant light flashed; Gwen was blind for an instant. Something struck the rock from the other side, jerking it in her hands three times, *tock-tock-tock*. Two more submachine-guns opened up, hosing the night with tracer bullets; Gwen leaped backward behind a concrete planter, crouching on all fours, blinking and shaking her head. Her eyes teared and then vision returned.

She could hear his footsteps and the faint metallic smell of his equipment, and beneath that the individual pungency of his body-scent, as unique as a fingerprint. He was retreating, back toward the ocean, as more of the guard force closed in on him. They were professionals, and not about to shoot each other by accident, but the volume of fire was building. *There*. He'd broken free and started to run.

"*Cease firing!*" she shouted to the guards, loud enough to shock them into obedience even through their adrenaline-rush.

She scooped the plasma gun off the ground and pursued in a blur of movement, faster than a galloping horse, hurdling planters and benches with headlong grace. The Samothracian stayed ahead of her, just. She braced and fired once as he flung himself into the waves, then again as he entered, hoping against hope that the shockwave through the water would kill. Thunder-crack rolled back from the water, then nothing.

Damn this museum-piece popgun. If she'd been wearing a modern, high-intensity weapon when all this started, it would have punched through the softsuit at least once. She'd been hoping it would overload the defensive field, but no joy. *That'll teach me to carry a four-hundred-year old pistol for sentiment's sake.*

She was panting; she slowed it to deep steady breaths, growling low in her throat with the rage of territorial violation and the need to kill. Her ears sang with the combat hormones coursing through her bloodstream, and she had an urge to throw herself into the sea in pursuit. Heat pulsed from her body.

Don't be ridiculous. She could swim underwater for fifteen minutes or so, but the softsuit could take oxygen out of the water and feed it to the wearer. He could *walk* to Nassau if he wanted to, along the bottom.

It was a minute or two before the guards arrived. Gwen dropped the plasma gun to the sand and covered it with a quick sideways motion of her foot; she remembered to hold the knife inconspicuously down by her side.

"The emergency's over," she said calmly, her voice pitched to spread conviction. They were staring . . .

Oh, the local nudity taboo, she reminded herself. She wasn't wearing anything but a slick film of sweat and some blood.

Gwen snapped her fingers at one of the guards. "Pierre, the jacket."

He handed it over, juggling the sling of his submachine gun. The Haitian was a hulking figure; the battledress fabric came down nearly to her knees. She belted it on and used the motion to retrieve and drop the pistol into one of the patch pockets; there was a slight smell of scorching cloth.

"Is François being seen to?" she asked. "Who else is hurt?"

"Philippe," a Dominican said. "Donna, he's dead. Ribs broke."

Several of the guards nodded. That would be the gas gun: very effective at close range; a good thing she'd been jumping when the charge hit her. Two more men panted up.

"Tom, Vulk," Gwen said, then raised her voice: "The rest of you, back to normal rounds. Take the casualties to the clinic. Be alert."

They walked away, murmuring among themselves. She recorded and sorted the conversations for future attention. Humans were extremely good at editing memories to suit their mental frame-of-reference; there were times when she wished she could do that herself. She heard *flare gun* whispered, *flame-thrower*—and more softly, *dupiah*, and *corps-cadavre*. It had been very dark, the whole action had only taken a little over five minutes, and most likely the guards would have the whole thing rationalized by morning.

Vulk Dragovic spoke: "What *was* that?"

She'd hired the Serbian in Santo Domingo, where he'd been vacationing after his previous career went bad. Most of the skills he'd learned in Mostar and Kosovo were relevant to her needs.

"A Samothracian," she said. "I told you about them, although I didn't anticipate one showing up here."

She looked out to sea. Very faintly, an IR heat-smudge marked the western horizon. Probably the boat the enemy infiltrator had swum in from—there were sharks in the water close to shore at night, but that wouldn't be any problem for her enemy, worse luck.

"Damn!" Tom said. "Everything was going so well up to today."

Gwen turned her head. "Tom, everything was *not* going well. Yesterday we had a very dangerous enemy that we didn't know about. Now we know he's here, and a good deal about him."

She examined her layer knife. The nick in the blade was small; she'd grind it out with an industrial-diamond grinding wheel.

"I could have sworn François hit him," Vulk said.

"He did—a full clip," Gwen said. "The Samothracian was wearing a softsuit. It's a single molecule, with field-guides and AI controls on the inner surface. When it's struck it redistributes the kinetic energy over the maximum possible surface, like a second skin of very strong steel with a frictionless surface. About . . ."

She paused fractionally to find a comparison that would make sense to the humans. " . . . about as resistant as a light armored car. You can broil or smash the body inside, or punch through with enough energy, but short of that he's invulnerable."

Vulk swore softly in Serb. Gwen went on: "The men did very well; they distracted him and it was crucial. We'll have to reequip the guard-force, though. Full-power semiauto battle rifles with hardpoint ammunition, .50-caliber machine guns, some of those .50-caliber Barrett sniper rifles.

"Tom," she continued, "I crashed the computer; he was hacking into it. Get rid of it, power up the backup and load from the tapes, but sever *all* outside connections. We'll have to use secondaries for those from now on; I'll give you more details in the morning. Go attend to that, and don't forget to check on our guests from New York. Reassure them if any of them noticed; it was dry thunder, or a wedding celebration in the village, or whatever."

"Yes ma'am."

Vulk licked his lips and reholstered the Walther in the shoulder rig he wore over his tailored safari suit. "That one—" He jerked his head toward the ocean. "Is he . . . like you?"

Gwen shook her head. "No, they have what amounts to a religious taboo against serious gene-engineering on their own stock. But he'll have a good deal of very capable equipment which about makes up the difference. A lot of it implanted in his body. Luckily, we know what he doesn't have."

"What's that?" Tom asked.

"No help, or they would have come together. And he doesn't have an antimatter bomb, or he would have used it and this island wouldn't be here now. They don't underestimate us, not anymore." She grinned, and Vulk paled slightly. "We taught them better than that."

"A nuclear weapon?" the Serb said, rubbing a hand over the sandpaper roughness of his blue chin. "Mother of God, that's —there are thousands of people living on Andros." He sounded more respectful than disgusted. Which was not surprising, considering what had happened in Kosovo.

Gwen nodded. "They're not significantly more squeamish than we Draka," she said meditatively. "Although they rationalize it differently. Hmmm. This whole thing smells of a stealth priority. Minimum energies."

She closed her eyes for a moment, concentrating. "Yes. I think I see. The physics . . . he's afraid that use of noncongruent energies will somehow make it easier for the Technical Directorate to home in on us here. And since his people could insert him deliberately, they know more about the molehole technology, and he's probably right to fear that." She smiled again, slow and savage. "That's an advantage."

She looked up at Tom. "There is one important point. Before, we weren't in a hurry. Now we are."

And I should have the fallback ready, she thought. There were a number of strategies open to the enemy; one of them would be to turn the local governments on her.

The answer to that was disposing of the human

population, or most of it. Not very difficult, but wasteful . . . and a little too much like fishing with grenades. Boring.

Still, at seventh and last you did what you had to do to win. A suitable plague and a deadman switch would be easy enough to arrange and hold in readiness.

"Be careful," Henry said. "You—"

The line went *click*, and then it was replaced by the steady hum of a dial tone.

"Shit!"

Carmaggio's thick finger stabbed for the pad, and then he realized that he hadn't the remotest idea of the number in the Bahamas. He glanced at the clock: 12:30. He swore, hauled himself into the bathroom—time, tide, and the bladder waited for no man—and then sank down at the kitchen table with the phone there and a pad and paper. Pushing aside a stack of pizza boxes and some fried rice still in the carton, he began.

"Hello, operator? I was in the middle of a long-distance call, from Andros Island in the Bahamas. I was cut off; can you—no, I *don't* know the number. Yeah, thank *you* very much for fucking nothing, too."

He laid the phone down and ran a hand through his hair, flogging at his mind and feeling the sand in the pipes. A nice juicy one had come up last night, a spousal just-can't-take-it-anymore ballpeen-hammer divorce, and kept him up; this was two days' sleep he was missing, and it got harder past forty. Hell, it got harder past thirty, if he remembered right.

Okay, Jenny used my call-in line. One of the few perks of this job at his level was that it made it easier to get two phone lines. *That'll catch it if she calls back.*

So . . . area code for Bahamas, no big deal.

"Hello, directory assistance?"

An accent this time. "I'd like the number of Ingolf-Tech Incorporated. No, not the Nassau branch, the headquarters on Andros Island. Thank you."

He jotted it down. Maybe a bit impolite to call this time of night, but fuck that. Five rings.

"*Hello. You have reached IngolfTech Incorporated. Our business hours are—*"

"Shit!"

He slammed the handset down into the receiver. "I can't leave a goddamn message. No fucking way I can let them connect to me. I shouldn't be calling as it is.

"Directory assistance? I'd like the home number for Ms. Gwendolyn Ingolfsson, Andros Island. . . . It's unlisted. *Thank* you very much.

"Bitch," he added.

Except that he had to do something; the knowledge was there in his mind, as definite as his own self. He stabbed more keys.

"Jesus? Yeah, I know what time it is. Listen, you still got that plastic piece?"

There was a silence on the other end of the line, and a sleepy woman's voice muttering in Spanish somewhere behind his partner. The gun was a curiosity, a little plastic-and-synthetics one-off they'd picked up a while ago. Technically Department property, but nobody was hurt by it going missing. The former owner had lost an argument; the way you did when your head tried to argue with a rifled shotgun slug at close range; and it hadn't figured in the evidence trail.

The interesting thing about it was that there was no metal except the ammo and the firing pin. It wouldn't activate an airport security scanner, not unless the scanner was set so it'd go off from the bridgework in your teeth.

"*Sí*, I've got it."

"I may need to borrow it tomorrow. Sorry about your day off."

"Can I help, *patrón?*"

"Yeah, you can cover for me; I may have to take some of that accumulated sick leave. I'll give you the details tomorrow. I just needed to know about the piece so's I could make some plans."

"Go with God."

"Same here."

He set the phone down more thoughtfully. Foreign forces got quite sticky about American cops wading into their jurisdictions—understandable; he wouldn't be entranced himself if some maniac came onto his turf waving a Glock and expecting the local wogs to genuflect. On the other hand, no way he was going to the Bahamas without a piece, if he had to go—he'd have taken an AK, if he could. The memory of what the warehouse and Marley Man's boys had looked like was unpleasantly vivid.

"I'm probably overreacting," he muttered, dumping coffee into the filter. "Jenny's a smart girl." Water gurgled into the pot and he poured it into the machine.

He was still going to be on that plane tomorrow if he hadn't heard something definite and couldn't get through. She was smart, but she didn't know how to handle this sort of situation.

Carmaggio remembered the heavy smell of blood, red meat turning gray with exposure to air in the terrible gaping wounds and smashed skulls, the stink of cooked brain.

If anyone knew how to handle it.

The lights flickered and came back on, but the telephone was dead; not even a dial tone.

Jennifer spent a moment jiggling the catch. "What the hell? Henry? Henry?"

She looked around. Nothing seemed different. *Calm. Calm down. It was just some sort of power out.* This was the Third World, after all.

"It's also a research facility," she muttered.

Computers and delicate, ongoing experiments that would be disrupted if the power supply went out. IngolfTech certainly had the funds to afford the best; the proof was all around her. She went out onto the balcony; the night was a little cooler, in the high sixties, perhaps, and she rubbed her arms with her hands. And why didn't the phones work?

Jennifer walked down the balcony steps into the garden, feeling her way along the balustrade; there were a few low-intensity blue lights up under the eaves, but they were scarcely brighter than starlight on the fountain that chuckled in its basin of Mexican tile. The pathway was checkerboard colored brick, between flowerbeds and young ornamental trees, leading her feet on toward the lawns and the slope to the sea. She bumped her toe in the openfaced sandals and swore at the sudden sharp pain.

Somebody shouted from the main block to her left. She turned and caught a glimpse of a running figure; shrank back into an alcove in a hedge of dog-rose, sinking down on a stone bench. *What's going on?* More shouting, down by the sea and left—south—away from the floatplane dock.

Crack. She blinked. A sudden blue-white flare of actinic light threw shadows and brightness across the gardens, a bright glare of color from a sheet of bougainvillea climbing a retaining wall to her right. *Lightning?* she thought? But it had come from the *ground*, not the sky—and the sky was clear, a frosted band of stars from horizon to horizon overhead. So clear she had been able to see the colors of the stars, earlier. The noise was like thunder too, only smaller somehow.

Crack. Again the flash of light. And a hammering chatter, flat and undramatic by contrast.

"That was a gun!"

She knelt up on the bench and peeked cautiously over the planter that backed it. More flashes and miniature thunderclaps, and more gunfire—a long burst from an automatic weapon. Then silence.

"My God, that *was* a gun! A machine gun!" *Breathe slowly. In. Out.* "We've been caught in a coup or something." Henry's words came back to her. "Oh, my God, we're being attacked by drug runners!"

CNN and the evening news flashed through her mind. WALL STREET FINANCIERS TAKEN HOSTAGE; the *Post* would banner-headline the whole thing. Connie Chung would do a special report. Jennifer's mother would have a seizure.

The pain in her fingers shocked her back into awareness. She had been gripping the coarse coral limestone of the planter hard enough to bruise. In the silence the loudest sound was her own breathing; she forced herself to take slow deep breaths, lowering her head until only her eyes showed over the edge of the planter and the low flowering vine within. From here she could see a corner of the main central block of the house and the darkened approachway and gardens before it. Tensely she waited. Nothing happened, for long enough that the night air cooled the sweat on her skin and brought goosebumps.

I didn't imagine that, she told herself. Then again, she hadn't seen anything except lights, either.

She heard the sound of feet on the crushed oyster-shell of the drive. There was a little more light there, enough to tell that a human figure was coming up from the waterfront. It turned and walked toward her; she shrank back. A man, two; black men, in gray uniforms, and each carrying a weapon. Some exotic-looking thing, one slung across the first man's chest, the other carried at port arms. They passed by ten feet away, heads turning alertly, heavy goggles making their faces insectile in the night.

They looked like soldiers, or policemen. *Or rent-a-cops*, she thought, relaxing slightly. *Yes*. There had been security guards around earlier in the day dressed like that—although *they* hadn't been carrying machine pistols, or weapons of any sort. The men passed by and moved further from the house, vanishing in the darkness.

More footsteps; lighter this time, and quicker. Another dim figure, this one moving at a quick gliding run. Bare legs flashed in the dim gloaming. *Ingolfsson?* Jennifer wondered. Impossible to tell for sure at this distance, and she—he, whoever—was turning away, toward the main block and the entrance. A few moments later there was another sound. A screech, like nothing so much as a cat out prowling for battle and fornication . . . except that it was far too loud, and somehow the modulation sounded like a voice.

"Weird," she muttered, rising.

Nothing cataclysmic seemed to be happening. She rose, feeling a little foolish as she climbed back through the balcony and firmly shut the french doors. There had to be some sort of rational explanation for all this. *Henry's paranoid, it goes with his job*. He was a dear, but she had to watch out for that us-against-the-world attitude, it was catching.

"Urk!"

Jennifer squeaked and jumped. The knock at the door repeated. She opened it a crack, to see Tom Cairstens smiling urbanely in the corridor outside. *I am not nervous*. She opened the door and stood aside, but the IngolfTech executive shook his head.

"Ms. Feinberg?" he said. "I noticed your lights were still on. Sorry about the noise just now. We've got a fair number of construction workers down by the new lab extension, and—well, they tend to celebrate a little hard, sometimes. It seems there was a wedding, or a christening, something like that, and the rum flowed a little freely, not to mention the firecrackers. Our security guards have everything under control, no need to call in the local police, even."

"Oh." *I feel silly.* "I thought I heard gunfire. And why did the phones go out?"

"One of the guards let off a few rounds into the air. Bad habits, I'm afraid—they're Haitians, you see, there isn't much local labor available for this sort of work. Good people, loyal as Dobermans, but a bit rough sometimes. One of them drove a backhoe through the cable to our satellite uplink; it's back in order now."

"Oh. I see. Thanks."

"See you tomorrow, Ms. Feinberg."

I feel really *silly.* Drug runners. Terrorists. Hostage-taking. *I watch too much CNN.*

Suddenly she felt sleepy, in reaction to the adrenaline perhaps, or just because it was late; after one, by now.

"Thanks, Mr. Cairstens." As the door closed, she remembered. "Ohmigod. *Henry.* The poor guy got cut off right in the middle of the call."

She dashed over to the phone and punched the number; a voice at the back of her mind noted dryly that she had it memorized by now. Jennifer told the voice to shut up; it sounded unpleasantly like her mother.

A voice growled in her ear on the other end of the line. "Jesus? No problem, I can get the ticket and you can tell the captain—"

"Henry, it's Jenny."

"Shit. Hell, sorry, I mean . . ."

"You were worried." She paused, and said softly: "You were coming *here*, weren't you?" An emergency flight to the Bahamas was not petty cash on a police lieutenant's salary.

A long silence. "Hell, I've got vacation time coming."

"You're a sweet guy, you know that, Henry?"

He snorted. "I'm a worrywort. Look, I don't want to crowd you, okay? I'm not looking over your shoulder or anything."

"Nothing wrong with a little of that." She gave an involuntary yawn. "We did have a little excitement here; it turned out to be some construction workers driving a backhoe around to celebrate something or other."

"Yeah? You can tell me about it when you get back."

"See you. I've got a working breakfast tomorrow . . ."

Kenneth Lafarge ignored the scuba gear that lay around the end of the knotted rope. Life was one footstep after another, until the cord was in his hands. Balance changed as the softsuit ejected its water ballast and inflated temporary air-cells to make him buoyant. A touch of the hands, and he floated upward along the rope. Weight caught at him, and he fought down a scream as he hauled himself over the railing of the boat. He fought back another as rough hands helped him.

"I'm . . . fine," he gasped, waving aside the crewmen. "Get going, *now*."

The boatmen were mercenaries; they shrugged and obeyed, leaving him to walk in a straight, slow line to his cabin. The boat's diesel blatted, then settled down to a steady burbling. He opened the door— anyone else trying that would get an unpleasant surprise—and let the softsuit fall to the floor in a thin puddle as he stumbled to the bunk. It collected itself and slithered to the table and up one leg, pouring itself into a container the size of a pocketbook to recharge and repair.

This time he *did* groan between clenched teeth as the air rasped at the burns and bruises that covered most of his skin. His right hand was swelling and red as boiled lobster from the two pointblank hits. According to the techs back home, a softsuit probably couldn't take close-range plasma bolts from a standard Domination hand-weapon. Apparently the United States of Samothrace built its agents better armor than they thought.

Enough better. Just. He staggered to the bunk and fell into it.

The suitcase clicked beneath the bed. He lay panting in the dark, his eyes swimming with the aftermath of the booster chemicals, as tendrils felt their way over and beneath him. They crisscrossed his body in a dense web, creeping into the corners of his eyes, nostrils, mouth. Things pricked his skin, and the pain diminished. Coolness soothed; there was a muted buzzing as dead skin was debrided away and replaced with temporary patches that would speed regrowth. Tentacles thin as wire and stronger than thought manipulated his gun hand.

no serious degradation of function, the AI said with indecent cheerfulness. **you will recover full effectiveness within five days, including metabolic stress from the combat drugs.**

Which took a little off your lifespan every time you used them—but it was better than being dead. His stomach twisted at the memory of the fight. Neural-link simulators could feed in scenarios of what it was like to fight a *drakensis* hand to hand, but there was still a difference when it was for real. His gut heaved again at the memory of the raw strength behind the grip that had spun him through the air, hearing again the guttural snarling of a tiger about to kill.

How can anyone mistake it for a human being? he thought. The face had been like a beast's, too; the sort of expression an antelope would encounter on the very last lion it ever saw.

it was not attempting deception with you, the machine answered pedantically. **presumably it takes more care with the local humans.**

I failed, Ken sighed. His hand tightened toward a fist until the twinges warned him. *I should have killed it!*

a scouting operation, the AI replied. **there will be other opportunities.** After a moment: **sleep.**

Thirty hours to the dropoff point near Miami. He could sleep the entire time. Darkness closed over him, as welcome as his mother's touch.

Gwen wrapped the weapons in Pierre's jacket and tossed them over the balustrade of her bedroom's exterior terrace eighteen feet above. Then she took two steps and leapt, hands clamping onto the rough coral rock of the balcony and swinging her over. Quicker than going up the stairs, and less likely to cause commotion. And her body craved movement.

Alice was waiting; she gave a jump and squeak of startlement as Gwen appeared. Then her eyes widened at the Draka's appearance. Gwen was still running with sweat, and there were bleeding grazes on her flank and one arm; they clotted with inhuman speed. Her chest heaved as lungs pumped oxygen into the bloodstream. Skin twitched as overprimed muscles sought release. She fought down another snarl.

"What *happened?*" Alice asked, crossing her arms on the breast of her robe in an instinctive gesture of self-protection. The Draka caught an edge of the creamy scent of fear; her mask had slipped a bit under the stress, and the other's subconscious was reacting to what it perceived.

"Bit of an emergency," Gwen replied, watching patterns of heat through the Australian's facial skin. They made her seem to glow from within, like a lantern. "It's over for now. I'll explain later."

"All right," Alice said, dropping her eyes. *Good, she's learning,* the Draka thought. She looked good. *Delicious.* Without looking up: "Do you still want to . . . ?"

Gwen nodded.

"That's fine with me." An uncertain smile. "You *are* very good at it."

"After four-hundred-odd years of practice," Gwen said, advancing, "I should be."

She pulled the blond woman's arms down, then stripped off the robe. Alice shuddered at the musky smell of her sweat, then again as Gwen bent and took a nipple between her lips. She cried out in surprise as the Draka put a hand beneath her buttocks and lifted her smoothly into a fireman's carry across her shoulder. And again as the fingers probed her openings, halfway between a moan and a protest.

"This will be a little different," Gwen said, as she strode easily across the terrace and into the bedroom. "More strenuous."

The scent was intoxicating; she bit at the thigh next to her cheek, just hard enough to draw a squeal.

"I had to go into combat overdrive and didn't have the chance to expend much energy. I'll have the jittering judders for days unless I work it off now."

The squirming within the circle of her arm had no more chance of dislodging itself than it would have from a similar thickness of steel cable; and in any case, it wasn't an attempt to escape. The soft helpless movement was extremely pleasant, like a kitten's paws batting at her hands. It helped flip the savage focus of killmode over into an equally directed urge: lust, but with an edge to it, raw and direct.

She tossed the other down on the bed and climbed onto her, straddling Alice's shoulders and linking hands behind her neck. The Australian's eyes were wide and her mouth trembled slightly. Her heartbeat hammered in Gwen's ears, nearly as rapid as her own pulse. The Draka's thumbs caressed the other's cheeks and the angle of her jaw, then drew her upward as she sank down.

"So play pony for me, Alice."

CHAPTER ELEVEN

Thomas Cairstens pedaled faster and looked down at the speedometer of the bicycle. *Twenty. For ten miles, the way she was going.* He'd cut across the circle of her course. *Jesus.* Gwen was loping along on the foot-trail beside the laneway, keeping pace without visible strain and hurdling boulders and logs with an easy raking stride. The scent of pine was strong in the cool dawn air, but the flicker of light in the east was bright enough to give a hint of the heat that would come later. The Draka moved through the dappled half-light with a wolf's concentrated economy of motion; he could barely hear her footsteps on the rocky limestone soil. She slowed as they angled back into the gardens, down to a trot and then a walk by the freshwater pool.

He dismounted and stood panting as she shed lead-weighted anklets, bracelets and waist-belt. "Impressive," he said.

Gwen was breathing deeply, and the sweat-wet exercise tunic clung to her. "Ironic," she replied. He raised an eyebrow.

"The way we're designed, we'd be the ultimate terrors in a world where wars were fought with rifles, or better still swords." She nodded toward the bicycle. "But on that, you're nearly as fast as I am; in a car, much faster. I can see in the dark—so can an IR scope. I can do differential equations in my head, but not as well as a computer, not even *your* computers. I've got a built-in drive to fight—and apart from some infantry mopping-up actions at the end of the Last War, it's been about as much use as an udder on a bull for four hundred years. Until now."

"What do you fight in your own world?" he said curiously. "You said it was very peaceful."

"Animals," she said. "Including ones we designed intelligence into, to make them more dangerous. And each other, particularly each other—*drakensis* are *drakensis*'s main cause of death."

She stripped the tunic off over her head and threw the sodden fabric to the stone pavement with a wet *smack*. The swimming pool was fed from a cast-bronze lion's mask set in a semicircle of rough stone blocks. Gwen bent her head into the stream of water from the lion's mouth and drank hugely. Cairstens felt his breath catch at the sight. Naked, she looked far less human; the sleek perfection of long bones and flat-strap muscle was somewhere between machine and animal. He caught the smell of her sweat, like musk mixed with flowery perfume, and gave an involuntary gasp.

Gwen raised her head. Her nostrils flared slightly, taking his scent. "You've been good," she said, and flicked her hand toward one of the loungers. "But quickly."

His fingers trembled slightly as he dropped his shorts and lay back on the padded deck-chair. He reached behind his head and gripped the framework as Gwen came to stand over him, her mahogany curls outlined against the rising sun.

"Another built-in drive," she said, and straddled him. Her hands clamped over his. The weight of her body

came down on him, always shocking; the denser bone
and muscle made it heavier than his, and hot—fever
hot with the superactive metabolism. Lips moved across
his as her tongue probed his mouth. Her hips moved,
and he felt his penis seized and clamped and held in
a warm internal grip just short of pain, like a wet
heated glove of flesh. The steel frame of the lounger
creaked rhythmically as she rode him, harder and
harder. She growled with pleasure as she moved, a
sound unlike anything he'd ever heard. The musk of
her scent and the crushing strength that held and
moved him brought an exquisite sense of yielding help-
lessness. When she stiffened and arched over him he
spasmed and cried out in abandon.

Gwen lay on him for a moment, smiling. "Best way
to start the day," she said kindly, chucking him under
the chin.

Cairstens lay limply. "God, I'm ruined," he said.

"Not at all," Gwen replied, picking him up and tossing him casually overarm into the pool.

He thrashed and sputtered for a moment as she
arrowed past him. When he turned, she was standing
on the bottom of the deep end looking up at him—
the sight was a little eerie, until you remembered she
was naturally denser than water. Then she crouched
and leapt and barreled by, her wake buffeting him
aside. They climbed out and put on beach robes; the
maid was there with breakfast, and Alice had brought
the files.

"No problems with the Belway people about the
other night?"

"Coleman and Klein didn't even wake up, according to the monitors. Feinberg was up, and went out
in the garden. I told her it was a minor disturbance
among the construction workers, and she bought it."

"She called her policeman friend again," Gwen said.
"I wonder just why he was so concerned. We'll have

to look into that." She grinned. "I think she's fonder of him than he knows, judging by her behavior in the bath after that."

Alice giggled. "Not quite as much the ice-maiden as she puts on."

"There's no conflict between libido and ambition," Gwen said. "Quite the contrary. Now. It's been a very productive week," she went on thoughtfully, loading her plate with johnnycake and local dishes—fire engine, chicken souse, slices of fresh avocado. She began to feed. "I think we've achieved a preliminary rapport with Primary Belway Securities."

"Got them around your finger, you mean," Alice said.

"Not exactly. Not yet. But their eyes are definitely full of dollar signs," Gwen said. She chewed thoughtfully on a piece of johnnycake. "Pass those grits, please. We'll need a secure line into Belway, somehow . . . definitely a hold on one of their executives."

"Which one did you have in mind?"

"The youngest, Feinberg. She seems to be more mentally flexible; that'll be useful if we can bring her fully on-side eventually. You humans tend to ossify mentally by forty."

"We've got a few months before the action moves to New York," Cairstens pointed out.

Gwen frowned slightly. "Yes, but that damned Samothracian is a complicating factor. I'll have to be very cautious there, with him around."

She murmured something in her native dialect; Cairstens thought he caught *damnyank*, but he couldn't be sure. It was too different from English as he'd been raised to understand it, and she rarely used it.

"You should set up a meeting with Amier and Lather," Cairstens said. "Their influence could be extremely helpful in the U.S. I think I impressed them, but you should consolidate it."

"An excellent suggestion," Gwen said thoughtfully.

"Speaking of risks, it's time to prepare a fallback strategy, just in case," she added.

"Just in case what?" he asked.

"Just in case the Samothracian manages to kill me," she said. Cairstens swallowed, feeling his stomach lurch. Alice had the same stricken look. "Oh, don't worry—it's a low probability. But it exists."

"What will you do?" he asked.

"Clone myself," she said. "I had Singh do up a viable embryo, and it's ready for implanting any time."

Cairstens frowned, searching for details; his background in genetics had improved considerably over the past few years, since that was one of IngolfTech's main lines. A clone was a genetic duplicate of the original, a cell-nucleus inserted into an ovum and stimulated to divide. This Earth still couldn't do it with higher animals, but he supposed it was routine in Gwen's timeline.

"But a clone wouldn't have your memories, would it? It wouldn't be *you*."

Gwen tapped herself behind the ear. "Not normally. But I can download a lot to my transducer," she said. "It's quasi-organic itself and the memory's stored holographically; we can extract a piece and implant it *in embryo* at about seven months, that's standard procedure, except that they usually use a blank one. That'll provide a lot of the background. No, it won't be me, a different personality . . . but it'll be fairly close. With the right upbringing, it—she—would be ready to start taking over in about twenty, thirty years. We mature about the same rate you do; the homeostasis doesn't kick in until then. I've drawn up a plan for a schedule of clandestine investments, safe houses, that sort of thing. You can start implementing it after the bankers leave. That way if everything goes sour, the clone can be reared in safety and have a base to start from."

Alice paused with a piece of pineapple on her fork. "Won't it be inconvenient, being pregnant?" she said.

Gwen chuckled. "Not for me, my dear. Not for me."

The Australian's fork dropped to her plate with a clatter. Her face went white around the eyes and mouth as the Draka reached over to pat her on the cheek.

"Don't worry," she said. "The procedure's painless, and once the embryo implants in the uterus you'll feel fine. Slightly euphoric, in fact. It's all designed that way. Special diet, of course—she'll need more minerals and so forth than a human fetus—but it's not dangerous if you're careful. And I can guarantee that you'll absolutely *adore* the baby. That's built-in too."

Alice stifled a scream. Gwen rose and pulled her to her feet, half-supporting her.

"It's all ready. No time like the present." She stroked the Australian's blond hair. "It's a very special relationship," she said soothingly. "Being a brooder for a Draka, that is. Come on now, don't fuss."

"Now, we have to keep this under careful control," the head of IngolfTech said.

Jennifer blinked. The sun threw sparkles of metallic brightness back from the water in the concrete holding tank. Sand gritted on the paving stones beneath her sandals. A succession of broad football-field-sized concrete holding tanks stood along the seafront, stepped down one from the other. There was a muted hum of pumps, and a hissing as bubbles rose through the water in the first four tanks; a heavy algae smell rose from them—but this last one was filled with something as transparent as distilled water.

Gwen dipped a glass into it and drank. "Try it," she said.

The Belway Securities executives followed suit. The water was sun-warm but nearly tasteless.

"Four days ago, that was sea water. A tailored algae-bacteria combination—solar-powered, bioengineered desalinization."

"You're serious?" Jennifer blurted. The other two executives looked at her, and she flushed. *Well, at least I'm not following her around with my tongue lolling out*, she thought. *Talk about* unprofessional, *give me a break.*

"Perfectly serious. The algae extract the sodium from the seawater, encapsulate it, sink to the bottom, then die. You drain the algae from the bottom of the tank, and the fresh water from the top. That's an oversimplification, of course; the technical data is in your briefing kit. Basically the algae produce a carbon-based ion-exchange polymer which holds the sodium and chloride ions in an insoluble chemical bond."

The managing director ran a handkerchief over his balding head. The Australian assistant made a hand motion, and a Haitian servant in a white jacket came forward with a tray of iced lemonade. Jennifer gave the blond a second's attention. Wearing a high-collared dress despite the heat, and looking rather peaked.

Back to business. "EPA approval might be a bit of a problem."

Everyone nodded. Gwen shrugged.

"It's not viable in the open ocean, no resistance to predators; and we built in a cellular failsafe to limit reproduction. Besides sun, it needs sulfur, nitrogen, and ammonia at much higher concentrations than in the sea. The bubbles"—she nodded toward the tanks—"are aeration. It's a photosynthetic process, of course, so atmospheric carbon compounds are a source and oxygen is a byproduct, just like any other plant life. The necessary nitrogen is taken from the atmosphere via symbiotic nitrogen-fixing bacteria, and two other bacteria also concentrate metallic salts. Incidentally, raw sewage would do fine as a source of bulk nutrients for the process."

"Ah," the managing director said. "And the byproducts?"

"Salts of various types. To be precise, a concentrated saline sludge with organic polymers. There's another process which recyles the sulfur and so forth for reuse, and the rest is chemical feedstock for a number of processes. In fact, the sale price of the byproducts would more than cover the installation costs—you could run this process at a profit *without* using the fresh water, just dumping it back in the ocean.

"But yes," she went on, "regulatory approval—particularly in the U.S.—may take some time. However, think of the potential once it is approved; and in non-American markets, as well. We've had expressions of interest from Saudi Arabia, among others. And Singapore."

"What are the costs?" Coleman said, swallowing.

"Minimal. Building the tanks, pumping, and adding the nutrients to the water. Then add the algae, stir, and wait. We calculate the overall cost to be less than five percent of conventional vacuum distillation or osmotic filter treatments. Cheap enough to replace any but the most abundant natural sources for coastal cities; cheap enough to use for irrigation anywhere under 100 meters above sea level."

Gwen was wearing a fairly conservative outfit, blazer and pleated skirt; she leaned one hand against the rough concrete of a lab building. The vice-president was still having trouble tearing his eyes away. Jennifer frowned in puzzlement. *Yes, he's a letch, but he doesn't let it get in the way of business*, she thought. Coleman evidently thought so too; or perhaps the implications had just begun to sink in, because he straightened and put a hand to his tie.

"Good *God*," he blurted, staring at the water.

My God, Jennifer thought. *My Greed!*

They all nodded. There were billions in that market, even if the costing estimate was overoptimistic by a factor of ten. If it was anywhere near accurate . . . Los Angeles alone would make the patent holder richer than J. P. Getty had ever been. Anywhere with bright sunlight and a shortage of fresh water. No energy costs, and no expensive tech necessary.

Damn, anyone *could use this. Places too primitive for* elevators *could use this.* She felt her face flush. If it really was cheap enough for irrigation, it could upset economies all over the world. Every low-lying coastal desert in the tropics could become a garden. Israel was importing drinking water by tanker from Europe— now the Negev would become wall-to-wall orange groves and wheatfields. Californians could water their lawns until they turned into rice paddies. Libya would become the Kansas of the Mediterranean.

"You have the patents?" she said, in a tone that held the hush of reverence.

"Pending, and I mean pending everywhere. Full proprietary rights, of course; this was done in-house."

"This looks . . . ah . . . too good to be true."

No overheads at all! Just send them packets of algae like baker's yeast! On the other hand, how would you prevent piracy? Forget that, this would be big even *with* piracy. Sit back and collect the royalties. Set them low, really low, so people would be less tempted to cheat, then get your revenue on high volume.

Jennifer looked at the vat of water with a feeling of awe. *I think,* she mused, *that this may just be the Perfect Investment.* It was a little like finding the Holy Grail.

Gwen nodded. "And things which look too good to be true generally are; however, you can study this to your hearts' content and you'll find nothing but hard, profitable fact."

*   *   *

Not bad, Lafarge thought. Martinique had places much more upscale than the one where he'd first met Captain Lavasseur. This one looked out over the hills of Fort-de-France with white buildings shining below, the foam-capped purple waves of the Caribbean beyond, mountains behind . . . and nobody was wearing a weapon as far as the AI could tell. He attacked the food with gusto. The *New America* had taken the genetic records of most of Earth's life-forms to Samothrace, but some just hadn't established themselves well. Lobster were among them. The *lagoustines* were delicious.

"You lookin' better," Captain Lavasseur said.

The schooner captain looked a little surprised. *I suppose I looked like death, a few days ago,* Lafarge thought. The local witch-doctors couldn't do anything at all to speed cellular repair.

"Well, I've had an attitude adjustment," Lafarge said. *When I finished kicking myself,* he added silently.

The problem was that he had no training for this at all. Insertion on the Domination's earth was a last-ditch emergency measure, with the agent's lifespan measured in hours or at most days—if he made it to the planetary surface, of course. You couldn't subvert a Draka, or a *servus,* and even the best-trained and prepared agent could only hope to imitate either for one or two brief encounters. Kenneth Lafarge could have survived in the vast wilderness reserves for months, or made a brief heroic attack on a selected target . . . but at infiltrating, suborning, coopting, he was a rank amateur.

"I've decided on a new approach to my business problems," he went on.

Like, I should have had a dozen mercenaries with me. Enough to neutralize the Draka's local servants, at least. That would have allowed him a clearer shot;

and there would be no signature of noncongruent energies. Or not nearly so much, at least.

Better late than never. He pushed across a brown paper envelope filled with something pebbly. Lavasseur took off his hat reverently as he accepted it; it wasn't every day that he handled twenty thousand dollars' worth of diamonds.

Odd that a particular arrangement of crystalline carbon was so highly valued. It was so *hard* for these people to make Nature yield what they wanted.

"Anytin' you want done, Antoine Lavasseur will do for you."

"I may take you up on that," Lafarge said. He handed over a business card. "I'll be in touch."

He had two great advantages here. If he *could* convince locals of the truth, it would be easier to get them to cooperate with him. *He* wasn't out to destroy them all.

The other was that the Draka was attempting to build something. All he had to do was destroy.

CHAPTER TWELVE

"Detective Carmaggio," he said, spitting the stick of gum into the wastebasket. It was his direct outside line; you couldn't have your snitches going through a switch-board, it made them nervous.

Sugar-free, he thought with disgust, looking at the crumpled wad of gum. It was like chewing rubber bands. What he really wanted was a smoke. About time to admit that gum didn't help the craving. Jenny didn't like the habit, either.

"It's about the warehouse killings, Detective," the voice on the other end of the line said. "You know what I mean."

Carmaggio brought his feet down from the desk and tapped one shoe onto the *record* pedal.

"Yes, I remember that. What's your name, sir?" The same motion activated the tracer. He kept his tone polite and calm, inviting the man on the other end to keep talking.

"That doesn't matter right now," the voice said.

Hell it doesn't. The usual influx of nutballs—confessing, or offering to reveal various conspiracies, or both—had died down long ago, it was better than three years since the murders. The voice was a man's, not old,

Standard American accent, perhaps a hint of Midwestern rasp.

"The murderer's name is Gwendolyn Ingolfsson," it went on. "It—she—is responsible for several other killings. She's currently resident in the Bahamas."

Excitement punched him in the gut. *Closed file, my ass.* This one really knew something. *Maybe she did have help. Maybe they're turning on each other.* He suppressed the speculation; facts first.

"How do you know this, sir?" Rodriguez came in, and Carmaggio made frantic *send a car to the trace address* motions at him.

"That doesn't matter either. What does matter is that she's coming back."

"Yes?"

"Back to New York. If you check, you'll find she's bought up the property where the murders took place, through front companies. She'll be coming to New York shortly, and dealing with an investment firm named Primary Belway Securities."

The Fischer killing. He'd been with PBS. *Hell, so's Jenny. Hell, she's in the Bahamas.* He suppressed a stab of worry. *Nobody's going to mess with a bunch of investment bankers.*

"It's extremely important that this . . . person not be allowed access to New York," the voice went on.

I am beginning to get seriously pissed off with this turkey, Carmaggio thought. The tone was desperately patient, the way you talked to a slightly retarded child. Plenty of people talked that way to cops; he was used to it. He got the feeling that this bird talked to *everyone* that way, however.

"We're always concerned with the safety of New York and its citizens," he said soothingly. "Why don't you come in and tell us all about it?"

The answer was a chuckle; the first hint there was an actual human being on the other end of the line.

"Not until we have an understanding, Lieutenant. I think you've figured out that this is . . . not a usual case, at all. I think you may be ready to understand what's really going on here. But it has to be in a way that doesn't endanger either of us. No contacts that leave any recordings, no involvement of higher authorities, and no meetings in places where we might be under observation."

Yeah, and I have to wear a rubber nose and give the secret handshake, Carmaggio thought. *If he's so paranoid, what does he think this line is?*

"That might be possible, sir. Where should we get in touch?"

"I'll contact you, in a day or two."

"Sir—"

"And Lieutenant . . . anyone in contact with Ingolfsson is in extreme danger."

"All right, you dickhead, I want some answers! Now! Stop bullshitting me or—"

The line went back to the dial tone, with no click of a broken connection. Henry Carmaggio sat looking at the receiver in his hand for a moment, then replaced it with exaggerated care. The alternative was beating it on his desk until the pieces were too small to hold.

"That was *just* the thing I fucking needed to hear," he said. "Jesus, you get the blue-and-white dispatched?"

Jesus Rodriguez's thin brown face came around the doorjamb. "No trace, *patrón.*"

"Fuck," Carmaggio said in a weary sigh. The new process was supposed to be automatic, with the number and location of the phone showing up on a map. "Nothing?"

"A glitch. It gives us our own number."

He tapped the pedal again, rewinding the tape. "Let's listen and see if there was anything I missed."

The tape hissed. Carmaggio waited, calmly at first,

then with a heavy sinking feeling. There was nothing on it, nothing at all.

The weird shit was starting again.

Kenneth Lafarge bought a soft pretzel with mustard and sat on the edge of the fountain in Washington Square Park. The wounds didn't hurt anymore.

It was a cold raw day, slush and lowering skies. A homeless man shuffled by, fingerless gloves holding two bulging plastic bags. Behind him loomed an off-white mock-French triumphal arch, and behind that a wedding-cake minor skyscraper. Pigeons hunched their wings against the cold. A man in chain-studded leather did too, his pinched gray face stubble-covered and shuttered. Two girls passed, talking and laughing; one wore a nose-stud. Ken smiled at them, at all the pulsing streams of people.

There were nearly as many people in this State of New York as in the whole of Samothrace. *I like it. I couldn't live here permanently, but I like it.* He'd been country-raised, and even the capital city of Jefferson was a manicured garden next to *this*. He remembered green-black tuftbush and Terran sage, riding down a canyon and the skin-winged majesty of a *gruk* arrowing by overhead, eyeing the herd of sheep but wary of his rifle.

"I'd go nuts here in twenty years. But . . ."

His scanner caught traces of conversations, checking for keywords: in Spanish, Chinese, Italian, in African tongues extinct centuries before the Last War in *his* history. Nobody on Samothrace had spoken anything else but English since the first generation of settlement. For that matter, every other language had been dying out on Earth by the end of the twentieth century— by compulsion in the Domination, through market forces and policy in the Alliance for Freedom.

I do like it here. These people were sloppy, restless,

childish, self-indulgent. They had no moral seriousness. *But they're alive in a way we never were*. Not even before the Last War. His ancestors' America had been an anxious giant, mobilized for generations against a menace that made the Cold War they'd had here look like a love-feast. Compared to this America his had been grim, puritan, uniform.

He imagined the Square broken and desolate, buildings shattered hulks. A weapons platform hovering in the Manhattan sky with the bat-winged dragon of the Domination blazoned on its side; a wolf-faced ghouloon trooper crouched where he sat, cradling a particle-beam rifle and gnawing on a human arm.

"Never," he said softly, getting to his feet and strolling with his hands thrust into his overcoat pockets. He attracted a few glances. By local standards six-foot, crop-haired blonds with his build in neat business suits were exotic.

The problem was the asymmetry of the positions. Ken looked at the glossy of the Draka's face again; his equipment had extrapolated it to a 3-D image and matched it against the files. This had to be one of the old ones; subtle clues in the bone structure marked it as the first or second generation of *drakensis*. Centuries old, then. Unbelievably experienced. And not limited by fear of detection. It *wanted* to be detected, to call the ghoul-horde through to feast.

"I can't let that paralyze me," he murmured.

An anchoring beacon wasn't all that difficult to make. The first expedition through a planetary surface-level molehole on Samothrace had managed to cobble one together from the equipment they'd brought. Then they'd broadcast until a new molehole was latched on— giving the USS a whole new Samothrace, in a solar system humans had never visited. As far as they could tell, in *that* continuum Earth had been scoured free of life sometime in the twenty-first century. Spaceborne

instruments could scan a planet fairly closely, even
across 4.2 light-years. The oxygen content of *that*
Earth's atmosphere had dropped far enough to make
it plain even the algae in the oceans were gone.

So the Draka here could mess up the landscape as
much as it needed to. The more the better, in fact—
it increased the possibility of a unidirectional lock-on
by the *drakensis* scientists working from the other side.

I'm only constrained in what I do, he thought meditatively.

"How much does this policeman have figured out?"
he asked himself.

Once he'd let the locals know, there was no going
back. And they'd be exposed; he'd have to push them
to the front, give the minimum of backup. The less he
interacted directly with the snake, the better. At all
costs.

"Well, Lieutenant Carmaggio," he said to himself,
"you wanted some answers. I hope you enjoy them."

Kenneth Lafarge smiled. The panhandler who'd been
about to approach the slumming businessman turned
on his heel and lurched away.

The snake is acting through locals. I can too.

There were three other people in Carmaggio's apartment: Jesus Rodriguez, Mary Chen, and the FBI agent,
Finch. It was cramped in the living room. Unlike a lot
of the Department, he believed in living where he
worked, which meant paying New York rents for zero
space. It was an old four-story walkup, mostly new
immigrants from Russia and a few old ladies in black
who passed the time of day with him on the stairs in
Neapolitan dialect.

"We don't have enough for an arrest," Carmaggio
said.

"That's an understatement," Finch said. "Not with
the evidence gone into a black hole."

The FBI agent fiddled with the buttons of her jacket and looked out the apartment window; it had a beautiful view of the fire escape on the building next door. "When will she arrive?"

Carmaggio shrugged. "Sometime in the spring, that's the earliest the paperwork will be ready. We don't know if she plans to come here personally at all. I've got a friend in Belway, but I can't badger her for the information. That's the impression I got, though."

He opened a folder. "But this company of Ingolfsson's has bought up or leased a lot of property. Close on twenty million dollars' worth, including the warehouse where Marley Man got wasted."

Silence fell for a long moment. The medical examiner broke it.

"We've got to face up to something," she said. "Henry, Ms. Finch . . . we've got to realize what we're facing."

"Which is?" Henry said. *You're the one with the fancy education. You tell me.*

Chen looked down at her hands, twisting the fingers together. "The genetics . . . nobody can alter mammalian heredity like that. *Nobody.* I did some discreet research. And nobody will be able to do it for a long time; fifty years, conservative estimate."

Henry grunted and looked away. "Hell," he said. "I never even watched *Star Trek* much."

Finch gave a violent shake of her head. "We can't afford to get ourselves caught up on labels," she said. "I think that's what the people at the Other Place— Langley," she amplifed, "Bureau slang for Langley— I think that's what they've done. It isn't ours, so it must be the Japanese or whatever. The more layers of committees they have to filter their data through, the more officially acceptable it'll get."

Henry nodded. That was how bureaucracies functioned; they were set up to hammer information into a few acceptable categories, and they did just that—

no matter how much violence got done to the data in the process. He'd seen enough men die in Vietnam because the raw intelligence conflicted with the approved version of reality.

"Okay," he said quietly, "we've got *National Enquirer* stuff here, only for real. Does that mean the spooks are right? We should back off and let official channels handle it? Concealing the information we've got is almost certainly an indictable offense."

Jesus Rodriguez spoke. "Like the lady said, I think they'll be looking for the wrong thing. And *patrón*— the stakes are high."

Chen looked up. "The . . . whatever it was . . . came armed. They killed and killed again. That doesn't argue for 'we come in peace,' Henry."

Her face went extremely blank. "And I don't care to be blackmailed. That sort of thing was what my parents took a very risky boat trip to avoid. So I'm not altogether convinced of the unarguable wisdom of the duly constituted authorities, right now."

Finch winced slightly. "Since Andrews and Debrowski came back from the Bahamas," she said, looking down at her hands, "there's been a fair amount of traffic that way. At a much higher level. Not those two. Whole delegations."

You didn't send wet-work specialists to negotiate, really. Even the sort of fairly sophisticated wet-workers involved, Amcits and on the official payroll. The accountants must have taken over, and the Government's tame scientists.

"They've clamped down harder than ever, and Dowding's been warned from higher in the Bureau not to even *think* about complaining again. They did some sort of deal, and they're excited about it. Very excited. And scared."

Carmaggio sipped his coffee. "Oh, lovely. Ms. Ingolfsson has become the goose that lays the golden eggs. She's teacher's pet."

"Right," he went on. "Now, let's see what we've got and where it gets us. There's that posse warrior with his head blown off at the eyebrows. Weapons are a hobby of mine, and there's nothing that could do it. Some sort of energy gun might. That's what the spooks said. They also said you'd need an eighteen-wheeler load of equipment. Our suspect had something no bigger than a rifle. From the later reports, I'd say it was the size of a handgun, small enough to carry concealed."

Chen pursed her lips. "I can think of several technologies that could produce a knife as thin and sharp and rigid as the one that inflicted the injuries in the warehouse," she said. "And was used to dismember Stephen Fischer. None of them available today, or will be for some time."

"When we've eliminated the impossible, whatever remains, however improbable, must be true," Finch said. Henry looked at her blankly. "Classical reference, sorry. What I mean is, I don't think it's aliens here. The—not exactly the MO—the stuff surrounding the incident is wrong. And the genetic material is human. Human, and animals from Earth."

"We sure of that?"

Chen tapped her own folder. "Extremely. Henry, the odds of a separate evolution producing that type of genetic correspondence is . . . well, getting hit by lightning is a dead certainty, compared to that."

"Time traveler," Finch said.

The words lay heavy in the pause that followed. Henry sighed deeply and ran a hand over his scalp, acutely conscious of the thinning hairs.

"Oh, shit," he said. He held up a hand. "Yeah, I know it's logical, I know it's probably *true*, but we've just bought ourselves a ticket to the funny farm if this ever leaks out to our respective superiors."

The idea lay like lead in his mind. *I've been chasing my own ass on this for three and a half years,* he thought. There simply wasn't any other explanation, nada, zip. Either he forgot the whole thing, or he went with this. And he just couldn't walk away from it. Like Jesus said, the stakes were too high.

"Something else," he said thoughtfully. "Okay, we've got a time traveler." He held up his copy of the Canadian RCMP fax. "A woman. One woman, armed, calling herself Gwendolyn Ingolfsson. And we got the arm of some *thing* with her. What's that suggest?"

"Something went wrong," Jesus said, flicking at his teeth with a thumbnail. "Accident, fuckup, *de nada.*"

"Not a woman," Chen corrected. "A female, yes. Related species, but not human. Probably from, ah, the future."

Henry sighed and loosened his tie. "Whatever."

"And she responded with a killing frenzy," Finch said. "That tells us something about the, the time and place she came from."

"Dropping into the middle of Marley Man's posse could send anyone into a frenzy," Henry said thoughtfully. "But the two apartment killings, yeah. Our Ingolfsson is seriously bad in both senses of the word."

Silence fell again. Finch broke it.

"Why buy the warehouse?" she said. "That seems to be important, somehow. Twenty million dollars worth of important. That's more than sentimental-souvenir money."

"We can't tell for sure, but it certainly looks like Ingolfsson *needs* the warehouse somehow."

"I've got—" Henry began.

"—a bad feeling about this, *sí,*" Jesus completed the sentence. "Unless she just wants to go home."

"Could we count on that?" Henry said. "No, I didn't think so. Let's think about the latest ingredient."

"Mystery Man," Finch said. "He's contacted you

several times, me once, and several people at this firm, Primary Belway Securities. He certainly doesn't seem to be operating with Ingolfsson. Trying to screw up her plans, evidently."

"Cop chasing perp?" Jesus said. "They sent someone back here to clean up the accident?"

"That's my gut feeling," Henry agreed. He looked over at Finch; the Medical Examiner wasn't in the same business, but the FBI agent was. "Mystery Man's got some gadgets too."

"Cop is a possibility," Finch said. "Or spook and counter-spook. He isn't necessarily a good guy."

"So far he's made a lot less in the way of footprints," Henry observed thoughtfully. "No trail of bodies, and no fancy gadgets apart from messing with our computers. Assuming he was sent back, you'd expect him to have more fancy stuff."

"But perhaps is more reluctant to use it," Chen said. The others looked at her. "If we have a time traveler, they could be—probably would be—careful about *changing the past*. And we would be the past, to them."

"Ingolfsson doesn't seem too concerned about that," Henry said. "Left a pretty heavy blood trail, and—"

He smacked himself on the forehead. "All that fancy high-tech stuff her company's been selling! *That's* where it came from!"

The future. The theory was starting to look convincing, not just to his head but to his gut, the place where ideas came from. He didn't know whether to be reassured or frightened. *Either I'm adjusting or going nuts.*

"Perhaps she *is* some sort of criminal under pursuit, then," Chen said, pulling at her lower lip.

Henry made a chopping gesture. "Let's not let the speculation get completely out of hand," he said. "You get too many preconceptions, it can foul up your ability to see things that don't agree with the theory you've built."

The others nodded. "What should we do about it?" Finch said.

"First, Mystery Man indicated he's willing to meet. Yes or no?"

Chen started to speak, but Finch cut her off. "Lieutenant, I don't think we can run this as a democracy. I think you should be in charge."

Christ, on point again, Henry thought. The others nodded.

"All right then. I *will* set up a meet with Mystery Man. When we've got more information from him, you'll all get to know. Which leaves us with the question of what to do about Ingolfsson."

Silence fell. "Right now, we watch," Henry said. "Right now, we can't pin any of the killings on Ingolfsson. Maybe she'll just vanish in the warehouse, maybe Mystery Man will get her, maybe she'll turn into a good citizen."

"And maybe the horse will learn to sing," Finch said.

Henry *did* recognize that one. He shook his head. "No, there'll be more killings, all right. And *then* we move in. Fuck national security; we'll blow this thing wide open and call in the artillery and nail Ms. Time Traveler to the wall. Fuck the consequences, too. Everyone with me on this?"

A circle of nods. He went on: "You all know what happens to whistle-blowers, don't you? Still willing?"

Nobody spoke. "All right, here's how we'll set it up. We keep everything word-of-mouth; and no more phone calls than we have to. Nothing on computers, absolutely nothing, and that includes notes to ourselves.

"When we move, we'll have to be able to move fast and big. Finch, you get onto your boss and bring him in on this. Chen, get me a list of those friends you've been doing the discreet research with, and we'll talk to a few of them. Jesus and I will sound out a few guys we know in the NYPD. Then we'll—"

*   *   *

"Hello," Carmaggio said.

The other man ducked his head in a nod and extended his hand. "Kenneth Lafarge," he said.

Henry gave him a once-over. Early thirties, he judged. Close-cut blond hair, blue eyes, a farmboy face—snub-nosed and tanned, square chin. Jock's build, broad shoulders and narrow waist. The hand fit that, slightly callused and very strong. Dressed in a suit and carrying an attaché case; sort of like a Norman Rockwell painting of an up-and-coming small town lawyer. Not heeled to Henry's experienced eye . . . *but he might be carrying a mininuke in a tie clip, for all I know. Christ, I wish I wasn't here.* For that matter, he wished all this wasn't happening, period.

Behind them the Mall was nearly empty, bleak and lifeless with winter. It smelled of wet earth, cold water, and traffic. Carmaggio had never liked Washington much: a marble veneer over a cesspit. Which was, he thought, sort of appropriate, all things considered.

"Detective Lieutenant Henry Carmaggio," he replied. *What do you say to a time traveler?*

"Thank you for agreeing to meet me, Detective Carmaggio," the younger man said. "A great deal depends on what we can do."

He spoke ordinary general American, but there was a hint of something underneath it; a formality of phrasing, that indicated it wasn't quite his native speech.

"Yeah," Henry said, hunching his shoulders. They turned and walked beside the gray surface of the Reflecting Pool. "Why here?"

"I'm apprehensive about what capabilities *it* may have in place in New York," Lafarge said. "A little extra caution never hurts."

"Look, let's be upfront." At the other man's lifted eyebrow: "Let's lay our cards on the table. You're from the future, right?"

The words hung heavy in the air. *Me and the Saucer People,* Carmaggio thought.

Lafarge nodded. "In a way."

"In *what* fucking way?"

The other man made a soothing gesture with both hands. "Four-hundred-forty-odd years in the future, yes. But the future of a different past."

"What?" Henry felt a dull ache begin between his shoulderblades and creep up his neck.

"I'm sorry . . . you know the concept? A battle turns out differently, a war, someone important isn't born, and things are changed?"

Henry nodded. "Lee wins the battle of Gettysburg, something like that?" There was no *end* to the weird shit.

"Yes, exactly. In my case . . . the differences start about 1779. By 1900 my world was very different from yours. By the 1990s, unrecognizable."

"What happened in 1779?"

"The Dutch Republic declared war on the British," Lafarge said. He ran a hand over his hair. "It's a long story. The British lost the war against us—against America—at about the same pace they did here, maybe a little slower. But they won the war against the Dutch, and that's where everything started to go wrong. They took the Cape Colony."

"South Africa?" Henry said. He'd done some research on Africa a few years back, when two branches of the Black Muslims had started killing each other over doctrinal points.

"Yes. After the war, they used it to settle the Loyalists—mostly the ones from the Southern colonies—and their Hessian mercenaries. The settlers they sent enslaved the locals. And they grew, and they grew. A century later the Draka—the colony was renamed after Francis Drake—were already a major power. In the Great War they took most of Asia; then in the Eurasian

War, something like your World War Two, they took the rest of Asia and Europe. There was a long cold war between them and us, the Alliance for Democracy, the U.S. and South America and the British, the Australasians, some others. The Final War happened in 1999."

"Wait a minute." Henry squeezed his thumb and forefinger on the bridge of his nose. "Okay, these . . . Draka?" Lafarge nodded. "They were seriously bad, right? Sort of like Nazis?"

"Worse. Smarter. In our world, the Nazis were a poor-man's copy of the Domination—the Domination of the Draka, that's what they called themselves. Call themselves." Lafarge shook his head. "I'm surprised your Nazis were so much like ours. We even had a Hitler, although he didn't look much like yours. Ours was taller, blond, and had an eyepatch . . . never mind."

"Wait a minute," Carmaggio said again. The tension in his neck was worse. "These supernazis, Draka, whatever, they *won* this World War Three, is that what you're saying?"

Lafarge nodded.

"Then who the hell are *you*, the French Resistance?"

"Space travel was commonplace by the time of the Final War," Lafarge said. Henry gritted his teeth at the heavy patience in the younger man's tone. "My ancestors escaped to Alpha Centauri in an experimental interstellar ship—slower than light, of course. There's a habitable planet there, you'll discover it yourselves as soon as you get some really powerful telescopes into orbit."

"Wait a minute—wait right *here*," Henry said.

He wheeled away, working his shoulders, then stopped and looked up at the spire of the Washington Monument. *From the future, from another dimension, and from another fucking planet, too,* he thought. *Jesus wept.* Wasn't someone like Arnold S. supposed to handle this sort of thing? Or a big-titted actress with a pair of glasses on to make her look like a scientist? Some morphing from Industrial Light and Magic to wow the kids, popcorn and Diet Coke. *Shit.* He remembered Stephen Fischer's head in the freezer of his refrigerator. That was all too real. So were the lab reports, so was the arm of that God-knew-what.

"Sorry," he said as he rejoined Lafarge.

"I realize this must all be a considerable shock."

"Do you? Do you realize how fucking consoling that is and how much better it makes me feel?" Henry jammed his hands down into his pockets and walked in silence. "By the way, how do I know you're a good guy yourself? You realize you've got absolutely no proof of anything you've said."

Lafarge shrugged. "If you can match what I'll show you anywhere in 1999," he said, "I'm the greatest liar since Judas Iscariot. As to who's the good guy . . . I'm not the one who left a trail of bodies through your city."

"There is that. There is that. What are we up against?"

"A *drakensis.* The Draka were . . . slavers, degenerates, mass muderers, but they were human. They didn't *want* to be, that was the problem—and they were very, very good at molecular genetics even then, it's how they won the Final War. A hundred years ahead of where you are now, by our 1970s. They created their own version of the Master Race, and it replaced them. Replaced true humanity entirely, here in the Solar System."

"Nothing left but the supermen?"

"*Homo drakensis* and *homo servus.*"

Henry winced. Servus. Slave. "That mean what I think it means?" Lafarge nodded grimly. "Tell me about the . . . whatever it is we got."

"It was an accident, if that's any consolation to you. We—the snakes and Samothrace—are developing a . . . faster-than-light drive. But if you do it wrong—

and they haven't got the control down yet—you end up with temporal instead of spatial displacement. I can't explain it to you, I'm a covert-action operative, not a physicist. And you're at least three paradigm shifts, three equivalents of Newton or Einstein, away. Could you explain a computer to a tribesman from New Guinea?"

"I can't even understand the goddamned manuals for PCs myself. Okay, what about our bad lady? What can she do?"

"It. Never forget that. It's not human. Do?" Lafarge shrugged. "For a start: it's fast, fast and very strong, with hyperacute senses. Very resistant to damage, reinforced bones, redundant organs, high radiation tolerance, tissue regeneration if it *is* hurt. Strong enough to rip a human limb from limb, hearing and sight and sense of smell like an animal. Utterly ruthless, fearless, and aggressive, with an inbuilt drive to fight and to dominate everything in its environment. A tiger with the mind of a man. Oh, and it's immortal—doesn't age."

Henry nodded to himself. Something in him wanted to add *what about the blue tights and the cape?* but the scene in the warehouse kept getting in the way. The memory of the heavy stink of blood, and the bodies tossed about like dolls, mangled the way a dog does a rat.

"That's for a start?" he said. "Make me even happier, Lafarge."

"Genius-level intelligence; in your terms, IQ of about 200, 220. Perfect memory. Idiot-savant mental abilities."

"Counting all the spilled matchsticks?" Henry remembered the movie well, although he doubted the killer was anything like Dustin Hoffman.

"Yes. They seem to be a little short on real creativity, but they're extremely smart. And then there's the control mechanisms. For controlling others, that is."

"Wait . . . you mean they can read minds? Hypnotize people?"

"Not quite. It can read body language and subvocalizations well enough to make it seem like a mind-reader, though. The control comes from pheromones. . . . You know what they are?"

"What makes the dogs howl when the bitch is in heat?"

Lafarge nodded. "They're more versatile than that. In us, in humans, they're becoming vestigial. The effects are subliminal. A *drakensis* has pheromones that are overpoweringly strong. Their serf race, the *servus*, are completely vulnerable. But on unprotected, unprepared normal humans, the effects can be devastating too. You wouldn't even notice them consciously; you'd just be bowled over by what feels like overwhelming charisma. Pretty soon you'd *want* to do anything the *drakensis* told you to. You'd stay awake nights thinking up ways to please."

"Shit." Henry stopped and sank down on a bench. *Would all this go away if I just hopped the plane back to New York and forgot about it?* Unfortunately, he knew the answer was no. He'd never been good at hiding his head in the sand.

He looked over at Lafarge on the opposite end of the bench. "Why do I get this really shitty feeling about all this? You going to offer us advisors and military aid? Like us and Moscow back in the old days? And sure, it's true we were telling the truth when we said some Third World schmuck was better off taking our guns. But by the time the elephants are finished their proxy war across his back garden, it's squashed pretty fucking flat."

"It's worse than that. We can't help you directly. The Domination holds the Solar System too firmly. Moleholes—it's the physics, I can't explain it. If the *drakensis* succeeds in making a beacon, they can open a gateway and flood through. You'll have about as much chance as . . . in your terms, as much chance as Australian Aboriginies with stone-tipped spears would against helicopter gunships and tanks. The Domination . . . they'll reduce you to domestic animals, playthings, and they'll gene-engineer you into *liking* it. That's one alternative."

"I hope there are others."

"If the *drakensis* can't establish a lock-on beacon here, it'll try to take over the planet by itself."

"Hell, there's only one of her. It, whatever."

"It's immortal, remember, unless it's killed. And it's a female."

"With no males, and a breeding population of one."

Lafarge shook his head. "They don't reproduce the way we do. They implant their fertilized ova in slave wombs—humans will do as well as *servus*."

Henry winced. *Jesus*. "Without a man—"

"Cloning. This is a cancer, an infestation, like maggots in your flesh. You have to get it all, no matter how deep you must cut." Lafarge grinned. "That's the bad news."

"You're the good news, right?" Carmaggio said.

"A big part of it. Myself, my equipment. And *it* has weaknesses. They tend to arrogance and over-confidence, and they're parasites, dependent on their slaves. Not really creative at all. And it's under-equipped, with nothing but its equivalent of street clothing."

"Good we've got you to ride to the rescue."

Lafarge let the sarcasm roll off him; Carmaggio suspected he wasn't long on irony, anyway. *Is it him, or are they all that po-faced where he comes from?*

"No, all I can do is *help* you. I'm incongruent with this reference frame. . . . Think of it this way: I stand out. Every time I do something that makes things different from the way they'd be if I weren't here, there's a . . . blip. An event wave. The enemy get a chance of detecting how-where-when we are."

"Damned if you do, damned if you don't," Carmaggio said.

Well, Chief Wampanoag, the Pilgrim Father said, he thought, *evil spirits hide in the iron tube. When you pull the trigger, they push the lead ball out.* . . . *Great Thanksgiving turkey, have another cup of mulled cider and now about that little land deal.* . . . He couldn't expect it to make any sense. In a way, that was reassuring. If it *had* made sense in his terms, he'd have doubted it. Four centuries—more, in terms of actual progress. Try explaining electricity to Sir Walter Raleigh.

"What can we do, then?"

"Act on my information. That'll still leave . . . signs . . . but less so. Muffled."

He held up a hand. "I can't direct you. Even *that* would be dangerous."

"Hey, jake," the Guard officer said.

"El-tee," Henry Carmaggio replied.

Actually Saunders was a National Guard major these days, but they went back a ways. Back to the delta. Carmaggio had been a plain garden-variety grunt; Saunders started out as a lieutenant and walked out a captain. To be precise, he'd been invalided out back to the World as a captain, with some exotic Vietnamese rot carried on a punji stake eating his feet. Still a trim little guy, dark—part Indian, from Oklahoma—looking more wrinkled and gray than they all had in '70, but hell, that was a long time ago. A small, smart man with a big nose, blue cracker eyes and a lot of oil money who still wore the uniform sometimes. Probably with as much conviction as he did the inconspicuously well-tailored businessman's suit he had on now.

"What can I do for you?"

Carmaggio looked around the office. *Nice.* At Saunders's level, weekend warriors had to have major pull; which meant their civilian jobs tended to be roughly equivalent to their military rank—and a lot better-paying than regular officers of the same formal status. A secretary came in with coffee in elegant bone-china cups. None of the lingering aroma of old socks and sweat you had down at NYPD headquarters, that was for sure. Pale carpet, pale pastel colors on the walls.

"El-tee—Christ, Mr. Saunders—"

"Bill, Henry."

"Okay, Bill. The first thing you can do for me is promise not to send for the guys with white coats and butterfly nets."

Saunders leaned back in his swivel chair behind the broad desk.

"Okay," he said. Time and money hadn't smoothed much of the East Texas rasp out of his voice. "I'm pretty damn sure you're not here to sell me tickets to the policeman's ball or tell me how you found the Lord. Shoot."

Carmaggio ran a hand through his hair. *Christ on a stick, this is embarrassing.*

"Right. About three and a half years ago, there was a big killing in a disused warehouse, twenty dead."

Saunders frowned. "Yep, remember that one."

"Here's what really happened—"

Twenty minutes later, he sank back in his chair, exhausted enough to let the thick leather upholstery cradle him in its Old Spice–scented comfort. Saunders looked at him silently; Carmaggio waited, sweat rolling down into the collar of his shirt and making his shoulder holster dig into his skin.

"Henry, that story leaves me one of three alternatives," Saunders said, clipping the end off a cigar. "Smoke?"

"Gave it up."

"Yep. Either you've started using the junk you confiscate, or you're seriously bullshitting me . . . or you're telling the truth. If you're tellin' the truth, you'd better have something to show me. I owe you one, but nobody's going to convince me the Gumbys of the Gods have landed without hard evidence."

The detective met the cold blue eyes. William Saunders might have ears like an old-fashioned milk jug and political ambitions, but he'd also brought his platoon through a year of bad bush with fewer losses and more done than anyone else in the district. He was listening for old times' sake, nothing more.

"Yeah . . . Bill. I realize hearing all this isn't like going through it yourself." A bleak nod answered him. "As it happens," he went on, taking a black rectangle out of his pocket, "I do have something fairly convincing."

CHAPTER THIRTEEN

"I don't know how you do it," Jennifer said.

The last traces of red and gold were dying out of the clouds on the western horizon, and a cool wind blew the gauze curtains through the open glass doors. Gwen sat with her head framed against the lingering remnants of sunset; some freak of the perspective seemed to make her eyes glint for a second as the lights came up automatically.

"Do what, Jenny?" Gwen said.

"Stay so *fresh*," she said. "And never get frazzled or get anything *wrong*."

In this business, nobody was lazy and most were workaholic. Gwendolyn Ingolfsson was . . . demonic, there was no other word for it.

"Ah, well, I just don't need much sleep," she said. "Never did, not more than three or four hours a night."

Oh, great, Jennifer thought. *What a week*. Even by the Street's insane standards, they'd been working like slaves. The other two execs had turned in earlier; she would herself, if she hadn't wimped out and had a nap earlier in the day. But it was about wrapped.

She looked down at some of the documents. There

was that seawater thing; another bacteria that fixed nitrogen on the roots of wheat and corn—GeneTech was going to *freak* when someone beat them to that— half a dozen things in thin-film screens, holographic displays, superconductors . . . no doubt about it, IngolfTech really *did* have the assets. Not just blue-sky laboratory stuff, but ready to roll, and three years of profitability from things already out. The biotech would need a lot of regulatory work, but even those were bankable if you knew they were real. The electronics could go tomorrow—some of it already had, commitments from companies that raised eyebrows all around the table.

"Well, you'll be a natural at an IPO circus," she said to the entrepreneur. "It'll be months before anyone sleeps."

"I expect Tom will be doing a good deal of that," Gwen said. "But yes, it'll be strenuous. Worth it, though—we're all very enthusiastic about the job you've been doing."

The initial float ought to bring in around two hundred million for a twenty-five percent offering at fifty a share, she knew. Say three and a half million shares, two and a half primary and a million and a half secondary founders'. Thirty days, and she could do her report. It was straightforward. Maybe *too* straightforward. As if they were being handed things on a platter; no tangled wires, no sloppy documentation, nothing that would scare anyone.

This was a candy store for venture-capital types; and with half a dozen successful licensing operations already.

"I noticed Ms. Wayne wasn't at the final presentation," Jennifer said. *I really should turn in.* Somehow she didn't feel sleepy, even though everyone had been keeping country hours while the Belway team was here. More prickly and restless. *Hell, it's barely midnight—*

and we're going back to New York tomorrow afternoon. Back to sleet, back to slush, back to her cat, who wouldn't forgive her for a week.

She forced down bitterness. *It's been a very successful week.* The problem was that now she had to go back to the workaholic scramble of a semi-upper-middle-class New Yorker's life. Where "life" was two hours of watching PBS between supper and bed, or a squeezed-in night at the opera; lately she might squeeze in a movie with Henry. And Ms. Gwendolyn too-perfect-to-be-true Ingolfsson was going to stay here in this goddamned mansion and pluck the plums of life as she pleased. Give or take a few hectic months while the IPO went through.

Maybe I should have stayed in med school. Then again, no. Doctors got even crazier than analysts, and they had to be around sick people all the time.

The secretaries began clearing away the documents.

"Well, that's all that can be done tonight," Gwen said. She stretched and yawned. "Let's get something to eat; and I'm going to go berserk if I don't hear somebody discuss something except due diligence reviews, draft registration statements, and the SEC."

The smile was infectious. Jennifer chuckled. "That's my life you're talking about. Odd to hear someone like you getting bored with business."

"It's a means to an end, as far as I'm concerned. This way."

This way was a small dining room, not the formal one downstairs. There were pictures on the walls; portraits. One of a woman with short blond hair and a face of delicate pointy-chinned beauty, dressed in a flowing off-the-shoulder gown.

"You might say that business doesn't run in my family," Gwen went on. "That's my mother, by the way— her name was Yolande."

"She looks sort of sad," Jennifer said.

"She had a hard life, in some respects," Gwen answered.

"What *were* your family in, if you don't mind me asking."

"My family? Well, soldiers, a lot of them. Gentleman-farmers, too." They sat and shook out their napkins. "The one thing I do envy you for living in New York," she went on, breaking a roll open, "is the opera and the galleries."

"You're an opera buff?"

"Mostly the older pieces. You know Delibes?"

"The one British Overseas Airways uses for their commercials?"

Gwen looked at her blankly for a second, then smiled. "I'd never thought of it that way," she said. "I had an aunt who was very fond of Delibes, though."

The servants brought in Jamaican jerk-pork soup, then steaks in a brown peppercorn sauce; the talk went from opera to design and back.

Jennifer took a mouthful of the steak. "That *is* good," she said.

"Buffalo," Gwen said. "Hump steak. I've been doing business with a certain TV magnate—he's probably going to be buying in heavily when we do the IPO—and he has a buffalo ranch, sends it over now and then. Nice of him."

That TV magnate? Jennifer asked herself. *Oh-ho*. "It may be blasphemy, but even the seafood here palls after a while."

"Yes," Gwen said. "Every once in a while I like to know that a higher mammal died for my dinner."

"You may not be an entrepreneur by choice," Jennifer said, "but that sounds quite sufficiently predatory of you."

Gwen looked up at her. "Predatory? Oh, you have no *idea*," she said, with a clear husky laugh.

God, she's strange, Jennifer thought, chuckling

herself. *Strange, but sort of fun. That charisma should get damned old after a while, but it doesn't. Just less noticeable. Come on, now, girl—where's your envy and resentment?* Gone, it seemed. *She'd make a great salesperson,* Jennifer decided. The "trust me" vibrations were strong enough to do double duty as an oboe in a symphony.

She glanced over at the painting of Yolande Ingolfsson again, then glanced back sharply. The background seemed to be a window-seat at first glance . . . it *was* a window-seat, but the curved glass behind it framed a landscape on the moon, gray and silver and a ragged crater wall. Above that hung the full earth.

"I can see that wasn't done from life," she said.

Gwen glanced over, tilting her face and looking out of the corners of her eyes. "No, I did it from memory," she said.

"You paint?"

"It's a hobby."

In your copious spare time, no doubt, Jennifer thought.

"You find me a little odd, don't you?" Gwen said.

Sharp, too. "A little . . . out of the ordinary," Jennifer said.

"Perhaps I'm an alien invader, then," Gwen said. Her green eyes sparkled. "From another dimension."

Jennifer found herself laughing harder. "Oh, right. And you prowl the back roads of America in your flying saucer, mutilating cows and performing proctologies on rednecks."

Gwen arched her brows. "Proctologies on rednecks?" she said thoughtfully. "Carefully selected rednecks . . . with the right prosthetics . . . perhaps occasionally."

Jennifer choked slightly on a mouthful of wine. "Who's Adonis there?" she asked.

The painting was of a youngish man standing on a

vaguely tropical beach; long white-gold hair fell to his broad dark-tanned shoulders. He was wearing only loose duck trousers, and sitting casually on a fallen palm-trunk, looking sleekly muscular and utterly relaxed; if the painting was anything like the person, heads would have turned. *Not a dry seat in the house, as Louisa says,* Jennifer thought.

"Alois, not Adonis. My husband."

The New Yorker set her wineglass down. "You're *married?*" she said. Somehow it was startling, unexpected, like a cat tapdancing. *And I could have sworn Cairstens and she were involved.* At least from the way the Californian carried himself. She imagined Gwen next to the man in the painting. *And I would have thought they were relatives. Maybe a cousin?*

"Was; Alois died . . . some time ago. Sporting accident."

"Oh." *Foot-in-mouth disease, Jennifer.* "I'm sorry."

Gwen sighed and shrugged. "It was some time ago. He—we both—had a taste for dangerous pastimes. If you do that long enough, it'll kill you. I've just been luckier, so far. In fact," she said, "eventually the universe kills everybody; one argument for taking a theistic approach to it, I suppose."

That which kills everybody is God? Jennifer thought. Perhaps not a tactful comment to make. Odd outlook.

"You paint a lot?"

"It relaxes. Let's finish this Merlot off."

"I shouldn't . . ."

"Work's over, you're leaving tomorrow."

"True. There, dead soldier."

The dessert was various tiny pastries of tropical fruits; the pyramid on the serving tray was as colorful as a peacock's tail or a flower market, and she felt almost guilty at disturbing it. Kiwi, mango, mangosteen, soursop, and the coffee was Blue Mountain.

"This is the life," she sighed.

Gwen leaned back with her cup in both hands, sipping. "It's a change from shark hunting," she said. "The Wall Street and finny varieties both."

"There are sharks in the water here? What a pity." The beach looked gorgeous, not that she'd had time for swimming. *Visit the tropics and stare at your computer,* she thought. *Sheesh. Bah, humbug.*

"They can be entertaining to hunt, when you feel like spearfishing," Gwen said.

Jennifer looked at her, trying to see if she was serious. "Not the Great White Shark, I hope," she said.

"No." Another of the white grins. "Although I've found some remarkably hostile things coming out of the water at me here," she added. "But enough about me. Tell me what life in New York is like for you."

Later, she stopped herself. "I'm babbling," she said. "You can't possibly want to know about my cat."

"On the contrary," Gwen said, finishing her brandy. "I adore cats. Let's go for a quick swim, then."

Jennifer hestiated. "Not with the sharks, I hope."

"I've got a perfectly good pool here."

She hesitated again. You had to watch out about getting too friendly with clients. On the other hand, why not? Nothing wrong with a swim, and Gwen was nice enough—weird, but nice. Also Klein and Coleman were pills. And she felt restless, as if someone were pricking her skin very lightly with invisible needles. The room swayed a little; she'd exceeded her usual rule of no more than three glasses of Chardonnay or something similar. They walked out to a terrace and down a flight of stairs; the pool was floodlit from below, lined and set among marble tiles and edged with a decoration of colorful Portuguese majolica. Water burbled from the mouth of a bronze lion, into a rock-edged basin and then into the pool itself.

"Which way's my room?" she asked, a little disoriented. "Got to get my suit."

"Why bother?" Gwen said, stepping out of her clothes. "Nobody here but us girls."

Jennifer gaped as the other hit the water in a perfect arching dive and with hardly a ripple. Her shape eeled down the pool, flashing into and out of the puddles of light thrown by the underwater sconces. She surfaced at the other end, mahogany hair plastered to her head, a flash of teeth and eyes.

"Chicken!" she called.

"Hell with that!" Jennifer called back. To hell with being sober and staid.

Hell with the extra ten pounds, too, she thought. She didn't have anything to prove. Still, she kept her briefs on as she waded down the steps. The water was barely cool to the skin, the stone smooth under her feet as she stood hugging herself. Fingers like steel wire suddenly gripped her ankles. She yelled as they heaved her upwards, catapulting her forward into the middle of the pool with a huge splash that sent water fountaining over the cool white and blue of the marble flooring. She whooped and thrashed her way back to the surface, glaring and sputtering.

"You looked so much like *September Morn*," Gwen said, surfacing not far away.

"Showoff!"

Carmaggio leaned back in his chair and watched the image of the earth spin slowly over the office table. It was the size of a large beachball, complete down to the swirling patterns of cloud; if you looked carefully at the edge, you could see a slight diffusion, where the atmosphere would scatter light. He peered closer. The detail got better and better as you approached. He had an uneasy feeling that if you whipped out a magnifying glass, tiny little ships and airplanes would be visible in the sky, and with a big enough microscope you could look in a window in a New York office building and see two men sitting on either side of a desk watching a holograph of the Earth. . . .

"I'd like to know how they do that," Bill Saunders said.

There was a slip of something the size of a business card underneath the image, on the businessman's desk table.

"I don't even understand TV, really," the detective said. "But I can switch it on or off. This quadrant," he added, raising his voice a little. "Enlarge."

The sphere vanished, to be replaced by a three-foot-square section. That flashed down and then down again, until they could all see the street outlines of a city; the buildings were perfectly to scale.

"Yep." Bill Saunders looked at the holograph again. "That's pretty damned convincing. You've convinced me, it's that simple."

He sank back in his chair, fingers steepled and eyes closed. *Taking it easier than I did,* Henry thought. But then, he hadn't been easily thrown back in Nam either.

"Okay," the businessman said after a moment. "Why not the government? I've got some pull with them; they owe me. Not least for staying out in '96, that was close."

"Lafarge thinks—and I agree, and our contact with the FBI does too—that we couldn't get anything done quickly. Too much incredulity. And anything the government knew, she'd know. By now she's probably got some influential people working for her."

"Yep," the Texan said again. "But with this, or a few things more, we *could* convince the necessary people. This Ingolfsson, the time traveler, she doesn't have much fancy gear, you say. We send in a Ranger team, and the problem's solved."

Carmaggio shook his head. He could feel sweat break out on his forehead. The more people in the know, the closer to disaster.

"Bill, that's just what we *can't* do. Lafarge says these Draka, they specialize in genetics—that fits what Ingolfsson's been doing with her company; yeah, plenty of electronics, but biotech stuff too."

"That oil-eating bug," Saunders said thoughtfully. "I *figured* that one was too good to be true. But I bought a piece of the action," he added. "Made a fair dollar. So, they're geneticists. So what?"

"So making a plague would be trivial work for her. That's how Lafarge puts it; trivial. They won their version of World War Three with something like that. Something that could wipe out ninety-nine point nine percent of the human race, leaving her to pick up the pieces."

"Judas priest," Saunders said. The words grunted out as if he'd been punched in the belly. He sat silent again for a full minute before barking: "Why hasn't the bitch done it already?"

"These *drakensis*, they're conquerors. As far as I could follow the explanation, they get a major charge out of making people truckle to them. You can't get much groveling time out of a corpse; and it would slow her down considerably, having to make components for her beacon instead of ordering them from working firms. But if Ingolfsson thinks her cover's been blown, she'd do it—Lafarge said he'd bet his life, literally, that something like that is in place right now and ready to roll."

Carmaggio wiped his mouth with the back of his hand. Lafarge had had some recordings of what Draka biobombs could do to organisms. Simple death, murderous insanity, hell, some of them had *dissolved*, rotting while still alive and fully conscious. . . .

"Damnation, this is like World War Three, only we've got our finger on the button," Saunders said, rising and going to the sideboard. "Speaking of which . . . a nuke? Drastic, but—"

"Lafarge is afraid there's a deadman switch on the bio-weapon," Carmaggio said. "His . . . he's got a computer, says it isn't conscious but does things no organic brain can do. And it says the probability of a fail-safe like that is over ninety percent now that he's here and she knows he's here, given what they know about enemy psychology."

"I don't know about you, but I could use a drink."

"I've tried it," Carmaggio said. "Several times since I talked to Lafarge. Doesn't help."

"Good thing you know that, but one won't hurt."

It was Kentucky bourbon; Carmaggio took a swallow of the sour mash and bared his teeth at the mellow bite at the back of his throat. He breathed heat, a little of it seeping into his soul.

"Yeah, El-tee, it just keeps getting worse. First I had a mass murderer, then a mass murderer who could do weird things, and then a time traveler . . . and now I've fallen into the script of a fucking—sorry"—Saunders didn't like swearing—"made-for-TV movie. As long as we don't start getting dreams about a little old black lady living in Kansas . . ."

"Mm-hmmm." Saunders was thinking with his eyes shut again; it emphasized the batlike ears. Then he opened them and looked at the holograph. "Heard about something like this in Hollywood. New gadget. Going to take a lot of expensive equipment, though." He nudged the black rectangle with one finger.

"So we can't call in the government," he said thoughtfully. "What can we do?"

"Play for time," Carmaggio said. "Stall—she evidently needs the warehouse, and she needs a lot of money for whatever she's doing there. Frustrate her without pushing her to use the . . . biobomb. And then when the moment comes, hit hard, take her out before she can do anything."

"Sounds like a longshot."

"Yeah. It is. What else can we do?"

"I'll think about that," Saunders said. "In the meantime, we could use some better intelligence." He paused. "Didn't you say that lady friend of yours who works for PB Securities was down there right now?"

Henry felt the tips of his ears flush slightly. "She's not my lady friend, exactly," he said. "Not yet. And we can't get her to pass information. That's the *last* thing we could do. Evidently it's impossible to lie to a *drakensis*, impossible to hide what you're feeling overall. No, Jenny's safe enough—as long as she doesn't know anything. Ingolfsson needs this stock deal too much to risk anything."

I hope.

Jennifer tucked her hands into the sleeves of her thick cotton robe. The wall panels of this upper gallery were murals, some still in progress, eight feet tall by twelve between latticed windows. The style was unfamiliar, a high-gloss realism but slightly stylized. Gwen came in, also still in her robe, wrapping a towel around her hair and then moving to the ebony sideboard by the entranceway.

"It just occurred to me," Jennifer said. "Ms. Wayne wasn't at the last presentation."

"Alice is not feeling well, I'm afraid," Gwen said. She smiled with a peculiar closed curve of the lips, her green eyes holding a secret mockery. "Bit of nausea. But we expect her to perk up in a week or so."

"I'm sorry she's ill," Jennifer said politely.

"She's important to our future," Gwen agreed gravely.

"These yours too?" Jennifer asked, nodding toward the walls and accepting a sherry.

"Yes. In the nature of a hobby," Gwen replied.

Jennifer looked at the mural. "What *is* this?"

The panel showed a street scene. Nineteenth century, perhaps, from the wide skirts of the women and the tall hats of the men; but the men wore swords, extravagantly ruffled shirts, and kept their hair in pony-tails; their coats were gaudily striped. Flowering trees thick with a mist of blue flowers arched over brick sidewalks; pillared houses stood back from the street behind wrought-iron fences and elaborate gardens with a hot, tropical look to them. Moving among the elaborately-clad strollers were blacks, in livery or ragged work-clothes, carrying burdens and pulling handcarts, sweeping the street, all kinds of labor.

Some weird part of the Old South? New Orleans? But there were cars on the street among the horse-drawn vehicles, big boxy-looking things with thin smokestacks and high iron-shod wheels.

"It's a historical piece, in a way," Gwen said, moving up behind Jennifer.

The New Yorker shifted uneasily; the head of IngolfTech seemed to radiate heat. She'd noticed that in the pool, an almost unhealthy warmth, like a fever. Obviously it wasn't, though. *I wonder what that scent is she's wearing.* Odd to put on perfume after a swim. *Sort of a musk, but flowery too.* Or was it a scent at all? Something that teased at the edge of perception.

The next mural was a sky view, clouds gilded by the sun. Across them swept the shadows of . . . airships, orca-shaped dirigibles. A fleet of them, dozens, perhaps hundreds. Biplanes were darting among them. Jennifer shook her head. *When did* that *happen?* The First World War?

A pastoral scene followed, vaguely Italian-looking. Hot sunlight on a dusty white road flanked by pencil cypress; vineyards snaking up a hill, the silvery-green of olives on the next, a line of Maxfield Parrish–blue mountains on the horizon, and a villa on a slope in the middle distance. In the foreground were a man and a woman on horseback, both in high-collared black jackets, boots, fawn trousers, wearing studded-leather belts with knives and heavy automatic pistols holstered at their waists. They were halted in the shade by the side of the road, leaning on the pommels of their saddles and talking to a group of men and women in peasantish clothing. *Italian, definitely,* Jennifer thought. The costumes were pure *cotadini,* working clothes from three or four generations ago. *But I can't place the context.*

"Tuscany?" she said, nodding.

"Chianti," Gwen replied. "It's a family connection."

"Your family lives there?" Jennifer asked, surprised.

Gwen's name and bone structure were both rather Nordic, despite her coloring. And there was something mid-Atlantic about her accent, sometimes. Of course, a lot of Brits had moved there—it was even called "Chiantishire" occasionally in *European Travel and Life,* which Jennifer read religiously.

"Not . . . now," Gwen said. "More of a . . . tradition."

The last panel was still incomplete, about three-quarters done. Jennifer blinked in surprise. The background was buildings, burning and shattered, under a darkened sky. The foreground was a hillock. Bodies sprawled about it, in unfamiliar uniforms and equipment but with an American-flag shoulder flash. On the hillock was . . . *well, a monster. Alien?* Something that looked like a cross between a gorilla and a wolf, at least. Much of its body was covered by futuristic-looking equipment, armor perhaps; the firelight caught at dull-red fur on the rest, and glinted off its eyes. One clawed foot rested on a human face; a huge curved knife was in one fist, a chunky-looking weapon throwing an iridescent beam in the other. The long jaws were parted in a fanged gape, long tongue lolling like a scarlet banner, serrated teeth gleaming. She could almost hear the bellowing snarl; the thing radiated a lust to kill.

"Now don't tell me *that* is historical," she said, glancing aside and out the tall windows.

"No, not in the present context. Although perhaps it might be someday."

"My God, what an imagination you've got!"

That closed-in smile again. "Actually I'm not very imaginative. It doesn't . . . run in the family, you might say."

Jennifer's mouth twisted. "It must have taken a fair amount of imagination to produce all this," she said, waving her free hand.

"No, just intelligence, memory, and application—not at all the same thing," Gwen corrected.

"Ms. Ingolfsson—"

"Gwen."

"Gwen, why do I get the feeling you are bullshitting me?"

"I'm not," she said. "I'm just not telling you enough to understand what I *am* telling you. The information's accurate, but radically incomplete."

Jennifer swung around, a spark of anger in her face. "In other words, you're bullshitting me. Look, I may be only a minor player—"

Gwen put the tips of her fingers on Jennifer's arm. The contact jolted her, a slight but perceptible shock. Her skin prickled again, and she felt flushed, as if she were coming down with the flu. The sensation startled her; she usually had better control of her temper than that.

"That's not necessarily true," Gwen said. She maintained the touch for a moment, then removed it. "I'm something of a judge of . . . human nature, and I think you're going to be a good deal more than a bit player. Otherwise I wouldn't waste time on you."

Jennifer finished the sherry. *And here I thought you wanted me for my body,* she thought sardonically—a suspicion which *had* crossed her mind, for some reason.

"That too," Gwen said tranquilly.

"I didn't say that!" Jennifer blurted in horror. She

stared at her glass. Two sherries and a couple of glasses of Chardonnay at dinner; she *couldn't* be that drunk.

"Not very loud," Gwen agreed. "But I've got excellent hearing."

"Look, I'm sorry, that was a joke." Her reputation would be ruined if she offended a client so gratuitously.

The alarm she felt was sluggish, somehow. She felt breathless, as if the Bahamian night was much warmer than it actually was. Sweat trickled down her face, and she could feel a pulse beating in her throat. And there seemed to be a hint of some unfamiliar scent from Gwen, something indescribable, like perfumed meat—except that it was wholly pleasant. Jennifer inhaled more deeply.

Gwen smiled and tapped rhythmically on the rim of her glass. "That's your heartbeat. You seem to be upset about something, Jenny. You don't mind if I call you Jenny, do you?"

"No." Her tongue felt thick. "My friends call me Jenny." *Why in God's name did I say that?*

"Jenny."

Gwen drifted a little closer, moving with that smooth dancer's gracefulness. Jennifer blinked; the other's green eyes seemed to be enlarging, filling her vision. Something touched her on either side of the neck, a soft light caress. Fingers. Moving with excruciating delicacy, barely touching her skin. Patterns of heat flowed after them.

"Look . . . ah—*please*—I, um, like men."

"Wonderful, that gives us something in common."

The fingers trailed down over her collarbones to the sensitive skin beneath her arms, stroking at the tender areas on the inside of her elbows. Jennifer shuddered, dazed. Lips touched hers; she responded instinctively, raising her face to the kiss. Off-balance, her arms came up and rested on the other's bare back. The skin beneath her hands burned hot, the muscles

beneath moving like sheets of living metal. Her eyes
jerked open in startlement. Gwen's tongue slid between
her teeth.

"Mmmmph!"

I can't believe *I'm doing this!* The only other time
she'd ever kissed a woman was once at university as
an experiment; she'd been drunk then, and even so it
had been about as exciting as kissing an arm.

Gwen leaned back slightly. "Lovely," she said.

"This is unprofess . . . ional," Jennifer said.

The top of her robe came down around her shoulders. Gwen's hands cradled her breasts lightly, fingertips
brushing over her nipples. She bit back a moan; it was
the most sheerly erotic sensation she'd ever felt, the
carnal equivalent of a mouthful of chocolate tiramisu.
Her knees quivered.

Oh, to hell with it. She put her hands behind Gwen's
head and kissed her again.

For a moment, Jennifer wondered where she was.
Then memory avalanched back in.

"Oh, my *God*," she mumbled.

The other half of the big bed was empty; it stood
under a ceiling fan, with French doors on three sides
leading to shaded galleries. By the quality of the pale
light, it was near dawn.

"Good morning, Jenny," Gwen said.

Jennifer flushed and pulled the sheet up under her
chin with both hands. Gwen took a glass of orange juice
from the wheeled tray and sat on the edge of the bed.
She was naked and entirely comfortable with it, something that Jennifer envied a little. *That's not all I envy*,
she thought. The head of IngolfTech had a figure like
a ballet dancer, except for the thicker arms and neck
and the fact that she wasn't flat-chested. *I feel like a
slug.*

"Isn't it a little late to be shy?" Gwen asked, offering

the glass of juice. "I mean . . ." She inclined her head toward the sheet. "Been there. Done that."

True enough, Jennifer thought, sitting up and taking the glass. She gave Gwen a quick peck on the lips and looked out the window as she drank.

"You make me feel self-conscious," she said after a moment. *And embarrassed. God.* She remembered more of the details. *I yelled and everything. I never lose control of myself like that.*

"What, about your weight?" Gwen said, and touched her lightly. "Ridiculous. Just pleasantly plump in the right places—what's the word, *zaftig?*"

She rose and belted on a robe, then pulled a medicine jar from a drawer. "But if it really bothers you, I'll put some of these in your purse." She picked it up off the chair—somebody had brought in her clothes, which made Jennifer blush again.

"What's that?" she asked, sipping at the orange juice.

"Metaboline, one of our products. Take one a week for a month, then one every month for a year." She came back and sat cross-legged on the foot of the bed.

Jennifer made a face. "Diet pills?"

"No, it's a metabolic adjustment. Increases your appetite, if anything—eat whatever you please—but it puts your body's static burn up even more." She smiled. "Trust me."

Jennifer blushed again, down to her breasts. Gwen watched with enjoyment, which made the flush worse.

"This isn't . . . ah . . . isn't like me," the New Yorker said, looking out the window.

Gwen made a graceful gesture. "Think of it as a matter of personal chemistry," she said. "No big deal. Besides, it had been a while for you, hadn't it?"

"Yes. You too?"

"No, I don't believe in passing up an opportunity for pleasure," Gwen said. She grinned. "You may have noticed. Come on, let's have a shower and then you can get back to your room before your colleagues wake up."

"Homesickness," Gwen said thoughtfully, looking down from her perch in the deep window, down to the dock where the Americans had boarded their plane.

That plan was launched, like a javelin—better, like a cunning shipkiller missile, with its own mechanical intelligence. It would strike or miss, and she would act accordingly. Dismiss it.

"I've been realizing how much homesickness must affect you humans."

"More than you?" Alice said from the lounger, looking up from her magazine, *Architectural Digest*.

"Much," Gwen said. "Your lives are so short, and yet this world you've made changes so quickly."

Something—perhaps the way the sun flickered through the bougainvillea on the coral-rock wall outside—prompted a memory.

First century, she thought. Back visiting on Claestum in Tuscany; she'd been . . . yes, a section-director on the Mars project then, glad of a break from space habitats.

Riding down from the hills, with a gralloched deer slung over the pack horse behind her. Rough slopes, the rutted earthen track and the slow clump of hoofs, the panting breath of the hound-beasts at heel. Summer smells of arbutus and thyme, leaf mold, horse, dog, the meaty scent of the deer carcass. Creak of leather and rattle of javelins in the holster before her knee; a flash of shy movement in the bushes, a glimpse of great brown eyes—a faun, still new and rare then. Stabbing flickers of light as she rode out into the valley fields, with the slow warm wind bringing her scents from miles beyond. Through an orchard of gnarled old apple trees—memory within memory, the sloping field new-planted with thin saplings—and into a grain field half reaped, the line of *servus* and the rhythmic flash of their sickles. Crimson poppies among the tall corn, the way the tunics stuck to the workers' flanks, the sweet mild smell of their sweat.

Three centuries ago, she thought. Yet—if only she could breach the wall of universes that separated her from it—nothing essential would have changed. Young oaks would have grown to great trees, the great-great-grandchildren of those reapers would reap the same bright-yellow grain in the same fields; the younger cousin who held that land would be at home in the manor. All memory was strong with her kind, but this one had more than vividness. The *impact* was still there, as tangible as the rich taste of the venison roasted with mushrooms, or the cool blue eyes of cousin Cercylas, the turn of his hand as he gestured.

"It's odd to think of you being homesick at all," Alice said.

Gwen looked up at her. Only three weeks since the embryo implant, not enough to alter her scent much. The language of her body had already changed, relaxed, tension draining out of the muscles around her mouth and in her neck day by day. It flattered her, and brought out the ripe-peach texture of her skin.

Also she thinks better when she's calm and happy.

"We're not altogether self-sufficient," she said gently. "We have our families, friends, likes and dislikes. Any social animal gets attached to their framework. For that matter, you're part of mine, now—it's a family relationship, in a way, and a fairly close one."

The Australian looked down at her stomach and traced it with her fingertips. "Yes, I suppose so. Funny, I can *remember* being upset about what you were doing to me, but I can't recall the *feeling* anymore. Everything just seems so . . . nice. I'm really looking forward to the birth, and having the baby to raise."

"So am I," said Gwen, uncoiling from the window-niche.

I must see that she has a few of her own, in a couple of years, she thought. *I'll breed her to Tom, perhaps.* Establish a brooder-line for the new infant, as a birth-gift. It would be her first clone, after all; Draka rarely cloned themselves. A little different from the traditional sperm-and-egg or egg-to-egg gene merging.

It was pleasant to be thinking of ordinary domestic matters like this; pleasant and a little premature. *Wouldn't do to forget this is just a little enclave of normalcy here,* she reminded herself. Beyond that horizon lay a vast feral wilderness to be subdued.

Gwen yawned and stretched. "Back to work. No rest for the wicked."

CHAPTER FOURTEEN

DOMINATION TIMELINE
EARTH/1
February 20, 445th YEAR OF THE FINAL SOCIETY
(2445 A.D.)

Tolya Mkenni had traveled a good deal via the Web—neural induction wasn't quite the same as being there, but it came fairly close. The last three years had been different: *physical* travel not just to the high-caste *servus* resorts of eastern North America but all over the planet on the Project's business, even to Luna. Not least to the clinic in Apollonaris where she'd been given the supreme honor of another lifespan. And now she was bound to Archona itself, to appear before the lords of the State. It was almost as thrilling as it was terrifying. She shifted slightly in the comfortable seat of the transport.

"Mirror," she said.

A space before her turned silver and then showed a three-dimensional image of herself. Not much different from what she'd seen for most of the past eighty years, except that the little signs of age—wrinkles at the corner of her gray eyes, threads of silver in her

shoulder-length wheat-blond hair—were gone or going;
the tone of her brown skin had turned youthfully
resilient. *Another three-quarters of a century,* she
thought. *I may see my great-grandchildren born.*
Amazing; only a few hundred of her breed had been
granted that, in all the centuries of the Final Society.
Woven into the left corner of her neat brown tunic
was a stylized circle with a gap, symbol of another
honor almost as great: Draka-level access to the Web
and unlimited personal mobility.

See that you deserve it, she told herself sternly.
Aloud: "Visual, external."

Walls and floor vanished from sight around her.
Atoms locked in powered stasis, the wedge-shaped hull
of the vehicle could not glow with heat. The air around
it could, and that was just fading as the speed dropped
from orbital to transonic. Below was the huge glittering of the Atlantic, empty save where sails marked plea-
sure-boats or once where the vast smooth curve of a
robot harvester slid by beneath the surface. They
passed over the coast, over what had once been the
Kalahari desert. The Race had long ago decreed that
it be lush green savannah and jungle kept inviolate for
the hunting they so savagely adored, empty of habitation save for the crumbled remains of ancient mines.

A minute, and cultivation showed below. Tolya leaned
forward with interest; this was the ancient heartland
of the Domination, where the destiny of the planet had
been hammered out and the Final Society born. Blocks
of cropland showed green and dull-gold, between
copses of forest and wider expanses of grazing. Widely
spaced manor-houses dotted the surface, each with its
dependent village of *servus* cottages; but the land
showed an archaic network of roads, even the long-
disused embankment of a railway. Abandoned cities
were woodland also above the ruins of home and forge
and factory, some showing a core of habitation still. Air

traffic was heavy, dots of silent brightness streaking past her transport.

Archona still stood huge, sprawling along the basin and ridge that separated the great highveldt plateau to the south from the blue distances northward. Twelve million souls had dwelt here when the city was at its height, back in the first century. Even then manufacturing had been moving spaceward, mainly a matter of automaton-machines; population followed more slowly, to Luna and the opening of Mars, the reclamation of the Americas. With the Web, there was little need for clumping together, and *drakensis* had a need for open space even stronger than their human-Draka ancestors. Still, this was the capital of the Solar System, cultural as well as political. Half a million of the Race lived here, many transients; six times that many *servus*, for their masters' multifarious uses and pleasures. Many of the buildings dated back four centuries or more, marble and colonnade and stained-glass domes amid avenue and grove and garden.

"Clearance," the machine said. "Clearance for private pad, Archonal Palace."

The vehicle made a neat curve and then sank downward. The tips of cypress trees dropped by on either side, and then a broad open field showed. Its surface was a dense tough mat of tiny flowers, blue and white and crimson; when the transport folded down a section of wall into a ramp and formed stairs, she could smell a faint scent of lilac and musk from the blossoms crushed beneath the ten-meter hull. A Draka waited below, in the high-collared black uniform of war. A gesture cut short Tolya's bow.

"Follow."

Tolya obeyed, stepping up onto the thin disk of the floater platform behind him. Even these last years such closeness was rare; she wiped the palms of her hands surreptitiously on the skirt of her tunic and adjusted her belt. The Master must be restricting his presence, since she felt no more than a tinge of the awe/fear/comfort it usually brought. The floater lifted to ankle height and turned, taking them through the field and up a long flight of granite steps flanked by sphinxes. Doors of fretted bronze opened; they slipped through corridor and courtyard and chambers.

I wish I wasn't so nervous, Tolya thought; the artwork and statuary moving by were almost enough to distract her, even now. The floater stopped in one last room, domed in carved rose-colored rock crystal; she stepped off at the silent direction, folded her hands before her and waited. Here at least it was no strain not to look about. The walls were murals in bas-relief, in gold and ivory and precious stones, scenes of the Last War and its aftermath; a Draka hand had executed those depictions of triumphant slaughter, rape, and butchery. It was fitting for the Masters to delight in such things, but hers was a gentler breed.

enter.

A soundless order from her transducer as the tall circular door dilated.

She walked through into a smaller chamber of audience; one central chair carved from a block of jadeite, flanked on either side by three more in a horseshoe-shape; the Domination's winged dragon on the wall behind, with the slave-chain of mastery and the sword of death in its claws. The light was a little low for *servus* eyes but enough to see the beings who sat at their leopard ease, in long robes of rainbow color or tight uniforms of plain black. She sank to her knees on the pad provided and covered her hands with her eyes, bowing her forehead to the cool marble of the floor.

"I live to serve," she said.

"And you've served us well," the Archon's voice said. "Raise your head."

She sat back on her heels, swallowing. The Draka

rested an elbow on the arm of his chair and his chin between thumb and forefinger; red-blond hair framed the hard-cut regular beauty of his face. Even then, her breath caught slightly at the sight of it.

"Exceptionally well, I understand," he went on, turning his head slightly to one side, toward one of his colleagues.

"Brilliant work," the head of the Technical Directorate said in confirmation. "Tolya's made some fundamental breakthroughs; without her, we'd be considerably further behind the enemy than we are."

Tolya shuddered. War flared beyond the orbit of Pluto; the ferals attacked, the claw of a universe cold and cruel, with only the Masters standing between her folk and oblivion.

The Archon made a single spare gesture with his free hand. "You needn't worry excessively," he said. "It's been too long since we had a war, but matters are well in hand . . . more or less. For now."

"For now," the Director of War said dryly. "And aren't you glad now, Alexis, that I and my predecessor insisted on keeping that 'useless' fleet updated and ready for reactivation?"

"Extremely glad, Chryse," Alexis Renston replied. "Gladder still that we had *some* preparation for the moleholes." He turned his eyes back to Tolya. "Legate Rohm informs me that we'll be able to duplicate the Samothracian technique shortly."

"Yes, overlord," Tolya said. "The energy expenditures will be very large, and you understand . . . the enemy will be, ah, watching for the other end of any macrocosmic molehole we send toward the Centauri system. I would advise a staggered series in interstellar space covering most of the distance."

"We'll consider that," the Archon said. "Damnation. At best, a restoration of the stalemate."

"Not necessarily," the Director of Colonization said.

"When we've beaten the humans back, it opens the universe to us. We anticipated thousands of millenia to bring the galaxy under the Domination of the Race. This will reduce the timescale by orders of magnitude."

"Something that the Archons of the colony worlds may not be entirely happy about," another Director mused. Since they were completely independent, now.

The Archon shrugged. "Needs must—and they *will* need us to defend against the Samothracians. For that matter, even with faster communications, interstellar government will never be very tightly centralized."

"I agree," the Director of Technics said. "Just because moleholes are fast, doesn't mean they're magic. You still have to expend the same energy for transport you would to put the same mass up to a high fraction of lightspeed, and over interstellar distances that mounts up. We'll probably end up using star-to-star hops and relaying for really long trips."

"How quickly our perspective changes," the Archon said, tapping his thumb on his chin. He looked back at Tolya. "This, I understand, will apply doubly to inter . . . universal travel."

Tolya bowed agreement. "Overlord, it's not only that a transtemporal molehole in the planetary gravity well will require even more energy to maintain the paramatter holding it open than one completely in the sidereal universe, but that energy has to be expended on a planetary surface. With fluctuations, unpredictable backlashes . . ."

Her voice trailed off. Energies that were a flicker in deep space could represent a planetary catastrophe on an inhabited surface. That was one reason most large-scale industry had long ago moved beyond the atmosphere.

"Plus the risk factor," the Director of Technics said slowly.

The others looked at her. "We're pretty sure there aren't any other technological species near us," she said.

Not unless they'd developed electromagnetic signaling too recently for the light waves to reach Earth, which was always a possibility.

"But we can be *sure*, after what we've discovered, that there are plenty of post-industrial civilizations near us in cross-time," she pointed out. "And we *know* that humans and derived post-humans are capable of developing them. Who's to say we won't run into more than we can handle, if we go exploring paratemporally? For that matter, we might—for all we know—hit a history in which that asteroid didn't hit the planet sixty-five million years ago, and end up fighting a ten-million-year-old civilization of intelligent dinosaurs."

Silence fell for a few moments. Tolya looked down at the hands folded in her lap again. Difficult to believe that anything in the universe could best these splendid predators. Intellectually she knew it might be a possibility, but her heart refused to accept it even as a hypothesis. *Keep your place,* she reminded herself.

"Which leaves," the Director of War said, "the question of what we do about Gwendolyn Ingolfsson."

The Archon's eyes narrowed. "How much in the way of resources would be necessary to continue the search?" he said.

"Overlord," Tolya replied, "no more than we've been using, but not much less. The odds of success are imponderable."

He thought for a moment. "Continue, then. We of the Race have our obligations, and we can afford that much." He smiled. "Especially considering that she held this chair herself, once. Chryse," he went on to the Director of War, "hold a legion in readiness. Inform me instantly of any breakthrough—I'll want to oversee it personally, if possible." He looked

from side to side. "I think that brings this matter
to a conclusion?"

Nods. He went on to Tolya. "*Servus* Tolya Mkenni,"
he said formally. "You have served your masters and
owners well; better than any other of your kind since
we created you."

"I live to serve, overlord."

"True, but we reward great service, nonetheless. You
will be given a third life—and you may ask a favor.
Not," he went on, "another lifespan beyond that,
though. That would be hubristic."

Tolya felt tears of joy filling her eyes; not for the gift
so much as for what it symbolized. Every *servus* child
for millennia to come would learn *her* name, *her*
accomplishment for the glory of the Race and the
subject-folk under their protection.

"I—" Her voice caught. "I, I am thankful that I can
serve the Race so well, overlord."

"The favor. Ask."

"Glenr Hoben, my lifepartner, overlord . . . if he
could be given another life with me also . . ."

The Archon canvassed his peers silently. "Granted."

Tolya bent her forehead to the floor once more. "If
the lost one can be found, we will do it, overlords," she
promised.

EARTH/2

APRIL 3, 1999.

"Damn," Gwen said mildly, looking down at the socket wrench.

The tough alloy-steel had bent under her impatient tug. Luckily nobody was looking, just now. She braced the tool against a corner and straightened it, before dropping it into the workman's box. *Finished, anyway.* Nobody else could install the power coil and drive-trains, of course.

Fun making them, she thought. Almost like reinventing them, to get Alfven-wave effects out of the components available. It had been a long time since she worked with her hands on machinery, not since duty on the primitive spaceships of the first century FS. This cobbled-together abortion was actually more advanced, in a sense—momentum-transfer systems hadn't been invented then, they'd still been using antimatter-powered reaction jets, or deuterium–boron-11 fusion pulsedrives.

The welded-steel cylinder was starting to look more like a vehicle inside by now. Conduits filled with cable snaked over every surface in view, and a heavy circlet of six-inch pipe had been mounted around the inner circumference of the hull in the middle of the twenty-meter length, to hold the power coil. Brackets for stamped-aluminum decking were already installed, left up while piping went in below. Curved consoles at the front would hold screens and controls. The air was heavy with the scents of ozone from the welding, with melted flux and phenol and plastics.

Gwen ignored the steel-rung ladder and jumped, hand clamping onto the dogging-lever of the roof hatch and swinging up to crouch on the platform just below it. There was a grateful rush of cooler air as she opened it and stepped up onto the scaffolding. The workmen were returning from their midday break, chattering and picking up their tools. The main contractor came over to her, averting his eyes from the way her sweat plastered the T-shirt to her breasts.

"All completed as ordered, Ms. Ingolfsson," he said. "Your own people shouldn't have any problem with installing the rest of the interior fixtures."

She shook his hand. "Excellent work," she replied. "Our little beauty should be joining the fishes soon."

The man looked at it curiously, the elongated teardrop of high-pressure steel lying in its timber cradle not far from the floatplane dock. Equipment littered sand churned up by heavy trucks, materials brought in from Nassau and even Miami, regardless of expense.

"You'd think you were building a *submarine* here," he said. "Not just an undersea research habitat."

Gwen and the others on the platform laughed with him; even harder, once the outsider had clattered down the steps.

"Lowe," she said. The young man, Captain Lowe's young nephew, came to an almost-attention. "How've you been doing on the simulator?"

"Fine, ma'am," he said. "Be easy, if t'computah is givin' me the right of it."

"Oh, it is." When you could apply thrust in any direction, vehicles did become easier to fly.

"Singh?"

"The onboard systems should be ready in another week," the Sikh said. His normally sour face was even sourer; engineering work was beneath his dignity.

"The flight-control computer is working out well." They'd used a surplus fighter-jet autopilot that the USAF wouldn't miss.

"Good," she said, satisfied. *A bit of an improvisation, but it'll come in handy.* "Lowe, I'll go through the simulator run with you after dinner. Everyone else, get busy."

She stayed, leaning on the railing of the scaffolding. Tom Cairstens lingered a moment. "You seem to be enjoying this," he said.

Gwen nodded. "It's nostalgic," she said. "As well as useful. It's been a long time since I worked with machinery this . . . discrete. Individual metal shapes, separate systems, that sort of thing."

"A bit like building a raft when you're a kid and playing pirate."

She looked at him in slight surprise. *Really quite perceptive, at times*, she thought.

"Exactly."

"How long will it be before Earth's . . . modernized?" he asked.

"That depends on how difficult it is to get things through from the other side," she said thoughtfully. "From what I've been working out on the physics, it'll be quite drastically expensive, even by our standards. Certainly we'll have to ship information and small knocked-down faber—fabricators—through first. And this planet is short of energy and raw materials until space is accessible. Several generations, probably, a long transition period."

"And in the meantime, you get to play with wonderful toys like this," he said, nudging the hull plates.

"What's life but play?" She looked at the metal oblong. "I think I'll call it . . . *Reiver*."

Gwen smiled. "I'll play with this. And with everything."

CHAPTER FIFTEEN

"Not bad," Henry said, dodging the crowds outside the theater.

Neon shone on the slick wet pavement; their breath showed in white puffs. He felt Jenny's hand steal into his and squeeze gently. Carmaggio grinned quietly to himself.

"What's so funny?" she asked.

"Dating again, at my age," he said.

"At least you got to stop for a while," she said, leaning against him slightly.

A panhandler approached them, opened his mouth, met Carmaggio's eyes and stepped back against the wall.

"How do you *do* that?" she asked.

"They can smell us," he said. "Eau de cop."

The line for the 9:45 showing was already around the block. "Lot of these look too young to have seen the first trilogy," he said.

"Go ahead—make *me* feel old," she said with a chuckle. "I saw the first one eleven times. The man's a magician; how did he ever get Kenneth Branagh to play Obi-Wan?"

"He had to—needed a Brit," Henry said idly.

Relaxed, he thought. *I'm actually feeling relaxed.* A minor miracle, considering what was coming down.

"Not bad space opera," he went on. "Despite the whooshing spaceships."

"I didn't know you liked sci-fi," she said, looking up at him out of the corners of her eyes.

"I've sort of gotten into it a little, lately," he said. "Can't read mysteries, after all."

She gave a gurgling laugh. *Damn, that's one fine woman,* he thought.

"No financial thrillers for me, either," she said.

They walked in companionable silence for a while. Even well east of Broadway the Upper West Side was fairly active on a Saturday night. *Yupper West Side,* he thought. *More sushi joints than Tokyo.* Funny; he'd been a beat cop here back in the seventies, when the area just ahead—Broadway and Amsterdam—had been about as shitty as anywhere on the island. Needle Park, and the name hadn't been a joke. Then almost overnight the renovators hit, and you were up to your ass in boutiques and expensive studio apartments. They turned left again, out toward Riverside Park.

Times like this you can forget what a toilet this town is, he thought. Behind them the towers reared up and disappeared into low mist, shining outlines of crystal and light. The buildings here were older, grande-dame apartment hotels like the Ansonia, terracotta swirls and mansard roofs.

"Did you know," Jennifer said, pointing to the Ansonia, "that Caruso lived there? And Stravinsky, and Toscanini?"

"I do now," Henry said. "Hell, I've even heard of them. Want to get something to eat?"

"Well—" Jennifer said. "Well, actually, if you can stand my attempt at Italian cooking, I have something ready at home. It's not too far."

*   *   *

"Dead slow," Gwen said.

Lowe grunted in reply. The water outside the TV pickups of the *Reiver* showed dark, ooze from the Hudson estuary welling up below the keel. Billows of gray sediment arched up, barely perceptible against the blackness, falling out of sight like silty snow.

Apart from a low whir from the ventilation system, the *Reiver* had an eerie quietness. In the control compartment the main light came from below, the glow of the video displays and digital readouts. Three swivel seats met the controls, for pilot and navigator and systems control; a little redundant, but Gwen didn't completely trust the glorified abacus known locally as a computer.

"Six knots," young Lowe said. His toast-brown face looked almost sallow in the bluish glow of the controls. "Depth one hundred meters, bearing six degrees north-northwest."

Gwen turned her chair and looked over to where Dolores was holding the navigator's position. "Tracking?"

"The yacht's half a kilometer ahead and dead in line," the Colombian said.

She closed her eyes and monitored the systems through her transducer. The interface was clumsy—the local equipment was pathetically slow in transferring data—but everything seemed to be going well.

"Turn it over," she said to Lowe.

"You have the helm, ma'am."

She slid into the control seat and took the stick. The drive couldn't thrust omnidirectionally, only over an eighty-degree cone to the rear, but that was sufficient. Power was at ninety-eight percent, good for two years of underwater cruising, or several hundred hours of flight; no sign of problems with the superconducting storage coil. *Although I'd hate to have to take this thing out of the atmosphere.* She eased back on the stick, and a slight elevator-rising feeling of increased weight followed. A touch on the pistol-grip accelerator on the control stick brought the speed up to twenty knots, and the *Reiver* broached smoothly through the surface of the Atlantic. Light showed on the pickup screens, the light of stars and moon on the endless waves. A slight pitching disturbed the previous rock-steady motion, sign that the craft was in the grip of powers even greater than the technics she had brought with her from the Domination's timeline.

"Hailing *Andros Adelborn*," she said.

A rooster-tail of spray fountained backward from the blunt curve of the *Reiver's* bow, surging almost to the forward video pickup. Radar showed no other vessels in the area, except for her own yacht dead ahead. The low shape of the surface ship drew closer quickly, yellow glow from the windows and the blinking navigation lights.

"*Andros Adelborn* here." Tom's voice; yet another Lowe was captain, and the crew were all her own Haitains, men who knew nothing and didn't want to know. "Ready for rendezvous."

Alongside the motor yacht; the *Andros* wasn't very large, no more than eighty feet at the waterline. She still bulked more than the submersible. Gwen throttled back, the yacht keeping pace until both vessels were motionless, rocking in the gentle swell. Then she locked the stick, standing with a slight feeling of reluctance. *Interesting,* she thought. Nothing quite like this had ever been built in her history; by the time Alfven-wave drives came along, materials technics had already advanced to the molecular-construction level.

"May I come too?" Dolores asked.

Gwen looked over at her absently, then took her scent. *Why not. I'll need somebody for the night.* She nodded.

"Can you handle it?" she asked Lowe.

"In my sleep," the young Bahamian said, grinning brashly. "It's no more trouble than ridin' a scooter."

"It will be in New York harbor," she said dryly. "Take her in extremely slow right in the *Adelborn*'s wake, and keep an eye on the sonar. Then down on the bottom and stay there, surface once a day to report. I'll send someone to spell you after a week or so, but I want the *Reiver* ready for emergency use at any moment. No monkeyshines. Understood?"

"Understood, ma'am," Lowe said, standing straight and swallowing. He might be brash, but he wasn't stupid.

She disliked punishing subordinates, even the locals. There was no need, back home. Nobody had to inflict pain on a *servus* to instill obedience. Humans were another matter, of course, and you did what you had to do to get results. Luckily they were usually frightened enough without direct action. *I miss the servus more and more,* she thought. They had a beautiful, supple, yielding quality that even the best-trained humans couldn't approach. As well as being generally more intelligent.

She ducked through into the open room behind the control cabin; it was rigged as a lounge-*cum*-communications center. The ladder to the deck-hatch was at the rear, where a bulkhead and corridor marked off a section of cabins and storage areas; the engineering spaces were in the stern. A man sprang to his feet as she entered, moving forward to take one of the consols.

"*Nueva York*," Dolores murmured. "I always did want to see it."

"We won't be doing much sightseeing," Gwen said. "Too dangerous."

Dolores's darkly pretty face grimaced. "That damned Samothracian! How I wish you'd killed him."

"So do I." With him gone, she wouldn't have to worry or hasten.

Gwen climbed the ladder and pulled the human up after her, standing with her feet braced on the coaming over the hatch. There was no superstructure, nothing to break the curve of the hull except a section of roughened metal to give feet a better grip. The air was chill with the northern spring, cool on her bare arms; cold salt spray touched her lips. The breeze brought a medley of odors: hot metal from the engines of the yacht, human, the distant land—itself tainted with burnt fuel and chemicals, but still green and earth-yeasty beneath. The joyous high-pitched squeaking of dolphins; their visible warmth was like leaping candles against the darker, cooler water. Heat billows plumed up from the *Reiver* and the *Adelborn,* a glowing background to the light-spectrum outlines. Overhead the stars arched in multicolored splendor, like a frosting of colored jewels across the sky.

She took a deep breath and shouted, a long wordless cry of exultation.

"A *what*?" Jennifer asked with a crow of laughter.

"A kangaroo," Henry said, grinning back at her. "So help me God, the MPs found 'em halfway back from the Honolulu zoo, hitch-hiking."

"How did they *do* that?"

"We never found out. Both of them were drunk as lords . . . and so was the kangaroo, or so the zoo people claimed."

That had been Gramsci and Dundas. They'd both been killed in that ambush about a week after they got back from the R&R; still, it was a good story, and they wouldn't have grudged him the use of it.

They'd have told him to make his move about now, he thought, as he watched Jennifer's pretty-wholesome face alight with laughter at the other end of the couch. *Christ, this is like being sixteen again*. He'd been married for fifteen years and divorced for two, and he'd

just gotten out of the habit. Especially with nice girls—
which Jennifer Feinberg was, old-fashioned phrase or
not.

The silence stretched slightly as the laughter died.

"You know, Henry," Jennifer said from the other end
of the sofa, "one of the things I like about you is that
you're a gentleman."

"Thanks," Henry said.

*Good thing you kept your hands to yourself. Oh,
well, it really was a great dinner.* Great dinner, fun
time. A relief being with somebody who wasn't a cop
but didn't have any hangups about the fact that he was.

He swilled the last of his Chianti around in the
bottom of his glass and looked around the room. Not
big, no bigger than his, although he shuddered to think
what it must cost up here on the Upper West Side.
More open; the bedroom just an angled section of the
L-shape layout. Books covered most of the walls; a
couple of prints, a good sound system with a stack of
movie disks for the new Sony flatscreen. A cat staring
at him resentfully from the top of a bookcase, hissing
occasionally at the invader of its turf. Not too much
in the way of frills and furbelows. It smelled like a
woman's place, though; of sachet, under the agreeable
scents of food.

"Henry, it's a good thing to be a gentleman, but
sometimes you can overdo it."

Henry put the glass down on the table and reached
for her.

"Slow," Vulk Dragovic said.

The Serb looked around warily as they walked down
the gangplank, his hand inside the pocket of his long
overcoat. That was not really necessary, although the
New York spring was chilly. The gun within probably
wasn't necessary either, but he didn't like taking
chances. The darkened wharf was eerily quiet, despite

the rumble of noise echoing in from Manhattan's towers. Cranes loomed above them like frozen metallic skeletons.

"Slow, coming in by sea. Why waste days?"

"Boats are harder to trace," Gwen said, coming up beside him. "And airports are easier to watch."

He could see her nostrils flare as she scanned the wharf. All he could smell was the foul water beneath. *She* could probably detect this Samothracian farting two kilometers away.

The green eyes turned toward him slightly. *Fool*, he told himself. Vulk meant *wolf* in his own tongue, but the Draka . . . *Watch what you think, always, always.*

She smiled at him, that slight curved turn of the lips. "Let loose the ants of war," she said.

Vulk turned and snapped an order to two of the Haitian servants. They carefully lowered the crate they had been carrying and opened the top with their prybars. A metallic rustling and clicking sounded within. Gwen's face went blank for a second; he recognized the expression, the look she took on when giving an order through her transducer. Dark six-legged shapes the size of a man's thumbnail poured out of the crate. The Serb pulled a foot back in revulsion as one skittered by him, suppressing an impulse to stamp on it like a bug. It *was* a bug, literally and metaphorically. A tiny self-contained android controlled by a vat-grown, gene-engineered version of an ant's nervous system implanted in a mechanical body. With a few simple imperatives: seek out a power outlet to recharge every five hours, proceed to designated locations and record, return to base to drop off the data. No transmissions, and virtually undetectable.

The pseudo-insects gathered into clumps and moved away; some into the night under their own power, others to the waiting cars to be driven nearer to their targets.

"It's a pity they can't breed," Alice said.

Vulk looked away from her. The six-month stomach was starting to show, which was disturbing. And the way she kept *smiling* . . .

"Too dangerous," Gwen said. Her head traced across the dock again, scanning. "We had to sterilize an entire habitat-city on the moon once, when we tried that. No way to stop them mutating. Selective pressure wiped out the implanted commands and they branched out on their own."

Vulk shook his head and concentrated on business. "We'd better get set up."

"You and Tom handle it," Gwen said. "I've got a few errands to run, first."

He opened his mouth to protest, then shut it. It was the humans who were in danger without her, not the other way round. One of the Haitians handed her a knapsack, anonymous black nylon to hide weapons and devices not of this world. She slipped her arms through the loops and walked off into the darkness, feet soundless on the concrete.

There were times when he wished he was back in Sarajevo.

"Hey, momma, you got the time?"

Gwen turned. There were four of them, none older than twenty. *A damned nuisance. Kill them all now?* On the other hand, she wasn't in *that* much of a hurry.

"It's 12:58, and far too late for you," she said.

There was a moment of shocked silence from the youths. That was *not* in their script for the incident. She smiled at the bewilderment on their faces. Anger started to spice their scents, mixing with the aggression and rut that had been floating to her for twenty minutes, since they began their stalk. Their leader reacted first. *Naturally. He can't be . . . what's the word?* Dissed, that was it. Dissed out by a female, in front of his followers. Her smile grew broader as he pulled out his gun.

Be careful now. A bullet in just the right place could kill her as finally as any human. She'd had friends who'd died because living through the centuries fooled their under-mind into thinking itself immortal. And there *was* no tearing hurry.

She stepped closer to the young man. The street was deserted except for the pack and its chosen prey, streetlights glimmering dimly on wet pavement. He extended the gun, holding it sideways with the butt level with the ground, an odd firing position.

"Crazy bitch!"

Then he screamed. Her fingers closed on the gun and the hand that held it, clamping metal and flesh together as irresistibly as a vise. The leather of his jacket ripped under her other hand as she held him immobile and slowly, slowly tilted the gun up under his chin. The flesh dimpled under the cold metal. *Sometimes humans can be very disagreeable.* This one's urine smelled bad. His free hand beat at her, and he screamed again as he broke his knuckles on the side of her head.

"Goodbye," she said.

Pumpf. The sound of the shot was muffled. Blood and brain matter spurted from the back of the mugger's head. It spattered into the face of the one behind him, and he clawed at his face, at bone fragments and clots of brain. Gwen reached out and plucked the weapon from his belt, then hit him sharply on the side of the head with the butt. He dropped and sprattled in a final galvanic twitch.

The third was running away into the darkened street, slamming into walls and stumbling in his panic. A plastic garbage can spilled aluminum and trash and a squeaking rat in his wake. Gwen examined the weapon in her hand. It was a Calico, with a helical fifty-round magazine mounted over the barrel and action. Not a bad design, considering the available technology. Nine-millimeter parabellum ammunition. She turned to the last of the pack.

"Better put that down," she said. His pistol dropped from shaking fingers.

"Don't . . . don't hurt me." His voice squeaked a little; he couldn't be much more than sixteen.

"Don't worry," she said. "Now about your friend . . . left knee."

She raised the pistol and fired. Two hundred yards down the roadway, the running man spun to the pavement. It took a moment for his scream to start. The flat elastic crack of the pistol echoed back from the empty brick walls. After a moment he lurched upright, pulling himself along the building.

"Back of the head."

Crack. Gwen buffed the grip and trigger assembly of the gun with her silk handkerchief. Then she chuckled and tucked the barrel into the dead hand of the mugger whose skull she'd crushed with the butt.

"Let them try to figure *that* out," she said, laughing.

The last mugger was staring at her, eyes enormous in the gloom. She reached up and flicked off the bandanna tied around his head. The hair beneath it was black and straight; he had smooth light-brown features and gold earrings in both lobes.

"What . . . what are you?" he asked.

"Your lucky night," she said.

Gwen pulled up the front of her skirt and tucked it into her belt. Then she skinned out of her panties, folding them neatly and dropping them into the pocket of her jacket.

"What you *doing*?" the teenager stammered, backing away as she rubbed herself. His hands came up, palms out.

"Exactly what you planned on doing to me," she said kindly. Her hands flashed out and clamped on his wrists. "Although the mechanics are a little different. But you're actually going to enjoy it, like it or not. Be good, now."

Gwen used one arm to hold him to her while the other circled his neck and its hand pinned his jaw, putting her scent next to his nose. He shivered and jerked in the immobilizing grip as she kissed him deeply. His mouth quivered when she drew back a little and stripped the leather jacket down over his shoulders. The T-shirt parted like paper under her fingers, and the man's jeans dropped shredded to the ground.

"Oh, you *are* being good," she crooned, taking the stiffening penis in her hand. *Wonderful things, phero-mones.* Not to mention the natural state of an adolescent human male, almost as susceptible as a *servus.* "Pity there's no grass, but this has its merits."

She pushed him back against the brick wall and pinned him with weight and strength, just enough to keep him from catching his breath fully, stroking his flanks and legs. Then she rose up on her toes and sank back, gripping him firmly inside her with a thrust of the pelvis and a rippling tug of her vaginal muscles. *Ah.* Rough and hasty, but pleasant. *Very pleasant*, she thought, growling contentedly into his ear as she rocked. His scent was heavy with fear and arousal, his sweat tasting of it; the sound of his heartbeat speeded to a frenzy. The gold earring dangled before her eyes; she lipped it and then bit the gold circlet through, spitting out the severed half. Her tongue explored his ear, and his whole body shuddered. His eyes were rolled half up into their sockets.

"Put your hands on my hips," she said. He obeyed, fumbling and then gripping with a strength that would have bruised a human. "Move to me. That's a good pony, rhythm now, rhythm."

Ah. It was a pity she had to hurry. *A long time since I took it this way.* Not since the killsweeps right after the War. *Now.*

Gwen quickened her movements. The boy's buttocks slapped against the brick wall behind him. Then she froze for a long instant, her only movement the heavy internal tug of orgasm. Clenched between her legs and body and the wall, the youth squealed like a dying rabbit and bucked in her grasp. Then he stilled too, gasping harshly, limp.

Gwen sighed, a throaty sound, and stepped back. The boy slid down the wall and lay half-fainting. She crouched beside him, tugging the remnants of his T-shirt free and wiping herself with it. Then she stroked his hair, turning his face around to meet hers. Conscious thought was returning to him, like something floating up through dark water. Thought, and fear.

"Sweet but brief, our little encounter," she said. "I'd like to spend more time riding you, but duty calls. The police will be here soon, and you'd better go. Understand?"

She stood and stepped into her underwear, smoothing down her skirt. The young mugger slid along the wall away from her in a crablike scuttle, then rose. The remains of his jeans pooled around his ankles and nearly tripped him; he kicked free and ran, throwing his shredded leather jacket behind him. Gwen smiled at the winking buttocks and flashing legs, then turned and walked quickly northward.

"Mmmmm." Henry Carmaggio muttered in his sleep, turning.

Jennifer woke and stretched, sliding out from under his arm. The bedroom was dim, but there was enough of the usual New York night glow from the window to see the pleasantly craggy contours of his face. She sat for a moment on the edge of the bed, smiling down at him.

"*You really* are *a nice guy*," she said very softly, before getting up and padding out to the bathroom.

It had been so long she'd forgotten about some of the messier details. *I feel good, though*, she thought. *Reassured, to start with*. The Bahamas just hadn't been like her. It was nice to know her wiring hadn't somehow gotten crossed up at this late date. Not to mention how nice it was just to be with someone again; and to know that he was just as happy about it. *Gwen didn't count. Put it down to happenstance.*

She turned off the bathroom light and eased back into the bedroom, her feet moving in an experienced scuffle—when you owned a black cat that liked to lie in the middle of the way, you learned that. Despite her care, Henry woke when she eased back into the bed.

"Hey, cold feet," he said as they snuggled close. She wrapped them around his. "Hey!"

"Warmth is a good thing," she said into the angle of his neck. "So share some."

"Damn, I find the woman of my dreams and she wants to use me as a heating pad," he grumbled, stroking her back.

After a moment she giggled. "Oh, so it's *true* what they say about Italians! Or are you just happy to see me again?"

"Damn," he said mildly, sounding surprised himself. "Must be something about having a beautiful naked woman in my arms. Even at four in the morning it—"

"Shut *up* and . . . oh, yeah."

Ten minutes later, the pager in his pants pocket went off. Carmaggio muttered a curse into Jennifer's hair.

"Ignore it," she said.

Damned right, he thought muzzily. He tried,

although after a moment he noticed that they were moving in rhythm to the *neep . . . neep*. That ended in a moment of gasping that collapsed into laughter.

"Now you know why so many cops get divorced," he said, kissing her and disentangling himself.

He rooted through the clothes scattered on the floor until he found the instrument, then stumbled to the phone. "This had better be important."

"Yeah, Jesus?" He listened for a moment. "You *sure?*" A resigned sigh. "Yeah, that sounds like it."

He turned to the bed. "Gotta go."

Jennifer wormed her way down farther under the covers, then threw them off and reached for her bathrobe. "Tell me about it tomorrow."

Not if it's like the usual, Henry thought. There were some details nobody was really interested in.

"I'll give you a call."

There were none of the exterior iron stairways so common here at the rear of Jennifer Feinberg's apartment. That was a minor inconvenience; Gwen reached up and clamped her gloved fingers onto the gaps between the bricks, pulled herself up and took a second handhold, and climbed straight up the wall. The ancient, dirty brick was a little tricky, since she had to be careful not to crumble it beneath her grip. It took her a full two minutes to reach the level of the bathroom window. She bent her ear nearer the window, and sucked air in through nostrils and open mouth.

Ah, probably not a good moment to drop by. Panting, creaking from the bed, and then a series of cries— interrupted by a shrill beeping sound.

"Ignore it." Jennifer's voice, sounding understandably aggrieved. Gwen grinned in the darkness as the sounds began again, to the counterpoint of the electronic signal.

The male eventually got up and turned the instrument off, then moved to the phone. This time Gwen's ears pricked forward in unconscious reflex.

Fast work, Gwen thought, as she listened to the telephone conversation; half with her ears, half with the transponder's electronic eavesdropping. *They must have found the bodies already.*

She shifted her fingers' grip on the wet brick outside the bathroom window of the human woman's apartment and hooked the edge of one foot onto the windowsill, still invisible to anyone who didn't put a head outside and look to the right. A trickle of command through her transducer, and a bug walked out of her sleeve onto her palm. Another, and it marched into the sill and began burrowing through a joint. She cocked her ears forward and checked the sound: not really audible to human-range hearing, but she commanded it to go more slowly anyway.

Why was this policeman concerned about Jennifer's business with IngolfTech? He couldn't *know* anything, or if he did he'd been very careful about saying it where anything electronic was listening. He had a reason to be concerned with Jennifer herself, of course: mating instinct. She rather approved of that—a healthy, eugenically sound emotion. Which left the essential question of whether anyone but the government agencies had any notion she was connected with the warehouse killings. The government itself was no great problem, since the dribble of miracles she was feeding them kept them far too greedy to risk killing the golden goose—at least, not for long enough that she could finish the Project.

Still, it was best to be sure. The Samothracian might be interfering.

surveillance, she commanded. **following parameters.**

Also best to be discreet. Public attention was

something she did *not* need, or anything that might scare off the investment community. She needed more of their resources to complete the beacon; several hundred million, and about four to six months of time.

The bug had its way with the ancient dried wood of the frame. Gwen closed her eyes for a moment, linking with its rudimentary senses; organic compound eyes for sight, a rudimentary tympanum for sensing air vibrations. Vision scuttled across walls and floors; a protesting hiss sounded as she passed a cat. The animal leaped back, and her 270 degrees of vision surged up a wall and settled on the top of a doorframe. She watched the two humans saying farewell at the doorway with amusement. Such a sentimental species, particularly this culture-group. Although—she inhaled to check the scent—they'd evidently been having a *very* good time.

The bug settled in. Jennifer stood by her bed, then hugged herself and did a little dance of pleasure; she picked up a large stuffed animal which had been turned face to the wall, kissed it and set it down looking out over her bedroom. Then she yawned. Gwen waited until her breathing and heartbeat settled to regularity before she leapt. Two stories' fall, with her jacket billowing out behind her; she landed on outstretched hands and feet, cushioning the blow until her chin rapped on the pavement, not too hard. The *smack* echoed slightly from the surrounding walls, but a moment's frozen alertness showed nobody had noticed.

She rose and began to trot south.

CHAPTER SIXTEEN

"This one shot himself?"

Mary Chen moved the corpse's hand, fingers sure and oddly gentle in their thin-film gloves. There was no stiffness to them; each digit was as limp as a rubber tube filled with slush.

"Not unless he managed to break all the bones in his hand while he did it," she replied. "There's powder burn all around the entry wound under the chin, yes, and there's distortion of the tissues where they flowed away from the pressure."

Most people didn't realize it, but even the spurt of high-velocity gas from a blank round could kill, at short ranges. That was a familiar story to everyone present; there were a few accidentals that way every year, and people trying to make it look accidental. Chen went on:

"The muzzle was in contact with the flesh when the round went off. Somebody wrapped their hand around his, bent his arm back until the gun touched skin, then clamped down hard enough to shatter the bones and pull the trigger."

Henry Carmaggio stuck another stick of gum in his mouth and walked over to the second body. "And this one beat out his own brains with the butt of his gun," he said heavily.

"*Sí, patrón.* After shooting the other victim," Jesus said, pointing down the street with the hand that held a pencil and a 9mm shell casing atop it. "Nice shooting, two hundred yards—in the dark."

The three of them moved unobtrusively aside, amid the crime-scene bustle, the traffic barriers and blinking lights. Carmaggio inhaled the stale cold smell of dawn, fresher than the body odors of violence.

"Not much doubt as to who *this* was," he said. He looked at the body with the dished-in head. "And she's fucking *laughing* at us. This was a message."

Jesus frowned. "Perhaps. Perhaps a chance thing. I do not think there will be fingerprints or blood types, this time."

Carmaggio shrugged. That *would* be asking too much. They all knew it took a good deal more evidence to haul in a multimillionaire than your ordinary punk: fact of life.

"I wonder what would happen if we just checked the hotels for her name and did an arrest?"

The tall blond man had walked up noiselessly, not making any particular effort to sneak but hard to notice all the same. The counterfeit ID hanging from the lapel of his overcoat were the best Carmaggio had ever seen . . . which was to be expected, of course.

"Bail would be made," Lafarge said quietly. "And then *it* would disappear, and we'd have to start all over again." He frowned. "Unless," he said thoughtfully, "I could kill it while you had it in custody."

Carmaggio forced down an instinctive bristling. Suspects had been known to fall down stairs and be shot while attempting to escape, but not on his watch. *On the other hand, this isn't your ordinary suspect.*

Lafarge held out a scrap of stained T-shirt. "I checked this with my moloscanner."

He nodded toward the brick side of a shuttered electronics store. There was a heap of shredded clothing there. Carmaggio hid a smile behind his hand, rubbing his jaw, taking the scrap. It had an odd musky odor, very faint.

"She actually fucked this gangbanger up against the wall?"

Lafarge flushed. *I think they breed them pretty straightlaced where he comes from,* the detective thought.

"The moloscanner reveals traces of human semen and *drakensis* . . . secretions."

"You can do that on site?" Chen asked enviously. Lafarge shrugged.

"Molecular analysis is fairly simple. My machinery is just much more compact."

"It doesn't help us much," Carmaggio said. "Not admissible evidence." Then he snapped his fingers. "Wait a minute! She left a *witness.*"

"*Sí,* but that's going to be one difficult *hijo de puta* to find. No witnesses to the incident; sure, we'll get some names of who the deaders ran with, but . . ."

Carmaggio held up a hand and looked at Lafarge. The . . . *man from Dimension X,* the detective thought . . . reached inside his coat. What he pulled out looked like a sheet of stiff paper. On it appeared an adolescent face; Puerto Rican, Carmaggio thought. The bandanna and earring fit the evidence left over by the wall.

"This is the face that goes with his genes. There may be acquired characteristics; scars, perhaps."

"Damn, but I'd like to have that gadget," Carmaggio said mildly. "How does it . . . never mind. Jesus, get this down to the office and see if it matches anyone known to run with the Lords. Then do up copies and have it APB'd."

"Grounds?"

"Material witness . . . no, make it assault, attempted murder, whatever. We'll find him and then do a talk-and-walk."

"It will take some heavy pressure to get one of the Lords to admit a *woman* tore off his clothes and screwed him," Jesus chuckled.

"Then we'll lean on him. Get on to it."

He looked down and noticed he was still smelling the rag of T-shirt. That wasn't the only thing that was happening, either. *Good thing I'm not wearing tight pants.* He grimaced and tossed the cloth aside. *Christ,* he thought uneasily. Suddenly what had happend to the gangbanger didn't seem so funny. Anything that could get a rise out of him tonight, at his age, was definitely bad mojo. He forced down an illogical silly smile.

"If we can find this little shit, we can pull her in," he said. "Manslaughter, at least."

"A good lawyer and she'd walk on that," Jesus pointed out, in police reflex. The NYPD was too over-loaded to bother arresting people who had a good chance of getting off. "Self-defense, even if she admitted anything. And *patrón,* our credibility would be shit, with a gangbanger's word against a respected business-woman with government connections."

"There's a forcible rape charge, too," Carmaggio pointed out. "Besides, what we want to do is slow her down and throw off her plans. She's gone to a lot of trouble to build up an image as a respectable business-woman. This would queer it."

Lafarge shook his head. "Your legal system is not going to make any impression on *it,*" he said. "Direct action . . ."

Carmaggio hunched his shoulders. "Our legal system is what we've got," he snapped. "We're going to use it. The alternative is six people with handguns trying an amateur hit. You think that's viable?"

"I don't think you're adjusting to the situation as it is," the Samothracian said carefully.

"I don't think you should assume that this is wogland," Carmaggio replied. "You know, the place where a white man with a gun can do whatever he wants?"

Lafarge blinked and looked away, ignoring the heavy irony. "I'm doing what I can to trace her operations," he said. "It looks bad. She's ordering components for a reactor."

The three New Yorkers swiveled to face him. "A *nuclear* reactor?" Chen asked incredulously.

"A fusion reactor. Early model, primitive . . . it will weigh about a hundred and fifty tons, in the three hundred megawatt range. Most of the components can be made locally, although nobody would know what it was for."

"How is she going to hide a set of turbines and alternators that large?" Chen asked curiously.

Lafarge shook his head. "I said primitive, not neolithic. Direct transformation of energetic particles to electricity or other input energies."

Carmaggio grunted and scratched at his chin through the heavy morning stubble. "Zoning violation?" he mused.

Chen shrugged. "I'm assuming there would be no way to prove it was anything but lab equipment?" she said.

Lafarge nodded. "Not until it was fired up. Then the neutrino flux would give it away, even to your equipment . . . but that would be too late."

"It would?" Chen said.

"I'm presuming the *drakensis* wouldn't activate the power source until the last set of tests needed on the signaling equipment."

He shrugged. "I'm also assuming it'll get the signaling device right—but under the circumstances, we'd better take the pessimistic interpretation." His head came·up. "I'd better go make sure you're not interrupted. I think . . ."

He turned and strode away.

Looping back on your own trail was good tactics. *Although now I wish I'd just outrun those ferals,* Gwen thought as she trotted southward, holding her speed carefully down to that of a human jogger—unusual in this neighborhood at night, but not totally bizarre. Her playfulness had gotten the better of her.

"This is war," she reminded herself. Not recreation, not hunting goblins or grizzly bears for the fun of it.

She slowed, walking through the night streets. There was a gathering of cars at the spot she had turned on the muggers; their heavy chemical stink made it hard to pick up individual scents, even downwind and as close as half a kilometer. Gwen looked around. The buildings were not too high here, mostly flat-roofed and built of brick. She crouched, leapt ten feet upward to clamp her hands on a metal bracket, then swarmed up the side and flipped over the parapet to land on the flat graveled-asphalt surface of the roof. Ventilator shafts and the square man-high covering of a stairwell dotted it. She bent over until the fingertips of her outstretched hands almost brushed the gravel, ran across the roof and leaped again to land atop the stairwell cover with her weight resting on fingers, thumbs, and toes.

Ah. She willed her sight into telescope mode, letting herself sink lower until only the top of her head and her eyes showed. *Yes, that's the policeman.* Her mind enhanced the images, branding close-ups of the faces into her memory and that of her transducer. *Odd about the policeman. He may know about me, but Jennifer certainly doesn't.*

Yes, that's him. The Samothracian was walking away from the flashing lights and huddled humans.

She snarled silently, a thread of saliva dangling from one lip. *Rush them?* She could be down from here in a few seconds, then charge out of the darkness faster than a racehorse, kill, vanish. Cut off the Samothracian's locally-recruited limbs. Literally; the layer knife was ready in the knapsack at her back.

No, too risky. Not while the cyber-warrior was nearby; and besides, there were too many humans there, too many videocameras. The last thing she needed was incontrovertible proof of her own existence flashed out over the news services.

Now, which way had the Samothracian gone? *Ah.* Along her original trail. The problem was that molecular machines could track the drifting particles of scent just as well as a gene-engineered nose. Better, in some respects. And she suspected that the Samothracian would have at least a small faber with him to manufacture what he didn't already have in his covert-operative kit.

Two can play at that game, she thought, reaching into a pocket and pressing the control stud of a small metal oblong. There was no audible hiss, even to her ears, but the molecules drifting out would bind to hers and blanket her scent very effectively. She wrinkled her nose slightly; it was a little like being invisible, the same sort of mental jar you would feel looking down and not seeing yourself.

Gwen leopard-crawled forward to the edge of the roof, filtering the noise background. There. That was the pattern of his walk, two streets over. It was only about ten meters from roof to roof, across the narrow intervening alleyways. She backed halfway across, braced, ran and *leapt.* The soaring was like being in zero-g again, but better, with the wind in her face. The thump of landing was soft as she used legs and arms to spring-cushion the impact, and the background noise was high. This time she kept well back from the edge, relying on nose and hearing and the knowledge of her own path the first time. She'd been high-scent then, sweating from fight and rut; easy for the enemy's sensor to follow.

Wait. Another leap. This time there was a human on the roof, cigarette frozen halfway to his mouth as he stared at her with a yokel gape. She came soaring down out of the night and landed next to him, twitched the tobacco out of his mouth.

"Those things are bad for you. And you didn't see me."

The Samothracian was disappearing into the darkened space beneath a highway, the river just visible to her right. She stuffed her shoes into the knapsack and then turned, slipped her legs over the edge and went down the face of the building in a controlled fall, breaking her momentum with snatch-grabs at cornices and window-ledges. The impact at the bottom was enough to bring a slight grunt, and then she was running lightly on the balls of her feet. Accelerating to full speed, fifty kilometers per hour, arm going back over her shoulder to take the hilt of the layer knife. Downwind from him to her, the slightly *off* scent filling her nose.

Time slowed, awareness expanded. The target was in local clothes, jeans, windbreaker, walking with his hands in his pockets. Undoubtedly wearing the softsuit under the clothes, but not covering his extremities. *One strong cut to the back of the head.* Reinforced bones or no, that would open his skull like topping a hard-boiled egg.

Something, the soft touch of her feet on the pavement or her breathing or the cloven air of her passage itself, warned him. She shrieked a long howling cry of frustration as the layer knife slammed into an upraised arm that shed it with a long *clang-hisss*. Shreds of fabric spattered for yards around, and the jarring impact shuddered up her arm and into the shoulder-joint with a force that would have shattered human bones. The momentum of her 195 pounds threw them both spinning, him backward. She turned the motion into a flying leap that ended behind a concrete barricade.

Crack. White fire lanced into the surface, and light battered her eyes as lime and steel burned. Ozone and combustion products clawed at her nose and throat, burning at her lungs.

Gwen skittered backward in a spider-crawl, over the asphalt, underneath a parked car, further back behind another lip of concrete at the edge of a parking lot. *Possibly I was slightly hasty,* she thought.

Crack, as the car she'd passed under took a bolt of blue-white light. Steel vaporized, the vacuum of super-heated air sucked fuel out into a mist of droplets and exploded. That turned the automobile into a fuel-air bomb of impressive size. Gwen tumbled backward like a scrap of paper in the breeze, twisting to keep the supernal sharpness of the layer knife's edge away from her own skin, thudding painfully into stone and concrete and metal. Her hair singed and stank; cars near the one struck by the energy bolt exploded, and then more in a chain-reaction across the parking lot. A pillar of fire was rising into the night sky, and sirens wailed in the distance. Lights swept up the Hudson under the whirring blades of a helicopter.

A lake of fire and twisted metal lay before her. Gwen spat blood to clear her mouth and resheathed the layer knife, willing away pain. *Nothing really damaged,* she decided after a brief check. Hearing slightly stunned, abrasions and burns that would heal, a little scorching to her upper lungs and bronchi.

Drawing the plasma gun from its sheath would expose it to the Samothracian's sensors, but right now she wanted a weapon with a little more distance effect.

She set it to needle-beam and waited, with the water to her back. Earth was cool beneath her.

The enemy came walking through the fire like an eyeless statue of living metal, his armor covering him in a fluid surface the color of mercury lit from within. Scraps of cloth flickered away from the softsuit's perfectly reflective surface in flame and ash. Her first shot struck the ground at his feet, lifting and toppling him backward. The second struck at the weapon in his right hand. The Samothracian curled around it protectively and rolled backwards into the fire, hiding himself in its heat and glow.

Damn. She keyed her transducer:

we've got to stop meeting like this.

A bolt out of the fire, gouging earth into steam near her face. She scuttled down the embankment and snapshot back at the transducer's triangulation-point of where the Samothracian was. He'd have moved too, of course.

the humans will be here momentarily, she went on. **shall we call a temporary truce? their government is more likely to believe my lies than your truth.**

Something small and dense arched out of the spreading pool of burning gasoline. Her wrist moved in a small, precise movement and her finger stroked the trigger, even as her other arm came around to shade her eyes.

The air picked her up and slammed her down again on the ground. The light was bright enough to hurt even through clenched eyelids and the flesh of her arm; that must have been visible all over the city.

Gwen fired again before the flash had died; this time into a large truck still intact at the edge of the lot. The liquid inside was heavy heating oil; it ignited and began to burn as it gushed out, a sweeping wave of thick black liquid four inches high as it poured over the shattered lot. The fire flared up higher, this time spreading a pall of thick tarry smoke.

have you no concern for your fellow humans? she asked, slithering backward.

The mental impression of a voice answered her, cold with rage: *more than you.*

then you must have realized the precautions I could take.

better the planet be depopulated than domesticated.

perhaps i've readied a kill-plague, she answered. **perhaps not. i've already started improving the place; check their fertility rates over the last two years.**

While she spoke silently she had been hyperventilating. *I'll leave him to think about that,* she decided, stripped off the hampering clothes, broke contact and slid backwards into the water.

The dirty liquid closed over her head. Her weight pulled her downward; she sculled gently with the current, heading out deeper and keeping her motions languid to conserve oxygen. If she was careful she had fifteen or twenty minutes before she had to surface to breathe, and he couldn't be sure where she'd entered the river.

Slap. Concussion jarred at her, a huge fist that squeezed at her chest and tried to force the precious air out into the water. She swam deeper and faster, lunging hands forcing the water behind her. The Samothracian was throwing minigrenades into the water. *Slap.* This time her vision blurred. *Slap.* Effort was draining her reserves of oxygen. If she surfaced, he might be in a firing position with the energy gun . . .

A huge dark shape loomed up out of the river's blackness. Lights blazed out from it suddenly, showing the teardrop hull and the *Reiver* stenciled across the bow. Her arms strained out and hands clamped onto a bracket as the bow-wave buffeted her aside. The hull turned and drove southwards, wrenching at her shoulder-joints. Gwen could hear her heart straining to beat faster as the last oxygen was scavenged out of her blood; when the vehicle surfaced she lay panting for a long minute until the strength returned to her body.

"That was close," she muttered, crawling over the upper curve of the hull and undogging the hatch.

"You all right, ma'am?" Lowe asked.

One of the Haitian crew brought towels and a first-aid box. Gwen waved it aside as she dried herself off; no point in bandaging, when you couldn't get infected and wounds clotted quickly.

"Never better," she said. "Just a little singed and scraped. Jacques, fetch clothing. Lowe, back to the dock."

She looked upward with a slight smile as the *Reiver* canted and turned, imagining her enemy's rage and frustration. Still, that had been too close for comfort. It was time to tighten up a little.

"I hope this isn't what you call subtle tactics," Carmaggio said grimly.

They were all sitting in a booth, and like nearly everybody else they were watching the TV. Every news channel in the city and the nationals besides were focusing on this one; it wasn't all that often that a section of the West Side went up in a giant ball of flame. The view from the helicopter had been on loop since he got up this morning; so had the interviews with dazed passersby, most of them swearing that ray-guns had set the cars on fire. Of course, a lot of them were also swearing that they'd seen the aliens with the ray-guns getting out of flying saucers, or into submarines in the Hudson.

The helicopter loop came on again. The beginning showed cars exploding across the lot, merging into a

single pillar of flame that buffeted the aircraft until the
picture jiggled with the updraft. And there were the
little straight-line flashes of light that had everyone
talking, flashes ending in explosions.

A talking head came on, some retired military type,
pointing to a freeze-frame:

"Definitely rocket launchers," he said. "Or rocket
propelled grenades . . ."

"If that dickhead ever saw an RPG fired, I'm the
Queen of Siam," Carmaggio said disgustedly.

He *had* seen RPG's fired, far more often than he'd
liked, back when.

I want a smoke. If it weren't for Jenny, he thought,
he'd bum one right now.

"Firefights with energy weapons are like that,"
Lafarge said. "I suppose the observers need some sort
of explanation to account for what they saw."

"Oh, that's all right then," Carmaggio said. The other
man nodded, then looked back at the policeman
sharply.

"It attacked me," he said. "I had to take the opportunity." His fist clenched. "I nearly *got* it. Damn, damn,
how did it get away underwater?"

On the screen a tiny metallic figure dashed through
the flames. A jerky close-up showed it hurling tiny
objects into the Hudson. Each time a shock-fractured
hemisphere billowed out of the surface as the underwater explosion punched the surface of the river. Then
the living statue dove into the water itself. . . .

Someone from a nearby booth blew a raspberry.
"Hell, I saw better'n that in that *Terminator* flick.
Who'd they think they're shitting?"

"I nearly *got* it," Lafarge repeated.

Which gives me a better sense of your *priorities,*
Carmaggio thought. The warnings about biological
weapons had been real enough, but if this character
got a chance to off Ms. Ingolfsson, he'd go for it.

"And I learned that it has already begun bio-bombing," Lafarge said.

"She *what*?" Carmaggio said, freezing with the beer halfway to his mouth. He felt his stomach twist and sweat break out on his forehead.

I am getting fucking sick of this sensation.

"Launched a biobomb. Not a lethal one; aimed at fertility. It probably feels the planet is overpopulated. Which it is, but that's no excuse for . . . never mind. I checked. Numbers of third and fourth births have started dropping all over the Earth, in the last two years. The pattern indicates an initial aerosol seeding at major airports in 1997, every continent, followed by rapid spontaneous spread. At a guess, it's a modified rhinovirus—common cold."

"It *sterilizes* people?"

"Women. After the second birth, for about seventy, eighty percent. Most of the rest after the third, and a very small percentage would be naturally resistant. It works by sensitizing the immune system so that it treats spermatic cells as foreign matter. Very subtle, by your standards. Nothing visibly wrong with the ovulation cycle, and the eggs could be fertilized *in vitro*."

"Urk." Henry finished the beer. He had been a fourth child himself. "Wait a minute; virtually nobody has more than a couple of kids these days. Except the Amish, maybe."

"Not here, but this virus is spreading *everywhere*. In areas with high infant mortality, population growth could go into reverse in a few years."

There was a choked sound from the other side of the table. Henry looked up sharply; Jesus had turned a muddy shade of gray, and his grip on the edge of the table was turning his fingernails white and pink. *Wait a minute*, the older policeman thought. *Yeah, he and the wife were planning on more kids.* He looked away for a moment; there were times when a man needed privacy.

"Now you see what we're dealing with," Lafarge said. "Something that looks at humans as domestic animals—or as wild game to hunt for pleasure."

"Yeah," Henry said carefully. The flush faded from his ears. He'd *known* this sort of thing for a while now, but for some reason that news brought it home. "You okay, Jesus?"

"*Sí*," Jesus said tightly. "I think."

"Goddam," Henry said. *We're probably going to have to go for a straightforward attack.* The risk was insane, but so was waiting.

"Well, if you'll excuse me," he said. Amazing how the rituals of daily life continued. "I've got to get some sleep today; hard night's work ahead tomorrow. *And* I've got a date."

Lafarge reached out and touched his arm. That was extremely rare with the Samothracian; Carmaggio stopped.

"Is that Miss Feinberg you're speaking of?" Henry nodded. "I don't want to . . . Please be extremely careful."

"Yeah, I won't let anything drop."

"Not just that. Nobody who's been in the *drakensis*'s presence for more than a few hours can be completely trusted. The dominance mechanisms . . ."

Carmaggio freed his arm with a slight jerk. "Thanks," he said flatly. "I'll certainly keep that in mind."

"And here's the list of subcontractors and component manufacturer's it's dealing with."

CHAPTER SEVENTEEN

Gwen looked down from the newly-installed overhead office, onto the floor of the warehouse, through air thick with a haze of dust. It was a maze of cables and sections of equipment now; her nose caught the heavy scents of ozone from arc-welders, smells of metal and oils and plastics, underlain with sweat and the omnipresent gasoline stink of the city. Behind her were several thousand feet of pastel-colored post-modernist office space, plus a suite for herself and rooms for staff and guards; all nearly complete.

Very different from the dusty abandonment she'd smelled that first night here. She remembered dropping into the midst of the humans and growled slightly.

The contractor looked at her and frowned. Gwen schooled her features and nodded at him to continue.

"Ms. Ingolfsson, I can build this," he said, tapping the computer screen, "but I'm damned if I know what it'll do."

Much of it was completely beyond local theory; and there were gaps in the CAD data, elements that were being hand-fabricated by Singh and Mueller down in the Bahamas.

Haven't these people ever heard of the concept "Do as you're told?" she thought. The contractor went on:

"I don't have the slightest idea what it *is*. And you'll need a pretty heavy set of capacitors to energize magnets like that."

She smiled without looking around at him. "Just put it together exactly as specified," she said. "It's . . . experimental equipment. We're planning to surprise the competition."

The man's jacket rustled as he shrugged. "It's your money. What I *can't* do is build it in the time-frame you're asking for."

The man took a half pace backward as Gwen's head rotated around to look him full in the eyes. She controlled herself with an effort, and he relaxed slightly, swallowing.

"Those were your own estimates," she said softly. "Why, exactly, are you changing your mind?"

"Look, ma'am, I'm only the prime contractor here. If subcontractors are willing to pay the penalty clause rather than deliver components to me, I can't send out a goon squad to take the stuff."

Gwen felt her hair rise and bristle, her ears lay themselves back. She forced down the reaction. Who else would be ordering rare-earth alloys in this quantity?

"Why are they willing to do that?" she asked, her voice still a deadly monotone.

"Because somebody else is bidding for 'em. Paying so much above market that it's worthwhile to forfeit. And those components are the bottleneck for the whole . . . whatever it is."

"Exactly," Gwen said dryly. "Well, let my people have the data on the defaulters, and I'll see what can be done. In the meantime, press ahead with the things you *can* do. That's all."

He nodded jerkily. "We'll knock off for the day, then."

Gwen stood, with her feet spread and her hands holding her elbows behind her back. "Dolores will see you out."

"The Samothracian?" Tom asked, when the door closed behind the outsider.

"Possibly. Possibly through a local agent. It's ingenious, in its way; but it smells local. Only the Samothracian could have identified the critical elements, of course, and we'll have to check everything that comes in with redoubled care."

She frowned. "I'm really going to have to have a talk with that man. This is becoming annoying."

Alice cleared her throat: "Another health inspector's notice," she said. The bureaucratic paperwork for having so many of the staff living on-site had turned out to be formidable.

The Draka turned and smiled at her. *Lovely scent she has now,* she thought. Almost as mellow as a *servus*'s. And a beautiful glow to her skin, as if the being within were shining through the human envelope. She patted the woman on the stomach with a surge of protective affection.

"Somebody's harassing us again," Gwen said, taking the paper from her. "Considering the sweeteners we've spread out, somebody with influence . . . or a great deal of money, or both."

Vulk Dragovic came through the door in time to hear her.

"The enemy?" the security chief said.

"Probably. It's a little subtle for one of them, though." She paused. "Again, he could be acting through local agents. I *did* leave a bit of a trail when I first came through, and no doubt he could convince some others. We know he's contacted some of the local police, although not how much he's told them." Another pause. "We'll have to look into that. There are certain obvious leads . . . that policeman, for instance. The computers don't show anything, but that's meaningless with a Samothracian involved. Meanwhile, get this paperwork squared away."

"I'll see to it," the Californian said, with a weary sigh. "It'd be easier on the west coast, or back in the Bahamas."

"Yes, but the signaler wouldn't *work* in either of those places, probably," she said, handing over the form. "Get right on it, Tom. Vulk, have you finished the postings?"

"Yes," the Serb said, jerking a nod. "All approaches covered. There were some difficulties, but the weapons will be within reach, despite the Americans."

Gwen stretched and rose. "Then that's everything for this evening. Go wait for me in the room, Vulk; I'll be having you tonight."

The Serb's darkly aquiline features flushed as he left the room, a combination of hatred and longing. Alice chuckled, with a touch of malice.

"I don't think Vulk likes being the girl," she said with a sly smile.

Gwen stopped for a moment. Then she laughed. "I see what you mean," she said. "Well, he's just lucky it wasn't a male of my species that got dropped through, isn't he?"

She was still laughing and unbuttoning her jacket as she walked through the door.

"You're having all that?" Louisa Englestein said.

"Damned right," Jennifer said.

She speared a french fry with her fork and ate it slowly, then took a bite from the pastrami sandwich, savoring the rich flavors. Chez Laurence *did* have them, if you asked. She hummed a little under her breath.

"Don't tell me," Louisa said. "You got laid."

Jennifer looked at a french fry with an elaborate expression of innocence, then ate it, slowly.

"*No.* Not the Italian cop?"

"Henry. And he's more than an ethnic identifier and a job, you know. He's a sweet guy. And smart."

Louisa rolled her eyes. "*Puh*-leez. Sweet? Oi vey gevalt, this is worse than I thought. Think of what your mother would say."

"Don't be sarcastic. He *is* a sweet guy; not only did he call, but roses, no less, today. Pass the ketchup."

Louisa looked at her. "How long have you been off the diet?" she said.

"A few months—since the Bahamas."

"But you've *lost* weight, I'd swear."

"Twelve pounds," Jennifer said, and patted her stomach. All from the right places, too. "And for once, it wasn't a 'tits go to China, tummy stays' loss, either."

"My god, how did you manage that?"

"My secret," she said, and nibbled on a pickle. "I've been working out more." She had, too—somehow she felt more energetic. "Maybe that's what I needed, fuel."

"So, how did the Bahamas turn out? You had a bad feeling about it."

"Strange. Really strange. Like a visit out of the world, somehow. But the money's there. This is going to be *big*, Louisa."

The pastries came, several of them. Louisa watched incredulously as Jennifer bit into one.

"What was the mysterious Ms. Ingolfsson like?"

"Even stranger. Really forceful personality, and die-you-bitch-die gorgeous. In a very odd way . . . sort of like the most dangerous jock elf you ever saw."

"Oh, come on now, Jenny—in Danielle Steel, maybe, you get gorgeous seductresses starting wildly successful companies and making a mint before they're forty. Even in the romances they're mainly in cosmetics."

Jennifer shrugged. *If you only knew how seductive.* There were some things, however, that you didn't tell even your best friends.

"Every once in a while, truth has to be stranger than fiction," she said.

"Welcome to the Fortress of Solitude," Henry Carmaggio muttered under his breath.

The reception room was empty except for standard office furniture, a stack of used magazines and one of the new voice-recognition computer receptionists. Henry hated them; it was like talking to an answering machine . . . although come to think of it, Lafarge probably had one that could do literary criticism, or even something really difficult like ordering Chinese and making sure the restaurant understood not to add MSG.

"Fortress of Solitude?"

The voice came out of the air. Carmaggio hid a start.

"Local reference," the detective said.

He went through the door behind the desk of the non-existent receptionist and through a corridor flanked by storerooms. Up a flight of iron stairs, and then past a plain bedroom and another, larger space fitted out as a gym. The workroom occupied most of the rear of the building, full of tables and conduits and enigmatic shapes on overhead trackways; Lafarge was bending over a mechanical shape held in a clamp. Something almost familiar lay on a cloth spread across a bench nearby.

"It's a plasma gun," Lafarge said, without looking up from the workbench. "I'm making a number of them."

Henry picked up a finished model, keeping his hands well away from the trigger assembly. It was about the length of a short rifle, with a butt-plate at the rear and a short stubby barrel at the front. He swung it up to his shoulder, and a LCD display just in front of his eye came live. A red dot appeared on the wall, moving as his hands pivoted the weapon.

"This'll bring her down?" he asked.

"Quite effectively. There's a range next door, and a target set up."

Henry took the hint. Lafarge's workroom gave him a mild set of the creeps, anyway. Not that he knew much about laboratory equipment, but he could *recognize* it. A lot of the stuff around him was perfectly ordinary high-tech gear. Among it were . . . differences. Melted-looking apparatus that gave no clue to its function except that things *happened*. One was about the size of an attaché case, with flanged pans on either side. The left-hand pan held an assortment of materials: coins, small ingots, bundles of wire. The pile shifted occasionally, as if bits were disappearing from beneath. Something was forming on the other pan, small and complex and precise.

"It's a faber—a fabricator," Lafarge said, following Henry's eyes. He could do that, somehow, without looking up. "Just a portable model. What I wouldn't give for a full-scale industrial type! As it is, I'm using it for the absolute essentials and relying on local components for the rest. I'll be through here in a minute."

The detective walked through into the long target range. A rack held local weapons, mostly highly illegal; a Barrett .50 sniper rifle, assault weapons, a couple of machine guns, high-capacity handguns. Ammunition was stored below. At the other end of the narrow room was a metal plate, with outlines sketched on it. Human figures, for the most part, and something that looked like a giant baboon with a knife.

He brought the plasma weapon to his shoulder. It balanced remarkably well, easy and precise. That put his eye behind what he'd assumed was an optical sight. Instead it was some sort of video display, very clear. The targets leaped up to within apparent arm's length of him, much more brightly lit than the rather dim background.

"Slick," he muttered. He steadied the red dot on the chest of an outline, and his finger stroked the trigger with remembered gentleness.

CRACK.

Henry sprang back with a yell, almost dropping the weapon. The sound was stunning in the confined space, but it was the flash that startled him, like close-range lightning. He swore and shook his head, pawing at his eyes and blinking at the afterimages and tears. The air stank of ozone and hot metal, a dry angry smell.

"Sorry," Lafarge said from behind him. "I forgot you didn't have implanted protectors. Here."

He held out a pair of goggles, each eye covered by a hemisphere of some nonreflective material.

"Golly gee, Batman," Henry growled. *If he had any sense of humor, I could* resent *that remark.* But he didn't, so presumably he really had forgotten.

The goggles were simply a pressure on his face, utterly invisible from the inside. *Not quite,* he decided after an instant. The ambient light level had gone up. He looked over at the target again, squinting . . . and jerked as the point-of-view rushed toward his focus, steadying at about six inches away. A fist-sized hole had been punched in the metal, the edges still glowing a sullen red with the heat. Something paler showed behind.

"What is that stuff?" he asked.

"An absorbent plastic for trapping solid shot, backed by an inch and a half of titanium steel," Lafarge said. "With a ceramic baffle behind that."

Henry's lips shaped a silent whistle as he looked down at the weapon in his hands. "Shit," he said reverently. "Now, that's *firepower.*"

He swung it up to his shoulder again. *Line-of-sight,* he thought. *That would make aiming dead easy.* "What's the range?" he asked.

"Several kilometers, depending on field-strengths in the vicinity."

"This would make infantry work real interesting," Henry mused. "Watch out."

He fired again. *CRACK.* This time the light was only a bar of brightness across his vision. The recoil was a lovetap, about like a .22 rifle. With this sucker you could snipe out tanks and shoot down fighter jets—no lead-off, striking in an absolutely straight line at the speed of light.

"This is sort of like the gun that Ingolfsson's got?"

"Very like, although a little more bulky. Both twenty-first-century designs, quite basic. I analyzed the impacts from the weapon in Bermuda, and it's an antique. Probably *it* was carrying an old model for sentimental reasons, or as a trophy. I did tell you it's one of the first generation of its kind?"

"Yeah," Henry said.

I just shot a fucking ray gun, he thought. Even now, every once in a while it came up and bit him on the ass.

"How many of these have you got?"

"Half a dozen," the man from the future said. "I can make a few more, perhaps twenty or thirty, in the next few weeks. The bottleneck's the components from my faber, and assembly; I have to do that myself. One torso hit with one of these should kill it. And I'm making some backpack shield generators. They'll offer some defense against its hand-weapon."

"That doesn't solve our basic problem," Henry pointed out, putting the plasma rifle down reluctantly. *One shot to the head. Sigh.* It wasn't that simple.

"I have to get at its systems," Lafarge said. "Here, and in the Bahamas. Simultaneously. To do that, I have to either get the *drakensis* out of its nest and immobilized for at least a few days, or I have to get someone on the inside to plant some devices of my own. With that, I can disarm the trigger system for the biobomb, and then we can kill it."

Henry grinned. "Well, kemosabe, your faithful native sidekick may just be able to help you with that."

Kenneth Lafarge walked through Central Park, his hands in the pockets of his overcoat. The AI scanned again, through the numberless sensors amid the vegetation and life all around him.

no anomalous presences, it said.

I wonder if I'm being foolish? he thought.

Unfortunately, that was not a question the quasisentients made of graven atoms could answer. Knowledge and logic they had, even a kind of consciousness, but neither wisdom nor folly. Those, only the non-algorithmic brains of organo-sentients could produce.

He took a deep breath, cold with the late-spring rains. It brought his attention back from the multiple feed of the nanobugs, like closing a thousand eyes. Even with only his own sight, everything had the laser-cut diamond clarity of the overdrive system laid along his neurons. He could hear the *drakensis* long before he saw it, hear its heartbeat and breathing. When he did see, it was almost shocking. Hardly different from any native human woman, sitting in slacks and roll-necked sweater and long unbuttoned coat. There was a book on the bench beside her.

It certainly looks human now, he thought; then remembered to clamp down on subvocalization.

Gwen cracked another peanut and flicked the kernel at the squirrel. The beady rodent eyes fastened on her suspiciously, and then it darted closer and scurried away with the nut. There was a raccoon not far away, sleepy but interested.

She leaned back and set the bag of nuts on the bench, crossing her ankles and her arms.

"It?" she said to the tall blond man. "It? Come now. I *am* a female hominid, if not exactly the same species as you. Surely I rate a *she*, at least."

He lowered his head slightly into his broad shoulders, motionless and silent as none of the primitives she'd met here could ever be. She enjoyed the sensation of danger for a second, a subtle pleasure, then sighed at his boulder-solid patience. He'd be thoroughly buffered against pheromonal dominance, of course. His scent was as odd as his body language: human, but with overtones of something else. Almost mechanical, in fact.

"Has it occurred to you," she said, after they had studied each other for a moment, "that our little conflict here is a paradigm for the past six centuries? Six centuries of our own history, that is, not this timeline."

He showed his teeth slightly. "It must be frustrating, never being able to get away from us pestiferous Yankees."

"There is that," she said, inclining her head. "But I was mostly commenting on the futility of it all."

His eyes shifted to the book. Wittfogel, *Oriental Despotism*.

"Odd choice," he said.

"You recognize it?"

"I've looked through the literature here."

"Interesting analysis," Gwen said. "Very acute. Nothing like it in our history, that I have data on; although if someone had come up with this back when, my ancestors would probably have killed him. They were an intolerant lot."

His brows rose. "You aren't?"

"We *drakensis* don't need ideology, much; we've got genetics instead. Our social order is hard-coded into our nervous systems." She saw the distaste on his face, an infinitesimal movement of his facial muscles.

"What is there to discuss?" he asked.

"We're neither of us constrained to obey the dictates of our societies," she said equably. "Even Draka have free will, of a sort."

"You're offering to surrender?"

At that she laughed, a clear warm sound. "No more than you, cyber-warrior. Come now, though; you must be an intelligent man. Why should we extend the feuds of our respective peoples here?"

"Duty."

She nodded. "Consider the implications, though. I've been giving this 'many worlds' matter some serious thought. There are a near-infinite number of variations on possible outcomes. Ones where I never came here; ones where you never came here. Ones where half of me got chopped off by the transition phase shift, like poor Wulfa's arm. Ones where I've already won, ones where *you've* already won."

"In other words, there has to be an alternate where every possible outcome occurs. What of it? That doesn't alter the fact that each of *us* has only one world-line to live on and it's the only one we get. The event wave is deterministic in retrospect."

"A point—yet we live in the present, not retrospectively, and anticipate the future. But it's also true that, practically speaking, nothing we can do here will ever affect our home time-line. Considering the physics . . . there has to be a substantial degree of fuzziness, somehow, in any world-line's location in the universe's wave function. You may well not be from *exactly* the same timeline that I am—if exactly has any meaning, in this situation. And if I succeed in building an anchoring beacon, the world-line I contact may be subtly different from the one I left. I'd probably never know for sure."

The Samothracian went very still, even by contrast with his usual state. *Aha,* Gwen thought. *I hit, with that one*. Her hypothesis on the physics must have been correct. That alone made all this trouble worthwhile.

"Interesting," he said at last. "But why set up a meeting to discuss the obvious?"

"Who else is there to talk to?" Gwen said. "The natives?"

He made an angry gesture with his head. "I might have expected you to underestimate them."

"Because they're human? Not in the least. I don't underestimate *you*, I assure you. I assume you've got some of them working under you—"

"*With* me," he corrected.

"—as I do. They're often quite intelligent. They just don't have our knowledge base. Look at the way they're wrecking the planet. It'll be uninhabitable in another century, at this rate."

"Only on a straight-line extrapolation. There are feedback mechanisms already at work to correct the negative trends; there usually are in an open system. Overcontrol is hubris. You snakes were always prone to that."

"A judgment call." She sat up. "Here's my point," she said. "You're here to prevent me from contacting the Domination, correct?"

"That's one of my mission priorities," he acknowledged.

"Well, then," she said, "why not divvy the place up ourselves? Easier on the locals than fighting over it. You get the Western Hemisphere, I get the Old World. That means you control my only access to the Domination timeline; and you can't access the one you came through, I'm pretty sure it's way off-planet."

Lafarge snorted. "You really don't understand humans at all, do you? For all that you exterminated them in the Solar System."

Gwen shrugged and tossed a peanut into her mouth. "My parents were human." She smiled at his slight

shock. "Par*ent*, really. I'm a clone. Yes, I'm that old.
I fought in the Final War; I saw your ancestors leaving
for Alpha Centauri, and wept with envy. . . .

"I'm not human, but my ancestors were; and what
they dreamed, we are. By our natures; but you have
more choices. Which is exactly what I'm offering you:
a choice."

"To let you wipe out humanity on two-thirds of
Earth?"

"Oh, I don't think I'd transform them to *servus*. Not
with unaltered humans around in numbers; it wouldn't
be fair, they couldn't compete, and I can't start up my
own race here in sufficient numbers to protect them.
Besides which, humans are a challenge. Have a peanut? No?"

"No," he said. "This is all a game to you, isn't it?
Moves and counter-moves and prizes."

"Of course," she said. "I'm *four hundred* years old.
Nobody lives that long without gaining a certain degree
of detachment. By the way, there's no reason why you
shouldn't live that long or longer, here. We're beyond
reach of Samothracian law as well as Draka."

He turned on his heel and walked away.

Humans, Gwen thought. "So emotional."

Worth it to get a sense of her enemy. *Strong will.*
She'd expected that, but not quite so much so. She
crumbled a handful of peanut shell, and tossed the nuts
among the squirrels. They squabbled and chattered
over the bounty, tails curled up. A bit rigid, though.
He should have played it out longer, probed for her
weaknesses.

What would I have done if he'd said yes? she wondered. A very low probability . . .

"I'd probably have gone along with it, for a while at
least," she murmured. "Would have been enjoyable."

She cast her mind back, reviewing every episode of
the past few weeks. *I've made some sort of mistake,*

she thought. No definite clue, but the gestalt had been wrong. *Ah*.

A squirrel came close to her feet; she flipped it into the air with a toe and grabbed it in one hand. The tiny heart beat against the skin of her palm, and the little animal squirmed in her grip. She held the tiny face close to hers.

"Be more cautious," she said to it. "It's a dangerous world."

Gwen tossed it underhand. It sailed through the air with its paws spread, landing on a tree about ten meters away; the gray shape clung for a moment, then vanished upward into the branches.

CHAPTER EIGHTEEN

"Dammit, it's my money," Bill Saunders said. "If I want to buy materials you want, that's my business and none of yours."

He glared at the Californian. *Slicker than snot*, he decided. Probably a faggot. Not that he had anything against queers as such, although presumably God didn't approve. There had been one in his company back in Nam who'd been the best hand with an M-60 he'd ever met. He just didn't like this San Franciscan snob. *Who is a traitor.* Not just to the United States, but to the human race.

Tom Cairstens leaned back in the chair across from the desk. "Mr. Saunders—you don't mind if I call you Bill, do you?"

"Yep. I do."

Cairstens's smile didn't falter for an instant. "IngolfTech has done a good deal of mutually profitable business with you. Why endanger it? *You* can't use those components."

"That's proprietary information."

Their smiles were equally false as Cairstens rose to go.

"Name's Laureano, and he runs with the Lords,"

Jesus Rodriguez said. He showed the picture to the barkeeper. "Laureano Gomez. Seen him lately?"

The barkeeper muttered something. It was easy to lose a sound in here; there were probably louder places in East Harlem, but not many. He didn't recognize the group playing, just that it was Puerto Rican, and cranked enough to warp the woofer. *Lot of good talent out there,* he thought. Nice that tight short dresses were back in. That brought a slight stab of guilt. *I'm married, not blind,* he told himself. Lot of very flashy-looking dudes, too. He was a little out of place himself, probably not enough to scream *policía.*

Certainly the boss would stick out if he'd come in himself; there weren't any Anglos here. The smell of sweat and weed was pretty thick, curls of blue smoke drifting up under the ceiling lights. The bartender stared at him silently.

"I can't hear you," Jesus said patiently. "But the health inspectors might."

The barkeeper wasn't the owner, of course, but he wouldn't want to piss him off, either. He jerked his head at a door.

"Stairway's there."

The interior one, at least; somebody might well be watching the outside doors to the aboveground part of the building. There were rooms on the upper floors, hourly and daily rents, real class. He should have backup for this. Instead all he had was the *patrón* and the . . . he didn't even like to *think* about Lafarge. The bartender's hand showed him a key: 613.

He went behind the bar and through the doors, touching one finger to his ear. It wasn't necessary to activate the little button, but it made him feel better, somehow.

"I'm going up," he said, in a whisper that didn't move his lips. "He's in 613."

"Be careful," Lafarge's voice answered. It sounded

like normal conversation, but he knew nobody else could hear a thing. Shit. "There are at least three other people in those rooms."

"I'm always careful," he answered shortly. "*Patrón?*"

"Ready out back," Carmaggio's voice answered.

The stairwell was dark and littered, smelling of urine and ancient dirt. He went up the stairs two at a time, the treads of his shoes making no sound; they looked like dancing leather, but he'd bought ones with composition soles. No sense in slipping at a critical moment. On the sixth floor he took a careful look both ways down the corridor. Nobody, and most of the lights were out. Perfect. He slipped his ID into one hand and the automatic into the other. The door was wood, with an ordinary Yale lock—low security, for New York. He kicked it flat-footed beside the knob, once, twice, and on the third time it flew open.

"*Policía!*" he shouted. "Everybody down, everybody down!"

The girl screamed—they always did. Just the two of them, on the couch, both in their underwear. The man wasn't Laureano—too heavy, a big beefy guy with a wisp of pointed beard. He backed up against the sofa with his hands at shoulder level.

"Hey, chico, no problem. Be cool," he said.

His eyes darted to a chest of drawers by the wall, covered in tossed-off clothes. Probably a piece there, or his stash. The girl was much younger, cowering back on the couch with her hands over her breasts.

"Down, *hijo*. Now."

The man went down. Jesus stooped and cinched his hands behind his back with a set of plastic manacles; great little invention, since you could put them on and tighten them one-handed. The girl stared at him as he went over to the door to the bedroom, standing wide of it.

"Police," he said through it. "Come on out, Laureano.

We just want to talk to you a little, is all, homes. Just a talk. Talk about a lady you met."

Four rounds blasted through the door—and through the outer wall of the suite and probably out through the side of the building, possibly through a couple of civilians on the way. The girl on the couch scuttled out the door on her hands and knees, grabbing bits of her clothing as she went and not wasting any more time on screaming.

"*Shit!*"

He curled back into the angle of the two walls beside the door, the hardest place to bear on from the inside of the bedroom. Two voices whimpered from within: women's voices. And the sound of heavy breathing.

"Man, you in trouble now. Don't make it worse. Come out without the piece and you can still walk away from this."

Bambambambam. Whatever Laureano had in there, it had a high-capacity magazine. And he was trying to hit; this grouping was much closer to the hinge of the door, and him. The prisoner over by the couch gave a yelp and Jesus spared him a quick flickering glance. One of the bullets had drawn a line of blood across his buttocks. The detective grinned. *Mierda.* This could get serious, though. Too many civilians around.

The heavyset prisoner was yelling at Laureano too; mostly insults.

"Shut up!" Jesus called.

He lay down and rolled on his back, inching quietly toward the door feet-first. Knees up, shoulders braced . . . *slam* and his heels knocked it open. He used the same motion to flip himself back up on his feet, automatic in a two-handed grip and pointed at the bed. His mouth opened . . .

. . . and closed as he saw Laureano's naked back vanishing out the window.

"He's on his way down, *patrón*," he said.

"Got him," Carmaggio said in his throat.

A dark shape coming down the rusty iron of the fire escape, into the piles of garbage bags and cans at its base. There was just enough light to see that he was naked; the gun was a black blur in one hand. The sour taste of danger at the back of his mouth was familiar, almost comforting, after the last couple of months. He tucked himself into the doorway, shoulders against the bars that covered the painted-over glass, inhaling the scent of garbage and stale urine. *Eau de Nouveau York*, he thought with a cold smile.

"Freeze; Laureano," he said. Not shouting, but loud and emphatic. "Put the piece down."

Shit! he thought, as fragments of brick spalled into his face. *The little fucker is fast!* The ricochet went *bwanngggg* across the alleyway and struck sparks from something on the other side.

Fast, but not very smart. Feet slapped on pavement, going away. Carmaggio surged out of the doorway, automatic out. He used the old one-handed grip; nothing wrong with the modern two-handed ones, but he stuck with what he'd been trained on.

"Stop!" he shouted, for form's sake.

Crack. The weapon bucked upward in his hand, and the spent shell pinged off iron somewhere to his right. Laureano went over forward as if he'd been hit with a sledgehammer. The detective broke into a lumbering run on the slimy pavement, gun held down. The fire escape rattled as Jesus plunged downward to join him. The gangbanger was down and squeezing his thigh with both hands as if he could force the ripped muscle and broken bone to unite. Both policemen stayed cautious until Carmaggio had toed the weapon aside. *Glock 17*, he noticed.

"Laureano Gomez, you are under arrest," Carmaggio

said, panting slightly. "You have the right to remain silent. . . ."

Actually, he was moaning pretty bad; the blood wasn't pumping the way it would if an artery had been cut, but it was trickling pretty fast. The ambulance should be here soon, though—and he'd have the usual ten miles of paperwork to fill out for a weapons-discharge. Shouldn't be *too* bad, though, what with the way young Laureano had been spraying 9mm from his Glock around. Only one round fired in response, and no fatalities. Speaking of which . . .

"You'd better get back upstairs," he said to Jesus.

"*Sí.* Laureano's friends, they don't like him too much, though. Say he's been acting crazy for the past few days, doesn't do anything but fuck like a bunny and beat up on his women. Also there's a quarter of a key of best-quality rock and some *muy malo* guns up there. Everyone's going to be real cooperative, real public-spirited citizens."

The younger man holstered his weapon and trotted back up the fire escape. A woman came to the exit, holding a bathrobe closed over her chest and peering downward into the darkened alley. When she saw the fallen gangbanger she began to scream Spanish obscenities at Laureano, a shrill counterpoint to the growing wail of sirens. Carmaggio knew enough of the language to follow those—highly imaginative, and mostly directed at the wounded man's putative masculinity.

"Man," the detective said, "I think you're going to be *real* useful."

"Push, Alice. *Push.*"

"I . . . *am* . . . pushing!" the human gasped.

Gwen stood between her legs. Expecting a brooder to deliver lying down flat on her back was one of the more curious local customs, which she had no intention of following. She'd had a proper birthing couch made. Alice lay with her torso up at a forty-degree angle and her legs out in the braces, body slick with sweat and panting like an engine. Her face knotted and the muscles of her swollen stomach rippled as she labored at her task. A shriek and the baby's head slid free of the birth canal. *Good, no complications.* No real tissue damage, no bleeding worth noting.

Gwen's strong fingers helped with the final heaves. Warm water stood by; she sponged the baby clean and wrapped it. The red infant face squalled, and she felt her heart melt with love. "There, my little one," she whispered. "It's all right. We know what you need." Her nostrils flared to take its scent, a clean sharp odor cutting through the heavy smell of human fluids.

She handed the infant to Tom, who held it dubiously while Gwen and Dr. Mueller saw to Alice and helped her into the waiting bed. The baby was crying again, sharp and demanding, craning its neck from side to side—smaller than a human newborn, but a little more coordinated. Reddish fuzz covered its head, and there was a trace of knowledge in the green eyes; the transducer would already have begun to trickle knowledge in, slowly and carefully. Neurons would be forming and knitting into patterns in the newborn brain.

"You can leave us now," she said.

The men left the small bedroom. Gwen put the baby to the brooder's breast; Alice gasped once sharply at the strong tugging, then relaxed with a contented little whimper. There were dark circles under her eyes, but she looked down at the small wiggling form with awed wonder.

"My little cuckoo," she said. She sighed and glanced up at Gwen. "That didn't hurt as much as I expected. It was sort of . . . exciting."

"Give us some credit for improving the process," Gwen said.

The brooder would be full of endorphins, to start

with. And being smaller, a *drakensis* infant did less damage coming out; the hominid pelvis hadn't adapted to the size of head an intelligent being needed, so the genetic engineers had done it the other way round and given the child a longer growth spurt programmed for immediately after birth.

"God, she's hungry."

"Well, she needs more nutrients than a human baby. Remember to take the diet supplements."

Gwen stroked a finger along the velvety cheek of her daughter, feeling the tiny muscles working against the brooder's nipple. *Take what you need, little one*, she thought. *It's a good start on life.*

"She'll sleep more than a human baby too, at first. You'll be up and around in a day or two, and we'll have a couple of house servants to help you with the details."

"I want to look after her," Alice said softly, a dreamy smile of pleasure turning her lips up. "More than anything."

Good old maternal instinct, Gwen thought, bending down to kiss the human's forehead as her eyes fluttered into sleep. The baby gave a small belch and slept as well with limp infant finality, head cradled on the brooder's chest. Newborns of her race triggered that inborn drive even more powerfully than human babies did, most strongly in the brooder but acting on anyone in close contact over time.

Gwen remembered her own brooder with nostalgia. She had never been quite as close to any other living thing.

"No more games," she said quietly to herself, rising and looking down at the pair. There was too much to protect now. She strode out into the feral world, a cold ferocity running through her with a taste like iron and salt.

*   *   *

"Yeah, Bill, I realize he threatened your family. No, we can't go after them right away—but Bill, there's some stuff you ought to see at the Fortress of Solitude. We may have to move soon. Meet you there, okay? Okay."

Carmaggio turned away from the phone and back down the corridor, dodging people and sipping at the lukewarm, oily-bitter coffee in the Styrofoam cup. It tasted about as bad as his mouth, badly in need of a morning toothbrush. For that matter, he could use a shave. *Have to take care of that.* He had the stuff in his locker, the precautions you learned after twenty years of irregular hours.

The interrogation room was plain and simple—one shaded overhead light, a deal table, some recording equipment carefully switched off, and chairs; it smelled of disinfectant, sweat and old cigarettes. Laureano was in orange overalls now, sitting sullen and resentful across the scarred deal surface, still in the hospital wheelchair. The bullet hadn't done more than chip the bone, fortunately. It would be a good while before the gangbanger was doing any sprints, but he could talk.

Luckily he hadn't asked for a lawyer, yet. Jesus was chatting, doing the good cop, offering coffee and cigarettes. Carmaggio came into the room with a carefully brutal expression on his face, and tossed his jacket over the back of a chair. That let Laureano have a good look at the piece that'd shot him.

"Laureano, you little motherfucker, you are in deep, deep shit," he said, turning the chair around and sitting down with his arms braced on the back. "We've got you on trafficking, we've got you on possession of stolen goods—you really ought to've filed the serials on those guns—assault, attempted homicide, on two police officers yet and in front of multiple witnesses. Incidentally, your fat friend Cesar is singing like he was on MTV. He don't like you so much anymore. According to him, he's an angel and you're the turd of turds."

"Hey, Lieutenant," Jesus said. "You don't have to come down hard on Laureano that way. He's not a bad guy."

"Not a bad guy for a pimping, crack-selling little shit who tries to blow cops away," Carmaggio said, enjoying himself. It wasn't often you got the opportunity to be completely truthful, and in a good cause.

Laureano recoiled slightly in his wheelchair, then flinched as it sent a stab of pain through his wounded leg. He was good-looking in a raffish sort of way, but there was a haunted look in his eyes that Carmaggio suspected had little to do with his wound or being in a police station, neither of which were new experiences for him.

"I want my lawyer," he said. "You gonna charge me, you got to give me a lawyer."

Both the policemen smiled. *Yup*, Carmaggio thought. *We would.* Good thing this was the late nineties; a decade or so before, they'd have had to use the juvenile system on little Laureano. Occasionally, legal changes did make things easier on the cops. Not often, but occasionally.

"Hey," Jesus said. "Did we say we were going to charge you?" He turned to Carmaggio. "Lieutenant, we don't really want to charge this guy, do we?"

"Oh, I don't know," Henry said. "Cute young chicken like this, he'll be real popular in stir once they put him in with the general population. He'll be the belle of the ball. Wouldn't want to deprive him of the experience of being sought-after."

That brought a reaction; more of one than Henry had expected. The young Puerto Rican was grimacing, clutching the arms of his wheelchair, sweating until Henry could smell the rank whiff of it. *Not normal.* Hardcases like this were in and out of juvie and then stir all their lives. Laureano had probably done his first killing around the time he lost his cherry. Prison wasn't more than a minor threat.

Jesus brought a cup of water from the cooler. "Here, *chico*, take this. C'mon, you'll feel better."

"I'm no sissy," Laureano said. "Don't you call me no sissy."

"Sure," Henry said. "You're a real man, *muy macho*. That's why you and your friends let a woman kick your ass up by Riverside last month."

Carmaggio tossed a glossy of Gwendolyn Ingolfsson across the table, a take from the prospectus Primary Belway Securities was putting out. The picture spun and settled before the gangbanger's eyes. *That'll probably get a reaction.*

Henry jerked back in surprise as Laureano screamed and tried to leap out of the wheelchair and across the table. The attempt failed as the wounded leg buckled beneath him; he caught at the edge of the table and screamed again as his weight fell against it, this time with pain.

"What the hell's going on in here?"

Captain McLeish broke through the door, watching as Henry and his partner levered the gray-faced suspect back into his wheelchair. His eyes narrowed.

"Carmaggio, that rubber-hose crap doesn't hold up in court, or hadn't you noticed."

Henry rose and dusted off his hands. "Laureano here just got a little excited," he said soothingly. "Neither of us laid a finger on him."

"He bleeding?"

"Nope, just jarred the wound a bit when he tried to get out of the wheelchair. No problem."

Carmaggio let the false smile slide off his face as the door closed behind his superior.

"All right, enough dicking around," he said. Laureano was hunched in the chair, eyes squeezed shut. "Talk, you little shit."

As McLeish had pointed out, beating confessions out of suspects was an exercise in futility, besides being a bad thing in itself. Any halfway decent lawyer could rip your balls off in court if you did anything remotely resembling the old third degree. On the other hand, they weren't trying to get Laureano to confess to a crime himself . . . and even the most modern practice didn't say they had to make him feel good.

"That wasn't a woman," Laureano said in a controlled hiss. "You believe me, it wasn't no woman. It just *looked* like a woman, maybe it was a *bruja*, I don't know, some sort of robot thing. José, he . . . She grabbed his gun and *killed* him with it, man, she just turned it around in his hand and blew his brains out. And she killed all the others, and she . . ."

Laureano put his face in his hands and began to sob. "I couldn't *stop* it, man, I couldn't do *anything*, I couldn't *stop* it, she just kept *doing* it and every time afterwards I touch a woman I see *her* and—"

Carmaggio looked away, embarrassed. Nobody should be stripped like that, not even a noxious little vermin like Laureano. Jesus was patting him on the shoulder, lighting his cigarette; he tossed his head toward the door.

Time for the Bad Cop to take a powder, Carmaggio thought, tripping the *record* switch and quietly slipping out of the room. The last thing you wanted to do was distract a talker once the dam had broken. He strongly suspected that this was the first time Laureano had said a word about his little out-of-this-world encounter on the mean streets. *And speaking of taking a powder . . .* Certain things reminded you of your age, and one of them was the bladder. He grinned at his reflection as he dried his hands. A signed, witnessed statement from Little Laureano the Alien's Pet, and they'd have a murder rap to pin on Ms. Ingolfsson. They might not be able

to make it stick, of course; they might not even be able
to hold her long. Riker's wasn't designed for superhuman
time-travelers.

But long enough would do. He remembered the
solid heft of the plasma rifle that Lafarge had made.
In, out, job done. Time enough to worry about the
consequences afterward. Henry Carmaggio had always
paced himself by the task at hand, anyway.

He was just outside the door to the interrogation
room when the first scream began. Not a long one, just
a sharp agonized grunt. Henry flipped the door open
and slammed it behind himself.

"What the fuck—"

Jesus had been sitting on the edge of the table,
leaning forward sympathetically. He put a hand on
Laureano's shoulder when the prisoner doubled over
with a squeal of pain.

The second scream was louder, and much longer.
Laureano reared up out of his chair, clutching at his
stomach. His eyes bulged, whites showing around the
rims. Henry started forward, and met an arching spray
of blood from the open mouth. Together the two
policemen caught the slumping, thrashing figure and
lowered it to the floor. The shriek coming out of the
gaping mouth was continuous and as nerve-shredding
as a nail across a blackboard. Blood spattered, in their
faces, on the walls, drops arching as high as the ceiling in slaughterhouse profusion.

Henry grabbed for the young man's chin, trying to
stabilize the mouth so he could see where the hem-
orrhage was coming from. It jerked in his blood-
slippery hand as the whole body arched and flailed. A
hand caught him alongside the head, stunning him. The
chin slid out of his hand, and Laureano bent until only
his heels and head were touching the ground. The
detective bored back in, shaking off the ringing in his
head, but before he could touch the prisoner the whole

body went limp with a boneless finality and fecal smell that were all too familiar.

"Dead," he said. "Son of a *bitch*. What—"

The dead man's head lolled. Something moved on the tongue, something that walked on six dainty legs and lifted a metallic head into the light. The dead mouth yawned wide, and a stream of them poured out over lips and teeth in a final gout of blood. One skittered forward, and Henry threw himself back with a shout of loathing, landing on his buttocks halfway across the room. His gun was in his hand, but there was nothing he could shoot at, nothing at all—and Jesus batted at one of the little monstrosities with an equally unthinking reflex.

"*Cristo!*" the younger man shouted.

Something glittering clung to his palm. He shouted again, pain in his tone, and slammed the hand down on the table. The shout turned into a scream when he lifted it again; the head of the *thing* that had killed Laureano was burrowing into his flesh. The legs waved, gripped, pushed.

Carmaggio felt his mind go cool and detached. He scrambled sideways towards the chair with his jacket, only taking time to come to his feet when another slick-black shape scuttled across the worn boards of the floor. His left hand dove into the inner pocket of the jacket, took out the button-sized black thimble and jammed it into his ear.

"Lafarge! Christ, we're under attack, *get moving*. Little things like bugs, they killed Laureano—"

"Coming."

Henry danced sideways like a bear on a hotplate as a metallic bug skittered toward his foot. He came down with all the weight of his two hundred pounds on his heel, and there was a *crunch* sound and a fat blue spark. He yelled himself as he tottered back; even through the thick leather he could feel the heat, and there was a circular scorchmark on the floor the size of a demitasse.

"Stop that, you're just driving it in like a nail," he shouted at Jesus.

He caught the younger man's hand and shoved the edge of his pistol-barrel against the thing chewing its way into his partner's flesh. Something snagged at the weapon. Tiny legs, clawing for a hold. He twisted hand and gun towards the wall and pulled the trigger.

Crack. The discharge was much louder in a closed room than outdoors. Chunks of plaster flew from the outside wall; there was brick behind that, thank God, and no ricochet either. Tiny bits of metal spattered the wall behind the bullet. Jesus snatched his injured hand away and hugged it to his stomach, cursing. He staggered and nearly fell. Carmaggio grabbed him under the armpit.

"Christ, watch it, there are more of them!"

"Coming fast. Hold on."

"Hold on my *ass*," Carmaggio barked.

The camcorder mounted on the table went up in a shower of sparks and smoke. Tiny shapes climbed out on the ruined casing, waving their feelers in triumph. More scuttled across the floor. The two detectives went back-to-back, kicking frantically.

Gwen opened her eyes. The transmission was a meaningless buzz to her transducer, but the origin . . .

samothracian patterns, the instrument said.

"Damn," she said mildly, cutting her link with the creatures inside the building above.

It wouldn't do at all to have her transducer open like that when Citizen Lafarge showed up. A pity; it would have been satisfying to finish them all off, but she'd made a good start.

The Draka pushed off from the wall of the police station and strode away down the street, whistling quietly and enjoying the mild spring air. For once New York didn't stink quite so badly, which was a relief. *I think I'll take a turn in Central Park.* Not too far away, and a place to rest her eyes.

At the corner she looked over her shoulder and smiled. They were probably *quite* unhappy, back in there.

They've stopped.

For one long second the crawling things hesitated. Then they turned and retreated; through the spreading film of blood from Laureano's corpse, into the baseboards, down through cracks in the flooring. Carmaggio staggered as the vise released his chest; he felt an insane giggle forcing its way up his throat. He straightened up out of his crouch and tried to reholster his pistol. That took several tries. Jesus was still glaring and waving his, with his hand dripping onto the floor half-covered with the prisoner's blood and fluids.

"I think they've stopped," Henry said.

He still jumped at a rustle, but it was only a fragment of tape going *thack* against the ruined recording machine as it spun. When the door burst open he jumped again, then stopped stock still with his hands in plain sight.

Captain McLeish was there, with half a dozen uniforms. They all had their automatics out, trained on him and Jesus.

"Freeze! Freeze right there!" McLeish bellowed. His gun jerked to follow Jesus's movements, and the younger detective laid his own weapon down with elaborate care.

McLeish looked down at Laureano's body. "Shit on fire, Carmaggio," he said softly. "I didn't think even *you* would pull something like this right in the precinct house."

*   *   *

"That videotape saved your *ass*, Carmaggio," Captain McLeish said.

"Yessir."

Henry watched Laureano die again, watched Jesus and his own image dance around the interrogation room while the body flopped like a gaffed fish. His mouth felt papery dry at the sight, at the memory that came flooding back like a great wave crashing over a seawall and sweeping away men and the works of men. The grainy image was too coarse to show the *thing* crawling out on the dead man's tongue. That was something to be thankful for.

"That and the autopsy. So you didn't shoot the little spic. Not unless one of your bullets has teeth and burrowed from his asshole out his throat, chewing its way along. But you did it somehow. I've known for years there's something weird about your and your faithful fucking Tonto too. If Internal Affairs doesn't pin this on you, I will—one way or another."

At any other time, that might have been a serious threat. Carmaggio stared sightlessly at the pictures on the Captain's walls. The words bellowed at him were no more real, *less* real than the politicians and their smiles.

"You're on suspension—your badge and gun stay *here*, motherfucker. And that goes for your partner, when they let him out of the hospital. Don't think you can go whining to the union. You had a suspect die on your hands. Don't try the press, either, or you'll regret it even more."

"No, sir," Henry said tonelessly.

Badges belonged to the old world, where metallic insects didn't burrow through men's flesh, eating them out from the inside. Right now that was the least of his worries. A gun he could get anytime he needed one. Last night he'd half-seriously considered putting one in his mouth, just for an instant.

"Get out of here, and don't come back until we call you. Get out of this building, get out of my life."

"Yessir."

He walked numbly out of the office, over to his own, went through the motions of getting the essentials out of his desk and responding to the bewildered sympathy of his friends.

Then his hands stopped. *Jenny.* Christ, it'd been bad enough before. And she was *working* with the thing who'd sent the . . . things.

"I've got to get her away from there."

CHAPTER NINETEEN

"What's the matter with you, Henry? You'd think I was taking you to an execution, not a party."

"Yeah, well . . . I've been sort of nervous lately."

"I know," Jennifer said quietly, and put a hand on his arm.

He'd told her that Laureano died in a fit. The papers had that much; what was more, she'd believed him without a moment's hesitation. The *Post* was hinting darkly at conspiracies. . . .

If they only knew, he thought, as the taxi passed 61st and pulled up in front of the hotel. A doorman hustled out with an umbrella.

He bit back a silent whistle as they went into the lobby. *Upper East Side with a vengeance,* he thought, jarred a little out of his introspection and welcoming the distraction from the icy bile taste of fear. An Art Deco space, full of evening dress and furs as the guests arrived for the reception in the upper ballroom. Brass, cream-colored marble, and bowing flunkies everywhere.

"Come on, it won't be so bad," Jennifer teased gently. *No, it wouldn't, if it was only social stress anxiety,* he thought. Right now he felt like one of the guys in those old stories, going into a monster's den with only a bronze sword, and smelling the rot of those who'd tried before. There *was* a monster waiting for him. He had backup—the black button deep in his right ear— but it was still as dangerous as anything he'd ever done.

Everything okay? he asked subvocally, as they walked up the curving staircase.

Standing by, Lafarge whispered. In theory Ingolfsson shouldn't be able to eavesdrop; the Samothracian's equipment had been designed to evade detection back on her home world, where the Draka had every sort of equipment. That was *some* comfort.

He shook loose his shoulders as they walked into the ballroom; no point in shouting how tense he was. His eyes took in the crowd with a jumping, flickering intensity. Financial types; he'd gotten more familiar with them since he'd become involved with Jenny. Old-fashioned portly ones, often with trophy wives several decades junior. Younger ones, male and female, lean and hungry-looking. Hangers-on from the Wall Street equivalent of the *paparazzi*.

"Why, if it isn't Jenny and her new friend," a voice said.

Time seemed to freeze as he turned. The voice was like nothing he'd ever heard, like a musical instrument with an undertone of vibrating bronze. She was taller than him, long-limbed and supple. The face he remembered from the pictures, but *alive*, it seemed to glow somehow from within, more alive than anyone else. Leaf-green eyes narrowed in mocking amusement, full of an ancient, innocent evil. Meeting them was a palpable shock, a physical tingling that ran down to gut and scrotum. Overlaid on it was the memory of insects vomiting out of a dead man's mouth.

He took the offered hand automatically. She smiled as she squeezed. Just enough to hurt a little; it was like having your hand in a velvet-padded clamp of braided metal wires.

"I've been looking forward to meeting you," she said.

"Yeah, I bet you have, Ms. Ingolfsson," Henry said.

"Gwen," she said. "Any friend of Jennifer's . . . And there's every reason we should cooperate to our mutual benefit."

Jennifer was looking from one to the other. "Is there something I should know about?" she said, with a little sharpness in her tone. "Have you met?"

"No, no," Gwen said. "I *have* heard of Mr. Carmaggio, of course. And now I have to run. Enjoy yourselves."

Carmaggio drew a deep breath as she walked away, conscious of how his palms were wet and how sweat was trickling down his flanks.

"A bit overwhelming, isn't she?" Jennifer chuckled.

"You could say that," Henry replied grimly. "Jenny, there *is* something you should know. My place afterwards?"

"Sure," she said, looking after Gwen with a thoughtful frown.

I hope it wasn't a mistake bringing Henry here, Jennifer thought, as she drifted off to circulate. She *had* to go—it was a business reception, when you came right down to it—and she was damned if she was going to look like she was ashamed to be seen with him. Particularly now, with that horrible thing happening to him at work. But he did seem nervous. Even if he looked adorable in a tux.

It was a relief to break out into the ballroom, decorated in a fantasy of peacock feathers and draped silk along the walls. The usual mill-and-swill, with a buffet along one wall, and the other was windows looking out on Central Park to the west. The mood was good, the launch had been a success beyond expectations. She frowned. *Beyond all reasonable expectations.* The way Lather Enterprises had jumped in was ridiculous; they'd had to split two-for-one right in the middle of things. *Talk about overallotment.*

She nibbled at things from the trays, sipped at a glass of Chardonnay, drifted and talked. A hour found her behind a piece of dreadful modern sculpture, out of sight and sound of the rest of the party.

"Well, hello," a voice purred behind her.

She turned, feeling an unaccountable looseness in her knees. *Damn, how does she do that?* Gwen was leaning one arm against the wall.

"I was starting to think you were avoiding me on the 'road show,'" she said. "Three weeks of touring, and hardly a word."

"Ah—" Jennifer hesitated. *I was avoiding you, of course.* "Well, we were all so busy."

"Tell me about it," Gwen said. She chuckled. "And then I thought your SEC would *never* declare the registration statement effective, not to mention the problems with the final prospectus. I thought this was a capitalist country?"

"You wouldn't think so, would you, sometimes."

A silence fell, evidently much more comfortable for Gwen than for her. Jennifer felt her skin itch, as if the room had suddenly gone up ten degrees and brought out a sweat. *Oh, God. Nobody else affects me this way. It's not fair!*

Gwen took a sip from her goblet, breathed the heavy, fruity scent of the brandy. Her head arched to one side slightly, with a play of tendons in her neck.

"All's done, though," she said. "You know, I don't have any murals here, but I do have some fascinating etchings."

Jennifer was excruciatingly conscious of the hangings brushing against her back and calves. She gulped for air. "Ah, that is—God, please—I don't want—"

Gwen swayed back. "Well, there's always tomorrow," she said, not unkindly. "You'll find I'm extremely good at getting my way. Good job on the papers to the bank syndicate." She fished in a small, elegant belt-pouch. "And if you reconsider over the next few days, do drop by—here's the admission code."

Jennifer slumped back against the wall as she left, fighting for calm. *What's* happening *to me?*

Damn, Carmaggio thought, repressing a start as Gwen came up to one side of him. *How does she do that? And in heels?*

"I place my feet down instead of tapping them the way you humans do," Gwen replied. "Steel can touch steel without sound, if you put them together without enough impact to start harmonics."

Carmaggio began humming soundlessly in his throat, hunching his head down into his shoulders and glaring. Ingolfsson stood hipshot, one hand holding the snifter and the other on her belt. That reminded him painfully of the fact that there was no belt holster at the small of his back. All things considered, it would have been nothing but a security blanket here, but that wasn't to be despised. *God, what a mantrap,* he thought. If you liked jockettes; not an ounce of spare tissue, except the smooth curve of breasts under the creamy silk. She reminded him of the old story about the statue that had come to life; you just couldn't look away from her. *I wonder what the impact would be like without the phero-mone blockers Lafarge gave me?*

Her nostrils expanded slightly for an instant. "Ah, I see our mutual Samothracian friend has been taking precautions with you—it dulls your scent. *And* makes life less pleasant than it might be. You people are scent-blind enough, without making it worse."

"I prefer to be my own man, thank you," Henry said

quietly, bracing himself against the force of personality that blazed out at him, as he might have against a physical wind. "And this isn't your place."

"Your own? Or the Samothracian's?"

She raised a slim eyebrow, the movement as coolly precise as everything she did. Habits of observation quirked at him. *She's got no tics,* he realized. *No waste movement. Nothing that isn't to a purpose or deliberate.* It made him feel heavy and clumsy and old, like some dirt-stained *cotadino* in the old country stumbled into a country-house ball.

"Have you," she went on, "ever considered that you might have been sold a bill of goods as to our relative merits? I doubt you'd find Samothracian society very pleasant either, you know."

Henry nodded jerkily. "He isn't trying to take us over. And he hasn't killed anyone here."

"He killed one of my guards, in the Bahamas," Gwen said reasonably. "He'll kill any number of you to get at me. A bit of a fanatic, don't you find? And no sense of humor at all."

Henry thrust down doubts. *She cannot read my mind.* "You've left a trail of bodies from the day you arrived. I'm a cop; it's my job to catch people like you— even when they aren't people."

"Will anyone miss Marley Man and his posse?" Gwen asked.

"You're not the courts. And there's Fischer, God knows how many others."

"Ah, well, that's war for you. You had a war of your own, didn't you, Detective Carmaggio? Didn't any bystanders get killed in that one?"

Henry felt sweat trickling down into his collar. "You're going to be stopped."

"Everyone's the hero in their own story, Lieutenant," Gwen said, smiling and shaking her head. "Think. This might be *my* story—in which case, I'll win, and you are a minor character." She paused, considering. "I *will* win. I've lived nearly half a thousand years, human, and I always *do* win. Don't sacrifice the few years you have smashing your glass against my iron."

He stayed silent. She nodded. "Yes, I can understand what Jennifer sees in you. Pity if she were hurt, wouldn't it?"

Carmaggio flushed. Then a movement caught his eye. *By God,* he thought. *That's* Captain McLeish, *by God!*

"Yes, a number of you have seen the . . . wisdom of cooperating with me. I could use someone like you in my . . . organization."

He looked into the clear green eyes. "I've done some, ah, questionable things, in my time," he said with quiet finality. "But I've never been on the pad."

She shrugged and turned. "Your choice."

Shaking, Carmaggio emptied his drink. *One more,* he thought. *Then we're out of here. Enough secrecy. Jenny has a right to know what she's facing.*

Even if it scared her shitless and risked her life.

Carmaggio's apartment was new territory to Jennifer. She'd assumed that was for the usual bachelor reasons; terrible housekeeping, for starters. Instead it was extremely tidy, in a ruled-off way, probably the result of weeks of intensive effort. The smell of wax and cleaner certainly hinted at that. Larger than hers too, although of course it was on Mulberry north of Canal, not the Upper West Side. She looked around as Henry struggled with their coats in an overstuffed closet. A couple of pictures, mostly photos. Family shots, and Henry as a young man stiff and self-conscious in uniform. Quite a few books, looking well-thumbed. A good computer off in a nook by the living room, with a rack of CD-ROMs beside it. A peek into the bedroom showed a folded exercise machine in one corner.

"Henry, there's something I should tell *you*," she began slowly, coming back toward the hallway. *I hate confessions.* How did Catholics do them all the time?

Henry smiled. "Not quite yet, I think. *Activate.*"

On the kitchen table lay a black rectangle the size of a business card. When he spoke, a twisting column of light appeared above it—a three-dimensional image, looking like an impossible moving sculpture of liquid.

"I—what *is* that?"

"I don't really know myself," Henry said. She looked over at him, feeling her eyes go wide. "But it's got some interesting qualities."

He spoke to it again. An image of Gwendolyn Ingolfsson appeared over the table: life-size, nude, and utterly indistinguishable from reality, except that it neither breathed nor moved.

"*Shit!*" Jennifer shouted, and scrambled backward.

She lurched into a chair and tottered, arms windmilling. Carmaggio leaped forward and caught her. An urge to push him away fought with an equally strong desire to cling, until all she could do was stand and shiver. After a while the blackness receded from her eyes.

"Wha . . . what *is* that?"

"Jenny." She turned and looked into his face. "Until you went to the Bahamas, I didn't have any proof—just some suspicions. And then I couldn't tell you because it'd put you in danger. You've got to understand that first. Understand?"

Jennifer shook herself. *Think, you cow,* she told herself. "I . . . I think so. What does it *mean?*"

Carmaggio took a deep breath. "Okay," he began.

"Pheromones?"

Jennifer stared at the skeleton the impossible machine was showing, rotating slowly to give an all-around view. She remembered more than enough of her premed

studies to know that the *skeleton* was impossible, too.
The flanged bones, the high-leverage double-acting
joints, the too-large nasal and ear cavities . . .

That isn't a human being. That isn't a human *being*.

"Yeah, pheromones, supercharged variety. Lafarge
says they can play games with your head."

"Oh, my *God*," Jennifer said. She put a hand to her
mouth. "Oh, my God, I went to *bed* with—"

Suddenly she was up and running, struggling to hold
back the bitter-tasting bile. Remembering fever-hot skin
tasting of cinnamon and salt, weight that crushed out
her breath, a growling chuckle in her ear. Vomit
splashed into the bowl as she knelt, heaving and retch-
ing uncontrollably; the raw physical misery was a relief,
crowding thought away. When she was finally conscious
of something else, it was Carmaggio standing beside
her with a towel and damp facecloth.

"Here," he said, helping her clean up. "C'mon, sit,
get your head down a little, try this."

She washed her mouth out with water and then took
a sip of the brandy, sitting on the edge of the bathtub and shivering. A hand rubbed her back and she
leaned into it gratefully.

"Don't sweat it," he said gently. "You're not to
blame."

"That's just *it*," she said roughly and took another
swallow of the brandy. "I thought I was seduced, and
I was *drugged*, I was *raped*—and I didn't even know
it. I was an accomplice!" She set the glass down carefully. Remembered words fell into place with little
mental *click* sounds. "The bitch, the bitch, she was
laughing at me all along. Laughing. I want her *dead*."

"Well," said Carmaggio, and put his arm around her
shoulders. "Yeah, that's the option we've been looking
at, actually."

"I think we have something!" Mueller exclaimed. The

words echoed through the huge empty spaces of the warehouse.

It was brightly lit now, with banks of overhead fluorescent lights; the interior was painted white, including the surfaces of the windows. Armed guards stood at intervals on catwalks around the upper interior walls, and another spanned the arch of the building. Below was the great circular ring of the fusion generator, man-high and twenty meters in circumference. Lying within that was another ring almost as large, smooth enigmatic metal with heavy fiber-optic cable junctions at its four corners. The air held a heavy electrical smell, overlain with new paint and hot metal.

The German scientist was standing at a console on the warehouse floor. Above in the glassed-in control chamber Gwen twitched her ears forward to pick up his voice, then glanced over at the display monitors.

"I think you're right," she said. "Get—"

CRACK.

The noise was deafening even here in the control chamber. The tragus clamped automatically across the opening of her ears to protect the sensitive inner mechanisms. Humans screamed down on the floor, clutching their hands to either side of their heads.

From within the center of the inner ring a thread of light too intense to see speared upward, cutting through the roof with hardly even a spark as the steel flashed into its constituent atoms and the atoms were stripped to ions. It was *thinner* than a thread, Gwen realized as she flung up a hand and glanced away, blinking at the line of darkness scored across her sight. She opened the door and stepped out onto the new metal of the catwalk, past a Haitian bawling in panic and fumbling with his heavy Barrett .50 sniper rifle.

Thinner than a thread and utterly rigid. The source was—her mind and transducer did quick calculations— a spot 7.32 meters above the exact center of the inner ring. Head height for her, now that she was out on the catwalk that spanned the transposition circle.

Her breath was fast and heavy; she controlled it, and throttled back the beating of her heart.

Below the thread of energy a spot opened. It swelled outward into a perfect circle a meter wide, and then flashed from silver to transparent.

"Well met," she breathed to the one who stood there. "Glory to the Race."

"Service to the State," Alexis Renston replied. "Sorry for the side effect," he went on, pointing upward to the beam. "Energetic particle byproduct."

The Archon was in a suit of powered infantry armor; it mimicked his form a few millimeters out, flexible as liquid and as strong as anything in the universe, set to a shiny jet-black at the moment. Molded lumps and protrusions told of engines concealed within, and weapons deadly enough to savage whole cities. It slid from face and hands as he tilted his head back slightly to take in Gwen, then glanced around at the interior of the warehouse. Behind him she could see others, and the hulking hyena-ape forms of ghouloons. The background was Reichart Station, but the forest beyond it had been cleared and the surface smoothed. Machines rested on it, waiting, and more hovered in the sky. The heavy iron was ready.

"I see you haven't been idle," the Archon said.

"Nor have you," she said.

There was a *servus* off to one side, operating some equipment. *Ah, Tolya.* The *servus* physicist looked . . . *younger.* Well, she deserved the ultimate reward.

datadump, she commanded her transducer. There was a barely subliminal hum along her nerves as it sent/received data at a rate far too high for conscious reflection. But it would be there, and here, when needed.

"Timeframe?" she went on, while the machines spoke to each other.

"This molehole is barely at the atomic scale," Renston said. "Proof-of-concept. Scaleup is proceeding rapidly and shouldn't present any problems, provided you keep the beacon in operation. Planetary Archon Ingolfsson," he added. They both wolf-grinned at the essential clarification of status.

"News?"

"The Samothracians attacked, with moleholes in place. We stopped them, but only just. We're making excellent progress on our own moleholes for interstellar travel."

"Gravitational effects . . . slipslide?"

"Exactly. Deeper into the solar gravity well than the Oort, and you go sideways. Very high energy costs, too."

"Acknowledged. I suggest we break off until you can establish full contact. The situation here's a little delicate; the enemy sent an operative through. He'll detect the spike . . . even the *natives* will detect it, and that could be awkward."

"Confirmed," Renston replied. His eyes had a slightly detached look, that of someone reviewing transducer-linked data. "Ahhh, good hunting there, grandmother."

"Very good. See you soon."

CRACK.

The thread of intolerable light disappeared, leaving nothing but the ringing in her ears and the memory of heat and light. With it went the holographic window. The humans were babbling and rushing about, some screaming or weeping, others exultant. Gwen stood rock-still; she'd have to see to them, but not in this instant of purest joy.

"I'll see you all, my brothers, my sisters," she whispered. "And we shall hunt together, forever."

Across New York, static seared radio and television. Instruments jumped and computers stuttered, data scrambled on electromagnetic disks. And nearly a million eyes saw a spike of intolerable fire slamming into the sky above Manhattan, like a line of blue-white light reaching into space and scoring the face of the moon. For six seconds it hung above the city.

When it ended, darkness fell as overloaded transformers shattered and exploded in fountains of sparks.

"What the *hell*?"

Carmaggio jumped up from the sofa. Jennifer stayed, but turned her red-rimmed eyes around while her handful of Kleenex fell unnoticed to her lap. The apartment lights flickered wildly, and the telephone rang— a single long note that went on and on. The computer in the corner of the living room switched itself on, flashed *system error*, and died. Then the lights followed with an abrupt finality; but the blackness that followed was only partial. An actinic blue-white light lit it, reflected off buildings and through windows. Thunder boomed in the distance.

Jennifer came to her feet. The two humans clutched at each other. For five long seconds the unnatural lightning-light lasted, until true darkness fell.

"What was that?" she asked.

"The end of the world, unless we're very lucky," Carmaggio said.

He fumbled in his pocket and pushed the tiny button into his ear.

" . . . working," Lafarge's voice—or his machine's— sounded. "The enemy has made a breakthrough. It's not a full-scale molehole but we can expect that soon. I'm coming to—"

The door burst open. A man-shape walked through, then lit to cast a background luminescence.

"There's no more time," it said. Glowing material ran like water down its face, revealing Lafarge. "No more time at all."

CHAPTER TWENTY

Work was piling up at the warehouse. There was no more time, and the outer circle of human servants was beginning to suspect something. She'd had to slap one down with a broken skull to get the others into order, of a sort. Gwen's lips lifted from her teeth when her transducer pinged an alarm at the back of her consciousness.

plasma gun discharge, the machine said. **location follows.** The antennas on the roof were big and clumsy, but they worked after a fashion, and the instrument behind her ear could interface with their input.

Gwen snarled, a ripping, guttural sound full of menace. The enemy must have made up a supply of energy weapons—easier for him; he probably had a small faber to do the difficult components. *Ah. Central Park.* Not too far away, and a good enough place to group for an attack. Why the discharge? It could be a trap; on the other hand, it was also likely that a cobbled-together group of hastily trained humans had poor fire discipline.

how many energy weapons? she asked the machine.

well stealthed, it replied. **indeterminate; not less**

than five, not more than thirty of the same class as the discharge.

"Damn," she said aloud. **detection anomalies? neural interfacer traces, possible.**

She couldn't take a chance on those plasma guns getting any closer. This building was shielded and ran off the power from the fusion generator, but that didn't apply to the surrounding neighborhood. A bad fire or brickwork collapsing on the fragile walls could ruin everything. And the Samothracian was with them.

"Listen."

Her humans looked up; it was safer not to make eye contact with a *drakensis* in the mood indicated by the sounds she'd made, unless you had direct orders.

"Vulk," she said briskly. "Get the perimeter out as we planned. The rest of you, Option Orange."

Tom's strained face turned to her. "What's gone wrong?"

"The Samothracian is desperate. He's armed a number of locals with improvised energy weapons, and we have to assume he's coming after us here. I can't allow that; too much danger to the apparatus, even with the shielding. I'll have to take them out. Hold the fort, and it'll all be over soon."

And if not, this planet gets scoured clean by the biobomb, she added to herself. A nuisance; her household were all immunized, of course, but they'd have to evacuate until bacteria took care of the bodies. Seven-million-odd corpses here in New York alone—a severe sanitation problem—not to mention the longer-term damage industrial spills and runaway nuclear power plants would do to the planet.

Needs must. She stripped and began putting on her blacks, while one of Vulk's men brought the backpack shield generator she'd cobbled together.

"Isn't that risky?" Alice asked. Dolores whimpered slightly, subvocally.

"Yes," Gwen said. "But at this stage, the maximum priority is protecting the signaling apparatus. The child comes second, and myself third."

She shrugged into the backpack; with the metal sheathing to protect it from mechanical damage, it weighed about fifty kilograms. A nuisance, but not enough to slow her down significantly.

"Hold the fort," she said, and trotted briskly away.

CRACK.

"Hell," Carmaggio said.

The oak tree toppled away from him, its trunk blasted into splinters by the bolt from the plasma rifle in his hands. The crash echoed through the park, sinking among the treetrunks. Flames licked up and caught, dancing reddish-gold among splintered wood blasted into kindling-dryness by the energy release. The firelight glittered over bodies and goggled eyes, extra brightness to the enhanced vision equipment from out of time gave him.

The others looked suitably respectful. They'd all practiced in Lafarge's shielded firing-range, but this was a lot more immediate.

He pushed the goggles up on his forehead, and night returned. Blacker night than any he'd ever seen in New York. You didn't realize how much ambient glow there was until it was gone; the stars were out over Central Park, a frosted arch across the sky. It was clear enough to see the *colors* of the stars. Quiet, too. A little traffic noise—not much, with the streetlights dead—and plenty of sirens. *A good thing I'm on suspension,* he thought dryly. *Probably lose my badge if I still had it, for not showing up in an emergency like this.* The policeman's part of his mind was shuddering at the thought of what it was like out there, with power down and communications scrambled.

There were about fifty men and women grouped

around him, in the woods just north of the pond and across from Bethesda Fountain. Saunders and his weekend warriors, in camo-patterned Fritz helmets and fatigues, all suited up with Kevlar body armor—much good that would do them. Finch and her boss and some FBI SWAT types. And Jesus Rodriguez and Mary Chen, of course. All with Lafarge's gadgets, shielding and plasma guns; which *would* do some good, and the little ECM pod which was supposed to fool the enemy's instruments into thinking Lafarge was here. He hoped.

Carmaggio took a deep breath of the night air, scented with trees and grass and earth, and now with burning hardwood.

"All right, people," he said. "You all saw that."

He jerked his head toward the Lincoln Tunnel, which was near enough where the spike of fire had thrust into the night sky.

"The bad lady is coming, and we have to hold her here. Otherwise it's all over."

He remembered a running translation he'd heard of a bad Japanese animated feature once—the Admiral up on the screen had talked to the hero for ten minutes, and this guy who knew some Japanese had said: *The fate of the Universe is in your hands, boy. Don't fuck up.*

And Jenny was walking into the tiger's den, with only this diversion to protect her.

"Keep together, keep alert, and don't shoot each other." Another deep breath. "Let's go."

Jennifer felt numb. *I'm a financial analyst, not a spy,* she told herself as she pushed through a panicked crowd in Lafarge's wake. *Financial analysts don't do this sort of thing.*

Nobody did this sort of thing. She stumbled over something lying on the sidewalk. Somebody. She looked down; there was just enough starlight to see the reflection on open eyes. Jennifer Feinberg had been born and raised in New York, mostly on Manhattan Island, and she'd prided herself on knowing the city in all its shapes. Until now. All at once there were no more people around her; maybe they'd all gotten sensible, and gone home to hide until things returned to normal.

She caught her breath, panting hard against the feeling of being squeezed beneath the diaphragm. If they—if *she*—didn't do something, there would be no more normal, not ever again.

"*Walpurgisnacht*," she muttered to herself.

Lafarge turned back and put a hand under one arm. She snatched it away. "I'm all right," she said. "Just keep going."

Keep going because if I stop I won't start again.

Financial analysts didn't—God damn it, nobody followed time travelers into deadly peril. That was for the movies. Nobody ended up in bed with genetic superwomen, either. Rage ground her teeth together and made the fluttering in her stomach recede. The fear that that column of fire had brought was still there, like a grace-note under the main theme, less personal but just as menacing.

A police car went by, siren wailing and lights blinking. Up ahead the metal bars on an electronics store had been torn loose and figures in hooded sweatsuits were carrying out equipment, laughing and prancing. The beams of their flashlights danced and jigged with them, sweeping circles of white light over windows dark except for the occasional candle. Shots sounded in the distance, a sudden crackle and then a series of slow deliberate *bang . . . bang* sounds.

One of the figures in sweatsuits turned towards them. A beam stabbed out and Jennifer threw up a hand to shade her squinting eyes. Voices rang harsh, threatening.

Lafarge moved smoothly in front of her. His right

hand twitched, and the man with the flashlight folded over and flew backward. He landed in the broken glass and lay utterly limp. His companions hesitated for a moment and then fled. Suddenly the street was filled with silence, quiet enough to hear a roaring murmur of voices not too far away. A helicopter went by overhead, probing downward with its searchlight, then skittered away sideways over the rooftops. Jennifer stumbled again when it was gone.

Without electricity, these canyon streets were *dark*. Dark as a closet with the door closed. She turned, fumbling for the wall. Where was she?

"You'll need this," Lafarge said.

Jennifer fought not to jump and closed her fingers around the warm metal tube he handed her. A flashlight. She turned it on, and nearly dropped it again. The man Lafarge had . . . *shot?* Struck down, anyhow . . . he was staring at her. At the whole world, rather, eyes and mouth open wide and unmoving in the dark-brown face. The light glittered on gold at his throat, on his hands, a puddle of operatic brightness against the deep velvet of the night. She could smell a heavy fecal odor that any New Yorker recognized, but it took her an instant to connect it with what she was seeing. Sphincter relaxation . . .

"You *killed* him," she said, her voice rising toward a squeak before she controlled it.

"He was armed; there was no time for half-measures," Lafarge said impatiently. "This way."

He was off again, head down and shoulders hunched. The posture reminded her hurtfully for a moment of Henry . . . who was God-knew-where in this madhouse of a city. *I desperately want to disbelieve all of this. I want it to have* not happened, *ever.*

She kept the flashlight on Lafarge's heels. That kept her from running into him when he stopped.

"We're two blocks away, south," he said softly.

He turned, and Jennifer jerked back slightly. The covering over his face had become a perfect nonreflective black that drank the light like blotting paper with ink, the only sign of features a writhing movement where his mouth should be when she shone the light directly on it.

"I have to go to maximum stealthing," he said. Somehow it was doubly horrible, that normal, rather pedantic voice coming out of the black mask. "*It* has left, but there are fixed sensors in place. This is our window of opportunity, and we've got to make the most of it."

"Why you say 'we,' white man?" she said, and turned on her heel to leave him blinking, baffled, in her wake.

You're the top of the heap, she told herself. "That's *Ms.* Bitch to you, Mister," she said aloud. Her shoulders braced back, and her sensible mid-heel office shoes beat out a tattoo on the sidewalk.

There was nobody in the block ahead. Nobody she could see, at least. The heavy arched wrought-iron door with *IngolfTech Inc.* on it stood over the main entrance to the ex-warehouse, just where it had been since the renovations started.

She'd been in a dozen times or more. Now it felt like the lion cage at the zoo. Her imagination insisted it even *smelled* like the lion cage, a rank predator's odor.

Jennifer stepped up onto the semicircular staircase and pressed the button. The smooth enigmatic object she'd been given to hide was only the size of a thimble and no thicker, lighter than Styrofoam . . . but it seemed to weigh like an anchor as she waited for a reply.

"What *was* that . . . light thing?" Finch asked.

She was scanning the approaches through the forest with slow, systematic care. Mary Chen was uneasily conscious of the fact that she wasn't trained for anything like this. *Wasn't trained to hunt superhumans, using plasma guns?* she scolded herself. *Who is?*

"How should I know?" she snapped. "I'm a forensic pathologist, not a physicist!" Then, with a slight feeling of guilt: "Sorry. I think it involved some sort of EMP, from the way it wrecked everything electronic."

"Like a nuclear explosion," Finch said thoughtfully.

"I certainly hope not."

They might all be dead from secondary radiation without knowing it, if it *was* like a nuclear explosion. She shivered and reached for the thermos tucked into her backpack; it was cold, for a May night. Thank God for camping as a hobby; she was used to being out in the country at night, otherwise she'd be completely lost.

Crack.

Blue-white light flashed through the trees, throwing her shape in a momentary cone of shadow over the thermos. She snatched up the weapon instead and fumbled her hand into the grip. The tiny device in her ear spoke, a man's voice, eager and excited.

"I think I hit—"

The voice cut off. Through her normal hearing she caught the beginning of a shriek, then silence. Then another scream, a long hideous ululation of fear and agony.

Gwen stopped the head rolling with a foot and held the body pointed away from her. The blood filled the night with its heady, exciting scent; she licked her lips unconsciously as she stripped the covering off the human's backpack with her hands and layer knife.

What a crazy hybrid, she thought in admiration as she bared the mechanism within.

Lighter and more efficient than the one which had just saved her life. *That* was already growing warm to the touch after a single bolt; the energy absorption factor was only a little over ninety-eight percent. This was much better, the guide coils and controller unit made by a modern faber rather than hand-assembled from purely local parts. Hers was slaved to her transducer, significantly reducing its capacities. What a pity she couldn't take one of these and abandon her own—this was still an elephantine pile of junk by fifth-century Draka or Samothracian standards, but vastly preferable to what she had. Not that she could, of course, any more than she could put one of the communications units in her own ear. She grinned in the dark to think of what would happen *then*. There were more attractive methods of suicide.

Instead she turned to the other human, the one she'd winded—or perhaps she'd broken a few of his ribs; she'd been in a hurry. Without his little goggles the night would be impenetrable murk to him, of course. His eyes were round, starting at every sound as he sat propped against a tree, his legs stretched out before him. He moaned when she whispered in his ear.

"Call for help, man. Call for them to help you."

Instead he tried to reach for a bayonet on his webbing belt. Impatient, Gwen caught the wrist and squeezed with brutal strength.

The scream went on and on as she worked her fingers into the shattered bone.

"Christ, that's Clarens! He's with Hadelman."

Carmaggio caught at Saunders's arm. "By the numbers, El-tee," he said softly. "We knew she could make a shield if Lafarge could."

Saunders nodded tightly. The cry trilled up into a squeal and then a gasping *"don't . . . don't . . ."* mixed with sobs.

Henry touched the disk attached to the side of his goggles. A heads-up display projected in front of his eyes, showing vectors and locations.

"This way," he said, and arrows appeared before the sight of every member of the little force. "Enemy's here." Another vector, like a compass needle pointing to the AI's best guess at location. "Let's go."

Spread out in a slight C-shape, they moved forward through the woods. *Back in the jungle*, Carmaggio thought with sour irony. *Back in the bad bush.* Big oaks and hickories, grass and shrubbery beneath, paved pathways—not too much like the Parrot's Beak, really. Except for the feeling in his gut and balls and the back of his neck; and that was different too. He was a lot older, his heart pumping harder in his rib cage.

The humans were moving in a staggered line, half carrying their plasma guns slung and M-16's or H&K's at the ready, half facing the darkness with the energy weapons. They moved at a slow deliberate walk; from what the equipment showed, Ingolfsson wasn't moving away from them. Henry paid attention to his feet. The light amplification was perfect, pretty much like a black-and-white image of a cloudy afternoon, but something was playing hell with his depth perception.

"Where the hell is she?" he whispered to himself. By the display, they ought to be right on top of her.

"*Looking for this?*"

A voice out of the dark, from somewhere above. He pivoted instantly on one heel, his finger squeezing at the trigger as the aimpoint cross from the indicator hung in front of his eyes.

Crack.

A treetop exploded in flame, a fireball in the night. His eyes widened. The beam shouldn't diffuse like that. She *did* have some sort of a shield. He caught a glimpse of a shape spreadeagled as it leaped, and then the vector arrow was quivering between trees. The one he'd hit was going up like a torch, every leaf and branch flash-ignited as the energy of the plasma spread around the circumference of the protective field.

Something arched out of the night at him as streams of tracer and plasma bolts raked the next tree into splinters. Dangerous splinters, from the way somebody was yelling. The object landed with a soggy thump and rolled to his feet.

Saunders recognized it before he did. "Clarens's head." The ex-officer raised his voice instinctively, despite the AI that would relay his words to every ear.

"Hold your fire until you've got a target! Keep moving."

They did. *Goddamn*, Carmaggio thought desperately, trying to follow the dots that marked out the schematic of the action. It was too *much*, too much information, slowing down his reactions—yet without it he'd be helpless. He worked his mouth and spat.

The dot that was Ingolfsson's *probable* location was skittering away ahead of them northward, moving at an estimated speed that raised his brows even now. A cross-country motorbike would be lucky to make that miles-per-hour in close terrain like this. And it was moving off to one side. . . .

"Flank left," he said. "Move!"

The ragged C of dots that marked his comrades started to move. Slowly, too slowly; it was like some computer game where you wrenched at the joystick and got reamed because the figures wouldn't *respond* in time—

"There—"

Mary Chen jerked at Finch's cry, even more at the stream of green-colored tracer from her submachine-gun. She leveled her plasma weapon, trying to bring the red firing dot on the vector her goggles were supplying. Something was coming out of the night, something moving like a coursing cheetah. Her beam smashed an explosion of steam and shattered rock out of the ground, and then the weapon was slapped out of her hands with a force that sent her spinning around like a top, throwing out her hands to try and keep from falling.

The blow turned her around faster than her own muscles could ever have done. In time to see a black-outlined shape running *up* the trunk of the tree that had been behind her. It had a human outline; she could see that much, and see that it held a weapon shape in its left hand. In its right was something long and slender with an edge of silvered moonlight. Then the run ended in a momentum-driven crouch and the figure leaped out and away from the tree, whirling in midair somersaults with knees drawn up to chest. In a long arch that took it back over their heads.

Help! I've fallen into a Ninja movie and I can't get out! The thought bubbled through her mind as she scrambled to get the plasma gun back.

Finch was snarling and slapping another magazine into her firearm, trying to track the target and jerk back the slide in the same motion.

Chen felt her whirl turn into a stagger that left her groping dizzily for the plasma gun. Something flashed. There was a huge cold impact across her stomach, and her legs dropped out from under her. Her hands felt numb as they groped for the wound, tried to hug the savaged, razor-cut edges of flesh back together and contain the slick wetness that bulged out. Her mouth opened and closed soundlessly.

Finch was off the ground, gripped from behind with an elbow-grip on her neck and an arm about her waist. Her own arms and legs kicked uselessly, the H&K firing off bursts into the night.

A voice hissed, every syllable as distinct as if it were cut from etched glass.

"Where is the Samothracian?"

"*Fuck* you!" Finch shouted, her fox-sharp features contorted with rage. The hillbilly accent was back, sharp and nasal.

"No time."

The arms wrenched and cast her aside. There was

a single squeal, as fierce and shrill as an animal turning in the owl's claws, then the body hit the ground with limp finality.

The figure in black took a long stride toward Chen. The dying woman tried to turn away, but all that moved was her head, rolling loosely to face her other shoulder. She remembered the heel marks on the necks.

Impact. Nothing.

"Move your *ass*," Carmaggio shouted. "Face left!"

The vector arrow was pointing back the way they'd come. All the friendly dots turned left and south, scurrying to try and make their formation face the enemy and give mutual support. All except for one dot that kept right on going away, as fast as he or she could move their feet—and Henry couldn't blame whoever it was one little bit. Saunders was cursing under his breath, voice a little shaky; Jesus did the same on his other side.

Sixty seconds since contact. Jesus fucking *Christ.*

A voice rang out from behind a statue-fountain set in a pool.

"Where's your Samothracian?" it mocked. If a battle trumpet could live, it would sound like that. Even at this instant, the beauty of it struck him. "Where's your strong protector now, humans?"

The sound firmed the attack vector to a brilliant dot. Bullets and a dozen plasma bolts lashed out. Bronze exploded into flying molten gobbets. Several thousand gallons of water also exploded, and the steam burst flung chunks of stone coaming right back in their faces. Something wet spattered Carmaggio over half his body, and a heavy limp weight struck him hard enough to send him staggering. He clutched at it automatically, and found himself holding Jesus Rodriguez—his body, since the top had been clipped off his skull by a knife-edged shard of rock. Bits of the granite still glistened among the pink brain and fragments, and his friend's body shuddered and flapped and bucked in his arms.

He thrust it away with an involuntary shout. Images flitted before his eyes and clawed at his attention.

"Regroup," he called out. The iron calm of his own voice shocked him, at some level far below the clarity that gripped and moved him. "Ten-yard intervals, circle formed on me."

The AI would show everyone where to go, if they kept their heads and did it. They *were* doing it. The enemy vector arrow was a blur, moving around his defensive position. Every now and then someone would shoot at it, but Ingolfsson seemed to know they were shielded against her plasma weapon—

She knows how to use these things and we don't, Carmaggio knew with deadly certainty. *And she's doing a better job of figuring out how to use them against us.*

A rock whined by his head and went *crack* against a treetrunk as it shattered into fragments—not even a superhuman could make an irregular object perfectly accurate. He didn't intend to stand up and see a trial of strength between this Fritz helmet and Ingolfsson's arm, though.

"Hit the dirt. And nail the bitch!"

Bolts lanced out through the woods. Trees toppled. Carmaggio felt a sudden something in his mind, a sensation like a mental *click*. He started to roll still prone, bumped into someone, rolled right over them despite their squawk of protest. As he did so another plasma bolt lanced out of the darkness, right into the mid-section of the tree he'd been under. The three-foot thickness of hardwood vanished in a meter-wide sphere of magenta fire, and the great crown of the copper beech toppled downwards. It crashed into the middle of their position, branches probing like spears.

Return fire lashed back at the firmed-up vector the

bolt provided for the AI. Thudding feet warned him that it didn't stay accurate for long. He was surprised the footfalls were so loud, but you couldn't move a hundred and ninety-five pounds up to greyhound speeds that quickly on soft little tippytoes, he supposed. Carmaggio went up on one knee, the trigger of the plasma gun sweetly responsive under his finger.

Repeated hits or a point-blank hit will overload the shielding, Lafarge's remembered voice said. *When that happens, the shield's energy storage coil will fail catastrophically.*

"And fry the bitch to hell and gone," he snarled under his breath. The sights were steady—

—and a stream of tracer snapping right by his ear with flat stretching *whackwhackwhack* sounds showed somebody had the same idea.

The bolt went wide, snapping out across Central Park—at that angle, it could blast a hole in concrete in one of the apartments over on the Upper West Side. Carmaggio rolled desperately, trying to get a new bead on the running, jinking figure. It was as if they were all standing still, or wading through honey, and she was the only normal person there.

"Shit. Shit, *shit.*"

The vector bead slid right across their circular position. People on the *other* side were shooting after her.

"Fuck, the captain's dead!"

Henry's head whipped around. Three or four of the National Guardsmen were standing shoulder-deep in the fallen beech tree, looking down. He forced himself to his feet and lumbered over. Saunders was lying on his back, and a stub of wood three inches around was through his chest.

"Oh, man, I'm outta here," one of the guardsmen said, backing away, his head shaking in an unconscious rejection of the scene before him. "Oh, man, I'm gone."

"*Shut up!*"

The AI blared it into everyone's ear in a shout that stopped them in their tracks.

"You want to be out there *alone* with that thing?" he went on. "And if you make it home, you want to wait there until it comes for you? Christ, if you're that anxious to die, eat your gun and do it easy and quick!"

Silence fell. "Get your attention back on the job." *Rollcall*, he whispered. Shock made him grunt. Chen, Finch, Jesus, ten more dead. Two run. And all in less than eight minutes.

The men and women faced outward. But the vector arrow had turned to a bead, and the AI drew him a schematic.

"She's going home," Carmaggio whispered. "We did it. I hope." Aloud: "Come on. We've got to get to the warehouse."

He walked toward the waiting vans parked along the edge of Columbus Circle. Past the bodies, past Finch lying like a pretzel, past shattered burning trees. *How many*— Two of the FBI types were kneeling by Dowding's body. He'd never really gotten to know Finch's boss, beyond the depressed-horse expression on his bony face. Now he was lying face-down, with a four-inch-deep cut running diagonally from left shoulderblade to right kidney. That must have happened as she left, running through their position.

The night smelled of death. Eighteen living humans followed him out of the park. None remained but the dead, as they walked toward the killer.

Jenny, he thought.

"Who's there?" a voice demanded over her head, after she punched in the code.

She pressed the button again. "Jennifer Feinberg for Ms. Ingolfsson," she snapped, putting her palm to the plate beside the door. "She told me to report here in an emergency. Now let me *in*."

A wait, while whoever was behind the video monitor let the computer confirm who she was and bring up its instructions.

Now she lived, or died. If the door didn't open, Lafarge attacked it himself—and he said the chances were better than five-to-one he couldn't defuse the biobomb in time. She closed her eyes and fumbled for a prayer, the first in a very long time.

There was a click. "Come through," the speaker said.

She did, into a lobby now dimly lit. Two tall black men stood by either side of the door, looking out through slits. They had rifles, absurdly huge spindly-looking things. Lafarge had said . . . *Barretts. Or something.* They ignored her. The one who'd let her in was a young Latina woman, with a wicked-looking machine pistol slung across her body, incongruous against the chic outfit.

"Hi, Dolores," Jennifer said.

"Buenas noches, Jenny," Dolores Ospina said. "Welcome to the Household. Glad you decided to be sensible." A flash of a smile. "Welcome to the harem, that is to say. . . . Come on."

Jennifer forced a sickly grin as the other woman led her down a corridor and into an elevator; the sheer *normalcy* of the closed-down offices was jarring, with plastic covers over the PCs and Post-it notes stuck to desks.

The elevator had glass panels on the other side, and they had a view of the main section of the converted warehouse as they rose. Nothing dramatic, floodlights and a few workers fussing around enigmatic machinery. She recognized Dr. Mueller—*his name should be Mengele*—and the Sikh in their white coats, bent together over a console. The elevator clicked to a stop at the third floor. Armed men patrolled the walkways, or stood around the outer wall in positions barricaded with curved shapes of heavy metal.

"We're parking everyone here," Dolores said,

indicating the door of a lounge down the top-floor corridor. "Just until the Mistress gets back, you understand." Excitment sparkled in the dark eyes. "They're actually going to take us through to the Prime Line, while this area gets pacified! I hope we get to see some of it."

"That would be fascinating," Jennifer agreed. *About as fascinating as a tour of Hell, guided by Beelzebub.* "How long?"

"Oh, not more than a couple of hours, she said." Dolores giggled. "And then it'll all be over. We can relax and never worry about anything again, just swim and feast and make love."

"Yes," Jennifer nodded. *Hours. I will not scream. I will not smack this repulsive little slut.*

She was very glad when the lounge door closed; it probably wasn't a very good idea to try and strangle someone with your bare hands when they had an automatic weapon. There were a dozen more in the lounge, and they raised an ironic cheer when she walked in. Jennifer smiled and waved, angling over toward the coffee urn and pastry tray, trying to look natural.

My God, that's Fred Lather! she thought. *Is he in on this?* And his wife. *My God, I've got five of her exercise tapes.*

Janeen Amier walked over. "Nice to see you again," she said, chattering nervously.

Jennifer took her hand. It felt dry against hers, which was damp with nervous sweat. The ex-actress didn't look nervous; more of an exalted expression.

"Did you know," she said, "did you know, the Mistress says Fred and I did so much, we can be made *young* again?"

That shocked Jennifer; enough that she really saw the aging woman for a moment, instead of her eyes skipping over the face in an unconscious search for danger.

"Young?" she said.

"Young, and beautiful. Gwen herself said," Janeen simpered and blushed, "that we'd be pretty when we were rejuvenated. How I envy you *that* experience."

"Yes," said Jennifer. She felt herself blushing. "Where's the powder room?"

"Just down the hall," Janeen said, skittering back to her husband's side. He was looking a little stunned himself, as if he couldn't quite convince himself that this was really happening.

It not only is *happening,* Jennifer thought grimly, *it's your bloody* fault, *you idiot.*

She sipped at the coffee and gave the others a quick look. A few politicians, some heavy-duty financial types, a black police officer . . . *My God, that's Henry's boss!* A Somali model married to a British rock star. An odd assortment . . .

"Souvenirs," she muttered. This was a collection of souvenirs. She remembered Gwen's words: *I look after my own.* Some weird sense of obligation, the sort you had to a dog. "And I'll look after myself, thank you very much."

She set the coffee cup down; it was Limoges; no plastic here. Nobody was standing out in the hall. She pushed open the ladies' and went into a stall.

Embarrassing. But it was the obvious place to hide something internally, and that little bit less likely to be detected, according to the expert. Henry had had the good grace to look embarrassed himself.

"I am going to have a talk with that man, when this is over."

If it got over. The thought heartened her, and she walked out of the room with an air of casual authority. *You belong here. Nobody will suspect you. Just another one of the souvenirs.*

Lafarge had given her a probable location, based on

his scouting and her descriptions of what went on here. "Drakensis psychology means the ultimate controls will be near its nesting site." That was just wonderful.

She palmed a featureless black rectangle from her purse, about the size of an old-fashioned cigarette case. Up a flight of stairs, and to a heavy steel door; she must be right under the roof in this section of the warehouse. A single guard, a Haitian. She didn't recognize him, but from the way he looked at her he probably did, perhaps from the Bahamas.

"Sorry, miss," he said, the submachine gun in his hands pointed down. "This off limit."

Jennifer raised the black rectangle with the business end pointed out between thumb and forefinger, and *thought*. There was a heavy tug in her hand. *Whump*. Pressure popped her ears in the confined space, two sharp little pains. The Haitian flipped backward as if punched in the face; his head gonged against the thick door, and he slid downward with his eyes rolling back in his head and blood running from his nose and mouth.

"I had to," she muttered to herself, keeping a fixed stare away from the man as she moved towards the door. "I had to do that."

She pressed the black cone against the electronic lock. *Something* pulled it out of her fingers, the last fraction of an inch. Crackling sounds came from beneath it. The door clicked; when she took the cone off the wall it came away easily, leaving the keypad riddled with tiny holes.

Into the inner sanctum. *Lifestyles of the rich and inhuman*, she thought. A series of big rooms, leading into each other open-plan. An office setup; a gym room with equipment like nothing she'd ever seen, and lead-weighted free weights of ridiculous, cartoon size. Bedroom. Huge curtained bed, and beyond it an elaborate . . . bathroom wasn't really the word. Bathing facility. She walked quickly over to a terminal set beside the bed and opened the cover of the CPU. Even a non-tech type could see that someone had been making heavy modifications; cables attached here and there, new circuit boards. Gingerly, she laid the black thimble down on the exposed equipment.

Tendrils the color of clear ice and thinning off to invisibility *grew* out of the instrument. They waved over the circuit board, hesitated a little, then pounced, burrowing.

Jennifer shuddered. There was something unpleasantly alive about the tendrils, in an insect-like way. Now they were a writhing net over the surface of the computer, and the black thimble was melting away, shrinking and disappearing before her eyes.

"Now to try and get out of here," she said, hurrying through the suite of rooms.

A man was waiting at the door. Medium height, broad-shouldered, ugly-handsome Mediterranean face with a heavy blue-black five o-clock shadow. The cross-draw holster showed under his opened jacket.

"Vulk," she said. "I was just—"

"Just what?" the Serb said. The Walther in his hand moved, and her eyes were drawn to the 9mm opening of the muzzle as if it were a cavern into night.

She moved back as he advanced, two Haitians behind him. He looked behind her.

intruder, the transducer whispered in Gwen's mind. **central interface units are compromised. attempting to contain.**

The knowledge almost froze her in mid-stride, moving through the enemy formation. Reflex carried her through; she slashed at a last figure as she ran, the layer-knife cleaving flesh as if it were jelly, bone with only a slight catch. Out into the night, dodging trees.

containment will fail in fourteen point seven three minutes, the transducer said.

The non-voice was slower than usual, too much of the quasi-machine's capacity diverted to the link with the human-built computers controlling the fusion plant and gateway.

Self-reproach was bitter as she ran. *Diversion.* One she *had* to respond to, but she shouldn't have stayed once it was plain the Samothracian wasn't there. He'd used the psychology of the Race against her, the tight-focused aggressiveness that had kept her there, killing like a lion in a herd of penned zebra. While the real enemy crept around behind her.

The streets ahead were pitch-black save for the headlights of an occasional car, and there were a fair number of humans abroad. With hormones pouring into her blood at maximum combat-load, she could treat automobiles and pedestrians alike as a series of static encounters. At times she vaulted a moving car, or used a walker as a resilient buffer at a corner, shedding momentum and turning her vector on them the way a billiard ball did on the padded edges of a pool table. Black against black, the passersby saw her only as a glimpse of movement in the night, a flash of light on teeth or the edge of her layer knife, a hurtling weight that left broken bone and torn flesh behind it. The screams were swallowed in the greater turmoil of the nighted city. Once she found a column of armored personnel carriers across an intersection, moving out from some National Guard armory to maintain order in the chaotic streets.

Crack. A plasma bolt slammed into the side of one vehicle, through the thin armor and into the fuel supply. Vaporized fuel sprayed inside the troop compartment and exploded. The turret with its 25mm autocannon flipped straight up, twirling end-over-end. The machine behind the one she'd shot tried to halt and couldn't,

ramming into the rear of the burning wreckage. The
smell of scorched metal almost overrode the roast-pork
stink of burning flesh. Gwen drove through the gap
between the wrecked APC and the one ahead of it.

"That ought to slow them a little," she said, to the
pulse of her breathing as she ran. Eighteen surviving
plasma guns were entirely too many to leave behind
her. Most probably the humans were too terrorized to
pursue, but there was no sense in taking chances.

seven minutes.

shield down.

The AI's voice sounded in his mind. Kenneth Lafarge
rose from his crouch atop the roof and pointed a hand.

Ptung. A thread-thin line spun out from the cuff of
his softsuit and whipped across the gap, slapping onto
the metal of a support on the warehouse roof, He took
a coil around a stanchion on the building he stood on,
pulling until the monomolecular thread came taut and
sank half a finger's width into the steel. Then he applied
the solvent; the thread cut off from the spool and
merged with the glob of ice-clear material that anchored
it there.

There were a half-dozen guards on the warehouse
roof, equipped with heavy slug-throwers and native
night-sight goggles. He recognized the make of weapon:
designed for long-range sniping and to penetrate light
metal armor. They would probably punch through his
softsuit with a square hit, and certainly do him no good
inside even if they didn't. With a slight sigh of regret,
he raised the plasma rifle.

Crack. Bits of flesh and metal spattered across the
rooftop. The guard's rifle and ammunition exploded
with a run of malignant crackles, like heavy firecrackers.
Vaporized metal and organic steam blossomed upward.
The others went to ground and began firing back.
Brave men, Lafarge thought. *Not very smart, but brave.*

Heavy bullets whipcracked through the air around him, or hammered into brick. Through brick, in most cases; the walls of the apartment building he stood on wouldn't stop hard-point rounds traveling at that speed. Others keened off metal closer to him, with each leaving a red-yellow flash of spark behind it.

He traversed the aimpoint of his weapon toward one set of muzzle flashes. *Crack.* This time the plasma released its energy on the thin sheet metal in front of a rifleman. The man reared up screaming, his face and torso ablaze from the finely-divided molten metal. Still burning, he plunged off the edge of the warehouse roof and into the street like a meteor through the night.

The others broke in horror and fled. Lafarge ignored them. Instead he sprang and hooked an arm and a leg over the thread between the buildings. It cut through the street clothing he wore over the softsuit as if the fabric were air, but the smart-armor gripped it in frictionless diamond-hard runnels. He slid down it in a long arching swoop, rolling over the parapet onto the flat roof and coming erect.

Ten meters away, the glass of a skylight shattered as a heavy bullet struck out from within. Reflex and the AI's prompting brought Lafarge around, weapon rising. Not even a cyber-warrior's reflexes could outmove a .50 round already fired, though. It hit him twice, glancing. The first on his forearm, smashing it aside and making the fingers fly open in reflex. The second impact nicked the plasma rifle.

do not fire, the AI said.

Lafarge looked down. The guide-coil of the barrel was cut. With an angry snarl he cast it aside and signaled for the vibration-knife. That chittered out, a yard of wire outlined in the shape of a sword. He slashed at the tarpaper and sheet metal beneath his feet, sending up gouts of sparks as he savaged the thin galvanized steel.

biobomb subroutine located, the machine told him with infuriating calm. **data follows.**

"Damn, there's a self-destruct sequence!"

Even the *drakensis* wasn't totally insane, then—there was a way to destroy it safely. He levered up a flap of roof and looked down. Fiberboard panels, forming the ceiling of a corridor below, with power lines and ventilation ducts.

"Good." *Initiate biobomb self-destruct sequence.*

initiated. three minutes, counting.

He leaped, relying on his weight to punch through into the space below.

five minutes, the transducer said. **following peripheral functions lost to enemy infiltration.**

No more than two blocks away. Seconds away. Her lungs stretched, feet hammered. Her human guards were firing from the roof of the warehouse. A plasma bolt arched out from another roof nearby, another, a third. One man plunged down, burning, and the rifle fire stopped. Something large and dark cut the angle between the two buildings in a swooping movement, dropped flat on the roof itself. Gwen's snarl was soundless, but it had the rage of territorial violation behind it.

He dares!

An object dropped from the roof and clattered at her feet as she reached the front entrance. A flick of the eyes took it in. *Plasma rifle*. Inoperable. She shrugged out of the backpack shield in the same motion; it was scorching-hot anyway, and wouldn't take another hit.

The ozone smell of the fusion reactor and the lingering, crinkling scent of the gateway's byproducts overrode all else in the building. The two guards cried out in relief as she charged through the door.

"Vulk!" she snapped, silencing them.

One pointed. Both followed as best they could.

"Get *out* of my way!" Carmaggio snarled.

The National Guard officer, under his helmet, looked much younger than the policeman. And much more frightened. The Bradley APC's of his company were still laagered around the wreckage of two burned-out models, with bodybagged shapes lying on the sidewalk. Nervous soldiers crouched in their shadows, fingering M-16's and rocket launchers. Searchlights from the APC's and Humvees played across the tall buildings on either side, probing through the darkness.

Disaster, Henry thought. That was obvious at first glance; you could smell it, too. There was something unique and unmistakable about the stink of human fat cooked out of bodies and pooling under a burned-out armored vehicle. It took him back, in ways he had no desire to remember.

"We're after terrorists," he went on. *Time-traveling extra-dimensional ones,* he added to himself. No sense in stressing this guy out, and no time to explain.

The officer looked at the two National Guard trucks. Carmaggio, in civilian clothes but Army body armor, well spattered with blood. He *might* have enough experience to know what brains looked like flecked out across cloth. The survivors of the FBI SWAT team. Saunders's guardsmen, carrying not only their own assault rifles but odd-looking weapons that would have been more appropriate in the hands of Obi-Wan or the Imperial Stormtroopers.

"Who the hell—"

"FBI," he said. One of the agents was still alert enough to flash ID. "We're after the ones responsible for all this."

"Yes *sir,*" the Guardsman said. "We . . . some sort of rocket attack, I lost . . . and we've got no communications, everything's out . . ."

"I know. We're in hot pursuit."

"Need any help?"

Carmaggio's brows went up. That *was* initiative, considering the circumstances. A lot of men would simply wait here until someone official came along and told them what to do.

"Hell yes, Captain." He gave the warehouse address. "Follow me and coordinate."

Jennifer screamed. Vulk Dragovic smiled as he ripped open her blouse and held up two alligator clips, then licked the metal to improve the connection. Thin wires ran back from them to a small portable transformer set.

"Soon you will sing, Jew bitch," he said quietly. "Sing like a diva."

His face was sweating, but his hands moved with an expert's emotionless skill as he stripped insulation from the wires and connected them to screw clamps on the transformer.

"This produced much good singing in Bosnia," he said conversationally; his Serbian accent was noticeably thicker. "And in Kosovo. All you needed to do to get those Turk-kissing Albaninan swine telling you everything you wanted to know was to take their sows and—"

The door slammed open. Jennifer bit back another scream. Gwen was there, but almost unrecognizable. Dressed in loose black, with her short red hair *bristling*. Her teeth showed, and the whites of her eyes in rims all around the iris. The wide eyes flicked to the gas-gun resting on a table in the cluttered storeroom.

"Computer?" she said. Vulk nodded. "Emergency. Samothracian. Upstairs. *Now*."

Jennifer blinked, and Gwen was gone. The Serb and his two Haitian assistants snatched up their weapons and headed for the door after her. Vulk was last, and he hesitated for a second. The fingers of his right hand were moving, and with a sudden chill that made her stomach feel cold and loose she realized that he was considering killing her right then and there.

"Later," he said.

The door slammed, and she heard his footsteps pounding away down the corridor. The beat of her own blood in her ears sounded louder. She strained against the cord binding her arms behind her and through the lattice of the metal chair; all it did was scrape the skin raw. It took a moment of that before she realized what Ingolfsson had said. Lafarge was loose inside the warehouse.

"Please," she whispered and prayed. "Please."

Gwen swarmed up the rungs set into the elevator shaft. Below her the twin circles gleamed with their internal heat, almost brighter than the reflected light in the visible spectrum.

three minutes, the transducer said. **all spare capacity diverted to holding reactor and gate functions.**

The lights died. Human voices yelled in panic; guards, Vulk, the roomful of pets on the third floor. The view changed only marginally to her eyes, but it took a few seconds for her followers to remember their night-sight equipment, and that was of primitive local make. The muzzle-flashes of the Barrett sniper rifles firing from behind desks and consoles and pieces of equipment all over the floor of the open section died down. A dark figure rose and darted forward toward the central catwalk. As he went he turned and slashed with his hand. Metal sparked and sang as it parted under the vibration-sword. The whole long weight of the catwalk lurched and shivered as one end of it came unanchored from the walkway that circled the building's interior at this height.

He means to drop it over the reactor and gateway, Gwen knew. To run down its length, snapping through the members that supported it from above.

That much weight of metal crashing down on the equipment would wreck it. And probably wreck any chance of a breakthrough from the Domination's timeline.

Gwen turned, holding her weight up by her renewed grip on the rung, and braced her feet against the wall of the elevator shaft in a horizontal crouch. With a long feline scream of rage she leapt, out across the empty space of the warehouse. *Impact.* Her hands gripped rough metal—*full circle*—and a whiplike surge of the long supple length of her body brought her up onto the shivering, moving surface of the walkway. She was alone on it except for the Samothracian and what scent told her was a cooling human body, cut open to the body cavity. Dolores's body, still clutching her machine pistol.

"*Come to me and die, human!*" she shouted, and charged.

Lafarge turned to meet her. The plasma gun in her hand flashed, *crack-crack-crack*, outlining him in white fire and burning the concealing native clothes to calcined ash. Then she was upon him. Layer knife met vibration-sword. There was no room for footwork on the swaying iron, and they grappled chest to chest.

CRACK.

Below and behind them the sky-spearing beam of light appeared again. This time the noise was loud enough to shatter glass. The light seemed to wash through her tissues, turning the conductive fabric of her blacks searing hot; the slippery surface of the softsuit under her hands went mirrored to reflect the energy. A lance of fire the thickness of a man's thigh speared upward. Below it the great circle of the gateway turned bright at a central point, then expanded outward to the rim. The brightness was like a pool of liquid mercury, rippling, distorting, and reflecting.

"You lose!" Gwen cried.

Her arms closed around the Samothracian. The softsuit had little protection against low-velocity impact, crushing force. His were about her with nearly equal strength. They fell to the walkway, rolling.

"You lose, human!"

Something was forcing its way through the silvery distortion that spanned the gateway's circle, the metallic-looking field giving way like water under surface tension. A domed machine was coming through, sleek and black, adjusting its adamantine bulk to fit the ten-meter opening between worlds.

"Cover us!" Carmaggio shouted.

Fifty-caliber bullets spanged and whinged off the glacis plates and turrets of the APC's as they faced in toward the warehouse. Their 25mm chain-guns and coaxial machine-guns answered, bottle-shaped muzzle-flashes of orange and white fire through the night. Something must be backing the warehouse walls at that point, heavy reinforcement, because the return fire continued. Someone was firing a grenade-launcher back at the National Guard vehicles, a heavy *chooonk . . . chooonk* sound, followed by the cracking detonation of the 40mm grenades. None of the armored fighting vehicles had been damaged, but both the trucks with Saunders's men and the FBI agents were burning. The survivors were around him, crouching in the lee of the armor.

The Bradleys felt huge and solid to him; he'd campaigned with the old M-113's, aluminum boxes. But he remembered what a single plasma bolt from a hand-weapon had done to one: ripped it like a C-rat can under a tread.

There was just no time.

Henry rose over the back deck of the APC and fired three times into the ground floor of the warehouse.

Crack. Crack. Crack. Metal and brick belled outward and upward as heat flashed steel into vapor and shattered the more resistant ceramic of brick into dust. Lime burned as the mortar ignited; lime, and human flesh beyond it.

"Follow me!" Carmaggio roared, and ran for the holes his weapon had punched. The fire from the warehouse slackened, stunned, but rounds still kicked up sparks around his feet. A wave of heat from glowing metal and he was through.

"Jenny!" he called.

It was the AI that answered, laying a green strip at his feet. He followed it.

Jennifer screamed again, half fear and half rage, and lashed out with her feet, the only part of her she could move. The dark figure grunted and staggered back.

"Christ, woman, what'd you do that for?"

She stared. *Henry?* "Henry?"

"Sure. Lemme—"

Hands found hers, and a blade sawed at the cords. "C'mon. Can you walk."

"Watch me *run*," she snapped. "Let's get out of this nightmare."

"I've got nightsight goggles. Here, take my hand."

They ran out into the corridor. That was growing lighter, bright blue-white reflections bouncing around corners and leaving knife-edged shadows. At the corner Henry's grip on her wrist turned to a heavy tug.

"Down."

She fell to the floor, shielding her eyes with her hand against the intolerable white light that came down the long stretch of hall leading to the centrum of the converted warehouse. That left her looking at Henry's face, contorted in a snarl as he aimed. The light didn't seem to be bothering him, through the goggles that covered his eyes like the two halves of a golf ball. He fired, and her hair crinkled from the nearness of the plasma bolts. Again and again, but the sound and light were lost in what was happening a few hundred feet away.

"That's all we can do." His hand squeezed hers. "Let's go."

"Not . . . this . . . time . . . you . . . don't," Lafarge gasped in her ear.

The loosened walkway shivered and bucked under them as they lay straining to snap each other's spines. Gwen locked her hand over her wrist and increased the pressure, ignoring the tightness in her own chest. The Samothracian was moving, scrabbling. She tried to lock his leg with hers, but there was no purchase on the slick surface, not without losing her leverage for the crushing hold.

The man's leg went straight. They rolled, toppled. Toward the roaring beam cutting into the night.

"Not this time!"

Gwen felt a last snarling howl of frustration escape her as they fell free. Her arms tightened, and reinforced bone cracked and splintered.

A moment of white light. Nothing.

"Get us the fuck out of here," Carmaggio shouted to the driver, half-throwing Jennifer up the ramp of the APC ahead of him. "Don't argue, just do it!"

The other Bradleys had already gone. Henry didn't know how many of the people who'd followed him into the warehouse had come out again; he'd sent the message to bug out through Lafarge's little earphones, and that was all he could do.

He crashed to the crowded floor of the Bradley's fighting compartment himself, half-landing on Jenny, gouging his bruised torso on the edges of seats and what felt like half a dozen metal projections. The officer in charge of the APC didn't give him any grief, at least. The diesel grunted and the tracks clattered on pavement even as the winch began cranking the ramp-door at the rear shut. The vehicle ran straight backward, lurching up enough to throw them all to the side as it ran up over the trunk of a parked car and ground it flat. It lurched again as the driver made a reverse turn, then accelerated backward away from the inferno.

Henry and Jennifer clung together. And—

—the interior flux of the fusion generator washed across coils severed by the policeman's plasma bolts. The system might have been able to compensate, but too much computer capacity had been compromised. Failure propagated in a feedback cycle—

—energy released, not into its own spacetime but into the molehole drawing greedily where its mouth protruded into Earth/2's—

—fluxing back through the entropy differential between the timelines—

—and into the vastly more powerful machines anchoring the paramatter that kept the molehole open. Boundaries blurred as it quasi-vibrated through the infinite event waves—

And *another Carmaggio pushed the remote button, staring at the TV. Nothing else to do but work, and nothing had happened to break the routine in more years than he liked to remember . . .*

And *another Carmaggio rolled the little cart down the alleyway, the stumps of his legs aching with the damp. They'd ached that way every year since he'd gotten out of the VA—since the claymore had smashed every bone below mid-thigh into gravel. He looked down in the cup. Thirty, maybe forty bucks. Enough for a couple of bottles . . .*

And *a thousand thousand Carmaggios blurred back*

*into the singular one that was all reality could contain,
the one he would have to live as if it were the singular reality of creation . . .*

White light shone through every crack and vision
block in the Bradley. The armor rang like a cracked
gong with heat expansion. It reared up as the wind
caught it, teetered, hesitated, dropped back on its tracks
with a shattering crackle of broken torsion bars. When
he became conscious of anything again, Henry
Carmaggio knew he was still clutching Jenny to him,
and that her arms were tight around his neck. Her
mouth moved, but the words seemed very distant.

" . . .happened?" she said. "What happened?"

"I think—" he began. *Jesus dead. Chen dead. Christ,
everyone in that building, and a block around . . .* "I
think we won," he said.

"Yeah," she replied, and laid her head back on his
chest. Tears dripped down onto the bloodstained Kevlar
of the armor vest. "We won."

CHAPTER TWENTY-ONE

The coffee tasted bitter, but it was warm. Henry sipped, watching the flames over the intervening rooftops, smelling the reassuringly normal stink of gasoline and ordinary, everyday burning. It was odd, having so much official stuff around and no role for himself. Odd, and fairly pleasant.

There was everything from APCs to fire-engines lining the streets. Even the press had shown up, although the city was still dark; luckily, they didn't seem to have any idea that he was involved. Helicopters went by overhead, and floodlights kept this section brilliant. There were even civilians crowding up to the police barricades where the uniforms kept the curiosity-seekers at bay. He sipped the coffee again, and looked across to where Jennifer sat on a park bench with somebody's jacket around her shoulders. Carmaggio smiled at her, and a faint turn of the lips answered him.

"I don't know," she said. "I don't know if it was all real, if I can believe it—or if I can ever forget it."

He crouched to bring their eyes level. "You won't forget it," he said. "But you're tough. You can live with it. Believe me."

"I do."

"Carmaggio?"

Henry turned and stood. So did Jennifer, clutching the coat about her and coming to stand by his side.

"Yup, that's me. And if it isn't Andrews and Debrowski, the Wet-Work Twins."

The two agents were in Army gear, camo BDUs and Kevlar, with officers' sidearms but no insignia. The ones behind them were the genuine article, though, Carmaggio judged; Rangers, at a guess.

Andrews smiled. "If we could talk?" he said.

"Sure," Carmaggio said. Jennifer stiffened, but moved with him to a spot where a little distance and the background roar of engines and voices gave some privacy.

"We'll have to debrief you both in detail," Andrews said. "But let's get one thing straight. It appears—appears—from the . . . information left on our computers by your friend—"

And he was, Carmaggio realized with faint surprise. *Damned if he was a likable sort, but he was a friend and a good one at that.*

"—that we misinterpreted the situation."

"Is that the royal 'we,' Mr. Andrews?" Jennifer asked coldly. "Or are you speaking for—"

Henry laid a hand on her arm. She cast him a doubtful look but shut her mouth with a snap.

"Well, all's well that ends well, hey?" Carmaggio said.

Andrews nodded, still smiling but his eyes narrowing. *That's right,* Henry thought. *I'm not giving you any excuse to use your tame gorilla there.* Debrowski was rubbing at his nose and glaring.

"Matters of national security are involved," the agent continued. "We'll be working out the implications of the technology we've acquired for decades. This incident will be handled with discretion. Otherwise it could destabilize the entire country; the entire world, come to that. I'm sure you see the necessity. And since most of the people involved . . ." He shrugged delicately.

"Are dead, yeah," Carmaggio said flatly. *So you can do a Grade-A coverup. I wonder who gets blamed for the explosions?*

Hopefully the *Jihad al-Moghrebi*. They deserved it. Debrowski stiffened slightly at his tone, then relaxed as the detective looked away.

"Yeah, no sense in getting people excited," Carmaggio said, letting his exhaustion into his voice. "We'll be glad to talk to you. And then maybe we'll take a vacation out of the country?"

"That'd be a good idea," Andrews said. He held out his hand. Henry shook it.

"We?" Jennifer asked sharply, as the two government men made their way through the uniformed crowds.

"We, if you want it that way, Jenny," Carmaggio said. "I had to send you in there."

"I did what I had to do. And you got me out," she replied. "What bugs the *hell* out of me is that those . . . those buffoons get to tie this whole thing up with string and put it in their safety-deposit box."

Henry looked after them, and then back at the woman. "Did I say that?" he said, a slow grin creasing his heavy-featured face. "Did I?"

"That's all then," the Bahamian lawyer said.

He shook his head at the American couple. "I've never seen anything quite like it in the way of wills, but the documentation's all in order. Net asset value—"

"I'll just take the papers, thank you," the woman said in a sharp, businesslike New York accent. "We've been over all this. Ms. Ingolfsson *did* follow all the formalities, and the probate's concluded."

He shrugged, and handed over the last manila envelope. Jennifer Carmaggio pushed her sunglasses up on her forehead, did a quick check-through and then nodded.

They stood hand-in-hand as the lawyer's car crunched away up the coral-rock driveway, then turned to look at the mansion. The hot Bahamian sun beat down, and the air smelled of sea and pine and sand, huge and clean. The sound of breakers on the reef came faintly over the roof.

"Amazing what Lafarge could do with computers and documents," Henry said, and tasted sweat on his upper lip. He shook his head, trying to make it seem more real. "And he *did* have a sense of humor. He would have loved this."

A tall black man walked up from the house; there was a suspicious set to the way he wore his loose printed shirt. Henry fished in the jacket slung over one shoulder and came out with an envelope. This one bulged pleasantly, crisp hundred-dollar bills.

"Captain Lavasseur," Henry said, extending his hand.

They shook, two big men old enough to forgo boys' games. "I think Mr. Lafarge would have liked you to have this, as well as the retainer."

Antoine Lavasseur took the envelope with a slight, white smile and a very Gallic shrug. "He was some man, him," he said. "But I smell death on him, from the first time." He checked the envelope with a pirate's lack of self-consciousness, and his smile grew broader. "*Bon*. Not too little, for come and watch the house, talk to police for a few weeks."

"You kept the staff from burning it," Jennifer said. "With what's in there, that could be very important— for the whole world."

Another shrug from the sailor. "You need this sort of help again—any sort—you call Antoine Lavasseur."

"We may at that," Carmaggio said. "And now it's all ours," he went on, when the man from Martinique was gone.

"I like to think of it as a trust, Henry," Jennifer said seriously.

He smiled down into her eyes. "That too. No reason we can't enjoy ourselves while we figure out what to do with it, though. Let's go honeymoon."

Hand in hand, they walked under the arched gateway. The ironwork Drakon flared its wings above, its empty eyes staring out into the sun.

EPILOGUE

Tom Cairstens leaned back from the controls and rubbed red-rimmed eyes. He looked back to where Alice nursed an infant with too much knowledge behind its green gaze.

Three hundred meters down and moving at a three-knot crawl, the *Reiver* ran deep and silent.

Silent, save for a baby's cry.

DAVID WEBER

Honor Harrington (cont.):

Field of Dishonor

Honor goes home to Manticore—and fights for her life on a battlefield she never trained for, in a private war that offers just two choices: death—or a "victory" that can end only in dishonor and the loss of all she loves....

Other novels by DAVID WEBER:

Mutineers' Moon

"...a good story...reminds me of 1950s Heinlein..."
—BMP Bulletin

The Armageddon Inheritance

Sequel to *Mutineers' Moon.*

Path of the Fury

"Excellent...a thinking person's Terminator."
—Kliatt

Oath of Swords

An epic fantasy.

with STEVE WHITE:

Insurrection
Crusade

Novels set in the world of the Starfire ™ game system.

And don't miss Steve White's solo novels,
The Disinherited** and **Legacy!

continued ☞

DAVID WEBER

PRAISE FOR
LOIS MCMASTER BUJOLD

What the critics say:

The Warrior's Apprentice: "Now here's a fun romp through the spaceways—not so much a space opera as space ballet.... it has all the 'right stuff.' A lot of thought and thoughtfulness stand behind the all-too-human characters. Enjoy this one, and look forward to the next." —Dean Lambe, *SF Reviews*

"The pace is breathless, the characterization thoughtful and emotionally powerful, and the author's narrative technique and command of language compelling. Highly recommended." —*Booklist*

Brothers in Arms: "... she gives it a geniune depth of character, while reveling in the wild turnings of her tale. ... Bujold is as audacious as her favorite hero, and as brilliantly (if sneakily) successful." —*Locus*

"Miles Vorkosigan is such a great character that I'll read anything Lois wants to write about him. ... a book to re-read on cold rainy days." —Robert Coulson, *Comics Buyer's Guide*

Borders of Infinity: "Bujold's series hero Miles Vorkosigan may be a lord by birth and an admiral by rank, but a bone disease that has left him hobbled and in frequent pain has sensitized him to the suffering of outcasts in his very hierarchical era.... Playing off Miles's reserve and cleverness, Bujold draws outrageous and outlandish foils to color her high-minded adventures." —*Publishers Weekly*

Falling Free: "In *Falling Free* Lois McMaster Bujold has written her fourth straight superb novel. ... How to break down a talent like Bujold's into analyzable components? Best not to try. Best to say 'Read, or you will be missing something extraordinary.'" —Roland Green, *Chicago Sun-Times*

The Vor Game: "The chronicles of Miles Vorkosigan are far too witty to be literary junk food, but they rouse the kind of craving that makes popcorn magically vanish during a double feature." —Faren Miller, *Locus*

MORE PRAISE FOR
LOIS MCMASTER BUJOLD

What the readers say:

"My copy of *Shards of Honor* is falling apart I've reread it so often.... I'll read whatever you write. You've certainly proved yourself a grand storyteller."
                    —Liesl Kolbe, Colorado Springs, CO

"I experience the stories of Miles Vorkosigan as almost viscerally uplifting.... But certainly, even the weightiest theme would have less impact than a cinder on snow were it not for a rousing good story, and good story-telling with it. This is the second thing I want to thank you for.... I suppose if you boiled down all I've said to its simplest expression, it would be that I immensely enjoy and admire your work. I submit that, as literature, your work raises the overall level of the science fiction genre, and spiritually, your work cannot avoid positively influencing all who read it."
                    —Glen Stonebraker, Gaithersburg, MD

" 'The Mountains of Mourning' [in *Borders of Infinity*] was one of the best-crafted, and simply best, works I'd ever read. When I finished it, I immediately turned back to the beginning and read it again, and I can't remember the last time I did that."   —Betsy Bizot, Lisle, IL

"I can only hope that you will continue to write, so that I can continue to read (and of course buy) your books, for they make me laugh and cry and think ... rare indeed."   —Steven Knott, Major, USAF

What do *you* say?

Send me these books!

Shards of Honor	72087-2	$4.99	☐
The Warrior's Apprentice	72066-X	$4.50	☐
Ethan of Athos	65604-X	$5.99	☐
Falling Free	65398-9	$4.99	☐
Brothers in Arms	69799-4	$5.99	☐
Borders of Infinity	72093-7	$4.99	☐
The Vor Game	72014-7	$4.99	☐
Barrayar	72083-X	$5.99	☐
The Spirit Ring (hardcover)	72142-9	$17.00	☐
The Spirit Ring (paperback)	72188-7	$5.99	☐
Mirror Dance (hardcover)	72210-7	$21.00	☐
Mirror Dance (paperback)	87646-5	$5.99	☐
Cetaganda (hardcover)	87701-1	$21.00	☐

Lois McMaster Bujold:
Only from Baen Books

If not available at your local bookstore, fill out this coupon and send a check or money order for the cover price(s) to Baen Books, Dept. BA, P.O. Box 1403, Riverdale, NY 10471. Delivery can take up to ten weeks.

NAME: _____

ADDRESS: _____

_____

I have enclosed a check or money order in the amount of $ _____

LARRY NIVEN, JERRY POURNELLE & MICHAEL FLYNN
Fallen Angels
A near-future cautionary romp by two *New York Times* bestselling authors and the award-winning Michael Flynn.

VERNOR VINGE
Across Realtime
Two Hugo-nominated novels in one grand volume.

ELTON ELLIOTT, editor
Nanodreams
Welcome to the world of the *micro*miniaturized future where with virus-sized self-replicating machines all things are possible—but only human wisdom stands between us and unspeakable disaster.